SENTINEL

by
Seb Woodland

This book is dedicated to my family and friends who
encouraged and supported me on this journey.

For Katree, who put up with my self-doubt-monster and
reminded me that it would all be okay.

For Candace and Taryn who helped me to feel inspired,
and to notice things I could improve.

And for my brother Bayden, and twin sister Ashlyn,
without whom this story could never exist.

One

The investigator sat across from me. She wore a black uniform and hat, with a sky-blue trim. She looked pristine, as though she'd never touched a speck of dirt in her life, which was curious since dirt is exactly what she was looking for. She placed a small computer on the desk in front of me, which I found interesting; why didn't she just use her holo-gauntlet?

I knew the answer. This way, I couldn't read whatever she was typing. She hadn't broken eye contact. But I did.

Silver light beamed in from the glass wall to my right. The moons were full, and the Toru nebula was in the sky tonight, glowing a striking purple. I took a deep breath in, and exhaled.

I turned to the investigator. "I appreciate you coming all this way, investigator; I am honoured. But I don't think I'll be of much help." I cleared my throat.

She smiled at me. "No need to be so modest, your highness. There's a reason I came to you, specifically. You have knowledge and experience that no one else has."

I shuffled in my seat. "Perhaps I should have someone bring us some refreshments?"

"I'm fine, thank you. I'd just like you to start from the beginning. This doesn't need to be a long process."

I glanced at the time on my holo-gauntlet.

"So, you'd like me to start from the beginning… of the Duhrnan incident?"

She shook her head. "We're not interested in Duhrnan. We're more interested in the Brotherhood's role in all of this."

"Well," I said, "I'm not sure where to begin…"

"Anywhere that feels natural. We can go from there."

"Alright," I said. I nodded slowly, but my mind raced back in time. There really was only one place the story could begin.

PAST

Two

Spending so much time with humans was certainly interesting. I had studied all about them of course, during my university years. Learned their language. Learned their differences from us, of which there were many, and their similarities to us, of which there were also a surprising number. Humans had always intrigued me, being the only friendly species us skythers had encountered in space. But it wasn't just that humans were the only spacefarers possible for me to be interested in; they were also undoubtedly complicated, emotional creatures. Though, I concluded that, like many skythers, many humans enjoyed pretending their emotions didn't exist. Or perhaps they enjoyed pretending they controlled their emotions. Personally, I had difficulty knowing what to feel at times, but that didn't stop the feelings from happening.

I looked up at the human soldier standing across from me by the mechanical doors of the dropship, shaking in my seat occasionally from the turbulence. He eyed me suspiciously, our heads at about the same level despite being seated myself. I nodded at him slowly, to remind him yet again that I was here to help, and that I was no danger to the vehicle or its crew.

Perhaps the most difficult thing about working with humans was that they had a very hard time reading my facial expressions. Maybe it was because of human mouths being so different than a skyther's; they had lips placed on the front of the face instead of mandibles underneath. And to humans, emotions seemed to have everything to do with the mouth.

Sarcasm was often wasted on them for this reason, but I found it hard to break the habit of cracking those kinds of jokes. I remembered a time several cycles ago when I applied for a cross-species cooperation program. It was a three Earth year program, and I was sent along with several other skythers all the way to Earth to the University of Victoria. It was one of the oldest universities on the planet, and the architectural history alone was quite fascinating. Thankfully it had its own private landing pad, which made it eligible for the program, and helped facilitate travel for field studies in other Earth ecosystems. I tried to make friends with my human peers, but they rarely understood my jokes. One time I said to someone "I will kill you if you touch these samples", and they must have taken it seriously. They never said a word to me again, until the program ended.

I was of course joking; at the time, I never imagined that I would one day kill a human, skyther, or any other creature. I was of course trained in the use of weaponry and martial arts by my mother, Queen Suranos, as all skyther princes and princesses are. But I never really expected I would have to put those skills to use.

Still, I carried an energy-pistol at my side just in case. You never knew what you might find when exploring ancient ruins, and hostile alien creatures have been known to be a threat in such locations.

While my mind wandered, I heard the human pilot's voice through the ship's speakers state that we had finally arrived.

The turbulence stopped with one final jolt as the ship landed, and the soldier in front of me stepped aside as the mechanical doors slid open. A blinding light cut through the apparently dim atmosphere of the ship's interior as I stood up from my seat. A chill air rushed inside the hull from the open door, and the white fur on my dangling ears ruffled as my foot crunched into the snow that covered the platform.

It was nice to feel the snow between my toes after spending so much time sitting still on the dropship. It reminded me of another curiosity about humans; human bodies are very susceptible to negative effects from "extreme" temperatures. And they wear shoes almost constantly, blocking the nerves of their feet from touching the ground and sending useful information to their brains. I understand it's to protect themselves from sharp objects. They seem, in many ways, fragile by comparison to us. I looked at the heavily armoured and padded boots of the soldier as he too stepped outside into the snow.

The fully armoured man began leading me across the landing pad we had just arrived on towards a large structure. It was snowing hard enough that he already had white flecks coating his helmet and shoulders, and even though we couldn't have been more than a few yards away from the entrance to the facility, it looked like a looming, hazy spire, blank and barren, any clear shapes or details obscured by the snow.

"Hey there, watch your step," said the soldier when he noticed my gaze wandering up to the top of the silhouetted building instead of looking down at the bridge ahead of us, safely railed, but suspended hundreds of feet in the air. Even a skyther wouldn't survive a fall from up here, and it was kind of him to say something in case I might eagerly throw myself over the human-sized railing by accident. Though, he may have sounded more scared for his job than for my life.

The landing pad we left behind was one of several attached to the facility here. I glanced back through the swirling snow as we were entering the door and noticed the pilot and a few other military personnel walking towards us from the small dropship.

I held the control to keep the door open for the other humans as they passed me. The pilot said, "Thanks," and again, I simply nodded in response. The door shut behind us with a hiss, and the blinding white atmosphere was replaced with a metallic, industrial hallway, lit by long white lights flush with the ceiling where it met the wall.

The floor was reflective and smooth, and the hallway was tall enough for me to walk comfortably. Thankfully this was standard design for the Terran Astral Union, as having architecture of this size made transporting large equipment manageable. It also made TAU-skyther interactions a lot more comfortable, if such interactions were to happen.

The soldier I had been watching stopped and looked up at me saying, "Alright, you should be able to find your way from here. The control room is on this floor, down that hallway." He pointed at a door off to the side of the entrance hall.

I assumed he was still wary of my presence, and wanted to part ways as soon as possible. While I found it odd that a soldier would harbour such irrational fears or discomfort, I wasn't particularly surprised to see it in a human after all my experience. Most humans who had tried to befriend me had a falseness to them, as though they were just seeking the status of someone brave enough to talk to a skyther. I had never done anything to harm a human in those days, so the fear seemed unwarranted, but after studying only a brief amount of human history it became clear to me that they often fear things that appear different from them, even other humans.

"Thank you very much," I said, nodding my head once again. "I can find my way from here."

He seemed to step back ever so slightly when he heard the words come out of my mouth, as though he was surprised to hear me speaking English. I supposed it would take him a while to get used to being around skythers, but since I was the only skyther on the planet, maybe he wouldn't need to. I figured that our brief interactions today might help set him on a path of acceptance… or maybe that was just wishful thinking.

I strode across to the door he had pointed to and stepped through as it opened automatically. It led to a long hallway with windows on either side letting the natural light of Voren's sun in. As I walked I looked to my left through the windows facing away from the rest of the facility, down to the icy plains far below the plateau this structure rested on. It was difficult to see anything of note; the snowfields of the planet Voren were like vast white blankets covering the ground. Nonetheless, the view was impressive from way up here, even through the thick falling snow.

I continued traveling through the facility, running into a few scientists, soldiers, and workers of another kind I couldn't identify. Most of them tried to hide their surprise when they saw me, though some clearly already knew I was coming today, or were used to seeing skythers, or were simply trying to be polite, and paid me little attention.

I think I may have gotten a bit lost on my way to the control room, as I shuffled awkwardly through a lab full of scientists and computer monitors, as well as a room full of people sitting around a table, discussing something of importance, before I found my destination. When I entered the control room it was noticeably darker compared to the outside hall, with blue lights on the ceiling and floor. The room was circular and fairly large with two levels. I entered on the top floor which circled the outside wall of the room and also had four spoked bridges to a central circular platform. At various points were ladders leading down to the bottom floor of the room, which like the top floor, was ringed with computers of various designs and functions. From the center of the tall ceiling a large robotic armature hung, and at its bottom was a set of four computer monitors, arranged in an upside down T pattern.

Workers wearing the TAU standard Earth-sky blue colours were stationed at almost every computer, and on the central platform on the top floor stood a man in a smoothly ironed uniform. He wore a hat signifying his position as Active Director. He had short, curly black hair, which hung down each side of his tanned face, and connected with his stubble, completely outlining his face with hair. When he noticed me he smiled, and waited for me to approach him on the central platform.

"Director Aali," I said, mirroring him as he reached to shake my hand.

"You must be Prince Talcorosax, am I right?" His grip was firm, and he shook my hand confidently. I nodded in response.

"When I was told they were sending a skyther to help us, it piqued my interest. You probably noticed that we currently only employ humans here." He turned away, pushing a few keys on a computer as he spoke, before turning back. "When I realized that you were the Prince of Astraloth, I was even more interested. I read your files. Graduated with honours in both fields of theoretical biology and linguistics? And I hear that the royalty of Astraloth is trained in martial combat as well?"

"Yes. It's tradition for skyther monarchs to teach their children the ways of-"

"You must have spent a long time in school," he interrupted with a slight smile, oblivious to what I had been saying. Had I been speaking quietly? I didn't think so.

I walked with him as he led me toward one of the walls on the upper level. The wall-plating rotated like industrial blinds, revealing a clear window as the mechanical plates automatically rose up into a stack above.

"...I spent many cycles studying many different fields," I replied, hesitantly. "I spent several years studying and living on Earth, in fact."

"So I read." He activated his holo-gauntlet, a tiny computer worn on the wrist, and a small holographic projection appeared above his arm as he tapped away on tiny buttons, manipulating some sort of data. He was clearly a multitasker. The sound of murmuring discussions and electronic whirring filled the silence.

"How long have you been working in the field?" he asked, pausing from his holo-gauntlet to give me a sidelong glance. "I've never worked with a loro researcher before."

"It's been three cycles- around four Earth years."

"Hmm..." he replied, gazing out the window. My ears drooped involuntarily. It was clear that after all, he really didn't care what I had to say. He pointed off towards the horizon. "I'll be sending you there to investigate the ruins. None of my people are qualified to examine them. We're a bunch of physicists, biologists, engineers, and soldiers." He turned to face me. "But none of us have any experience with the loro civilization, and most of us only speak one language."

"Well, it's good that I am here to decipher whatever we find there," I said plainly.

"Yes," he replied. "Talcorosax, do you have much experience working with others? I want to send a mercenary with you, one we've been working with for some time."

This was news to me. I had assumed I would be going alone, and I didn't understand why I might need a bodyguard.

"Do you expect there'll be trouble out there? Dangerous wildlife?" I asked, and then hesitantly added, "have you encountered any valicorr here on Voren?"

The Director looked out the window again and sighed slightly. "It's nothing like that. It's just the way we do things here. No one takes unnecessary risks. There are some dangerous predators, though they usually only come out at night." He hesitated. "We haven't seen any valicorr here... yet. But having such a well-stocked facility, full of fuels and valuable resources... and of course the thing valicorr love to take most: human life... well, I would be lying to say the valicorr threat wasn't on everyone's minds." A look of genuine concern passed over the Director's face.

When the valicorr first appeared to us twelve cycles ago, most humans and skythers alike thought the talk of space piracy was just a hoax. They were the second living spacefarers that either of our species had encountered. The first reported attack was on a skyther cargo transport, but they soon discovered humanity as well. And it seemed that once they discovered us, they decided to pour all their efforts into raids against us. For the past twelve cycles, the valicorr had been a constant threat to both the TAU and skyther authorities. Maybe it's because many of my people were already speaking English at the time, but soon enough the valicorr began to speak using the same words, though often only to intimidate us or make demands. A lot of human hotheads started throwing around the phrase "the only good valicorr is a dead valicorr". I can't say I supported the message, but I also can't say I blamed them. I'd never heard of a good valicorr; their very species was synonymous with destruction.

I contemplated what he'd just told me, and replied. "Director, if you're concerned there's a chance I might be ambushed by a valicorr raiding party amidst the snow, I hardly think sending one mercenary will save my life." I didn't phrase it as a question, but the Director got my message.

He smiled weakly, and said, "Well, the mercenary I spoke of is... special. A mutant, with superhuman strength. Grown to be a weapon of some kind by... some unsavoury group, but made too powerful. When she was found by the TAU, she had evidently broken free from her laboratory restraints without much effort."

I waited expectantly for the story to continue. It did not. Apparently Director Aali thought this was a good enough explanation, so I decided not to press the matter. It was likely that other details about this mysterious mercenary were classified anyway, just like the details about the facility we currently stood in. My sole purpose here was to investigate the loro ruins they'd accidentally discovered, and it was becoming clear that Director Aali was a busy man, who's facade of welcoming was growing tired.

I shifted my weight from leg to leg as I stood idly by, watching the Director work on his holo-gauntlet some more. "Director Aali, is there any place in this facility where I might eat- maybe have a shower- before I begin the expedition?" I knew it may have sounded like a strange request, but I wasn't eager to leave the station just yet.

He gave me a look of bewilderment, as though the thought that a skyther might wish to be well-fed and clean was absurd, but quickly regained control and resumed his false smile. "Ah, food, yes," he muttered. "Lucky for you the showers and kitchen are on the same floor, two above us." He paused briefly. "Though, uh, you might find the showers to be a bit low for you."

"That won't be a problem," I responded. "I'll contact you if I need anything in regards to the expedition."

"Please do," he said. "But you should know I've already made arrangements for a ground transport for you and Kay to take to the site, whenever you're ready of course."

"Kay? The mercenary, I presume?"

"Yes." He looked outside the window, then back to his holo-gauntlet, turning his body completely away from me. It was clear that his patience was entirely spent at this point, and he wanted to end our interaction. "Just head down to the ground bay when you're ready to leave. I've given instructions; just tell them you're there for the expedition."

I wasted no more of the Director's time, and after saying thank you, I left the control room, searching for the nearest elevator or stairwell. I found the stairs first, so I started to climb.

Three

"I'm sorry to interrupt, but could you perhaps skip ahead?"

The investigator was staring at me, blankly. It seemed my story was boring her. She brushed down her black suit jacket, straightening it out.

"Excuse me? I thought you wanted me to start from the beginning. Or at least, wherever felt natural." I tapped my fingers on the table.

She leaned back in her seat and took a deep breath. "Yes, I did. But we're really just interested in the Brotherhood, and Kay. Can you tell us more about that? Can you tell me what happened to her? These details aren't necessary." I was having a hard time reading her expression in the moonlight.

I sighed. "Investigator, you asked me to recount this story."

She nodded.

"My people have a long cultural heritage of oral storytelling. I can recount the tales my grandmother and father told me, word for word."

She continued staring at me, looking unimpressed, as though hearing this upset her.

"Word for word?"

"Yes, word for word," I said. "I mean, no one is perfect, but-"

"So if another skyther heard you telling an old story, they'd be able to tell if you got it wrong?"

I paused. My orange eyes flickered in the moonlight. The investigator was poised at her computer, ready to type. With one hand, she grabbed a stray bit of blonde hair between her fingers and tucked it up under her hat.

"Yes, I suppose," I said. "Sometimes us skythers gather for days at a time to hear and share our tales. This is a story I haven't yet told, not to anyone. Please, let me do it justice. The first telling will shape how the story is remembered for generations."

She nodded, and remained silent. Her blue eyes narrowed at me subtly. I gazed out through the window at the four full moons, glowing against the purple nebula. I almost thought I saw the nebula pulsing.

"My ancestors are watching tonight. They're listening to the tale just as you are, etching it in the stars, and they deserve to hear it in full."

The investigator followed my gaze. "Ancestors?" She looked me in the eye, and raised an eyebrow. "I thought you were a scientist."

I clenched my fists.

"Please," I asked, "let me tell my story. You may not understand the significance, but if I'm to tell it at all, it is of utmost importance to me that I get this chance to tell it correctly." I paused, and then added, "You said it wasn't urgent, anyway."

"Yes, I did *say* that." She paused, and looked around the room, before making a few notes in her computer. I felt tension building in me. I was anxious about telling this story, and yet, once I had begun, I felt that I needed to continue. She said, "I think some refreshments would be nice, actually." She forced a smile. Something I said had upset her.

I nodded to her, and lifted my ears, pressing a button on my holo-gauntlet. "Right away. But I would ask you, please, do not interrupt again unless you must. It will be a long while before it's over."

She sighed quietly, and nodded. "Of course. So… you were climbing the stairs?"

A skyther assistant entered the room, and handed us each a beverage, equipped with a straw. I thanked them, and sipped the fizzy drink eagerly.

"Yes," I said, "I was climbing the stairs."

Four

The stairs circled up a glass cylinder on the outside of the structure, and once again I got to look outside at Voren's blank-canvas landscape. It was difficult to imagine why the loro civilization would have chosen such a desolate place to build their structures. It's true that finding life on any planet is incredibly unlikely, which made Voren's natural ecosystems (although barren by comparison to my home planet Astraloth, or Earth) stand out like a bright star amidst the blackness of space. Nevertheless, the joint efforts of humans and skythers in the last twenty cycles alone had discovered many planets more fertile and lively than Voren. Why would a species so advanced like the loro choose this planet?

Perhaps any sign of life was reason enough for them to explore, study, and settle. What I knew of their culture was that they strongly valued the seeking of knowledge; loro scholars sought to uncover the truths of the universe, and why shouldn't a planet such as Voren play a role in the tapestry of our galaxy? The loro were all gone now, either dead, or according to a favourite theory in the loro research community they had ascended to some extra-dimensional form. And if so they had far surpassed us, skythers, humans, and valicorr alike, in technological terms at any rate.

No, I thought. It wasn't the presence of the loro ruins which was unsettling me. I could understand their motives from a cultural, and even spiritual standpoint, assuming I hadn't been basing all my research on something horribly misinterpreted in early loro studies. And even if I didn't understand their motives, I could only assume that was because the loro possessed a greater wisdom than I currently grasped. What I couldn't justify was the presence of the very structure I stood within.

I reached the top of the stairs, and stood there for a moment in a hallway, vaguely aware of people walking past me, giving me strange looks. The TAU hadn't picked this planet because of its wildlife. That seemed unlikely, given that there were much more biodiverse ecosystems on planets which were more accessible from Earth. But they had picked a livable planet for a reason, or they would have chosen somewhere else. It was clear that the purpose of this outpost was at least partially scientific… it was biologists who had uncovered the loro ruins I was to investigate in the first place, or so I had been told...

I shook my head. I was always eager to uncover mysteries, and simply being at a station with classified functions made me feel overly suspicious. I took a deep breath and told myself to calm down, get some food, and take a moment to clean up as I had told the Director I would. I straightened my back and walked down the hall, looking for a sign to point me to the showers, deliberately avoiding eye contact with an engineer who was staring up at me, wide eyed. Yet, all the way to the showers I kept catching myself visually scanning the hallways, peering into rooms as doors opened, looking for something, anything that I might not be meant to see.

When I finally found the showers, I was thankful to be allowed to use them. I found that the running water helped my mind focus, even if I had to crouch uncomfortably to wash my ears. It was relieving to feel the steaming hot water on the skin of my face, arms, legs, and back. And I was glad to get a chance to try out some new shampoo on my fur; ever since spending those years on Earth, I had been looking for the perfect shampoo. This shampoo had a fragrant but tasteful scent of lavender...

While I was appreciating this brief moment I had to myself, my mind wandered back to the upcoming task, and I began speculating about the mercenary, Kay.

So, Kay was some kind of mutated human with incredible strength. I would have to assume that this included super-resilience to physical trauma. If she was designed to be some kind of bio-weapon, as the Director had implied, then it would only be natural that she could withstand blasts from an E-gun. Otherwise, why not simply build a robot? A well designed combat drone could easily be stronger than any human in terms of weight-lifting capacity and resilience to weaponry.

I paused, inhaling the steamy air, savouring the warmth of the room.

So it would be more logical to build a robot… unless Kay's strength could outmatch anything a robot of the same size could achieve.

I started subconsciously miming punches, my eyes narrowed deep in focus.

I began to recall my studies of the planet MM094, more commonly known as Malum. It got the name from an ancient human language, known as Latin. The word translates to "evil," which was fitting considering the hostile environments and wildlife of the planet's surface. The humans who discovered it, and the skythers who followed in their place, generally agreed that they were not yet prepared to sacrifice lives in the name of exploration on that planet, though it did have a breathable atmosphere.

My mind was wandering. Why had I remembered Malum? There was a species I had studied briefly in school known as myroks. Myroks were incredibly dangerous creatures native to Malum; the apex predator across all regions they appeared, or so we believed from the little data we had on the planet. Myroks had beaks which could drill through bone, and tails which could discharge electric energy into a scorching long-distance projectile like an energy-gun. But in addition, myroks, in all stages we'd witnessed of their complicated metamorphoses, possessed not only some of the toughest hide skythers had ever encountered on a creature, but muscle mass to strength ratios which could not be quantified when compared to any other creatures we had studied.

I began stroking my mandibles as a human might stroke their chin. If Kay's biology shared similarities with that of a myrok, then perhaps it was possible that creating a bio-weapon would prove stronger than a robot of current human technology. This was all assuming Kay's creators were human; I hadn't considered that they might have been skythers.

I turned off the water. Perhaps Kay was in fact a mutated skyther? But the Director had described her abilities as "super-human", though it was possible that he was simply using a familiar phrase.

I stepped out of the shower. No, I was ignoring another detail. The Director stated I was the only skyther on the station. So either Kay was a mutated human, or the Director didn't consider her human *or* skyther. But I was beginning to decide she was likely some form of human.

I stepped into the body dryer, and waited as the air blades slowly moved up and down, my eyes closed. I had to crouch a little to fit inside the cylindrical chamber. I always found it took a while to dry my chest fur, so I ruffled it with my hands to encourage faster drying.

The more I thought about Kay, the more questions I began to have. What did she look like? I started imagining all kinds of humanoid creatures, mostly hulking, menacing beings.

Her name, however, seemed odd to me. It didn't sound like a name she would have been given by her creators. I couldn't come up with a reason to name a bio-weapon so personally. But it also seemed too obscure of a name for the TAU to have given her when they found her. They would have most likely chosen a common name, to make her feel welcome. Something like Ashley, or Sarah. Or something based on one of their ancient myths; the TAU loved to name things after myths. Of course I was just speculating, and for all I knew, Kay was a common name among the TAU, or perhaps it was a name of one of their mythical figures after all.

But she was apparently a mercenary, meaning she was not officially part of the TAU. If so, that reduced the chances that she was named by those who discovered her, which would be more likely if the TAU felt like they had ownership over her. There was a chance that she had chosen her own name. *No,* I thought, *it's more likely that the name Kay was indeed given to her by her creators.*

Finally dry, I stepped out of the body dryer and began putting on my gear, starting with my legs. Aside from the shower itself, the room was small, with a full body mirror covering the wall opposite the shower. A comb was waiting for me in a small metallic drawer to the side of the mirror, and I began combing my white fur as the mirror quickly began to defog itself automatically.

I took in a deep breath through my cat-like nose, and gazed into my own amber eyes, noticing how focused my expression was. I had always found it odd that human eyes had white sclera, instead of black, like skyther eyes. I wondered if Kay's eyes would be different.

Kay… her name was given to her by her creators. There must have been a reason this name was chosen.

I would have smiled with my lips when I thought of it, if I were human. Her name was not an English name, or a mythological name, or even a human name. It was an English letter: K. Which, I concluded, meant she must have been the eleventh experiment to be named, being named after the eleventh letter of the alphabet. Of course I was making an assumption, but I had already convinced myself it was the truth.

I was pleased with myself. I doubted I would be able to determine much more about her without talking to her. It was clear though, if she was a mercenary by choice and was rescued by the TAU as was implied, that despite being bred for war, she had a personality and mind of her own. What that personality was remained to be seen.

It had been an interesting day so far, my first time on Voren, and if I was hesitant about traveling to the loro ruins with another person before, now I could only say I was looking forward to it. I had a feeling things were going to get a lot more interesting as the day passed.

"K," I said quietly to myself. "I look forward to meeting you."

Five

I finally found one of the kitchens, which was arranged more like a cafeteria than anything; a great, wide room full of stools, tables and chairs, reflective floors, and like the rest of the facility's architecture, massive windows from which the bright atmosphere of Voren painted the room. Despite the size of the place, when I hesitantly entered I saw no more than ten humans in various uniforms at the tables. I didn't pay them much attention at first, instead turning my gaze towards the walls which were lined with machines designed to dispense food and drink.

I grabbed myself a plate and a tall glass and started dishing up some food for myself, conscious of, but trying to ignore, the attention my presence was attracting. I made sure to grab a fork; I learned the hard way while at a restaurant back on Earth that humans usually found it rude to see skythers using their mandibles instead of their hands. I wished to avoid another awkward social encounter like that, and ever since I'd been conscious of how I ate around humans.

The food dispensers didn't require any credits, thankfully. It was a reminder that this was a government funded station, the purpose of which was more than simply to make money; whatever was going on here, its cause was worth the risk of failure and losing resources. This was the only settlement on Voren, and unless you were going off-world just for lunch, you'd be out of luck if the station didn't provide food. I was sure they had food synthesizers installed for an operation like this, since importing food out here would have been quite an ordeal. I was honestly impressed at the selection and quality of the food as well. Though they of course didn't have any skyther dishes, they had some of my favourite human foods, including synthesized rice and chicken. But skythers need much less food than humans. Liquids are our main source of energy, especially sugar water. So when I noticed that they had root beer, my favourite human drink, I let out a stifled "yes!" I was sure to grab a straw, as was customary for such a drink.

I poured myself a root beer, enjoying the sound of the dispenser and the rising pitch of the liquid filling my glass. I moved my ears forward so they dangled on either side of the dispenser to get a better listening angle. Perhaps it was just my personality, but I found that I was often captivated by things which others referred to as mundane.

When I was young, I would eagerly tell my mother that my curiosity made me a perfect explorer, and she always responded the same way. "If there's anyone who can explore," she would say, "it's my son, Osax." I often wondered if she really meant it, encouraging me to try new things, or if she was simply too afraid of disempowering me with a more honest outlook. From her perspective, I had a lot of expectations to live up to, being her son, and the Prince of Astraloth. But she hated to force them on me, otherwise I never would have gotten to where I was: drinking root beer at a classified TAU station on Voren, graduated from schools on both Astraloth and Earth, on a mission as a loro archaeologist.

I wasted no time afterwards looking for a place to sit, preferring those near the windows. It was at that moment, after I had gotten my food, that I noticed a human sitting alone, silhouetted against the bright light from the outside. She was looking straight at me.

As I approached and her figure became clearer to me, I realized she was different from the others. I wasn't sure how I hadn't noticed her sooner. She could only have been K.

Her skin was an azure blue colour, the light from the window shining off its texture. Her overall body, though shorter than mine, was larger than an average human, probably taller than six feet, and with a muscular build. She didn't look like a body builder (and I was very familiar with what body builders looked like; I had studied the concept in my free time because it intrigued me), but her muscles were nonetheless very well defined, and looked well prepared for all practical uses. She was wearing tall combat boots, pants, and some kind of sleeveless armoured vest. Though her body was symmetrical overall, she had bone-like horns of a light blue colour jutting from her shoulders, forearm, and fists, which appeared different on each arm.

Despite this, her head appeared fairly symmetrical, with two bull-like horns protruding from the top sides of her head above her ears. From the top of her nose bridge began a jagged ridge which traced a central line up her forehead, and I assumed continued down her spine. She had no hair on her head, aside from thick, dark eyebrows, and at the corner of each eyebrow extended more small horns. Her cheeks were slightly rounded, and her jawline was sharp and pronounced. Two of her teeth stuck out over her top lip from her bottom, her mandibular canines judging from their placement.

Her face told me that she was angry about something. Still, she was staring at me, and I knew it would be more awkward if I didn't say anything at all.

"Are you K, by any chance?" I tried to speak in my most nonchalant voice. I was eager to see how she would respond.

Her deep orange eyes, an unusual colour for a human, shifted between each of my own. She seemed to loosen up a little, and leaned back in her seat, putting her arms behind her head. At last she spoke, after eyeing me up and down for a good long while.

"What's it to you?" she asked, bluntly. She continued to stare at me. She was testing me, and she knew I was doing the same to her.

I decided to take my chances and sit down beside her. She seemed mildly impressed at my lack of manners, a slight smile flashed across her face for a second.

"My name is Talcorosax," I said, "I came here to investigate the loro ruins." She seemed uninterested. "And though I thought I'd be going alone," I added, "Director Aali informed me that he would be sending you along with me."

She stayed fairly motionless as I said this. Her eyes looked away briefly. Then, she sat forward, put her arms on the table, and looked into my eyes again. She was waiting for me to continue.

I leaned a little closer as well, trying to meet her unspoken social challenges. I decided I would challenge her as well. "What's your problem with skythers?" I asked, knowing it was a risky thing to say upfront. Without waiting for a response, I began casually sipping on my root beer, narrowing my eyes a little. I hoped she could sense that my aggression was partially a show; I didn't want to accidentally get on her bad side by pushing too far.

She relaxed a little, leaning back once more. "No problem with skythers. Never seen one in person until now." She paused for a brief moment. "My problem is with people who think they can figure the world out just by looking at it." She raised an eyebrow at me, questioningly.

"And I suppose you think I'm that kind of person?" I said, and then added, "Just by looking at me?"

She thought for a moment, motionless. Then, she started chuckling quietly, and picked up her glass, before saying "Ah shit, I'm no good at these mind battles." She took a sip. "You should challenge me to an arm wrestle, see who wins that."

I relaxed in my seat, and took another sip of root beer, my other hand attempting to spear some rice with my fork. "A pleasure to meet you, K. I was a little worried you wouldn't want to talk to me there, so I had to break the ice."

She looked up at me after stuffing some food into her mouth and mumbled "You're assuming I want to talk to you now?"

"I'm assuming if you didn't want to talk, you wouldn't be."

She shrugged. I think the words she said next were "fair enough," though it was hard to understand her with her mouth full.

With her mouth finally empty she said, "So, what's your deal? You think you're some sort of detective, here to solve the world's mysteries? Is it mandatory that as soon as anyone finds some ancient junk, they gotta send some expert to come over and show us idiots what's going on?"

"Well," I responded thoughtfully, "as part of the treaty between Astraloth and Earth, it is mandated that any discoveries pertaining to ancient space faring civilizations, of which so far we've only discovered the loro, are reported back to both TAU and skyther authorities as soon as possible. It's a sort of insurance so that neither group discovers some advanced technology and-"

"And uses it to destroy the other?"

I thought for a moment. "Essentially, yes." I took a bite of 'chicken' before continuing. "After talking to the Director, I'm sure he wishes that weren't the case. It seems he doesn't want any outsiders interfering with operations here, and would have rather kept the loro ruins secret, or dealt with them himself. It's not like if he broke the law it would warrant a Code-Alpha emergency or anything... nothing *that* extreme. But he's smart enough to know that breaking a law like that, once discovered, would seriously ruin his career, possibly result in jail time, and probably put the station here in jeopardy." I leaned forward. "What exactly goes on here anyway?"

K looked deep in thought. "Well, I probably don't know much more than you, and to be honest, what I do know is pretty boring. It's a multipurpose station, for all sorts of science-y things." She waved her hands in the air, vaguely. "I don't know. They study the planet, do experiments, and other things."

"Then what do you do here?" I asked.

She laughed. "That's a damn good question." She picked up her drink and began swirling it around, before taking a sip. I had a bit more of my own drink. "We have soldiers here mostly to protect against pirates. An installation like this has a lot of valuable equipment in the eyes of a scavenger."

She looked outside. "Me personally, when I'm not wasting my time sitting around, or arguing with the Director, I'm getting sent off to escort scientists like you in the snow." She looked at me with a mischievous smirk on her face. "I think the Director just doesn't know what to do with me, and prefers the peace and quiet of the place when I'm gone."

"Well, have your services been helpful in your time here?"

She let out a laugh, though I'm not sure what she found funny. "Oh yeah, from time to time. I've had to kill my fair share of dangerous predators on the surface. Nothing too dangerous, though." She leaned forward once again. "If you ask me, this place is a lot more boring than it's made out to be."

I got the sense K was being genuine, but it only increased my suspicions of the place.

"So what'd you say your name was again?"

"Talcorosax," I replied.

She shook her head. "How about Talco?"

"You can call me Osax, if you like."

"Alright," she said. "Osax. That's a much better name, where'd you get it?"

"Well, my mother used to call me that."

"Your mother?" K chuckled. "If she came up with the name Osax, why did she choose to name you Talco-bo-so, or whatever." She sipped some of her drink, still eyeing me. "Osax is a much better name. Short and sweet."

"Well," I replied slowly, "it was my father who named me."

"She shouldn't have let him!" K folded her hands together and stretched out her arms. My eyes were drawn to the pale blue spikes on her shoulders as her muscles flexed. I was formulating an opinion of her, and it was so far mostly positive. Intriguing, if nothing else.

"Well," said K, "nice meeting you too, Osax." She gestured to shake my hand. I placed my drink on the table, and returned the gesture, careful not to wrap my relatively long fingers over the spikes on the back of her hand- not that they were sharp.

Her grip was incredibly tight, and I winced, letting go long before she did. When she noticed my eyes squinting and my ears peeling back, she released me. Her face flashed an apology, then hardened. She looked away.

A hollow feeling crept into my chest. I rubbed my crushed hand as the pain slowly receded. Despite her appearances I had almost convinced myself that she was normal, but I began to realize just how little I understood about her. I tried contemplating what it would be like to exist as the result of an experiment. But I couldn't imagine it.

After a long moment of silence, K turned her body to me again. She looked down at her glass and picked it up. She shook its contents a little, peering into her nearly empty drink, before finally raising it to her lips and emptying it completely. When she put the empty glass back on the table and finally looked at me, she was smirking slightly.

I mindlessly sipped my root beer. "Well," I said, "when are you prepared to leave?"

Six

I felt uncomfortable as K and I stood in the elevator heading down to the vehicle bay at the base of the cliff. She didn't speak. And despite my curiosity about her, I didn't speak either. I felt as though it wasn't a good time to be probing her for information, particularly about her past. I watched her standing beside me in the rectangular elevator; she was gazing intently at the doors.

My gaze wandered toward them as well. It was clear that she had difficulty judging her own strength. I wondered if that had caused her many problems in the past. I wondered why she was here.

The elevator slowed to a halt. My insides felt strange from the shift in momentum.

When the doors opened, K motioned for me to follow her and she led the way into the halls. We were now well below the landing pad I had arrived at, and the cliffside that the main portion of the station was built on. Down here, the halls were darker, with few windows, and the walls appeared rough, unlike the refined design of the station's upper levels. Clearly these halls were designed with practicality in mind, but not luxury.

I followed K through the lower levels of the station. We passed by several technicians, some of which were working on repairing a set of light fixtures in the hall. They nodded at us as we passed.

K strode ahead confidently, her head and chest held high, and I followed behind her quickening my pace to keep up. The closer we got to the vehicle bay, the more excited she appeared.

We entered the hangar to the sound of echoing machinery and voices. Staff moved this way and that in the large chamber. Open, box-like hover-lifts glided across the smooth floor and over thick power cables which ran along it. Work lights were set up on tripods to illuminate a damaged all-terrain vehicle while three mechanics worked noisily repairing it.

"Wait here a minute," said K, before darting away, weaving between machines and workers, and out of sight.

I stood amidst the bustle of the hangar, not knowing which way to go. A whirring sound grew closer behind me, and I ducked aside to let a shouting hover-lift driver skim past me. Everywhere I looked, the people down here were staring at me, their expressions ranging from mild discomfort to disgust. I frowned with my eyes, though they probably couldn't tell.

I glanced around in time to see the three mechanics had paused their work to stare at me. When I caught eyes with one of them, the other two went back to work, but this man stood up, and strode toward me. Had I not hesitated, I would have had time to walk away, but I suppose my curiosity got the better of me; instead I turned fully to face him.

He wore a mechanic's uniform with TAU-blue colours, though it looked stained with oil. He appeared to be in his fifties, with hair that had just begun to grey. He had short stubble outlining his face, and I thought I detected anger in his eyes.

In an instant, he was a mere foot away from me, his hand pointing powerfully, accusingly, at my face as he looked up at me. "What are you doin' down here, huh, skiller?"

I blinked.

He continued, shaking his finger. "You tryin' to play dumb? I'd tell you to get lost, but it looks like you already are."

The other two mechanics were now staring at us, and so were several others. I took a deep breath in, and replied "My name is Talcorosax, I'm here because-"

"You don't look like a mechanic to me. Or a human, for that matter." He lowered his hand, but seemed to stand up taller. "This is a TAU station. *Terran. Astral. Union.* Not skyther. Not Astraloth."

I raised my hands slowly in defense. "I understand. You must not be used to seeing skythers-"

"Not *used* to 'em?" He laughed in bewilderment. "Girl, I've seen what you skillers can do. How much hate your kind has for us. How much joy you get from killin'."

A spark of rage ignited inside me. I stood motionless. I wasn't sure how to respond to this accusation. Not to mention being misgendered. This man clearly had no idea about us.

After a moment of silence, he continued. "Get out of here. You're making us all uncomfortable."

I trembled. "You… don't know what you're talking about. We don't hate humans; well maybe some skythers, but-"

"I won't say it again! Get out of here, or I'll call the Director."

The noise of talking in the chamber had ceased. All eyes were on us.

My blood felt hot. I stepped toward him, trying to look intimidating. I stood a few feet taller, towering over him, and a voice jumped out from within me. "We aren't like that! What's wrong with you?!"

He stumbled back, a look of terror on his face. "Help! It's threatening me!" He backed up, and made sure the space between us was sizable. No one made any motion to help him, but I noticed then that no one stood near me either.

I glanced around the room, hoping to see a sign that someone was sympathetic, that someone knew what I was trying to say. Each face I turned to looked away, and slowly everyone returned to their work.

My heart sank a little. I wasn't sure what to feel.

The mechanic, who had made his way back to his friends, uttered "It shouldn't be allowed to have that E-gun in here…" The other mechanics talked to him more quietly, seemingly urging him back to work.

I wanted to tell him I was a Prince, and that meant my duty was for peace, but I felt the focus slowly drifting away from me, and gave my body a quick shake, trying to reset myself and clear those thoughts. I wasn't here to start fights, or to finish them. Not even in the name of truth and understanding.

"Hey, Talcorosax?"

I swung around to face the sound of the voice. The woman was standing behind me, and stood about five and a half feet tall. The first thing I noticed about her was her hair; the left side of her head was shaved, the rest of her hair sprawled out in short, purple dreadlocks. Her left cheek had a purple spiral tattoo emblazoned on her dark skin. She was wearing silvery blue armour plating, with a large E-gun of some kind slung over her back, an E-pistol at her side, and what looked like a retracted molecular sword. I was relieved when I noticed she was smiling.

Despite the relief, my ears drooped backwards in embarrassment. "I- Sorry. I'm not usually like that." I cleared my throat and twitched my mandibles.

She raised her hands up to me, shaking her head. "It's okay, it's okay. You're the loro researcher, right? How about we take a walk?"

Glad to leave that mechanic, I nodded and followed. She led me toward the bay doors, so we were further from most of the mechanics and other staff, now standing surrounded by several vehicles of various sizes. The sounds of metal clanking and workers chatting echoed through the room.

She stopped, and I gestured to shake her hand. "You already know my name. What's yours?"

"Joëlle Weidman. Round Table." Her grip was confident.

I paused for a moment. "What brings an RT to an establishment like this?" I tried to sound less interested than I was when asking the question.

She eyed me carefully, the smile still on her face. "You… don't know what they're doing here, do you?"

I shook my head.

She sighed. "Well, neither do I. I was hoping you'd have some more information."

I chuckled. "I understand, I'm incredibly curious about this place." I tilted my head to the side. "You didn't answer my question though."

"Right. Well, I wasn't just trying to get information from you, I actually also wanted to give you a bit of a warning." She paused, and squinted slightly. "Talcorosax, right? That is your name, just making sure."

I nodded again. "Yes, you had it right the first time. What kind of warning? It's not about being unwanted in a TAU operation, I hope?"

"No, it's not that. That guy was just being…" She exhaled. "I don't know. That's not important right now. Just a few days ago, TAU authorities received communications from a civilian transport which had found its way into the system. They claimed their sensors picked up some kind of ship but couldn't identify it, and it wouldn't respond to their hails. In fact, when they tried to hail the vessel, it warped out of the system. Apparently it spooked them enough to activate their distress signal."

My interest was piqued. A mysterious ship? I stroked my mandibles thoughtfully. "That is strange… what else is going on?"

"Well," she said, "TAU control forwarded the sensor logs to Round Table, and my team and I happened to be in the area, so that's why I'm here. We're meant to wait around here, to make sure if anything bad happens we can counteract it. And if we're lucky, to find out what that ship was." She scanned the room with her eyes. "That ship, whatever it was, it didn't look like anything from Astraloth or Earth. We suspect the valicorr." She locked eyes with me. "And if it was a valicorr ship, that's not good… because it's bigger than any ship I've ever seen."

I gulped, and looked around the room. "So, your team is here on

Voren with you, just in case this ship shows up?"

"Exactly. I wanted to warn you because, if it is valicorr, there is a small chance they're here on Voren somewhere. If they've been monitoring the station…"

I nodded, understanding what she was implying. "They might know about the loro ruins; they might even be there already. Why didn't Director Aali inform me? I asked him about the valicorr and he acted as though there wasn't any concern."

Joëlle shook her head and sighed. "I'm not sure. But I guess he didn't think it was worth mentioning. We're only theorizing that it might be a valicorr ship. Whatever it was, it might not even show up again in this system. Nonetheless, the Director was pretty evasive when I was speaking with him as well."

"How did you even know I was coming? From what I've seen, I doubt he volunteers much information about anything."

She smiled. "Well, we've been here a few days. He's not the only person to talk to on the station, and a lot of people were talking about you. They're surprised that a skyther was sent to investigate the ruins. I think some people don't trust that you have the credentials."

"Well," I said, narrowing my eyes as I looked back at the angry mechanic at the other end of the room, "I do in fact have the credentials. I've studied the loro quite extensively, and as a registered member of the loro researcher's society I'm qualified to interact with loro remnants under the treaty."

She nodded. "I understand. Some people just wish they sent a human." She caught herself, and raised her hands in defense. "I- I'm not saying that's okay! Or, it's not okay?"

I tilted my ears forward in attempt to calm her, before remembering she might not understand the social cues. "No need to worry. I am used to others being… xenophobic."

"Okay. I-" She breathed out. "Never sure what to say. I've met quite a few good hearted skythers and I don't want it to come across as though I'm prejudiced."

I noticed K approaching us from the side, armed with an E-pistol and what looked like a large, retracted molecular sword on her back. She squinted, and brushed something off her cool blue forehead, and for a brief moment the bony ridges there caught on the spikes jutting from her hand. She shook her hand before stopping right next to us, giving me a quick look, and then turning to the RT.

K's orange eyes pierced Joëlle's brown ones. Joëlle cleared her throat and glanced at me.

A little flustered, I hesitated, before saying "K, this is Joëlle Weidman, an RT. Joëlle, this is K. She was sent to escort me to the ruins."

"RT?" asked K.

"It means Round Table," I said. "They're a branch of the TAU military, but they operate outside of normal protocol, mostly governing themselves. And their primary directive is to protect the innocent, and uphold the peace."

"Right, like Arthur's knights, I get it," said K.

Joëlle forced a smile, and reached out her hand toward K in greeting. "It's a pleasure to meet you, K."

K spoke as she turned her body away from her, and half-heartedly raised her hand in a wave. "Hey."

Joëlle slowly lowered her hand and looked between me and K, as K continued. "Osax, let's head. I'm dying to get going."

I nodded. "Alright. Do you know which-"

She walked past me, heading for a hover-car that looked swift and big enough for a skyther to be comfortable. "Yeah, I do. It should even have the ruin's coordinates programmed into the navi-system, or so the supervisor just told me."

K was already getting into the vehicle when I turned back to Joëlle. "Sorry," I said, "we'll have to continue this conversation later."

She smiled as she began walking away. "If I'm still around, I'd like that. With any luck, high command will deem this system safe and we'll be on our way. In any case, good luck out there." She winked.

"Thank you." I lifted my ears in a smile.

"Oh!" she said, before raising one arm up across her chest, then waving it to her side as she bowed. I returned the gesture, and warmth filled my heart. Not many humans knew that skyther goodbye.

◆

I secured my seat belt in the hover-car's tall cockpit. K was already seated to my left, and she'd positioned the steering control armature in front of herself. Her eyes gleamed as Voren's stark white atmosphere flooded into the chamber while the bay doors lifted open, and she grabbed the controls. Blips appeared on the navi-system and quickly calibrated to our position, with a clear marker flashing, representing the loro ruins, far away from the station and deep in the cold, harsh atmosphere.

I peered into the white blizzard, and the flashing marker seemed to beckon me. What was out there?

Turning back to K, my body began to fill with adrenaline. Her entire body was poised for our craft to lift off, as the doors lifted higher and higher. A smile crept across her face, and her head tilted down as she stared through the windshield.

"All systems online." The hover-car's onboard computer reported.

I tilted my head slightly, my furred ears dangling at a skewed angle. "I thought I was going to drive."

K tightened her grip on the controls, and shot me a glance. Her eyes were on fire, and a wide grin emphatically displayed her determination; fangs, tusks and all. She spared only one word for me then. "Tough."

And without any more warning, her eyes locked forward, and at a blistering speed we tore into the open air.

Seven

"Why not just go by Sax?" K's orange eyes glanced toward me, as she smirked. She didn't exactly need to keep her eyes ahead of her since we were in a particularly flat area, and our car hovered a few feet above the ground. Ice was forming on the edges of the windshields, and snow shot past us at an incredible speed.

I found her question amusing, and returning her glance, I responded. "My name is Talcorosax. My mother called me Osax. Sax just seems…"

I was trying to find the words to express my thoughts, but K interrupted, turning her focus back to the landscape ahead of us. "Oh, or you could just go by 'O'." She glanced back to me, mouth open in a silly smile.

I realized I hadn't responded for a few seconds, and began, "Well…"

K began chuckling to herself and looked back at the road, shaking her head. I narrowed my eyes, absentmindedly scratching my chest-fur. "Are you okay?"

It seemed that my questioning triggered something in her and she snorted another laugh, clearly trying to contain herself. Curious, I persisted.

"You know, I actually have a sense of humour too. What's so funny?" I was suppressing a chuckle, despite having no clue what she was laughing about. Her laugh was infectious.

She glanced at me briefly before turning her attention ahead. "Well, I just thought-" She chuckled, "I- I just thought if you were 'O', I'd be okay with that." She looked at me expectantly, her eyes wide matching her grin. "Because… I'd be- I'd be 'O' 'K', with that. 'Cause- Do you get it?"

I laughed and shook my head. What a fascinating person, created for combat, yet so amused by such a simple pun. My ears lifted in a smile. "I think I get it."

She raised an eyebrow. "Why'd you shake your head then?"

"I…" I continued laughing, "I'm not sure."

In an instant I noticed a flash of fear in K's eyes, and a fraction of a second later we swerved jarringly to the right. My ears peeled back and my fists clenched. I saw through the left windshield amidst the bright snow, a dark, towering shape. My adrenaline spiked. And then it was gone, left behind us as we glided on.

The cockpit was silent other than the straining hum of our vehicle's engine, the icy snow pelting the windshield, and our panting breaths. After a few moments my heart rate began to slow again.

"Did you get a good look at that?" I gasped.

K shook her head, panting. "It didn't look like a rock…"

The sun was blaring behind us, coming in through small windows on the back of the cockpit. I shoulder checked to see if I could glimpse the object, but we must have been going too fast. All I saw was the blinding light of the sun, dispersed through the mass of snow. I spun back toward the front of the vehicle.

I rubbed my face. "It probably was nothing," I said.

The sound pierced the hull of our craft with a suddenness that made me jump. It lingered in the air, engulfing us in a shrill tone before descending to a growl, and finally leaving us in silence. K and I locked eyes.

"You still think it was nothing?"

I shook my head, my heart pounding. "Some kind of creature..."

I held my breath. My ears slinked back, dangling, as a thunderous thumping sound repeated on itself, each second. It was getting louder, closer, and the hover-car was shaking from each reverberation.

K looked frantically from side to side, checking over her shoulder, then back ahead. "I- I can't see anything!"

I was breathing quickly, staring at the controls in K's hands. "I take it you haven't encountered something like this before?"

K shook her head, unable to look at me. Her horned shoulders were tense, and I noticed her breathing rate had increased. *Interesting,* I thought, *my respiratory rate is also increasing.* My mind was losing focus.

I glanced back over my shoulder, trying to get a glimpse of what was chasing us.

Boom. Boom. Boom. Boom.

A figure was taking form, dark, monstrous, and lumbering closer at an alarming speed. I couldn't tell if it was dangerously close, or just startlingly large. I barely glimpsed its gargantuan maw opening, as one of its limbs hurled something toward us.

"Look out!" I screamed, and K swerved to the left.

The massive snowball crashed into the ground just ahead and to the right of us, splattering shards of ice and snow against our windshield. I spun around to get another look at the creature, which I swore was unnaturally closer to us than when I had last looked. But just as I peered out to get a better view, K flicked a switch on the ceiling controls and a thick metal plate slid over top of the rear window.

She glanced at me with intensity in her eyes. "If it hit the windshield, we'd be dead!"

With a crash from the rear, the hover-car lurched forward, dipping its nose downward, and the interior lights flickered for a second. Some electronic coils were sparking in misalignment, and I began to smell ozone.

K steered the vehicle back into position, and accelerated. The pitch of the engine began to rise.

"Does this thing have any weapons?" I asked, eyes wide.

Another snowball exploded in front of us, and K pulled the controls back, gliding over the debris. She leaned forward, beads of sweat forming on her forehead. "Yeah, but, they're forward cannons," she said, "no turrets." She paused, clenching her jaw, and slammed the dashboard with her hand in frustration. A crack appeared where she'd hit. "Shit!"

I covered my cheeks with my hands, shaking my head. "Can you- can you try facing it head on?"

She looked at me like I was insane. Just then, the world outside appeared to darken, the thundering gallops almost upon us. And then I realized why.

K scanned the horizon, then flicked more switches with one motion of her hand. "Shit!" Metal panels slid over the front and side windows, and the noise from outside was muffled. The light from the snow-covered fields was choked out of the cockpit, and we were left illuminated only by the dim, flickering interior lights. The small emergency display flared to life, giving us a few narrow views from the cameras positioned on the vehicle's exterior, flickering in time with the lights. I leaned forward to get a closer view.

"This isn't good," said K, steering now by the display. We were completely in its shadow, and looking at the rear view camera, all I could see were the edges of four massive legs covered in dark fur, tailing us.

"Try changing direction!"

K curved left and right, trying to confuse the creature. The display was hard to view, as it flickered and swerved, but the thing was still right behind us. Eventually K stopped turning. She shook her head with a grunt.

She grimaced. "I-"

She squinted and raised one hand to her head, her face contorting in pain. The veins on her forehead were pulsing viciously.

"K?" I stammered, "K, what's wrong?!"

Boom. Boom.

She didn't respond, and her steering was becoming sluggish. The right facing camera went dark in a blur of motion, and I heard something heavy hit the side of the car. The vehicle groaned as the right half began tilting upward. K wasn't doing anything, her arms slowly becoming limp.

My heart was pounding, and my amber eyes darted between the display and the controls. Breathing heavily, I wrenched them from K's hands, and positioned the armature in front of me. I angled the ship to the left and started pulling up, breaking free from the thing's grip with a shudder, peeling away from it. My body shook as the car's front end bounced off the ground before levelling out again. The right camera was clear at last, but as I strained my eyes to see the display, I noticed to my horror that the front camera had been damaged when I collided with the ground. Static was all I could see.

K's face was blank, her eyes barely open, and she was motionless. I jostled her. "K?! Are you injured? K!"

A bolt of adrenaline hit my veins as I looked down at the rear camera, and noticed between flickers that the creature was upon me again. Its legs were spread so widely apart, it must have been gigantic. The booming sound of its steps only grew more terrifying as time went on.

Both hands firmly on the controls, I looked once more at K. In the flashes of light I could see something wet on the dashboard in front of her seat. I noticed thick blood trickling down from her forehead, her eyes closed. I couldn't tell if she was breathing. My chest felt constricted.

With one hand I covered my ear, and winced as the creature cried once more, this time deafeningly close. The ship dove downwards in a jolt as the monster must have pummelled its nose. The metal covering the windshield barely sustained the hit, and as the car leveled out once more my eyes landed on the energy cannon controls.

I took a deep breath in and started charging the weapon. The cannons began to hum in the eerie ambiance of the cockpit, punctuated by the creature's booming footfalls, and I glanced down at the emergency display. While I held the trigger for the guns, building up as much firepower as possible, I reangled the vehicle and watched carefully.

My heart skipped a beat. My body jerked forward, ears swinging, as I slammed on the breaks, launching the vehicle between the creature's legs. For a second the thundering was all around me, and the next I was tossed to the side in my seat, swerving out of control for a moment as the car clipped one of the monster's feet.

I held my breath. Flipping a switch, searing light filled the cockpit as the protective shield disengaged from the front window. I regained control of the ship, the hum of the cannons blaring, and when my eyes adjusted to the light I centered the creature in my view. It was gigantic and furred, with two pairs of legs and a long wide tail. Its body contorted upward almost like a centaur, and two lanky arms with black, webbed hands trailed at its side. It was skidding to a stop and rotating to face me, it's long head tilting like an owl. Four massive white eyes gazed at me and it screeched once more, revealing a set of pale-blue teeth, as long as swords, dripping with saliva. And in that moment, I fired.

I exhaled. The energy blast arced in a shining blue pellet toward the creature, bursting with a mighty crack on its body. The thing recoiled from the hit, smoke rising from the impact. But my vehicle was still moving toward it.

I steered away just in time to miss the monster's legs by a meter, then one of its hands came down from above and knocked my vehicle off course. The vehicle spun as I tried to break, losing altitude and skidding roughly in the snow to a halt.

The navi-system blinked innocently. After catching my breath for a few seconds, I deactivated the other blast protectors so I could see out all the windows. The creature was a fair distance away from me, on the left of the vehicle, and appeared to be motionless.

I closed my eyes, and rested my head on the controls for a second, trying to control my breathing. But a second later, my heart jumped.

"K?" I said, turning to her. She was sitting limply like a ragdoll.

I unbuckled my seat belt and reached under the dashboard, opening the emergency compartment, my heart still beating quickly. My long fingers frantically removed the adhesive bandages, and once I had one secured, with a cloth from the medical kit I wiped the blood from K's head. She had been bleeding from a patch of skin on the top-right of her head, but at a glance the wound didn't appear deep at all. Hastily, I slapped the bandage on her forehead.

I looked at the wet spot on the dashboard and in this light could determine it was blood. She must have hit her head on the dashboard the same moment the front camera broke.

I grabbed her hand, pressing my fingers to her wrist, feeling for a pulse. Her skin was too thick to detect anything, so I tried her neck. Her heart was beating steadily.

I let myself rest for a moment, knowing at least that she was alive, and tried to clear my head so I could better focus. *You are okay. You're alive.*

When I calmed down, I realized her head wound was probably not an issue, as alarming as it had been to see her bleeding. Though I wasn't sure about K's exact physiology, I knew from my education that humans bled disproportionately from head and scalp wounds compared to other parts of the body, due to the high concentration of blood vessels. She probably only suffered a minor cut. But why had she fallen unconscious?

I looked at her still body, breathing lightly, with a pained expression in my eyes. I rested my gaze on her face.

She opened her eyes, and blinked. "Mm… what…"

My eyes lit up. "K! Are you alright?"

She sat up slowly, looking around. "Wh- where... what happened?" She looked confused. A second later fear crept onto her face, and she looked me in the eye. She said to me, "Are you hurt?"

I shook my head slowly. "I got thrown around a bit, but I'm just a little shaken, that's all."

She closed her eyes again, her expression morphing from relief to frustration. She put her head in her hands. "So, you got us away from that thing."

"Yes." I said, looking out the left window at the creature's enormous body in the distance. K followed my gaze.

"Holy shit." she said under her breath, and for several seconds we sat in silence, the navi-system blinking softly.

She shifted in her seat, still gazing out the window away from me. The silence stretched on. The smell of ozone filled my nostrils. I turned back to her.

"Are you okay?" I asked once more. She turned to face me, her expression stern.

"Yeah, I'm okay. Let's keep going." She reached across my front and swung the control armature back to her side, and without a second thought engaged the hover systems. The car stuttered for a second, before lifting up a few feet off the ground, as it should, and leveling out. Her eyes glanced down to the navi-system.

"Wait," I said, gesturing to her. "You- You really think you should drive?"

"You got a problem with that?!" She whipped her head around to face me as she said this, and glared at me. My ears recoiled.

The bandage I'd tried to apply to her dangled in front of her eye. In my rush to help her I had misplaced it across some of her horns. She tore it off and stared at it, before throwing it to the floor of the cockpit and looking forward. "I'm fine," she said gruffly. Her eyes trailed down to the crack on the dashboard she had caused during the chase, and I noticed her body tense. So did mine.

She said at last, "We're closer to the ruins than the station. May as well make this trip worth it."

I hesitated, and in that moment K spun the vehicle around, and began speeding off toward the point on the navi-system. I decided to save my breath for now, but I was very conscious to buckle in my seat belt.

Eight

I trotted over ancient debris in the dim light. Each time my foot knocked aside a broken rock, each time I took a step, sand-coloured dust rose in a slow, billowing plume, accompanied by the crisp sound of crumbling stone which echoed in the dark cavern. We each wore a headlamp, and our holo-gauntlets were equipped with flashlights. The dust seemed to glow in the cones of light we emitted as we traversed the depths of the ruins. We had no reason to believe there was anything dangerous within the ruins, aside from Joëlle's suspicions about the valicorr, but we hadn't seen any signs of them outside the site. I decided not to tell K about her theory, because she didn't seem to want to talk, and Joëlle herself had said nothing was certain. Even so, since our encounter with the beast in the snow fields was still fresh on our minds, K strode around with her molecular great sword in her hands, extended and ready for battle. The blade was thick, and at least a foot wide. It looked like I could stand on its edge in a full suit of power armour and it wouldn't break. The sword looked unreasonably heavy, but K held it as though it was nothing. She was avoiding eye contact with me.

I stopped for a moment and looked around at our dark surroundings. We were deep underground, which I was used to. Many loro sites were built into the ground, often using materials such as stone or clay in favour of more advanced metals and alloys. This perplexed many scientists; why would they intentionally forego sturdier, more reliable materials in favour of more natural building blocks? No one had a clear answer, but it was evident in the carvings on the walls that these structures served some kind of artistic and perhaps spiritual purpose, that might not be the same with more advanced technology. My people had created similar monuments in our early history, using wall carvings to depict the rise and fall of leaders, and heroes, and to tell stories of loss and of victory. I was lucky enough to visit some sites on Earth which were similar to the loro ruins as well. It seemed primitive to us, humans and skythers, because such carvings reminded us of our history, when technologically we were less advanced. But I knew to presume the loro as primitive would be foolish. Their same symbols, their same architecture and statues spanned several star systems, and that was only what we had discovered. We had discovered some of their computers, though always with a fair amount of memory corruption. How many more sites had these people stood upon? They had once traveled the stars, and they had stories to tell.

Most of the inscriptions and carvings on the walls were damaged, either partially or completely, due to age. I was hoping to find a database I could access somewhere within the ruins, though not all loro remnants housed one. But my mind was hardly focused on the ruins, as wondrous and mysterious as they were. A more urgent mystery was on my mind.

I inspected K once more. She seemed to be doing fine, if distant. She had donned a thick fur suit which had been stored in the hover-car. I took note that the cut on her forehead was already hardly visible. She caught me staring at her, and I turned away, continuing down the uneven stone floor.

I was wearing a thermal outfit to keep warm, but the water vapor from each breath of mine condensed and dispersed into the chasm. I glanced back at K, who was now looking the other direction at the walls. I counted the time between her breaths by each wisp from her lungs- around seventeen breaths per minute, I guessed. That seemed to be within a normal range.

"What are you looking at?" She spun around, her sword trailing behind her.

"I-" I looked away, but quickly looked back, knowing that it wouldn't solve anything. "I'm making sure you're okay."

She snorted, and looked away. "Well, I am okay. So, drop it." Despite her hostility, looking at her eyes, I thought I could sense sadness, not aggression.

I obliged, and we continued on in silence for a while, until we entered a large chamber. I recognized this type of architecture. As we stepped inside, shining flashlights on the intricately carved walls and pillars, I led the way toward the center of the cylindrical hall. Wide stone steps led up to a large pillar in the center of the room, and eagerly I clamoured up to it.

When I reached the base of the pillar in the center my headlamp illuminated a metal panel on the wall. I wracked my brain for a moment as K caught up behind me. I remembered the symbols on the buttons from my studies, and began punching in commands. Each button press was accompanied by an electronic beeping sound, which echoed calmly in the chamber. After a few button presses, a green light emanated from the terminal, and just as I had predicted, began tracing it's way up the pillar in the grooves of the carvings, spreading out like water flowing through canals as it spilled over into every etched detail on the ceiling and walls. When the light reached the tops of the other pillars, as it passed by them it began snaking down each one until the darkness of the room was expelled completely by the now luminescent walls, pillars, and ceiling. The lights were dim enough as to not be blinding, but since the green glow came from all directions, the room was now well enough lit that even the far end could be seen.

K had been staring in awe as the light spread and now that it had completed its activation, she turned to face me, wonder in her eyes. "Whoa."

I lifted my ears in joy. Wonders like these were what had drawn me into the loro research community. I remembered the first time I encountered a control room like this, with other researchers at a loro site on Ki-Luum. I was speechless for a long while, and not much help to the others, honestly.

I pulled out a device from a compartment on my armour, and began searching the terminal for a port.

"What's that?" said K.

"It's a device for interfacing directly with loro computers. Thankfully, in our research we discovered they had their own universal design for data ports."

K just nodded slowly, looking confused.

"Once we figured that out..." I grunted, straining to pull off a panel which had become stuck closed, presumably after ages of being left alone to slowly warp and contract underneath the main buttons. K stepped forward and gestured for me to move aside, so I did.

I watched curiously as she knelt down, reaching a horned blue hand to the panel, turquoise in the light, and with one effortless motion pulled the panel off. Normally it would have swung open, if it were working correctly, but with a crack the entire thing came off, as easily as if K had simply brushed aside a pebble. She stood up, awkwardly holding the panel, and stepped aside looking at me. "You were saying?" she said.

"Ah, thank you." I stepped forward, and knelt down, holding up the device so K could see. "Once we figured out that they had a universally designed physical interface, it was just up to the researchers to design a device that would be able to, well, interface with it. So they came up with this." I plugged the device into one of the slots hidden behind the terminal, and it generated a blue hologram, displaying some text using skyther symbology.

I stood up and brushed some sand and dust off my legs. "That should copy any uncorrupted data from the computer to itself. It'll take some time, but from there, it can be downloaded onto another computer, for further study."

"Cool." said K, though I noticed the wonder and interest fading from her face. She turned around, taking in the surroundings of the strange, luminescent room. She breathed deeply and tossed the panel gently down the stairs where it bounced with a clank.

I looked back at the hologram, which told me it would be a while until the process was done. I walked over beside K and sat down, looking up at her. She glanced down at me, and sat on the stair as well. She was frowning in the silence.

I scanned the room, trying to think of what to say, but she spoke first.

"So, Osax." She sat with her sword resting between her legs and across her shoulder.

"Yes?"

"These loro guys, I guess they're all… gone now."

I nodded, looking at her, though she was staring down the steps. She continued.

"How long do you think it took them to build this place?"

I paused, trying to make an estimate. I wasn't really an architect and I knew little about construction. "I'm not sure. I suppose it all depends on their tools, how many people were involved... But it probably took them quite some time, given the detail." I looked up at the ceiling, noticing the intricate glowing artwork depicting a four-armed loro standing on their digitigrade legs, battling some kind of creature with a whip-like weapon. The creature looked similar to the one that had just tried to kill us outside.

I pointed up at the image. "Look, that creature- it looks similar to the one we encountered in the snow, only smaller! They must have been here for countless generations."

K strained her eyes to see. "Huh." After seeing the picture, she lowered her head.

I waited, staring at her.

She didn't look to me. Humans were puzzling.

I took a deep breath. "K," I said at last, "you fainted just a while ago. It could have been caused by any number of things, but I get the feeling you already know the cause."

She remained silent, tightening her jaw.

"Why won't you tell me?" I said, and then a brief moment later I felt my fists clench. "Why won't anyone tell me anything on this damn planet!" I was surprised to hear myself so agitated. Apparently, skythers were puzzling too.

She shot me a look, still frowning. "Why do you care?" The question seemed genuine.

I wasn't sure how to respond. "We almost died. And that's partly because of whatever your condition is that caused you to faint." I wasn't trying to accuse her, and I wasn't even sure that was why I was curious. In fact, I knew her fainting hadn't really put us in much more danger than we were already in. I simply was curious about her… but how could I explain that? Shouldn't every feeling, every thought have an explainable, justified cause? And if not, then what?

She shot back angrily. "Hey, it's not like I decided to faint! It's not like I decided to be like this!" She stood up as she spoke, staring at me with unmasked anger, gesturing to herself. Then she pointed at me. "You're alive!" She yelled. "Isn't that good enough for you?!"

I stood up slowly, my arms raised defensively. "Hey," I said calmly. "I'm sorry, I wasn't trying to agitate you."

"Well nice job!" She spun around and walked a ways down the steps. I followed slowly.

"K-"

"Why do you care?" She whipped around, orange eyes almost glowing. "Why do you care about any of this? None of it is going to last!"

"I…" I hesitated, not quite sure what she meant. I guessed she was referring to the ruins. "It will last if we preserve it." I motioned to the interface device.

She shook her head. "Osax, you don't understand."

"No, I don't," I confessed. "So will you enlighten me? What's going on? You're a bio-weapon, but how did you get here on Voren, working as a mercenary at a classified TAU station? Who found you? Why are you inexplicably fainting? How long has that been happening?" I paused for a moment, K's eyes narrowing at me. "And you bled so easily, for a weapon. Why didn't your creators just make a combat robot? Why did they make *you?*" My words cut through the air, leaving a vacuum.

Holding her sword in one hand, K ground her teeth, took a step closer to one of the pillars, and tightened her fist. "I. Don't. KNOW!"

My heart skipped a beat. In a blur of motion her spiked fist collided with the pillar. Instantly, a large segment of the pillar cracked and discharged away from K, slamming against the wall in an explosion of dust and debris. Luminous green fluid began spilling out from the ceiling and out of the pillar, and the whole room shook. A second later, the top of the pillar began collapsing in chunks, and a strange odour began filling the room. K stepped back from the pillar, disbelieving, and I lunged for the interface device.

My heart was pounding, the light in the room slowly pouring out of the ceiling and down the stairs. Everything shook and I heard the echoing sounds of stone collapsing. The hologram told me the transfer was 85% complete. If I disengaged now I might corrupt the files.

I glanced back at K, who was staring up at the ceiling and staggering backwards. I caught a glimpse of her eyes for a moment, and she looked terrified. Cracks were spreading in the ceiling, and more of the glowing fluid began dripping down from them, along with columns of dust.

I looked back at the device. *87%.*

I heard K exclaim, "Goddammit!" I turned to face her and saw she was already at the exit. She glanced back at me. "What are you doing? Osax!"

My mind raced. I glanced back at the device. *88%.* I slammed my hand on the side of the central pillar as I knelt there. "Come on…" There was no way to know what knowledge this archive held. It could be the key to understanding why the loro disappeared, or how they advanced so far. It could be anything. I wasn't about to give up now. I wasn't about to screw this up.

I held my breath. I could feel my heartbeat.

The rumbling continued, and a drop of the green fluid splashed on my arm, but I kept staring at the hologram. *89%. 90%. 91%.*

I heard K's voice from the edge of the room. "Let's go! Grab it and run!"

I yelled back, "Go!" I didn't turn.

92%. As soon as it was complete, I would dash out of here. I thought about the mechanic who had harassed me in the vehicle bay, and my blood boiled. I needed to succeed. I was the right person for this job. I deserved this.

My eyes widened. There was an awful lot of fluid dripping onto me from the ceiling. I looked up.

I froze. The cracks had stretched out to the ceiling above me, and with a roaring crash a huge stone from the ceiling began hurtling toward me. I couldn't move away.

Suddenly dust burst from the center pillar, and debris fell all around me, but I wasn't crushed. When the dust cleared, protruding from the column several feet above me I saw K's molecular sword, shielding me from the falling debris. I spun around to face K, and saw her standing near the exit with her body forward and her arm to the side, following through on her throw. Electricity sparked from the pillar, and looking at the hologram I noticed it had turned to a red colour indicating a major error. After all that, everything was probably lost.

But I was alive. I pulled the device from the slot and sprinted down the stairs, almost slipping on the pooling, glowing liquid. To my surprise, K waited for me, and when I reached her we ran together through the dark ruins, headlamps and holo-lights guiding our way. A few moments later, I turned back, and saw the room's entrance collapse. And then, without another word, we continued, until we burst into the bright, icy world outside.

Nine

We could still hear the rumbling, leaning against the ice-lined hull of our hover-car, catching our breaths, panting heavily. Slowly the rumbling ceased, and I gazed toward the temple-like structure, half-collapsed from age, and now also from our meddling. Despite the size of the entrance and the surrounding obelisks, the snow was so thick that the sandy coloured stone was almost invisible. K's fur coat was picking up snow incredibly quickly, and she turned to me with a strange half-smile. I wasn't sure why she was smiling. A moment ago, she was so angry. She'd punched a pillar across the room. She had put us both in extreme danger, and likely destroyed any chance at recovering data from the ruins.

"I'm freezing like hell," she said. "Let's get inside."

I nodded, and we both opened our doors as the wind picked up and ice pelted our faces. We hurried inside and closed the doors, this time seated on opposite sides, the howling wind outside now muffled by the insulated hull.

I turned to her, my eyes narrowing, my breathing strained from the exertion and the cold. "Why are you smiling? We almost died," I said.

Her smile faded as she stared at me. "I- Because we escaped, that's why."

I continued, "The transfer device malfunctioned when your sword hit the pillar." I held the device in my hand, staring at it as my ears lowered. "I don't think it retrieved anything."

K's face hardened. "What the hell is wrong with you?" She glared at me. "I saved your life! And honestly, that was a pretty impressive throw."

I felt a pang of guilt, but I persisted. "You saved me, and it was very impressive," I conceded, "but you were the one who put me in danger in the first place."

She scoffed in disbelief. "Look, I may have caused the ruins to collapse. That was an accident. But I didn't save you from me, I saved you from you!"

I was silent. She continued.

"I didn't mean to make the ceiling collapse, but you *did* mean to stick around while it was happening. You could have run, but instead you stayed in the middle of a collapsing cave. And for what? Do you really care about research more than staying alive?"

She had a point. I had put myself at unnecessary risk.

As I pondered this, a hollowness filled my heart. I stared out at the frigid, barren wastes, and I felt guilt. I knew from my first encounter with K in the station that she had difficulty judging her own strength. I glanced down at the dashboard in front of me, my eyes landing on the crack from her hand. Of course she hadn't meant to destroy the ruins. Perhaps I was being unjustly harsh to K.

"I'm sorry," I said, "I was being unkind. I agitated you in the ruins, by prying too much. I am a curious person, and sometimes I can't help but be frustrated by secrets. You saved my life. Under any circumstances, that is worthy of my utmost gratitude." Despite her anger and recklessness, she put her own life in danger by staying around to make sure I got out. I bowed my head low. "Thank you, K."

K stared at me. "Yeah. Well, you're welcome." She scratched the back of her head. "Sorry I ruined the mission… and put you in danger."

I raised my head, and we sat in silence for a moment. After a few seconds, I decided to take the controls and the car came to life with a hum. The interior lights flickered. To my surprise I let out a laugh, and immediately my solemnity was replaced by gratitude for being alive.

"This mission has gone absolutely horribly," I said, smiling.

K let out a chuckle, rolling her eyes, and replied, "Yeah, glad you agree. Honestly, what the hell happened today?" She shook her head, amused at the absurdity of it all. "I mean that creature; no one ever told me the wildlife could get so massive on Voren. I honestly was not prepared for that. We should have been given a more well armed transport. Definitely with some gun turrets." She turned to me, her face puzzled. "How did you shoot that thing anyway, I never asked?"

I scanned the horizon as we sped onward. "I'll- I'll tell you later. It is strange though. Perhaps we were the first to encounter that creature since the facility was constructed."

K rubbed her chin. "Yeah, maybe. But, I don't know." She seemed to be gazing out into the distance. "Wouldn't someone have found at least some sign of those creatures? Shouldn't we all be driving around in tanks for safety?"

"You're right… a creature of that size and mass would leave its mark. Trails in the snow as wide and deep as this vehicle. But it's possible that the creature simply had never wandered close enough to the station to be noticed." I wasn't sure I was convincing myself. "Then again, this facility, it is impressive in scale. To construct and maintain such a place… this facility must have been in operation for several months, at the very least. Perhaps years. If we are to believe the Director that the loro ruins, all the way out here, were discovered by biologists, than we must assume that for as long as the station has been equipped with ground transports and thermal outfits, biologists from the station have been exploring the wastes outside, searching for signs of life." I turned to K, concerned. She mirrored my expression. "You'd think that they would have encountered such a creature…"

K looked away, clearly deep in thought. We kept driving for a few moments. Had the people at the station intentionally let us leave unprepared?

"Then again," I said, "that creature moved incredibly fast, faster than our hover craft's maximum velocity. Which means, it is capable of travelling great distances in a short time. So it's possible that until very recently, it was living too far away from the station for any away teams to catch wind of its existence, and only recently sprinted into the vicinity." I looked over to K, and brushed a sizable amount of snow off her coat. "Plus, we know how quickly the snow cover builds up out here. Any tracks, even massive ones, might be invisible within hours. In order to find its tracks, you'd need to be in exactly the right place during a very small window of time, unless the weather cleared up."

"It practically never does," said K. She looked a little uneasy. "You're probably right."

After a brief pause, I slapped my head, feeling silly. K looked at me, one spiked eyebrow raised.

"What?" she said.

I reached forward to the dashboard and began pressing some buttons. "The ship's communicator- we could have contacted the station at any time. I had completely forgotten about it. I should inform them of how the mission went; and maybe we can ask some questions."

K began to smile in a sly way, nodding along with me. "Aw yeah, let's get some answers. I'm tired of being left in the dark."

I felt empowered having K at my side. It was nice knowing I wasn't the only one who felt out of the loop, and also, having K with me might make my case stronger. How can you run an operation if your agents aren't being given all the information they need? The communicator began connecting, and I waited eagerly for someone to pick up. A flash of dread hit me when I remembered I'd have to explain that we destroyed the ruins… but I shook it off. I figured I could lessen that news by playing up how we were almost killed by that monster earlier. In fact, I wouldn't really need to exaggerate anything.

K's arm shot out and canceled the call. I spun to face her, and noticed a franticness in her eyes. "Don't- don't tell them I fainted," she pleaded. I hesitated, before nodding. I wanted desperately to ask her about that, but considering how it went last time, I decided to wait. Her breathing slowed and she relaxed in her seat a bit. "Knew I could count on you, Sax."

"Please don't call me that." I said, though my ears were smiling.

"Okay O," she said, the smile returning to her face. "'O' 'K'."

"Just call me Osax, K."

"Was that like, 'K', or like, 'kay?'"

I turned and punched her arm, jokingly. Then she, laughing, punched me back. I could tell she was trying very hard to do it lightly.

Nevertheless, my heart raced as I tried to regain control of the vehicle. We swerved several meters off course with a jolt. After a second, K laughed heartily.

"Whoops!"

"Just let me drive."

"Hey, if you punched me and I was driving, we'd still be gliding straight as an arrow." Her smirk was charming. She had so much life in her, but I couldn't always understand where that energy was being directed. She held a lot of anger and resentment, and it seemed as though she was far more comfortable joking around than letting herself be vulnerable.

I realized that was true for me too.

"Seriously though," she said, "can I drive?"

I was concerned I'd have to take over for her, in case she started to faint again. I looked at the longing in her eyes. She really wanted this.

I moved the armature over to her side, and she grabbed the controls eagerly, the fire returning to her eyes. No sooner than she held the controls did we accelerate to our top speed. I had to hold onto my seat while we were accelerating, but once we hit our maximum velocity, I punched in the communication code and waited for the call to connect.

Beep. Beep. Beep.

It was taking longer than I would have expected for this kind of planetary comms device. I turned to K.

"Does it always take this long to connect?"

Just then the communicator flashed crimson. "Unable to connect." The computerized voice continued. "Unknown Error. Make sure you are using the correct code. If the error persists, try resetting your device." It continued to drone on, repeating the error message, until I shut it off. I tried again, but to no avail.

K looked at me. "Maybe it got damaged when we were running from that thing?"

"Maybe..."

Just then, something dark blotted out the sun above us for a second. I craned my neck to peer out the front window. It was something flying across the sky, some kind of bird perhaps, headed the same direction as us.

I caught sight of a tiny trail of light behind it, and realized it must have been a spaceship of some kind. It kept flying steadily ahead of us.

"Did you see that?" I said to K. She shook her head.

"No, what?"

"Some kind of ship, flying toward the station!" She stared at me. "I wonder what it was..."

Then I remembered Joëlle's warning, and my mind began to race. A mysterious ship was spotted in the system just weeks ago. Apparently it was larger than anything she'd ever seen. Looking up into the sky, I had no way of judging the ship's size. But its appearance was somehow foreboding. I couldn't really make anything out, but I felt uneasy.

"We'd better hurry back, just in case."

"Well, I'm already going top speed. We'll get there when we do." K looked at me. "You don't think... it's valicorr, do you?"

I shook my head. "No, of course not." My ears folded back and I began twiddling my thumbs. "I'm sure it's just another TAU ship."

K obviously didn't believe me, but she didn't ask any more questions. She did however mutter to herself, "Wish I still had my sword..."

And after that, we drove on through the snow.

I liked her. Maybe every emotion didn't need a logical explanation after all. At the very least, I was starting to think that my quest for logical emotions was in vain- something I should have realized long ago, given the blatant contradiction of words. Even if some emotions came from evolutionary roots which I could justify, I knew well enough that they often manifested in unusual ways. But the desire for companionship was almost universal, at least it was shared between skythers and humans. I hoped when we got back that K and I would spend the evening sipping root beer and laughing about the day, getting to know each other better. But somehow, I didn't think that would happen. My eyes trained on the black shape in the sky, getting slowly smaller, drifting into the distance ahead of us. Things were about to change.

Ten

It's a good thing the navi-system was still working after our craft took damage. On our way back, a thick storm blew in and before we could reach the facility the snow got so thick that we could barely see ten meters ahead of us. Without the navi-system, not only would we have been lost, but we wouldn't have been able to call for help since the comms were malfunctioning. The craft was built to survive in such conditions, thankfully, and we decided to activate the external heating, even though it was a drain on power, so that the hull remained above zero degrees and we didn't get frozen inside. After driving for a while the smell of ozone became stronger, which was unpleasant. It indicated something was overheating, but there wasn't much chance of us conducting any repairs, at least not out in the snow. We'd likely freeze before making any progress, and if we accidentally made things worse we might not have had the vehicle to seek refuge in from the elements.

When the conditions got bad enough that our visibility was significantly affected, I told K she'd better slow down, just in case we ran into another unexpected object, or creature. She obliged, begrudgingly, but after a while seemed to lose interest in driving altogether and passed the controls over to me. For a long while I piloted the hover-car, mostly in silence, as the sun began to set. K fiddled with the audio system, which I had failed to notice, and began playing some quiet music in the background. It sounded like jazz.

I considered how K's presence hadn't actually kept me safe in any way; quite the opposite in fact. She had destroyed the ruins, and likely damaged any information my device had attempted to retrieve, though I hadn't actually checked yet. And she had damaged the car as well, though only minorly. Yet, looking at her sitting beside me, unnatural eyes gazing into the fog of the storm, I felt comfort in our companionship. She was misunderstood. Outcast. And from my years on Earth, I could relate to that.

She shot me a glance, her eyes matching the orange glow of the sunset, diffused by the fog, and I wondered what she was thinking. She showed a small smile, and I felt contented.

I found myself wondering about her fainting, and what might have caused it. She appeared to be in pain just before passing out from some kind of head trauma. But there was no obvious cause for her symptoms. Perhaps this was just something she lived with, being a biologically-engineered creature. I had no way of knowing what was normal for her; there were no other K's I could point to for reference. I was aware that some brain conditions in humans could cause unpredictable seizures. I suppose this was similar, in a way.

It could have been a product of the high stress situation we were in at the time. Once again, it made me question why she had been created. She should be equally, if not more effective in high stress situations than a human. And, spontaneous fainting is a particularly undesirable trait for a soldier. It's entirely likely she didn't meet her creators' vision, whatever that was.

I shook my head to myself. Of course she didn't come out as intended, or she wouldn't have broken free from her lab restraints as the Director had told me. And no one in their right mind would create a weapon with such emotions.

All that considered, she was unreasonably strong. No robot of equivalent size should have been able to demolish that pillar with such force, not even with a full body slam. All it took from her was a single punch. I was beginning to think my theory about the strength of the myroks was correct. Maybe the scientists who created her had somehow gathered samples from the planet Malum, and used myrok genes in her creation, in attempt to replicate their disproportionate strength. They would have needed to retrieve samples from the caves of Malum, in which myroks took shelter from the heat of the planet's surface. Whatever they did, they succeeded. Her strength was incomprehensible considering her mass.

"What are you thinking about?" asked K. Despite her being at the forefront of my mind, I had almost forgotten she was there.

We drove on through the sunset coloured fog and snow, as a calm trombone solo played in the background.

I cleared my throat. "I'm thinking about the people who created you."

Her face was solemn, and she stayed quiet. After a moment she replied, "Well, what about them?"

"Hm…" I kept my eyes forward. "Well, they must have been crazy to think they could control you." She actually grinned at this.

"Yeah, that's true. I don't remember much before the TAU found me… but I'm sure it wasn't pretty for my 'parents.'" She folded her arms behind her head. "You can't contain this. I'm a free agent."

I chuckled. I had expected this conversation to go worse; this was a good start. "So, what's your earliest memory?"

She tilted her head to the side, a look of intense concentration on her face. "I guess the earliest memory I have, I'm sitting in a white room. There's a glass wall, and people are watching me on the other side of it. I'm fully grown but, I don't know what anything is. I hear people talking about something but I can't understand any of it. I think I'm wearing a jumpsuit." She scrunched up her face.

"That sounds interesting." I waited for her to continue.

"Yeah. I guess. Eventually, somebody comes in. I think they're wearing a lab coat, and they've got dark hair, and a headset, or visor, or something, and they bring me some food. I remember it tasted awful, but I was really hungry. Everybody was talking quietly, but urgently. I looked at them, and they looked away from me. I tried saying some things to them, but they just stood there, staring…"

"These were the TAU people who found you?"

She nodded slowly. "Yeah, I think. Eventually everyone started walking away, leaving me alone, and I got scared. When they closed the door, I just punched through the glass wall. They started freaking out, which just made me more scared. I- I didn't know what to do."

"What did you do?" I asked.

"Well," she sighed, "I didn't really do anything. Some more people came in, kept me company. I calmed down eventually. I felt like they were going to abandon me, but I remember they kept someone near at all times after that."

"That's good," I said, my mind stretching to imagine what that must have been like.

"What about you?" She asked. "What's your earliest memory?"

I hesitated. "I'm not sure…"

"Come on, Sax-O. I just told you mine."

I gave her a nudge with my elbow and my ears twitched up. "That's not my name, *Ayk*."

"'Ayk'? Where'd you get that name?" She smirked.

"It seemed like fair play," I said. I kept my eyes on the horizon and exhaled. "I don't know if it's my earliest memory, but it's one of them. I'm not totally sure, but I think I was maybe two, or three cycles old. We were sitting in the shadow of the floating spheres above the Great Temple, on Astraloth. Way beneath them, at a park, at the base of the temple."

"We? Who?" K asked.

"My guardian and I. I guess she had taken me out to the park to play."

"Is that all you remember?" K asked.

"No," I said. "There were other families there. Skyther parents conversing as their children ran across the grass and leaped up onto large stones. A ball was being tossed around."

K leaned forward. "What were you doing?"

"I wasn't playing... just ripping up the grass. None of the other children approached me."

"Why not?"

I shook my head. "I think they were all terrified of my caretaker."

"Why? Was she mean?" K asked.

"Well- No, she wasn't mean- a little cold, maybe- just... she was my babysitter, I guess. But she was hired by my mother, who was... very powerful, to say the least. My family is... I don't like talking about it, because I find it changes people's perspective of me- I like to be seen for who I am, not my blood- but my family is kind of... a big deal."

"Fair enough," said K. "I think... I kinda get that. Wanting to be seen for who you are."

I lifted my ears a little.

"Well," she continued, "what else do you remember?"

My ears drooped. "Well, as I was sitting I remember I looked across the field. In the distance I saw a group of young skythers following someone even younger. My eyes were fixed on them as they closed the gap on this terrified boy." Unconsciously, I gripped the controls of our vehicle tighter. "They started shoving him, pushing him around..."

K was watching me silently.

"They were right next to an old building. I think they pushed him inside, or maybe they were pushing him behind a corner... And I just remember being so confused... and scared. I guess I was wondering what they were doing? And why they were hurting him. But I didn't have the words to understand.

"My guardian was telling me about the great floating spheres above the temple, and how they supposedly held the power to protect Astraloth.

That the spheres contained the energy to shield Astraloth from harm. That with the spheres, not even time could destroy Astraloth. But if they had some magic power to protect Astraloth, why couldn't they help out that poor boy?

"I thought someone would help; I thought one of the parents at the park would notice and protect him. But when I looked around, they were just talking. The children were laughing and playing and yelling and having fun. And no one saw them disappear, except for me."

"Did you do something?" asked K.

"I started crying, and my guardian came over to me. She picked me up and spoke to me, asking me what was wrong. The more I began to sob the more worried she became, and pretty soon she was carrying me back home to the temple. But as she pulled me away I lost even more control. No one knew what was happening, no one saw the boy or, I guess they were a gang, and I couldn't do anything to help him. He was getting hurt, and I couldn't do anything.

"I couldn't sleep that night. I was just terrified- Not of being hurt, but of watching as someone else was. I was terrified that those skythers were still shoving him around, beating him up, hurting him. And every time I started calming down, and the tears started going away, I thought he might still be in pain. He might be getting hurt right now. He might be crying right now, as I'm trying to relax and get some sleep.

"I couldn't ignore it. For the next few weeks I thought about it every day. I couldn't have fun anymore. I felt like no one was noticing the things that were going on in the Temple or around me. I was scared that no one was noticing. I felt so small and powerless and insignificant. Everyone was just acting normal, like nothing had happened, like they had no responsibility, like it didn't matter..."

"Why didn't you explain what was happening?" asked K. She looked perplexed.

"I wanted to, but I couldn't. I… was a late talker, I guess. It took me longer than most skythers to start talking."

"Really?" asked K. "I find that hard to believe." She snorted and shuffled in her seat. "How long ago did this happen?"

"Over twenty cycles ago, that's for sure. Maybe twenty-three."

We sat in silence, and I appreciated the calm nature of the Earth music playing on our speakers. It helped take me out of those memories.

I wanted to change the subject, so I asked K, "How about you? Do you remember when you were in that white room and broke the glass?"

"Around a year ago."

My mandibles dropped, and I caught myself staring at her, dumbfounded. Her earliest memory, before she could even speak, was less than a cycle ago? She couldn't have been much more than a cycle old, in that case, unless she suffered from significant memory loss.

"You-" I struggled to find the words. "You must have learned everything so quickly!"

She exhaled, and nodded. "Yeah. When I started being able to understand words, the people looking after me told me that my growth was incredibly accelerated. I was able to learn things super fast, but my brain couldn't handle all of it. It took a long time for my memories to stabilize, so, I don't remember much about growing up. In fact most of my memories are after I chose to become a mercenary."

"What made you choose that, anyway? You could have done anything."

She shook her head. "Not really. I was always breaking things, and around when my memories began to stabilize, my learning slowed down a lot. I still probably learn faster than most people, but it's not fast enough for me to pursue something else. Fighting, reflexes, athletics- They come naturally to me. And besides, they needed people to go protect away teams and such. It was a logical way to help out and feel useful at home."

I lifted my ears in surprise. "Voren- This planet is- You've lived your whole life at this station?"

She nodded. I couldn't believe it, but she continued nonchalantly.

"Yep. Surprised you didn't hear that from someone back at the base. I was brought here after the TAU found me."

My mind was racing. "So, you've never seen a forest? Or an ocean? Or a moon? You've never been on a spaceship?"

She looked at me like I was clueless, and replied, "No, I've never been on a spaceship, but I know what a forest looks like. I was given a lot of learning material in my youth."

It seemed strange that someone less than a cycle old could have a youth at all, but under the circumstances I understood it.

"Then, how long ago did you decide to become a mercenary?"

"Around eight months. Hey, watch where you're driving, okay?"

I stopped staring at her, but I was shocked. Her stream of consistent memory only lasted zero point five cycles. She'd been alive for maybe a cycle. I had lived around twenty-six times longer than her, which I found hard to believe.

"Well, I'm glad the sound system wasn't damaged," said K, relaxing in her seat once more.

I nodded slowly, and let the smooth jazz piano fill the ambience. Despite being incredibly strong, she was so young, and this facility was her only home. My mind returned Joëlle's warning and the mysterious ship I had seen in the sky, and I could only hope that her home was safe.

It wasn't.

Eleven

"Why haven't they let us in?"

We were idling a mere five meters from the doors of the vehicle bay, at the base of the massive cliff on which the facility was built. Because we were driving slowly, by the time we arrived the sun had set, and the snow had almost stopped falling. The fog was thick, pierced only by the cones of light angled down at us from above the metal bay doors, and our own headlights. I turned off the music and tried the comms system once more, for good measure.

Beep. Beep. Beep.

K looked at me, concerned.

"Unable to connect. Unknown Error. Make sure you are using the correct-"

I shut off the comms device and sighed. Something was wrong. My body was tensing.

I unbuckled my seat belt, and said to K, "I'm going to get out, and see if I can determine anything." She nodded, and started doing the same.

We stepped out of the vehicle into the freezing fog. Looking behind us, I could only see a few meters into the distance before the snow faded into a black veil of mist. In front, the overhead lights provided some much needed illumination, but looking up the cliff I couldn't see much higher than the light fixtures. On a clear night, this would have been a beautiful, open space, but now, it felt claustrophobic. We left the hover-car idling, hovering a few feet off the ground, and pointing its lights at the frozen doors.

K folded her fur coat over herself, and we both crunched through the snow until we reached the doors. We shared a glance, and then I knocked on the massive vehicle doors with my hand. Each hit reverberated along the metal sheet.

"Hello?" I had no idea if they would be able to hear us, but I thought it was worth a try.

We waited for a response, but all we could hear was the moaning wind as it whistled past the cliff. K grunted.

She was clutching the side of her head with her hand, eyes closed.

"Are you okay?" I asked.

She nodded slowly, looking at me. "Just- Just a headache."

I gazed back into the dark snowfields and felt my heart rate increasing steadily. I remembered the sound of the creature in the snow, howling, and my ears twitched. "We should get inside as soon as possible."

K, rubbing the pale blue ridge on her forehead, asked hesitantly, "Do you think they're... okay in there?"

"I..." I trailed off. Her eyes were full of fear. "I'm sure it's just a malfunction with the vehicle bay camera system. Combine that with our faulty comms system, and we just need to find a way to communicate with them through the door." I continued knocking on the door, and calling out.

There was a sound from inside. Something shrill, echoing through the chamber. I could barely make it out.

"What was that?" asked K.

There was the sound again, this time louder, and followed by the unmistakable sound of an E-gun blast. Then all was silent.

"We have to get inside, now!" said K. She squatted to the ground, and tried finding a place to grab the door and lift it. Not finding anything, she took both fists, and punched two large indents into the door with a clank, using those spots to get started.

I watched in awe as in her desperation she clenched her jaw, and began slowly lifting the door. It must have weighed at least 500 pounds, and it might have weighed significantly more. Once she got it high enough, she positioned her body under it, and motioned with her head for me to step inside. I drew my E-pistol and it flared to life with a brief electronic whir, a dim red glow emanating from the barrel. I crouched low to get under the door, and felt a wave of heat hit me as I stepped inside. My mandibles dropped, my arms limp at my side, and my heart began pounding.

With a thunderous crash, the door closed behind us, and K stood up next to me, clutching her head, clearly in pain. When her eyes adjusted to the sight, she stood motionless too.

It was chaos. The main lights were inactive, red emergency lights blaring. An alarm could be heard faintly crackling through damaged speakers in the far side of the room. Massive vehicles were turned over, and the floor and walls were scorched and misshapen from energy blasts and explosions. Oil fires were burning all over the room, and in the dim lighting, I could make out bodies of technicians and mechanics strewn about. Some of them were thrown atop supply crates and vehicles, with smoke rising from their bodies. One was leaning over the controls of a hover-lift; she had been driving it around when the attack started.

I started walking through the middle of the room, slowly. Fire crackled and warmed my skin, and I could smell burning rubber. The bodies were all human, and they all wore TAU outfits. I stood in the middle of the room, scanning the carnage, E-pistol in hand.

K, with a great deal of difficulty, made her way over to me. She was still clutching her head. "Osax…" she said, shaking her head in disbelief. "What happened?"

I knelt down next to one of the bodies, and started examining it. His eyes were wide open in surprise, and his clothes and the floor were wet with blood. He had no weapons on him. My body trembled.

I stood up, and my eyes caught the reflection of firelight in a pool of liquid. It wasn't oil, or blood, at least not human blood. It was a thick, greenish colour. I activated my holo-gauntlet, and began scanning the substance, though I was almost certain I already knew what it was. My hand quivered, and I hoped I was wrong.

K walked past me. "I'm going to head for the elevators. We need to get to the control room."

I spun around. "K, wait! It could be dangerous!"

"It will be. But I'm not wasting time!"

"Alright. I'll be right behind you." I turned back to the substance, as K jogged her way to the exit and left the room.

My holo-gauntlet was analyzing the data. Comparing it to known substances. And with a beep, it was done.

I stood up quickly, alone in the dead room, my heart racing. I was breathing fast. That was valicorr blood. Of course it was; who else would have done this?

I jumped, and whirled around, my gun trained on a hover-lift several meters away from me. Something was moaning, and it was coming from that direction. I looked toward the exit of the room, where K had gone. *I should follow her…*

I turned back to the moaning. Cautiously, I stepped around an oil fire, over a smouldering body, towards the broken hover-lift. The moaning grew louder as I got closer and closer, my pistol aimed shakily at the vehicle.

I started pacing around the lift, trying to be as silent as I could with my breathing.

Suddenly, a burst of red light shot out from behind the lift. The silence broke with an energy blast and a startled scream, and I clasped my shoulder. I let out a skyther curse. Searing pain shot through my right arm and I dropped my pistol clamouring to the floor. The gunshot grazed me, and my thermal suit had torn off at the shoulder.

I fell to the floor and exclaimed. My eyes were staring down the barrel of an E-gun. The man's lower half was stuck, crushed under the weight of the broken hover-lift. His body was twisted to the right to face me. His left arm was trying in vain to move the lift, his right holding the gun. His TAU-blue outfit was covered in oil, and his face was lined with short stubble, his hair beginning to grey-

I blinked, staring at his face in the red emergency lights and the glow of the fires. He was the mechanic who'd harassed me.

"Jesus!" he cried, holding the gun steady.

Wincing in pain, I let my right arm rest as best as I could, and cautiously raised my left arm. "It's okay-" I closed my eyes, the pain in my shoulder flaring up. "I'm here to help."

"Get back!" His eyes were full of fear, beads of sweat on his face. "Get back or I'll shoot!"

I started slowly reaching my hand toward my E-pistol on the floor. In an instant, he blasted my pistol away with a gunshot.

"Whoa!" I yelled, raising my hand up in defense.

"You were reachin' for a gun!" he cried, his voice almost breaking.

I was beginning to sweat. "I wasn't going to shoot you! There might be more valicorr around!"

A metal crate tumbled behind me, and I turned to look. I couldn't see anything, but dread filled my chest.

I looked back at the man. "There's something else in here."

"How do I know you aren't on their side?!" I saw a tear drip down his cheek. He was shaking.

A blur of motion in my peripheral. I saw the shadow of something moving, cast on the wall by one of the flames. Then it was gone. The man turned his gun in the shadow's direction.

He was looking around frantically.

I noticed movement behind the hover-lift. I urged him, "Don't move!"

The man looked at me and hesitated, still trembling. There was a sound of movement from the other side of the hover-lift. I glanced behind me to see if I could find another weapon. There was an E-pistol, a few feet away from me, next to a scorched body. If I could just reach it...

Fear gripped me. Crawling over the hover lift, the dark shape of a figure slinked closer to the man. It had a thin body, and was around seven feet tall. It had six long fingers on each hand, and digitigrade legs with sharp talons. It wasn't holding any weapons that I could see, but horrifyingly, its jaw opened, revealing a set of needle-like teeth. The firelight reflected off of its three pitch black eyes.

I moved toward the gun, and the man yelled. "Don't move!"

I froze, my arm outstretched toward the gun, staring back at the man, and the thing, which was now leaning over him, mouth wide open. He was pointing his weapon at me. He hadn't noticed it yet. I was shaking, leaning on my injured arm.

"Above you!" I cried.

"Shut up, skiller!"

The creature leaned its mouth in closer to him. The man's gun was still trained on me. I couldn't take it anymore.

I lunged for the gun; my arm couldn't hold me, so I collapsed, now lying sideways on the floor. But the gun was in my hand.

The man fired a shot at me, but it soared overhead, missing by an inch. I fired at the creature and red energy bolts raced toward it. I hit one of its arms, but with a hiss it scampered aside behind a crate. The man, finally noticing it, screamed and tried desperately to get out from under the hover-lift.

With some difficulty, I stood up, and raised my gun toward the crate. I was still shaking a little. I heard the sound of what must have been an E-gun powering up. I started charging a bolt of energy and got ready to dash for cover, the tip of my pistol glowing brighter as the energy hummed.

In a flash of motion, the valicorr cried, leaping toward me over the crate, firing a spray of yellow energy bolts from an arm-mounted cannon. Their legs were powerful and allowed them to jump meters into the air. I vaulted over another crate and ducked, sparks bursting from the bullet impacts all around me.

I was breathing heavily. In front of me was a parked hover-lift. I could see the valicorr in the reflection of its smooth hull. It raised its arm cannon toward my cover, and from its other wrist, a shimmering red plasma blade appeared, as it took another step forward. The sword sparked and buzzed, and it hissed.

I shivered.

My weapon was beginning to overheat, the red glow intensifying. Sparks of red energy were flitting out of the barrel. I'd have to release the energy soon.

I saw the valicorr dash towards me in the reflection, and without thinking I rolled to the side.

The plasma sword sliced deep into the crate where I had been hiding. Noticing it missed, the valicorr angled its gun toward me. Summoning all my strength, I swung my right hand to knock its aim to the side as it fired three bullets of energy that ricocheted off the hover-lift.

I held my breath, and fired my weapon. A wide beam of energy impacted the alien, and it was blasted back several feet from the explosion. Its weapons powered down, smoke rising from its body. It was dead.

I stood there panting for a moment. My shoulder was still in a lot of pain from the mechanic's gun. I turned to face him, raising my ears. He was staring at me wide eyed, mouth open, still holding his gun in my general direction. I walked over to him, and he lowered his gun.

"You…" he tried to speak, but seemed to be having difficulty, tears welling in his eyes. I knelt down beside him.

"I'm here to help." I said, and then putting the gun down, tried to lift the vehicle off of him with both arms. My right arm seized with pain, and I had to take a break.

If only K hadn't gone ahead, I thought, and then I squatted next to the vehicle and hooked my hands under it again. I only needed to lift it enough for the man to crawl out.

My blood was pounding in my head as I lifted with every fiber of my being. The man was trying to lift too. We angled it up just enough that he started sliding his way out from underneath. I was straining to keep it lifted as he used his hands to crawl out.

At last he was free, and I dropped the hover-lift with a thud. I felt like my right arm was about to fall off.

The man tried to stand, and I helped him up. He was leaning against me for balance, and we stood amidst the wrecked, flaming vehicle bay. His legs didn't look too crushed, thankfully.

He spoke at last. "Th-Thank you." He wiped away some tears from his eyes, though he still looked to be in shock.

"Don't mention it," I said. For a moment, I felt anger for this man. He deserved my anger; but he also deserved my help. He was a living being. "I'm going up to the control room. Let's find someplace safe for you to hide."

"I…" he looked around the room, then back into my eyes. "I'd rather stick with you, ma'am."

"Actually, I'm male."

His cheeks flushed. "B-But your ear fur… I thought-"

"Male skythers can have ear fur."

"I- I didn't know."

I started leading us toward the exit, not before picking up the E-pistol again. "It's fine," I said, and then added, "You can call me Osax." *Osax?* I thought. I hadn't introduced myself as Osax since I was a child. I guessed that spending all day with K, such an informal person, reminded me that I liked the name. My thoughts drifted to my mother...

"I'm Waylon," said the man. He seemed to be calming down, which was good.

"Alright, Waylon," I said. I grimaced as I rubbed my shoulder, then tightened my grip on the pistol, narrowing my eyes. "To the control room."

Twelve

"There you are!" K looked relieved to see me, and my ears lifted.

"Talcorosax!" My eyes dashed to Joëlle, who'd been talking with K in the hall junction. She was wearing a helmet with a blue tinted T-shaped visor, but I recognized her voice and armour. "K was just about to go looking for you."

K turned to Waylon. "Who's this?" I noticed Joëlle raise an eyebrow in confusion through her visor when she recognized the mechanic, and him leaning against me for support.

"I'm Waylon. You've gotta be K, but who're you?" He gestured to Joëlle with his gun. I didn't think he was trying to be threatening; clearly he'd never learned proper gun protocol. I lowered his gun with my right hand, then winced.

Joëlle was about to speak, but K rushed over to me first. "Osax, you got shot! Are you okay?"

"I- I'm fine, I was only grazed." The pain was quite intense, and I struggled to keep it together.

Joëlle nodded at Waylon. "My name's Joëlle Weidman, I'm a Round Table operative." She was holding her E-rifle, keeping it aimed to the floor.

I jumped. A deep explosion was heard somewhere far above us in the structure, and the ground shook. Lights flickered, despite this hallway being relatively undamaged.

K had a grave expression, looking between all our faces. "Well, now that we've all gotten friendly, let's stop wasting time! We have to stop the attack!"

Joëlle turned to me, breathing quickly. "Talcorosax, you probably already guessed this, but we were right; it was a valicorr vessel! And it's here, at the station!"

A rush of adrenaline hit me. Even a small valicorr ship would have been a serious threat.

"K's right," I said, "we have to stop the attack, and that ship if possible." I looked to K's desperate expression. "We'll fix this."

◆

The elevators were offline, so K, Waylon, Joëlle and I made our way up the winding stairs. The glass wall let me stare out into the black night, but there wasn't much to see. The ground rumbled as we ran, and I stopped to grab onto the railing, and Waylon, so neither of us tumbled back down the steps. K turned to me to make sure I was alright, and then we continued. We were running as fast as we could.

A yellow laser bolt shot past us, and I tried to duck to the side. Before I could see what happened, Joëlle whipped her rifle to the target, and a smouldering space pirate collapsed to the floor across the hall. She signaled for us to keep going, and continued leading the way.

We turned a corner, and saw two valicorr; one of them was dragging the corpse of a third into a doorway leading to a landing pad. Valicorr never left their dead at the scene, if they could help it. No one knew exactly why, but most assumed it was to intimidate anyone who might arrive later at the site, and to hide how many attackers there had been.

When they saw us, they fired on us, and we all ducked back behind the wall, aside from K. I leaned around to get a shot, and managed to hit the one pulling the corpse right between its three eyes, killing it. K charged forward and let out a war cry. She punched her hand into the wall, violently tearing off a metal panel as she ran. Yellow bullets sparked off her chest armour, and my heart stuttered.

But she kept running, unscathed, and slammed the valicorr with the metal plate with so much force that its head broke through the panel, and it crumpled to the floor. K was breathing heavily, and clearly just getting started.

As we rounded the corner once more to follow her, she turned and sprinted toward the landing pad. When we got to the doorway and looked outside, I saw a purple valicorr dropship, hovering just above the platform. It was starting to take off, and K drew her pistol and began firing at it, non-stop. I leaned Waylon on the wall, and stepped onto the platform, shooting the dropship as it took off. Neither K's nor my blasts were effective, and K hurled her pistol after the ship in rage.

Joëlle stepped forward, and as she aimed her rifle at the ship, the sheets of metal shifted and it transformed into a shorter, wider shape. The gun lit up with red and blue lights, and began charging. The drop ship was getting smaller in the distance, but Joëlle knelt and braced her gun. I noticed behind her visor a tiny holographic targeting display lit up.

"Shoot it!" K pointed with so much force, I almost thought her finger would destroy the ship.

A second later, Joëlle fired the gun, and blue and red energy beams coiled around each other, piercing a hole through the ship. It exploded in flashes of fire, and tumbled down the cliffside.

K rocketed her fists up into the air. "Woohoo! Yes!" I heard Waylon cheering from the doorway.

Without pause, Joëlle lifted her hand to the side of her head, and began responding to some communications coming through her helmet. "Yes- The eastern tower, top floor? Can you climb down? They're at the doorway. I see. I'm headed there right now; we're going to try to regain control of the base and restore power. I'll send someone over. Hang in there, okay? Remember your training!" She paused. "Hold your ground, I'll get you out of there."

We were all staring at Joëlle, who stood, and led us back inside the base.

"What was that about?" I asked. I grabbed Waylon, and we began moving as fast as we could.

"The rest of my squad, they're under fire at the top of the eastern tower. They've got twenty valicorr coming up the stairs, and the elevators are down."

My ears peeled back in shock. "What are they doing up there? How badly are they outnumbered?"

"It's me and five other RTs, but one of them's badly hurt. Too hurt to fight. They were going to man the anti-aircraft battery positioned on the tower, try to take down the mothership which is flying high in the sky right now." She shook her head. "Problem is, the AA guns run off the station's power, and that's down right now, so they can't even use it." She skidded to a halt as we met yet another junction. The four of us exchanged glances. "If you take this right, the hallway should lead toward the eastern tower."

The stations shook again from another explosion. I blinked, and stared at Joëlle. "What are you saying?"

She took off her helmet, purple locks spilling out, and looked me in the eye. "You're clearly trained in combat, Talcorosax. I need you to head over there, buy them some time. K and I will head to the control room, and bring back the power."

My body was full of adrenaline, and I nodded.

K glared at Joëlle. "Who said you were the one in charge?"

"You're a mercenary. It's your job to follow orders. We can't reach the Active Director, so I'm the highest rank here."

"But you don't even work here!" K spat.

"Stop complaining! I know what I'm doing, and if you want to save the station, then you should help!"

"You shouldn't order Osax around! Just because he's a skyther-"

"It's not because he's a skyther!" Joëlle shot back.

I stepped between them. "It's okay, I agree with the plan." *I can do this.*

"What about me?" asked Waylon, his eyes full of fear. K rolled her eyes, and marched over to us.

"I can carry you; you'll be just as safe with us." She wrapped an arm around him and hefted him up to her side with ease. Waylon cried in surprise.

I turned to him. "Don't worry. K will keep you safe." I turned to K, and looked her in the eye. "Right, K?"

She snorted, and gave me a smirk.

Joëlle shot K a glance. "You *will* be careful with him, right?"

K raised an eyebrow at her. "Yes sir." She saluted her lazily with one hand.

"Don't listen to her," I said to Waylon, gesturing to K. "Joëlle, I'll see what I can do for your squad. You can count on me."

She smiled as she fitted her helmet back in place with a pressurizing hiss. "Good. They're my family, Talcorosax. Take care of them."

"I will. And, call me Osax."

"If I'm still around, I'd like that." She winked, and I quickly bowed a skyther farewell, which she mirrored. She continued running down the hall. K began to follow, before stopping and looking back once more.

"Osax?" she said.

"Yes?" She was gazing into my eyes. Her expression was stern, and she opened her mouth to speak, before shutting it. She blinked. At last she spoke.

"...See ya." She waved, and with that, she bounded after Joëlle.

◆

Heart pounding and mind racing, I sprinted down the other hall, my furred ears trailing behind me as I ran. Pain flared up in my right shoulder, but I tried to shake it off, tightening my mandibles.

I dashed through the dim halls, lit only by emergency lights. Blast marks covered the walls, and a few bodies of TAU marines were strewn across the hall. I took one look at my E-pistol and holstered it at my side, bending down to take a carbine from one of the fallen soldiers. His faceplate was broken, revealing one startled eye, and blood trailing down the side of his nose. *I'm sorry,* I thought, *but with this, perhaps I can avenge you.* I activated the gun and it buzzed to life.

I kept running, until I heard the sound of valicorr speaking to each other around the next bend. Instinctively I froze, and stopped just before the corner. Their voices were raspy, and they spoke in a language I couldn't understand.

The voices were coming closer, and if I didn't act soon, they'd get the drop on me, instead of the other way around. I started charging a volley of bolts and felt my breathing constrict in fear with each second. I could feel the blood pumping through my veins.

I waited several seconds until the red sparks began spewing out the barrel of my gun, and then ducked out from the corner and fired my weapon across the room. Three valicorr were in the hall, none of them had seen me, and the red energy darts shot across the hall horizontally. I'd hit all of them, and each one fell.

I noticed I'd been holding my breath, exhaled, and began running past their bodies in the hall.

Suddenly, blistering pain shot up through my right leg, and I saw my own reflection in the floor speed toward me. My carbine clattered to the ground as I slammed my face on the floor. I spun around, prone, to see the third raider lying on the ground with his arm outstretched and a plasma sword extended toward me. He snarled and hissed as he rose, and began limping to me.

I almost couldn't think from the pain in my shoulder and leg, and my face was aching as well. The pirate stepped closer, using the wall for support, and pointed his shimmering energy sword at my face as he approached. His mouth opened, revealing his needle-like teeth, as he snarled. The emergency lights flashed across the hall illuminating him in a nightmarish red.

I began crawling backwards, and tried drawing the pistol with my right hand, but I couldn't close my fingers tightly enough around the handle without hitting a wall of pain. The valicorr's wrist cannon smoked, damaged from one of the bolts I had fired earlier. He was almost upon me.

I grabbed the pistol with my left hand, and with a whir it lit up and I aimed it at the valicorr. But to my horror, I realized if I shot him now, he might fall onto me, and his sword would pierce deep into the floor, straight through my chest. I hesitated, and all I could hear was my heartbeat. My heartbeat, which in a second, would be silenced forever.

I altered my aim just slightly, and sparks burst from his sword emitter as my bolt collided with his wrist. The plasma sword dissipated, and he cried out. I readjusted, and fired multiple times into his body, and he collapsed on top of me.

I shoved him off, panting, and began to stand. My right leg was cut, I wasn't sure how badly, but it hurt too much to stand on, so I limped along the wall as fast as I could toward the eastern tower. I decided I needed both hands for this, so I left the carbine behind. Another explosion shook the floor, and the lights flickered.

◆

I was beginning to doubt I'd be much help to Joëlle's squad, as I struggled to get across the hallway. *No,* I thought, *they're counting on you. They're trapped, and they need your support!*

Flickering orange light emanated from the next bend in the hall, and I heard the sound of crying, and fire crackling. As I clamoured around the corner, I saw fires burning in the hall, and several bodies of soldiers. The outer side of the hall was entirely made of glass, overlooking the cliffside. I could see the eastern tower from here through the window. The fog was beginning to clear up, but snowfall replaced it, swirling around outside the windows. I was very close.

On the outer edge of the hall was what looked like a door to a glass elevator shaft. Standing in front of the closed door was a woman wearing a lab coat, her eyes welling with tears. When she saw me, she jumped back in fear and exclaimed.

"I won't hurt you, I'm here to help!" I tried to sound as confident as possible. She stared at me as though she couldn't believe it, and continued crying. I limped my way closer to her, and she didn't back away.

Through sobs, she started talking. "He- He's stuck! He's stuck in the elevator!"

I reached the elevator doors, and tried peering down the side of the shaft through the window. I saw the elevator car, suspended motionless about thirty meters below us.

"Who's stuck?" I asked.

"Solomon, my- My husband. He was coming up from the Bio-labs, we were going to meet up here…" she was struggling to pull herself together.

I nodded. "How do you know he's in the elevator?"

"I-" She sobbed, "We were down in the labs when they came and started shooting. He was close to the elevator, I saw him go inside with some of the others. I tried to tell him I'd meet him up here- I ran up the stairs as fast as I could, but then I heard shooting in the hallway, and I thought they might have found him…" She was having difficulty speaking, losing some balance as she cried. I reached my left hand toward her and she held onto it. "When I thought it was clear I came out, and I saw that he wasn't here, but the power had gone out and- Oh god, what do I do?"

I looked out the window toward the eastern tower, and my heart skipped a beat. A valicorr gunship swooped in and was now circling the tower. I could see there was a landing pad armed with a defense cannon just a few doors down between here and the tower, but there was no one to operate it. I figured I could get there fast enough…

The woman's crying pierced my thoughts, and I turned to her. "I'll help your husband, and whoever else is trapped in there." I glanced up toward the valicorr gunship, which was hovering, scoping out the tower.

"Thank you so much!" She kept crying, and backed away from the door a little, letting go of my hand.

I tried the door controls, but they weren't working. I tried prying open the door, but my right arm was almost useless. The woman, seeing this, came over to my side, and with both hands pulled on one of the doors, while I pulled on the other. I saw out of the corner of my eye the gunship had begun firing on the tower in rapid-fire spurts of yellow energy.

The glass elevator doors slid open with a lurch, and I almost fell into the chasm, catching myself with my left hand. Peering down the shaft, I noticed an emergency exit hatch on the top of the elevator, and a metal service ladder on the inside wall of the shaft. The elevator was suspended by six thick cables grouped together in the center of the elevator.

I looked around, and grabbed one of the dead soldier's carbines. I activated it, and passed it to the woman. She looked stunned.

I lowered my ears. "In case any more valicorr show up."

"Right…" she nodded slowly.

"You'll be alright. Hide down in that room, I'll be back up with everyone in a minute."

She nodded, and backed away, ducking in behind one of the other doors on the inside of the hallway. I turned to the ladder, and began my descent.

I was rather slow climbing, both my right arm and leg feeling weak. I grit my mandibles to try to ignore the pain, and slowly, steadily, lowered myself through the shaft. Halfway down, I looked out the shaft toward the tower; the gunship was flying near the top, still firing. I saw an explosion burst from one of the top windows. I wasn't going fast enough.

I dropped down onto the elevator, and heard startled noises from the passengers inside as the thing shook. I fell down on my right knee in pain.

My heart was pounding. I twisted open the emergency hatch. Inside were six humans. One of them appeared to be a soldier, wearing TAU armour and carrying a carbine. The others, all scientists.

The soldier aimed his gun up at me, and said "Get back!"

"I'm here to help!" When he lowered his gun, the people started murmuring to each other, and I braced my body with my right arm, reaching down with my left to help someone up. One of the scientists grabbed my hand, and I started pulling them up.

My body quivered, and my breathing was laboured. Once she was high enough, she grabbed onto the roof of the elevator and helped herself up. The two of us helped the next one.

One by one, we worked together to get everyone out of the elevator. The soldier was last, due to the weight of his armour, but with a few of us helping we managed to pull him out.

I ushered everyone to begin climbing, the soldier first. I would go last. They all thanked me as they went, one by one, grabbing hold of the ladder.

Then, yellow bullets began falling from above. I looked up, and two valicorr leaned out the doorway. One of them was aiming its wrist gun at us, and the other had its plasma sword extended, reaching for the elevator cables.

With a shudder, one of the cables was cut. The elevator shifted slightly, and I looked up and saw the cable falling down the shaft toward us. There was one scientist who hadn't grabbed hold of the ladder yet, and without thinking I pushed him against the wall, shielding him with my body.

The cable struck the roof of the elevator, barely missing my back. Instantly, I stepped away from the wall and drew my pistol. The soldier, who was climbing the ladder, fumbled with his rifle, trying to get a clear shot.

I shot the valicorr who was slicing the cables, and he rolled forward, past the ladder, careening into the elevator's roof. It shuddered from the impact.

The soldier fired at the remaining valicorr. It retaliated, hitting the soldier once in the shoulder, though his armour absorbed the impact. A second later, and it was tumbling down the chasm from the marine's energy rifle.

The last scientist started the climb as the soldier continued to lead it, and the valicorr's corpse hit the elevator, causing it to shake once more. I glanced outside toward the eastern tower, clutching my shoulder. The tower shook from the gunship's laser blasts, and I noticed just how much I was sweating.

I looked up, hearing a shrill cry from above. Another valicorr came into view, peering outside the doorway, and in one horrible motion, melted through the five remaining cables with its sword.

I jumped. The elevator lurched downward, cables trailing behind it, as it began to screech and spark down the chasm. I was suspended in midair, gasping. I dropped the pistol in my hand and reached for the ladder as I began to fall. My fingers traced past a rung, then two, before finally finding their grip. My body slammed against the ladder.

Gasping for air, I looked up, and saw the soldier fire at the valicorr, hitting it directly. The space pirate collapsed forward, and began falling into the chasm, but it was still alive. With one flailing hand, it clawed one of the scientists as it fell past, and he lost his grip with a scream.

The valicorr flew past me, chasing the elevator car to the depths of the shaft.

I felt my heart nearly stop as the scientist fell from the ladder. I reached out my hand toward him, trying to grab onto anything. I needed to save him. What if this was her husband?

My hand felt contact, and I clutched his arm with all my might. The weight of his falling body jerked me down. Then my right arm exploded with pain, and I realized I'd grabbed onto him with my right hand. For a second I held on, and he swung back toward the ladder, but my grip was so weak with pain; a moment later, he slipped from my grasp.

My eyes widened in horror as I saw the man fall deeper into the shaft, until he was engulfed in darkness.

I felt my chest collapse. He was dead.

I had to keep climbing.

I made it to the top of the ladder, and everyone was in shock. The woman was stepping out of her hiding place, and the soldier was calming everyone down. She looked frantically around at the faces. But she didn't smile, and her eyes welled with tears. Our eyes met, and I felt something break within me.

I sprinted for the landing pad without looking back. Stepping into the frigid air I heard the wind whistling and the hum of the gunship's engine. I saw the defense cannon, and made a break for it.

Missiles flew from the gunship. Blinding light flashed from the base of the eastern tower, as massive explosions sent chunks of metal and debris flying in all directions. I stood motionless, stunned by the spectacle. Heat waves crashed into me as I stared unblinking, my ears peeled back, and I collapsed on my wounded leg. The massive tower, slowly, terrifyingly, tilted away from the cliff, and began tumbling to the base of the mountain, with Joëlle's team still inside.

I couldn't look away.

I had failed.

Thirteen

I ran past the group from the elevator, pain spiking through my leg with each step. I couldn't bring myself to look at anyone's faces. The woman was crying, embracing two of the other scientists. The others were talking quietly. I wanted to apologize to her. I wanted to say something, but I couldn't. I'd already wasted enough time, and I knew nothing I could say would help.

My eyes were beginning to water. I tried not to think about it, clenching my fists as I ran through the station. Tears started streaming down my face. I rubbed them away.

I had no weapon. I scanned the halls ahead until I found another soldier's body, and took his carbine. I was shaking, but I kept going, limping through the facility.

My thoughts turned to K. Was she safe? The control room was probably crawling with valicorr, otherwise it likely would have been reclaimed by now.

I thought about Joëlle, pausing to listen in on her headset, hearing the screams from her squad. She'd said they were like her family.

I stopped moving, and shook my head fiercely. I had to get that image out of my mind.

I imagined K and Joëlle's bodies on the floor of the control room.
No.

I picked myself back up, and wiped away my tears. With my injured arm I braced myself on the wall, and trekked down the hallway. Another explosion shook the floor, and I paused to catch myself before continuing. I wouldn't let them die. I had to save them.

I turned a corner to another long hallway, lined with large windows. I stared outside, and noticed a dark, massive shape, gliding down from the sky. It was dotted with orange lights, and the shape was hard to make out, but it looked long, with thick protruding limbs all along the sides and bottom like some kind of gargantuan insect. I couldn't tell how close it was or how large it was, but its giant hull covered the station like an umbrella. A low growling sound pierced the air like thunder, coming from the ship. This could only have been the mothership.

As I continued to run, staring out the window at the massive thing, I was having difficulty swallowing. I was like a pebble and it was like a mountain, but somehow, I knew I couldn't give up. There was a way out of this.

◆

The signs of battle and destruction grew ever more present as I neared the control room. I could hear gunshots just beyond the door, and I burst into the room on the top ring. Bodies were strewn about, and some of the computer terminals were smoking from laser damage. I gripped the marine's carbine tightly, and began charging a blast as I scanned the room, lit only by emergency lights. Arcs of light sped around the room causing mini explosions. Several valicorr, I couldn't count them all, and TAU troopers were spread across the room, exchanging bullets. My ears lifted when I saw K, standing on the far side of the circular balcony. She was engaged in melee with a valicorr.

Energy bolts shot toward me and I ducked down behind the railing of the upper circular balcony that ringed the room. I noticed Waylon, hiding there beside me, breathing heavily, clutching his pistol.

"Waylon!" I yelled over the sounds of gunfire.

He spun his head toward me and aimed at me, panting. "Oh!" He lowered his gun.

"What are you doing in here?! Why aren't you outside?!"

"I- I wanted to help! Damn bastards killed my buddies." He shook his head and grimaced. "If I'm gonna die, I'm gonna do it fightin'!"

I hesitated, then simply nodded. I peered over the edge of the railing, and noticed that a few of the window blinds had been lifted. I could see the dark shape of the mothership, getting closer to the station. Flames erupted from a computer terminal beside us that had just been shot. I looked around at the chaos, and tightened my grip on the carbine as it continued to charge. Director Aali's body was lying on the central platform, beneath the hanging computer armature. I couldn't tell if he was alive.

I put my hand on Waylon's shoulder. "Look, you're not going to die!"

"How can you say that?!"

"No one else has to die!" I shook him with my arm, and he just looked at me bewildered. I knew I wasn't making sense, but a fire ignited within me. I leaned over the railing and aimed my gun, firing at some valicorr on the lower level. My bolts connected, and two of them fell to the ground. I turned away from the ledge.

I found the wind suddenly knocked out of me. A valicorr had snuck around the upper level, and jumped me, thrusting its fist into my chest. I met its black eyes, and it opened its mouth wide. Its wrist gun was aimed directly at my heart.

Before it could fire, Waylon let out a cry, and let his weapon loose. Smoke rose from the space pirate's body as it was cast to the side from the impact.

"Thank you." I lowered my ears in gratitude.

"Yeah," was all he said in response.

I leaned over the railing and took a few more shots. I noticed Joëlle on the lower level finish off another valicorr. I heard K's voice exclaim, "Osax!"

The sounds of combat ceased.

K and I ran to each other, meeting at the central platform with the director's body. K looked relieved. Without warning, I was wrapped up in her blue arms, gasping for breath.

"Ahg!"

She let go, and stared at me, her face apologetic.

I rubbed my right shoulder and squinted. "Glad you're okay."

Joëlle and the other marines looked up to us.

K nodded, her face hardening. "Yeah. You're not dead, I'm impressed."

One of the marines spoke first through his helmet. "Is the Director alive?"

I took a deep breath. I knelt down beside him and pressed my fingers to his wrist, then his neck. He had a wide, charred black hole in his uniform about his chest.

I stood up slowly and shook my head. "There's no pulse."

Everyone remained silent, exchanging glances for a few seconds. Waylon stood up from behind the railing and looked at us.

The Director was dead. I'd never get to learn the secrets of this station after all... at least not from him, and I didn't know who else to ask, or who would tell me. I looked down at his face. His eyes were closed peacefully. I wasn't sure what to feel. What was going on here? Why was the station's true purpose classified? Perhaps the valicorr knew, and they wanted something from the station. Something secret. Perhaps that's why they attacked in such force.

"Osax, what about my squad?" Joëlle stepped forward, gazing up at me. I felt my palms beginning to sweat.

I shook my head slowly, feeling my heart pounding.

"I lost contact with them…" She gestured weakly toward me. I was glad I couldn't see her face through the helmet from up here.

I trembled. "They- The tower was destroyed."

"*What?!*"

She lowered her head, and stood, motionless. I wanted to reach out to her, to say something to help, but I was frozen too.

One of the marines climbed up the ladder and removed his helmet, placing it on the platform. "Let's get the power back online. We should be able to reboot the station from this control console." I stepped aside and let him use the computer hanging from the ceiling. K picked up the Director's body and carried it to the edge of the room before coming back.

The marine shook his head. "Dammit! This isn't going to work."

K stepped forward. "What the hell do you mean it's not going to work? Wasn't the plan, 'get to the control room and restore the power'?" She crossed her arms, which were cut up pretty badly.

The marine's face was stern. "The assumption was, the invaders broke into the control room and manually shut down all power to the rest of the station. Apparently, even though they took control of this room, the real problem is they somehow broke through security to the generator, and disconnected the powerlines. There isn't any power for the control room to use, aside from the auxiliary power the emergency lines have been using."

"They broke through the rest of the station's security, it can't be that surprising that they made it into the generator," I said.

K replied, "The generator is so essential to the station, it's probably the most well guarded room in the whole place. It's got three shielded doors, and if an unauthorized breach is detected in any one of them, then the Director is immediately notified. If they attacked there first-"

"That would explain how the station was caught so unawares," I mused. Another mystery. "All they needed to do was somehow deactivate the power undetected, and they could take out scanners, elevators, shields…"

"And our biggest anti-aircraft guns, apparently," said K.

The marine responded, "The cannons need to draw power from the station, or else they wouldn't be able to fire. Those guns are strong, but they take too much energy to operate on individual power cells."

I felt a flash of selfish hope. "So, even the defense cannons run on station power?"

He shook his head. "No, those weapons are much smaller. They're fitted with their own power supplies. If only we'd had more warning, we could have had those in operation."

So it was my fault. I could have taken out the gunship before it destroyed the tower. If I had just left the people in the elevator...

I looked at Joëlle. She hadn't moved. I felt hollow.

But those people were stuck in the elevator. I needed to help them. I needed to try. *Right?*

K shot the marine a sarcastic glance. "Well, that was well designed. Let's make all our essential systems linked to one power source, with no backups."

The marine shook his head. "They shouldn't have even known about the base. But that's not important right now; we need to secure the generator, assuming it's undamaged."

"If they were going to raid this station, why would they leave the generators undamaged?" I asked. "Wouldn't it be better for them if we had no way to restore power without conducting repairs?"

K brushed past, saying, "I don't know, Osax. But who cares. Let's hope they just disengaged the power cells, cause then we still have a chance to restore power."

One of the marines on the lower level spoke up. "Captain Orion, I'll head to the western tower. I'll wait at the cannon until you restore power to the station."

The marine put his helmet back on. "Good. Karl and Tweezer, you two watch her back. I know none of us were expecting action today, but that's why we're here!"

"Yes sir!" The three marines saluted, before rushing out of the room, the sound of their boots fading into the distance.

"Everyone else, with me. That includes you K, we could use your brute strength." K nodded.

The marine turned to leave, then paused. "Actually, we need someone to reboot the control room once we restore power."

"I'll stay behind," said Waylon, and the marine spun to face him.

"So will I." Joëlle spoke up, but didn't move. I felt my voice suppressed by something. I didn't know what to say.

"Alright," said the captain. "Move out!"

Everyone filed out of the room, except for Waylon, Joëlle and I. K lingered for a moment, and I reassured her I'd be right behind them.

Waylon looked between the two of us.

"Joëlle..."

"Just go!" She whipped her head up at me. "We've got this. You're needed elsewhere."

"I'm... I'm sorry." I felt a tear run down my cheek.

"Go!" Her voice was breaking.

I trembled. I nodded at Waylon as I passed him, trying to present an air of composure as I limped out the door.

Fourteen

"I'm going to have to stop you there, Talcorosax."

I paused, staring at the investigator.

"What's the matter?" I asked.

She took a deep breath. "This story, it's all very interesting…" She paused, and adjusted her hat. "But, it's getting quite late." She looked me in the eye.

I tilted my head to the side. "It was late when we started."

"Yes, it was. That's exactly my point. You haven't even mentioned Duhrnan yet. Aren't you getting tired?"

"Tired?" I looked her sternly in the face. "Investigator, I assure you, I have stayed up much later than this."

"I'm sure you have." She yawned. "Well, I'm getting tired. Too tired to continue."

My ears drooped. "There's so much more to tell. Aren't you curious about what happens next? About how we try to save the station?"

She stood up and adjusted her uniform. Her voice was almost monotone. "You are a great storyteller, Talcorosax. But I'm too tired. Besides, without being able to interrupt and ask questions, my being here is a little redundant."

"I thought you wanted to hear the story?"

She sighed, and rubbed her eyes, before looking at her holo-gauntlet. "Looks like it's past my shift anyway; I hope they pay me overtime for this. I'll keep the recording going, if you really want to keep telling the story." She motioned to the computer. "I'll be able to tell if you tamper with the recording at all, so don't do anything like that."

"Why would I do that?"

"I don't know." She glanced outside the window, then back to me.

"Tomorrow, I'll listen to the recording, and I can follow up on any questions I might have about it tomorrow night. How does that sound?"

I nodded slowly. "That is acceptable. Thank you."

"Thank you, Talcorosax, for letting us stay here."

"Of course." I bowed my head solemnly.

"I'll speak with you in the morning."

She turned away from me, and then paused. I looked at her expectantly. She glanced back over her shoulder. "I was wondering about something, Talcorosax."

"Yes?"

"Do your people have records of other stories? For instance, other recordings of tales you or your mother told?"

I thought for a moment. "Yes. The library is located on the bottom floor of the temple."

She smiled. "Great. Do my people need any special clearance to access it?"

I paused. "No."

"I see. Thank you, Talcorosax. I'll speak with you tomorrow."

She walked away from the table, and left the room, closing the door. It clicked when it shut, and I found myself alone in the quiet ambiance of the room.

I looked toward the nebula and the four moons. *Shall I continue?*

I thought I saw some movement in the stars. My ears lifted.

I turned back toward the table, and lowered my head, closing my eyes. I took a deep breath in.

Fifteen

I tried not to think about Joëlle's squad, or that woman's husband. The doors to the generator room were all open. They were each about a foot thick, and stood a meter apart from each other in the entrance hall. I could see signs of energy weapon fire on the doors. None of us hesitated, guns at the ready, and we all charged into the dimly lit chamber.

Our footsteps echoed on the metal catwalks which spidered out into the room. The room was huge, and cylindrical. It had no windows, and was lit by small orange auxiliary lights dispersed throughout the room. In the center was the generator itself, a giant cylindrical tube that extended from the ceiling all the way to the bottom of the dark chasm below.

Halfway to the catwalks that ringed the center tube, pain arced through my leg. My eyes widened as I tumbled to the side, catching myself on the edge of the catwalk.

"Whoa!" I said. I imagined the man falling down the elevator shaft as my gaze fell into the pit below me, and my head started spinning.

K glanced back to me, pistol in hand. "Be careful!"

"At least they installed railings," I said.

Everyone made it onto the central catwalk before me, and when I caught up they'd already assessed the situation.

Captain Orion spoke. "They removed two of the power cells, here and here." He pointed to two empty cylindrical slots in the tube. "That's why the power isn't working."

I tilted my head to the side. "Only two? That's all it takes to shut this thing down?"

He turned to face me, voice muffled by his helmet. "It's assumed you never let hostiles into this room. The fail-safes are minimal once you get inside. The energy can only flow through the machine if there's at least one of those two power cells inserted in the row, and it'll work better if we get both."

I scanned the room. The station rumbled, and we all grabbed onto the rail for balance.

One of the marines began. "Captain, how are we supposed to find these power cells? They could be anywhere! And I don't see any valicorr in here."

I stared at the tube. It had two columns of power cell slots running down the front of it, and the empty slots were across from each other on one row at about eye level. I asked, "So, there needs to be at least one power cell in each row?" The Captain nodded, and I pointed toward the next row, which had its full set of two power cells. "Why don't we just borrow one of the other power cells to complete the circuit?"

"Good idea! It won't be as efficient as if we had the proper number of cells, but we should be able to restore most of the station's power."

One of the marines began removing a power cell from the next row down, twisting it by the handle. If they wanted to sabotage the base, why didn't they do more damage? This was just about the most benign way of shutting down the power they could have done. And from the sounds of it, getting into this room in the first place must have been an ordeal; why didn't they make the most of it?

The marine removed the blue canister with a hiss, and stepped forward to begin placing it in the empty row.

Suddenly, he screamed in pain, and my blood started pumping adrenaline. He dropped the power cell on the catwalk, and it started to roll towards the edge. Sparks were shooting from his chest armour, and a hole was getting bigger. It looked like some kind of shimmering red energy was beaming out from the hole, a few inches from the edge of the armour, before fading away.

We all stared, and backed away, our guns pointed in his general direction. My heart was pounding and my ears were pulled back, and I stumbled on my bad leg. The soldier shook, and the red energy disappeared entirely. He stopped sparking, but the hole in his armour was smoking, and he stepped backward quickly losing all tension in his muscles.

Captain Orion was on one side of him, the rest of us on the other.

My eyes widened. The marine tumbled backward, over the railing and into the chasm. I noticed the power cell rolling closer to the edge, and so did the captain.

He held his rifle in one hand, and lunged for the power cell with his other.

I held my breath. He collided with something in mid air, and grunted, being pushed back upright by some unseeable force. But there was nothing there. Then, the power cell, which was about to fall off the edge, flickered, and faded out of sight, as it began to levitate in the air.

Everyone gasped in surprise, and the Captain was thrust against the railing. He dropped his rifle which bounced off the rail and into the abyss, and seemed to be wrestling with something. At the edges of his hands, some dark shape was barely visible, pushing against him. One of the marines called out to him.

I aimed my pistol toward him. I didn't know how, but it must have been an invisible attacker. But when I trained my sights on the captain, I trembled.

I heard K call out, "What the hell's happening?!"

I couldn't bring myself to fire. What if I was wrong, and I accidentally shot him in the head?

He was being pushed against the railing, breathing heavily, his body leaning back over it. My finger rested on the trigger.

Out from around the bend of the central tube, a red laser bolt shot out and sparked off of the invisible shape wrestling with the captain. I jumped in surprise, and a few more shots hit the thing.

The captain pushed the thing off, which sparked and flickered into view. It was a valicorr after all, wearing a dark outfit with dark metal rings on its shoulders and limbs. Its body collapsed to the floor, and it dropped the power cell it was holding.

I lunged forward, and caught the cell just before it rolled off the ledge. The captain was panting, and the remaining marines ran over to him, asking if he was alright.

I stood up, bracing myself on the railing as I did, with the power cell in one hand and my pistol in the other. I aimed the pistol around the cylinder, anticipating the captain's saviour to reveal themself, but I was hesitant.

"Who's there?" I asked.

Slow footsteps reverberated through the metal catwalk, and a figure emerged from hiding. His gun was slick and black, still smoking and glowing a faint red as he held it down. He was wearing a white and black outfit, his coat was long, almost like a lab coat, trailing behind him. His height was about 5'8, with an athletic build, and his shoulders bulked out with dark grey armoured pads. His forearms and boots were armoured as well, and he had a plate of armour covering his chest. His hair was short and dark, spiked up and to the side. His cheeks were rounded, and his jawline well defined. He sported a thin, dark moustache.

But of all these details, what caught me off guard were his eyes. His left eye was a striking orange colour, and his right was replaced with a metal plate, and a robotic eye with a faint red glow.

He looked at all of us, his lips pursed, but when he laid eyes on K, his jaw dropped. I noticed him tilt his pistol up toward her slightly. His organic eye widened, and the aperture on his cybernetic one followed suit.

K stomped towards him, and before he could get a shot off she grabbed him by the collar with her free hand and lifted him up off the ground. He dropped his pistol and gagged.

"What the hell were you doing hiding back there?!" Her eyes were narrowed and she bared her teeth.

"Gak!" The man struggled to get free. "Put me down!"

"K!" I yelled, limping forward. The marines all had their guns trained on him. "Put him down!"

She shot me an annoyed glance, and obliged.

The man collapsed to the floor, coughed, and then stood slowly, retrieving his pistol and adjusting his collar. He resumed a more collected facial expression after standing upright, and stood with dignity.

He spoke, his voice now calm. "I came here to see if I could fix the station's power issues." He glanced at me, as I began screwing the power cell into its new place on the empty row. He chuckled. "I started looking for the cells- When I heard you coming in, I was too suspicious of you to come out of hiding." He pointed toward the power cells with a black-gloved hand. "I wish I'd known I could have just rearranged them."

The captain stood, and reached to shake his hand. "I'm Captain Orion. Thank you; you saved my life."

The man smiled, and shook his hand firmly. I kept screwing the cell in place.

"Pleased to meet you, captain. I'm sorry you lost one of your marines to that thing."

The captain sighed. "Not the only one we've lost today, but thank you."

K spoke up. "How did you know to shoot that valicorr?"

He gazed down at the body, the smile fading from his face. "When I heard the struggle, I peaked around the corner but I couldn't see anything. I thought it might have been a cloaked valicorr, so I activated my thermal vision, and sure enough, there it was." He pointed to his robotic eye as he said this.

The canister finally clicked into place with a hiss. "I've replaced the cell, we should be able to restore power now."

The captain raised a hand to his helmet, and began speaking through the communicator. "Come in Joëlle. Affirmative, you should be able to reset the power…"

I stepped toward the man over the valicorr's body, and reached out my hand. My ears lifted in greeting and he gazed up at me, looking a little stunned.

"My name is Talcorosax," I said, as he took my hand hesitantly. "If not for you, that valicorr may have killed all of us. It's a good thing you stayed hidden."

He smiled, and shook my hand. "Ah, well, I'm glad."

"What's your name?"

"Oh, my apologies. I'm Jonathan Wellsworth, Head of Biology."

I nodded, "I'm a biologist too."

"Are you? Interesting. Quite a fascinating field, I think. And relevant, since we're all living things, aren't we?"

K spoke up. "So, we're just glazing over the fact that this valicorr was invisible? I thought that shit was impossible."

Jonathan turned to K, eyeing her suspiciously. I couldn't blame him; the first thing she did was nearly hoist him into the abyss. Hesitantly he spoke. "They're called shadow scouts. Only elite valicorr agents are equipped with them- the cloaking devices, I mean. Clearly this valicorr was sent ahead to infiltrate the base and sabotage the generator." He began rubbing his moustache. "After the generator was taken out… the assault force could approach the station undetected, and unhindered by our defense systems."

I nodded. "We figured that much out, which is why we came here."

The captain finished his call, and suddenly the auxiliary lights were replaced by bright white ones. The power was restored and the entire room hummed and whirred to life.

I glanced around at everyone. "Come on, now that the power's back, let's head back to the control room."

My suggestion was met with nods of agreement, and we ran out of the generator room.

◆

Though my heart was still pounding, and my wounds aching, I felt hope running through the well lit halls. We heard the faint sounds of a massive energy cannon firing somewhere above us, and stopped to peer outside the glass wall. This part of the station was built on top of a ledge which stretched out beyond the window, level with the floor.

The air was quiet around us. Light splashed across the black sky and falling snow as we gazed up at the valicorr ship hovering above us outside. K and I stood next to each other, and exchanged glances. The light reflected in her orange eyes. Jonathan stood back from us. His mouth was open slightly, and his eyes scanned the ship.

We could see blasts of energy firing from the western tower. *The anti-aircraft battery!*

We all held our breaths, watching bolt after bolt explode against the ship. Ten seconds passed, and the ship hovered, unflinching.

I turned to face everyone else, hoping my eyes were playing tricks on me as the gun continued to shoot. Someone must have seen the ship take damage from the cannon; it couldn't have been invulnerable.

Everyone's gaze was on the ship, and I could tell from their expressions they were thinking the same thing. This couldn't be happening.

"It must be doing something," I said.

K clenched her fists, and grimaced.

"Captain, what should we do?" one of the marines asked.

"I… I don't know." The captain shook his head slowly.

Jonathan gulped, but remained silent.

K bared her teeth, and screamed. "Why can't you just leave us alone?!"

I shielded my eyes as shards of glass burst out from the window, and snow gusted inside. K stood, her fist where the glass wall used to be.

The marines stepped back in shock. Jonathan stood his ground, coat trailing in the breeze, his brow furrowed at K.

"Rein it in, K!" Jonathan stared at her.

K's eyes were full of anger. "Why don't *you* rein it in, jackass!" She stepped outside onto the snow covered ledge, and ran toward the ship.

"K, wait! What are you doing?" I sprinted after her, and skidded to a halt a few feet behind her, my ears blown to the side in the wind. Ice spun around us as her fur coat flapped. She was staring up at the massive ship. I turned my head away from where the eastern tower would have been. I couldn't look that way.

I glanced up at the AA gun on the western tower. It was firing white beams of energy at the ship, but it still seemed ineffective.

K aimed up at the ship and started screaming in rage, firing her pistol in vain. Spit frothed from her mouth. She winced, and with her other hand clutched the side of her head.

I looked back and saw that Jonathan and the marines were still standing inside, looking out at us, and the ship.

K's arm started to go limp, and I noticed her losing her balance. She stopped screaming, and my body tensed.

"K!"

Moaning, she started to collapse. I lunged for her. I grabbed her arms and pulled her back so she wouldn't fall off the ledge. We landed on our backs and crunched into the snow. I sat up and leaned over her, and I could see she was still partially conscious.

"Osax..." she said, eyes half open. The sound of the AA gun echoed across the cliffside.

She reached a hand up to me, and clutched my arm. "...I can't take this." Tears were forming in her eyes, and she scrunched up her face, trying to suppress them. I was breathing hard.

"You'll be okay. You'll be okay." I had no idea what was going on. It didn't matter. She needed me. "We're in this together. We're okay, remember? 'O' 'K'?"

She shook her head, eyes closed.

Jonathan ran up to us, and knelt down beside her. "What's going on?" he asked.

I shook my head. "I'm not sure. She fainted earlier too; there was no obvious cause."

K mumbled, "You said you wouldn't tell."

My heart sank. "I'm sorry K; I'm just trying to help you!"

Jonathan pulled out a small scanning device from his coat, and began scanning K's head. His expression was stern. "Still suffering from random blackouts..." he muttered.

K croaked, "I'm dying."

I shook my head, as the sky flashed with another blast from the cannon. "No, no you're not, K. You're not dying."

I looked into Jonathan's orange eye. His expression was grim.

Suddenly, a red light began to glow from the bottom of the ship. A few seconds later, red energy, like a lightning bolt, flashed toward the AA gun. The top of the tower exploded into debris and flames, and abruptly, the sound of the cannon ceased.

"No..." K groaned, and tried to sit up.

"Take it easy K," I said, helping her sit up. I gazed up at the ship, looming overhead. Jonathan stared at it solemnly.

I noticed out of the corner of my eye a valicorr dropship flying away from the ruined station, and up toward the mothership.

"It looks like they're leaving," said Jonathan.

"What?" I blinked. The ship disappeared in the shadow of the cruiser, and I noticed a few more dropships returning to it. Then, slowly, the mothership began to ascend.

Snow fell into my eyes, my ears chilled in the frigid wind. K staggered beside me and followed my gaze. We stood, motionless. The black shape accelerated toward the sky, getting smaller until it disappeared in the darkness.

I let out a sigh of relief, and lay back in the snow, letting myself rest. The situation was grim, but at least for this moment I could relax. We were safe, and it was time to assess the damage.

Sixteen

The sun was high, and the sky was blue and crisp, free of any clouds. I gazed out at the station and the ice fields beyond from my perch on the mountain, my eyes tracing the line where the white below met the blue above. I dug my toes into the snow, and breathed in slowly and fully. The air was fresh and pure. I exhaled. It was clear enough that I could gaze off and see the white mountains far off in the distance. I lay on my back and gazed up at the clear blue sky.

My shoulder and leg were both feeling much better. Last night, after the valicorr retreated, we got the station's medical wing working. I was lucky enough to have my wounds treated by a doctor who'd worked on skythers before. She gave me some class-6 medical gel for my injuries and it was already doing its job. I was thankful to be alive in an age where medicine was so advanced. I flexed my right arm and hand as I lay there, and felt my strength had already returned. There was still a little pain in my shoulder, but it wasn't too bad. My leg would take a bit longer to heal, as the cut was pretty deep. But even so, it was incomparably better feeling than it was last night. Getting a good night's sleep was a bonus too. I'd expected the stress of the attack to keep me up all night, but as soon as I lay down to sleep I practically blacked out.

With the Director dead, and much of the station destroyed, it was agreed that arranging an evacuation transport was the best course of action. Joëlle contacted TAU authorities and had arranged for a nearby cruiser, Kronos, to stop by Voren and retrieve all of the survivors. They estimated they'd be here around midday on Voren. I noticed Joëlle hadn't spoken to me directly since I left the control room. Captain Orion led his remaining marines through the night, helping out survivors. I'm not sure where Jonathan or Waylon went off to.

K, after regaining her strength, was distant. She spent most of the night away from me, and everyone else. I'm not sure where she went off to, in fact, but she said she wanted to be alone. Actually, she said, "Screw off!"

All the fighting had made me tired, so I went to bed after I heard that the Kronos was coming to pick us up the next day. When I woke up, I went to the showers, but they weren't working, so I went straight to the kitchen. Bodies lay in some of the halls, since there hadn't been much time to clean up. I sat in the kitchen alone. Somehow, the root beer didn't taste the same.

I knew I needed to decompress from the chaos of the last thirty hours, so I donned my thermal gear and found one of the exits that led to the top of the cliffs. I spent the morning hiking up here, to clear my head and get a moment of peace.

I took a deep breath. I still didn't know why the station's directive was classified. Maybe I never would know. But I had so many questions about what was going on here.

How had the valicorr known of the base, and why did they attack? Perhaps just as importantly, what caused them to leave? There goal evidently was not to wipe out the station, or they would have seen that through. They easily could have...

My thoughts drifted to the loro ruins, the reason I had arrived at Voren in the first place. I still hadn't checked the transfer device to see if I'd recovered any information.

I wasn't sure my brain could handle any more mysteries just then, so I pushed that thought aside. There'd be another time for that.

I closed my eyes, and stretched. When I opened them, I saw a TAU cruiser warp into the sky far above. Tiny dropships were flying toward the base.

◆

I stepped onto the landing pad. The dropship doors were open, and a soldier stood outside in the bright sun, carbine in hand. His face was covered with an armoured helmet, and his helmet was ringed by the fluffy fur of a hood. He beckoned me to come inside. "Looks like you're the last one, big fella. Come on!"

I took one last look at the inside of the station. My ears sank. It didn't feel right leaving this place in such a state, but I knew there'd be no use in sticking around.

"Hey, wait!" K rushed onto the platform from inside the station.

The marine jumped back at her sight. "Sorry, I thought the skyther was the last one unaccounted for."

K stopped beside me, glanced at me, then back to the marine. "Uh, nope." She shrugged.

"Good to see you, K," I said.

"Yeah, you were gonna leave without me." She punched me on the arm, smiling. I cried out in pain.

"Shit, sorry."

"No worries." I said, holding in another groan.

We boarded the dropship, and the soldier followed. I noticed there wasn't anyone else on the dropship except us.

The ship shuddered and hummed, and began lifting off into the sky. The protective shields were down, so we could look at the station through the windows as we flew away.

"We'll be docking with Kronos in ten minutes," said the marine.

K blinked. "It's that fast?!"

The marine nodded, and we were silent. The station grew smaller and smaller in the distance as we flew. I sighed.

"So, you're feeling better this morning?" I asked K.

She raised an eyebrow at me. "I don't even know what you're talking about."

I shuffled in my seat. "I mean, you weren't doing so well last night. Nobody could blame you."

She put her hand on my shoulder and looked me in the eye. "Sax, I'm fine." She looked away.

I shook my head. "K, we've been over the whole 'Sax' thing."

"We've been over the whole 'me being fine' thing, Osax."

"Fair enough." She was gazing out the window.

It didn't take long for our ship to breach the atmosphere. K stood up and put her face right up to the window. Slowly, Voren became a giant white orb, shrinking as we flew, and a million stars shone just outside the window, reflected in her eyes. I stood next to K, and we both gazed out at the stars.

"Holy shit…" she said. I smiled, and lifted my ears.

After a few moments, she spoke again. "Makes you just wanna step out onto the ship and stare up at the planet from the hull." She was smiling in wonder.

The marine spoke up. "Doesn't make *me* wanna do that."

"Shut up." said K.

He did. Though, I imagine he probably complained about us to his friends some time later when we arrived at Kronos. Rightly so.

◆

Kronos was a Titan-class battlecruiser, named after a figure from ancient human mythology. Our dropships flocked to it, docking at one of its massive hangars. Though it was fitting of the Titan-class, Kronos seemed small compared to the valicorr ship that had attacked the station. It was long and grey, with rectangular shapes on its hull. Blue stripes lined its exterior, and the word KRONOS was painted on its side in black.

The hangar was full of noise and motion as the survivors from the base on Voren spilled out of the dropships. Fighters and other military ships were suspended in the air, ready for launch. Marines and officers in sky blue uniforms ushered us around, organizing us into groups and leading us out of the hangar into the halls of the ship, toward the ship's various amenities. K and I stuck together; she was gazing around at everything in wonder. Some wounded people were taken directly to the medical bay, others to the ship's lounge for refreshments and a chance to relax. Most of the people here were still shocked by the attack.

K and I, along with a few other groups, were brought to the lounge. I was happy to be guided around for a while; it meant I could keep my thoughts to myself and I wasn't put in a place where I needed to make many decisions. But when we arrived at the lounge, which was a wide room with with several tables, a bar, and some computer screens mounted high on the walls, I started trying to determine what to do next.

Two marines were positioned outside the entrance, and the place was filled up with scientists, engineers, and marines from the planet. K and I took a seat together at the bar, which was currently unattended, and glanced out across the murmuring crowd, and beyond the windows into space. I noticed several of the people in the room staring at the two of us. I slouched a little and my ears folded back involuntarily, and I turned away from the crowd.

K was tapping her fingers on the counter, and shot me a glance. "What's up, Osax?"

I narrowed my eyes a little. "What do you mean?"

She shuffled in her seat and turned her body toward me. "Aren't you glad we made it out? What's with you always being so moody?"

"I'm not always moody. I don't know where you got that impression."

She raised an eyebrow at me. "You take things so seriously all the time. Why?"

"Not all the time-"

"Whatever, you're taking what I'm saying and making it dumb. You look concerned. What's up?"

I glanced toward the crowd once more. "I…"

K waited for me to continue. I faced the bar once more.

"I'm fine," I said at last.

K nodded slowly, smirking. "Sure. Okay. Fair enough."

We remained silent for a while. The crowd was fairly tense, but I could sense the relief everyone was feeling from being off the planet and on a well armed and armoured TAU ship.

"I need to know what that station was all about."

"What?" said K.

"The station, most of its functions were classified. If I never get to find out what that was all about, I think I might explode."

"Why does it even matter?" asked K. "There's so much more world out there. Look at the goddamn stars out there; there's more than I can count. You're never gonna know everything, so why worry about something you know you can't know?"

I turned to face her. She was an intriguing person. But she didn't understand.

"It's a big deal, K. That installation was impressive, it must have taken the TAU a lot of resources to construct. And the fact that the valicorr didn't destroy it completely; they wanted something from that base. And whatever it was, they got it. I need to know what it was."

"But Osax, why? Why do you care about that at all?"

"Because people died!" I said. "And I couldn't save them! I tried- I tried, but I couldn't!" I felt tears welling in my eyes, and I continued, my voice breaking. "I failed. I failed at everything."

Tears streamed down my face, and I put my head in my hands. I noticed the murmuring had quieted, and I felt eyes on me. My ears trailed onto the table.

"Shit, Osax." I couldn't see K, but I knew she was still looking at me. "Hey, at least you didn't destroy the loro ruins."

I kept crying. I'm sure it was a strange experience for the humans in the room; I doubt many of them had seen a skyther cry before. And there I was, crying in front of all those people.

"Look." K put her hand on my shoulder. "This isn't over yet."

"They destroyed the base. They succeeded at whatever their mission was. The Director is dead, Joëlle's team is dead, I couldn't save the man in the elevator, the ruins are destroyed-"

K shook me with a jolt. "But *you're* alive! So your life isn't over. Get it together! It's not over yet, unless you give up. Or something. Right?"

I took a deep breath, and wiped my tears. I was being told to get it together by the person with the temper so huge they could destroy a temple with a single punch. I figured in that case, I should try to listen.

"I'm sorry."

"Never apologize," she said. I didn't know how to respond to that, so I just remained silent.

K noticed how everyone was now silently staring at us, and she turned to face them.

"Mind your own shit!" She aggressively shooed them away, and everyone went back to their own conversations.

I collected myself in the next few minutes. I felt better, having had the chance to release some tension there. But I knew I'd have to talk to Joëlle about her team. Then I imagined K saying, "Well you don't *have* to do anything." But I felt I needed to. Hopefully I'd get a chance to before we parted ways.

A few minutes later, the entrance opened up. A woman stepped into the room, along with two marine guards wearing black and blue armour, with black fabric trailing down from the waist. These were elite guards, and their faces were covered by black helmets with blue visors. They each held a short rifle at their sides.

The woman was wearing a smooth black uniform, with grey cuffs and details, and blue accents. She wore a black hat over her short blonde hair with a large silver TAU emblem on the front. My ears lifted at the sight of her. Her right pant leg was rolled up to her knee, revealing a dark metal cybernetic leg. She only wore one boot, over he left foot; her right one didn't need protection. Similarly, she wore a glove over her left hand, but her right was also robotic, like her leg. At her side was an E-pistol, and a molecular sabre.

She smiled slightly, and surveyed the room, standing at the head of it.

Her voice was gruff and commanding. "Welcome to Kronos. I'm Admiral O'Kane. I wanted to personally welcome you all onto my ship. I'm sorry about the circumstances under which we're meeting, but I hope to be as accommodating as I can be while you're all here.

"We're heading to the Olympus system; from there, each of you should be able to secure transport to wherever it is you must go. I've already contacted Olympus and they're expecting our arrival. In the meantime, you're welcome to use the ship's computer to make calls, and of course help yourself to any food or supplies you need. If you need anything, don't hesitate to contact one of my crew. All I ask is that if one of my officers asks you to do something, or *not* to do something, you listen. This is a military ship, and we have to keep things running smoothly in case we do run into any danger.

"If you're injured, you should have already been led to the med-bay, but if not that's alright. I can escort anyone there who needs medical attention, as it's my next destination."

There was some quiet chatting amongst the survivors. The admiral spoke again. "I'll be heading that way in two minutes. Don't be afraid to come up and introduce yourself."

The conversation resumed, and I stood up from my seat. K gave me a look.

Admiral O'Kane's eyes landed on me, and she paused. Then, she smiled and stepped forward.

"Well, what do we have here?" she said, extending her arms out in greeting.

I bowed my head slightly, my ears lifting. "A pleasure to see you again, Fiona. I hadn't known you were promoted to admiral!"

She clasped me on my shoulders. K was staring at her suspiciously.

"Well," said the admiral, "I hadn't known the great Prince Talcorosax was still off exploring the galaxy. When are you going to get your life together and head back to Astraloth?"

K leaped from her seat, knocking her chair to the floor.

"Wait- You're a *prince?!*"

Seventeen

"You never told me you were a prince!"

I swung around to K, smiling. "Well, it wasn't relevant."

The admiral laughed. "You always were humble."

K stared at me, her eyes wide and her mouth hanging. "You… you…"

I laughed. It felt good to laugh. "I'm sorry if you feel betrayed K; I wasn't trying to keep it secret, it just never came up."

She furrowed her brow. "Yeah, that's because people don't go 'hey, nice to meet you, are you royalty?' I think you need to volunteer that kind of information. Besides, when you were talking about your family, you never mentioned it! Don't pretend you weren't trying to avoid the subject."

I shrugged, suppressing some more laughter, and Fiona stepped closer to K.

"Don't worry," she said, "Talcorosax just doesn't like thinking about it. He'd rather be a scientist or a hero than a political leader, so he pretends he isn't one." She grinned at me, and I shook my head.

"It's not that…" I said, but the thing is, it sort of was.

"Well what is it then, huh?" K started chuckling and went to punch me on the arm, and instinctively I leaped backwards. Her swing missed.

The admiral stared at us, and we both started laughing.

"That was close," I said.

"Sorry, I keep… I don't know," said K. "It just feels like the thing to do."

The admiral extended her hand toward K. "A friend of Talcorosax is a friend of mine," she said, "and since you're apparently the only friend he has, this is a special occasion."

"Hey-" I said, but K cut me off, shaking the admiral's hand.

"My name's K."

The admiral winced in pain, and pulled her hand back. She stared at K with an intense expression. "You've got quite a firm grip. Guess I shouldn't be surprised judging by the look of you." She sized her up. "You look like quite the hardy one."

I noticed a flash of empathy on K's face, but she just nodded, and resumed a stern expression. "Yeah, I'm pretty hardy. Didn't realize you could feel pain through that robot hand."

"I can turn the pain off, if need be. Technology is amazing," she said. "What's your story, K? I've never seen anyone like you."

K crossed her arms. "I'm a mercenary. Worked on Voren."

"...Interesting."

"Yeah. Actually, with the Director dead, not sure how I'm gonna be paid for the past few weeks of work there. I'll need to contact somebody about that I guess."

The admiral nodded. "Yes, well as I said, feel free to use the ship's computer for making calls." She glanced at her holo-gauntlet. "I should go. Glad to see you, prince; and you, K."

"Wait," I said. "How are you and Reinhardt doing?"

She rolled her eyes. "You know how it is with him, Osax."

"On again? Or-"

"Off. Definitely off." She shook her head. "Anyway, I really must go." She smiled at me.

K nodded, and I bowed a skyther farewell. "It's a pleasure to see a familiar face," I said.

The admiral left the room with her guards, leading a few of the people to the med-bay. I turned to K.

"I'm curious, what do you do with your pay, anyway?" I asked.

"Hm?" She chuckled. "Well you wouldn't understand, you royal, rich piece of shit."

"Wh- Hey!" I exclaimed. "That was uncalled for."

K nodded, smiling. "Yeah, but it felt good."

I shook my head.

"Hey, I was just joking around. Lighten up, you're a good guy."

I lifted my ears slightly, but squinted at her.

She sighed. "I've just been saving my credits, you know."

"For what?"

"You know, getting a place somewhere nice, maybe. Getting my own ship. Going to the amusement parks on Gamralt, for like, months, or something. Or just getting away from everything." She paused. "I guess you could probably just give me some of your family's wealth and I wouldn't have to work."

"That's… not exactly how it works," I said. "My family is wealthy, but my mother has been very selective about funding for me. Mostly for my education."

K scoffed. "Yeah, sure, but at least your mom has things to select. You're full of it if you think you aren't privileged."

"I know I'm privileged," I said. "Maybe that's why I don't like advertising my bloodline."

"Why not?"

"Because, it makes all my accomplishments look like they were handed to me."

"Well, if I know anything about how money works, they kind of were, so…"

I shook my head. "Whatever."

"Hey, it's not a big deal," said K. "Nothing wrong with appreciating what you got. Just don't pretend that you made yourself rich." She paused. "I mean, I didn't make myself strong, or resilient. That's supposedly my best trait. Gotta be okay with that somehow, while I'm still alive."

I nodded. "I suppose so."

◆

I turned a corner while heading to the admiral's room and Jonathan slammed into me.

"Oh, excuse me," he said, brushing down his coat as I recovered my balance. He stood up straight, then looked me up and down. "Ah, it's you."

"Jonathan," I said, and bowed my head. "Headed down to the lounge?" I crossed my arms. "Where have you been anyway?"

He smirked. "I was just exploring the ship. Quite fascinating; I used to serve on board a Titan-class cruiser like this one."

"Really?" I asked, and my ears lifted in interest. "What ship?"

"Several years ago, I served aboard the Asteria. When I was in my early twenties, I was a TAU marine."

"That explains your skill with a weapon," I said. "I assumed you just practised at a shooting range."

He pointed to his robotic eye. "You don't get scars like this at a

99

shooting range; not unless something goes horribly wrong, at any rate." He chuckled, and shook his head. "No, I've seen my fair share of combat. Mostly with valicorr."

I nodded. "And that explains why you knew about the shadow scouts."

"Yes." The aperture of his cybernetic eye narrowed. "In fact, it was one such thing that took out my eye in the first place."

Silence hung in the air for a moment.

Unexpectedly, Joëlle passed us in the hall, heading toward the admiral's room as well.

"Jonathan," she said, nodding to him. He nodded back.

"Hey Joëlle," I said. She didn't even look at me as she turned the corner.

"Ah, that's her name," he said. "Joëlle." He ran his fingers through his hair, and exhaled. "I couldn't remember it."

My ears drooped, and I tightened my fists. "Yes," I said, watching where she had gone, "she's quite a friendly person."

Jonathan nodded in agreement though he clearly wasn't listening. "You know, and I'm quite sorry, but what was your name again?"

"Talcorosax," I said, and added, "but, if it's easier, you can call me Osax."

"Right! I'm sorry, I really am terrible with names." He laughed. "Us scientists tend not to be the most sociable of people."

I squinted slightly. I guess I could see what he was saying, but I quite liked interacting with others. Though, I suppose it may have stemmed from a scientific curiosity about human and skyther behaviour; similar to the curiosities that led me to become a biologist in the first place. So, I nodded in agreement.

He continued, "You know, I do think I've heard that name before. Isn't there a famous skyther named Talcorosax?"

"Well..." I began, and he stepped back, staring at me with a slight smile.

"You can't be... *prince* Talcorosax, are you?"

I nodded and my ears lifted. "Yes, I am. It seems everyone is finding out today."

He chuckled. "Well, had I known I rammed into a prince a few moments ago, I would have responded with much more pleading and apologizing, and perhaps a bit of grovelling."

I shook my head, and sighed. "That's- That's not necessary."

"Good," he said. "Well, I won't keep you any longer, Prince Osax."

He bowed, and I responded with the skyther farewell.

Jonathan seemed like a kind fellow. I hoped I'd be able to get to know him better some day, but I had business with my friend, Admiral O'Kane. I hadn't seen her in many years, and there was a chance she could help me out.

I entered her room. It was fairly small, with a window pointing to the front of the ship. From here, you could see most of the entire hull of the ship, and the stars gave it a mystical vibe which offset the practical military aesthetic. The admiral was standing on the other side of her desk which was placed in the middle of the room, gazing out the window. Joëlle stood facing her, standing at the desk.

"You don't understand, Admiral!" Joëlle leaned over the table. "The mothership is a threat to any and all TAU colonies. It's even a threat to Earth! It has to be stopped!"

Admiral O'Kane's voice was cold and unflinching. "I'm not disagreeing with you, RT. But I will not follow the ship."

"We don't know where they're headed next, but there's still time to follow their trail. If you wait too long, the slipspace emissions will dissipate too much; you won't be able to track them!"

The admiral turned her head, looking back. "I am not planning to track them. Not while Kronos is full of civilians. If the ship is as strong as you say it is, do you even think we'd be able to make a dent in it?"

"At least give me a team! I- I can't work on my own!"

The admiral spun around. "I'm sorry that your team was killed, but I will not just assign members of my crew to your suicide mission! If you want to track them, that's your imperative, RT. You have your own ship. But Kronos is headed for Olympus, and unless I get word from the Fleet Admiral, I'm not changing course."

I cleared my throat, and they both turned to me. Joëlle's face was full of anger and disbelief.

"Talcorosax, welcome," said the admiral.

"Admiral Fiona, I'm sorry to interrupt," I said.

She raised up her hand. "You aren't interrupting."

"Yes, he is." said Joëlle.

My ears shot back. I had hoped we could be friends, her and I. She was so kind to me when we first met. But I let her down. I tried to keep my composure, but I thought about the attack, the man in the elevator shaft, and the tower exploding, and I trembled.

Fiona looked concerned, and took a few steps toward me. "What's wrong, friend?" Joëlle looked between us, and pursed her lips.

"Nothing's wrong," I said, "I'm fine." I stood up straighter and lifted my ears to a neutral position. "I came here seeking information. I thought, being an admiral, perhaps you knew some details about the base on Voren. Such as, what might have attracted the valicorr to it in particular, or why it was stationed in such a remote location."

Joëlle tapped her fingers on her leg. "I'd like to know too," she said, "since I'm planning to hunt them down."

The admiral glanced out the window, and then slowly paced in the room. "Well," she began, "after receiving word about the attack last night, I thought I'd do some research on the station. And you're right, Prince, I was able to access some of the classified information." She paused, looking at us. "Since you're my friend, and the Prince of Astraloth for that matter, and you're a member of Round Table, I feel it's okay for me to divulge this information to you both."

Joëlle turned to me. "...Wait, you're Prince Talcorosax? I thought you just happened to have the same name as him."

I would have said something, but I was eager to finally hear about the station from Fiona, and I didn't know what to say since Joëlle was acting so cold to me. I didn't want to hurt our chance at friendship by saying the wrong thing.

"Yes, he's Prince Talcorosax," said Fiona. She sighed. "Now, there's no way to put this that makes it sound good. The base on Voren, among other functions, was a secret research lab... developing a weapon of mass destruction."

My heart skipped a beat. So that's why the valicorr had attacked.

"A weapon?!" exclaimed Joëlle. "What for?"

Fiona shook her head. "Unknown. What I do know is, they called it the 'Shade Beam'."

"The Shade Beam..." I said. The valicorr must have come for the plans, or prototypes, of this weapon; and whatever it was, that was bad news. "I don't understand. Why did they have so many biologists and scout vehicles there if the real purpose was to design weaponry?"

"Well, the base served many purposes, according to TAU records. The Shade Beam happened to be classified, and for good reason."

"How many of the people working there knew about this?" asked Joëlle.

"I don't know, the records didn't go into detail about that. Apparently, the Shade Beam is a kind of disintegration weapon."

My eyes widened. "Disintegration?"

She nodded solemnly. "Yes. Apparently, they had developed a

working prototype for a handheld cannon that could completely vaporize a target. The drawback was, the weapon requires a rare element, diffusionite, to turn into fuel for the weapon."

Joëlle spoke up. "Admiral, this doesn't sound like much news. A handgun that can kill isn't anything new, even if the method is more thorough. But you called it a weapon of mass destruction..."

Admiral O'Kane tapped a few buttons on her desk, and a holographic blueprint appeared. It looked like a blueprint for a massive cannon. "Well, they made a prototype that was for infantry. But they were designing the technology for a much, much larger scale."

"How did you get access to the blueprints?" I asked.

"If you look closely, you'll see these aren't real technical schematics. It's only a concept, meant to illustrate what the Shade Beam might become when finished." She closed the hologram. "The real blueprints, the real designs, must have been kept safe on Voren where the weapon was being developed."

"And what might it become?" asked Joëlle. "What kind of mass destruction are we talking about?"

The admiral turned to face the window, and remained silent for a few moments. "The Shade Beam, once completed, would have the ability to generate a field around an entire planet, and disintegrate it completely. It would only have to fire once, and the planet, and everything within the field, would be destroyed."

Silence hung in the air. The stars twinkled outside. My fists clenched, and I stepped forward.

"What were they thinking?! Who needs a weapon like this? Since when did the TAU need to destroy *planets?*"

Joëlle and Fiona looked at me.

"I can't believe this!" I yelled. "Did Astraloth even know about this? Did a *single* skyther know?!"

Fiona frowned. "I don't know, Talcorosax. I'm baffled too."

"And now," I said, fuming, "the valicorr probably have the plans, and the prototype." I shook my head, and tried to concentrate on my breathing. The valicorr, who in all the time we'd known about them never once displayed a friendly, let alone neutral disposition toward us, had the keys to a weapon that could potentially destroy billions of people in the blink of an eye.

Joëlle turned to Fiona. "How- How can you refuse to go after them, even knowing they probably stole the plans to the Shade Beam? How come you won't provide a team for me at the very least?!"

Joëlle and I jumped back. "I will *not* put my crew at unnecessary risk!" She yelled. "I'll speak with the Fleet Admiral, once Kronos is safe at Olympus. But I will not assume I know the best course of action in this very unique and precarious situation! I am not willing to risk throwing all of our lives away, metaphorically speaking, attacking a fortress with a dagger."

"But this is Kronos!" said Joëlle. "It's a Titan-class battlecruiser! The TAU doesn't *have* ships that are stronger than this!"

"Well, from what you've told me, one ship won't be enough."

"Fine," I said. "I understand your reasoning, Fiona. Thank you for filling us in."

"Of course." She had a stern expression on her face. "Now, I need to get this journey underway. You're both dismissed."

I could see Joëlle ball her fists, before storming out. I bowed to Fiona, but she was clearly in a bad mood. She waved curtly, and turned to face the window. I decided to leave my old friend be, and left the room, chasing after Joëlle. I needed to talk to her.

Eighteen

"Wait, Joëlle!"

I caught up to her in a hallway with windows facing the back of the ship. A few moments later, and I noticed the space outside began to distort as though it was pooling into a drain directly behind the ship; at last Kronos had entered into slipspace.

Joëlle was staring outside too. "Dammit!" She pressed her hands against the glass. "I can't take off from Kronos while it's in slipspace."

I stopped beside her, and between pants, said, "Theoretically it's possible, just incredibly dangerous."

"Shut up!" She spun toward me, her brow furrowed. After a moment of silence, she asked, "What do you even want?"

I took a deep breath. "I want to help you. I want to travel with you in pursuit of the valicorr mothership. I want to take back the Shade Beam before they can turn it into a real threat."

"No."

"But- You said you need a team."

"*No!*" She was glaring at me.

I stepped forward slowly. "Why not?"

"Because you let my team die, and now I'm all alone!" She spat. "I trusted you! I don't know why, but I trusted you!"

My ears dropped. "I tried to save them! But I got caught up helping some other people on the way-"

"Some other people?!"

I was finding it difficult to swallow. "Yes, some other people. They were trapped in an elevator. Her husband-"

"Trapped in an elevator?" She took a step closer, looking up at me. "Was the elevator in danger?!"

"There was a woman, she was crying, trying to save her husband who was stuck in there." I bowed my head. "I had to pry the doors open, and climb down the shaft to help them."

"Anyone could have done that!" She shook her head in disbelief. "Not anyone could have taken out that gunship or bought us enough time to restore power, so my team could get out of there. But you're a skyther prince. You're combat trained, you should have been doing that!"

"Wait- The valicorr started attacking us in the elevator! I had to defend them!" I raised my hands defensively.

"In the elevator? You mean after you'd opened the doors?" She shook her head. "Do you really think those valicorr would have even known people were in their if you didn't leave the doors wide open for them to see? *You* put them in danger, by trying to help!"

I noticed the beads of sweat forming on my cheeks and palms. Maybe she was right. I made the wrong call… maybe if I hadn't tried to help, the valicorr wouldn't have noticed them, and no one would have died. I would have run to the defense cannon and shot down the gunship, and then I would have found some way to distract the valicorr who were blocking her team's exit, until the power was restored.

My eyes were beginning to water. "I assessed the situation and made a choice," I said.

"You made a bad choice! Why didn't you just do what I asked and help my team?! Now I'm all alone!" Her voice was breaking, and I saw tears forming in her eyes. "Why couldn't you save them?!"

"I don't know." I stared blankly at the floor.

Joëlle wiped her face. "I need a team. People I can trust."

"You can trust me!" I said. I felt a spark within me.

She shook her head and frowned. "I can trust you to what? To go back on the plan? To get people killed? What can I trust you to do?"

Slowly I closed my fists together, and I stood up straighter. I lifted my head, my ears, my eyes. I looked at Joëlle. I took a deep breath.

"You can't trust me to save everyone," I said. "You can't trust me to be perfect. Honestly, you can't even trust me to stay out of other people's business." I stepped forward. "But you can trust me to try, and not to rest until that mothership is neutralized. I'm not happy about what happened at the base. Honestly, I'm devastated. I let people die. But I just want to do what I can to make up for it. And this Shade Beam needs to be stopped, before it's functional." I reached out a hand. "So please, I'm volunteering to put my life on the line with you, in the name of protecting the galaxy. Please accept my help, and my friendship."

And my friendship? I thought. *Whatever, the rest was good.*

She was looking at me with more sympathy, but I could tell she was holding back tears. I held my hand out for what felt like ages, listening to the sound of us breathing and the ship's hum. Finally, she grabbed my hand, and shook it, looking me in the eye.

"I'm sorry," she said.

"So am I. I am so sorry."

She bowed her head. "Well… we have to wait until Kronos arrives at the Olympus system. Which means we've missed our window for tracking the mothership via slipspace emissions. I won't let that stop me from trying though; I will find it."

"So, we definitely won't be able to track the slipspace emissions?" I asked.

"Not necessarily," said Jonathan. Joëlle and I jumped back at the sound of his voice as he stepped around the corner. "I'm sorry for eavesdropping, but I must say I'm very intrigued by the sound of this 'Shade Beam'."

"What- I thought you were going to the lounge?" I said.

He smirked. "Did I say that? I don't think I did."

Joëlle spoke up. "So, you didn't know about the Shade Beam?"

"Only rumours about a planet destroying weapon. I assumed it was nonsense." He shrugged. "I guess it wasn't."

Joëlle rubbed her eyes. "So, you think there might be a way to track the slipspace emissions, even after flying to Olympus aboard Kronos, and back to the Voren system in my ship?"

He nodded confidently. "Yes, if I were able to operate your scanners, and modify them a bit, I've been working on such a device in my spare time. One that would be able to detect even minuscule traces of slipspace radiation. It's technically complex, so you might need my expertise to use it." He manually adjusted his cybernetic eye.

"You… want to come with us?" I asked. Joëlle shot me a glance.

"Yes, I do," he said. "All my research on Voren, well, it's going to be put on hold indefinitely unless the TAU decides to construct a new research base there. But, if word about the Shade Beam gets out, I doubt they're going to fund another station there. It'll be associated in the eyes of the public with secret weapons testing, which is not a wonderful image." He paused, and his smile faded as he stood upright, his coat trailing. "The valicorr killed my coworkers… and friends. I want to do what I can to help stop them." He turned to Joëlle. "And I was just telling Osax about my history as a marine. I'd be good help in a fight, when inevitably it comes to that." He smiled weakly.

Joëlle slowly nodded. "Alright. I can work with a team of three. Five would be ideal, though four would be better than three…" She trailed off, then turned to Jonathan and shook his hand. "Welcome aboard, Jonathan."

"Thank you," he said. He smiled strangely.

My ears lifted and I sighed in relief. The valicorr had a seemingly unstoppable ship, and now the means to construct a weapon that could destroy an entire planet. But, we were forming a team to counteract it. It seemed foolish, but that thought brought me comfort.

"I was thinking as well," said Jonathan, "we should get K in on this."

"I was hoping K would be interested," I said, and my thoughts turned to her. I had no idea what she was planning to do, now that her home was destroyed. I wasn't even sure how much she cared… her mood swings were so extreme. But I had a feeling she'd want to join us.

Joëlle nodded. "Yes, K would be an extremely valuable asset," she said.

"Well," I cleared my throat. "I'll go find K and talk to her about this. Shall we regroup when we arrive at Olympus?"

"Yes," said Joëlle. "When Kronos exits slipspace, let's meet in hangar D; that's where my ship is."

Jonathan stretched his arms and shoulders. "Getting a bit nervous. I didn't expect to be doing this." he said, and chuckled.

I looked him in the eyes. "No one expected this."

◆

I found K alone on one of the observation decks. It was a dome-shaped room which you entered via stairs leading up to it. The dome was made up of windows, and K was lying down on a couch, staring up at the stars streaming past in a distorted blur. Her chest rose and fell slowly with each breath, and her orange eyes gleamed dimly in the light. She was humming a song, with a simple melody I had never heard before. It was enchanting, and flowed smoothly like a waltz. When she noticed me, she tilted her horned head to look my way, and waved casually.

"Hey." She turned back toward the stars. I could tell she was deep in thought.

I approached her, and sat down on a chair nearby. "How are you doing, K?"

She exhaled. "Great."

I gazed up at the stars. "Me too."

She looked at me and raised an eyebrow. Then she chuckled to herself. "You're funny, Osax."

"So are you, K."

We sat in silence for a while longer.

"So," I said, "do you know what you're planning to do, now that you're out exploring the galaxy?"

She sighed. "Yeah."

"Can I ask what you're going to do?"

She snorted. "Yep."

"...What are you going to do?"

She closed her eyes. "I'm gonna lie here."

I waited for her to continue, but of course she didn't.

"So-"

"Osax," she interrupted me. "Uh, you go ahead."

"No, it's alright."

She sighed. "Okay, so… I just was wondering..." she turned to face me. "Why... are you still talking to me?"

I titled my head to the side. "I don't understand." She didn't look angry.

"I mean, we're done the mission. And I royally screwed it up." She shook her head, and chuckled. "Actually I guess you royally screwed it up; I normally screwed it up, just, more than usual."

I remained silent, and she sat up.

"Look," she continued, "we don't have to work together anymore. We were assigned to a mission, we almost died, we found the station under attack, and we tried to save it and kind of succeeded. But now, don't you have princely things to do? Other people to talk to about scholarly things and ancient alien bullshit?"

"Alien bullshit?"

"I meant loro stuff, not skyther stuff. Mutual aliens."

I raised one of my ears. "Would you rather me not talk to you?"

"No!" She said, and then turned away, chuckling nervously. "No, I just don't get it. You don't have any reason to want to, and you have plenty reason to leave me alone. You must have other friends."

I paused. "Do I need a reason to want to talk to you?"

She stared at me puzzled. "Uh, don't you?"

I thought for a moment. "I just enjoy your company."

She looked at me dumbfounded. "Ha, ha," she said sarcastically.

"Really," I said, "I enjoy being around you."

"Why?" she was eyeing me suspiciously.

"You're headstrong, you're funny. You have a heart somewhere in there; you tried to cheer me up when we were in the lounge, and the stress of everything was getting to me. You're curious about things, like me."

She scoffed. "I might be curious about things, but not like you, you nerd."

I shook my head, ears lifting. "You know, I'm trying to compliment you."

"Yeah, that's the best time to insult people. Catches them off guard." She flashed a toothy grin at me. "Besides, now that I know you have feelings for me, I can manipulate you."

I laughed. "What the hell is wrong with you, K?"

"I have no fricken idea. You're the first person who's gotten close enough to me to ask that, and still wanted to talk." She looked me in the eye, her tusks framing a warm smile. "So, does this make you my friend?"

I felt my chest get lighter. "I hope so. I'd like to consider you my friend."

She grinned.

"And actually, I don't have many friends," I said. "I've traveled so much, much more than most people, skythers and humans alike. It makes it hard to maintain friendships. Fiona is one of the only friends I still have, and even then this is the first time I've seen her in ages."

"I guess I shouldn't be surprised a nerd like you is so lonely." She said, smirking. For whatever reason, I found her teasing endearing.

"What about you? You must have had some friends on the station…" I trailed off, realizing that even if she did, they may have been killed in the attack.

She shook her head, and the smile began to fade. "No, not really. When I was growing up, the doctors and scientists took care of me. But, none of them really cared about me, I guess. I think I scared people too much."

"Yeah?"

"Yeah." She shrugged. "Scaring people isn't all bad."

"I know I scared some people on the station," I said.

"Those people were cowards, if you scared them."

"I was trying to say I sympathize, and you turned it into an insult. Come on, K. Why?"

"I don't know. You're the one who wanted to be my friend." She was smiling. "So, I interrupted you a while back."

"Yes." I said. I relayed to her the information about the Shade Beam, and how Joëlle and Jonathan and I were planning to go together to try to stop the mothership. "So," I continued, "we wanted to know if you would come join us."

She looked at me with a startled expression. "Osax, that's insane."

I nodded.

"No, like, that's really insane. The AA guns couldn't even dent that thing."

"So, that's a no?" I asked.

"No? No!" She grinned. "It's a yes. I wanna get back at those bastards. Besides, once we're heroes I'm sure there'll be fame and money in it." She crossed her arms.

I smiled. "Yes, I guess so. I'm glad you're on board."

"I'm *so* on board. Honestly, I had no idea what I was gonna do since the base got destroyed. Was thinking of stealing a ship and flying after it, or something."

"K…" I said.

"Hey, I was just thinking about it, I didn't do it!" She paused. "Hey, also, do we have to go with Jonathan?"

"Yes, we do."

"Fine."

"What's your problem with him?"

"I don't know," she said. "I just don't like him."

I shook my head. "Well, we need him to track down the mothership."

There was a long pause, and I listened to the hum of the ship. Then she spoke again.

"…Do we have to go with Joëlle?"

I put my head in my hands.

Nineteen

Olympus was the name the TAU gave to the planet which served as their primary military base. The planet was also home to the largest human settlement outside of Earth.

When Kronos arrived in the system, K and I were still sitting on the observation deck. We emerged from slipspace to see the green and blue planet, and a large fleet of TAU ships. K and I both sat up at the same time, gazing out at the ships in wonder. There were two other Titan-class ships; one of them was grey with yellow stripes, and the word ASTERIA on its side. The other starship was black against the glow of the planet, and I could see the word HADES written in white on its hull. Blue energy faintly glowed from the engines of the ships, and the space in front of us was dotted with smaller ships and transports flying to and fro.

Kronos drifted close to the planet, in between Asteria and Hades. K and I trained our eyes on small TAU fighters which flew overhead in a blue streak, inspecting Kronos.

"Wow," said K. I forgot for a moment that she'd never left Voren before, so of course this was an amazing sight to her. I'd visited Olympus several times in my life, and even so it still filled me with wonder. The light of Olympus' star reflected off each hull, igniting the edges of each craft in a warm orange glow.

"Pretty impressive, isn't it?" I mused.

K closed her mouth, which had been hanging open. "Yeah, it's alright." She smiled at me knowingly.

"Come on," I said, and stood up. "Are you ready to go?"

She flung herself out of the couch, and stretched. "Yeah, I'm ready. Not much time to relax though, huh?"

"Unfortunately not. Any second that mothership is out there with those plans, the Shade Beam could get closer to manifestation." I lowered my ears. "And the closer it is to manifesting, the closer our planets are to disintegrating. I don't think I even believe it's possible, honestly, but I think at the least we need more intel on that ship."

K nodded. "Alright, sounds good. What about your wounds though, how are you holding up? You got kinda messed up back there."

I touched my shoulder. "I'm healing well, it only hurts a little."

I glanced up at the lush planet in front of us, and I felt a longing to land there and relax for a while. But then I thought about Joëlle, and how I failed to protect her team because I didn't follow her orders. I thought about my mother, about Astraloth, about Earth. I thought about how the valicorr had come and killed so many on Voren, and I knew that was only the beginning.

But even thinking about all that didn't quiet my mind. *Forget about this,* I thought. *I came to Voren to research the loro ruins. That's it. And I still haven't even checked the transfer device to see if I got anything. I could just head back to Astraloth, say hello to my mother, rest for a while, and study anything the transfer device may have saved.*

"Uh, Osax? You sure you wanna do this?" asked K.

"I…" I squinted.

There was another reason I *did* want to follow the mothership. Valicorr had never attacked in such a coordinated way until now, and certainly had never been seen with such an imposing starship. We didn't know anything about how their government worked or how their military was organized, but this seemed like an emergence in their behavioural pattern. A new curiosity. A mystery. And the starship itself, the Shade Beam too, was enigmatic. I felt myself getting excited at the prospect of uncovering its mysteries. Was I more interested in learning about the Shade Beam than preventing its existence?

I shook my body, trying to reset my thoughts.

"I'm fine," I said, and lifted my ears. "You head to the hanger; I want to say goodbye to the admiral first."

"Alright," said K. "I'll see you there."

◆

I entered the admiral's room once more. The window revealed Olympus and the TAU fleet.

"So," she said, looking up from her desk, "the prince is off again?"

I took a deep breath.

"Yes, and I'm going to be helping Joëlle track the mothership."

Fiona paused, and stared at me.

"You know, Talcorosax, I'm going to be mentioning this to the Fleet Admiral. I'm going to do what I can to get the gears turning. If you just wait a bit, you won't have to go."

I sighed. "That's not good enough." I wasn't even sure what I was saying… but I'd already decided I wanted to find that ship. I had to.

She scoffed. "Not good enough for a prince, maybe, but it's the best I can do. I'm not sure how the higher ups are going to deal with this, especially considering the conspiratorial nature of the base on Voren. It's got a lot of mystery surrounding it. But there's a lot on the line if I push the Fleet Admiral too hard on this." She paused. "To be honest, I'm worried. I'm worried they won't like that I learned about the Shade Beam."

I remained silent, and after a brief moment she continued.

"I just don't want you to get into any trouble, but I know that's exactly your plan."

I shook my head. "No, the plan is to prevent the valicorr from being able to do any more damage with that ship, or with the Shade Beam. Getting into trouble is avoidable."

She sighed, and stood up. "I don't think so. But, it's your decision." She reached out a hand to me. "You can contact me anytime. I might not be able to do much, but I can try."

I shook her hand. "Thank you, Fiona. It was good to see you again.

She had a grave expression. "You too, Talcorosax. Don't die."

I turned to leave, but she called for me to wait.

"I forgot to ask…"

"What is it?"

"I don't mean to be rude, but where did that blue one come from?"

I tilted my head to the side. "You mean K?"

"Yeah, that's the one. Is she going with you?"

"Yes, she is. So is Jonathan Wellsworth, a scientist. We're all going to help Joëlle."

"K's a bioweapon, isn't she?"

I nodded slowly, my ears drooping. I still knew so little about her.

"She is," I said. "She was found by the TAU, broken free from her restraints in a secret lab somewhere, and then brought to Voren."

The admiral raised an eyebrow. "Really? Where was she found?"

"I don't know. K doesn't remember, and the Director, who seemed to know more, is now dead."

"I have a theory about what organization may have created her," she said.

I perked up a bit. "Really?!" I asked. "Who do you think created her? I've been trying to figure that out."

"Well, to me, this has the Brotherhood written all over it."

I was taken aback. "I thought the Brotherhood was just a hoax."

"Really?" She asked, looking surprised. "Well, it's true they're secretive. But unfortunately, they're also real. Not enough is known about them, except that they want to bring down the TAU, and they don't have a love of skythers either it seems."

"They're a group of human terrorists, right?"

"They'd want you to think of themselves as revolutionaries, but they're brutal, violent, and cold. The Brotherhood is the epitome of, 'the ends justify the means'. Perhaps true in some cases, but not when you're killing innocent people. The few times we've had encounters with them, they've been outfitted with some special kinds of beige armour. Often carrying spread-shot energy rifles, equipped with molecular bayonets."

My eyes widened. "That sounds deadly; where are they getting this equipment?"

"If the TAU knew, we'd shut down the supply at the source. It's unlikely they're using conventional methods to acquire the gear. They have enough funds and resources to run research labs, and experiment with bioweapons, which is why I thought they might be behind K. It's likely they've set up their own methods for manufacturing their gear."

"Hmm," I said. I'd heard rumours about the Brotherhood over the past year or so, but hadn't realized they were actually real. A group of humans, operating in secrecy with excessive resources, trying to bring down the TAU. I was not happy to hear that the rumours were true, especially not when the valicorr threat seemed to be more prominent now than ever with their new mothership. "Well, thank you for the information. I should probably get going."

"Before you do, there's one more thing I wanted to say, and I hope I'm wrong about it." She looked at me with concern in her eyes.

"You're worried that K is a sleeper agent, aren't you?"

She exhaled. "Yes, I'm worried about that." She put a hand on my shoulder. "Keep an eye on her, alright? Especially if you notice anything strange happening with her."

Immediately, I thought about her unexplained blackouts. I cleared my throat. "I'll keep an eye on her. Thank you."

I turned to leave, but my thoughts were dark. I didn't know what I'd do if K betrayed us, but so far I had no reason to think that would happen. *Right?*

◆

The hangar was loud and busy, with many of the survivors from Voren boarding dropships. The dropships animated and whirred, and flew out of the hangar's containment field, which was a mostly transparent wall of energy which kept the air and pressure of the hangar intact, while allowing ships to pass through. Over a crowd of crew members, I saw Jonathan and Joëlle standing, talking to each other. Jonathan's orange eye flashed in the sunlight bleeding in through the containment field. I saw K just ahead of me, slowly approaching them as well.

"I thought you'd be at the ship by now." I said.

K turned to me. "Oh, hey." She rubbed her head. "Guess I got a headache. Didn't quite feel like bookin' it down the halls."

"Fair enough," I said, and my thoughts spiraled, thinking about her mysterious condition yet again.

We pushed through a crowd of people and made it up to Jonathan and Joëlle.

"K!" said Jonathan, with a mischievous smirk. "I'm glad you decided to come."

K shrugged. "Well, whatever."

Jonathan raised an eyebrow at her and sized her up, but said nothing.

"Osax, thanks for offering to help." Joëlle was looking up at me. She didn't look happy, but she didn't look angry either, which was good.

I said, "You're welcome," because I didn't know what else to say.

K's eyes lit up. "Holy crap, that's your ship?"

Joëlle smiled at her, and I followed her gaze. Several meters away, docked on the floor of the hangar was a black gunship. It looked large enough for ten or so people to stay in, but no larger than necessary. It was rounded and smooth on the top, with two bulky wings on either side of the cockpit, which was front and center. Shallow fins traced the top of the ship like a spine. The windshield was wide and lined with a vibrant red colour, matching the detailing on the rest of the ship, which was otherwise black. The sunlight glinted off the hexagonal grid texture of the hull. Four large weapons of some kind stuck out from the front, two on either side.

"Yeah," said Joëlle, "It's my ship. She's called the Firebrand."

"So, I take it you're a good pilot?" I asked.

116

"Yes, I was the designated pilot for my team." She frowned. "We all flew in this ship, when it made sense for us to, anyway. It's a home away from home."

"If I'm not mistaken, that's a Ranger-Class gunship, correct?" said Jonathan, his eyes flashing between us. "An all-purpose vehicle… fast, agile, resilient, and with decent storage." He grinned. "A triple-redundant Tetryon-generator for energy; multiple bunk beds… a spacious interior with ample head-room. Oh, and it's got a dedicated kitchen, doesn't it? With cupboards and everything? Perfect for running away in, and living amongst the stars."

Joëlle nodded, her lips spreading slowly to a smile. "That's all true. Where'd you learn all that? Were you thinking of getting one yourself?"

"I was considering it, actually," he said. "Some time ago."

Joëlle flicked some stray locks of hair from her eyes with a twist of her head, and smiled. "Well you've got good taste, Mr. Wellsworth."

Jonathan's cheeks flushed a little. "The colour palette absolutely agrees with me; that must have been custom painted. I think *you're* the one with excellent taste."

Joëlle smiled, and lowered her head slightly. I thought I could see some red in her cheeks as well. K stared at them impatiently.

Jonathan continued. "Well, I'd like to get shown inside, take a look at the scanners. I'm eager to see what I can do with them." His lip twitched into a half smile, and Joëlle led us inside.

The ship was well lit on the inside, with multiple rooms and beds. The ceiling was, thankfully, around nine feet tall, giving me ample room to stand up straight. There were several rooms and amenities. Despite being a gunship, it was also designed for long excursions into space. It was clearly a multipurpose vessel.

We were led to the cockpit, which had five seats; three in an arrowhead at the front of the ship, and two more behind them, one on each side. Jonathan, Joëlle, and K all took seats at the front, one at a time. I stood, watching over their shoulders as Jonathan began to work.

"Can you work on the scanners while we're flying?" asked Joëlle.

"Yes, of course."

"Then, everybody, this is your last chance to bail." She looked at each of us for a few seconds. None of us said anything, or made a motion to leave.

At last K spoke up. "What, do you think we'd really just leave? We all saw what that mothership did. Shade Beam or not, I wanna get some vengeance."

I nodded in agreement.

"I think we all know the risks," said Jonathan.

"Getting blown up?" asked K.

"Uh- yes." said Jonathan, before turning back to the scanner. He ducked under the control console and began fiddling with things.

"Alright, we'll head back to Voren's orbit. If Jonathan's right, we can start tracking the ship from there." said Joëlle. Her expression hardened as she gripped the controls from the central pilot's seat. "Let's go."

The engine began to buzz and the ship lifted off the floor of the hanger smoothly. I wouldn't have even noticed we were moving if I wasn't looking outside the window. Slowly, the ship began to spin around, and I felt a pang of anxiety. For a moment, I was back on the snowy ledge, clutching K in my arms. The massive black ship was on top of us like an umbrella, humming deeply. It reached an arm of blood red energy to the AA cannon. Like cracking a whip, it lashed out, and the cannon shattered like glass. I shivered.

The Firebrand pointed out of the hangar, and started to accelerate, in sync with my heart rate. Silently, we passed through the containment field, into open space. We left Kronos behind, and slowly the planet Olympus, and the fleet too. A thousand stars stared back at us, unblinking in the blackness of space.

I sat down on the seat to the left, next to K, and gripped the armrests tightly. K and I exchanged glances. My heart was pounding. *Are we really about to do this?*

As if to answer, "Of course we are," K flashed me a smile, and the stars ahead of us began to warp and shift as the Firebrand accelerated, and drifted into slipspace.

Twenty

Eight days passed. Jonathan was apparently having difficulty getting the scanner to work, so we were exploring space more based off of educated guesswork than hard facts. According to Jonathan, we had some leads, but I wasn't totally convinced. K lost most of her enthusiasm by the end of the first day, and Joëlle was struggling to stay optimistic, but not one of us uttered any word of complaint, or any hint that we should give up. Not even K. I think we all knew that to hear another person explicitly express their doubts might shatter our resolve, and bring us all to the brink of a listless sadness. To my surprise, Jonathan was holding our spirits together. He had the strength to offer up words of hope and encouragement that we weren't far behind the ship in moments of silence, even though we all knew the more time passed, the harder it would be to track the mothership.

In a way, I was glad. We didn't exactly have a plan for what to do once we found the ship. In the first day at least, Joëlle informed us that the Firebrand was equipped with a unique, experimental cloaking device. It didn't literally turn the ship invisible, like the valicorr shadow scout that attacked us in the generator room. Instead, it made it impossible to detect via most scanners, meaning the mothership would have to spot us visually, from a window. If we kept our distance, that would be very unlikely in the vastness of space. The downside was, the ship's weapons couldn't fire while the cloaking device was active. Still, it comforted me that if we ran into the mothership, it wouldn't instantly notice us and obliterate our spacecraft.

We'd agreed to sleep in two shifts. K and I were one shift, Jonathan and Joëlle were the other. There were several hours of overlap where everyone was awake, but this way, there were no times when we were all asleep. Since we were out in space, we had to set our own schedules anyway, with no sunrise or sunset to guide us. I noticed over the course of the week that Joëlle and Jonathan seemed to be getting along well. They looked at each other often, during the hours when the four of us were awake, and Jonathan even made Joëlle laugh every now and then. I realized I hadn't heard her laugh until then, at least not since the attack on Voren at any rate.

Jonathan also talked to K a fair amount, often asking innocuous questions about her. She mostly shrugged them off or gave half answers, and seemed much more comfortable talking to me when we were alone. Joëlle and K seemed comfortably distant. I think Joëlle tried to be friendly with K, but K didn't really respond to her much. It got me wondering about why she had opened up to me as much as she had. K made some jokes, but continued to seem fairly reserved. I didn't notice her suffering from any more headaches or fainting, which was good. I tried to push away any thoughts that she might be a sleeper agent.

The Firebrand was equipped with a galactic communicator, and I'd been contemplating calling my mother, but something kept holding me back. My mother was the queen of Astraloth. She rarely had any time for me these days, though she tried to be supportive of my work as a researcher and scientist. She hadn't ever outright said it, but I could tell over the past few cycles that each time we talked, she was more uncomfortable. I believe she was concerned that if I continued down this life path of exploring and putting myself in danger, that I might die, and there might not be an heir to the skyther throne. My father had passed away many years ago, and I was an only child, so it probably brought my mother great stress to think about me, and how I wasn't with her to learn more about our people's ways, and what it meant to be king. I was grateful that she had never explicitly told me these concerns, because if she did, then I'd have to tell her the truth; I didn't want to be the ruler of Astraloth. It's a beautiful planet, and a wonderful place to live, but I was called by the world beyond our planet. My heart was drawn to the stars. But if I was being honest with myself, that wasn't the only reason I didn't want to acknowledge my lineage. It was also because I knew I was unfit to take my mother's place. I wasn't a leader.

I found myself alone lying on a bottom bunk bed in the left wing, where K and I had been sleeping. K was piloting the ship right now, or at least watching to make sure the autopilot functioned correctly. We were traveling through slipspace to our next destination, one Jonathan was "absolutely certain" was the right trail, but none of us were convinced.

I'd connected my holo-gauntlet to the Firebrand's communications system, so I could make calls using my gauntlet as long as I was within range of the ship. My hand hovered over my mother's number. I had no idea if she was busy right now. I had no idea where she was on Astraloth or what time of day it would have been where she was. I had no idea what to say to her. I just felt as though, maybe, I should talk to her, and update her on what I was doing, and the attack on Voren.

I shook my head and deactivated my holo-gauntlet. I didn't want to have to explain what was going on just yet. I still felt like my mind hadn't settled down enough. And I had no idea how she would react, but we didn't always get along.

Instead, I took out the transfer device, sat up, and went over to a computer console. I plugged the device in and ran a diagnostic. After a few seconds, the computer beeped faintly at me.

My ears lifted. Apparently it had salvaged some information from the ruins after all. Most of it seemed compromised, but I started decompressing the data. The computer screen flooded with images and text files and symbols. Immediately, I remotely connected with the loro research servers and began uploading all of the raw data, updating them on the findings so that they could study it themselves. I took a few minutes to fill out a report of the mission on Voren, making sure the information was sent in full to the TAU and Astraloth. When I was satisfied, I returned to browsing the data the transfer device had recovered for my own interest. I was fairly skilled at translating loro languages, but not all of them were the same. I didn't know what to look for, but I decided since nothing else was happening on this expedition so far, I may as well spend my time deciphering some of the data. I was happy to have something familiar to do. It was relaxing, and also exciting. Each piece of data recovered from the ruins hadn't been seen by anyone since the loro vanished from the galaxy. I was the first person, right there, on that small spaceship, to gaze upon these pieces of loro history.

I paused on a photographic image of a loro. It wasn't the first image of a loro that had been recovered, but nevertheless it was exhilarating to see. This loro was standing, holding a double bladed sword of some kind in her two left hands. She was wearing some kind of ceremonial garb, and a mask covering her face, which was typical of the loro. To my knowledge, no one had yet found a picture of a loro whose face was uncovered. It was standing outside a temple or structure in a lush jungle. The structure had what appeared to be large laser turrets on the top of it. The image was colourless, like all loro photographs. They didn't appear to have words for any colours in their language, at least not that anyone had yet deciphered. The belief among researchers was that the loro were completely colour blind. But even in greyscale, the image was striking. The sun was in the sky, and upon looking closely I could see two much smaller stars next to the primary star. From the look of things, this planet orbited in a unique looking trinary star system. I couldn't recall any loro ruins being discovered in trinary star systems... which meant this was a clue to finding more undiscovered loro remnants.

I spent the next few hours parsing the data from the transfer device, and translating anything I could. I wanted to find the planet; I thought it would be a good way to keep myself entertained. Eventually I was able to link some coordinates to the image I was looking at. I uploaded the data to my holo-gauntlet and walked into the cockpit.

K was leaning back on the front left chair, with her legs propped up on the central one. Her holo-gauntlet was active, displaying a holographic screen several feet in front of her. Some kind of three dimensional virtual world was displayed on the screen, and in her right hand was a holographic gun, which she aimed at the screen. Faint sounds of virtual gunfire sounded through the cockpit, and she had a look of intense concentration on her face as she played the game. Her left hand held a holographic controller.

She looked up at me, startled at first, and then smiled. "Hey, Sax, help me out."

"With what?"

"I'm playing 'Defenders of Earth'. It's got a drop in coop feature, apparently."

"Huh." I said, and sat down beside her. "I came here to use the ship's navigational computer, actually."

"Oh," she said as she kept playing. "Well, that's boring."

"I'm trying to conduct some research."

"Yeah, boring," she said, smirking. I shook my head, and started inputting the coordinates and timestamp from the image into the navigational computer.

"It's quite exciting, actually. I'm trying to find the location of some potentially undiscovered loro structures. By plugging in the coordinates and timestamp from a picture I recovered-"

"Oh hey, so I didn't destroy all the data after all!"

I paused. "No, you didn't. Can I finish?"

"Sure."

"I can use the navigational computer to retroactively determine what planet would have been at those coordinates in relative space at the time it was taken."

"That sounds complicated."

"Yes, it is. That's why I'm getting the computer to do it."

I wasn't totally sure if it would work.

"Is that gonna take long?"

I glanced at the progress bar. "Yeah, looks like it will."

She turned to me. "Alright, come on." She beckoned me.

I lifted my ears. "I'll play, if you admit that research is both valuable, and interesting."

She groaned. "Come on, I've never played this game coop. No one has ever wanted to. Everyone at the station either was really busy all the time or just didn't want to spend their free time with me." I felt a twinge of sympathy.

"Well, you have to be nice to me if you want to hang out."

"Actually," she said, "we're kind of stuck together on a tiny spaceship. I don't really have to do anything to hangout."

"Alright," I said, and I stood up to leave.

"No, Osax!" she pleaded, and then laughed. "The computer AI sucks! I need a real person controlling the gun turret at this part. I haven't been able to beat it."

I turned to her and stared at her, lifting my ears. I put my hands on my wide hips.

She sighed. "Fine. Research is good and not boring."

"Thank you," I said, and then laughed. K chuckled too. I sat down next to her and activated my holo-gauntlet.

"I'll send the game to you. Oh, let's pair our holo-gauntlets!"

I raised a brow at her. "Pair our holo-gauntlets?"

"Yeah!" she said, excitedly. "That way we can send each other files whenever we want. Our computers will be directly connected!"

"Why not just request a file transfer? I'll approve it... If our holo-gauntlets are linked, won't that mean that you'll be able to access my holo-gauntlet remotely?" I asked.

She crossed her arms and smirked. "Well, yeah... but come on, I wouldn't do anything to mess with your gauntlet. And if I did, you could do it right back! Not that I would," she said. "...And if I did, it would only be for fun." I sighed. "Not that I would," she added.

"Well, alright," I said.

We paired our holo-gauntlets, and then K sent me "Defenders of Earth."

"Thanks. You'll have to teach me how to play."

"Okay." She shook her head, chuckling. "You're probably bad, I don't know why I wanted you to join me."

"We'll see." I narrowed my eyes and booted up the game. A holographic screen faded into view, and controls appeared in my hands. I didn't really feel like playing, but I wanted to help keep K entertained. I felt a bit bad for leaving her alone in the cockpit for the past few hours. I connected to her game, and started helping her fight virtual alien enemies.

◆

"Calculation complete," said the computer.

I practically leaped out of my seat. "Finally!"

K lifted her arms in frustration as my holographic display disappeared, and hers displayed the text, "Game over".

"You could have saved me from that sniper!" said K, staring at me.

"No I couldn't have, I didn't even know there *was* a sniper," I said, honestly.

K turned off her game. "Fair enough, I guess. You weren't too bad after all. That sniper was ridiculously well hidden."

I blinked, staring at the navigational computer's screen. It had indeed found a planet to match up with the picture, but it confused me.

K noticed my motionless, puzzled expression, and stood up out of her chair, taking a step towards me and leaning over my shoulder. "What's up?"

"Apparently that picture was taken on MM094, or at least that's the closest planet the computer could find," I said.

"Osax, you just said a bunch of letters and numbers. Should I know what you're talking about?"

I looked at her. "Malum. The planet is also known as Malum."

She raised an eyebrow at me.

I continued. "Malum got its name because of how incredibly dangerous and hostile the environments on its surface are. Creatures with hide that can resist E-guns, and strength beyond what should be possible for them. There's already so much that makes Malum a significant point of interest, but now, apparently there were once loro structures there as well. That means, there probably are still loro ruins. It makes sense that the loro would be interested in such a place…"

K pursed her lips. "Well, wouldn't the wildlife have destroyed all those structures by now, if they're so hostile? Even by accident, can't the growth of plant life degrade structures?"

"Hmm," I stroked my mandibles. "Possibly, but maybe not. I suppose we'll never know unless we go there."

"We?" she asked, smirking.

I sat up straighter. "I guess I'm getting ahead of myself."

Abruptly, K clutched the side of her head. She closed her eyes and scrunched up her face in pain again. I reached out a hand to stabilize her, and surprisingly she didn't recoil, letting me clutch her arm.

"Are you alright, K?" I asked, trying to sound calm, but my mind was racing.

The veins on her forehead were pulsing noticeably. She groaned.

"I'm- I think I'm okay." With difficulty, she lowered her hand and tried to sit up straighter. Slowly, the pulsing veins faded until they were flush with her head.

We sat in silence for several moments, as K looked out the window.

"We're almost at our next destination," said K, looking at the navi-computer. "Should probably wake up Jonathan, so he can redirect us."

"K…" I said, my ears lowered in concern. She gave me a look, and I could see concern on her face. She sighed and looked away, tapping at the computer console with her finger.

"Look," she said, turning back to me. "You want to know what's going on with me?" she asked, her orange eyes fixing me with an intense stare.

I nodded. "Yes, I do."

K paused for a moment, before at last speaking again. "I told you already, but you didn't believe me."

I tilted my head to the side and raised and ear. "What? Really?"

She nodded. "When we were on the ledge, outside the base, underneath the mothership. I told you I was dying, but you didn't believe me."

I stopped breathing for a moment. Slowly breath returned to me. "You- I was trying to calm you down. I thought you were just having a panic attack of some kind. It's something I deal with from time to time…"

She looked at me as though she didn't know what that was, but then continued. "No, I'm dying." She took a deep breath. "The doctors who raised me… they told me that because of all of my accelerated growth, I was at risk of dying prematurely. As I got older, they changed their diagnosis; I am dying. Something a little like cancer, they said, but then they also said it's nothing like cancer, so I don't know. If it was cancer they'd have been able to treat it in some way."

The air felt cold and still to me. "Do you know how long you have?"

She shrugged. "They said they didn't know. Anywhere between a few weeks and a few years." She began touching her hands and rubbing the spikes protruding from them. "Apparently my growth is so unpredictable, they can't really give an estimate." She shook her head and furrowed her brow. "Not that an estimate would really be helpful anyway. It's not like I can change when I die."

Her expression was solemn. Her skin was a beautiful shade of blue, and even the horns growing on her arms and face were not unattractive. Her orange eyes were mesmerizing. I felt an urge to show her the galaxy; to take her through my own life's journey and share with her all the wonder and heartbreak and insights that I was able to experience in my time in this universe. But beyond that, I could tell she had a complex inner life. Emotions and thoughts and new discoveries all swirling around in her brain, not like a bioweapon, but like a human. Not just any human. *My friend.*

I noticed tears streaming down my face.

She looked at me. "Are… you okay?"

I sniffed. "No," I said, my voice breaking. "*We* are."

She smiled, but she still had the weight of sadness over her. "Yeah. We are." She patted me on the arm, and I winced. "Gah, sorry. I was just trying to-"

"I know," I said. "I know." I wiped away my tears. "Is there anything I can do to help you?" I asked.

She shook her head.

"Let- Let me study you," I said. She looked at me, as if to say "Osax, just give it a rest," but I persisted. "I'm a biologist. I've extensively studied alien zoology, and theoretical biology. Maybe if you let me study you I can figure out what's going on! Maybe I can help you!" I lifted my ears and leaned forward. "My holo-gauntlet is equipped with some high-end bio-scanning technology."

She shrugged. "If it makes you feel better…"

I activated my holo-gauntlet and began scanning her body. She sat fairly motionless, and the room was quiet aside from the hum of the scanner and the buzz of the ship.

"I'm going to get a detailed scan of your brain, if that's alright," I said.

She sighed. "Yeah, that's okay. Thanks, Osax."

I slowly moved the scanner around her head. "Of course. You've been getting a lot of headaches, so it's likely that there's something wrong in your head."

She chuckled. "Yeah, you could say that."

"I mean biologically. If you don't mind, I'd like to scan your head area every day or so, that way I can compare data over a period of time and see the fluctuations and changes in your body. From that data I might be able to find a cause, for your headaches and fainting, and once I find that, I might be able to cure you!"

She looked at me, apologetically. I looked into her eyes and could imagine what she was thinking. *I'm glad this is making you feel better, Osax, but I've already accepted that I'm going to die.*

I thought back to when she fled the ruins with me. She clearly has a sense of self-preservation. She couldn't understand why I had put my life at risk for the research data. And why would she understand? I've spent years of my life focusing on the goal of research; it's become part of my identity. But to her, it seemed like a waste of life. From her perspective it made no sense that someone like her, who might only live for a few months, or less, would desperately guard their own life, but someone like me who potentially has decades, countless cycles left to live, would risk it for something like that. She had some wisdom.

Suddenly the silence was broken by the voice of the Firebrand's computer. "Distress signal detected."

Twenty-One

K, Jonathan, Joëlle and I were all seated in the cockpit when the hum of the slipspace drive dissipated and the view outside the window unstretched back into shape. Our ship had arrived at the origin point of the distress signal.

To our left was a large red nebula. It looked like a titan had poured a star-system's worth of red ink into a glass of water, started stirring it, and then froze the ink in time and vanished.

Ahead of us we could see the tops of two ships: a Titan-class battlecruiser, drifting above a massive black shape. It was the valicorr mothership, and it was attacking the TAU ship.

"We found it!" I exclaimed. *And in the middle of another crisis, too...*

Laser bolts and missiles flew between the two vessels. As we got closer, we could see starfighters had been deployed from each force and were dogfighting each other and attacking the larger vessels. The TAU battlecruiser didn't seem to be doing any damage to that thing.

"It's bigger than I remembered," said Jonathan, staring at the mothership.

"Should we get in closer?" I asked.

Joëlle grabbed the controls. "Already on it. Jonathan, you keep scanning that ship, give us any useful information."

K rubbed her hands together. "Alright. What's the plan, are we going to fly in close? Board it? Take it out from the inside?" She paused. "We have that cloaking thing, right?"

Joëlle nodded as we sped toward the battle, swooping under the mothership. Its massive black shape blotted out the top half of our view. "If we can find a place to board it, that might be our best bet."

My heart was beating quickly. "You know, we shouldn't rush into this, that ship is probably crawling with valicorr." The magnitude of the situation was beginning to settle on me as we crested the mothership and the TAU battlecruiser was revealed. Starfighters flew back and forth in a dizzying motion, like a swarm of bees. I noticed a red glow, appearing on the mothership, and a moment later red electricity blinked across to the TAU ship.

There was a flash of an explosion where the energy connected, and to my horror a massive chunk of the TAU ship detached from itself and began drifting off into space.

We were all staring at it.

Jonathan shook his head. "There's no way we can stop this thing," he said.

"Shut up," said Joëlle. "There has to be a way."

"I can't see one." said Jonathan.

Joëlle handed me the controls and leaned over to look at the scans of the mothership, trying to find a weakness. I kept us hovering under the shadow of the mothership, my heart racing.

Suddenly, the ship's communicator started flashing. Someone was sending out a general hail. We all exchanged concerned glances, before Joëlle spoke up. "They don't know we're here, but we can listen in. I'll make sure they can't hear us." She flicked a few switches, and then connected to the call.

Two images appeared on the communication-console's screens. We all crowded around to look at it. The right image must have been coming from the TAU cruiser. We could see what looked like the bridge of a Titan-class ship, with emergency lights flashing and flames burning. An officer of some kind was standing in front of the camera, eyes wide with fear. There were a few other people in the background, assessing a body. I thought I could make out an admiral's outfit on the body.

The other image was dark and unchanging. Dim purple lights filled the screen, surrounding a throne-like chair, barely illuminated in the light. A humanoid creature was sitting in the chair, casually resting its head on its hand, but it was too dim to make out any details. I couldn't see any other creatures in the image.

The voice of the TAU officer rose, shakily, and breaking in static. "What do you want?"

I held my breath. We could hear the muffled sounds of people moaning in pain, and the fires crackling coming through the TAU communicator. A few seconds passed, and an alien voice emanated from the mothership, though the figure remained completely motionless, in shadow. My eyes were fixed on it.

"How are you?" it said.

The TAU officer spoke. "What?!"

Silence.

"What do you want?!" he said again.

"How *are* you?" it said again, slowly. I felt a chill run down my back.

The officer was shaken. He spoke slowly. "Call off the attack, and then- Then we can talk."

"Alright." said the creature. I glanced outside and saw the valicorr ships starting to retreat.

"All starfighters, return to dock," said the officer, over his communicator. The TAU ships returned to the cruiser.

K spoke up. "What the hell is happening?"

"I don't know," I said.

"So, how are you?" said the creature.

The officer shook his head furiously and tears welled in his eyes. "How do you think?! You've destroyed a quarter of the ship! You've killed our people! You attacked us completely unprovoked!"

"So, not doing so well, I see." The creature began to chuckle in a strange, disturbing manner. Its voice didn't sound like a valicorr... I didn't think it was human either. Could it have been a skyther?

Jonathan and Joëlle were quiet, watching the screen. I fixed my attention on the communicator.

The TAU officer remained silent, glaring at the camera. Two other officers approached and stood behind him, looking at the communicator.

"What. Do. You. Want?" repeated the officer. I didn't like where this was going.

"Perhaps some music would ease your mind?" The creature moved one of its arms, and pressed a button. A second later, some kind of classical piano music began playing throughout the communicator, eerily calm, and definitely of human origin.

The TAU officers looked at one another. "What the hell is this... where did you- How did you get this recording?"

The music played over the ambient sounds of the burning fires. We exchanged glances once again, none of us knowing what to say, as our ship continued to hover in the shadow of the mothership. Jonathan's expression was unreadable.

"This," began the creature, "is Bach's prelude in C major." It laughed again, and then sighed dramatically. "So calming, this 'piano' instrument."

One of the other officers spoke up, taking a step forward. "What are you?! Who do you think you are?"

There was a long pause, where the creature remained motionless. The music played, and I glanced out at the ships through the window. The TAU cruiser was in bad shape, the large chunk which had discharged continued to drift away. How many countless lives were stranded, dying, on that chunk of debris? They were probably dead already, with the entire section now devoid of power, and depressurizing. I clenched my fists and trembled. What was this monster?

At last it spoke. "Who do *you* think I am?"

The officers glanced at each other, bewildered. "You are the captain of your vessel, are you not?"

"I am. But I am much, much more than that." There was an air of pride in its voice. "I am the leader, the Emperor, of the valicorr. I am Duhrnan. Have you heard of me?"

The Emperor of the Valicorr? I thought. *Duhrnan?*

"N- No, we've never heard of you. We didn't know the valicorr had an emperor."

"Well they do." He laughed, and began tapping his armrest, though his body was still mostly obscured in darkness.

"We have to stop this," I said, looking to my companions. They returned my glance.

"How?" asked Joëlle. Jonathan and K remained silent. I glanced at the weapon controls, but even I knew there was no way we could damage the mothership if a Titan-class cruiser was ineffective.

The creature, Duhrnan, continued. "It would be much less fun if I outright told you, so, let me ask you this, in response to your other question. What do you think I am?" At this, a large shape of something fell to the floor from the ceiling, behind Duhrnan's throne. It started moving around, making some amount of noise. The officers looked stunned.

The officer in front gulped. "You are a valicorr."

Slowly, the creature began to laugh. He leaned forward, towards the camera, out of his seat, and light illuminated his body.

My heart skipped a beat. He had two wide eyes on either side of his long face. He had two slits for nostrils on his pale snout, and a tall, wide row of teeth which grinned menacingly. My mandibles dropped in disbelief when I saw his extra set of arms; four in total.

Grinning up to the camera, with that chilling shape moving in the darkness behind him, he spoke. "Wrong!"

The mothership's energy weapon fired again, taking out another chunk of the TAU ship in a bolt of red electricity. My heart jumped, and I stood up out of my seat. Consoles erupted in flame on the TAU bridge, and I saw the officers gripped with fear. I clenched my mandibles.

Another bolt hit the ship, and it broke again. Then another, and another. The piano music continued to play as Duhrnan grinned, and the TAU screen snapped to static. Again and again, the mothership lashed out with its energy weapon, tearing the TAU ship apart.

"No…" said Joëlle as we all gazed out at the window. The mothership closed communications, and the music cut off abruptly.

"He's a sadist!" exclaimed K, standing out of her seat. "Holy shit!"

Jonathan said nothing, and stayed motionless. Finally, the ship stopped attacking the debris.

"Joëlle, is it possible to fly close enough to the mothership to catch a ride in its slipstream?"

She nodded. "Yes, it is."

Jonathan spoke up. "Are you crazy? We'd have to be practically touching its hull. Even if it was a friendly ship that would be dangerous, we might collide with it, but it's not a friendly ship. If it notices us, we'll surely be destroyed."

"Well, it's one way to ensure it doesn't get away from us," said Joëlle, flashing Jonathan a sympathetic look. She tilted the Firebrand toward the mothership, and flew in closer until the hull practically engulfed the entire view.

"I can't believe we're doing this…" said Jonathan, exasperated.

"Me neither," said K, though she sounded excited. I looked at her and she gave me a confident smirk.

"Do you think they'll hang around here long? Or are they heading somewhere?" I asked.

Joëlle was about to speak, when we noticed the space around the ship begin to distort and felt ourselves pulled jarringly forward. Normally the ship's stabilizers and artificial gravity would compensate, but we were catching a ride on the mothership's slipstream; the Firebrand wasn't designed to do that.

Joëlle spoke. "I guess they're in a hurry."

"And now, so are we," said Jonathan, shaking his head.

Twenty-Two

Joëlle was concentrating, keeping our ship within the mothership's slipstream. We'd been in slipspace for about twenty minutes, and Jonathan had been conducting more thorough scans of the mothership, trying to glean some more information. In order to do a complete scan however, we'd be emitting signals that would be easy for the mothership to notice, so we were fairly limited. Nevertheless, over that time we managed to take very detailed scans of its energy emissions, which were certainly unique.

I was sipping on some root beer from the Firebrand's food synthesizers- a set of boxy metal machines against the wall in the kitchen- to calm my nerves, and K had her own drink of some kind. Unfortunately it wasn't really working; my whole body felt tense.

"They knew where they were going," I said.

K took a sip of her drink and looked at me. "Well, we know where they're going too."

"Yeah," said Joëlle, "to the heart of the nebula. We should be arriving soon-"

Joëlle's eyes filled with fear as the mothership slightly changed course and suddenly we were speeding towards the hull. My heart jumped and I clutched my seat.

She wasn't fast enough.

We all lurched forward, root beer spilling all over the cockpit. With a crash, the lights flickered, and we all held onto our seats as tightly as possible as the Firebrand somersaulted away from the hull.

With a thunderous shake, we tore out of the slipstream and tumbled through space at an incredible velocity. The view outside the window was incredibly dizzying as stars and red gas from the nebula whipped around us. Joëlle began trying to stabilize the ship. The spinning slowed, until finally we were flying straight. We all took a moment to catch our breaths.

"I told you," said Jonathan, shaking his head. "We shouldn't have tried that."

"Everything's fine," I said, trying to calm him down, though my heart was racing.

Joëlle looked at me in annoyance. "No, not everything is fine, Osax." She pointed to a flashing light on her dashboard. "Our oxygen recycler is having some kind of malfunction."

Jonathan gulped. K stood up and leaned over Jonathan to get a look at the display. "What do you mean it's got a malfunction?!"

Jonathan was shaking his head. "We need to turn back, and find someplace to repair the ship."

"Or what?" K asked.

"Or we're going to die."

I was breathing heavily. "How much time do we have? Where's the nearest base? Or refuelling station? Or planet with a breathable atmosphere?"

Joëlle was examining her instruments. "Well, it's hard to tell how much time we have…"

"Until what?" asked K. "What's going to happen?"

Jonathan turned to her. "Our oxygen recycler is what keeps the air within the ship breathable. If it's not working properly, it's only a matter of time before we all suffocate." He sounded surprisingly calm.

K on the other hand, was beginning to quiver. "We're going to suffocate?!"

Joëlle glanced between us. "Everyone, try not to get too agitated. We'll have more time if we expend as little oxygen as possible." She met my gaze. "Osax, it's okay. Try not to hyperventilate."

I tried to slow my breathing. K started shaking her limbs and jumping up and down a bit, trying to calm down. Joëlle put a hand on her arm for a second.

"K," she said, "every time you move a muscle, you're spending some oxygen. You should sit down, and just try to relax."

She shook her head in disbelief. "Try to relax?"

Jonathan calmly pivoted in his chair toward her. "You'll be alright, K." His organic eye was lined with concern, contrasting his cybernetic one, which stared blankly.

K looked to me, fear in her eyes. I tried to speak, to comfort her, but felt frozen. I gazed out at the red nebula which enclosed around us. There was a line through the nebula as though a giant arrow had pierced a cloud of smoke. Already the gas was shifting and slowly the line was fading away.

"Look, we can still track the mothership," I said, pointing at the physical trail it had left behind.

K sat down slowly and stared at me, shocked. "Aren't you concerned about the whole dying thing? Are you ever concerned about that?"

Joëlle looked up from her instruments. "It looks like we have at least a day or two of air, between the four of us, as long as the recycler keeps working at its current capacity, and we keep our cardio levels low."

K sighed in relief. "Well, that's not too bad."

"I guess not," said Joëlle. "But, the nearest planet that is confirmed to be breathable is over one and a half days travel in slipspace."

Jonathan remained silent. K spoke up. "Well, I don't want to cut it too close."

"Neither do I," I said. "What planet is it? I'm not even sure where we are in space right now."

"Actually," said Joëlle hesitantly, looking up from the navi-computer, "it's Astraloth."

I blinked. I hadn't been home in many months, and I wasn't expecting to see it again any time soon. The nebula we were in must have been the Thala nebula, which was visible at times from Astraloth, during the night. My thoughts turned to my mother, and my home on Astraloth, and the Great Temple.

"Oh," I said. "Well, that… is good news."

"That's great!" said K, "There's no question that they'll be able, and willing, to help us then."

"Yes…" said Joëlle. Her eyes narrowed, and she took one more look at her instruments before piloting the ship toward the fading arrow in the nebula.

"What- What are you doing?" asked Jonathan, suddenly agitated. "We should be docking somewhere, and repairing. We shouldn't be putting our lives in unnecessary danger!"

"Yeah, Jonathan has a point," said K.

"The nebula interferes with scanners, which means we wouldn't normally be able to track or find anything in here. We're lucky that we can follow this trail visually since it's so fresh," said Joëlle.

"But, we should go to Astraloth!" Jonathan furrowed his brow. "This makes no sense; you're putting all our lives at risk!"

I took a deep breath. "We still don't know what the mothership was looking for. It makes sense to follow it for a while, to see if it was heading somewhere in the nebula, for a specific reason."

Joëlle said, "Osax, I actually agree with you. That's why I'm taking us in."

Jonathan shook his head violently. "I must protest!"

Joëlle looked at him. "I'm going to allow us a four hour margin of error, which doesn't give us much time to track the mothership. But I have a feeling they were already close to their destination when we got ejected from the slipstream; we shouldn't be far behind."

"No," said Jonathan. "I won't allow this."

Joëlle just glared at him. K and I exchanged glances.

"Shut up, Jonathan, it's a good compromise," said K.

He turned to face her, shaking his head. "I'm trying to look out for all of us, you especially, K."

"Yeah, I know. But it's okay. I'm good now. I'm okay with this." She nodded at him, and held a confident expression on her face. "Besides," she added, "I didn't ask for your help, or your sympathy."

We all remained silent.

Jonathan stood up. "I'm going to rest in my room for a moment, clear my head." He walked slowly out of the room.

◆

Some time later, we emerged from the red cloud into a wide clearing in the nebula. The mothership was hovering, like a menacing black spider suspended on a web. Just in front of it was another structure, and I gazed in disbelief.

The structure appeared to be a ship. It was massive, grey, and surrounded by construction supports. It looked strikingly similar to the Shade Beam battlecruiser concept design. Could it have been that the TAU were already constructing the weapon in secret?

"That looks kind of like the concept for the Shade Beam super weapon," I said. Joëlle nodded, her mouth hanging open in surprise.

K leaned forward. "Wait a minute." She started pointing out the window to the ominous meeting of the two massive ships. "You're telling me the TAU was already constructing the big version of the gun?"

"I…" Joëlle couldn't find the words.

We drifted closer toward the ships. Duhrnan's ship had sent out smaller vessels which were cutting off the construction clamps on the device.

"If they've been constructing it, it would make sense to hide it in a nebula," I said, hesitating. "But, why would they build it here, so close to Astraloth… unless-"

"No," said Joëlle, shaking her head. "No, they wouldn't. The TAU would never…"

K had a thoughtful expression. "But, they might." She looked to me and Joëlle. "What makes them exempt from evil?"

I lowered my ears, and frowned. "No, it doesn't make sense. Why aren't there any TAU ships protecting this?"

I gazed out the windows, mesmerized as the construction clamps drifted away from the Shade Beam, and the mothership slowly approached it, clamping its limbs down onto the cruiser.

"I'm picking up another large object behind the Shade Beam on the scanner…" said Joëlle, glancing down to the control console.

My eyes were darting around the cockpit. "Another ship?"

K got up and came over to the scanner, inspecting it. "Huh, looks like a blob. Not very helpful."

Joëlle sighed. "The Shade Beam is too thick for the scans to get an accurate reading from this angle, especially if we keep our cloaking device active. Which, we definitely should."

"We need to get around the Shade Beam, get a better look at that object." If it was indeed a ship, who's ship would it be? A TAU ship that had surrendered to the threat of the mothership? Or perhaps another valicorr ship that had been waiting here. It couldn't have been a skyther ship…

Joëlle was about to take us in closer, when the oxygen recycler's emergency light began flashing and beeping at a faster rate.

K spoke up, breathing quickly. "Is that- Did the recycler just get worse?"

Joëlle nodded slowly. "Apparently. We don't have time to check this out."

"No!" I said, standing up. "But we're so close to getting another clue about what's happening!"

Joëlle gave me a sidelong glance. "We're also close to dying, Osax. I'm setting a course for Astraloth."

My ears drooped as we entered slipspace once more. I was less concerned about our oxygen running out, and more dismayed at this new unsolved mystery of the object which was just out of sight behind the Shade Beam. Not to mention, Duhrnan clearly had a plan, and it looked like it was so far unfolding unhindered. I shuddered.

Everyone was breathing slowly, and trying not to speak too much. That was good, it meant we'd be saving more oxygen. I was glad Jonathan had decided to get some rest and calm down. I hoped he was asleep, and would wake up to find us well on our way to a safe haven. K seemed to be deep in thought, her eyes focused on a random point on the controls. And Joëlle just sat back in her chair and let out a big breath after engaging the slipspace drive. It was on autopilot, so we could all just relax. I thought about getting some sleep, but knew I wouldn't be able to. Either way, I decided to head to my room.

Jonathan was walking into the kitchen from the back of the ship as I entered it. He gave me a startled look, before exhaling.

"How are you doing, Jonathan?"

He looked around. "I was just pacing, trying to calm down."

"You shouldn't be moving more than necessary," I said.

He nodded. "Right. Sorry, Osax."

I raised my hand to calm him down. "It's alright. We've set a course for Astraloth now. The oxygen recycler is in worse shape than we thought, but I think we'll make it if we all just try to relax."

He scrunched up his face. "Alright. Good. Thank you."

"My mother will surely help us out and provide a nice place to regroup and collect our thoughts."

"Ah, yes. Queen Suranos..." he said, thoughtfully.

I approached the bedroom, but he spoke up again.

"Excuse me Osax, this may not be a good time, but I was wondering…"

"Yes?" My ears lifted slowly. I could guess what he was going to ask.

"They say Queen Suranos is a powerful psychic. That she has the power to sense thoughts or emotions, and move things with her mind. Is that true? Can your mother… really do that?"

I nodded. "Psionics are rare in humans-"

"Practically non-existent," Jonathan interrupted.

"...but less so in skythers. Still, my mother… is definitely the most famous psychic of this cycle."

"Is it hereditary?"

My ears drooped. "Can we continue this conversation later?" I asked. "How about when we're not worried about our oxygen use." I sounded more agitated than I intended to.

He shut his mouth and nodded.

"Alright." I left the room.

I lay down on the bed, and folded my hands over my chest. I couldn't sleep, but resting my body felt good.

Twenty-Three

The Firebrand touched down on the wide landing pad of the Great Temple.

K's orange eyes met mine as she spoke, and the four of us stood up slowly from the cockpit. "Not much air left… you sure Astraloth's air is breathable for humans?"

I replied, "Yes. It's true, we last longer in depressurized environments than humans, but we breathe the same kind of air." I patted her shoulder, forgetting that it was covered in spikes. Luckily they weren't sharp. "You will be fine."

"Let's open the hatch as soon as possible," said Joëlle. "The air is pretty stale in here."

We all hurried over to the exit ramp positioned on the bottom of the ship. I trailed behind everyone else as the ramp extended downwards and light filled the ship from Astraloth's atmosphere. The sound of ships flying overhead and skythers talking echoed into the Firebrand, and we all took a deep breath as the fresh air rushed inside. I caught myself brushing my ears with my fingers, and ruffling my chest fur.

I was apprehensive. It had been months since I was home, and the last time I spoke with my mother, I had gotten into an argument with her about my life abroad. Honestly, I couldn't even remember what details were said, only that it had happened. I hoped she had forgotten, but even if she had, she might be able to sense my thoughts, and remember it through me. It was hard to keep secrets from her, which may have been a factor in why I decided to study on Earth and work away from home.

She'll be able to sense that I'm thinking about her ability to sense my thoughts, I thought, and then shook my head quickly and took a step outside, past Jonathan.

Joëlle and K were already standing on the platform, and I stood next to them. The Great Temple loomed above us, a collection of white pyramids with several giant red spheres suspended atop each point. The spheres seemed to defy physics, though I knew they were suspended via something akin to stasis technology. The pyramids themselves were made of a pearly solid compound, with evenly spaced balconies adorning the slopes. Long, straight staircases and perpendicular water canals (which collected rainwater to use for the temple's amenities) crisscrossed each other along each slanting wall, and in all of the space between verdant flora bloomed. Trees and bushes and fruit grew in a lush rooftop garden, more like a forest, which covered each pyramid, providing much of the temple with ample shade and fresh air. There was a large city below us surrounding the temple on all sides, and vehicles flying through the sky, above and below us. The platform we stood upon protruded from a section of the Great Temple which was less than halfway up its side, but even so, hundreds of feet in the air. Above us, at the midpoint of the Great Temple, an entire floor was cut out and exposed to the open air. If you looked at it from the side you would be able to see straight through the temple. The two halves were held together by a grid of pillars, and staircases and elevators which took you from the open floor to the floors below and above. Beyond the city stretched jungle, mountains, and ocean, as far as the eye could see.

"Wow…" said K. "You… don't tell me you live here?"

I chuckled. "I grew up here, yes."

Joëlle took a few steps forward, gazing at the incredible vista. The sun glinted off her armour and made her purple hair appear to glow. "I've been to Astraloth before, but never to the Great Temple. Apparently, I made a mistake!" She turned to me and winked. I lifted my ears slightly.

Jonathan peered outside, and spoke softly. "Marvellous…" He paused, and I turned to face him. K and Joëlle were preoccupied with the view, so he spoke to me. "Osax, I'm just going to get a head start on the repairs."

I tilted my head to the side. "Are you sure, Jonathan? You don't want to come inside and rest first?"

He smiled weakly. "I'll feel much better once the oxygen recycler is repaired."

Joëlle caught the conversation and chimed in. "Do you even know how to repair one of those, Jonathan?"

He smiled, and nonchalantly spiked his hair to the side. "Actually, I do. When I was a marine, I took on some special ops missions-"

"Wait, you were a special ops guy?" asked K, smirking, and stepping towards him. "So, you're not completely uncool after all! Your moustache still is, though."

Jonathan shut his mouth and furrowed his brow, glaring at K. "You should remember, I saved your life back on Voren."

K scoffed. "Yeah, from what, one guy? I could have taken him."

"An *invisible*… 'guy'," said Jonathan. He rolled his eyes as he said "guy."

Joëlle lightly grabbed K's arm. "Leave him be, K." She pulled her away, glancing back to Jonathan. "Well, if you know what you're doing, go ahead. Just don't wreck my ship!"

Jonathan bowed his head slightly. "Of course not, my lady. I shall treat it with the utmost respect." I sensed a playfulness in his voice.

Joëlle glanced back at Jonathan with a face that seemed to say, "Stop being an idiot." But I caught a slight smile when she turned away from him.

We stepped toward the temple, and three skythers stood in front of us, ready to greet us. The two on either side stood near to my height, around eight feet tall, and each wore full suits of armour. The armour was white, with red accents. Though the armour was surely protective, it was designed with ceremony in mind, not combat. They each held plasma spears, though the edges were inactive. Red woven fabric dangled in the wind from the base of the spearheads.

In the center of the three stood my mother, her arms outstretched. It was good to see her smooth, round face, her yellow eyes squinting warmly in the light. Her ears hung calmly, without tension, and she wore a gold, white, and red ceremonial outfit. Her mandibles were tucked politely under her face, which was tattooed with intricate black and red designs. Her furred torso was bare, but she wore flowing sleeves and jewelled necklaces befitting her title of queen. Fabric billowed from her waist in layered sheets of gold, white, and red, each sheet embroidered with the next colour.

Without thinking I tugged at the functional but plain armour piece on my forearm. I felt underdressed.

"Mother," I began, stepping forward. Joëlle remained quiet, and I was surprised to notice that K did so as well. "I'm so glad you're here."

She stepped forward ahead of her guards, and gracefully, reached her arms toward me. I felt awkward in my movements by comparison, jerking my arms up to hold her hands.

She spoke to me in our traditional language, Skorali, but I will translate what she said. "Oh, Osax," she said, lifting her ears and clasping my hands. "It's been too long. I had a feeling I would see you on this platform today... I thought I sensed you coming."

I responded, also in our language. "I... am glad. We needed to dock for repairs. We are on an important mission."

She pulled me in for a hug. She was a foot taller than me, and pressed her head on top of mine. Awkwardly, I put my arms around her and returned the hug.

I heard K mutter, "I didn't realize Osax was so short," before snorting a laugh.

I felt my cheeks getting hot, and my mother let me go, holding me by the shoulders. She spoke again, in Skorali, looking me in the eye. "I'm sorry, Osax, I didn't mean to embarrass you. It's just been so long since I saw you."

"Mother, it's alright." I rubbed my arm absentmindedly.

She glanced toward K, then back to me. "Do not worry, K is feeling more self conscious than you are. She's just trying to hide it."

"Mother!" I said, stepping out of her grasp. "We've talked about this-"

"Oh, right. Sometimes I forget that you aren't interested in other people's feelings."

I clenched my fists. "It's not that-"

"I know, dear. I can sense just how interested you are- You just think its rude for me to share other people's feelings with you."

"I think it's rude to-"

"To listen to their thoughts in the first place, I know." She sighed. "Just, forget I said anything."

I took a deep breath, and my mother turned to K and Joëlle who were looking at us expectantly. She spoke, this time in English.

"K, Joëlle, welcome to Astraloth. I know you are only stopping here for repairs along a... perilous quest. But I hope the nature of your mission will not prevent the four of you from relaxing while you are here. It's been many cycles since Osax has brought any friends home."

"Mother..." I said, my cheeks flushing.

"Thank you," said Joëlle. "It is an honour to be in your presence, Queen Suranos." She bowed in a skyther style, and my mother returned the gesture.

"Yeah," said K, before trailing off. "Nice place." She nodded after a brief pause.

"I hope I will get to meet Jonathan in person once he is done with the repairs," said the queen. "In the meantime, let us all head inside."

My mother turned around gracefully, and began walking up the stairs of the temple. Her guards followed, and so did we.

K walked close to me. "So, she... actually reads minds?" She looked concerned. *Rightly so,* I thought, even if I was used to it.

I nodded. "Yes, yes she does."

K started shifting her eyes around, and tapping her fingers together as we walked. "So... that doesn't mean... you... *you* can't read minds though, right?"

My ears lowered. "No, I can't. Why do you ask?"

She shrugged. "No reason. I just... was curious." I noticed she wasn't making eye contact with me.

I shrugged it off. I had too much to think about already. The Shade Beam battlecruiser had already been under construction, and now, however far along it was, it was being stolen by the valicorr. Not only that, but what was that mysterious shape just out of sight behind the Shade Beam? It must have been some kind of spacecraft, but of what origin?

I gazed out across the breathtaking landscape around us as we continued to climb higher up the white staircase. The sun was shining high in the blue atmosphere, bright enough that you couldn't see the nebulas in the sky, though I knew they were there. We were entering the shadow cast by the red sphere suspended above our pyramid.

Who is Duhrnan? I thought. The image of his body and face flashed across my mind. *How did he get involved, and above all else, what is he? He certainly isn't a human or a skyther, and he isn't a valicorr either. He has four arms, but that couldn't mean-*

"A loro," said my mother, pausing and looking back over her shoulder. I glanced up at her.

K and Joëlle spoke simultaneously. "What?"

"Duhrnan must be a loro, Osax." My mother turned to face me, and so did K and Joëlle.

I shook my head. "I had considered the possibility, but that's impossible." I clenched my fists. "Besides, I'm the loro researcher. I would know."

She bowed her head. "You do know, Osax. You're just having a hard time accepting it."

"But," I said, looking down at the steps, "their culture is all about respecting, cherishing, and valuing life, and the universe. They were observers of, even protectors of life. They definitely weren't sadists!"

"Uh, and they're all dead, right?" said K, glancing between us.

"That too," I said, "though… we don't have proof that they're all dead. There's just a significant lack of proof that they're still around." I felt my heart beginning to race. "But if Duhrnan is a loro, then… there's so much we could learn from him. So much we could learn!"

"Osax, listen to yourself!" said Joëlle, shooting me a fiery glance. "I don't care what kind of things we could learn from him, I still wouldn't let him live."

"What?"

"You saw what he was like; you can't be suggesting that we try to talk to him, can you?"

"No, I…" I paused, trying to slow my breathing. "I'm not suggesting that, necessarily. I just, never- Never in my dreams did I imagine that I might encounter a loro who was alive. Imagine the kinds of knowledge he might have!"

K stepped in between us. "Hey, we don't even know he is a loro. All we know for sure is he's damn messed up." She turned to Suranos. "So, I guess if you know about Duhrnan already, then you know about-"

"The Shade Beam… yes." My mother sighed. "I'm sorry, I was trying not to pry, but you're all thinking about it with such energy that it was impossible to ignore." She turned to Joëlle. "Don't worry, Joëlle, this doesn't mean I won't let you all relax here. I still believe, even in times of crisis, rest is essential."

Joëlle let out a sigh of relief. "Th- Thank you, Queen Suranos. I think I'd feel better if we didn't talk about this for a while."

"You need rest, I know." She paused, and shook her head slowly, looking at Joëlle. "You need not fear being alone, Joëlle. Look around you; you are not alone, even if you may feel that way."

Joëlle's expression hardened, and she lowered her head, gazing at the steps in front of her.

My mother turned back around, and continued leading us up the steps. "Come along, everyone. Yes, K, you can stay here as long as you like, though Osax would rather leave as soon as possible."

K looked startled, and gave me a glance. "Why do you wanna leave so fast? This place seems great!"

"I just…" I trailed off. My eyes drifted to the sky, and I thought about Duhrnan, the mothership, and the Shade Beam, off somewhere in space, out of reach. *Could he really be a loro?* I thought. *What else could he be…*

I turned to K. "I'm surprised you don't know."

Twenty-Four

"That's odd," I said, hovering my hand above K's head. She was seated in a dimly lit section of the temple, and I was standing next to her. Rays of orange light coated the walls and carpeted floor, streaming in from the windows. K, keeping her head as still as possible, looked up at me.

"What is it?" she said.

My brows furrowed. I was cross-checking the data I had taken from scanning her head the other day.

"Well, even just compared to when I last scanned you, I'm noticing a few growths forming on your brain. There are two noticeable spots on your frontal lobe, and one larger one on your parietal lobe. It's odd how much change there has been in such a short time."

"Huh," said K. Her gaze fell to the floor. "So, my brain is getting bigger?"

"Well," I said, moving my hand around her head, continuing the scan, "not exactly. That implies an equal distribution of growth. This growth is seemingly random, only affecting certain places. Not unlike the spikes growing on your exterior."

K nodded slowly. "I guess that makes sense."

"I'm going to check your cerebellum, the other day I noticed a small growth. I wasn't sure if..." My ears lowered. "The growth there seems to be gone..."

"Okay... so my brain is getting smaller?" K looked up at me with an eyebrow raised.

I shook my head. "It's almost as though your body is developing tumours at an abnormal speed, but also disintegrating them. There's no sign of the growth I noticed before."

"Huh..." said K.

I deactivated my holo-gauntlet and began rubbing my forehead. "That kind of explains what your doctors meant, about it being like cancer, but nothing like cancer."

"I suppose it does. I don't know why they never told me the details about it though."

I squinted my eyes. "Well, you were only how many months old at the time? I think it must have been hard for them to know how to relate to you… or how to treat you."

K stood up and stretched, walking over to the window. She took in a deep breath, and I caught the beams of light sketching a bright outline around her face and body, and the spikes jutting from her arms and head.

"They never really cared about me, I guess," she said. "But I don't remember them very well." She kept her back to me. "So, does this information help you treat me?" she asked.

I sighed. In truth, this discovery was extremely unhelpful. I had no idea what would be causing her brain to change so drastically and so randomly in such a short time. It wasn't even a "simple" matter of removing a brain tumour, because they were disappearing almost as quickly as they were appearing, so what good would that do? Operating on her would be needlessly dangerous, even for a proper surgeon. I had hoped I could use my skills as a theoretical biologist to come up with some kind of a solution; a theoretical solution which could be posed to someone more equipped to perform an intervention, whatever it ended up being. Perhaps if I was lucky I'd be able to concoct some kind of medicine to halt the progression of her condition, or alleviate some of the symptoms. Though I didn't have that much experience with pharmaceuticals.

Furthermore, I noticed something odd glancing down at her scans. There was a decently sized section of her brain, which, across all of my scans, showed no elevated signs of use. The tissue was clearly alive, but the neurons there weren't firing properly. I had no idea what it meant, and debated whether to tell K or not. I wasn't really an expert on brains, after all.

K turned to face me and I saw the fear, and hope in her eyes. Her lips were pursed in anticipation. "Are you gonna be able to help me?"

I struggled to remain composed as a bolt of anxiety hit my chest. I had no idea what was wrong with her. Something about her genetic makeup, her accelerated growth and learning, must have been linked to the growths. But I had absolutely no idea how to help her.

"I'm sure if we keep up the scans, I'll figure something out. I'm already forming some ideas…" my voice caught in my throat, trying to squeeze the lie out through my constricted breathing.

"I knew I could count on you, Osax!" she said with a smile. She came over to me and hugged me, grinning. The wind was knocked out of me in an instant and I felt my arms being crushed by her strength, and her anxiety transferred to me. "I never… I never thought I had any hope. But now… just knowing I have a chance, that maybe I'll get to live a normal life… That's-"

"You- You don't have to say any more," I coughed out. She let go of me.

"Sorry, Osax."

I caught my breath. "No worries. Let's… let's get something to eat."

K nodded, her expression returning to normal, before flashing a slight smile.

My body felt heavy, and not just because Astraloth has a stronger gravitational pull than Earth, Voren, or the artificial kind on TAU ships.

◆

That day, my mother gave Joëlle and K a tour of the Great Temple. I followed from a distance as she led them through the ornate halls, and Joëlle spoke to her politely and graciously. K couldn't seem to decide if this place was incredibly exciting to her or incredibly dull; it seemed as though every new room she entered she'd flip a coin before reacting. She kept glancing back at me and smiling though, and every time she did her mood seemed to lift. And every time her mood lifted, mine plummeted.

I wandered through the halls of the temple, of my childhood, passing people, priests, and guards, who were all kind enough to give me space. Even those who recognized me as the prince, despite my armoured outfit, were observant enough to see that I wasn't quite in the mood for talking. I wasn't good at speaking to multiple people at once, and there was already a great discussion being staged in my mind.

At last I settled on a balcony overlooking the city surrounding the temple. The sun was setting, and a large orange bird perched on the railing. I was so withdrawn from the world that when I stepped forward and leaned on the rail the bird didn't even twitch at my presence.

Then my holo-gauntlet flashed and flared to life without warning. The bird cawed and took off. I glanced at my arm. K had opened up a text document on my computer remotely from hers. I shook my head and chuckled to myself. Why had I agreed to pair our gauntlets? I knew I couldn't trust her not to mess around.

The text document was blank for a second, then words appeared. She could have just called me; instead she opened a text file which we were both editing in real time. It was certainly creative.

were are you, sax?

I smirked, and manipulated the cursor. I replaced 'were' with 'Where', then added an 'O' before 'sax.' New words appeared.

Where are you Osax? haha, xD

I typed into the document.

Where are you Osax? haha, xD I'm just spending
soasdjslgkdsfgdlhgmdsfjlsdhgeds;fjsdkfjtdskfljdsfi
asldkmsadljesd adsakd;lksdfdsodsfnedsfg

As I was typing, K started mashing keys. I paused, watching the garbled text continue to expand. After a while, she deleted everything.

sorry

I lifted my ears.

It's okay, it was kind of funny. I'm just spending
some time alone, while we're on the planet and
not all cramped together in Joëlle's ship.
you mean you dont like being all cramped
together for days? :P
Sometimes I just need space. I'm gonna delete
this file.
ok

The file closed, and I sighed. I was so glad we were friends, and I didn't want to mess that up. I told her I could help her, but that wasn't the truth.

I had no idea how to help K.

◆

My holo-gauntlet beeped while I walked down a long hall of the temple that evening, startling me out of my circling thoughts for a moment.

Click.

"Hello?" I answered.

"Osax, hello!" Jonathan's voice scratched through the communications device, much to my surprise.

I took a long breath before responding. "What is it, Jonathan? Need a hand with the repairs?"

I heard him chuckle with a nervous edge in his voice. "No no, the repairs are going just fine. We should be in good condition for space travel in just a few hours."

"Great!" I exclaimed, surprising myself with the desperate tone of my voice.

"Yes. I appreciate the enthusiasm!" There was a moment of static before Jonathan spoke up again. "That's obviously not why I'm calling."

"Obviously. So why are you calling?"

"Well, I was just calling to let you know that I won't be staying in the temple tonight."

"That's fine," I said, "but if you don't mind me asking, what's stopping you from joining us in the temple?"

I heard him sigh. "To be quite frank, Osax, it's your mother. I don't like the idea of having my mind read."

So that's why he was so eager to start the ship's repairs when we landed.

Without a second thought I started walking down to the hangar the Firebrand was docked at. "That makes good sense to me."

Jonathan chuckled. "Thanks for understanding. I had a feeling when we were talking out in space that you weren't exactly comfortable with your mother's powers. That your relationship was… strained."

"Well, you're right, I guess." As I said this, I turned a corner and bumped right into my mother.

Even if she somehow hadn't heard our conversation, she could read my thoughts. I swallowed.

Jonathan's voice came through as my mother stared down at me, her ears slowly drooping. "In any case," he said, "contact me when you've had enough of your mother. We can head out again just about any time now."

My eyes lowered to my gauntlet, though I could feel my mother's gaze still on me. "Okay. Goodbye." I hung up the call, and quickly began walking around my mother, not looking up.

I got a few steps past her in the otherwise empty corridor before suddenly, against my will, my limbs slowed to a halt and I was frozen in place mid step. I could still move my neck, so I turned my head around, glaring at the queen. Her eyes were glowing a dim white.

"Mother, let me go!" I exclaimed. "I'm not a child anymore!"

Slowly she stepped toward me. "What's troubling you? You have so much on your mind, Osax-"

"What, is that not allowed? Is that illegal now? I have to be apprehended for having thoughts?!" I struggled to break out of the force field hold that she was projecting with her mind.

At last she let go, but I no longer wanted to run. All the tension that had been building in me since arriving on Astraloth- since arriving on Voren, even- was rising to the surface in the shape of anger.

I marched toward her. "Who do you think you are?!" I screamed. "You may have raised me, but I'm almost twenty-seven cycles old! I'm a warrior, a scientist, a loro researcher, and yet you treat me like a child. Always interrupting me, telling me what I'm thinking instead of letting me do it for myself! Telling me how I feel instead of hearing what I need! And always with the air of a concerned, protective mother. But instead of protecting me, you're just smothering me!"

I paused for a moment as she recoiled. I was panting.

"Osax-"

"You have no idea what I'm going through! I don't care if you've been through your own things, I don't care if you think you can sense my feelings, or my memories. You don't get to decide for me anymore! Even if you think you can see what I see, and you think you're wiser and smarter and more experienced." I swung my arms emphatically. "You don't get to decide for me!"

My mother remained motionless and a calm expression fell over her face once again. My blood began to boil.

"You always do this! You always act so calm and stoic. You say you can sense my feelings, but you have no sense of empathy!" I felt tears welling in my eyes. "Why? Why can't I just walk away from you without you stopping me, trying to get your own word in? Trying to tell me who I am?"

Her voice was quiet, almost defeated. "You can."

"Thank you!" I said, before turning around and storming off.

Twenty-Five

I yawned.

The sun was beginning to rise. It was already 'tomorrow', and if I was to be awake when the investigator was ready in the evening, I'd have to sleep during the morning.

Becoming aware of my surroundings again, I hesitantly spoke four words. "That's... all for now."

I stood up from my chair, looking at my long empty cup of root beer forlornly. I felt so much calmer than I had back in the moments I was reminiscing about. But thinking about how I acted with my mother... it didn't make me feel like a proud warrior. I didn't exactly regret it either. It just made me feel sad. Like all our emotions were needlessly confused.

I walked over to the window and gazed across the landscape, the orange sun slowly rising. A large orange bird flew across my view in the distance.

Slowly I turned to the computer the investigator had set up on the table. I walked over to it and sat down, looking for the button to stop the recording.

The door behind me hissed open.

"Hey!"

The investigator took a few steps forward and leaned in over my shoulder, hitting the stop button on the recording. She wasn't wearing her uniform and her hair looked messy, and in her hand she was holding a coffee mug.

"What were you doing?" she asked quickly.

I stood up out of the chair and dusted myself off. Calmly, I replied. "I was simply pausing the recording."

She blinked, and scanned me over suspiciously. "You... you were recording the story all night? Until just now?"

I nodded.

She shook her head and scoffed. "I guess it'll take me several hours to listen through it all then."

I shrugged. "That is accurate."

"Did you stay up this whole time?" She asked incredulously.

"I've stayed up longer in the past."

"Yeah, yeah, I'm sure you have," she said, taking her seat in the chair.

"Well, I must sleep now if we are to continue the story this evening. I hope what I've recorded so far helps."

"Me too," she said. "Goodnight- Er, morning… Have a good sleep. Let me know when you wake up, assuming I'm finished listening to this."

"I will."

I stepped out of the room as I heard the click of a button, and my own voice began, staticy through the speakers. *"I tried not to think about Joëlle's squad, or that woman's husband. The doors to the generator room…"*

I wandered back to my room. Each step I took, I felt like I was getting farther and farther from the past. The sun was rising, but the shadows were long, and the room seemed to stretch. It was probably just my tired brain, but with each footstep I felt like my mind was also stepping simultaneously toward and away from infinity. Away from and toward so many memories of a time not so long ago, and of friends. But here and now, I was alone.

◆

That evening, after a good amount of rest, I wrenched myself out of bed, and got some breakfast and a morning tea, steaming and minty. I took a stroll outside the building, breathing the fresh air in through my nose. TAU ships were scattered across the sky and landed on the ground between skyther ones, and patrols of soldiers of both factions marched across the landscape, mingling with civilians. The TAU ships seemed to be in good condition, and great numbers. I was pleased to offer them a safe haven in this region of space, though at a glance they didn't look like they needed it.

"Talcorosax," said an unfamiliar voice.

I spun around to see a TAU captain, fully armed and armoured. His armour was just like Captain Orion's, from Voren, and his face was completely obscured by his helmet.

"Yes, Captain?" I replied, standing tall.

"Investigator Mercedes wishes to speak with you," he said plainly.

"Alright." I said, gazing off into the distance. "I'll be there in a minute."

He took a small step toward me. "Immediately."

I looked him up and down. The rifle in his hands was neither active, nor aimed my way, but I got the sense there was a reason he was holding it. Slowly, I nodded.

"Right this way," he said, and I began to follow him.

◆

I entered the room once again, and the doors shut behind me. My empty cup of root beer from the day before was still placed on the table. The investigator was sitting in her seat, once again looking pristine in her uniform. She looked up at me as I entered. Two TAU soldiers were standing on either side of her. The window's blinds were closed, and the room seemed strangely dark. The Captain stood behind me as I sat down.

The seat creaked as I leaned into it. "What's the matter, investigator?" I asked, calmly.

"Nothing's the matter," she said, smiling slightly. "I'm just eager to ask you some questions."

My heart rate was beginning to rise. "Ask away."

She leaned forward slightly. "This whole time, in your story, you're acting like you didn't know about Jonathan. Is this true?"

I paused, briefly. "At the time, I didn't know."

She continued, "And K, you admitted to considering that she might have been a sleeper agent?"

I took a deep breath. "Yes, the thought crossed my mind."

She continued pressing further, "You admit to trying to help K-"

"Of course," I said, agitated. "K is my friend."

"Is?"

"...Was." I said, grimacing. *What was she getting at?* I thought. "You heard the story so far. I thought you'd understand."

She leaned back. "We thought *you'd* understand, Talcorosax, that we aren't interested in your life story. Arguing with your mother, circling in your own head about what's right and wrong, true or false, laughing and crying, we don't care. We don't care about you, Talcorosax. All we want to know is the Brotherhood's role in all of this mess."

I paused, drinking in the silence of the room. If she didn't care about me, she could have gone to anyone else to get their side of the story. She was particular about speaking to me, specifically. So why was she lying?

"You didn't need to seek haven here, did you?" I said, my eyes narrowing and my ears peeling back. "You just wanted an excuse to station your ships in the atmosphere, your troops on the ground, because you think I'm a member of the Brotherhood. You think I'm somehow working with them." I gripped my empty cup tightly. "And you're afraid that I might attack."

The investigator paused, smiled, and shook her head. "No no no, nothing like that. We wanted to seek haven here, for the time being, to restock and rest for a while. Fleets this big need significant time for repairs, and the crews need shore leave. It was just convenient that you were here to give us some information about the Brotherhood."

I snorted. "I seriously doubt that I have any information which you don't already have about the Brotherhood."

"Just, tell us what happened to K," she asked, clearly agitated, but masking it with a smile. I noticed the two TAU soldiers behind her exchange glances.

"No." I said quietly.

"No?" Her eyebrows raised, and her smile faded.

"I don't care what your reasons are for being here, you're still guests." I said. "And I will not *just* tell you what happened to K. I made it clear what is right for my culture, and what is right for me. And that is to make sure I do what is right for this story. I won't leave out details. I won't skip ahead."

I heard the investigator groan as she put her head in her hands. "Please make it as quick as possible," she said. But I was watching her intently. Behind her fingers, I noticed her shielded lips twitch into a slight smile. *She actually wants to hear the whole story?*

My skin began to crawl. I looked up at the soldiers, my eyes shifting between everyone. Had she been using reverse psychology on me? What did she really want?

Body tensing, I closed my eyes briefly, trying to mask my newfound nervousness. Even if I didn't know, I knew I had to take some control of the situation.

"I don't think those soldiers will be necessary. You aren't scaring me."

One of them spoke up to the investigator. "Sir?"

She met my gaze, and for a few solid seconds we shared in an unspoken staring contest. "Just go," she said. "You too, Captain."

"Of course," he said, motioning the other soldiers to follow him out of the room. The door shut behind them.

"I'm opening the windows," I said. I moved to let in some light, and exhaled deeply as quietly as I could.

The room was filled with light, though the sun would be setting soon. I had slept through most of the day. I took a seat again, pressing a button on my holo-gauntlet. She looked slightly amused, one eyebrow raised almost unnoticeably.

"Would you care for any refreshments?" I asked the investigator, trying to sound as pleasant as possible.

"Please," she said halfheartedly.

"You know," I said as a skyther brought me a fresh root beer and another drink for the investigator, "There's nothing forcing you to listen to this whole story."

She remained silent for a moment until the skyther left the room, and I sipped my drink, eagerly anticipating her response. "Actually," she said carefully, "I was lying."

I blinked. She was eyeing me closely, gauging my response.

"I *do* have orders to get this information from you, because you *are* under suspicion of working with the Brotherhood."

I froze.

"Of course," she said, "I don't believe it. To be honest, I don't even want to be here."

"That's not obvious at all," I said.

"I wouldn't normally open up like this to someone I was investigating, but this is a special case. We've all heard the story about you in one way or another. It's just... it's hard to believe you'd be working with the Brotherhood. I guess I feel like this whole thing has been a waste of time."

My brows furrowed. "Well, to be honest, it has been greatly helpful to me to have an audience for this story... a reason to tell it. So, I appreciate it."

She smiled. "I'm glad something is coming of all this. But since your people value storytelling so much, why haven't you just recorded this story on your own?"

I walked over to the window and gazed up at the sky. "And how do you know I haven't?" I asked. I was glancing at her reflection through the window.

Her hand darted to her chest for a second. The question seemed to catch her off-guard.

"Well," she began, "you said yesterday that you'd never told this story to anyone."

I turned to her. "I never said I made no records of it."

The investigator remained silent. When I looked at her she was shaking her head. "Okay," she said. "Well, in any case, I'm not leaving until I have a recording of you explaining what happened to K, and to-"

"I get it," I said, raising my hand as I returned to my seat. "And I promise, I will get to that part. But as I've said before, I must tell the story properly. The first telling will shape the future tellings, even if you are the only one to hear it."

"Yes," she said, removing her cap and placing it on the table. "Well, take as long as you need." She clicked a button on her computer, and gestured to me to begin the story again, as she leaned back into her chair trying to get comfortable.

I eyed her intently and she returned my gaze. She wasn't being fully honest with me. But I had a suspicion that the only way I could find out her true motives was to play along. And if truthfully, she was just here on TAU authority to investigate any connections I might have had to the Brotherhood, then I'd best tell the story properly to dispel any suspicion. Either way, she had me where she wanted. I knew I had to keep talking.

Twenty-Six

That evening I considered staying in the temple, but decided to sleep aboard the docked Firebrand instead. When I arrived, Jonathan was sitting in the cockpit. I told him I was also going to spend the night in the ship. He seemed to understand, commenting on how the Firebrand's beds were surprisingly comfortable for a starship. We didn't talk much.

That night I had difficulty sleeping. Even though we were just outside my home, I felt no comfort from it. I was anxious to leave. The room was silent, punctuated only by my own breath. I lay on the bottom bunk as I had before, but without K's presence I felt strangely alone, even though Jonathan was just a room or two away. I shut my eyes and tried to control my breathing, but in the blackness of my mind I kept seeing arcs of red lightning; a wide set of teeth was smiling at me through the red storm. And then there was K, writhing in pain.

I shot up and stormed out of the room, half-awake, but too unsettled to sleep.

Panting, I ran in the moonlight. I wasn't sure where I was going, I just needed to move. My entire body felt constricted. My ears trailed behind me, and my fur was ruffled in the cool wind. Each breath I took filled my nostrils with a fragrant, invigorating scent of the flora surrounding the temple. I ran down the stairs of the temple, out into the winding paths and streets of the city. I ran past trees and buildings and orange lamp posts. My eyes shot up to the temple, to the surreal floating orbs I knew so well from my childhood, as I darted down toward the ocean.

I ran across a wall overlooking the beach as sea breeze air filled my lungs. The dusty stone beneath my feet awoke my senses as I traced the edge of the wall.

I stumbled down the side of a hill toward the sand, and the rippling waves, reflected in the starlight. My toes kicked up the sand as I got ever closer to the crest of the water. A wave rushed toward me and for a moment I hesitated, before increasing my speed.

My lungs gasped. Cold water splashed around my legs as I waded into the ocean.

I was already half submerged in water, so I committed in a split second and lunged forward with my arms outstretched.

The sound of the waves gently crashing against the beach was like a soothing melody for my ears. I waded in the water, enjoying the shock the cold was giving to my senses. I was awake.

I looked up to the night sky- Astraloth's sky- and in that moment I was no longer afraid. Birds quietly soared above, and I caught sight of a shooting star. And on the horizon, I saw the red nebula, the Thala nebula that had hidden the Shade Beam, and I simply stared.

"Great night for a swim!" I heard a voice call from the beach in Skorali. I could barely see their figure, so I swam closer to the shore.

"Yes… the water is quite nice tonight." I said to the silhouette. I was fairly close, but I still couldn't make out their figure. It was a skyther, I could tell that much from their voice and outline.

"Not many people come down and swim here this time of year," said the voice in a low, friendly tone. "I admire your spirit."

"Th- Thank you,"

The skyther began walking away down the beach, calling out a few more words as they left. "So many people these days, too caught up in machines, and the future and the past. Nice to see a fellow present-liver. To live so carefree, swimming in the calm of the night... Must be a good life." They paused briefly, before finishing. "Enjoy this moment, alright?"

I felt conflicted for a moment, and I was about to protest, but they were already too far for me to yell to them.

They were right about one thing, though. To be so carefree, even for a few minutes, was what I needed. It was nice for a change, being in the moment.

◆

All moments pass however, and soon the sun was shining and the valley was filled with the sounds of the city awakening. Joëlle and K were just returning to the Firebrand as Jonathan made himself some coffee and I drank some root beer in the small kitchen of the ship, the smell of our two drinks mixing as they filled the room.

"Joëlle," I said. "Good to see you."

"Morning!" said Joëlle with a smile on her face as she stepped in the door. I felt my heart lift instantly, seeing her happy for a moment. She must have had a good night in the temple.

Jonathan raised his mug to her and smiled. "The lady of the castle has returned!" he said.

Joëlle tilted her head. "It was a *little* charming the first time, but don't make a habit of calling me lady, okay?"

Jonathan's smile flickered for a second. "Ah- My apologies."

She chuckled. "Don't worry about it. Just don't do it."

He frowned, and nodded. "Fair enough." Then his smile resumed as he took another sip of his coffee.

Joëlle passed through into the cockpit as K entered the room. She was clutching her head, and I noticed Jonathan's smile fade.

"Hey Osax," K said, smiling weakly as she groaned.

I stood up and went to her side. I was going to do everything I could to help her, starting now. "K, how are you feeling? Why don't you take a seat?" I said, guiding her to one of the chairs.

She sat down and looked me in the eye. "Uh, thanks."

Jonathan spoke up as I went over to one of the cupboards and K continued rubbing her head.

"So, having a migraine?" he asked. His mouth was thin and his eyebrow raised just slightly.

K looked at him suspiciously. "I guess."

"I've got something to help with your problems!" I said, quickly. I retrieved a bottle of small white pills from the cupboard, and unscrewed the lid.

K looked at the pills, then back at my face. A smile crept up. "What are those?" she asked. Jonathan was eyeing me, his expression unchanging.

"They're…" I stumbled over the words. "Th- Just something I synthesized last night, using the food synthesizers. I was looking at the scans of your brain, trying to come up with something to inhibit the changes…"

K started nodding. "So, this'll help my headaches? And my blackouts?"

"Yes, it should," I said, lifting my ears and smiling as best as I could with my eyes.

Jonathan said, "You never said you were a pharmacist, Osax."

K looked at him with a sidelong glance "Never mentioned he was a prince either, but hey! He's Osax. He's full of surprises". She grinned.

"Well…" I began, feeling my cheeks flush.

"Not that being a prince seems to mean much to you. You just do whatever you want, no extra responsibilities or anything! I guess you become king once your mother dies, right? Then you gotta lead your people." She snorted, stretching her wrists as she extended her arms out. "Being free sounds more fun."

K… One minute she would be brooding, the next she'd be so lively. I may have had a hard time living in the moment, but K had trouble getting out of it. Maybe that's why we bonded; we each had something the other lacked. *The star is brighter on the other side,* I thought.

"Here," I said, bringing over a pill and a glass of water. "Why don't you try it, let me know if it helps?"

K picked up the pill between her blue fingers and held it to her eye. "How long does it take to affect things? You know, to work?"

I tapped my fingers together. "Well, I don't know for sure, but it should help if you take one every morning. I expect the effects will show up within the day, even if it's just minor. The pill is designed to counteract the growth development in your brain."

"Growth development?" said Jonathan, quietly.

K glanced at the glass of water. "You want me to swallow it?"

I nodded.

K hesitated for a brief moment, before tilting her head back, opening her mouth, and holding the pill between her lips. She pressed her finger and thumb together and crushed the pill into dust with ease, brushing it onto her tongue. Then she picked up the glass and washed it down.

Jonathan and I were staring at her, and she stared back.

"What?" she said. "I don't like swallowing pills."

She slammed the glass on the counter, and stood up.

"Well… the headache seems gone for now," she said. She took a step toward me, as if she was going to give me a hug, then paused, and lifted her fist toward me.

I returned the fist bump.

"You're alright, Osax," she said, smirking confidently. Jonathan kept watching us. "See you in the cockpit."

K left the room, following Joëlle. My heart was racing.

I began following her, but Jonathan grabbed my arm as I was passing him. I looked down at him and he pulled me in close, glancing toward the cockpit.

"I'm impressed that you were able to create such a pill on such short notice, with such little information," he said, his voice as low as the hum of the ship.

I gulped, nodding. "I- It was a challenge. I stayed up last night making sure it was perfect- Well, as perfect as I could make it with my limited knowledge."

He nodded slowly. "So, that's what you were doing at the temple," he said, staring me in the eye. His fingers felt tight around my arm.

"I…"

"Or were you doing it somewhere else? You certainly weren't working on it in the kitchen, or in your room."

"Wait," I said, my eyes narrowing, "were you watching me last night?" I pulled away from his grip.

He sighed, and his expression softened. "I'm sorry, I must be coming on quite strongly. After our conversation last night, I couldn't sleep. You seemed to be acting a little bit strange. On top of that, when I checked my spare eye…"

"You have a spare eye?" I asked. "An extra cybernetic one, I presume?"

He was flustered. "Yes. I- I don't have a spare *organic* eye, that would be absurd. Anyway... well, I seem to have misplaced it… ah, never mind. It just- Things felt a little bit off. Maybe I was just feeling paranoid." He shuffled his feet. "Anyway, when I wandered around the ship and noticed you were gone, even though you made a point of staying here instead of at the temple, I admit I was perplexed. And just now, you were acting rather suspicious. I want to make sure you know what you're doing if you're feeding drugs to K." His robotic eye flared in intensity as it narrowed, and his orange one was as sharp as a spear. "What do you know?"

I noticed my mandibles were clenching. "It's okay Jonathan, I… I know what I'm doing."

"Really?" He said, "Because I don't recall drug synthesis being part of the curriculum for theoretical biologists." He glared at me. "I would know; I've studied theoretical biology as well. And I doubt skyther Princes are all trained in the arts of manufacturing medicine." He stood up. "So you better be sure you're not feeding her poison, because if you are-"

"Jonathan!" I exclaimed, before whispering, "It's just sugar."

Jonathan's eyes widened slightly. For a moment he looked startled, then slowly his lips curved into a shallow smile.

"What's going on back there?" Joëlle's voice echoed through the ship.

"Just spilled a bit of coffee on accident, and it startled Osax, that's all!" said Jonathan.

"Well, make sure you clean it up! Not only could that be a slipping hazard, but I don't appreciate messy teammates!"

Jonathan smiled. "Will do. I'll be in there in a minute!"

"You won't tell K, will you?" I pleaded.

Jonathan shook his head. "As long as it's not hurting her, I see no reason to hurt her myself."

I felt a pang of guilt in my chest. I was lying to K after all, but what else could I do? I promised I would help her.

"I'll see you in the cockpit," I said plainly.

◆

While alone in the hall leading to the cockpit, I jumped. My holo-gauntlet flared to life without me doing anything. My heart was racing. It was displaying a holographic image all on its own…

I tilted my head to the side, perplexed. It was a watermarked photo of two humans hugging. Then some white text appeared.

> didnt want to hug you in front of Jonathan. feels
> weird with him staring. granted, this is probably
> weirder. didnt really think that through…

The text started deleting itself, followed by the image.

I entered the cockpit, and saw K fiddling on her holo-gauntlet. She glanced up at me, and smiled guiltily, scratching the back of her head.

"Uh, hey," she said sheepishly.

"K," I said. "Just because we paired our holo-gauntlets doesn't mean you can use mine to open random files. If you want to talk to me, just do it in person, or give me a call."

Joëlle glanced back at us. "You two paired your holo-gauntlets?"

K deactivated her holo-gauntlet. "What of it?"

"Well," she said, "that's not really meant for two people. It's more for one person who has two holo-gauntlets, and needs to be able to remotely access them. That's why it bypasses all of the security features."

K and I looked at each other. She shrugged.

"Just, don't overdo it," I said.

"Just trying to show my appreciation," she said, awkwardly.

I took a seat on the right side of the cockpit and spun the chair around to face them, lifting my ears with a little effort.

"So, Osax, your mother was worried about you last night," said Joëlle.

I sighed and leaned forward, resting my elbows on my knees. "We don't always get along. Unfortunately, yesterday was one of the times we don't."

"In any case, we're ready to set out. I just figured you'd want to say goodbye to your mother before we leave."

I looked out the window of the cockpit toward the Great Temple. My mother was somewhere there. I didn't know when I would see her next, but I was still so furious with her. *Maybe I should call her,* I thought.

"It's alright. I'll see her again, after the mission," I said.

K and Joëlle were silent for a moment.

"Well," said Joëlle, "I'm glad you're confident you'll make it out of this alive."

K nodded. "Yeah, as long as you remember to run away from falling debris."

I lowered my ears at K, as she smirked at me.

"Anyway," said Joëlle, "Queen Suranos was kind enough to give me this." She tapped a plate-sized metal device which was fitted to the scanning console. "This is a rare quantum extender, one of a kind; it will increase the range of our scanner by… well, by a longshot. It only works for very specific energy signatures, but we should be able to use it to track the mothership- Duhrnan's ship- from nearly anywhere in the galaxy." She smiled confidently. "Well, as long as he's not hiding in a sensor-scrambling nebula."

"It's that precise?" I asked.

"Yes, but only because we got close enough to get some detailed scans on the ship's energy output. So, we won't be able to track the Shade Beam itself with that kind of accuracy." She activated the scanner and it flared to life, displaying a distant coordinate in the emptiness of space. "But it seems to be working on the mothership."

K chuckled. "Well who cares. Duhrnan should be shaking in his boots. He may not know who we are, but he will when we come crashing through his front door."

I nodded in agreement. "We still don't have an attack plan, but since this scanner upgrade works, we should get going at once. At the least, by following him we can keep unraveling his plan."

Jonathan stepped into the room. "So," he said, "I guess we don't need my scanning abilities anymore."

"Probably best not to rely on you anyway, what with your directional deficiency," said K. Then she surprised us all by adding, "I'm just kidding."

"So, nothing left to do on Astraloth?" asked Joëlle. "You all still have the option to leave."

I thought about my mother, and my ears twitched.

"We're coming with you," said K.

Jonathan and I nodded.

"Right." said Joëlle, spinning her chair around to face the controls. The ship began silently and smoothly lifting off the ground. My eyes fell on the shrinking temple below us. "Last night I contacted Admiral O'Kane. I told her about Duhrnan and the Shade Beam."

"And?" asked Jonathan nervously.

"She relayed the information to the other Admirals. It sounds like they're not eager to take any actions just yet. And from the sounds of things, they're more worried about the public finding out about the Shade Beam than about stopping the valicorr."

"Hmm," said Jonathan.

"So," I said, staring down at my home, getting ever smaller as we breached the clouds. "We're on our own for now?"

Joëlle nodded. "For now."

Twenty-Seven

We had been out in space chasing down Duhrnan's mothership for days when we received the signal. The day had been rather uneventful until then; I had been giving K her "medicine" each morning and she seemed grateful. Jonathan seemed wary of me doing so. I wasn't sure why, but he seemed very protective of K. All the while, Joëlle was acting a bit more cheerful than she had been before staying at Astraloth. Once a day she would ask me about my relationship to my mother, but I felt so tense that I always avoided the question. It just wasn't what I wanted to be spending my energy on at the time. I hadn't really realized she was just trying to bond with me, something which she hadn't attempted since before the attack on Voren.

We were in the overlapping hours of our sleep schedules, and all four of us were awake, sharing a meal in the cockpit.

Joëlle smirked at me in the silence only broken by the sound of my slurping straw.

"Why root beer?" She asked.

I lifted my ears away from the straw. I had been entranced by the sounds of the root beer in the glass and straw. "What do you mean?"

"Why do you always drink root beer, isn't that unhealthy?" she asked, brushing aside a lock of purple hair.

K leaned forward in her seat, taking a big bite of a sandwich and mumbling through her mouthful. "Yeah, I don't think I've seen you drink anything else since we met."

Jonathan chimed in, sipping a cup of coffee. "If a human were to drink that much root beer, they'd be unfit for missions, to say the least." He relaxed in his seat.

I exchanged glances with all of them, laughing and raising my ears. "I just like root beer. And while sugar is destructive to human physiology, it's actually pretty healthy for a skyther. Liquid sugar is an essential part of our diet… unlike humans we metabolize sugar much more effectively and-"

"Maybe so," said Joëlle. "but I keep seeing you with your ears down, practically surrounding your glass when you drink, or when you pour yourself a glass."

Jonathan turned to her, saying "It's probably ASMR."

Joëlle and Jonathan started laughing, and K and I locked eyes.

"What is that?" I asked.

"Autonomous sensory meridian response," Jonathan replied. "Essentially, it's a calming reaction to sensory input, usually a gentle kind of stimulus. It means certain sounds are pleasurable… maybe even make you feel tingly." He was smirking.

Joëlle shot me a glance. "It's just… kind of cute."

"Cute?" I said, tilting my head to the side. I admit, certain sounds and sensations did make me feel tingly.

Jonathan said, "It's something experienced in humans fairly regularly, but-"

"It's cute to see a skyther experiencing it," said Joëlle. Her smile disappeared in a flash and she covered her mouth with her hand. "Oh- I'm sorry, I wasn't trying to be… I wasn't trying to…"

K glanced between them with her hands raised. "Look," she said, before swallowing a bite. "He just likes root beer. Does he need to explain why?"

"It's fine, K," I said. I sipped some more root beer, savouring the taste and the sound. "It's just something that helps me relax and slow down my mind."

Jonathan glanced to Joëlle. "Not sure about skythers, but I'm pretty sure there are countless studies which would suggest the opposite of that is true."

They shared a warm laugh as K and I shrugged to each other.

Sudden noise drowned out the laughter. Unease rippled out through my body. My ears twitched. A screeching signal cut into the cockpit, and I saw my companions start in surprise. The communications console in front of Joëlle blinked urgently.

Eyes locked to the console, I placed my drink on the counter beside me and stepped from my seat. I reached to answer the call.

I paused as Joëlle's hand gently touched my outstretched arm. Her eyes were full of concern. "Osax… wait."

K mumbled through a mouthful as she put her sandwich aside and leaned in. "What's going on? What's that noise?"

My heart rate was steadily rising as the significance of this sudden event began to sink in. The sound kept screeching throughout the cockpit.

Jonathan's mechanical eye flickered and he quickly raised his fingers to it. "It-" he said, distracted as he fumbled with his prosthetic, "It's the alliance Code-Alpha signal."

K frowned. "What alliance?"

Joëlle slowly retracted her hand and her gaze fell. "The alliance between humans and skythers. Between the TAU and Astraloth." She grit her teeth, and I understood why she had stopped me from answering the call. None of us wanted to hear the broadcast.

I found myself breathing heavily, but I tried to speak anyway. "It's not just any emergency, K. This signal represents the highest level of threat to our civilizations. And the only people who have the authority and the means to use this channel are the Cardinal of the Terran Astral Union, and the Queen of-" My voice choked up as I thought about my mother, and what kind of situation she would have to be in to use the Code-Alpha signal.

After a brief moment where none of us spoke, Jonathan pointed his hand toward the row of consoles in front of us, beneath the wide windshield. "Answer the call, Osax" he said sternly.

My muscles tensed. Joëlle's mouth formed a straight line and she held her breath, closing her eyes. Jonathan lowered his hand and frowned. K blinked once, looking my way, and smirking as if to shrug, but without moving her shoulders. I lowered my left hand to the metallic console in front of Joëlle from which the lights and sounds of the alpha signal emanated. My finger traced the plastic button that would answer the call, allowing us to hear the emergency message in full. I applied some gentle pressure, but not enough.

I glanced to my side at the navigational system. With the help of my mother's quantum extender our scanners could track the valicorr mothership to a solar system anywhere in the galaxy, and right now it was in an inconspicuous star system far away from any notable human or skyther settlements.

I could feel the blood pulsing through my finger as it rested on the button. Only the sound of the signal beeping and screeching filled the room. I drew a slow breath.

"We don't know what he's done with the Shade Beam," I said. "It could be anywhere."

Jonathan twisted his jaw, his lips firmly closed. K frowned. Joëlle looked up at me, and I saw a flicker of hope in her eyes. She grabbed my hand, and decisively pressed my finger into the button.

The screeching stopped, and was replaced by the sound of calm music. Joëlle sat in the central seat, with K seated next to her on her left. Jonathan left his seat and stood behind them, leaning in over their shoulders, and I hunched beside Joëlle as she clutched my hand. The blinking light faded and a holographic projector flickered to life.

I felt Joëlle grip my hand tighter, and gasped. Duhrnan's unmistakable grin plastered his face as he spoke, and shimmered in the glow of the hologram.

K spat. "How the hell is this bastard on here? Didn't you just say only the leaders of-"

"Yes," I managed to force out through clenched mandibles, "he shouldn't have access to this channel."

"This is being broadcast to every quantum communicator in the galaxy that can tune to this signal," whispered Joëlle. "What does he want?"

Duhrnan was speaking to us from the same dim, purplish room we had seen him in before. He rested his long muzzle on two fists, his remaining two arms gesturing casually as he spoke. Behind his chair I could make out something moving in the darkness. A creature of some kind, large, playing with something, like a canine with a bone. I leaned my ears forward, trying to listen to Duhrnan's words, and the freakish growling of the monster he seemed to keep as a pet.

"...is not important." His voice seemed to slither out through his teeth. His eyes were wide slits, and he watched the camera in a way that I could only describe as predatory. "All that matters is that by now, most of you should be tuned in and listening. Hopefully watching as well, though I understand not everyone has access to visual communicators." He laughed to himself. "Now it's rude of me not to introduce myself, so I'll waste no more time."

Duhrnan stood up out of his chair, and waved his hands in an exaggerated human greeting. "I am Duhrnan, emperor of the valicorr." He bowed, his fangs stretching wide across his face. He wore dark coloured robes, accented with solid black armour plates. The reds, browns, and purples of his attire all mixed together in the haze of the hologram. When he stood back up he nearly shouted. "And as of this moment, emperor of this galaxy!" He lifted his top set of arms to the ceiling as if he had just won a prize, while his bottom two began clapping.

K clenched her fists. "You're not *my* emperor!"

Jonathan tapped her on the shoulder. "You know he can't hear you, this is a one way broadcast."

K scoffed. "Yeah."

I tensed, closing my fingers around Joëlle's. The creature in the back rolled into view. It was furred and built like a massive elongated wolf, sporting an extra set of legs. Its fur was black and blue, with a few red accents. Its tail was tipped with a razor-sharp barb, and its eyes were white and soulless. In its snarling jaw it chomped at something fleshy, tearing and stretching it with its plate-sized claws.

"You all must be thinking now, 'oh no, but this isn't an emergency! Doesn't our new emperor understand that the Code-Alpha signal is only to be used in dire situations which threaten our very existence?'" Duhrnan was a bad actor, but he was having more fun playing his role than any performer I had seen before. He struck a pose with his mouth hanging open and his eyes wide in feigned surprise, his two left hands covering his mouth as he brushed his forehead with the back of his right hands.

"I didn't know I could hate someone this much." I felt the words coming straight from my mouth as I heard them repeated in K's voice. We glanced at each other, and somehow, despite myself, I was able to feel a tingle of amusement and comradery. But it was like a drop of water in a vat of oil. In a second it was indistinguishable from the black, volatile fluid that was coursing through my veins.

Duhrnan dropped his pose and his smile faded too. His gaze fell to the floor, and his shoulders drooped as he shook his head, suddenly sullen. "This gets boring very quickly," he muttered, before he perked up. "Alright, onto the point." He reached out toward something beneath the camera, and the image changed.

The broadcast was now displaying a view from the hull of a spacecraft of some kind, looking at a beautiful planet.

Duhrnan's voice came in through the speakers. "This, for you humans who don't know, is Astraloth, home of your friends the skythers."

I couldn't breathe. I wanted to find something in the image which proved that he was wrong, but every detail on the planet's surface, the moons, and the nebula behind it confirmed that he was right. We were looking at Astraloth. I only noticed my hand was shaking when I felt Joëlle struggle to keep me still. My thoughts spiraled to my mother, Suranos.

"Wait-" said K, getting up out of her seat. "He's not… that's not the-"

"We're looking at this beautiful planet from the hull of the Shade Beam!" Duhrnan exclaimed.

"Oh no," I said. "Oh no no no no no…"

He continued talking, but I began to lose focus on his words. Joëlle turned to me, but my eyes were glazing over with tears. She was saying something. K was speaking too, yelling even, but everything was just becoming noise. I slumped onto my knees, gazing straight into the hologram with limp arms, one hand still resting on the console, held by something.

"…to demonstrate my power, courtesy of the TAU government." his voice continued.

I felt like my heartbeat was a ticking bomb, and I could feel each second as it passed me, but once it had it melted into ambiguity as I struggled to keep focus.

"Is there nothing we can do? We can't jam the gun somehow?" asked K.

"We're light years away," said Joëlle, "and even if we had some way to get a signal from the Firebrand to the Shade Beam, I have no idea what we'd have to do to neutralize it."

"We have to try, dammit!" K screamed. She slammed her fist on the weapons console in front of her, and a chunk of metal snapped off and onto the floor with a spark.

Joëlle spun to face K, and raised her voice. "K, there is nothing we can do from here!" Vaguely, I noticed the feeling of her hand still pinning mine to the console.

I realized Duhrnan had been silent for several seconds. The silence continued, and it gave me a chance to try to return to my senses. All I could manage to do was close my eyes and breathe.

"I apologize for that interruption." His voice was sharp in the silence. "As I was saying, this weapon was courteously constructed by the TAU. Why? I don't know and frankly it doesn't matter. They are what has allowed this moment to happen. In exactly twenty seconds, I will fire the Shade Beam at Astraloth, and it will be disintegrated, ceasing to exist." His voice was calm. "I'll start the countdown. Twenty."

"No," I said as his voice droned on.

K turned to me with frantic eyes. "Osax, it's going to be alright, okay?"

"Seventeen."

"No," I said, shaking my head as the tears began to obscure my vision again.

K walked around to my right side and grabbed my free hand. "Suranos was telling me about the spheres of the temple," she said enthusiastically.

"Fourteen."

Joëlle was staring at K as she continued to speak. "Osax, they're for the defense of the planet, right? She said they could protect Astraloth from invaders. They could save Astraloth from destruction, when it was most necessary. She was telling me about the secret defense system."

"Five."

I clenched my mandibles as tears streamed down my face. K was crushing my hand, but I could barely feel it. "It's just a myth," I said, staring down.

"Three."

K's face contorted in shock. "What?"

"Two."

"She lied," I said, looking up at the hologram. My home.

"One."

There was a flash of dark energy from the hull of the Shade Beam, a firing mechanism which was out of sight. It almost looked as though the planet vanished before the energy even struck it. And then it was gone. Silent, and gone.

"I'll be firing this at Earth in exactly seven days," said Duhrnan. His voice was cold. A timer appeared on the hologram. "Try to stop me."

Twenty-Eight

Duhrnan flashed back onto the hologram for a few seconds more. It was just enough time for him, grinning viciously, to bow farewell in the skyther style. And then he disappeared, and all that remained on the display was a ticking timer, set for 7 Earth days, counting down by the second.

Blood dripped through K's fingers from my right hand onto the console. She let go, and exclaimed, "Shit!"

My eyes were locked to the timer. The numbers were a blocky, solid white.

06:23:59:53… 06:23:59:52… 06:23:59:51…

"Osax, god, I'm sorry!" K hesitantly held her hands toward me, but didn't dare to touch me.

Joëlle held her breath and gazed at the timer, and my bleeding hand.

As if in perfect rhythm with the timer, pain gently pulsed up from my palm. I couldn't take my eyes off the countdown.

K kept apologizing and asking me if I was okay. Joëlle turned to the doorway of the cockpit and said, "Where have you been?"

I heard Jonathan's voice from behind me respond, "I- I'm sorry. I didn't know what to do, I tried to make some calls-" His voice caught in his throat. I'd never heard him sound so shaky.

My eyes fell to my right hand. It looked like a crimson mess, but the sight of it didn't seem to affect me at all. I felt like I was vibrating at a somehow stable wavelength.

Jonathan's footsteps came closer. "That looks bad," he said. "It looks broken."

K glanced toward him. "I'm sorry! I was trying to help!"

Joëlle looked at the sparking weapons console, and the chunk of it which lay lifeless on the floor of the cockpit. She said, "It doesn't matter, it was an accident. Jonathan, get the medkit!"

I heard him shuffle to the back of the room and fumble with something. The quiet hum of the ship's engine filled my senses in the space between each painful heartbeat. I looked out through the window at the black veil of space, dotted with stars, and squinted.

"Osax, are you okay?" asked K.

I felt Joëlle gently squeeze my left hand. "Osax?" she said, quietly.

Jonathan came over to me, stepping between K and I, and knelt down beside me with the medical kit in hand. He began tending to my hand, cleaning the blood from it, and prepping some medical gel. His organic eye was facing me and I gazed into it.

"Osax?" he asked hesitantly, pausing his work. K and Joëlle were silent. I noticed through the haze that his hands were shaking, and his eye was red, as though he had been crying, but I didn't remember hearing him cry. After a moment of silence, he tightened his lip, and turned back to my hand, rubbing it with medical gel.

Seconds passed, and I knew exactly how many staring at Duhrnan's timer, each second simultaneously too fast and too slow.

K bowed her head. "Osax... I'm so... sorry."

Joëlle sighed. I blinked, gazing at the timer.

"I can't believe this happened," she continued. "Your planet... your home..."

Jonathan paused and looked up at me for a brief second, before returning to his work. I sat motionless.

Joëlle shuffled in her seat. "I wonder what's happening back on Earth now. Everyone knows that the Shade Beam was created by the TAU now... I wonder how people are reacting. And with this timer... they're probably terrified. Humanity has never faced something of this scale."

K balled her fists. "He's gonna pay. He's gonna pay!"

Joëlle let go of my hand and leaned forward, gazing out into space. She grimaced. "This is perfect for the Brotherhood. Astraloth is out of the picture... faith in the TAU will be completely destabilized."

"The Brotherhood?" asked K.

Jonathan spoke up quietly. "They're a group of revolutionaries, mostly human, seeking to destroy the power-balance of the galaxy, in order to rebuild a more just civilization." He gave K a sidelong glance. "I'm surprised you've never heard of them."

"They're terrorists," said Joëlle.

K shook her head. "Well, who cares about the Brotherhood. Astraloth just got destroyed! What about Osax?"

Joëlle shifted around so she was leaning in front of me, looking into my eyes. I didn't meet her gaze. "Osax, are you alright?" I was silent. "It's okay if you aren't…"

"No, it's not okay," said K. "He's gotta be fine. He *is* fine." She placed her hand on my shoulder. "You're fine."

Jonathan swiped her hand away with his arm. "Careful!" he commanded.

K recoiled. "I- I just want to make sure he's okay!"

"He's clearly not okay!" Jonathan spat, quivering. "But it's okay," he said, regaining his posture. "Everything happens for a reason."

"Yeah?" said K. "And why did this have to happen, huh? Why did Astraloth have to be destroyed? Why did billions of people have to die?"

Jonathan's eyes flickered as he worked on my hand. "Maybe… you just wouldn't understand." His voice was quiet and precise.

"Why wouldn't I understand?!" K shouted.

Joëlle interjected. "I think he just means, maybe it's not for us to understand. Maybe there is something good to come of this…"

I glanced down at my hand. Jonathan had cleaned up all of the blood. I tried to flex my fingers, but they barely moved, and searing pain shot up my arm.

"Careful not to move," said Jonathan. "This kind of wound will take some time to heal, even with medical gel. You've got broken bones."

I shut my eyes tightly, trying and failing to numb out the pain. It was growing stronger and more unbearable each second, and I found myself suddenly struggling to breathe slowly. With my eyes closed, images of my mother spilled into my mind. She felt so distant, but she felt alive. She couldn't have been dead.

Tears started silently streaming down my face. The temple was gone. The bird on the balcony, the royal guards, the town, the mountains, the stranger at the beach: all gone.

"This means," said Joëlle, hesitantly breaking the silence, "that Talcorosax is the King of Astraloth now."

"How can he be the king of Astraloth?" demanded K. "Astraloth is gone!"

Joëlle sighed. "Well, he's the official ruler of any skythers who respect the authority of Astraloth."

K shook her head in disbelief, and looked at me. "Osax… you're a king now." I couldn't bring myself to look her way, and she noticed. "Come on, why aren't you looking at me? Why aren't you talking?"

"Give it a rest, K, he's not well!" Jonathan growled.

"Doesn't mean he can't talk, or give us a sign," said K.

"We can't make Osax do anything, K," said Joëlle, brushing her purple dreads to the side and sighing. I looked down at nothing in particular on the console in front of me, and she continued. "We have to decide what we are going to do though."

"What the hell are we gonna do?" asked K. "We can't bring Astraloth back…"

Jonathan closed his eyes and froze for a brief moment.

Joëlle stood up from her chair, and turned away from the window, taking another huge sigh and raising her hands to her head. "We can contact the TAU fleets, see if they have any plans."

"You think they'll be able to come to a decision now? From what Admiral O'Kane told you, they were too worried about making the wrong move or revealing that they were responsible for the Shade Beam to actually give us a hand in hunting Duhrnan down before… why would they feel different now?"

"Astraloth is destroyed. I doubt even the TAU expected the Shade Beam to be functional so quickly, it's probably got them scared. And Duhrnan's threat, and the timer… they're probably planning how to stop the Shade Beam right now!"

"They're probably scared," said K, "But that doesn't mean they're ready to fight. You know, it's actually the fight, flight, or freeze response. There's a two out of three chance that-"

"When did you get so interested in probability?" Joëlle snarked. "We should return to Olympus and meet with the Admirals in person. We'll need a fleet to stop Duhrnan and the valicorr."

Jonathan cut in. "You think that fighting Duhrnan in a head on war will work? Even a Titan-class cruiser was little more than light rain to the mothership. And you can bet the Shade Beam will be outfitted with whatever armour and shielding Duhrnan can equip it with."

Joëlle put her hands on her hips. "Well then what do you suggest? Each second passed is a second wasted, and if there's a way to stop Duhrnan, the fleets will figure it out."

My eyes glanced to the scanner still tracking Duhrnan's mothership. It was in a strange solar system.

I furrowed my brows. I recognized the solar system, but I wasn't sure what its significance was.

Jonathan replied. "I'm not sure what to do, but I know the fleets will be crushed against the Shade Beam and the valicorr mothership. And that's not even factoring in any other valicorr ships he might have under his command."

"Wait," said K, with a puzzled look on her face. "Why would he wait seven days to destroy Earth anyway? I mean sure it takes some time to travel between Earth and Astraloth, even with the fastest slipspace drive available, right? But way less than seven days."

Joëlle shrugged. "He's sadistic. He wants everyone to be afraid, and in pain. By drawing it out, he's only increasing everyone's suffering, and his enjoyment." She shuddered.

K shook her head. "No, that doesn't seem like enough. I mean I agree, he's twisted beyond anything, but that can't be the only reason."

Jonathan let go of my hand. "That's all I can do for now," he said, but I didn't look his way. He sighed. "Well," he said, turning to K, "the Shade Beam is powered by a rare fuel source, diffusionite. It's possible he needs to reload it."

"And that takes seven days?" asked K, unimpressed.

Jonathan frowned. "No... though I hear the weapon has a long recharge period, perhaps days long. Maybe-"

"How do you know that?" asked Joëlle.

"I heard rumours while working on research at the base on Voren," he replied.

"Why didn't you mention this earlier? Maybe you know something-"

"I swear, I would have volunteered any rumours if I thought them believable or useful enough to mention."

"Who shitting cares?" K exclaimed. "Look at us... Look at Osax. What are we going to do?"

"We're going to go to the fleet." said Joëlle.

"Don't be an idiot," said Jonathan.

"Then suggest something else!"

"We could... find the Shade Beam," said Jonathan with little conviction.

"How?" said K.

"We can't." said Joëlle. "It could already be anywhere by now... we have no idea how fast it is or where it's headed."

"What about the mothership? We can attack him there!" said K.

"Same problem as the fleet," said Jonathan. "We simply cannot expect to win in a fight against him."

"Then you're just suggesting we just give up?!" shouted Joëlle.

"No..." said Jonathan hesitantly.

Joëlle took a step toward him. "Then what do we do? Unless you're about to reveal some mystical technique of yours for tracking the Shade Beam, this far from Astraloth and without any clear sense of its energy signatures, then I suggest you give us an alternative."

"Yeah," said K. "If you're so sure that this all happened for a reason, then tell us why. Tell us what we're going to do about it."

I stood up from my chair.

My heart was beating calmly, and my eyes trained the floor, but I could see the three of them staring at me, in silence. I looked up at my faint reflection in the window, and something glimmered in my eye. My ears were held still and I stood up straight enough, with my head angled down just a little.

"Osax…" said K.

I inhaled. "Duhrnan *wants* the fleet to unite against him. That's why he gave a time and a place for his next appearance: Earth, in seven days."

They remained silent.

"Which means to go to the fleet would be a waste of time," I continued. I lifted my right arm to my chest, and rubbed my wrist with my left hand. "Astraloth is gone…" I said, gazing at my hand. I looked up at the stars. "We aren't."

I could feel a glow of energy inside me coming into focus. I could feel it building in the room between us.

"He was sending that message from his mothership, far away from Astraloth, and to his knowledge, completely hidden. He must expect the TAU and skyther colonies to send ships to Astraloth, looking to confront the Shade Beam." I took a deep breath. "Meanwhile, he's hiding away on his mothership."

"What do you mean?" asked Joëlle.

I stepped away from them back toward my chair, and continued. "He's scared. That's what I mean; he's scared. Somehow, despite all the grandeur, he knows he has a weakness, and he's betting that no one will figure it out. He's distracting everyone with the Shade Beam and assuming that no one will be able find him out there on the mothership."

Jonathan slowly chimed in. "I don't understand."

"He thinks no one can track him. He never knew that we got so close to him in the nebula."

Jonathan persisted. "But even so, why would he hide? The mothership is, for all intents and purposes, invulnerable."

Fire was kindling inside me. I whipped out my left hand to the glass of root beer I'd left on the counter, and snatched it up, whirling to face Jonathan and the others as my ears lifted and my eyes narrowed in a confident smile. "Exactly. He would only hide if he had a reason to. A weakness."

Joëlle's eyes glimmered, and Jonathan looked at me with hesitant appreciation. K's mouth was open, slowly morphing into a smile.

"He's confident in every way, except about this one weakness!" I said, gesturing to the scanner. "He's-"

"And what is that weakness?" interjected Jonathan.

"I don't know," I said. "I don't know what the weakness is, but we may be the only ones who can find out."

"How do we do that?" asked Joëlle.

I narrowed my eyes, and took a long drink of fizzy root beer. "We follow him. We find the mothership, we find out what he's doing on Malum, and we find out how we can use that knowledge to stop him for good."

"Malum?" asked K.

"That system he's in," I said, pointing to the scanner, "the only notable planet there is Malum. And he's a Loro. And remember the picture I salvaged from the loro computer on Voren?"

"It was taken on Malum!" said K, grinning. Joëlle and Jonathan glanced between each other.

"Precisely," I said. "He must have a reason to be there… and it must have to do with the loro."

There was a moment of silence. Joëlle glanced at the timer. "Well," she said, reaching for the controls of the ship, "we have six days, twenty-three hours, and fifty minutes, give or take. Let's stop wasting time."

The stars peeled back around the Firebrand as once more we kicked off into slipspace.

Jonathan stood up, moving past me to head to the kitchen with a sigh. "You know, this is a huge gamble."

"You're a scientist," I said. "Sometimes, you just have to test your hypothesis."

He smirked at me, and his gaze pierced mine for a second. His long coat trailed behind him as he exited.

I took a deep breath, drink in hand, and looked out the window. K stood up, smiling. Her eyes darted down to my bandaged, broken hand, and her smile disappeared. Tears started forming in her eyes and she brushed them aside before they could.

"Osax… you know I'm so sorry. I- I was only trying to comfort you…"

I felt strangely balanced. An incredible weight lay in my heart and I knew everything had changed in the galaxy, but something had also changed in me, and in that moment I felt an equally powerful force raising me up to meet the collapse of things. I knelt down and opened my arms for a hug, and K hesitantly opened her arms, and wrapped them around me as gently as she could.

With my face next to hers, I closed my eyes, and whispered to her. "Never apologize."

Twenty-Nine

My eyes fluttered open slowly. I twisted, and the smooth grey covers I was wrapped in rustled lightly. My head rested gently on the feathery pillows and I yawned blearily. White lights dimly illuminated the room from the corners of the walls. The sleeping black computer and chair to accompany it were all that filled the room, aside from the bunk bed I found myself sleeping on. Everything was quiet except for the faint, low hum, gently vibrating through the hull. A vaguely metallic scent brushed my nose, followed by something sweet.

My eyes landed on a figure, and a smirking blue face came into focus. K's lips curled up around her tusk-like teeth, and her brows lowered. She was wearing a long-sleeved black leather jacket underneath her usual armoured vest, and rugged, fingerless gloves. My eyes lazily scanned her arms, noting the holes she'd cut (or ripped) into the outfit about her shoulders, arms, and backs of her hands, letting her pale-blue growths stick out, leaving the outfit free to otherwise fit snugly to her toned arms. About her neck and shoulders she was wearing a dark grey cloak, unripped and draped carefully over her spikes. It fell to the back of her waist, and sported a hood, which she wore down. It would be difficult for her to wear it over her head anyway, given her horns. At her side was a retracted molecular sword, and a sleek black pistol was holstered across her chest for quick access.

She was humming a song, the same melody I heard her hum back in the observation lounge on Kronos. She raised up one of her hands which held a clear glass of a bubbling dark liquid, equipped with a bendy straw.

I sat up slowly, and rubbed my head. "What time is it?" I mumbled.

My throat felt dry. When I touched my right hand to my head, it began to ache dully. I looked at it, and tried flexing my fingers. I was able to flex them, though it hurt quite a lot. The medical gel was doing its job. K's music quietly wafted into my ears.

K handed me the drink and I began to sip it as she responded. "It's time for you to get out of bed. We just made it to Malum." She sat down on the bed beside me as I threw my legs over the side. "We would have woken you earlier but… we all thought it was best to let you sleep, while you were able to."

"Thanks," I said. "And thanks for breakfast."

◆

Joëlle sat alone in the cockpit. I stood beside her as I looked at the planet in front of us, centered in the frame of the window. Joëlle was already wearing her silvery-blue armour, with her helmet resting on the console beside her. I ruffled my chest fur with my fingers.

The planet was reflected in her helmet's smooth visor. Malum was primarily orange looking from up here, with several notable storm clouds raging about the surface. Green and blue splotches dotted the landscape. My eyes narrowed on the blocky text of the timer. It had taken us nearly a full day to get to Malum from where we were when Duhrnan sent the broadcast.

"From here," I asked, "how long would it take us to get to Earth?"

Joëlle glanced up at me. "Slipspace travel is fickle… I'd feel comfortable giving us a full twenty-four hours, if we want to be safe."

I narrowed my eyes, staring at the planet below.

"So, the plan is to find out how to stop the mothership, stop it, and then intercept the Shade Beam when it arrives at Earth in six days, and stop it too?" she asked.

I nodded. "Precisely."

The planet started getting bigger as we approached.

"It's a good thing you knew about Malum's connection to the loro," said Joëlle, "because while you were sleeping the mothership disappeared from the scanners.

"So it's emissions got scrambled?"

"Exactly. But we know where to look." She winked at me.

"Malum is one of the most hostile planets either of our species have discovered," I said. I remembered hearing that the atmosphere of Malum scrambled several types of signals; it was just one of the many dangers we would face upon landing.

"I wanted to thank you," I said, looking her in the eye.

"For what?"

"For holding my hand," I said.

◆

I suited up in a black undersuit, and my familiar armour. My right hand was still bandaged, and I probably wouldn't take the bandages off for another day. Joëlle gave me a black cloak like the grey one I'd seen K wearing. I asked if I could cut holes in the hood for my ears to fit through, and she said it wouldn't be a problem, so I went ahead with my DIY project.

She also gave me a pistol, smooth and silver, designed specifically for charged shots. She'd explained that the pistol she gave to K was actually an automatic gun, claiming it suited her combat style better. She described her as "an unchained lion," and while I thought K was more akin to a wild athurlist of Astraloth, I agreed with the statement. *Besides,* I thought, *as of yesterday, the athurlist is extinct.* I wouldn't let the same fate befall the creatures of Earth.

The smell of coffee wafted into my nose. The kitchen counters were all bare and reflective, illuminated by a white light centered in the middle of the ceiling, complemented by strip lights in the four corners of the room. Jonathan wore his usual getup, a stylish black and white long coat with grey armour plates on his chest, shoulders, and boots. He had his own pistol, black and reflective, holstered safely at his hip. He was wearing the same black gloves I'd seen him in when I first saw him in the generator room, his fingers wrapped around a coffee mug with a TAU symbol of Earth on the side. He gazed at his mug with a forlorn stare, as he leaned back onto one of the counters.

K was seated at the table in the center of the room, with a glass of water at the ready. She clutched the side of her head with one hand, fingers laced around her bull-like horns, and winced in pain. I stepped over to her, handed her a pill and activated my holo-gauntlet. Ritually, she tilted her head up and crushed the pill into her mouth, washing it down with the water, while I added today's scan of her brain to my growing collection of data that I had no idea what to do with. I met eyes with Jonathan as he held his mug to his lips, and his expression was unreadable, as usual.

I lowered my eyes, looking at K. "It's bad this morning, is it?"

She burped, generating a chuckle from Jonathan. "Yeah," she said, "but since I've been on your medicine I haven't blacked out, so, I think it's working."

Despite my best efforts to keep them raised, I felt my ears sag a little. "Well you- Your scans are looking good…"

My heart was beginning to race. I glanced up at Jonathan.

He exhaled in satisfaction as he lowered his mug. "Good thing you've got Osax looking after you, K." He smiled, his robotic eye closing a little.

K rubbed her temples just in front of her horns, and looked at him. "We look out for each other," she said. "And you've got nobody, Jonny. You're just jealous."

"Trust me," he replied, "I am not jealous of you." He took another sip. "And don't call me Jonny, it makes me sound so unprofessional."

"If you ask me, your moustache is unprofessional."

"So," I interjected, "we'll be in landing range of Malum's surface in just a few minutes. We've got no time to lose finding out where the valicorr went, and what Duhrnan wants here. Better finish that coffee, Jonathan."

He nodded, downed the rest of the mug in one swig, and placed the mug on the counter beside him. Then his body shook a little, and his lips became a frown, his eyes turning to a thousand-yard stare.

My brows snapped down, and I hesitated. "Are you… alright?"

He blinked, smiled, and looked me in the eye. "I'm fine," he said. He stepped away from the counter and brushed his coat down with his gloved hands, then proceeded to adjust his prosthetic eye. "Why do you ask?"

I stared deep into his eyes and felt a chill run down my spine. His organic eye was red and irritated, as if he had been crying. There was something he was holding back, something painful that I sensed he wanted to tell me, but couldn't.

"No- No reason," I said.

"Don't worry about me, Osax," he said, stretching his arms to the ceiling. "We've all got to worry about ourselves… and isn't that enough to do?"

I took a long breath in through my nose, and looked to K, who met my eyes, oblivious.

"We're entering the atmosphere," said Joëlle, her voice coming closer.

She stepped into the room, wearing a long hooded cloak of a grey-blue colour, as she fitted her helmet to her head and it pressurized with a hiss. She was wearing her E-pistol and molecular sword, and the transforming multipurpose rifle she had been using on Voren. She casually tossed something to me and I fumbled to catch it; it was a retracted molecular longsword.

"You ever fight with swords?" She asked, her voice muffled slightly through her helmet.

I nodded. "Actually, I was one of the top duelists back at the Great Temple, back when I was taking lessons from my mother," I said, "I just prefer to keep my distance from my enemies if possible. Well, I prefer to avoid fighting, actually..." I held the handle of the deactivated sword in my right hand, weakly. I was right handed, but until my hand fully healed I'd probably be better off using my left hand. "Skyther swords are somewhat different... they're longer, thinner, curved, and usually-"

"Osax, how many more things can you do?" K said. "You're a biologist, a linguist, a duelist..." She laughed. "You know, if you'd opened with that back when we met on Voren I'd have warmed up to you a lot faster. You must know so much stuff!"

I shrugged. "Well, I've lived around twenty-six times longer than you," I said, lifting my ears.

Joëlle proceeded to toss Jonathan and K each a small black earpiece, which they fitted to their ears. "We can all communicate via holo-gauntlet, but with these earpieces we can keep our hands free, and it'll be a little less conspicuous if we run into trouble and need to make a call." Jonathan and K nodded. I looked at Joëlle and she smiled, revealing another device for me.

I caught it, and glanced at it. It was a headset, fit for a skyther, with a wire that wrapped around the base of the ear, and a silver strip which outlined the left side of my face. I put it on, and a green holographic eyepiece materialized in front of my left eye. I blinked, getting used to the device's HUD, which could recognize and pinpoint my comrades as living beings distinct from the inanimate objects around us, outlining them in green.

Joëlle stepped up to me. "An old friend gave that to me," she said. "He thought I might find a use for it someday, so I've kept it until I might find a skyther who could make good use of it. It's also connected to our communications, like those earpieces, but it's obviously got some special features." She motioned to the E-gun she'd given me earlier. "The targeting system is linked up to that pistol."

I drew the gun and powered it on with a whir, careful to keep it aimed away from Joëlle, Jonathan, and K, the tip glowing a faint green. Immediately I noticed a new detail on my headset. Wherever I aimed the gun, I could see through the holographic display a straight green line like a laser-sight extending out from the tip of the pistol to my target, overlaid on top of my surroundings.

"Keep the sword just in case," she said, "but this should help you keep your distance from things." She smiled through her helmet, and tapped a button on the side of my headset, which deactivated the holographic display.

"Thank you," I said, and bowed. I deactivated and holstered the E-gun.

"Hey, why don't J and I get those sweet targeting headsets?" K said.

"Don't call me J," said Jonathan. "That feels very wrong..." He paused, then waved his hand dismissively. "It- it's not very specific with Joëlle around."

Abruptly my insides lurched to the side as we all stumbled toward the walls of the room, away from the center. The Firebrand shook violently and I slammed my head on the table, barely bracing myself with my injured hand. Jonathan fell to the floor on his hands, and K held on to the edge of the table, crushing it between her gloved fingers. Joëlle leaned her elbow against the wall. An alarm started blaring throughout the ship's speakers, and the lights changed to a red hue.

"What's going on?" cried K.

"We've been shot by something!" Joëlle exclaimed.

I gripped the table and with a concerted effort pushed myself to an upright position against the force which was pulling me to the side. The ship was spinning. I glanced up to Joëlle, who, bracing herself against the wall, was stumbling toward the cockpit. I stood up to follow her, and was thrown against the door frame to the cockpit with another shake of the ship.

Somehow, the valicorr must have discovered us as we entered the atmosphere. I knew coming to Malum would be dangerous, but I hadn't expected for us to be thrust so quickly into a life and death situation. It seemed odd to me that they were able to snipe us out of the sky so quickly and efficiently. Even if they had noticed us as soon as we breached the atmosphere, wouldn't they have needed time to assess their scans of us, to determine if we were a threat or an enemy? Then again, the valicorr may have considered any unidentified vessel an enemy; it would be consistent with their known behaviour. In any case, they were right to shoot us, but I felt like it all happened too fast.

The four of us stumbled into the cockpit. The view was dizzying in the daylight. The sky was a bright greenish colour, and the line where it met the orange rocks of the surface was spinning clockwise at an alarming speed. Joëlle struggled into the pilot's seat, and wrestled control of the ship against inertia, leveling us out. We all stumbled to the side when the ship became balanced at last, our bodies readjusting. But the Firebrand was still descending at a staggering pace.

Joëlle glanced around at the ship's instruments. "The engines were hit directly!" she stated. "I'm not reading any power from them."

I felt my head aching from the stress as I sat down on the seat to her right. The smell of burning rubber assaulted my nostrils. "Where's the attacker?"

I glanced at the scanning console, and through irregular blips I could pinpoint an energy source of some kind above us. I leaned forward and craned my neck to see a black spidery valicorr starfighter soaring smoothly away above us, as if it had lost all interest in us after its initial strike. Why didn't it finish us off? I looked ahead at the ground which was steadily rising to meet us and considered that perhaps it didn't need to.

Jonathan took his usual seat on the far left, and buckled in. Joëlle and I took a hint and did the same.

Joëlle struggled against the controls, and lifted the ship up a little so it was gliding more smoothly through the air, but still dangerously fast.

"We have to take out that fighter!" said K, stumbling into the seat between Joëlle and Jonathan. She looked down at the remaining half of a weapons console in front of her, and muttered, "Oh, right."

My heart was pounding. "Buckle up, K!" I shouted. The sandy orange rocks below us were getting larger and larger until they filled the entire view of the cockpit, and the Firebrand was whirring and humming in a way I had never heard before.

Lungs ready to explode, I screwed my eyes shut, and dug my fingers into the armrests of my chair. The air ahead of us whistled and screeched desperately in the last few seconds it could spare scraping against the windshield before the solid rocks below would take its place.

Thirty

A dull pain pulsed through my whole body. Blinking, with a groan, I pushed my hands against the console in front of me, sitting up as straight as I could with the Firebrand's nose dipped so low. The sound of tiny stones tumbling across the ship's exterior slowly faded. The bottom half of the windshield was completely submerged in orange-brown dirt and rocks, but it remained unbroken. Some wiring must have been damaged because I could smell metallic and rubber fumes from somewhere. The Firebrand was angled down nearly forty degrees; I braced my toes in the corner between the floor and the bottom of the console in front of me so that when I unbuckled my seat belt I didn't tumble forward.

I stood in the off-kilter cockpit and stretched my neck and shoulders. Joëlle and Jonathan seemed to be alright, wincing, but slowly following my lead and unbuckling out of their chairs. K on the other hand never had buckled in, and was sprawled across the half-broken weapons console with her arms out in front of her touching the edge of the window and her right cheek planted on the console. The horn on the right side of her head had speared the remains of the weapons panel, half-buried in metal and plastic. I grabbed hold of the leathery back of the pilot's chair with both hands and climbed up and around it, and slid a few inches down the tilted floor toward K.

I grabbed hold of her arm just as she was beginning to stir. "K, are you hurt?"

She wiggled her arm out of my grip, and tugged her head away from the console once, though it remained stuck. She paused, then pressed both hands on either side of the console and pushed. The metal sheared away with a screech, and she stood upright, taking a moment to stabilize herself on the sloped floor. A chunk of the console was pulled away, touching her face and still speared to her horn. She turned to face me, blood covering her forehead and nose, and lifted both hands to the chunk of debris, tearing it in half like a piece of paper, freeing her horn. She dropped the clanking bits to the floor, and wiped some of the blood from her forehead. Then she smirked, and laughed.

"I'm good, Osax," she said, her orange eyes full of life. "Ready for anything."

◆

I hopped a few feet down from the landing ramp, which due to the angle of the crash was sticking out parallel with the ground, suspended in the air. My feet hit the warm, amber stones. The ground was rough, and rocky. My cloak blew behind me in the wind as I marched forward out from under the Firebrand's shadow and into the light of Malum's trinary star. Sandy dust grazed my cheeks as I squinted my eyes and raised my hand to shield them from the sunlight which came at me directly ahead of the Firebrand's exit ramp, which faced away from the front of the cockpit. We had crashed at the edge of a mesa. Ahead of me was a vast desert speckled with large rock spires, and a pale-green sky. The clouds were wispy and thin, but in the far distance I could see a storm brewing. I took a few more steps away from the Firebrand, waking up my thighs as I bounced up and down the uneven terrain, and spun around, the breeze playing with my cloak. The air smelt fresh, and somehow alive.

Just ahead of the Firebrand's nose, and to the right, a looming cliffside rose up from the mesa. The cliffs continued on to the right for quite a long way. Had the sun been in a different section of the sky, we would easily have been in the mountain's shadow. To the front and left of the Firebrand, there was another cliff, this one inverted, dropping down a long way into a lush jungle. We were well above the treeline on the plateau. Beyond, on all edges of the horizon, distant mountains both barren and lush covered the landscape. There wasn't a hint of civilization in sight.

The wind whistled calmly and echoed across the mesa and against the cliff walls. I gazed up to the sky and activated my holographic eyepiece. Far off in the sky across the desert the valicorr fighter continued, a faint glow behind its shadowy body.

I deactivated the eyepiece and switched on my holo-gauntlet, tuning into the Code-Alpha broadcast. Despite the atmospheric interference which would be distorting certain signals, the timer appeared instantly and unwavering.

06:00:01:38

I took a deep breath and continued to scan the horizon as K, Jonathan, and Joëlle stepped onto the ramp behind me.

I spun around and looked up at them, huddled on the ramp in the shade of the Firebrand's smooth black exterior. "Could you get the food synthesizers working?"

"No," Joëlle shouted at me. "We've got three major system failures. Firstly, food synthesis. We need that to survive. Secondly, the engines. We need that to get off this planet. And thirdly, the weapons system..." She looked to K, then back to me. "Well, we don't necessarily need them, but if we can get the engines back online it would be nice to be able to defend ourselves."

K lowered herself down the ramp with one hand, and touched down onto the rocks. She glanced up to Jonathan and Joëlle before making her way over to me, squinting slightly in the sun. She was dabbing the last of the blood away from her face with a white cloth that she then cast aside, blown away in the wind to litter the ground somewhere. Her skin had already stopped bleeding.

"Any ideas, Osax?" she said.

"Well," I said, activating my holo-gauntlet and raising it up for a general area scan. "No sign of civilization on the surface so far. And no sign of the valicorr other than that fleeing starfighter." I pointed off to the horizon. Then I spun around to face my comrades. "Priority one is ensuring our own survival, which means securing food and water. Everything else comes second. At the very least, we can use the Firebrand for shelter, even if we don't get it moving."

"That's a good short-term goal," said Joëlle, "but in six days Duhrnan will destroy Earth."

"I know," I said. "We have to take things one step at a time."

"Agreed," said Joëlle. She removed her helmet and brushed her purple dreads out of her eyes.

"To maximize our chances of survival, I think we shouldn't leave any solutions unattempted." I said. "We should try to make repairs to the food synthesizers as soon as possible. If we get those finished we can work on repairing other parts of the ship. In the meantime, somebody should go looking for a water source in case we don't fix the synthesizers by tonight." My mouth felt dry. I regretted not drinking more at breakfast. "And one more thing; we should try to get some help from the TAU. They might have some soldiers to spare, or at least a transport with supplies."

"Good thinking," said Joëlle. "Well, Jonathan and I can work on repairing the synthesizers. K, are you any good with fixing-"

"Nuh-uh," said K, raising her hands defensively. "That's a definite no."

Joëlle nodded. "How about you, Osax?"

I gazed out at the vast landscape before us. I wasn't particularly skilled at repairing starships, and I knew next to nothing about food synthesizers, but I did want to help Joëlle. At the same time though, we were standing on Malum. So few people had been here, how could I not want to explore? The thought of stumbling across a loro structure seemed exhilarating. And beyond that, if I somehow ran into Duhrnan...

My blood boiled.

"I think I'll be on the exploration team." I replied.

"Alright," said Joëlle. "You and K can stick together." She hesitated, then said "I'll be right back, I've got something you might be able to use, just need to find it."

She disappeared back into the Firebrand, and I noticed Jonathan who had been standing quietly this whole time gaze at her forlornly. Then he stepped to the edge of the ramp and sat down, dangling his legs over the edge and gazing blankly out into the desert, his gloved hands gripping the edge of his seat. I furrowed my brows and my ears lowered. I turned away and took a few steps from the Firebrand further into the sunlight.

K stepped up beside me, her blue skin shining in the sun. We were several meters from the Firebrand. We gazed out at the alien world together in silence.

"Ah-" she grunted, and shook her head, covering her temple.

"Headache?" I asked.

She nodded, and then shook it off.

"I don't understand," she said.

I tilted my ears at her. "You don't understand what?"

She bent over and picked up a baseball sized stone. Her eyes pierced the clouds. She hurled it off into the distance, impressively far. "Well, a lot of things I guess. But I'm thinking about..." She turned to face me. "Why would Suranos lie to me?"

My heart sank. I lowered my eyes to the ground, and picked up my own stone, unease soaking into my limbs. I spun around and threw the stone as far as I could; barely a tenth as far as K's throw, and the rock was much smaller.

"Maybe she was just trying to be a good host. Sharing interesting stories..."

K exhaled, and her eyes trained the ground. She kicked a few rocks casually. "She didn't seem like she was lying. But... obviously..." She sighed. "Obviously those spheres didn't save Astraloth."

"I always loved the story about Astraloth's ultimate defense," I said. I took a deep breath and gazed up at the sky. Images of my mother filled my mind. "She would tell me not to be afraid of danger, because Astraloth would always be safe. I would ask how, and she would tell me it was a secret. But that the red spheres of the Great Temple weren't just extravagant decorations... they housed a power capable of saving Astraloth from destruction." I felt my fingers clenching into fists. Behind my eyes I could sense tears, and heat flowing to my cheeks. "Deep down I always knew it was just a story she made up, to cheer me up, but..."

"But she told me that story," said K. "I didn't need cheering up..."

I rubbed my eyes.

"You know," I said, "The last thing I said to her was... to leave me alone. I yelled at her. I said she was smothering me... and I *meant* it." I grit my mandibles. "But at the end of the day, I don't know if any of that mattered, even if it was true."

The subtle, persistent wind filled the silence.

"Is it really worth lying to someone just to make them feel better?" said K.

My breath caught in my chest.

She looked at me with utter confusion in her face. "Life is too short for lies. I'd rather have shitty truth than perfect lies." She frowned, and crossed her arms. "I don't know. Why complicate things, right?"

"Right..." I said, my heart pounding. I could feel Jonathan's gaze on the back of my head, as though his thoughts were drilling into me.

"But hey," she said, her lips curving into a smile, "at least, even after all this shit, both our homes destroyed, doomsday knocking on our door... we're stranded together, right?" She grinned and carefully placed a hand on my shoulder. "Never thought I'd have someone watching my back, besides me."

I swallowed hard. "K," I mumbled, "I don't know how to say this, but-"

"You two, come over here!" Joëlle's voice called out to us.

We jogged up to the ramp, and I shoved that thought deep into the back of my mind. Jonathan was still sitting there, and Joëlle tossed us two hard grey backpacks, made of some kind of plastic. The backpacks each had fabric pouches on the back and sides for quick access over top of the hard exterior. K and I slid our arms through the straps, and I helped K get it over her shoulder spikes.

"Those bags are full of empty containers you can fill with water, if you find some."

She then tossed K and I each a small rectangular device as wide as my palm and as long as K's forearm. Equipped with arm straps, we started putting them on.

"Those are wrist cables," she said. "They're quite strong, and should help you if you find yourself in any precarious… vertical situation."

K aimed hers at the bottom of the Firebrand, grinning, and fired. A thin, gold-coloured cable shot out from the wrist-mounted box, whiffling through the air. The tip unfolded into a three-pronged grappling hook, and ricocheted off the bottom of the hull.

"It doesn't work," said K, frowning and retracting the cable into its case.

Jonathan interjected, "It has to have something to hook onto. Shooting it at a ceiling won't do you any good."

"That's not how they work in Defenders of Earth. In that game, you just shoot at whatever, and *fwip!*" She flattened her hand and shot her arm diagonally to the sky. "You just got propelled."

Joëlle smiled and laughed, and I suppressed my own giggle. Jonathan smirked. But it seemed like it was forced.

"Anyway," said Joëlle, "I forgot to mention that each of our earpieces are equipped with a tracking device." Jonathan's gaze snapped to her before she continued, and his smirk faded. "Just in case somebody gets separated, we should be able to track one another's locations."

"Great," I said. I adjusted my black cloak at the neck, then glanced at my holo-gauntlet.

05:23:55:41

My ears lowered. "Alright, let's stop killing time. You ready to head out, K?"

She nodded.

Joëlle said, "I'll contact the TAU, see if I can get anyone to come by and help us."

Jonathan stood up. "Actually, I think I should contact the TAU." He glanced between us, frowning. "You know your food synthesizers better than I do, you can get a head start on the repairs. I'll see if I can call for help."

"Alright," I said, "Well, we're going to check out the jungle down that cliff. For the plant life to grow there, there must be water," I concluded.

Joëlle nodded. "Okay. Stay safe, you two." She bowed farewell to me, and I returned the gesture.

"We're on Malum," I said sarcastically. "We'll be safe."

Thirty-One

Our descent into the jungle was treacherous. Using the wrist cables, we carefully propelled down the side of the cliff ahead of the Firebrand. After securing our hooks to the top of the cliff, we plunged into the shadow of the plateau. The cliff ledge was an overhang, so the first step of our descent had us dangling in open air, meters away from the wall. Our cloaks billowed out from under the sides of our backpacks, and my ears twitched when a bird-like caw broke free from beneath the jungle canopy in the distance, amplified by the resonant cliff. For the most part only our own cables rubbing on the cliff made any sound as we gingerly descended, relying on the strength of our devices, and our arms to hold on. The cliff began sloping back toward us, and at last we touched ground; even at a nearly ninety degree incline, it felt much more stable, and thankfully the rock wall was rough and littered with hand and foot holds.

Stones tumbled under our feet and echoed across the deep green roof of the forest as we found a thin ledge where we could stand for a moment, bodies pressed against the wall, panting. We'd both run out of cable length, so we detached them and found new holds for our hooks at this lower level. Stray purple-tipped brambles latched onto the edge of the steep, rocky cliff, and K and I were extra cautious to avoid being pricked by them in case they were toxic. As we got closer to the shadowed, saturated branches of the forest, the cliff slowly started to level out. Thick purple and green vines snaked up the amber wall. The leaves of the trees were massive, and swayed slowly in the slight breeze. Dust wafted through the open air from the plateau above us, and tiny particles of sand gently grazed the tops of the trees. I looked up at how much lower we already were from the cliff ledge, and began to worry about how we'd manage ascending it on our way back, and with packs full of heavy water, too. *One step at a time,* I thought. Perhaps we'd have to find an easier section of cliff to climb. Duhrnan's timer had spurred us on to take whatever chance we could get coming down.

Slowly climbing down the steep slope, K turned to me. "So, you were going to say something to me earlier?"

I paused to catch my breath, and looked across to her. In that moment I didn't have the time or energy to worry about anything other than getting to the forest floor. "I- Sorry, I don't remember what you're talking about," I panted.

"Fair enough," said K, and we continued down the wall. But as we edged closer to the forest, something nagged at the back of my mind- something I had read about the jungles of Malum.

◆

My nostrils furrowed at the scent of fresh spores, and something I can't describe. Sunlight snaked in through the thick net of leaves above us. Barely illuminated, the forest floor was thick with bushes that brushed our legs, and the noise of creatures moving and chittering underneath. The earth was a grey-brown colour here, and the foliage was a blend of green, purple, red, and blue. There were faint blue glows coming from some low, bioluminescent plant life, giving the place a distinctly alien feeling, completely unlike Earth, and I tried not to let it remind me of the few bioluminescent plants of Astraloth.

Spiny creatures littered the landscape like sea urchins, nestled against the gnarly off-colour roots of thick trees, and resting gently atop buoyant green moss. At a glance they appeared to be part of the plant life, but I noticed one wiggling and moving slowly after staring at it for a few seconds. The trees were tall, but their branches hung low and I had to duck my head to avoid clipping the claustrophobic ceiling of the jungle. Thankfully, there were no large creatures in sight. I kept my eyes peeled for myroks; I had never seen one in person before since I had never been on Malum, but I had seen the few pictures and videos available in the university's computer system. They were nearly as strong as K, and possessed an unusual organ which enabled them to discharge energy blasts from their tail like their were firing a gun. Not only that, but their beaks were shaped like ice picks, and could puncture bones with ease when combined with their immense strength. If we encountered just one, even with our weaponry and armour, we might be outmatched. Of course it would all depend on what stage of metamorphoses we found it in. And luckily for us, I knew they preferred the caves of Malum to the surface, though I couldn't remember why...

K trailed behind, her sleek black pistol active in her gloved hands, red sparks flitting out of the barrel every few seconds. She kept it trained on the ground, flinching every time she heard a new creature beneath the foliage. Her eyes were narrowed.

I withdrew the silver molecular sword and extended its blade. The sheer metal plates rang as they shifted and solidified into place as one solid, ultra-sharp edge. I used the sword like a machete to hack away at vines and brambles which blocked our path. Traveling this way was slow, and took a lot of energy, but the blade made things much faster.

Adrenaline trickled into my bloodstream. Beads of sweat dotted my face, and I could feel myself sweating under my armour. The jungle was like a thick blanket, trapping in the heat of the sun, and my body was trying to cool off. In practice, all I was doing was dehydrating myself even faster.

I stopped. If it was hot enough for me to be sweating this much, K must have been having an even harder time. Skythers have a much higher temperature tolerance.

She had removed her gloves and tucked them into her belt, and was wiping away sweat from her forehead. Her sleeves were rolled up, and her skin was so reflective it looked like she had just dipped her forearms in oil. She was breathing heavily, through her mouth.

That was what had been bothering me on the way down. I recalled hearing about how the trees of Malum acted like a super-effective greenhouse, trapping in all the heat that hit them from the sun, and all the heat expelled from the creatures which crawled about the forest floor. And that's why the myroks preferred the caves; they were more adapted to the cold, not the intense heat of the jungle. Even dead plant and animal matter as it decomposed would emit heat that, given the biology of the forest, would remain trapped inside its tightly-knit leafed shell for an extended amount of time. Even though the plateau the Firebrand had landed on was hot in the sunlight, the breeze and open air made it significantly cooler than the muggy interior of the forest.

K staggered and caught herself on a tree trunk, pausing to catch her breath.

"Ouch!" she exclaimed. She pulled her hand back, shaking it. She had accidentally poked her hand on one of the spiny creatures which had been camouflaged against the tree. She took a step to the side and leaned up against another tree, rubbing her stung hand.

I shouldn't have brought her along, I thought. *I should have known this was dangerous!*

I stepped over to her, deactivating and replacing my sword. My ears lowered as I looked into her face; she was clearly losing focus.

"K?" I said. I placed both hands on her shoulders. "K, are you alright? Talk to me."

She panted. "It's too hot," she managed.

I nodded, sweat trickling down my face. "We have to find you someplace to cool down."

She shook her head. "I don't know if I can make it back up the cliff."

I grit my mandibles, and tightened my grip on her shoulders. "Okay. Then we're not going back. We're going to find some water to get you hydrated, and someplace to cool off."

I left her leaning against the tree and panting for a second, activating my holo-gauntlet and scanning the area. The scans flickered. The atmospheric interference wasn't as bad in the forest, but the physical interference of the trees limited my scanner's range. I was looking for a cave, or clearing in the forest where we might sit in the shade but with open air above us, when I noticed a faint energy signature not far from our location ahead of us, blinking in and out as the scanner struggled to work.

Wiping away some sweat from my head I spun back to K. "There's an energy signature not far from here," I said. "It could be anything… chances are it's dangerous, but, it could be a loro structure."

K blinked blearily. "Okay..."

"I'm going to go scope it out."

"Sure." K slid down the side of the tree into a sitting position.

I tapped her on the shoulder. "You just sit tight. Keep that pistol armed just in case."

She nodded a few times slowly.

I turned away toward the direction of the energy signature and began creeping toward it, trying not to make any sound. Thankfully the forest was loud with the noise of creatures buzzing and rustling around, but the foliage trapped the sound so well that there was hardly any echoing between the trees, which made each sound sharper.

With each second I got further from K, and closer to the energy signature. I weaved between trees and over and under fallen and twisted trunks. I wrapped my bare left hand around the side of a tree for leverage as I pulled myself over massive roots and between two trunks, but my hand got pricked by something.

The side of my hand stung, and I twisted my head to get a look at what I'd accidentally shoved my hand into on the tree. It was one of those spiny, sluggish creatures. It was purple with red splotches, and it was moving slowly around the curve of the smooth, mossy trunk. I rubbed my hand absentmindedly, but the pain wasn't going away.

I tried to shake it off and kept moving to the energy signature.

I was almost upon the energy signature, and it appeared to disperse somewhat, as though the scan was picking up multiple smaller signatures clumped together. I heard movement ahead of me through some thick red vines which wove together. And then the sound of breathing, muffled by the forest. *No,* I thought, *muffled by a helmet.*

I stepped up to the vines and crouched low, cautiously sliding my fingers into them at eye level and gently pulling them apart so I could see through.

Adrenaline jolted me awake. In a clearing only a few meters wide, fully immersed in shade from the tall trees, stood five figures. Each figure stood upright on two legs, and wore a full suit of beige power armour, adorned with small green lights. The helmets they wore had green visor-plates which stretched across their face. They each wore an oxygen tank on their right thighs, with a thick grey tube running from it to the muzzle of the helmet. Their helmets were equipped with lights on either side which shined wide beams of light that illuminated the spores and dust floating around the air in white cones. They each held in their hands a thick, dark E-rifle, equipped with a molecular bayonet protruding from the tip. Their shoulder pads were wide and rounded, and a white skull insignia was emblazoned on the left shoulder of each one.

My eyes darted between them as I struggled to breathe as quietly as possible. Casually, one of the soldiers lifted his gun toward a spiny-creature resting on a stone. For a half second the rifle whined in a rising pitch before it yelped. In a single click of the trigger his gun fired three purple energy bolts, long, thin and parallel with the ground like arrows, vertically aligned and evenly spaced from the tall tip of the gun, detonating like miniature bombs on impact. In a flash the creature was blasted apart. A tangy smell wafted my direction. Smoke rose from the three barrels of his gun, faintly illuminated by the purple energy bubbling in the core of the weapon. The group snickered ominously.

I shut my eyes for a moment, feeling my heartbeat in my throat. These must have been Brotherhood soldiers.

They matched the description Admiral Fiona O'Kane had given me, but why would the Brotherhood have soldiers out here on Malum? Were they also trying to stop Duhrnan? No, that didn't make sense. We were presumably the only people who were able to track Duhrnan's mothership to Malum. Unless they already knew Duhrnan would be here by other means.

That still didn't make sense. It was my understanding that the Brotherhood's main purpose was to dismantle the power-structures of the galaxy, specifically the TAU government. If Duhrnan succeeded at his goal, then the TAU would be destroyed, which would help the Brotherhood. But surely the Brotherhood didn't want to destroy planets, and kill billions of people… unless they were sure it would lead them to their desired world-state.

I stared motionless at the soldiers, my ears peeled back. What if, somehow, they were working with Duhrnan?

"Where the hell is that loro site?" one of them said. "Jackie, check the scanner."

I tensed. If their scanners were tuned to the right frequency, they might be able to pick up on the energy signatures of my devices, and if it was accurate enough they'd be able to discern my shape behind the vines. I tried to remain completely motionless.

Jackie, presumably, took out a hand scanning device and glanced at it. "We should be close by, not more than ten minutes walk from here. The cave entrance is just…"

He paused. "Huh… Sir, I'm picking up something strange." He looked my way, his face completely obscured by the reflective green mask of his helmet.

I moved my hand to my pistol, and drew it slowly. I would have to move quickly to get the drop on them, and any chance of success in a fight.

I was poised to push through the vines and take them out. My holographic eyepiece blinked into view and connected with my pistol, which I activated. The soldiers all began turning toward me.

I ducked my head, ears back, and pushed through the red vines with both hands, my left tightly gripping the E-pistol. My feet dug into the ground, and my legs tensed and pushed against the plant life, before lifting off for the next step. I brushed most of the way through, my arms pushing past the plant-matter when I felt a force pulling them back, and I slowed down.

The soldiers all squatted slightly in a battle pose, guns aimed at me, fifteen barrels of purple energy aimed directly at me with five simultaneous electrical whines. I pulled my arm to aim at one of them, but found it was stuck. The red vines crept around my limbs, lacing inbetween my arms and legs, holding me in place and slowly tightening.

"Wait," said one of them, holding up his hand to signal the others to lower their weapons. He snorted and closed the gap between us nonchalantly, while the other soldiers exchanged glances.

I stared up into his helmet, which he pushed close to my face.

"What are you doing here?!" I spouted.

The soldier paused, holding his face in front of mine for a few moments in silence before speaking. "What's a skiller doing on a planet like Malum? A live skiller, for that matter?"

I grit my mandibles and struggled. "You're part of the Brotherhood, aren't you?"

He chuckled. "Aww, our little skiller knows his symbols!" He tapped the skull on his shoulder. "Good for you, kid."

"I'm twenty-six cycles old," I said.

"That's like fifteen years, right?" he said, incorrectly. He laughed, pulling his face back. "Too bad, that's pretty young to die."

He powered up his rifle and aimed it into my eyes, and the vines continued tightening around me. I turned my head to the side, squinting.

"Wait," I said, "Have you tuned into the Code-Alpha emergency signal? I'm here to stop Duhrnan. I know his mothership is here. You might not like the TAU, but do you really want Earth to be destroyed? Because if not, then we can help each other out. I've got friends with me here; we can all work together."

He lowered his gun, and paused. Panting, I looked to him.

One of the other soldiers said, gruffly, "We're not going to help you, skiller."

"Yeah," said the one next to me, "but we won't kill you either."

"Malum will do a good enough job with that."

I tugged against the restraints.

"See if you can't find one of his friends for us, Jackie."

I gulped. The five soldiers began making their way out of the clearing. Jackie said, "Sir, I'm picking up a faint energy signature not unlike that skyther's over this way. Possibly some kind of energy weapon."

"It's probably one of them. Why don't we go introduce ourselves?"

Sweat dripped down my cheek as I struggled against the red vines in the heat. I just put K in grave danger. The soldiers disappeared from the clearing, heading back the way I had come, and I felt the prick on my left hand sting. I closed my eyes. I had to get free.

Thirty-Two

Out from the canopy two gold objects shot past me, and sliced the vines at their bases. They lost there grip on me and I caught myself with my hands on the cushioned ferns at my feet, panting. My right hand still ached from being crushed on the ship the day before, but by now it was a fainter pain than the stinging from my left hand. My ears hung to the floor, and gently rustled the plants beneath my face. The saturated greens and purples beneath me filled my senses as I caught my breath for a moment in the humid air, wondering what had set me free. Whatever it was, it must have been intentional. The vines were cut in one swift motion, in exactly the correct spot to render their restraint useless.

I raised my eyes up and scanned the forest. Luminescent plants scattered away into the distance, giving the forest a sense of scale with their bluish glow. But I couldn't see anything ahead or behind me, aside from stout, curling trees, and more of those spiny creatures.

I glanced behind me at where the gold objects landed. Sticking out of the ground, half-covered by the grass and low bushes, I saw the two weapons, distinctly star-shaped like an Earth shuriken. Each star's blade-edge was glowing a faint orange. The plasma edges quickly fizzled out into small plumes of smoke.

I looked ahead once more, and gradually got to my feet, sweat still beading all over my skin from the heat. A warrior with that kind of accuracy would easily be able to target my vital organs and kill me.

Despite this, caution got the better of me and I bent over to pick up the E-gun I had dropped. Gun at my hip, I panned across the clearing ahead of me where the ninja stars must have come from. Chirping and skittering filled the silence from nearly everywhere around me.

Not more than a few meters away from me, the creature fell down from somewhere up in the trees, landing gracefully on the grass in a low crouch, releasing a cloud of spores and dust. I leaped back in surprise, raising my weapon instinctively towards the creature.

It was bipedal, humanoid, and with a flat face. Its skin was a pale bluish-green colour, almost iridescent, and it had large, reflective black eyes. Its mouth was almost humanoid, but its edges were angular. With its lips closed, its mouth formed a straight line which dipped down into a 'V' shape on each side. It had no discernible nose; in its place was simply smooth, spotted skin.

The spots accented its forehead and bare-shoulders and the backs of its hands. It had no hair, only a smooth, bald head, with a low ridge which began partway up the forehead and traced a line to the top back of its neck. It balanced on the balls of its feet, which were bare, four-toed, and shaped like paws with angular claws. It almost looked digitigrade, though it was hard to tell at a glance. Its body was very thin, but clearly athletic, built with a smooth, elegant form, and densely woven muscles.

It wore black, skintight clothing on its torso and legs, and silver-gold bracers. Sprouting from the base of its spine was a long, smooth tail which flicked back and forth and looked incredibly flexible. The tail shifted to a red colour as it flared toward a wide tip.

My mandibles dropped in shock and wonder at the creature as I continued to take in its appearance. I had never seen anything like it.

I was beginning to think it must have been a species native to Malum, when I noticed its equipment. It wore multiple belts across each shoulder and its smooth hips. The waist was covered in gold shurikens like the ones it had thrown at me, but lining one of the shoulder belts was a series of powerful grenades, of TAU design. Slung over its back was a TAU grenade launcher, painted black. I could tell its arm bracers also hid some kind of devices; I assumed they were concealed weapons, but I couldn't be sure.

I slowly lowered my pistol to the ground. It locked eyes with me and its lips widened and twisted upwards in what could only be a strange, charming smile. Gracefully, it rose to a standing position, and stood around five and a half feet tall, notably shorter than me. It made no move to draw any of its weapons, and it kept its arms ready at its side.

"Do not be afraid." Its mouth moved revealing a reddish tongue. Its voice was androgynous, somewhat nasally, and almost monotone, but it managed to convey an air of compassion. "You are not my enemy," it said.

I powered down my gun, and wiped away some sweat from my face with the back of my right hand, conscious that the creature seemed not to be perspiring at all in the heat. "You saved me," I panted. "Without your help I'd still be stuck in those vines. Thank you."

It simply nodded. It maintained eye contact, but kept its distance from me.

"What are you?" I asked.

"Now is not the time for questions," it said, activating a tiny hologram from its wrist and glancing at it. It looked like a local-area scanner. "The Brotherhood are almost upon your companion. I must stop them."

Without any more hesitation, it leaned forward into a run and darted past me. I glanced around quickly, before falling into step with it, trying to keep up. "Wait!" I exclaimed. "What's your name?"

Halfway through vaulting over a giant root, it stopped and glanced back at me with its black reflective eyes. Its lips stretched into a smirk.

"Omega," they said. Then they faced forward once again and continued to bound through the trees.

I struggled to keep up, ducking under and jumping over obstacles as I followed close behind them. Omega seemed to sift through the terrain like water through a storm drain. They used all of their limbs to get around, grasping with their hands and clawed feet, and even using their tail to swing and push off the ground. Effortlessly, they managed to avoid getting pricked by any spines, or tripped up by any snags in the terrain. And since they were smaller than me, following them was difficult because I had to make course corrections for myself to avoid accidentally lodging myself somewhere I couldn't fit.

Omega was unlike anything I had ever seen. Where had they come from? I was trying to piece it together as we closed the gap on our enemy, hoping to intercept them before they could ambush K in her defenceless state.

Waves of dizziness crashed into me and I stumbled against a tree, groaning involuntarily. My vision blurred, and I suddenly felt nauseated. Lines of sweat dripped from my face down my mandibles, mixing with some fowl tasting saliva I struggled to keep inside my mouth.

Omega stopped and stared back at me. I looked at my palm; my skin was turning blue where I had been poked. I coughed up some more saliva.

Omega was by my side before I could react. They took my pistol from my hand, powered it off, and latched it back into my holster. I felt their arms wrap around me, and despite their size they swung my weakening body over their shoulders.

My eyes fluttered closed as, disoriented, I sensed my body jostle up and down as they carried me. The sound of the forest seemed to echo further and further away from me. I told myself to stay awake.

◆

I awoke in a cool, azure cave. The sound of running water filled my ears and bounced off the smooth, glistening walls. I breathed slowly, and felt life returning to my muscles.

I sat up. K was lying next to me, motionless. Our cloaks, backpacks, and outer-gear were all set aside and folded neatly. Our weapons were arranged next to them. My fingers pressed into the cool ground beside me. The cave was made up of a smoky-blue crystal. On the other side of the cavern, the ground dipped into flowing water. It was an underground stream which intercepted the cave. Blue light dimly glowed from the walls and ceiling behind the crystal.

I bent over to K and gave her a gentle prod. She didn't react, but she was breathing calmly with her eyes closed. I sat up straighter.

My left hand was no longer hurting, and had returned to its normal colour.

Something swung down from the ceiling in front of me, and I nearly fell onto my back. It was Omega, hanging upside down. I looked up at the ceiling; their tail was adhering to it somehow. I looked back at their face. Their lips were curved in a smile.

"You saved us," I said.

Omega nodded. Then they reached their arms to the floor and twirled around as their tail let go of the ceiling. They halted, sitting cross-legged in front of me.

"How?" I asked. "I must have been poisoned by that spiny creature-how did you stop it?"

"I rubbed the antidote on your wound. Your body accepted it and fought off the poison," they said.

Was it luck that they had the antidote? Or something else?

"You are not part of the Brotherhood," they said. Their round eyes blinked and they tilted their head to the side.

"No. We don't like the Brotherhood," I said. I sat forward. I knew now that I could trust Omega, but I didn't yet know why. "You don't like the Brotherhood either?" I questioned.

Omega shook their head. "They are the enemy."

I glanced to K, then back to Omega. "You could have left us alone.

Why didn't you?"

"Why would I?" said Omega.

"Well..."

"Would you have?" they asked.

My eyes trained the reflective floor between us. "No. I would have tried to help too. I'm just trying to understand you."

"Why?" they asked.

"I- I suppose I'm curious. It's in my nature. Wouldn't you be curious about your saviour, if you had one?"

Omega looked up at the ceiling for a few seconds, before looking back at me.

"I do not know," they said. "I have never been saved. I do not know if it is in my... nature... to be curious."

Our eyes met and we sat in the meditative quiet of the cavern.

"What happened to the Brotherhood soldiers?" I asked.

"I eliminated them."

There was a pause.

"I noticed you carrying TAU gear... They must have sent you to Malum. What's your mission here?" I asked.

"Peacekeeping," they said.

"Peacekeeping?" I said. "But, there are no settlements on Malum. None that I'm aware of."

"There are no settlements here. None except for Brotherhood outposts. I am here to eliminate the Brotherhood. If any member of the Brotherhood remains, the chance for peace in the galaxy is zero percent. I must keep the peace."

Their voice was almost monotone and their smile disappeared. I felt a chill run down my spine. They were talking about killing like it was nothing. I simply nodded. I was glad they were on my side.

"I also noticed you carrying TAU gear," they said to me. "They must have also sent you to Malum."

"Well, not exactly," I said. "We're working with members of the TAU, but we weren't sent by them."

"What is *your* mission?" they asked, and tilted their head to the side.

"Our mission? We're here because-"

My heart skipped a beat. How long had I been unconscious? I flicked my holo-gauntlet on and tuned into the Code-Alpha signal.

05:07:10:26

"Shit!" I exclaimed. *Over fifteen hours!* The heat, dehydration and poison had gotten to us.

I started back by the sudden movement as K lurched from her rest, and glanced around. Her eyes were bloodshot, full of fire, and locked onto Omega.

"Get away from Osax!" she cried, and lunged toward them with both arms forward. I fell back onto my hands, holo-gauntlet deactivating. K's hands grasped thin air, but Omega sprung into a backwards cartwheel and landed on their feet. K growled.

I stood up and jumped between them. "K, it's alright! They're with us!"

K panted, and slowly eased up. "What happened?" she asked.

"Omega saved us," I said.

"Omega?" said K. Her brows were twisted with concern. "You mean that... thing?"

Omega nodded, seemingly unaware of K's judgment. "I am Omega," they said.

K began pacing back and forth. "You saved us, huh? What even are you?"

"I am a bioweapon created by the TAU to destroy the Brotherhood," they said.

"Bioweapon?" said K, raising an eyebrow.

I took a step back, and Omega approached K. K stood above them, bulky and awkward by comparison. I couldn't help but notice the stark contrast between the two; K's bony ridges and horns made her appear so much more imbalanced than Omega, who looked like they were printed by a finely tuned machine.

"What are you?" said Omega.

K clenched her fists. "A bioweapon."

"Created by the TAU also?"

"No. I dunno. Probably not." she said, before taking a few steps away.

"What were you created for?" said Omega.

K looked back over her shoulder, cracking her knuckles. "I- Why do you care?"

I stepped up to K, and gently placed a hand on her back. "K, it's fine. We can trust Omega. They're with the TAU."

She sighed. "If you say so," she said, and turned around. "I'm glad you're safe."

"You too," I said, my ears lifting.

Omega stepped up next to us and we both turned and looked down at them. Their black eyes sparkled in the light of the luminous crystals. "What is your mission here... Osax, and... K? Perhaps we can help each other."

We sat in the cave for a while as I explained to Omega what had happened since I arrived on Voren. K tried to call Jonathan and Joëlle, but the signal couldn't reach them through the cave walls and the atmospheric distortion. Instead she filled our packs with water from the stream, mostly ignoring our conversation. I told Omega about the attack on Voren, about Duhrnan, and about Joëlle and Jonathan and how the Firebrand had crashed. They seemed interested at every part of the story, but not excited one way or another. I told them about Astraloth… and the Shade Beam, and Duhrnan's threat to Earth.

"Duhrnan must be stopped," they said, after a moment of silence. "If Duhrnan remains, the chance for peace in the galaxy is zero percent. I must keep the peace."

K rolled her eyes. "How dramatic."

"But probably true," I said. "We know that Duhrnan's mothership is somewhere on Malum, and we know that he's probably aboard it. The trouble is we don't know where, or how to destroy it." I fixed my eyes on Omega. "You weren't sweating in the heat of the jungle."

K scoffed and leaned forward. "So what?" she said.

"You were made specifically to survive on Malum, weren't you?" I asked.

Omega nodded. "Yes. The TAU discovered Brotherhood presence on the planet, and created me to be an undetectable agent who could sabotage their plans and remove them from the planet."

"That's how you had the antidote too… The TAU put their best into designing the perfect agent with all the knowledge, skills, and physical prowess and coordination needed to not only survive alone out here, but to take out the most deadly of the Brotherhood soldiers."

Omega nodded.

K raised her hands in defense. "That's so cool," she said, sarcasm dripping from her lips. "We should all admire the fancy bioweapon."

"There is no need," said Omega. "I was not created to be admired."

"Ha! Yeah, me neither," said K, rolling her eyes.

"Omega," I said, "Can you help us get back to our ship? It's up a cliff a ways off-"

"I know where it is," they said. "I saw it crash. I assumed everyone aboard to be dead, so I did not initially investigate. But I know how we could get up the cliff."

"Well, great!" I said, hoisting my backpack onto my shoulder. "We shouldn't waste any more time- I don't want to leave Jonathan and Joëlle to themselves any longer."

K stood up, ready to go. "Yeah. Osax, we gotta get back to them. They might be in more trouble than-"

K winced and clutched her head. Omega stepped forward.

"What is wrong?" they asked.

"Nothing!" said K, clearly louder than she intended. "Just a headache." She rubbed her forehead.

"Head… ache?" said Omega.

"Oh, of *course* you don't get headaches," K spat.

"I was... not created to get head aches," Omega said.

K's jaw tightened and her brows lowered.

"K," I said, my ears drooping, "let's just get going."

"Yeah, yeah," she sighed.

We all moved to exit the cave, and I winced as I gripped my shoulder strap with my crushed, bandaged hand. K looked at me remorsefully.

Omega stepped up to me, hands outstretched. "I can carry the pack while your hand recovers."

"Actually, it would be nice to rest my shoulders. Thanks," I said, and gave them the backpack.

K stood there staring at us, unimpressed. "Hey, Omega, would you mind please carrying my pistol for me too? I'd really, really appreciate it," she said in a sarcastically high voice.

I was about to say something, but Omega stepped up to her and simply said "I would not mind."

K handed them the gun. "Oh, thank you. How kind, and sweet of you. Isn't Omega just the best?" She looked at me with a fake smile.

"K," I said.

"Come on, Osax-" K began.

We both stopped and stared as Omega turned away from us, and without hesitation spun K's pistol twice on their finger, before flinging it up into the air. The pistol almost hovered for a second as Omega took a step, and it began to fall. Another step forward, and the pistol slid perfectly into the pouch of the backpack Omega was wearing on their back with a satisfying *fwump*. Omega continued walking away from us, oblivious to our gaping mouths and wide-eyes.

Thirty-Three

"Oh no," I exclaimed, looking at the time on my holo-gauntlet.

"What is it?" asked the investigator after a brief pause.

I stood up and glanced outside. The sun was sinking below the horizon and the sky dimmed. "I just remembered I have some errands I needed to do before sundown," I said. I looked to her face. I was trying to figure her out, and she looked like she was doing the same with me. "I'm sorry to cut this short, but I really must be going."

She hesitated, and slowly stood, stopping the recording. "It's nothing to be concerned about, Talcorosax. You've been very cooperative."

I raised an ear. "Have I? I thought you wanted me to cut to the chase about K and the Brotherhood. But I've refused to do so."

"I-" She chuckled, and looked up at me with a strange smile. "I suppose… I've become somewhat invested in the story." She crossed her arms. "I hope we'll get to continue the story tomorrow morning?"

"I don't know," I said, checking my holo-gauntlet absentmindedly.

"I see. Where are you off to now?"

"I need to stop by the market… I'm picking up some groceries."

She snorted. "Being the King, I assumed your errands would be more urgent."

I was rushing out the door, when I said to her "Everyone needs to eat. Goodnight investigator!"

The door hissed closed behind me, and she called out "See you soon!"

I made my way through the hallways and with each passing step my shoulders began to sag further toward the ground. My ears went limp. My fingers had no tension. My eyes trained the floor. My pace slowed.

I stopped by my room, and lifted my arm up with the minimum effort required to the clothes hooks which lined the wall of the door, and paused. I was reaching for a long red coat, but on the hanger next to it was a black hooded cloak. The sight of it made me tense. I retrieved the coat. I put it on and glanced at the tall mirror against the wall.

I was startled. Someone was standing in the room. Their eyes were swollen, and their face looked wrinkled with exhaustion. Their mandibles hung slightly, and they slouched forward almost like a zombie. There was no life in them, yet there they stood.

I took a step forward and reached out toward them. My fingers met theirs as they touched the glass of the mirror. I pushed my face close to the mirror and looked deep into their orange eyes, damp and reflective in the dim light of the room.

"Who are you?" I muttered.

◆

The night air was crisp and almost freezing. I wrapped my jacket around my body to keep warm, and anxiously checked the time on my holo-gauntlet. My bare foot sunk into a puddle on the paved road. Rain poured down on the street and the buildings and stalls of the market. It was mostly skythers, but some humans too were walking around the market with umbrellas or hoods worn tightly over their heads. My jacket didn't have a hood, so water streamed down the skin of my face and dripped off my mandibles and my soaking wet ears. It was difficult to hear through the rain, but I listened for the sound of sizzling food and watched the chefs working their magic from behind counters and windows on either side of the market. It was almost like a neon canyon, with massive buildings on either side covered in advertisements and glowing signs, and the evening market crowd bustling around at the base of them. It should have been a center for community, but the people were almost drowned out by the corporate advertisements which blared from the skyscrapers above.

I heard my own voice reverberating off the buildings through the rain from some hidden speakers, and I looked up. On a massive screen I could see myself sipping from a can of root beer. I was decked out in combat gear. The can was labelled in bold English print, *Galaxy Root Beer.*

"Nothing beats a can of Galaxy Root Beer! Galaxy Root Beer, you're a life saver." I exclaimed, before holding up the can to the camera.

Rain pelted my face as I strained my eyes to watch the ad. I remembered filming in an empty room, but they had digitally created a set. I was drinking root beer in the middle of a scorched and smoking battlefield.

The shot cut to me lifting an unreasonably sized piece of rubble as humans and skythers of different shapes, sizes, and colours climbed out from underneath. Then I was handing out the drink to them one at a time as a masculine human voice came over the speakers. *"Galaxy Root Beer: It's a real hero, for a real hero."* The final shot was an image of me winking to the camera, with the Galaxy logo next to my head.

Just as quickly as it had started, the image changed to another ad. Inspirational music played from the speakers as it showed humans in all sorts of exhilarating environments and activities, before jump-cutting to a shot of a sleek hover-car.

I rubbed some of the rain from my face with the back of my drenched sleeve, to no avail, as the sounds of commercials fought to steal my attention. There were so many lights and sounds here that the city felt so alive. But, muffled by the rain, I felt detached. I barely noticed what was going on around me, trying to keep my eyes forward to my destination. My eyes caught a skyther, huddled in the corner of a building, wrapped up in a blanket, shivering. In front of them they had a bucket, and a sign written in Skorali asking for charity. And below the skyther text was the same thing written in horribly broken English.

I narrowed my vision, away from the struggling soul.

I stepped up into the warm light of the vendor's stand, glancing at the time on my holo-gauntlet once more.

An old skyther with grey skin and fur and a stained apron leaned over the counter and peered at me. She was sheltered from the rain under the canopy of her establishment. She spoke in Skorali. "We just closed. Come back tomorrow."

"Please," I said, stepping forward. "I was caught up all day, or I would have come sooner-"

"You must know how it is," she said. "If I spend a second more with the store open tonight I might not have time to prep and rest for tomorrow. Can't make exceptions for anyone these days. If you don't run an airtight show then the big corporations are gonna stamp you out like an insect."

She turned away, but I persisted. "I need to buy two weeks worth of rations. I can ensure it's worth your while." I lifted my holo-gauntlet up to her, and showed a large sum of credits. "I can send this right away."

She eyed me suspiciously. "You sure about this?"

"Yes," I said.

She stepped up to me and handed me a device. "Just tap here."

I touched my gauntlet to the device and heard a sound confirming the transaction had gone through.

"Alright," she said, staring at me in mild disbelief. "I'll grab a crate of rations for you."

I hesitated. "Actually, can you put it into two containers?" I asked.

I shuffled my feet as she went inside her store room to grab the preserved food. My eyes scanned the streets. The sun was beneath the horizon now, and people were mostly vanishing from the market. Already it was much less busy, but the ads continued to play above and around me. The lights of the stores were shutting off one by one.

I grabbed each metal box of rations by the handle and thanked the vendor, retracing my steps down the street.

The skyther was alone, still huddled against the wall of the building, with their eyes half open, still shivering. I slowed down, and walked up to them cautiously.

I knelt down and placed one of the boxes of rations next to them. They opened their eyes and glanced between me and the box.

"I brought some food," I said in Skorali. "It's made to last, so it shouldn't go bad. You can eat it whenever you need to."

They sat up, still quivering. "Th- Thank you," they replied.

"It's not much," I said, as they removed the lid and grabbed some dried fruit and vegetables and nuts. "Oh, make sure to keep it dry," I said.

They slid it under the small overhang of the building to shelter it from the rain. "Thank you so much!" Their voice was shaky.

I shimmied out of my coat and wrapped it around them. "This might help keep you warm. It's pretty cold out tonight." I paused. "I didn't bring water but… you know you can use the fountain at Tolo Square, just down the street, if you get thirsty. It's free for public use, all day and night. It's not sugar water, but…"

They nodded, their mandibles hanging open in surprise. I turned to leave, but I felt them feebly grab my hand. "Please, it would be nice to have some company," they said.

My heart sank. "I'm sorry," I said. "I have to go."

Their ears lowered. I stood up and started walking away. I looked back at them, wrapped in their blanket and my coat, some food in their hand. But they looked so tired. "Thank you," they said once more.

"Take care of yourself," I said.

"Wait!"

I glanced over my shoulder back at them. The skyther scanned my face.

"You're the one from the commercial," they said, in a disbelieving voice.

I struggled against a sudden, powerful desire to hide my face. I nodded, unsure of what to say.

The skyther's face contorted into one of confusion as they continued to drill me with their sullen gaze. "You're the real Osax? The King?"

I shut my eyes and spoke. "Talcorosax. Yes, I am. I must be going."

"Have you retired or something?"

My eyes fell to the rippling water beneath me. "No."

"But where have you been?" they asked. "You said that after the fight was done you'd honour your mother's position, and work on helping the people. But nothing has changed. What have you been doing all this time?"

"Surviving," I muttered.

I looked at the ragged, starving skyther, and guilt pierced me like a knife. I wondered who I was, to say such a thing in my position. Without another word, I turned away, unable to look at the skyther again. Unable to apologize, for I thought I deserved no forgiveness. I bowed my head, clutching the remaining box of rations to my chest. I choked back a sob. He could recognize the face of Osax through the rain and darkness of the night. But the face he saw was like a lifeless mask: a snakeskin I had outgrown, but was unable to shed. I was merely a ghost; I wouldn't let myself be anything more.

I tightened my jaw, squinted through wet eyes, and marched away through the streets. Despite my efforts to block them, emotions of regret and longing churned in my gut and turned to thoughts. An invisible weight pushed down on my heart, heavier than the world, squishing the voices in my head together into an indecipherable chorus. The more I thought about this weight, the more I felt responsible for it all. I thought no reason could be good enough for me to feel so anguished. Nothing had happened. Everything was supposed to be fine now.

I gasped for air, and my eyes darted around the streets, crying silently for someone to see my pain, to reach out and tell me nothing was wrong. To tell me I was enough, because maybe if I heard someone say it I would believe them. To tell me it was all going to be okay.

But no one was there, and a single unfocused thought broke through the weight on my chest. Words which rested precariously above the discordant bed of emotions in my heart. Words which repeated deafeningly in my thoughts, over and over as I walked.

I miss you.

In the shadow of an alley, covered by the sound of rain, they ambushed me.

I dropped the rations to the floor and flung my arms to my neck. My hands grasped at the arm grappling me from behind. The skyther was strong. Two more skythers came into view in front of me, approaching slowly as I flailed, gasping. They wore dark clothing, and cloth obscuring their faces.

I gagged. Adrenaline fuelled my muscles as they expanded, and I punched at my captor. It was futile. He wrenched my arms together and pressed them up against my chest, holding me in place with both of his arms wrapped around my arms and torso.

I clenched my fists. One of the skythers in front of me raised their hand. They were holding some kind of syringe, with a long reflective needle, aimed at my throat.

I shut my eyes, and jumped up. I leaned back on the one who had grappled me with my legs tucked in. Then as I began to fall I kicked my legs forward and pulled him to the ground.

I ducked as I hit the wet pavement, and water splashed around us as I flung him over top of my body and onto his back. The two other skythers recoiled in surprise, but only for a second as I began to stand. I grabbed onto the handle of the steel rations case with my right hand.

The syringe-wielding attacker lunged at me. The needle was held tightly in his right fist, and it was headed straight for the side of my neck.

I inhaled sharply, and took a step toward him, slamming the inside of his wrist with my left arm. I grabbed his wrist and twisted. The side of the needle caught on my arm as I rotated his hand and his body contorted, and he dropped it. The syringe clattered on the ground.

Heart pounding, I turned to my right as the other skyther came at me with a raised fist. Without thinking, I hefted my right hand toward his face and with a thud the metal case connected with his mandibles. He stumbled back and exclaimed, clutching his bleeding jaw.

I was still holding onto his arm when the skyther who had tried to stab me tried to pry my hand off with his free hand.

I grimaced, and yanked him down toward my knee as I shot it up towards his chest. We both shook from the impact, and he let go. I let him fall to the floor with a splash.

I took a few steps back, keeping my eyes trained on the three of them.

Two were out of commission for the moment, but the third one had finally risen, and I heard the unmistakable rising pitch of an E-gun activating. A faint red glow appeared in his hand against the shadow of his body.

I ducked my head and held the rations case with both hands in front of me as a shield. My eyes shut and I braced myself for pain as I stumbled backwards toward the end of the alley, lacking any grace.

Red light flashed as the energy blast sped toward me, then a sound cracked, and my arms shook. Metal sheered and dried food spilled out onto the slick cement beneath my feet. My hands, each still gripping a side of the now smouldering case, fell away from each other as it completely collapsed from the explosion of the energy blast.

I dropped the warped metal remains, and bolted.

Thirty-Four

Shivering a little, I took the last few steps to summit a small mountain overlooking the city. The adrenaline from the encounter with the skythers had shocked me out of my depressive thoughts. I was fairly certain I had lost my attackers as I fled the streets, and there were no public paths that led up the mountain; I had discovered my own way long ago. The rain clouds lingered over the city ahead of me but above me the sky was clear. The skyscape was full of an unfathomable number of stars. The moons hung in the sky, the Toru nebula sticking out like a great swathe of purple paint on a black canvas. I could see my breath in the moonlight. TAU ships dotted the sky above the orange glow of the city, where I gazed. I sat down on a large rock, legs aching from my impromptu run. Behind me forested wilderness stretched on for miles, and a breeze blew past me like the breath of a massive creature hiding in the dark, beckoning me to run away with it, away from the light and into the vast, welcoming shadow. But I knew I was alone.

I clenched my fingers together as my hands rested beside me on the rough stone of the summit. I had spent the past two days living in the past, but getting ambushed in the alley was a good wake up call.

I rubbed my hands together. Why did they attack me? I had nothing of great value on my possession; even the rations case I carried was not expensive under normal circumstances. I figured they weren't after money, unless they recognized me and hoped to ransom me.

Then there was the matter of the needle. They must have hoped to drug me, probably to knock me out for a good long while so they could capture me. That would make sense if they wanted to hold me for ransom. But if so, why did the skyther shoot at me with an E-gun? Perhaps he was trying to cripple me so I couldn't escape, but the blast completely destroyed the rations case, and I was covering my chest with it. If I hadn't done so, he would have shot me right in the heart and judging from the power of the weapon I would have died.

I furrowed my brows. It was likely that he meant to cripple me, and just had poor aim. It's a good thing I had that case to protect me. But I wished he hadn't destroyed it.

I stood up, and retrieved a pen and paper from my pocket. I turned around and leaned over the rock I had been sitting on and began writing.

"Due to complications, I regret that I couldn't bring any supplies tonight. But come back tomorrow night. I'll have some rations for you then."

I took a few steps toward the forest. I approached the usual tree, and slid the paper snugly into the crevice of a branch, making sure it wouldn't blow away in the wind. My eyes caught movement in the darkness of the woods, and my ears lifted.

A small creature scampered up a tree, and then there was nothing.

I sighed, and began my journey back to the city.

◆

"So glad you decided to continue the story," said the investigator.

I nodded, and lifted my ears slightly. Even after a night's rest, my legs still ached from running the night before. I hadn't been very active in recent days. We were back in our usual room with light cascading in from the large window to my right, and the whole routine of the thing was starting to feel strangely normal. A skyther came in with our drinks and some breakfast, placing them gently on the table before leaving through the door at my back. I sat in the same seat with the investigator wearing the exact same black and blue suit, sitting across from me with her computer ready to record and her hands ready to type. Her smile seemed as fake as ever, and I couldn't help but wonder how I had gotten into this situation.

"Well, I wouldn't want to take up two days of your time and then abandon you before the conclusion." I leaned forward slightly, gazing at her face. "Especially since you said you've become invested in the story."

She laughed strangely. "Well, I hope you had a good time at the market last night," she said. "Did you get what you wanted?"

I nodded slowly. "Yes, I did." She was staring at me intently.

"I'll admit I was surprised that you bothered to buy groceries at all when I remembered that the temple is outfitted with food synthesizers.

You must have wanted something special that the synthesizers can't create, right?"

Her gaze was intimidating, and I cleared my throat. My hands absentmindedly flexed. "I did. I had been… thinking about getting some artisanal dishes. I've been growing a little tired of eating synthesized food every day."

She pointed to my plate of chicken and rice. "That looks just like what you had for lunch yesterday; wasn't that synthesized?"

"It is- I'm saving the good stuff for later."

"Lunch?"

"To be honest, I haven't decided yet," I said. I scratched my forehead, and felt a bead of sweat. She was pressing me too hard, and I had to turn the tables. "So before we dive into the next part of the story, I had something I wanted to talk about."

"Oh?" she said. Her eyes narrowed ever so slightly.

I took a sip of my drink. "To be honest, I don't fully understand why you're here conducting this investigation."

"Like I said yesterday, I've been sent here because the TAU suspect you of working with the Brotherhood. They want to know about your involvement with them…"

"Okay. But you've been giving me mixed signals. It seems like you want to hear the story in full, otherwise why would you be going along with it? But you've repeatedly asked me to cut ahead and complained about me taking my time. Which one is it? Do you really want me to just talk about K? Or do you want me to give the complete story? I would imagine that for an investigation such as this, one in which the goal is to determine a powerful authority figure's allegiance, that more detail would always be better. Yet on the first day in particular, and before admitting to your true mission yesterday, you continually implied you wanted me to skip ahead. Yet clearly, that isn't true. Can you see the contradiction?"

Silence hung in the air. I breathed calmly. Her eyes fell away from mine as she considered how to respond. I knew something was up with her.

At last she looked up at me. "I wanted to see how you would react," she said, confidently. "It's… a fairly standard procedure."

I folded my arms. "So, this whole time you've actually wanted to hear the full story?"

"Yes," she said, and smirked.

I believed her; it only made sense that all along she had wanted to hear all the details of the story, employing reverse psychology initially and feigning disinterest. But it still didn't fully make sense. Her methodology seemed a little too erratic, and a little too malleable. Over the past few days she had acted in strange ways. The only consistent behaviour that I could see was that everything she said, and every action she took, she was always trying to look inconspicuous. Even in this moment. And once I realized that, I knew that either her intentions were sinister, or she didn't really trust me at all.

My ears lowered as I stared at her. None of this made any sense. She adjusted her hat, emblazoned with the TAU symbol of Earth. Had they really sent her to test if I was affiliated with the Brotherhood?

"Well, that clears some things up," I said, lifting my ears and trying to look relaxed. "You know, we might have gotten along better if you had just been upfront about it from the beginning."

She leaned back. "Yes, I know… but I was sent here to test you. Part of that means… withholding some information. But for what it's worth, I trust you."

Her smile was so close to genuine this time, but not quite. *She's offering me trust so that I will do the same.* I didn't know what her intentions were. But I knew that I had to keep playing along if I was going to find out. And I was determined to find out.

"Thank you," I said. "Are you ready for the next part of the story?"

She clicked a button on her computer, and looked up at me with a wicked smile. "Of course."

I narrowed my eyes and leaned forward, grabbing my drink. "Well get ready- this is where the story gets interesting."

Thirty-Five

"Hey Omega, can I have my gun back?" asked K.

Omega had led us, carefully but quickly, through the steamy jungle and halfway up to the plateau along a natural sloped path which outlined the cliff. The lithe bioweapon turned back to us, unfazed by the exertion as K and I panted from the climb. Their hairless, freckled face smirked awkwardly in contrast to their apparent grace. The three suns of Malum had set and risen since K and I left the Firebrand, and they were low in the sky, lighting up our odd trio and our path up the cliff.

Omega retrieved K's pistol from my pack with their dexterous green hand, and gave it to her. "Your gun," they said. K took it and holstered it.

The three of us had remained mostly quiet as we journeyed to the Firebrand. I wondered what had happened to Jonathan and Joëlle, hoping they were safe and that they had managed to call for help from the TAU and repair the food synthesizers, at least. But if not, I was glad we had enough water to last a few days, and we'd made a new friend, or at least an ally against our enemies. But as we walked I kept looking at the time on the Code-Alpha channel.

05:06:06:56.

Time was ticking away, and we still hadn't even located Duhrnan, let alone determined how we would stop his mothership. The Shade Beam would of course be the final challenge, but once we regrouped with Jonathan and Joëlle we would need to spring into action against Duhrnan and the ship which stole the Shade Beam in the first place.

At last we crested the edge of the plateau, and in the distance ahead of us was the unmistakable black and red starship I'd come to think of as a second home. And with Astraloth gone, I thought it might as well be my only home.

At the sight of the ship, K and I both exclaimed in relief. It was no longer nestled into a bed of rocks from the crash, and its landing gear was firmly planted on the rocks, meters away from the crash site. It was parked deliberately, level with the ground, and that meant that they must have gotten the engines working since we'd left.

K started jogging through the dusty plain toward the ship, and I followed behind, my heart racing. Omega kept up, but stayed behind us.

The sun glinted off the black windshield of the Firebrand. Below the windshield someone was standing, wearing a welder's mask and ducking around, working on the four cannons on the underside of the ship. It was Jonathan, and it was strange to see him without his white and black long coat. Instead he was wearing a dirty white jumpsuit, with leathery pads on his knees, shoulders, and elbows. He wore thick black gloves and boots, and his sleek black pistol was holstered on his hip. He stood up and turned to us, lifting the mask from his head, and his robotic aperture twisted as his eye fixed on us. He looked shocked to see us.

"You're alive!" he called out, genuine relief in his voice.

We closed the gap, and stood under the shadow of the Firebrand. Jonathan looked exhausted, with a noticeable bag under his left eye, as though he had barely slept. Omega and Jonathan locked eyes, and his mouth hung open.

"And I see you've... made a friend?" he asked, staring straight past K at Omega.

"Good to see you too," scoffed K.

Omega took a single step toward Jonathan. "You must be Jonathan Wellsworth, head of biology. Ex TAU special forces."

Jonathan gave me a confused look. "Yes… they told you about me?"

"Yes we did," I said. "Their name is Omega. They're a bioweapon created by the TAU. They saved our lives."

Jonathan nodded slowly. "Oh… kay…" He lifted a hand up to his ear and pressed a button. "Joëlle," he said, "Osax and K are alive, they just made it back."

K smiled, and I lifted my ears. Jonathan winced as Joëlle's voice screeched through his earpiece, loud enough for us to hear. *"Oh my god! Bring them inside! Ah ha ha!"* I could hear the smile in her voice.

Jonathan removed the earpiece and held it an inch away from his ear. "We'll be inside in a moment. And, we have a guest."

◆

With the five chairs of the cockpit finally filled, I couldn't help but feel as though we were meant to encounter Omega here. The smell of coffee filled the room, as the ship hummed. From left to right, if you were to look at the cockpit from the entrance door and out towards the window, sat K, then Jonathan next to the still broken weapons console, Joëlle in the pilot's seat in the center, Omega at her side next to the communications panel, and I on the outer right seat. Our seats were all angled toward the center of the semicircle. K was shovelling a freshly synthesized burger behind her tusks, half ignoring the conversation, while Joëlle, wearing a dusty blue jumpsuit, slowly picked away at a bowl of rice with a pair of silver chopsticks. Omega was fidgeting with the earpiece Joëlle had just given them, which was connected to our communications channel. After a moment, they fitted it to their ear. They sat with their legs crossed on their seat, hands resting on each bare paw-like foot, and their tail coiled around their legs. Jonathan sipped coffee greedily, and looked worse than I'd ever seen him before. I would believe it if the coffee was the only thing keeping him awake. I flexed my right hand, and felt the strength returning since K had crushed it. I gripped a glass of root beer, and exhaled deeply, relaxing into my seat. The sound of slurping filled my ears, and for a wonderful moment, I let myself be at peace, and feel the full relief of finding myself back in the comfort of the Firebrand, with my friends.

Joëlle's brown eyes locked with mine. "...So while you were unconscious and Omega was taking care of you, Jonathan and I were working on the repairs."

"You didn't get much sleep, did you?" I asked, my eyes turning to Jonathan.

He shuffled in his seat. "Well, I tried to. Couldn't really though." He sounded almost frail. "Just a lot on my mind."

Joëlle glanced into his eyes, and gently placed her hand on his knee. His hand fell on top of hers, though he didn't look relieved. In fact, he appeared more sad at the gesture, lowering his head slightly. But he forced a smile.

"A- Anyway, Joëlle, you were explaining..." Jonathan said, moving to hold his cup with both hands. K munched loudly, and Joëlle pulled her hand back.

"Right," she said, scanning the room. "Well, when you left, Jonathan called the TAU for reinforcements."

He nodded, eyes down.

"Meanwhile I began work on the food synthesizers. He came in and told me he contacted an old group of special forces units he used to work with, and that they were on their way to help as soon as they could. They would contact us as soon as they arrived at Malum."

"Great!" I said. "So, we've got Omega to help us, and now we have TAU soldiers on the way. That will be incredibly helpful once we find Duhrnan. Who knows what kind of forces we will need to stop him."

"Awesome," said K. "Hey, do you think the TAU guys are gonna be bringing any awesome weapons? Ooh, how many are coming, anyway?"

Jonathan cleared his throat. "I could have tried to arrange a large force, but there were two reasons I thought it wouldn't work. One, a fleet of ships would alert Duhrnan to our presence, and we would lose any chance at surprise we had. And two, the TAU are already mustering their fleets to defend Earth when the Shade Beam arrives in five days, so they don't have many ships to spare."

"Well, wouldn't Duhrnan already know that we're here?" I said. "The valicorr ship that shot us down..."

"Shot us down," said Joëlle. "In all likelihood, they think we're dead. At the very least, we aren't considered a threat as the small strike force we are, or they would have come back to make sure we were extinct by now, right? Duhrnan probably knows we arrived on Malum, but I'll bet he thinks we were destroyed too."

"Right," said K. "So anyway, how many?"

"They're sending a dropship of twenty soldiers," said Jonathan.

"Well they'll definitely be able to help us if we need to fight our way onto the mothership, or attack one of these Brotherhood bases Omega was telling us about." I said.

"Exactly," said Joëlle, taking a moment to chew some food. "So, I assessed the damage to the synthesizers and determined that some fluid from the cooling lines had leaked into the central processor. In order to drain it and repair the system, we would have to first bring the ship to a balanced angle. Which meant fixing the engines first."

"Okay, so you determined some nonsense stuff about some science-y, technical things, and you fixed the engines and the food synthesizer. Is that it?" said K.

Joëlle hesitated for a moment, staring at K. She chuckled. "Yes, I guess the short story is just that. We fixed the engines and the food synthesizers. Jonathan and I made a great team," she said, and smiled at Jonathan, who returned it weakly. Seeing this, her smile faded. "Though we have had no luck with the weapons. We... we thought you two were in danger, or dead, but... we didn't want to try searching for you until we were certain that we could use the Firebrand for food and shelter. Once we fixed the engines and the synthesizers, it was well into the night, and we both tried to get some sleep. I think I had an easier time than Jonathan," she gave him another concerned glance.

Omega's head tilted slightly, gazing intently at Jonathan. "There is a connection between the REM stage of sleep and eye movement. Could the presence of your robotic eye interfere with your body's ability to rest during sleep?"

Jonathan shook his head hesitantly, but couldn't resist a smirk at Omega's odd conversation choice. "I don't think you understand how sleep works… but I guess I'm not a sleep scientist."

"REM is connected with dreaming. Do you find since losing an eye that you have had less frequent dreams? Or have you-"

"Omega," interjected Joëlle, "let's continue this discussion another time. More pressing matters?"

Omega nodded. "Of course, commander."

Joëlle raised an eyebrow, and a smile slowly spread across her face. "Commander?"

Omega's angular lips formed a slight curve. "You are a member of Round Table, the previous leader of the squad, and the Captain of the Firebrand. K and Osax are not members of the TAU. Despite Jonathan's previous experience in the military, he is now primarily a scientist. You are the highest ranking TAU officer on the planet. I am a servant of the TAU; you are my commander."

Joëlle grinned. "Well, I'm happy to have you on the team, Omega." She gestured to them. "But, if you're comfortable enough to sit cross-legged on a chair in front of your commanding officer, then you're comfortable enough to just call me Joëlle."

Omega's smile faded, and their neutral expression resumed. After a few moments of silent hesitation, they unfolded their legs and tail, and sat normally on the chair, with their back straight and their claws brushing the floor. "I understand your point, commander."

Joëlle paused, exchanging glances with me. She looked back at Omega. "Actually, I'm… not sure you do." Omega tilted their head to the side.

"Anyway," said Joëlle, "I'm so glad you're both safe."

"I'm glad we're all safe," I said.

"Yeah, me too," said K, mumbling through the last bite of her sandwich. "But, we gotta make an action plan or something, cause at this rate Duhrman's gonna disintegrate Earth while we're just sitting around chatting."

The room fell silent, save the hum of the ship. The five of us exchanged glances.

"Alright," said Joëlle. "Omega, how long have you been on the planet?"

"Would you like it in Earth years, or Skyther Cycles, or-"

"Earth years are fine," she said.

Omega blinked. "I have been here for exactly 1.3751 Earth years."

Joëlle nodded. "I'm guessing that means you've had time to identify major Brotherhood outposts and other points of interest."

"Yes." they said. "I was designed to be undetectable by life sign scanners. That has made it easier for me to keep track of Brotherhood activities."

Joëlle paused. "Wait, do you have a vehicle somewhere, or do you do all your travelling on foot?"

Omega said, "I do some of my travelling on foot. Some travelling on hand, and some travelling on tail."

Joëlle and I snorted a laugh, to Omega's confusion. Then K stood up from her chair.

"Hah ha ha, what a hilarious, weird little dude we found." K's voice was sharp with sarcasm. My body tensed looking at her expression. "But can we please stop wasting time and get to the point?"

Joëlle spun around to K. "Sit down, K. I am getting to the point- If you ever actually listened to me you might have noticed."

"I-" K winced, and began to growl. "Yeah, I'll sit down... In the kitchen, where I can take some medicine." She stomped off toward the exit, my eyes following her. "Let me know when this meeting is over."

"K-" I began.

The door slid shut behind her.

Joëlle spoke under her breath. "What is her problem..."

"Well," I said, "she suffers from chronic headaches and blackouts. And she's dying. That's got to put anyone in a bad mood."

"I know, you told me that a while ago. But ever since we met she's mostly either ignored me, or talked back to me." Joëlle brushed her purple dreads to the side, revealing the spiral tattoo on her cheek.

"It's not just you," said Jonathan, adjusting his cybernetic eye. "She does that with me too, despite my interest in her."

Joëlle turned to him. "You're interested in her?" she asked. "That's..."

"No no," he said, raising his hands in defense. "I meant academically.

Academically.”

Joëlle chuckled loudly. “It’s alright, I’m not here to police people’s feelings.”

“It’s true. I don’t really have time to develop feelings for people, anyway,” he added.

“Yeah,” said Joëlle, turning away from him. “None of us do.”

I tilted my head to the side, though neither of them noticed. They were an odd pair of friends. I glanced to Omega, who seemed to be observing with silent curiosity, still sitting perfectly upright.

“But she seems to like *you*, Osax,” said Jonathan. Something about the way he said those words put me off.

“Yes, her and I are friends,” I said. “I mean, I consider all of you to be my friends,” I said, before taking a small sip of soda.

Joëlle smiled warmly, and said “Thanks Osax. I… guess we are.” My ears began to lift, but at the same time I noticed Jonathan had frowned, and turned his face to the floor.

“...Jonathan?” I asked. Joëlle and Omega turned to him.

He took a deep breath in. “Well, maybe K just likes you because you’re giving her those pills.”

“That’s not it- We became friends before that. I think if you want to be her friend, you just need to… open up to her. Give her the benefit of the doubt.”

“Well, what you’ve been doing for her is certainly admirable,” said Joëlle. My ears began to sink. “Making all the medicine for her… it’s sweet.”

Jonathan leaned back in his chair. “Yeah, even though it’s just sugar.”

My heart began beating quickly, Joëlle turned to him with her mouth open and brows furrowed. Then she looked to me. Beads of sweat were forming on my cheeks, and just above my eyes, and I lurched forward with my hands raised. “Shh! Don’t- Don’t tell K,” I said.

Jonathan looked a little startled, and to my surprise, a little guilty, when he realized what he had said. Joëlle just stared at me, silent.

Omega looked at me with their round black eyes. “Why can we not tell K?” they said, loudly.

“Because! She thinks the pills actually have medicine in them!” I whispered urgently.

Joëlle frowned. “You don’t actually know how to help her...”

I shook my head.

“So,” she continued, “You were hoping that placebo would be enough to make her feel better.”

I sighed, and nodded. "Please," I said, my heart beginning to relax, "just keep it a secret. I should be the one to tell her."

Joëlle and Jonathan exchanged glances, and she nodded. "Alright."

Joëlle hesitated for a moment. "Well, I need to keep talking with Omega, to find out what she knows that can help us-"

Jonathan elbowed her, and said quietly, "I think Omega is male."

Joëlle's cheeks flushed. "Oh, Omega, I apologize…"

Omega spoke. "Apology accepted. Male and female has not been a concern for me in the past… I have not spoken with anyone in a long time who might be confused. I have not spoken with anyone in a long time until I met Osax and K."

"Right," said Joëlle. "Well which pronouns would you prefer?"

Omega thought for a moment, their tail flicking absentmindedly. "Which pronoun is better?" they said at last.

Jonathan, Joëlle and I shared a look. "Neither is better," I said. "In fact, you don't need to pick between those two. In my language, we don't even use gendered pronouns."

"Thank you, Osax. I will not pick between those two."

Joëlle shuffled in her seat. "Okay, then I'll just… refer to you as they?"

Jonathan shook his head impatiently. "It's not that hard, Joëlle. No need to get awkward. Haven't you met a non-binary person before?"

Joëlle looked at him. "Sorry, I'm just… not totally used to it. I know it's not unusual, it just wasn't common in my circles, I guess.

"Anyway," she continued, "as I was saying, I need to find out what you know that can help us right now, Omega."

"Alright," I said. "Let's make some plans."

"Actually," said Joëlle, turning to me. "I'm tasking you with ensuring our team doesn't collapse."

I blinked. "Oh?"

"Yeah," she said. "As we were just saying earlier… You're the only one K has a real connection with. Which means, you need to come clean about the medicine."

I grit my mandibles.

"If K feels betrayed by you," she continued, "it might break apart our team."

She was right, of course. And perhaps I needed her to point it out for me, but I didn't want her to.

"Jonathan, Omega and I will discuss plans against Duhrnan. But right now, I need you to keep K's spirits up, and not by lying to her. I know what it's like to lead a good team and a bad one, and the good ones always start with trust."

Jonathan looked away from her.

"So come clean. You said it yourself; you should be the one to tell her."

I stood up and sighed. "You're right, Joëlle. You're right."

She smirked. "There's a reason I became a leader."

"Yeah," I said. "I'll go… take some responsibility for this."

"Good luck," she said. "So, Omega…"

Her voice trailed off as I opened the door and headed for the kitchen. I clenched my fists. I wanted to help K so much. I was terrified of admitting that I didn't know how to. My palms were sweaty.

I entered the kitchen, and she was nowhere to be seen. I could hear the low hum of the ship as I scanned the room. The white lights illuminated the counter tops, and my eyes landed on an object resting on the far counter, crushed and deformed. It was the bottle of pills I had synthesized for K, completely squished together, with powdered dust scattered around it like it had exploded out the top from pressure.

My eyes widened, and I became uncomfortably aware of my own heartbeat.

"K?"

I ran into our room. She was gone. Her gear was missing.

I sprinted down to the exit ramp of the ship. It was wide open, and the dusty atmosphere of Malum wafted in, howling in the wind. Heavy boots printed in the dust on the way down the ramp. I raised a hand to my earpiece.

"Joëlle…" I muttered. "K's gone."

Thirty-Six

The Firebrand hovered smoothly over the jungle. Jonathan was peering at the scanner, which had honed in on the tracking device in K's earpiece. It blinked hazily on a holographic map of the area, which fizzled in and out due to the atmospheric disturbance of Malum.

Joëlle's hands gripped tightly onto the controls of the ship, smoothly piloting just above the roof of the forest. A flock of blue birds burst up from the trees just ahead of us, and Joëlle pulled back on the controls, stopping us for a moment, breathing heavily. After a few seconds she tilted the ship forward and we sped on.

Green and purple foliage streamed by beneath us, and I stood gazing out across the landscape. I readjusted my black cloak, wrist cable, and weaponry.

Jonathan's eyes were narrowed in an intense focus. His lip was a straight line.

Omega sat in the far right chair of the cockpit, legs crossed again. They were observing the scene, but clearly unsure of how to help, so they stayed quiet.

"I don't understand," said Jonathan, staring at the scanner. "There's no way K could have made it this far, in this amount of time."

I glanced at the scanner. "We're just about on top of her… Joëlle, can you bring the ship any closer to the roof of the forest?"

She looked up at me confidently. "This ship is like a second skin. Of course I can."

I couldn't feel the change in velocity, but I could see us begin to lower even closer to the leaves below us. We were almost touching them.

"Why did she run away?" asked Omega. Their face was puzzled.

"Because…" I began. I closed my eyes, and breathed slowly. "She must have heard our conversation." I shook my head, and cursed in Skorali. "Because I let her down, and I lied to her."

Jonathan cut in. "We're right on top of her. She's not moving right now."

I tapped my earpiece. "K?" I called out for her.

I waited a few seconds, but there was no response.

I took a deep breath. "K... I'm sorry. I didn't mean to hurt you." I had to shut my eyes to stop them from tearing up. "I only wanted to help. I'm really, really sorry."

Joëlle glanced back at me, and Jonathan and Omega watched quietly. The engines thrummed faintly.

"Are you there, K?"

Nothing.

"We're worried about you." I turned away from the window, and squatted, covering my head with my hand. "I'm worried about you."

I sat there for several seconds.

"She's not responding," said Joëlle. "Osax?"

"I'm going to propel down to her," I said. I stood up and marched toward the door.

"Alright," said Joëlle, looking back to the window.

I walked through the ship, to the exit ramp. I reached out my hand to the wall panel and pressed a button. The ramp began to whir and fold open, and the dim room was splashed with light reflected off the trees. Air whistled into the room, ruffling the fur on my chest and ears, and filling my nostrils with a strange smell.

I turned around and activated my wrist cable, hooking it onto a handle on the side of the wall. I gripped it with both hands, and looked back down at the forest. I began slowly inching my way down the ramp, holding tightly to the cable.

I reached the bottom of the ramp, and the wind seemed to glide across the tops of the trees. It sent my ears dangling to the side. I felt the edge of the ramp with my feet, and reached a hand over to my holo-gauntlet. I activated and calibrated the scanner. A holographic image appeared, directing me to K's tracker.

Omega stepped into view just as I began lowering myself to the ground so I could climb down safely.

They looked at me and spoke over the sound of the rustling leaves. "Can I assist you?"

I shook my head. "It's my fault K left, and I'm gonna bring her back," I declared.

Omega simply stood and watched as I flung myself carefully over the edge. My legs were touching the treetops and their over-sized leaves.

"How're we doing back there, Osax?" Joëlle's voice came through my earpiece clearly.

"Fine," I said. "Just keep the ship steady, and we should be alright."

"Roger that," she said.

With one hand, I lowered myself slowly into the rustling branches. I strained to look at the scanner on my holo-gauntlet.

I paused, staring at the image. I had only descended just below the treeline, but already the scanner was showing me below K.

I deactivated the scanner and grabbed the cable with both hands, climbing back up so my torso was just above the trees.

A large insect buzzed onto my arm, and I flicked it aside. My eyes focused and scanned the leaves ahead of me. The cliffside was a ways off behind us. And K was nowhere to be seen.

Then my eyes caught it; nestled atop one of the huge leaves of the tree ahead of me was a tiny black device. K's earpiece.

I shut my eyes tight, and reached a hand up to my own communicator.

"K's not here," I said. "She ditched the earpiece… must have thrown it away from the plateau." No wonder we had flown so far trying to track her. Jonathan was right, there was no way she could have run this far in this short of a time. I grabbed her communicator swiftly and stuffed it into a pouch on my leg.

"Dammit!" I heard Joëlle exclaim in response. I heard Jonathan sigh.

Then my body froze. Glancing back at the plateau, I saw several dark shapes in the sky above it. Too large to be birds.

"Oh no," I said.

"What is wrong?" Omega asked.

My skin began to crawl. A shadow fell over the plateau.

"Osax, you'd better get inside!" Joëlle exclaimed.

I scampered up the side of the ramp, leaving the trees behind. I gazed out toward the plateau, and the giant black bug which lowered down to it from the sky like a spider.

"I know," I said. "I see it."

"Well," said Jonathan shakily through the communicator. "At least we found Duhrnan."

"No," I said, withdrawing my pistol from my holster. The flock of insect-like fighters began to turn toward us and accelerate. Yellow-tipped energy cannons burst to life on the fronts of the black ships. "He found us.”

Thirty-Seven

The ramp hissed to a close behind me, and I rushed past Omega, pistol in hand. The scent of the forest spores lingered in my nose as we sprinted through the halls of the starship into the cockpit where Joëlle sat. Jonathan was there beside her, leaning over the control consoles with a hand resting on her shoulder, his long coat hanging on the back of his seat.

The quantum extender flickered every few seconds, struggling in the atmosphere to pinpoint the location of the mothership, desperately, as though it was trying to warn us that Duhrnan was nearly upon us.

The sky was bright, and clouds of dust billowed around us. Joëlle pulled the controls upright, and the ship began lifting from the treeline, and rotated so that the plateau was ahead of us. I saw the dark shapes of at least ten valicorr attack ships changing course to intercept us, all of their weapons charging. They left trails of dust, disturbed in the wake of their speed. And looming above, behind them was the mothership. Its limbs flexed slowly like a gargantuan arachnid. Somewhere aboard was Duhrnan, I thought. The one who was responsible for stealing the Shade Beam, and for killing countless on Voren. The one responsible for destroying Astraloth. For killing my mother. My knuckles turned white as I squeezed the handle of my weapon.

Joëlle snapped forward with a deliberate energy, violet strands of hair flinging to and fro. She flipped a switch, and glanced down at the remains of the weapon controls which K had destroyed earlier. Her eyes narrowed, and her nose twitched as she looked up at the attack force.

"We have no weapons," she said, flatly. "We have to flee."

Jonathan squeezed her shoulder. "We have to get out of here, now!"

Joëlle was about to turn the Firebrand around and flee... and she would have if I hadn't seen K just then. She was unconscious, and three valicorr carried her toward a dropship that had landed near the precipice between the plateau and the greenery. My skin prickled at the sight of her in the hands of our enemy.

"Wait!" I cried. I leaped forward, pointing down to the plateau. "Stop the ship!"

Joëlle and Jonathan followed my gaze, and froze. Heatwaves still wafted from the valicorr dropship's cylindrical engines. Several valicorr soldiers stood about the landing site. Three more were dragging K's limp body toward the shuttle craft. Joëlle halted the Firebrand, and I strained my eyes to see if they had hurt her, but we were too far to be able to tell.

"We can't leave K!" I said. "They'll kill her!"

"She fled into the forest, and then had a blackout!" Jonathan exclaimed. "Of all the bad times!"

Joëlle was breathing heavily but steadily. I looked at her face as she stared out the window at K and the valicorr captors. They were several meters away from the dropship.

I felt something warm on the back of my arm and jolted around. Omega was standing right behind me, their breath grazing my arm. Their black eyes were darting around the scene, jumping between enemy targets. Their lips were still, but they gulped silently, calculating the situation. The heat of the jungle didn't faze them, but here in our air-conditioned vessel I noticed a drop of sweat rolling down their freckled cheek.

I turned back to the window. The valicorr fighters were encroaching on us. In a few seconds, they'd be well within firing range.

"They're going to take her up to the mothership!" I shouted. I dug my fingers into the back of the pilot's seat. "We have no time. We have to save her, now!"

Jonathan gestured to the window. "If we try to save her, they'll shoot us down in an instant! We're sitting ducks out here!"

"Sitting… ducks?" asked Omega.

Joëlle cut in. "They might not be able to hit us…" She shot Jonathan a desperate look. "The valicorr have good scanners, but the cockpits of their fighters have low visibility. If the atmosphere of Malum wasn't enough to scramble their sensors, I just activated the Firebrand's cloaking device. Since we can't use the weapons anyway…"

"So they'll have to aim manually?" I said.

Joëlle nodded. "There's a small chance…"

"Take it!" I thrust my hand forward, gesturing to the dropship. The cannons of the valicorr fighters began to spark with energy.

Joëlle inhaled. "Alright everyone- Hold on tight!"

The cockpit lit up with the light of energy blasts streaking past the window, casting warped shadows on the inside walls. Joëlle took us into a steep dive, and suddenly the forest floor was speeding toward us. The valicorr fighters broke formation, scattering around us like a flock of birds. I flinched; the ship was about to faceplant into the trees. But just in time, Joëlle pulled up, and the Firebrand skated across the treeline, sending a trail of leaves and twigs up into the air as we flew.

K was centered in the view from the cockpit, her unconscious body being carried by three valicorr, one holding her legs, and one more for each of her arms. They were only about fifteen feet away from the valicorr dropship, which sat waiting with its side-door open, the inside inhabited by well-armed pirates. Bright yellow bolts rained down upon us from the sky, and the trees around us began to ignite in bursts of amber flame and smoke. We were approaching the cliff at a dangerous speed, and Joëlle would have to pull up quickly to intercept the landed dropship and K's captors.

"What's the plan? What are we doing?!" yelled Jonathan, who had plopped down into his seat and was clutching the sides of his chair. "We have no weapons, how are we expecting to come out of this alive?"

Explosions rumbled around us. "Osax?" said Joëlle.

I activated the targeting hologram of my eyepiece, and my E-gun whirred to life. I stepped back towards the door and flung the black hood over my head. "Drop me next to K. I'll get her!"

"Got it!" yelled Joëlle.

Omega said, "Does this vessel have an escape hatch?"

"On the top of the ship, yes!" Joëlle shouted, leaning into the controls, picking up speed toward the dropship and swerving to evade laser fire.

Omega sprung up, startling Jonathan, suddenly standing with their grenade launcher in both hands, armed and ready. "Open the hatch," they said bluntly.

Joëlle glanced at them for a fraction of a second before spinning back to the windshield. "Jonathan! Show Omega to the escape hatch!"

He bounced out of his seat, and flung his long coat on. "I can do that!"

Jonathan and Omega rushed past me out of the cockpit. I grabbed hold of Joëlle's seat for stability as she steered the Firebrand up just a little so we were heading straight for the shuttle, and began to decelerate.

The barrage of lasers had stopped briefly, as all the valicorr ships were circling around behind us getting ready for another assault. My eyes trained down to K and I backed up toward the door. They'd lifted her torso onto the platform, and two of the valicorr had already gotten inside. The third one was lifting her legs into the ship, and ready to leap aboard.

"What are you waiting for Osax?!" Joëlle shot her hand back toward me. "Get to the exit ramp! Go! Go! Go!"

I heard her command loud and clear. My blood boiled, and I bolted back to the exit ramp.

As soon as the ramp opened, wind gushed into the room and knocked me aside. I clutched a handle on the wall and leaned into it, stabilizing myself as my eyes struggled to keep up with the speed of the terrain moving on below me. The ramp faced the back of the ship, so I was able to look out to the horizon behind us. We had left a trail of spot fires, blazing where valicorr energy blasts had missed us and ignited upon the treetops. The valicorr fighters had just finished circling around, and accelerated toward us once again. In a matter of seconds they would begin shooting.

We crested the edge of the plateau and sandy rocks shot by in my vision. Joëlle started slowing the ship so that I could leap off. My eyes locked to the valicorr on the ground. K was just put inside their shuttle, and the last valicorr leapt up into the ship. Then K, the dropship, and the cliffside were engulfed in the shadow of the impenetrable mothership as it moved overhead.

My mind raced, calculating as the Firebrand slowed and lowered to the ground at exactly what speed and distance I could safely jump.

An explosion of heat shocked my body when a charged projectile from one of the starfighters impacted the ground just below the ramp, and I disregarded any notion that I had time to make a plan. The Firebrand was moving too slowly. Waiting for me to jump off made it too easy to hit. If Joëlle couldn't focus on evading the valicorr now, everyone aboard would surely perish. So pistol in hand, I dived out of the ship into the open air, squinting my eyes against the dust. The hum of the Firebrand fell behind me and my senses were filled with the sound of the wind surfing across the plateau and the forest rustling beside it. The engines of the valicorr starfighters groaned in the distance. I held my breath, arms and legs outstretched, body tense, arcing forward with each second. I could feel the blood pumping in my throat as I soared with nothing but air below me, and questioned why I thought this was a good idea. I sped toward the ground, and tucked my head in. I closed my eyes, and braced for the impact, trying not to imagine the roughness of the ground beneath me, painfully aware that in a moment I wouldn't need to.

The wind was pummelled out of me as I tumbled a few meters onto the stones. Pain glowed dully all over my body, and I struggled to sit up, still clutching my pistol. My eyes began to focus again, ears dangling limply, and then I felt pain flare up from the scrapes on my palms, forearms, shoulders, and knees. I gazed up at the Firebrand gliding slowly away, and whipped my free hand to my earpiece and shouted. "I'm free! Get moving!"

Joëlle heard, and the dark gunship dashed forward, peeling up into the sky. It flew upwards toward the shadowy underside of the mothership, who's limbs stretched outward, before darting to the side. A second later I lost track of it, as it camouflaged against the dark battlecruiser, but where the Firebrand had been just a moment earlier a hundred beams of energy hurtled past with a buzz, electrifying the air around me.

The dropship doors were beginning to slide closed, slowly blocking K's prone body from my view. I scrambled to my feet, wincing in pain. I had landed several meters away from the shuttle; I only had a few seconds to reach it.

My feet dug into the amber rocks and sand, and I kicked off with all my strength, sprinting as fast as I could toward the closing door. Heatwaves hung above the engines of the craft, which started to glow. The vehicle started to gain height, rising five feet above the ground.

I ducked down. A massive gust of wind pushed against me as the flock of starfighters screeched by in the air above me, hunting the Firebrand with ferocity. Their energy cannons were deafening in the naked air of the planet's surface, especially being fired in such rapid volleys. But even while I thanked the stars that none of them had targeted me, my eyes caught a valicorr who had seen me from the closing gap of the dropship doors, and armed their gun, snarling through needle-like fangs. The barrel of their weapon flared with light.

I dove to the side. A plume of smoke rose where I had been standing. I caught myself in a somersault, wincing as my bruised arms and back hit the ground. I had no time to hesitate. I locked my pistol to the valicorr, and lined up the holographic laser-sight with its torso. The trigger dug into my finger and clicked; an electric gunshot rang out, and a green light flashed from the muzzle. The bullet of energy sparked against the space pirate, and it keeled over, just as the dropship door snapped closed. My palms were sweaty.

The stones were hot against my feet as I hurried the last few steps to the ship. My ears peeled back reflexively as I approached the shuttle and the growl of its massive engines crescendoed. Its bottom was already at my eye-level, and it was accelerating upward. But still I reached my free hand onto the lip of the platform.

The engines were blasting air onto the plateau which, with nowhere else to go, shot outward in a disc and shook my fur and clothing. My fingers felt a smooth, cold surface- the rim of the doorway which stuck out like a four inch ledge- and I tried to hold on. My entire body stretched upward with the rise of the starship as I tensed my arm, trying desperately to cling to the edge.

My fingers slipped, and I stumbled forward, air escaping from my lungs. I wiped a line of sweat from my face, and glanced up. The ship was out of reach. And I was stuck alone on the ground of a dangerous planet, below a squadron of valicorr fighters and the largest battleship I'd ever seen. Gunshots echoed from the starfighters between the mothership and the plateau. The Firebrand zoomed by, outrunning the pursuing energy bolts and starfighters, which zigzagged around. A second later I was knocked off balance by a gale of dust in the wake of the ships. The mothership hadn't fired a single shot yet. I looked back to the dropship's bottom, covered in pipes, fuel-lines, and other unidentifiable machinery. I thought of K, and what they might do with her. I remembered the way Duhrnan played with his victims when we first intercepted his communications. I wasn't going to let that happen again. Not to my friend.

I holstered my pistol, and aimed my wrist cable up at the ship. I shot the hook toward a grate on the underside of the ship. The cord whiffled through the air, missing the mark by a foot, but miraculously it looped around a pipe. Before it could unhook itself and fall back down to the floor, I pressed a button on the bracer to extend the prongs of the hook, and it lodged securely to the shuttle. Despite myself, I laughed, astonished that it had worked.

"Osax!" Joëlle's strained voice yelled in my ear. "What's the situation?!"

I glanced up at the mothership above. The Firebrand was swooping low to the surface of the ground. The valicorr ships were disoriented, each flying on their own separate path now instead of as a unified group. They almost looked like giant wasps, spitting spears of yellow lightning each time one caught sight of the Firebrand in the frantic, deadly dance.

Then my shoulder lurched upwards, and my feet touched nothing but air. I swung my free hand onto the cable and held on tightly with both hands for dear life.

I tapped my communicator quickly, regaining my grip. "The situation is..."

What the hell are you thinking, Osax? I thought.

Dangling about twenty feet below the valicorr dropship, and at least thirty feet above the ground, I trained my eyes on the Firebrand, which screeched past below me before curving up and to the side. I strained my eyes- Was someone standing atop the ship?

That's why Omega asked about the escape hatch!

Like a tiny action figure glued atop a model spaceship, Omega stood on top of the Firebrand. Their head flicked around, scanning for the nearest valicorr fighter. Their legs were widely spread, each foot gripping the surface, and they crouched low with one hand forward on the roof and the other aiming their TAU grenade launcher into the sky. The red tip of their tail adhered to the surface, stabilizing them. Their clothes were skintight, eliminating as much air resistance as possible, but I was still astonished by their spider-like grace and ability.

"Osax?!" Joëlle shouted.

The wind whistled in my ears. "Sorry! I'm-"

A valicorr fighter broke out from the swarm and dashed for the Firebrand. Omega perked up, then spun around, lifting and replacing each limb with an uncanny dexterity. A half-second later Omega fired a grenade, and a second after that flames erupted from the valicorr vessel. Chunks of smouldering debris arced away from the explosion down to the surface. Trails of smoke and flame dotted the sky, and as the flames cleared in the wind, all that remained of the aircraft were gravity-bound components.

"Woohoo!" I cried, ears lifting into a smile. I thrust a fist toward the sky. Then my adrenaline spiked as I lost balance, and I brought my hand back to the cable. A wave of vertigo hit me as I realized how much height we had already gained.

The Firebrand swerved up and out of sight, evading more projectiles from the swarming ships. Jonathan's voice called out. "That explosion- Did Omega just take one of them out?"

Omega's voice sounded through the communicator, unreasonably calm. "Yes."

"It was incredible!" I said.

"Hold up!" said Joëlle. "Where are you, Osax? The dropship left the landing site… Did you get K out of there?!"

The shuttle's engines blared above me, and I gazed up at the twenty feet of cord between me and its underside, swinging back and forth as the ship continued its course up toward the mothership where Duhrnan waited. I clutched the cord tightly.

"Not yet," I replied, tightening my jaw. Sweat trickled down my cheek. Carefully I held the cable with my dominant hand. I wore the device on my right wrist so I wrapped my hand around it for extra support. Then, I let go of the cable with my other hand, and pressed a button on the device. With a small jolt, the cable began to retract, with difficulty, pulling me slowly up to the hook and the base of the ship. The infinite horizons of the planet encircled me, saturated colours of purple and orange and green all mixing together in an abstract form as my mind tried to concentrate on the task at hand. But the sheer vastness of the open air, and the deadly energy bolts crying past made me feel incredibly vulnerable. *I just need to get to K,* I thought. *One thing at a time.*

Joëlle spoke up. Dread was dripping from her voice as it came through the speaker. "Oh no… You're not…"

"Osax is hanging from the bottom of the dropship." Omega said over the screeching winds.

"What?!" Jonathan blurted.

"It's alright!" I yelled. "I have it under control! Sort of!"

Suddenly, smoke and sparks flew from the arm-mount of the wrist cable, and I yelped. I stopped ascending. Half of the wrist mount fell away from me, shrinking into nothing below, and the other piece swung freely, dangling from the cable I held in my hand, but detached entirely from my wrist. An energy bolt had shot it, fired from an E-gun above me. I grabbed the cable with both hands. I was now relying entirely on the strength of my hands to keep me from falling to my death.

Waves of heat seared my face and arms. I craned my neck to see the dropship. A valicorr soldier was clinging to the ship, with their face and one arm peeking out from the side of it. Its three jet black eyes were trained on me, and it flexed the six long fingers on its hand, manipulating the wrist-mounted weapon on its arm. Glowing bolts of energy sprayed past me.

I fumbled, adjusting my grip on the cable, as I swung to the side and the ship continued to climb. I gasped when a laser bolt clipped my torso and seared my clothing. I spun helplessly as I dangled, losing sight of my assailant behind me. At last I found purchase on the cable with my left hand bearing most of the weight, and I reached my dominant hand down to the pistol holstered on my leg. When the soldier spun back into view, my arm was outstretched, aiming.

I pulled the trigger. With the holographic laser-sight aligned I managed a hit. The pirate fell out from behind the bottom of the ship, and I couldn't look away as it descended past the dogfighting ships below me to the dust clouds of the plateau. I shut my eyes briefly, then holstered my pistol.

I was breathing heavily, and my hands were sweaty which made the climb all the more terrifying. But each second, I put one hand above the other, and pulled myself up a few inches. I only had about ten feet to climb before I reached the bottom of the ship.

My cape billowed violently in the turbulence, and a confidence filled me. Probably from the endorphins my body was releasing as I worked my arms more than I had in months. But even as I closed the gap on the dropship's underside, it closed in on the mothership. If I was able to get aboard and commandeer the vehicle, I might be able to save K, and myself. But if it docked with the battlecruiser, we'd probably get stuck inside. I became aware of the pressure changing in my ears, but forced myself not to look down.

The Firebrand soared past a valicorr fighter. Energy arced through the air. Omega fired. The valicorr ship burst, and careened like a tumbling set of fireworks into the surface. It was a miracle that Joëlle had been able to avoid getting shot down so far, or a testament to her unbelievable proficiency.

I reached the base of the shuttle with aching muscles; unfortunately I couldn't rest them yet. I slipped my fingers into the cool metal grates and pipes of the ship, letting the grappling hook hang. Breathing heavily, I started inching my way across to the edge of the spaceship. I was slow, but it was taking nearly everything I had to keep holding on. One accidental glance at the now hundreds of feet between me and the ground sent my head spinning. I shut my eyes and tried to regain my balance. My arms wouldn't last much longer.

I spoke hesitantly into the communicator, and I felt my face getting hot from the stress. "Joëlle, I-" I exhaled. "I'm not sure how much longer I can hold on."

Another valicorr ship exploded. The Firebrand looped around, and started slowing below me. Omega glanced up.

"Osax, you better not let go!" Joëlle commanded.

Straining, I reached out for another handhold, but my sweaty hand slipped. I caught myself, panting. "If I do, it won't be by choice," I said.

The Firebrand danced around below me, and Omega took out yet another fighter. Then Joëlle steered the ship below the shuttle, and matched its speed, trying to hover directly below me. She said, "Omega, you're doing a great job! Now keep those fighters away from us while we spot Osax!"

Omega replied, "Yes, Commander," and fired another shot. A few seconds later and another attack ship was down.

Joëlle's plan seemed crazy, but no more than mine. I doubted their ability to catch me if I fell. Now that they were hovering I was terrified for their safety from the fighters. But that just pushed me to keep climbing.

I swung myself forward just like I was swinging on monkey bars at a human playground. I was only a few feet from the side of the ship, but I had to be careful making my way.

Each second Joëlle gained some altitude, shortening the distance between the ship and me. A valicorr fighter dove in and launched a burst of energy bolts. Omega was like a sprung trap, and blasted the attacker instantly. The ship splintered into debris, but the Firebrand was smoking, grazed by a bolt.

"Joëlle! You're hit!" I exclaimed.

"It's nothing," she said. "Only superficial!"

Even though I should have been climbing forward I was watching the Firebrand. I had to make sure it was okay. When the smoke cleared, the escape hatch had just finished closing, and now, standing shakily next to Omega was Jonathan.

Omega barely turned their head to face him, focused on the battle. "Jonathan, have you come to help?" they asked.

He knelt down atop the ship, keeping his center of gravity low. His tone was grim. "If we die, we die! But if we survive, I'm not going to be the only one who did nothing!"

His long coat flapped, and from underneath it he revealed Joëlle's rifle. He'd transformed it into the artillery mode which she had used on Voren to take out a valicorr dropship.

Joëlle's voice cut into my earpiece. "Jonathan? Are you on top of the ship?!"

"Yes!" he exclaimed. He lifted the rifle up to his robotic eye, and began scanning the sky around him. Omega was doing the same. "Just doing my part-"

"Omega can stick to ceilings!" Joëlle screamed. "You can't! Get back inside before you slip off!"

"Just... try not to make any sudden movements!" he replied.

"We're under attack, you idiot! I might need to take evasive maneuvers!"

Blue and red spears of energy flashed from his rifle, intertwining as they flew. At the same time, Omega fired a grenade in the opposite direction. The energy pierced straight through one of the starfighters, and Omega's shot connected with another. The two smoking ships curved to the side and smashed into one another.

Joëlle's voice was shaky. "I'm not going to lose you!"

"Joëlle... I..." he trailed off.

I panted. I had almost made it to the edge of the ship. Just a little further!

"Omega, make sure Jonathan doesn't fall!" Joëlle exclaimed.

"Yes, Commander!" they replied. I looked down below me at the Firebrand. Omega lifted their hand off the ship, and grabbed Jonathan by the bicep. They exchanged looks.

"Alright," said Jonathan, bracing the gun up to his shoulder and taking aim once more.

I lifted my head up, and screamed. A valicorr swung down from the side of the ship right in front of me. Without thinking, I dropped my right hand to my pistol and yanked it from its holster. I struggled to hang on with one arm. They hung with one hand wrapped around the edge of the ship, and opened their horrifying maw with a hiss.

I flung my arm up and pulled the trigger, but with their free hand they grabbed the barrel of my E-gun and twisted my arm so it fired uselessly into the air. I began kicking at them as we struggled over the gun, and I stared into their empty eyes.

They lunged their mouth toward my hand, razor teeth chomping in the air. I flinched, and pulled my hand back, letting go of the pistol and grabbing onto the ship. A drop of blood fell through the air and a sharp pain pinched my hand like a paper cut, but I had avoided any serious damage.

The space pirate swung side to side, twisting the pistol in its hand. It took another bite at me, and I swung backwards. Then as I began to swing forward again, I pulled my body up with all my strength, and tucked my legs in. At the peak of my swing I kicked forward, planting both feet firmly on the valicorr's shoulders. It lost its hold on the ship, and tumbled down through the air. I took a second to regain my balance as my eyes followed its trajectory. And then I froze.

The valicorr slammed directly into Omega, who let go of Jonathan and tumbled backwards out of view off the top of the ship, flinging the grenade launcher into the air. Jonathan's rifle clattered onto the roof of the Firebrand and he slid backwards, collapsing onto all fours. He stopped just on the edge of the ship's curve, and clawed his hands against the hull with a grimace.

The valicorr scrambled to its feet, slowly rising with an injured leg. It screeched at Jonathan, and flicked its arm to the side. A shimmering blade of plasma burst to life, extending from the creature's arm.

"Look out!" I cried.

Jonathan rolled to the side. The plasma blade sliced into the hull of the ship. Sparks were tossed aside in the wind, and the Firebrand tilted slightly, moving through the air.

Jonathan yelled, and pulled himself up, charging straight for the valicorr. It swung the blade toward him, but he caught both of its wrists in his hands. The two of them wrestled atop the starship until at last Jonathan swiped a leg under the valicorr and tripped it. The valicorr landed on its back, having released my pistol from its grip. Jonathan held it, and stood up tall with his jacket billowing in the wind. He yelled, and drew his own pistol from beneath his coat.

Both weapons fired simultaneously, and Jonathan kicked the smouldering body. It rolled and slid down off the windshield.

"What was that?!" asked Joëlle. "Are you okay?! Jonathan!"

"I'm fine!" he replied, clearly strained.

"What about Omega?"

Omega's voice rang through the speakers. "I am alive."

"Good!" said Joëlle.

"Just hanging out." they said.

The three of us were silent.

"W- Was that a joke?" Joëlle asked.

"...Was it not funny?"

"Just climb back up!" yelled Jonathan.

I reached my hand around the side of the dropship and grabbed onto the lip. We were getting closer to the mothership; it almost seemed to blot out the sky.

Below me, Jonathan shoved the pistols into his coat pockets, and lunged for Joëlle's gun as it had begun to drift toward the edge. He caught it, and fired at the valicorr fighters, keeping them at bay. I noticed they were being more cautious now, keeping some distance from the Firebrand. Perhaps they were afraid, after seeing how many ships Omega and Jonathan had already destroyed. Omega inched their way back to the top of the ship, adhering to the hull.

Against all odds, I found a vertical handle next to the side door, and used it to pull myself up. At long last, I rested my feet on the lip of the dropship, and though I was still clutching the ship, I could give my muscles a brief rest. I sat there, panting, giving myself a moment before I tried to pry open the door and get to K.

"I made it to the door," I declared.

"Alright! Get inside, and do your thing!" Joëlle said.

I reached down to the molecular sword at my hip. I thought I should be able to use the blade to cut or pry the door open. I swivelled my head, body pressed flat against the shuttle. Then something caught my eye: a red glow coming from the mothership, growing brighter.

That's why the fighters were staying away from the Firebrand.

"Joëlle! The mothership!"

"Shit!" she responded.

I looked below. The Firebrand spun to the side. Jonathan screamed and began slipping off, but Omega pounced him, trapping him beneath their body as they latched onto the surface. The ship whirred and flipped, and a thunderclap shook the air. Red lightning arced down from the battlecruiser, missing the Firebrand by an inch. The bolt crashed into the plateau below, and sent stones and dust high into the air.

"Is everyone alright?!" I asked.

"Somehow!" Jonathan replied.

"Yes," said Omega.

"For now!" said Joëlle.

I thrust the sword deep into the crack of the door, cutting downward into the latch which held it closed. I cringed at the sound of metal sheering and scraping together. But I had cut through.

I flung the door open. K was prone on the ground in front of me, her arms and legs now bound by thick metallic cuffs. A single valicorr stood in the room and raised its arm cannon toward me.

I ducked low and pulled myself into the ship with one arm raised for defense. A bolt of heat flew over my head and sparked against the inside of the ship. A second later, and I drove my sword into the pirate, grimacing.

I dropped the corpse to the floor, and there I could see the back of the pilot's seat in the next room. The pilot glanced back at me, and vocalized something. Then the ship tilted violently to the side. The floor sloped down toward the open air, and K's body tumbled toward it.

I dropped my sword clattering out of the ship and lunged for K. My arms stretched and I let out a cry. I held tightly onto a handle inside the ship, feet planted firmly on the tilted floor. With my other hand I held K by the arm. She hung freely outside of the ship, and my arm felt like it was going to tear. Images of the cold elevator shaft on Voren invaded my mind.

"Joëlle!" I screeched.

"Holy crap!" she replied. The Firebrand curved around and accelerated up towards me and K. "Omega! Catch them!"

The ship was level again, and Omega stood up, leaving Jonathan to crouch on the top of the ship. The dropship was spinning, trying to shake us off, and Joëlle tried desperately to match its movements, inching slowly closer each second.

Suddenly, K cried out. She glanced around frantically, eyes wide, spinning her horned head every direction. Her face was filled with terror, but when her eyes met mine, she squinted in confusion, then grit her teeth.

The Firebrand wobbled back and forth just a few meters below us. K wriggled, then her arms burst free from the handcuffs. They were made of thick metal, but it wasn't enough to hold her back after all. She twisted her body, and grabbed onto the floor of the dropship, and created her own handholds by digging in her fingers and warping the metal. I let go of her arm, and we both gazed at the Firebrand, calculating the jump. Jonathan fired the rifle below, keeping valicorr ships at bay.

"I will catch you, K!" Omega said. They stood with perfect posture and outstretched arms.

K glanced down, then swung herself a little and let go. I wanted to shut my eyes, but I was transfixed watching her glide through the air. She landed just beside Omega, on the edge of the Firebrand, and lost her footing a little. Omega reached out an arm to her, and instantly she swatted it aside with her hand.

"I can do it on my own!" she growled.

"K, get inside the ship!" Jonathan commanded.

She glanced up at me briefly. The look in her eyes chilled my soul. But she hopped down the escape hatch into the vessel.

I wasted no more time. I pressed my feet against the platform and leapt toward Omega, but just as I did so the dropship shifted away from the Firebrand.

I hadn't jumped far enough.

I stretched my arm out as I descended. My cape and ears shot straight up.

And my hand met Omega's.

My body swung into the side of the ship, and the wind was knocked out of me. Omega hoisted me up, and spoke to Joëlle. "We have secured Osax and K."

"Great!" She cried. "Woohoo! Everyone! Inside! Now!"

Jonathan took one last shot before slipping into the ship, coat trailing behind him. Omega held my hand, helping me to the hatch, then jumped inside. I glanced up at the mothership, and noticed a red glow. I dove into the hatch.

The Firebrand's engines flared to life. Crimson energy cut through the air as we retreated.

But we were unscathed. Jonathan and Joëlle cheered. Omega was silent. K looked away from me. And I shut my eyes, took a slow, deep breath, and soaked in the feeling of resting my aching muscles, sitting against the wall in the corner. I was riding wave after wave of relief. And I laughed. We survived.

Thirty-Eight

"There is *absolutely no way* that all of that is true." The investigator's voice was firm, disbelieving.

I chuckled. "It is true."

Her mouth hung open in disbelief, almost disgusted. Annoyed at the very least, that I had the tenacity to say such a thing was true. She regained some composure, and stuffed a stray blonde lock beneath the rim of her dark hat.

"You must be lying," she stated.

I shook my head. "I am not lying."

She eyed me cautiously. "So you're telling me that you jumped out of a moving starship onto the ground, then grappled to the bottom of an enemy ship, and while hanging there, shot down a valicorr, climbed up the rope and had a hand to hand battle with another valicorr while hanging beneath the ship, which you kicked off onto-"

"Hey!" I interjected. "What did I just spend the last half hour explaining?"

She scoffed.

I continued, "I'll have you know, this isn't even the most unbelievable thing that happened to me."

"I don't believe you," she said. "This can't have been what happened."

"Fine," I said quietly. I leaned forward. "I'll tell you what *really* happened."

She smirked, and eyed me confidently. "I knew it."

I leaned back. "So, I pointed out K on the ground beneath us, and Joëlle flew the Firebrand down toward the valicorr. Omega and Jonathan and I had created a myrok disguise by jury-rigging the food synthesizers to create a costume. Joëlle faked a crash near the dropship, which startled the valicorr into dropping K. Because I was tallest, I was at the front of the costume and operated the myrok's arms and head. As the ramp opened we fired some flares to make it look like the ship was sparking and exploding from damage.

"We rushed outside, with Jonathan in the middle of the costume and Omega at the back, operating the back legs, and the tail (with their tail, of course) and we all gave our best impression of a myrok howl. The valicorr turned and ran back into the dropship, leaving K's body on the ground. They flew up into the air, and when they were sufficiently far, I picked up K and shoved her into my fake mouth. The valicorr pilots, terrified, followed the dropship back into the hangars of the mothership. And then we ran back inside the Firebrand and took off, flying low, to get away from them before they realized what had happened."

The investigator raised an eyebrow at me, and we shared in an unspoken staring contest. I was fuming.

At last she snorted, and spoke up. "Did that really happen?"

"No!" I cried. "Of course not!"

She leaned forward, her brow creasing. "Why are you wasting my time with these lies?"

I tilted my head to the side, in a mock pose of contemplation. "Oh, what a good question? I hadn't considered that. Why am I wasting your time?" I stared at her. "Why do you think I would waste your time with lies?"

She paused. "I don't know."

"Ah, I see. You probably don't know because there *is* no reason for me to lie. What was the point in me telling you that nonsense about the myrok costume? Where did it get you? What justice did it do for my story? There was no point, except to illustrate to you that it was pointless. So why would I spend thirty minutes explaining in detail fabricated events? I wouldn't. I'm not telling this story for you. I'm telling it for me, and for my people. So stop being so adversarial. You are a guest in my home, and I can have you removed if necessary."

She sighed. "I'm not the one being adversarial," she said. "The TAU would not be happy about that. I can't help but find your story difficult to believe, and it's important that I get the exact truth."

"Well it's the truth," I said. I crossed my arms. "Do you want me to continue the story? Or have you had enough? You've been nothing but disrespectful to me. I think I've been playing your game long enough."

I surprised myself by standing up from my seat. I couldn't figure her out. I knew something was wrong… but I was growing very tired of trying to determine what it was. Why was she here? I turned my back on her and stepped away from the table.

"Wait, Talcorosax!" she called out. "Where are you going?"

I stopped, and looked back at her. "It is, quite plainly, none of your business," I said.

She stood up, slamming her chair into the table. "You can't just lie to me and then walk away! You're under investigation by order of the TAU authority under suspicion of association with the Brotherhood. As the king of the skythers you should know the treaty between Earth and Astraloth is at stake if you-"

I planted my palms onto the table. "Am I really?! Is that *really* why you're here?!" I shouted.

She fired right back. "You know that's why I'm here! I already told you!"

My ears twitched, straining to detect the smallest waver in her voice. "You've been pretty contradictory so far," I said. "All I'm saying is, between the two of us, we both know that you lied, one way or another, about your mission. I'm not the liar here."

She shut her eyes. Sunlight poured in from the windows. "Fine," she conceded. "I misled you. I was ordered to do so."

"Right," I said.

"Maybe… maybe we should take a lunch break," she said calmly, as though neither of us had just been shouting.

"That's an excellent idea," I said. "We can reconvene in a few hours, if you really want to."

"Alright," she said.

I inhaled through my nose, and stepped toward the door.

Then her voice broke into my thoughts. Her tone was chilling. "Enjoy your artisanal dishes, Osax."

My ears twitched. I whirled around. My voice was cold. "*Don't* call me Osax."

I left the room with the image of her sly smirk stamped on my mind.

◆

I patrolled the ornate halls of the temple. Royal skyther guards stood at nearly every corner, bowing to me as I passed. Sunlight painted the floor and walls in a crisp, cool glow. Leaves rustled in the trees outside. I stepped out onto a balcony, and watched the bustling city below. Despite the sunshine, the air was cold. The presence of the TAU ships in the sky above me felt suffocating. Could she really be telling the truth?

White clouds gently drifted along the horizon. It was so picturesque. A bright sunny day, with humans and skythers mingling together. Flocks of birds soaring overhead, beneath the starships which hovered above. Skyther and TAU military officials teaming up and sharing resources. And the investigator and I hiding away each day, prying at each other's brains.

I furrowed my brows. My fists clenched on the railing. My eyes landed on the market district way off in the distance. Even from here I could see the massive billboards and advertisements. If the image was of a beautiful utopia, then beneath the paint, the canvas revealed a darker picture. Innocent people struggling to survive. Corporations and impersonal powers pulling strings and dictating the price of rights. Muggers and mercenaries killing for credits. And emotionally detached leaders, doing nothing but applying fresh coats of beautiful paint and pretending to be alright.

I was supposed to be a hero. I could risk my life for others. I could battle the valicorr and the Brotherhood. And people revered me as a hero, painting the world in white and black, putting me firmly on the good side and my enemies on the bad. But what good did that do? I was the hero I always wanted to be, but all that meant was becoming a corporate sellout and having people too busy admiring my image to notice my pain. But who was I to complain? I was ashamed to seek comfort. I could see others struggling and suffering, despite all my efforts to save them, to protect the galaxy. Their pain must be greater than mine. Even after everything my friends and I had fought for, there was so much pain in the world. So much wrong with it. So much I could never fix. So why bother? I had risked everything I had and barely survived, but for what? The galaxy would always been in danger. And we would all lose everything eventually.

I felt like I needed someone to talk to. I opened my holo-gauntlet and scanned my contacts. There was only one I thought might pick up.

I called Fiona. I took a few deep breaths, listening to the dial tone.

"Hello,"

"Hey Fi-"

"I'm not available to take your call right now."

I shut my eyes, and dug my hands into the railing.

Her voice continued. "But considering that you're calling my personal communicator, and not my work, that means you're probably a friend or family member, in which case feel free to leave a message and I will return your call as soon as I can. Or of course, you might be a robo-caller, in which case… Hello! Now you know how it feels to talk to a pre-recorded message. Except probably not, because you're a robot, and robots don't feel anything. Actually, I beg to differ… my prosthetics can feel things. But I digress. Uh, I've never been good at recording these answering machine things. This is probably going on too long. So anyway, if you're a friend or family member, feel free to leave a message after the beep. If you are in fact Reinhardt Taylor, then feel free not to leave a message. I told you not to call me. Thank you!" A few seconds after she stopped talking, I heard a faint mumble, which was cut off by a beep.

"Uh-" I began. "Hi, Fiona. It's me. Talcorosax." I trailed off. "I… wasn't really calling for any particular reason. Just, dealing with some weird stuff. I thought it might be nice to chat. But you're clearly busy. You've been busy a lot these days. I understand, I've been pretty busy too. We both have, I guess. A- Anyway, I… I just wanted to talk, that's all. Nothing urgent. Call me back if you feel like it. Goodbye."

I hung up, and put my head in my hands.

◆

A good while later, we were seated again, her with a coffee mug and I with a glass of soda. I was annoyed at the interruption, apparently more annoyed than I thought I would have been. I was eager to get back to the story, but I was genuinely angry with the investigator. I tried to relax, but it was challenging.

"No more interruptions," I stated. "No more accusations. If you want the story, then you have to cooperate."

She shot me a glance, severely annoyed. "I have only the utmost respect for you, King Talcorosax. But you're treating me very poorly."

I shook my head in disbelief. "You must be more self aware than that. Each time we speak our interactions become more uncomfortable. And I'm going to wager that I'm not entirely to blame for that."

"But you are partially to blame," she said. Her lips twitched into a wicked smile. "Fine. I won't interrupt. And you won't lie. That seems fair, right?"

I sighed. The way she was staring at me was incredibly uncomfortable. But even so… my plan was working. The further along I got into the story, and the more impatient I became, so too did she become impatient.

And her impatience revealed more cracks in her mask. She was not my ally, that much I was certain of now. But I would only know exactly how and why she wasn't if I finished the story, and got to the details she was looking for. I would have to watch her with extreme scrutiny to figure her out. The only trouble is, her plan was working too. Whatever she wanted to do with this knowledge, she wanted me to keep talking. Our eyes met, and we both knew. Someone was going to spring a trap, before the end. How, when, and what kind of trap, I didn't know. But a fire burned in my eyes. Maybe the world was a mess. Maybe it was futile to try to help it. But all that mattered to me now was solving this last puzzle. The puzzle of the investigator. I had given up on finding happiness; despair was more comfortable. But this challenge, this dark deceit, made me feel alive. And I was going to hold onto that, even if everything else had slipped from my grasp.

Her mask was cracking. I was determined to see what it revealed.

I lifted my ears in a feigned smile. "That seems fair."

Thirty-Nine

It took us hours to make absolutely sure that we lost our pursuers by flying swift and low across the surface of the planet, zigzagging around cliffs and mountains. Every time we thought we lost them, a valicorr fighter would fly in overhead. For much of the flight, we were silent. Eventually, a turbulent storm rolled in, and our visibility was limited by thick rain and flashes of lightning in the daylight. Fog seemed to seep out from the forests below. Searching for a place to hide, Joëlle found a massive ravine nestled in a mountain made of deep blue and purple stones. The Firebrand's headlights activated, and we slowly entered into a vertical fracture in the steep mountain range. The light glistened against damp stones and luminous crystal formations. Sky-blue vines covered in tiny circular leaves snaked up the interior walls of the mountain. The ceiling began to close in on us, and Joëlle lowered the ship carefully into the mountain.

We emerged in a massive cave shaft. The walls dripped with liquid, and the cavern was strangely lit with randomly placed glowing crystals. As we descended, the trickling water on the walls met up with hidden streams within the cave. Waterfalls, sparkling in the crystal light, poured down on each side. The five of us gazed in wonder at the beauty of it all. And as we watched, it became more apparent that this cave was teeming with life. Bugs buzzed, spiny creatures shimmied up the walls, and something bat-like flew around us, investigating our ship. At last we reached the bottom of the shaft, where the cavern opened up far into the distance where no crystals glowed and shadows overtook the path. The Firebrand's landing gear touched down on damp rocks, a wide, flat platform almost like a landing pad, with deep water on all sides but one. There was a path in the rocks ahead of us, heading into the darkness of the cave. Cones of light from the Firebrand's nose scraped at the shadow, to little effect.

"We should be safe here, from the valicorr and the storm at least." said Joëlle.

We all agreed that it would be best for us to take this time to rest, and sleep if possible. We were on a time crunch, as the Code-Alpha signal made so painfully clear. We shouldn't be flying in a storm like the one which raged outside unless absolutely necessary, and with nothing else to do, sleeping in preparation for when we might not have a chance seemed like the best option. We figured that after eight hours, we could check to see if the storm had passed.

If not, we would just have to brave it. In eight hours time, we would only have approximately 4.7 days left to figure out how to destroy both Duhrnan's mothership and the Shade Beam before the valicorr attacked, and destroyed Earth. Due to the unpredictability of slip space travel, Joëlle figured we should give ourselves 24 hours to fly from Malum to Earth. That meant once we woke from our rest, we would have closer to 3.7 days to destroy the mothership and figure out our plan to stop the Shade Beam. When I pointed this out, Joëlle and I agreed that maybe we would have to live with 6 hours of sleep each, enough to keep ourselves somewhat functional, but bumping our window of time to stop the mothership and plan for the Shade Beam to around 3.8 days. Thinking about it made sleeping all the more difficult. That, and the fact that by the time we were trying to sleep, K and I had only woken from our unconscious states close to 5 hours ago.

It didn't help that K, who was on the bunk above me, had barely said a word to me since running off earlier, and we certainly hadn't talked about the pills. The room was dark, and quiet save for the low hum of the ship and subtle creak of our beds each time one of us made a movement. I could hear her breathing. It didn't sound like she was asleep. I was painfully aware of the silence between us. The longer it went on, the more difficult it became to ignore it. A heaviness pressed on my heart. I didn't know what to do.

I rolled over onto my back, resting my hands on my stomach and staring up at the bottom of her bunk. Then I shut my eyes. Minutes passed, and I tried to focus on my breathing, but I could only focus on hers.

Out of the quiet, a soft melody began. K was humming to herself, that same tune I had noticed her humming twice before now, once on Kronos and once as she brought me breakfast on the ship. The melody was enchanting, and I was surprised to find tears welling in my eyes. I shut them, and wiped the tears away, trying to be quiet. She kept humming softly.

I waited for a minute. She kept humming. My chest was filled with a warm kind of anxiety.

"What is that song?" I asked, quietly.

She paused. I heard her body shift onto her side above me. "Why do you care?"

Silence filled the room. Seconds passed. Everything was still.

"I'm curious," I said.

She took in a slow, deep breath. "I don't know. It's just a song. Guess I made it up," she said, softly.

My eyes slowly circled the room.

"I'm sorry," I said at last.

We were silent.

"Is that all?" she asked, a slight edge in her voice.

I sighed heavily. "I'm… I'm also glad you're okay," I said. "Really, really glad." I almost choked.

She remained quiet. I screwed my eyes shut, heart beating in my head.

I fought back a sob. Then another. Pretty soon, I was crying softly. I placed my hands over my face. My arms were shaking, sore from the stunts I had pulled earlier, and weak.

Once I started, I couldn't stop. What felt like an eternity passed.

Then K leaned her head over the edge of the bunk, and stared at me upside down, frowning. Our eyes met, even as I kept whimpering.

She exhaled shortly. Then she crawled over to the ladder and climbed down quietly. She went over to the counter, and fumbled in the dark. Then, she tossed a device onto my lap, and plopped down onto the bed beside my legs. Her holo-gauntlet flared to life, and she adjusted the brightness levels and turned the volume down. I sat up, and wiped my eyes. Then I faintly heard the opening music of "Defenders of Earth" from her holo-gauntlet, and I saw her grip a holographic gun and controller in each hand. The virtual screen hovered in front of her.

"Come on," she said. She didn't look my way.

I put on my holo-gauntlet, and booted up the game. I sighed. "I guess we really are the defenders of Earth," I said, shakily.

She kept her eyes trained on the screen, and replied, her voice gentle, barely more than a whisper. "Not right now," she said. "Right now, we're just friends."

Groggily, I shuffled out of bed. K was already up, and there were sounds of chatting coming from the kitchen. I could smell spices, and some kind of sweet sauce. My fur was a mess. I picked up my holo-gauntlet and checked the Code-Alpha signal.

04:20:08:31.

My ears drooped.

I rubbed my eyes. My stomach growled, and I decided I had better see what was going on in the kitchen.

Considering our dangerous mission and current location on a hostile, relatively unknown world, I decided I should gear up before getting breakfast in case something unexpected happened. I left the cloak in my room, but donned my armour. After getting ready, bleary eyed, I walked into the kitchen. Apparently Omega was thinking the same thing, already suited up. That, or they hadn't slept at all, but if that were the case they seemed very well rested despite the sleep deprivation.

Omega and K were crowded around Joëlle, who was eating a bowl of stir fry. It smelled delicious, and was nearly empty. She was picking at it with silver chopsticks, a look of intense concentration on her face. As I stepped into the room, out of no where her and K exclaimed in disappointment. Omega tilted their head to the side, looking at them curiously.

"You *almost* got it," said K. She rubbed the bony ridges on her forehead with both hands, clearly invested in whatever was happening.

Joëlle ran her fingers between her dreadlocks. Then she leaned forward, staring intently into the bowl, and continued fiddling with the chopsticks.

When she noticed me, she smiled. "Good to see you up, Osax. Looks like you're ready to get going."

"Hey, Osax," said K, softly.

I lifted my ears. "Good morning… or evening. I can't remember what time it is here on Malum." I rubbed my forehead. "What are you doing?"

"Joëlle's trying to see if she can pick up a grain of rice," said K.

I nodded slowly. "That seems doable."

Joëlle shot her a sidelong glance. "You forgot the important part, K. I'm trying to pick up a single grain of rice, lengthwise. With chopsticks, of course."

I lifted an ear. "An… interesting challenge." It was so strange to see her and K just killing time after the intensity of the last few days, especially considering Duhrnan's timer. But, strange or not, it was a welcome thing. I suppressed a chuckle.

I walked over behind them and peered over their shoulders, standing much taller than any of them. All our eyes trained on the chopsticks and the grain of rice, singled out in the center of a mostly empty food dish. But no matter how hard she tried, Joëlle could not manage to grab it.

"Damn!" she exclaimed, sitting back and giving it a rest. "Maybe if the rice were stickier…"

"It's that sauce you used," said K. "Makes it lose its stick."

"May I attempt the mission, Commander?" Omega interjected. K and Joëlle stared at them. K's expression was a lot less friendly than Joëlle's.

"Uh, sure, Omega. Why not?"

Omega took the chopsticks from Joëlle, and stared at them intently. They manipulated them between their fingers, testing out the weight. Then, once they were satisfied, they leaned their spotted face over the bowl with their chopsticks poised. In one slow, graceful motion, they grabbed the grain of rice lengthwise. It was bending generously, but somehow Omega had done it.

They lifted it up into the air, and held it at eye level. The rest of us were silently staring in awe. Joëlle's mouth was hanging open, eyes wide. K had one eyebrow raised. After a few seconds, Omega awkwardly twitched their head to us. Then, unsure of what to do, they slowly moved to put the grain of rice in Joëlle's mouth.

Reflexively, she pushed their hand aside, and began to clap, laughing. "Wow, Omega!"

Omega placed the chopsticks on the counter. "Was that satisfactory?"

Joëlle chuckled. "You made it look so easy!"

"Yeah, they sure did," K grumbled.

Omega's lips curved into a slight smile. The light seemed to sparkle in their black eyes. "I did not know I could do such a thing… I was not created to pick up a single grain of rice lengthwise using chopsticks as implements."

"Well, Omega," I said, "that's one of the gifts of being alive and growing. You get to discover new things about yourself, and test your limits."

"I am more used to discovering new things about the Brotherhood," Omega said. "That is one of my assignments." Their voice held the faintest concern.

"We know," I said.

"Hey, Omega," K said, loudly. "I know you like showing off… how about we see who wins an arm wrestle, huh?"

Joëlle and I gave her a frown. Omega blinked at K, intrigued.

"I have never arm wrestled before. How does one perform such a maneuver?" they said, innocently.

"I'll show you," said K, pressing her elbow onto the counter, her forearm raised toward Omega, ready for the test of strength.

"K," I said. "Is this really necessary?"

She rolled her eyes at me. "No. Was lying to me necessary?" She stared at me. "Well you did it anyway. So sometimes people do things."

I bowed my head. Of course she hadn't completely forgiven me. Yet still when I was crying she had comforted me. It would probably take a lot of time... and honest communication for her to forgive me. I felt like an idiot for thinking that I could keep the truth from her.

Joëlle said, "Well, you know Osax was only doing it because he wanted to make you feel-"

"I know why he did it!" K shot her a glance, her eyes on fire. "But I still hate it. It was a horrible thing to do. He was a bad friend."

I guessed she didn't know how to say it directly to my face... So instead she was saying it to Joëlle, with me obviously within earshot. It hurt, but if it would help repair the rift between us, I welcomed it.

"I agree with you," said Omega. "Osax made an unethical choice to keep the truth from you while claiming to be helping."

I grit my mandibles.

"But, Osax risked his life to save you!" said Joëlle.

"You all risked your lives to save me," said K. "Osax was just going along with it."

"You know that's not true," Joëlle said.

"Why are you defending him?!" She spat. "Don't forget that he betrayed you too! He didn't follow your orders, and he got your team killed."

Joëlle stood up from her seat, silently. She was shaken.

"K. Stop." she said quietly.

"It's... alright," I said.

"Not really," said K. "Whatever! That's not even the point!" She turned her attention back to Omega. "Omega! Let's see who's the strongest. It's real simple, we just keep our elbows on the table like this, grab each other's hands, and push. Whoever's hand touches the table first loses. Got it?"

Omega nodded.

Joëlle took a step back. "Omega, you don't have to prove anything."

They looked up at Joëlle. "No," they said. "But I can prove something."

I furrowed my brows. "This isn't a good idea," I said.

Omega mirrored K's position, and grabbed onto her hand. Their eyes met. My heart rate quickened.

"We'll start on the count of three," said K. "One, two, three!"

Crack!

Joëlle and I flinched. Omega yelped. Omega's forearm was slammed onto the table instantly. Their elbow twisted unnaturally, and their skin had torn. I looked away from them, and shut my eyes.

"Oh my god..." K said, letting go of Omega's hand. Her expression was deeply shocked.

"What did you do?!" Joëlle cried, covering her mouth.

Omega's eyes shifted between their mangled arm and the three of us, but they were silent. Their eyes narrowed, and their lips tightened, suppressing the pain.

K stood up, staring at what she had done. Then she looked down at her hands with wide eyes, and I felt a pang of sadness. Tears were forming in her eyes.

"Osax," said Joëlle, "hurry and get the medkit!"

I nodded, and turned to run for the medkit, but Omega interrupted me. "No need," they said.

We all stopped, and turned to them. They forced a smile, their tail flicking behind them. Our eyes fell to their broken arm. Miraculously, the bone seemed to be resetting itself beneath their bloody, iridescent skin, which slowly stretched and reconnected. Within a matter of seconds, Omega lifted their arm, and was able to move it and flex their fingers. There was no sign of damage, though the colours of their skin seemed to shift and pulse for several seconds more before finally resting. The blood which had landed on the table remained, but Omega's skin had absorbed all of the blood which was on their arm back into their bloodstream. They pulled their legs up into a cross-legged position and rested their hands on their clawed feet, staring at us with a smile.

We were all surprised and relieved, but K looked the most confused. "What- How did-" She struggled to speak.

Omega stretched out their just-broken arm toward K, and touched their finger to K's sternum. "You win," they said.

K snorted, astonished. Joëlle and I exhaled in relief, and she began to laugh.

"You truly are incredible," I said. "In all the creatures I've studied,

I've never seen such an effective and instantaneous process of self regeneration. Truly astonishing."

"It must be unbelievably useful when you get into fights with the Brotherhood," said Joëlle, grinning.

"No," said Omega. "Its usefulness is believable."

I noticed K lower her head slightly. Their face and eyes fell into a frown. "Glad you're okay," she mumbled.

"I am glad you are okay, also." Omega said, their voice almost monotone. Then they grabbed the sides of their head, and closed their eyes. "Regeneration requires a lot of energy… I require… breakfast."

Joëlle smirked. "Well, if breakfast means your arm's okay, then it's coming right up! After I clean the counter." She turned to grab some towels and a sanitizer, and started scrubbing the blood off the table.

K stood up from her chair, rubbing her forehead. She was clearly in pain, suffering from another headache. She kept her gaze away from me. "I'm gonna… be in my room," she said.

"Alright," said Joëlle. "Hey K," she said, but K had already left the kitchen. She shook her head and sighed. Then she turned to face me. "Osax… will you keep an eye on her?"

I sighed. "Sure, but… I think she needs her space right now."

Joëlle replied. "Alright. Fair enough. I just want to make sure our team is as happy and prepared as possible. I know we have had some… well, some tension to say the least. And she's clearly hurt. But some space might be good. You know her better than I do."

"Sometimes I think not that much better." I lowered my ears. "But trust me… I want to make up for what I did. I'm going to try."

She offered me a soft smile. "You're good at heart, Osax. I know we haven't always seen eye to eye. But that's not the point. Keep on trying, learn from your mistakes, and we should be good."

I sighed. "When K mentioned your team from Round Table-"

She raised a hand. "Hey, Osax- You and I, we don't have to live in the past right now. If we stop Duhrnan, then we can hash it out. Let's not waste the time we have right now."

I nodded slowly. "I only hope our team is good enough to do so," I said. I activated my holo-gauntlet and glanced at the Code-Alpha signal.

04:19:57:44.

She paused, staring at the timer. Then she put a hand on my shoulder and looked me in the eye. "We had a rough start. But now, we're five strong. And honestly I think we might be some of the best people for this job in the galaxy." She smirked. "Since getting to know Jonathan more, and Omega joining the squad, I'm confident we can pull this team together. No one can predict the future. We might fail, but if we do our best... well, what more can we do?"

I lifted my ears slightly. "Thank you for the inspiring words, Joëlle."

"Of course," she said. "Once Jonathan gets some better rest, and K cools her head a bit, I'm confident we'll be right on track for stopping Duhrnan. As much as we can be."

Joëlle and I operated the food synthesizers which beeped cheerfully. She showed Omega how to use them, and they promptly downed three meals of food and several glasses of water while I ate my breakfast and thought about our circumstances. I could hardly believe that Omega's body could fit so much food in it at once... their slim figure bulged noticeably from the sudden ingestion of food, but they didn't seem uncomfortable. Their skin began changing hues, and over the course of my breakfast I noticed waves of heat emanating from them. Their body returned to its normal shape, though they looked exhausted, and the colour of their skin became static, notably less saturated than before. I asked if they were okay, and they informed me that it would take some time for them to recover. Apparently, the process of near-instant regeneration was a little more complicated than it initially appeared.

After I finished my breakfast, I asked Joëlle about the current plan. She informed me that the ship's scanners could still pick up the disturbance from the storm, bouncing distorted signals down from the sky outside through the crevice. The storm had almost passed, but she wanted to give us some extra time to wait.

"I forgot to say, I received word from the TAU reinforcements," she said.

"Oh?" I replied.

"They'll be arriving on Malum within twenty minutes, maybe sooner. I already sent them our location... I figured this site was as good as any to use as a temporary base of operations, and the platform down here is wide enough to fit a TAU shuttle next to us."

"Excellent," I said. "It will be good to have some extra help."

Omega spoke up. "I am eager to meet them."

"So am I," I said. "Hey, by the way, where is Jonathan?"

"Jonathan?" said Joëlle. "He's already had breakfast. Said he wanted to explore a little. I told him not to go too far. He should be just outside the ship." Her expression became concerned. "He's been there a while actually... Would you mind checking on him for me? Since we're on Malum, after all."

I sat up and pushed my chair in. "Of course. I want to check on him anyway."

"Thanks, Osax."

◆

The stones beneath my feet were cool and damp. Each footstep and breath echoed through the chasm with the sound of the waterfalls. I took in a deep breath, my nostrils filling with a scent akin to seaweed and salt water. The stone platform was surrounded by deep water on all sides, with creatures moving beneath the surface. A stone bridge extended out from the landing site, into the darkness of a cavern ahead. The walls and ceiling seemed to be converging together down that direction, but it was too dark to see anything beyond a certain point. I gazed up at the open tower, made of blue stones and glowing crystals. Purple and blue vines snaked up and around the cave. Water poured into the pool surrounding our ship from streams high up in the walls.

Jonathan was standing alone at the water's edge. Though smaller creatures crawled about the walls and floor, he was given a wide birth. It seemed odd to me that the crystals of light grew in the shaft, but not down the tunnel which was shrouded in darkness. He stood at the precipice of light, on the left side of the bridge. The glare of the crystals and the Firebrand's lights illuminated his long white and black coat. His left half faced me, his orange eye gazing into the water. The other half of his body was cloaked in shadow, save for the red glow of his robotic eye. He twisted his body and cast a stone into the water. It skipped twice, then sank.

He was humming softly to himself as he tossed the stones. In the ambience of the waterfalls he hadn't yet noticed me. I could see his face was strained, concentrating. He knelt down, looking for rocks to skip across the pool, and then his soft melody acquired words, which he sang quietly.

"...Show me a place where the people are free, the shackles of justice are nowhere to see..." The melody was enchanting, and flowed smoothly like a waltz. "...Break up the treaties and take up a stand, pave me the way to an anarchist's land." The melody seemed familiar to me somehow, but I couldn't put a name to it.

I stepped toward him, and he glanced over to me, silencing his music. His lips twitched into a half-smile, and his eyes locked to me. He looked conflicted. He glanced back to the water, and tossed another stone. It hit the water hard, and sank with a splash.

As I approached, he wiped his gloved hands together, then squatted to the ground, his eyes scanning for stones. I squatted beside him.

"Come to check up on me?" he asked. He picked up a stone.

I grabbed a stone of my own, and we both stood. He tossed it into the water, and it skipped once. I threw mine, and it splashed loudly.

"Joëlle was getting a little concerned," I said. "And I hadn't seen you yet this morning. Or since waking, at least."

He kept his attention on the stone skipping game, and I played along as we chatted.

"Fair enough," he said. He exhaled, and ran his fingers through his spiked hair. "How… how are you doing, Osax?"

"I've had less stressful weeks," I said. "But I'm alive. I'm anxious to get going. I can't help but feel like we're running in circles though."

He frowned. "Yeah?"

I knelt down, and grabbed another stone. "Joëlle seems confident in the team, despite our conflicts. But the fact is, at this rate, we are never going to stop Duhrnan in time. We need a game-changer. Something big." I tightened my grip on the rock.

Jonathan's eyes fell to the floor. We tossed our stones silently. At last he replied, "I've been thinking the same thing."

He turned to face me. "Osax, I- wanted to talk to you about something." His lip formed a straight line.

I tilted my ears. "What about?"

He took a deep breath and sighed, before turning to face the pool. "It's… hard to talk about," he said.

I shrugged. "You can tell me, Jonathan. Whatever it is."

He clenched his jaw.

I put a hand on his shoulder. "Look, Jonathan, I've been worried about you," I said. "You've been… obviously distressed for a while now."

He sighed. "I guess it is obvious, isn't it…"

"Well, yes, it is. I think everyone's been thinking it."

He shut his eyes.

I hesitated. "Is it… about Joëlle?"

He spun to face me. "What?"

I removed my hand from his shoulder. "You know, Joëlle. You two…" I began fidgeting with my hands. "It's… kind of obvious."

He took a step back. "What is- What's obvious? What?" His cheeks were turning red.

I looked around the cave, then back to him. "You two sit next to each other, you share the same shifts while we're out in space, you flirt with each other. I mean, it's pretty clear that you both have feelings for each other."

He stared at me in silence for a few seconds, before putting his face in his hands. I guessed he was embarrassed.

"Are you… worried about how that will affect the mission?" I asked. "Have you two-"

He cut me off. "We have not. Whatever you were going to ask, no, we haven't." He looked at me, dumbfounded. "Osax, that is *not* at all what I was going to talk to you about." He chuckled nervously. "I mean, sure, she's very admirable and kind..."

I raised my hands in defense. "Sorry, I shouldn't have assumed..." I wasn't sure I believed him.

"Besides," he said, "you and K do most of the same things as Joëlle and I. You even paired your holo-gauntlets! You must trust K a lot, sharing access to each other's personal computers."

I laughed. "Well, we don't flirt with each other," I said.

"Are you sure?"

I nodded. "Positive. Well, maybe in a friendly sort of way..."

"Maybe that's how Joëlle and I… flirt," he said, his cheeks turning red.

"You make a fair point," I said. "Sorry."

"No… no worries," he said. He picked up another stone and tossed it into the water.

I followed his example and skipped a flat rock across the water. "On the topic of Joëlle, I'm not sure if she told you, but she got a call from those TAU reinforcements."

Jonathan spun to face me, surprised. "Oh?"

"They should be arriving soon. Probably within five or ten minutes."

The blood drained from his face. "I... see," he said, turning once more to the water.

I furrowed my brows. "Are you alright?" I asked.

He seemed distracted. "I'm fine. Just, quite fine."

I stared at him. At last he turned to face me once more, and glanced up at me. He exhaled, and smiled. "You know Osax… I don't think I've told you how much of an honour it's been working with you, and getting to know you. You've been a real inspiration to me… the way you have taken the loss of your home in stride. It's unbelievable, the strength you have. Truly. I've been lucky to know you."

I lifted my ears, cautiously. "You too, Jonathan. I don't think I got the chance to tell you just how brave you were, fighting atop the Firebrand." I locked eyes with him. "That was heroic stuff."

He frowned. "I don't know about heroic," he said. Then he reached into his long coat and retrieved my pistol. He handed it to me. "I forgot to return this to you earlier. I suppose you might need it."

I holstered the pistol. "Thanks, Jonathan. I'm glad it fell into good hands."

"Well, I had to pry it from bad ones," he said.

He turned away and squatted, looking for more stones. I eyed him carefully.

"Do you believe in destiny?" he asked.

I paused. An interesting question. But given the dramatic scale of our mission, I could understand what prompted the thought. I took a long look out into the blackness of the cave, then back toward the light of the shaft.

"I don't know," I said. "It's hard to believe in destiny when so much bad happens. But at the same time, sometimes badness leads to good. Is everything predetermined? I don't think so. But does that mean everything is just pure, indifferent chaos?" I paused. "I like to think of life as something a little random and a bit unpredictable, but in a magnificent kind of way. Just looking at all the strange creatures and planets out there. In the face of it all, I like to think that we are more than just actors following a script. I like to think that we choose our own destiny."

He stood up. "I used to think that," he said.

"And now what do you think?"

He frowned. "I think that destiny is like a net of flowing rivers, each heading to a certain fate." His robotic eye twisted. "They connect in certain places, and they separate, and the water eases up in areas and constricts into rapids in others. You are always given a choice of what direction to swim, with or against the flow. But if you miss a fork in the river... you may find yourself stuck being propelled downstream." He looked up behind me. "And perhaps sometimes, the stream leads to a waterfall. And try as you might, unless you're an angel, you have no wings to carry you from the abyss."

I followed his gaze to the TAU shuttle which was descending into the cave. It was sleek, silver, and its landing gear was extended. Their engine whined to a halt as they touched down on the surface next to the Firebrand and sent tiny creatures fleeing into the water.

"Looks like they're here early," I said, lifting my ears.

"Indeed," said Jonathan. "Get the others… tell Joëlle to prep the ship. I'm sure we'll want to leave as soon as possible, now that they're here."

I nodded to him. "Sounds good. And thanks, Jonathan, for the kind words."

He smiled.

"Go on," he replied. "I'll greet them."

Forty

"The TAU soldiers are just organizing before they leave the shuttle." I said. "Jonathan suggested that you get the ship prepped for takeoff while we all meet them outside."

Joëlle gave me a confused look. "Immediately? I know we're on a time crunch, but I'd rather us all go out and meet the reinforcements." She smirked. "Besides, as Omega so kindly pointed out, I'm the highest ranking TAU member around. I should be there to greet them."

I shrugged. "I agree. Jonathan just wanted me to pass that along."

"Alright. Go get K, Omega and I will head outside."

I nodded. Omega stood up from their seat in the kitchen and dusted themselves off gracefully. The colour had returned to their skin and they looked fine, as though their arm hadn't even been touched by K. Joëlle was wearing her jumpsuit but opted to leave her weapons inside. The two of them marched out of the ship, and I walked into the room with K.

She was sitting at the desk next to the bunk beds, fully geared up with her grey cloak and armoured vest over her dark leather jacket. Her gaze was low.

I stepped up to her, and realized I had forgotten to return her communicator until now. I reached into my pocket and retrieved the earpiece, handing it to her. "I meant to return this," I said.

She looked at it, surprised for a moment. "But, I threw that..." She trailed off. She took it lazily, and fit it to her ear. "...Thanks." She turned away from me.

"The TAU are here," I said quietly. "Want to come out and meet them?" I asked.

She sighed. "What's the point?" she asked. "Probably better if I stay inside."

I squinted my eyes. "What's the matter?" I asked.

"Nothing," she said. "I'm..." She closed her eyes.

I waited for her to continue.

"I'm sorry," she said, "for earlier. For lashing out."

I sat down on the bunk facing her. The ship hummed faintly.

"You apologized," I said.

She snorted. "Yeah, don't expect it to happen again though." She crossed her arms and looked away from me.

"No, I mean… Thank you." I said. "But you were- are- right to be upset with me."

She sighed. "That's why I hate apologies." She flung her hands into the air. "You already said sorry, but I'm still kinda… hating you right now. And now I feel bad for being angry, because you said you were sorry, and I should forgive you, and I thought I could, but I don't know, it's complicated! You're kind of my only friend."

She frowned. I looked away from her.

"But you lied to me," she said, "you said you could save me, and had me going along with the stupid medicine thing like an idiot… But I *know* you were doing it to make me feel safe, so I should feel grateful, but instead I just feel betrayed."

"Honestly, I think you should be feeling exactly what you're feeling right now," I said. "I apologized to you because I regret what I did, and I care about you, and I wanted you to know that. I didn't do it because I thought it would instantly fix everything. Everything you just said makes sense."

She shook her head, and clenched her fists. She began to growl. "But I broke Omega's arm!" She put her face in her hands, clawing at her horns. "The only reason you and Joëlle let that go is because of Omega's surprise regeneration powers. If it had been someone else… how do you think you'd be looking at me right now?"

My ears lowered. "You're right. K... what you did was awful. You could kill someone if you aren't more careful-"

"I know! I fucked up!"

"You did!" I said. "But people do that! People mess up, sometimes really badly! You did... and I did too... So we have to do better. We have to *be* better now. And hope that our team mates can learn to trust us again."

She groaned, slowly rocking in her seat. "How do I start being better?" she asked.

"Maybe start by going and telling Omega how you feel. And yes... in this case, maybe apologizing would be beneficial. Hopefully, that will be enough for them to forgive you, eventually.”

K curled up even tighter. “Yeah. Okay.”

My chest tightened. I placed a hand on her shoulder. “K… come on out with me to meet the reinforcements. It would be good for you. You’re part of the team.”

“But you don’t need me,” she said, shakily. “You’d be better off without me.” Her voice was breaking. I’d never seen her like this before.

“K?” I said. “Are you okay?”

“No I’m not okay!” she exclaimed through clenched teeth. “From the day I was made, I’ve never been okay!”

I didn’t know what to say. She fumed, quivering in a mess of anger and sadness and panic.

“What have I contributed to the team?” She asked. “Think about it. I haven’t done anything. I’ve been nothing but a pain in the ass, that no one wants around.”

“That’s not true,” I said. “We all want you here-”

“But what have I done to help?” she sobbed, lifting her face from her hands for a moment to look me in the eye. “What good have I done?”

My eyes darted between hers. “Back on Voren, you helped fight off the valicorr. You helped keep people alive.”

“Back on Voren!” she cried. “Back on Voren I blacked out in the middle of driving you to the ruins. I broke part of the vehicle- Hell, I destroyed the ruins and almost got you killed!” Tears streamed down her face, and she inhaled sharply. Her orange eyes were damp and reflective. “I broke the weapons on the Firebrand… I crushed your hand! And- And…”

She screwed her eyes shut. I rubbed her shoulder as she covered her eyes with her hands.

“It’s okay,” I said. I tried to be as soothing as possible.

She kept crying. “I couldn’t even help you in the jungle. And I just… I ran away and then my stupid blackout happened. I couldn’t even do anything about it… I can never do anything about it. That’s how useless I am.”

I felt tears forming in my eyes as I stared at K. “K, It’s not your fault that you have blackouts-”

“I can’t imagine what danger you went through,” she said, “just to save me. But I don’t know why you even bothered, since I’m just going to die anyway!”

“K…” I said.

"For a while there I believed you," she said. "I thought for once I had a chance at a normal life, after all of this danger passed. I thought you could cure me. It was too good to be true! And it was. I never was going to be cured. I've always known, deep down, I was born to die."

I stared at her face deeply.

"Sometimes," she said, "I think about dying, and I wonder why it hasn't happened already. Sometimes, I think it would be better if I didn't exist at all."

I pulled my hand away from her slowly. She sobbed into her hands, shaking in utter despair. Every few seconds she paused, inhaling, as if she were going to speak, only to violently cry. I gazed at her solemnly as my insides twisted into knots.

"I wouldn't know what to do if you died, K. You're one of *my* only friends."

"Well it's going to happen," she said, lowering her hands to her lap. "Even if I make it through until Duhrnan's attack, do you really think we're going to stop him? We're all probably going to die. You know that."

I grabbed her hands, and squeezed them tightly. She looked down at them, then into my eyes. "Probably isn't definitely," I said. "And I thought you lived for a challenge? For excitement?"

"I don't know what I live for," she said. The crying began to subside.

"You... don't need to," I said.

"Why do you even care about me, when Omega is part of the team now? They are so damn perfect at everything."

I shook my head. "But Omega isn't you."

"But Omega can do so much more than me. And they know why they're alive. To stop the Brotherhood. Even if I knew what I was supposed to do, I don't think I could do a very good job of it."

I squeezed K's hands, and stared into her damp eyes. Seconds passed in silence. Her lips were curved downwards. Her brows were furrowed slightly.

"You're right about one thing, K." I said bluntly. "You are going to die. So am I. We all are. And no one knows, not even you, when, or how. Maybe the doctors on Voren were right, and maybe you've got an incurable genetic ailment. Maybe you're going to get killed on this mission. And I don't want to think about that moment. But you knew that when you agreed to come along. You were maybe the most excited about the mission. And here's the important thing... You are alive."

She lowered her eyes, breathing heavily.

"You are alive!" I exclaimed. "Right now, you're alive. And now is all we have. It isn't over until it's over, right?"

"Right..."

"Promise me you won't give up," I said.

She looked me in the eye. "But-"

"I won't give up on you," I said, "So neither can you. Not until Duhrnan is stopped."

"Osax," she said. "I don't know if I can…" She pulled her hands away.

"You know," I said. "You know you can." I offered my hand for her to shake.

She sighed.

She lifted her hand slowly. "You promise you won't give up on me?" she said.

"I promise," I said.

"And you won't lie to me for any reason?"

I shook my head. "I won't."

"Even to make me feel better?" She asked, an eyebrow raised.

"I won't lie to you," I said. "Prince's honour."

"King's honour," she said.

Her words stung, though I didn't think that was her intention. I hesitated briefly, then replied.

"King's honour," I repeated.

"Alright." She grasped my hand, and took a deep breath. "I will not give up until Durhnan is stopped." She shook my hand. "But," she said slyly, "I can reconsider if there's a point in life afterwards."

I lifted my ears. "So you do have some hope."

She smirked. "I figure, as long as one of us has it, we should be good. Let's get outside."

Forty-One

"Finally," said Joëlle.

Steam hissed from the ramp of the silver TAU shuttle, parked just beside the Firebrand. The blue glow of the crystals lining the cavern bounced off the ship's hull and the damp surface of the stone landing. Joëlle stood powerfully with her chest held high. She looked relieved. K and I fell into position beside her, exchanging glances with the others. Omega's bare feet splashed into a puddle, though they didn't seem to mind, and they contorted into a side stretch before straightening out once again with a gently flicking tail. Jonathan's eyes bounced between the ground and the ramp as he paced back and forth a few feet from us. He bit his lip. I caught K frowning, but when she noticed me looking she flashed me a smirk.

We all watched the shuttle's ramp hit the stone, and armoured boots marched down out of the ship.

One by one, twenty marines walked onto the platform. They were each covered in sky-blue armour, similar in design to Joëlle's, though she wasn't wearing hers at the time. The cavern echoed with heavy footsteps. They marched out in formation and formed a semi-circle around us. They each held a rifle in their hands, pointed to the sky and close to their bodies. They were fully prepared for combat. They each looked so similar in appearance, I began to wonder if they had a leader.

"Marines," said Joëlle. "Welcome to Malum."

She took a step toward them confidently. "Where is your captain?" she asked. "I'd like to speak with them."

Everyone was still. The only thing that moved aside from the falling water was a small creature which skittered into the pool.

Joëlle smirked. "At ease, soldiers. I take my job seriously, but I'm not a hardass."

The marines remained motionless.

I started to feel queasy.

"Hello?" I asked.

K and I exchanged glances. She looked just as confused as me.

"Perhaps they were not made to speak," said Omega, glancing to Joëlle.

"Um..." said Jonathan uneasily.

Joëlle scanned their helmets, frowning. "Well if being casual isn't your thing… I order you to speak! Where is your captain? Tell me."

After a moment of silence, one of the soldiers spoke up. Their voice was cold. "Now, sir?"

"Yes," said Joëlle. "Now."

The soldier's head turned slightly. He hadn't been speaking to Joëlle.

"Now," said Jonathan.

Suddenly the air was punctuated by the sound of energy rifles being armed. The TAU soldiers aimed their guns at us. Each barrel began to glow a faint red. Joëlle stumbled back in shock. Omega's eyes narrowed. K gasped. And Jonathan calmly retreated to the shadows.

"Nobody move!" one of the soldiers shouted.

I was petrified. Twenty guns were trained on us… all of us except Jonathan. I looked at his face; his lip was perfectly straight, his eyes blank- *almost* blank- as he looked at us. We met eyes, and his lip twitched. He clenched his jaw and furrowed his brow.

Joëlle followed my gaze, and the look on her face was nothing but heartbreaking confusion. "Jonathan?" she asked quietly, but couldn't say any more.

He screwed his eyes shut, and turned his face away.

K looked to me for answers. "What the hell..."

Omega faced Jonathan. "You are a liar," they said. "You told Joëlle you called the TAU. You did not." Their skin seemed to sparkle and shift hues, getting warmer.

I didn't know what to say.

"But," said K, "The uniforms!"

"...Just a disguise," I said at last. I saw the TAU symbol on their armour, sure enough. But Omega was right. These weren't the TAU.

A knot was tightening in my stomach. There was only one thing this could mean, though I didn't want to believe it. There was no other explanation. They were all members of the Brotherhood.

And so was Jonathan.

My head was spinning. Jonathan betrayed us. He had been spying on us for the entire journey. Where had I first met him anyway? In the generator room of the TAU facility on Voren. *Of course.*

"The Brotherhood is working with the valicorr," I said. "Aren't you, Jonathan?"

Joëlle looked at me, wide eyed, then back to Jonathan. "You… You *are* with the Brotherhood, aren't you?" She sniffed.

"What?!" K cried. She bared her teeth. "You bastard!"

Jonathan winced. He paused. He inhaled. He opened his mouth to speak.

"*I trusted you!*" Joëlle screamed.

"Sir," said one of the soldiers, eerily calm. "What should we do with them?"

Jonathan hesitated. "Secure them, and the Firebrand. Bring them to the mothership… Duhrnan can decide their fate." He locked eyes with me, then looked down at the pistol on my hip. The one he had just returned to me. He took a deep breath. His eyes met mine once more. He frowned, and his voice was low. "It's too late now…"

I shook my head in disbelief, mandibles clenched. Even though I stood a few feet taller than all of the marines, I knew they could easily overpower me in this situation.

I had to suppress my spiralling thoughts about Jonathan. If I survived, there would be time to puzzle over it later. *Stay in the present moment!*

The soldiers slowly encroached upon us. K was frantic. Joëlle and Omega stood motionless.

"You're my friend, Jonathan," Joëlle said. "Aren't we friends?!"

He gulped, staring at her. "We weren't supposed to be."

"Drop your weapons, now!" shouted a marine. The glowing rifles were a good incentive to obey, but I had to think of something. I had to make a move.

But I didn't like my odds. Slowly, I removed the pistol from my holster. I looked to Jonathan.

"I don't know what you expect me to do," I said, bitterly. I cast the gun to the floor.

Joëlle simply raised her hands. She was already unarmed. Omega stayed motionless.

Three of the soldiers approached Omega. "Hey!" said one of them. "Drop your weapons, or we'll drop you!"

Then K roared. She bent forward, her horns aimed directly at Jonathan, and charged. She was more bull than human in that moment, though she reached down to her belt and grasped the hilt of her sword. With her other hand she drew the pistol holstered on her chest. Her cloak soared behind her as she closed the space between her and Jonathan before the marines had time to fire.

But Jonathan thrust his hand forward. He stepped back. His holo-gauntlet activated, and a holographic image appeared in front of his glove. Abstract patterns and symbols flashed on the display, and he held it in front of K's eyes. She slowed to a halt mere feet away from Jonathan, and dropped her weapons to the ground.

"I'm sorry, K. I didn't want it to come to this."

K's eyes glazed over, mesmerized by Jonathan's symbols.

My blood boiled. "What are you doing to her?!"

Two of the Brotherhood soldiers lunged for me. Each one grabbed one of my arms. Their rifles dug into my sides. They were about to do the same to Joëlle and Omega. The marines picked up my discarded weapons.

Jonathan gazed at K. "Just as a literate eye that sees words cannot refuse to hear them in the mind… you must know what the symbols mean, K. You are awakened." Despite the gravitas of his statement, he sounded defeated.

I struggled against my captors, and the marines grabbed Joëlle. Jonathan powered down his gauntlet.

K slowly turned and looked to us. Her expression was blank.

"N-No," I stuttered. A chill rippled down my spine, and I felt my body begin to shake with anxiety. K wasn't herself anymore. She wasn't human anymore. She was just a weapon. She had been activated.

But I didn't have any more time to think when Omega sprang into action. The three marines harassing Omega were almost touching them when they thrust both hands and their tail to the underside of each soldier's barrel. The guns fired too late: their bolts soared harmlessly through the air, and Omega wrenched the rifles from their hands in a swift motion and cast them away. Without a moment's hesitation, Omega withdrew two grenades from their shoulder-belt, armed them, and tossed them to our attackers and their parked ship.

I blinked as flames erupted. People shouted all around. My body was engulfed in heat. The ground shook, and everyone stumbled into plumes of dust, smoke, and steam. The marines let go of my arms, and a second later the stolen TAU shuttle, which was caught in the initial blast, hissed. It cracked and flashed, sending chunks of charred metal through the air. The hull was replaced with thunderous fire, and the air was clouded with debris.

My nostrils were filled with smoke and the smell of burning plastic. Red energy bolts arced through the dust, and Omega was hit twice. But still they managed to leap safely somewhere out of view. I ducked low to the ground, and stumbled on all fours toward K through the smoke. I had no idea what to do, but getting to her seemed like a good idea.

The stones continued to rumble. I collapsed, and came face to face with a Brotherhood soldier who had fallen onto his hands. He looked up at me through a broken visor, our faces only a foot apart. I could see only anger in his eyes. No fear. He scrambled to his feet, ready to shoot, but I lunged for his rifle.

My fingers wrapped around the barrel and stock of his gun, and I pulled and spun with all of my weight. I knocked him off balance and threw him to the side. The rifle was in my hands.

Out of the corner of my eye, I saw Joëlle being forced back to the Firebrand with half of the marines aiming their weapons at her. I was about to change course and run to her when Jonathan's voice pierced my mind.

"Stop Omega!" said Jonathan. "Subdue them!"

I spun around. K and Jonathan were standing meters away from each other, and not far from me. Soldier's bodies lay near them, dead, killed instantly from the grenades.

K turned toward Jonathan slowly. He frowned.

"K! Stop Omega!" he commanded, pointing into the smoke.

I took a step forward, and the earth groaned beneath me. Everything shook, and I caught myself with both hands on the wet stone. I looked up to see K and Jonathan stabilizing themselves, still standing.

K's voice was robotic. "I have my orders," she said.

"Osax!" Joëlle's voice called out from behind me. I spun around. The Firebrand's ramp hissed closed, with her inside, held by the marines. Then the engines flared to life, and it rose up out of view. But the cave was still shaking. Shards of glowing crystal splintered and rained down the shaft of the cavern, bouncing off my back like hail.

"Then follow your orders!" Jonathan said. "Stop Omega!"

A boulder fell from the cavern and breached the surface of the pool. I flinched as a huge clap of water splashed up into the air. A spray of thick droplets pelted my back. The cave was collapsing.

"You," K said, "are not my master."

"What?!" Jonathan cried. "I *made* you!" His face was a mix of terror and outrage. He was beginning to panic.

K took a step toward him, and he kept his distance.

I began to cough uncontrollably. My eyes stung from the smoke.

"K, stop!" he shouted, his voice breaking. "What are you doing?!"

K advanced, raising her hands. She glanced at the pale-blue ridges jutting from her knuckles. "The Director said you know too much," she said. She curled her hands into fists.

The ground shook once more and I fell face first on the ground. The wind was knocked out of me. The rifle slipped from my fingers and clattered away. I looked up, struggling to breathe. Jonathan yelped. Helplessly, he fell onto his back. He winced in pain. K lost balance, but stayed upright. A large stone careened toward her from above, but before it could hit her she forced her fist through it, smashing it to dust with ease. The brunt of the tremor passed, and her gaze fell to him. He was frozen with fear. She stepped above him, and lifted her fists above her head. She was going to kill him.

"Just do it, then!" Jonathan spat, shaking. "End this already!"

Crack.

Just in time, I grabbed the rifle and fired at K's shoulder. Her fists slammed limply to the floor as her body smacked onto the ground. Smoke rose from her shoulder. I exhaled. Jonathan's eyes were wide with shock as his gaze followed the energy bolt's trail back to the glowing tip of the rifle in my outstretched hands. He was unharmed.

I mustered all of my energy and charged for Jonathan, dropping the still fuming rifle. I grabbed him by the arms and dragged him onto his feet, pulling him into the darkness away from the landing pad and into the shadowy cavern. I glanced back, since there was no use in looking forward into the abyss; it was too dark to see anyway. The smoke was clearing. The TAU shuttle was in pieces. The Firebrand was gone. Omega was nowhere to be seen. And K's body, strewn between the corpses of the Brotherhood agents, shifted. She began to slowly rise. Her orange eyes seemed to glow in the cavern.

Then the roof shuddered, and stones crashed violently to the floor, sealing the light out, and me and Jonathan in.

Forty-Two

The dust and shaking settled long before the two of us stopped coughing. It was utterly dark, save for a few tiny shards of blue crystal on the floor, but even their glow seemed to be dimming, as though their luminescent energy was drawn from the walls of the mountain shaft. The only other light was the dim red glow of Jonathan's cybernetic eye. It was a tiny spot in the black void that surrounded us.

Jonathan and I stood next to each other, trying to catch our breaths. I wanted to activate the light from my holo-gauntlet, but I hesitated. I didn't know if I could look him in the face right now.

I was reeling. Jonathan had betrayed us. He had been part of the Brotherhood all along. How had I not seen it before?

The air was musty and stale down here. With the shaft closed behind us, I wondered about how much air we would have. For all I knew the cave system branched out into multiple exits, but perhaps not. If not, then we wouldn't be able to stay there forever, or we would run out of oxygen…

The oxygen recycler! Back in the nebula, when we were aboard the Firebrand our oxygen recycler was damaged. But right after Jonathan left the cockpit, it got worse…

"You took advantage of the damaged oxygen recycler, and sabotaged it further, didn't you?" I asked. My voice was low and calm, though I didn't bother trying to hide my anger.

Jonathan's arm began to glow as he activated the lighting system on his holo-gauntlet. We were illuminated in a small sphere of white light coming from his wrist, casting long shadows on the walls. I could see Jonathan's breath puffing into tiny clouds.

His eyes met mine briefly, before he looked away and sighed. He sat down on a boulder next to the caved in wall. He kept his eyes trained on the floor, and began to slow his breathing.

"Yes," he said at last. "I did."

I stared at him. Weakly I gestured with my arms, before turning away from him, shaking my head.

"That's why you wanted to fix it yourself. You knew that one of us might have noticed the sabotage. That's why-" I smacked myself in the forehead. "Of course. You didn't want to meet my mother… because you knew you couldn't hide your thoughts from her. She would have found out that you were part of the Brotherhood, and she would have exposed you."

I balled my fists. My heart quickened in anger.

"What the hell did you do to K?!" I exploded in rage, and spun to face him. He looked up at me in alarm. I expected him to be defensive, but instead he just looked ashamed.

He was with the Brotherhood. He betrayed us. He was in league with Duhrnan. He let my planet be destroyed. He let billions of people die. My body began to shake.

Then my arms went slack. My eyes glazed over. I remembered the look in Jonathan's face when Astraloth had been destroyed. He had been crying. It was the first time I had seem him look so distraught, but not the last. Ever since then he had appeared exhausted, tormented by something. He hardly slept. There was something he couldn't share, because it meant telling us what he had done. What he had let happen.

I still couldn't trust him.

I knelt down beside him and grabbed his coat. Before he could do more than exclaim in surprise, I reached into his jacket and retrieved his E-pistol. He didn't bother trying to fight me for it. I took a few steps back, and held the gun at my side, powered off and aimed at the floor. He glanced at me, his eyes shifting between my face and the gun.

"If you are going to try killing me," he coughed, "then why did you save me from K?"

My ears lowered. "I don't want to kill you."

"Because you want answers?" He asked.

I shut my eyes, and took in a deep breath. I breathed it all out, then opened my eyes and holstered his gun on my hip. "You were my friend, Jonathan."

He pursed his lips. He ran his fingers through his spiked hair, and looked away from me. His hands were gloved, as usual.

He had been wearing gloves when I first met him, in the generator room on Voren. He claimed that he had been trying to restore power, but… He was the Head of Biology at the station. The bio-labs were on the lower levels of the facility, far away from the generator. Why would he have been there? How could he have gotten there so fast after the attack, unless he had been there before the attack started?

The generator is so essential to the station, it's probably the most well guarded room in the whole place. It's got three shielded doors, and if an unauthorized breach is detected in any one of them, then the Director is immediately notified. I remembered K's words. And I remembered how the doors were ajar, with only minor weapon damage. I didn't consider it then, but the damage to the doors was superficial. It certainly wasn't enough to open them. It was probably caused by a small weapon, like an E-pistol. And besides, if the doors were breached, then the Director would have been notified like K said. If the Director had been aware of the breach, he probably wouldn't have waited around to be killed in the control room. I found his body just feet away from his station; he had been killed while he worked, trying to maintain control during the power outage.

No. Jonathan had opened the doors to the generator room himself. As Head of Biology he clearly was in a high class at the outpost; he must have gotten authorization to enter the generator room. He wore gloves so that when he handled the door controls, or anything for that matter, his fingerprints wouldn't be found. And he gave the doors a few blasts with his pistol after opening them to make it appear as though they had somehow been damaged. He had removed the power cells, only two, making sure to break the circuit and cut off power to the entire base. He did it with a surgical precision befitting his position.

He looked at me, as if to say "I know what you're thinking." I blinked in the dim light. I took a moment and activated my own holo-gauntlet's light, just in case he decided to cut the lights and try to surprise me in the dark. But gazing at him, he didn't seem like he was about to make a move against me. He just looked tired. So tired.

He had said only moments ago, before the collapse, that he made K. Whatever he meant, it was clear now… Fiona's suspicions were correct. K was a sleeper agent; a bioweapon created by the Brotherhood. But how did the TAU find K, and bring her to Voren? And more importantly, why?

Don't be stupid, Osax! I thought. That was the story I had been given, yes, but there was no proof that it was the truth. I was beginning to doubt just about everything I knew.

I figured that Jonathan wasn't about to attack me, and with him now disarmed just to be safe, I wasn't afraid. So I began to pace a few meters away from him as he sat against the wall. His eyes followed me warily.

"Who was the Director K mentioned?" I asked.

Jonathan hesitated. "I… am not certain."

"Come on. Who do you think she meant?"

"She… must have been referring to Aali."

"I knew it! And those Brotherhood soldiers that were pretending to be part of the TAU… that was real TAU gear, wasn't it?"

Jonathan nodded.

"The Brotherhood has infiltrated the TAU. For how long?" I waved my hand aside. "Forget it… that doesn't matter right now. But the base on Voren… it was being run by Director Aali, a member of the Brotherhood, right under the noses of the TAU. And you- How many of the people there were part of the Brotherhood?"

Jonathan coughed, and cleared his throat. "Not everyone. Some of the people were what they appeared to be. Members of the Terran Astral Union. And in a way, so were we all. Just, some of us had other obligations."

"I don't understand… if the Brotherhood was pulling the strings there, then why didn't you ensure only Brotherhood spies were stationed there? Wouldn't having outsiders put your operations at risk?"

Jonathan nodded. "Yes, it was risky. But, you're not considering the whole picture." He stood up slowly. "If, to continue your analogy, the Brotherhood is pulling the strings, then so too is the TAU. Even with the TAU infiltrated, we never had direct control of everything, including personnel assignments and the like. If we are all puppeteers, Brotherhood and TAU alike, then it would be dangerous to take too much control of any one part of the stage… not until ensuring that we held all of the puppets."

I growled. "The TAU aren't puppeteers. The TAU is built on trust, and open communication."

Jonathan frowned and shook his head. "I'm afraid you don't know what you're talking about, Osax."

"What do you mean?"

"I mean it's not a story where they're the angels and we're the demons. The TAU aren't saints. No one is."

"Still," I said, "how did you manage to keep the Brotherhood secret on Voren?"

"Actually, it's precisely because not everyone was in on it. When the higher-ups of the TAU took a look at our facility, they engaged with those who knew what we wanted them to know about it. But, for the most part, not with us. If you look at ten people, and five of them are being truthful, and the other five are not, but they all appear to be working towards the same goals… How can you tell them apart? Genuine, oblivious people only strengthen the validity of those who hide in the shadows. If you were to notice a contrast in behaviour, you might simply attribute discrepancies to personality. You might say, 'Oh, she isn't so talkative'." He lowered his gaze. "Besides, everyone has secrets. Anyone reasonable knows it. And if you know everyone has secrets, how can you tell the harmless secrets from the nefarious? Well if you want to be a good leader, you treat everyone with the same respect. And if most of your people have no hidden agenda, then for the most part, you won't see one."

I was in near-disbelief. "The Director arranged for our transport in the snow, just before the attack," I said. "We were attacked in the snowfields by a massive creature, something we weren't warned about or prepared for. We didn't have weapons appropriate for such an encounter. And our communicator was malfunctioning. Do you think…"

I didn't know why I was asking Jonathan, as if we were in this together. He had betrayed us all. But he looked concerned.

"It's possible," he said, "that the Director had been ordered to eliminate you."

My spine tingled. "Ordered by whom?"

"Ryner."

"Ryner?" I asked. "Who is that?"

"He is the leader of the Brotherhood," he said. "He's the one who gave me the order to let the station get attacked."

"So it was you," I said.

He shut his mouth, and nodded solemnly. His voice seemed frail. "He said to make sure the Director was killed in the attack. I informed the valicorr of where he would be…"

I stared at him, dumbfounded. "But if you were all members of the Brotherhood, why would this Ryner guy want you to kill Aali?"

Jonathan looked away. "The same reason that he wanted Aali to kill me," he said.

"What?"

"That must be why K tried to kill me," he said, a look of sudden revelation spreading across his face. "K was told I knew too much… that's exactly how Ryner described Director Aali to me. It's the justification he gave to me for letting him die. Ryner must have told Aali to have K kill me. I wouldn't have seen it coming." He frowned. "I... didn't see it coming."

"But," I said, slowly piecing it together, "if the Director was going to use K to kill you, why would he send her with me on the expedition- the expedition which he had rigged to kill me? If Aali wanted K to kill you, then he wouldn't have wanted K to die with me in the hover-car." I paused. "K couldn't have killed you if she was dead." I said bluntly.

"True," said Jonathan. "But, the Director and I were somewhat... rivals. I never liked him, and he hated me. But he especially hated K... he only kept her around because I refused to let her die."

"You?" I said, surprised. "You protected K?"

He nodded. "Aali saw an opportunity to get rid of her and sent K to her death with you. Or so he must have planned. He must have released the monster and set it after you. And, likely, with K gone he would have used that as an excuse to deal with me in a more... personal manner." Jonathan grimaced. "He did like taking things into his own hands. But I let him die first..."

"So... wait, wait, wait." I said. "Ryner, the leader of the Brotherhood, tried to get you both to kill each other?"

Jonathan stared at me intensely. "Yes. I should have known I meant nothing to him."

I paused for a moment. "You... you have a lot of explaining to do," I said.

Jonathan appeared apprehensive.

I walked over to the rocks and sat down.

"Uh," he said, "shouldn't we try to find a way out?"

"No," I said. "Take a seat."

He paused, then walked over beside me and sat down on a crumbling stone.

I continued. "Why did you do it?"

He was silent.

"Why did you betray us?" I looked him in the eye. "Why did you join the Brotherhood?"

I felt a strange excitement swelling in me.

Was I really so driven by curiosity? The man had betrayed my trust, he was involved in the deaths of countless people and allowed many more to be killed through his inaction. He twisted K's mind with his holo-gauntlet, turning her into a puppet of the Brotherhood by activating some suppressed part of her brain. He had been sabotaging our every move, hadn't he? And yet I was excited to hear him talk. I couldn't help myself… the search for truth was too compelling. And I had a feeling I was about to get the answers to many of my burning questions.

He looked away, and carefully removed his gloves. He slowly adjusted his robotic eye, and did up his coat. Despite all that he had done, somehow looking at his face, a face I had put so much trust in, I could see the humanity in him. We sat together, uncomfortable in the cold, rocky cave, huddling by our dim lights. At last he spoke.

This is what he said.

Forty-Three

I always looked up to my father.

William Wellsworth. He was a strong man. Indeed, both strong of heart and body. He had the most fashionable moustache too… Bushier than mine; though I inherited some of his good looks, I wasn't blessed with such thick facial hair…

Sorry.

I know it's- It seems weird to be talking about this. But if I'm going to tell you what happened… Well, you have to understand, I loved and admired my father, more than anyone in the world.

He was an example of the perfect dad, at least that's how I felt. He had a hearty laugh, was well-dressed, well-spoken… Whenever he gave me a hug, he gave me the tightest squeeze he could. He said he would give no less to his little girl. Of course I told him I was a boy, like him. He asked me if I was serious, and I was. He told me to talk to him about it if I still felt like a boy the next day.

Well I did. And I wasn't too old before I realized that being a boy wasn't about being like him… It was just about being myself. But he was so accepting; he told me about people he knew who were transgender, and non-binary. He told me that as I got older I could make more decisions about what I wanted for my body. He was so accepting… more than many of my peers. And of course, I took those opportunities to have the body I wanted and present the identity I knew I had. It was so freeing to be me, Jonathan. I always wanted to be like my dad, but that was just about being me. Of course, it did make me feel lucky that people started comparing us more after the transition. I liked that. It was a nice perk.

He was also a soldier. He worked with the Terran Astral Union. He was strong and skilled and disciplined. He was so good, in fact, that he became involved in a special forces unit. Some people had recommended him for his fast learning, adaptability, and team-oriented nature.

I always wanted to be just like him. My mom loved him. Everyone loved him.

I'm getting distracted.

I followed in his footsteps and joined the TAU military when I was old enough. Cliché, I know. Though, I actually had a harder time deciding what I wanted in life than it sounds. To be honest, I've never really felt as though I've known. But doing this made sense to me. He was like... a beacon of honesty, and genuine goodness. He was a hero in my eyes. He fought for the good of us all, and he never let it get to him.

I also thought I might get into science, and study biology, because I'm fascinated by life and all its forms. Also, my mother was a bio-engineer, so she liked to teach me things. After my surgery, I became curious about what technology we humans had developed to manipulate our bodies for medical, or cosmetic reasons. What other ways could we influence life? These bodies we have are just crude vessels for our souls; that's what my mom would have said, anyway. She was a bit of a poet.

That led me down some very interesting paths studying gene manipulation, psychology, enigmatic creatures... among other things. But all the while I continued on my path to become a marine. I wanted to be a good man, like my father.

◆

By the time I was working as a special forces member, my dad had retired and was living with my mom in a colony on the planet RS833. Colloquially known as Rose. I didn't spend much time with them those days. This was only a few years ago now.

It was around that time that I lost my eye, during an attack on the colony. We were trying to defend-

Actually, that part isn't important, as traumatic as it was. You already know I got a cybernetic replacement. No one I knew was hurt during the attack, not my parents anyway, and I didn't think much of the situation at the time. It was a small colony, and it was upsetting that the valicorr had attacked. But it wasn't unusual.

A few weeks later, and my team got a classified message from high command. Apparently the attack unearthed some information about illegal activities taking place at the colony. And the public was not happy.

In all of the reporting of the valicorr raid, it was revealed that there was a weapon being developed in a secret research lab at the colony... a weapon of mass destruction, endorsed by the TAU. High command claimed they knew nothing of the project, and that it was being funded using stolen credits. There were connections between some of the colonists and the research and development project... including my mother and father, who apparently were working on this weapon in secret, or at least working with the people who were creating it.

The weapon? It was the Shade Beam, though it never came to fruition. It was an earlier version that was never completed. The aim was still the same: to create a weapon that could destroy an entire planet in the blink of an eye.

I was utterly broken. I couldn't believe that my parents were involved. It had to be a mistake. Why would they be working on this? Especially in secret? My father had gutted my trust... He was working on something outright evil. I admired him so much; I dedicated so much of my life to following in his footsteps. I couldn't understand why he would do this.

My world was shaken. But the worst was yet to come.

The message ended with our new orders: to destroy the colony and wipe out the 'terrorists.'

Did high command even know those were my parents they were asking me to kill? Did they even care? It was so hypocritical... so horrendous. They claimed they knew nothing of the project, but how could they be so blind? The colony was full of high-ranking TAU members. They must have known about the Shade Beam. But as soon as it became clear that the secret was out, that the weapons development was happening there, they flipped. They wanted to save face. And they must not have wanted the skythers to find out. To build such a weapon would defy the treaty between Astraloth and Earth. Yet they wanted to construct it. My parents had betrayed me, but the TAU had killed me.

We bombed the colony. There was nothing left but ashes and glass. No one survived.

I quit the team. The TAU said that they highly respected me and would love to have me back. I doubted I would return in any capacity. I decided to focus on science. I wanted to help people. I tried not to hate myself. My mother and father had been evil, hadn't they? I told myself that. It was the only comfort I had, and it offered me very little. The TAU said everyone living on that colony was evil. That they were terrorists involved in a plot to destroy civilization. But the TAU were heartless. They were just trying to cover themselves.

My grandfather was my only living relative. I spent a year with him, before he died, on his farm. He lived on Earth, in Norway. He was the only one I could talk to about my distrust of the TAU. We talked for hours about how backwards our entire civilization was. We talked about what true freedom would be like. We talked about how the common citizen of the TAU was blinded by false promises and distractions. We talked about how much better the world would be if everyone were free from the constraints of our corrupt government. And he shared with me a song that he sang, almost daily. It was a song of rebellion against the world order.

"Show me a place where the world never turns. Bring me the light of a star as it burns. Where nary a soldier is there to command, take me away to an anarchist's land.

"Show me a place where the people are free, the shackles of justice are nowhere to see. Break up the treaties and take up a stand. Pave me the way to an anarchist's land.

"Fight your commanders and fight for a voice, where governments distant aren't given the choice. Where all life is equal and no deaths are planned, live with me safe in an anarchist's land."

That song became my anthem of hatred for the TAU. It became my comfort that I was doing what was right. I continued to sing it long after my grandfather passed, and I was alone as the last Wellsworth.

◆

That's why I joined the Brotherhood. Because I had lost all faith in the TAU. I saw a corruptness in it that I couldn't unsee. I had done things under their orders that I couldn't undo.

When Ryner contacted me, I was skeptical. He said he knew what I had done. He said that he knew why I had done it. He said that he knew what was wrong with the TAU, and more importantly, he said he knew how to bring them down.

He asked me to join the Brotherhood. I said we would have to meet in person first. To my surprise, he agreed, and we took a long walk together, talking quietly about his group. He was young, and incredibly smart. He was pale, tall, and thin, with wispy hair and a clean face. He had a simmering menace to him… I didn't like him. But I agreed with what he was saying. It was time for the power-balance of the galaxy to shift. If the people were freed from the control of their rulers, then the world would be a better place.

I know it sounds insane now. Looking back… I don't know why I ever thought it was a good idea to help. I should have killed him then and there, had I known what I was getting into. It would have been a lesser evil than he would have me do. But he told me that he learned the TAU were restarting the Shade Beam project. That piqued my interest. And it made me so angry. How could they *dare?*

I wanted to stop them. I wanted to expose high command, but Ryner hushed me. He ensured me that playing the long game would be much more worth it. He told me about the base on Voren, and that his operatives had already acquired positions there. He said that there were enough members of the Brotherhood there to influence, and ultimately take control of the entire Shade Beam project. And he had a plan to influence the TAU to fast-track production of the full-scale super-weapon as they worked on the smaller prototypes on Voren.

The plan was to allow the TAU to create the Shade Beam… to help them even. To make the public see what their leaders were truly. And, in a worst case scenario, to take control of the Shade Beam and use their own weapon against them, threatening the galactic leaders to surrender their control.

Like a fool I agreed to help him, and he managed to secure me a spot as the Head of Biology at the base on Voren.

He assigned me a special project, noting my knowledge and skills regarding genetics. He wanted me to work on creating a bioweapon from cloned DNA, that could be grown and taught in as short a time as possible, and that could be imprinted with programming. Essentially, he wanted soldiers that could act as spies, unaware of their true allegiance until activation, at which point their true nature would be revealed and they would follow whatever orders they were given by their master. There were many layers to the task, but I was up for the challenge.

He said he trusted me, and would only give me orders if absolutely necessary. So, I started coming up with ways to fulfill his request. I knew a bioweapon would have to be strong, so that was my second goal, after working on accelerated growth and learning. To find a way to create a more powerful, more resilient clone of a creature. At first, we cloned the fauna of Voren, manipulating their DNA.

There were countless prototypes. Most of them failed, but with each success and failure I gained knowledge to apply to the next. Eventually I had figured out a way to manipulate myrok genes and create muscles of an unreasonable strength and durability.

Then my team started work on the final step. The ability to create a clone which, at the flick of a switch, could be completely controlled by its master. Ryner called it the "Sheep's Clothing" project. We knew we had to start working with human clones. I was so eager… I used my own DNA to begin the experiments.

K was one of them. The eleventh experiment. But not the last.

The Director at the base on Voren, Director Aali, was annoyed with my experiments. He didn't understand why I was given so much freedom at the station. He felt it was his duty to oversee operations and he should have been given more control over the bioweapon project, but Ryner wanted me to be in charge.

Of course, he was just using us both. He probably wanted us to resent each other, so that when he finally gave us the orders to eliminate one another… we would.

When K was awoken, she went into a panic. None of the previous experiments had survived. But her… she was alive, frantic, and emotional. She was tearing apart the lab, and I knew it was my duty to kill her. I held the gun in my hand, and aimed it at her. I almost pulled the trigger. But I just couldn't do it. I knew everything about this was wrong… The least I could do was give her a chance to live.

The Director was furious, but I convinced him to let K live at the station. We would fabricate a story for her, not far from the truth, saying the TAU had discovered her. The doctors on the station, most of whom were members of the Brotherhood, would train her, and watch over her. It was clear that she had a strong personality, but I assured the Director that keeping her alive would be more useful than having her killed. Really, I just couldn't bear to let her die. I felt responsible for her existence. I was responsible.

I was too responsible. I had to distance myself from her, so I made a point not to talk to her. Ever. But from early on it became clear that she suffered from random blackouts and headaches. I felt the pull to help her. But that feeling scared me. It was something like family, something I hadn't felt in years. It was terrifying and comforting and that made it all the worse. I kept my distance, and the other doctors did what they could. No one knew how to counteract the side-effects of her accelerated growth. And we very quickly determined that her lifespan, while unpredictable, was going to be very short. I was at once mortified and relieved to know that sooner rather than later, she would be gone, and I would be free of these distracting thoughts. *I must remain focused,* I thought. I wanted to be heartless, I had to be, so I numbed myself.

Ryner informed me that we would proceed with the "Sheep's

Clothing" tests on her. I reluctantly agreed, but I didn't oversee it. The only way it could work was if the "Sheep's Clothing" was integrated during the early phase of accelerated learning... it wouldn't have worked on a normal human.

I was given the trigger, a set of visuals which, when she saw them, would activate her. I never thought I would need to use it. I hoped she would get to spend the rest of her short life on Voren, oblivious to everything that was going on in the shadows. She was given jobs around the station to keep her busy. Surely, some of the TAU members there were genuine to her. But her life was a lie. And I was responsible for it.

Then one day, Ryner told me that the Brotherhood was working with the valicorr's new leader, Emperor Duhrnan. I was stunned, but he demanded that I believe him. He put me in direct contact with Duhrnan and his valicorr, and ordered me to coordinate a strike with them on the Voren base. I asked him why, and he said it was all part of the plan. Well, you were there. You know what happened.

I immediately regretted my actions when I disabled the generator. People were dying everywhere, and it was only because of me that it was happening. But I thought, some sacrifices must be made. That was the lie I told myself over and over again. The TAU wanted to create the Shade Beam. They had us destroy the colony on Rose. The one comfort I had was knowing that once the valicorr retrieved the plans for the Shade Beam, they would retreat. I made sure only to minimally disable power to the facility... I would need to restore it to ensure that the secret labs where I conducted my experiments stayed powered after the attack.

It seemed ridiculous to allow an enemy to steal the Shade Beam... if we wanted to use it, why didn't we do so ourselves? Well, Ryner believed it was always better to remain hidden, he said. Duhrnan seizing control of the Shade Beam meant exposing the TAU's involvement in its creation, which would destabilize people's faith in the TAU. Astraloth and the skythers would be outraged, as would most humans. And Ryner informed me that he had a plan to betray Duhrnan when the time was right. That was when we would reveal ourselves... the world would see the error of the TAU, and they would see the heroism of the Brotherhood. We would be revered as saviours, and with galactic faith in us, we would tear down the old societies and build something new. Something free. So when he had me disable the facility, he also had me send Duhrnan the access codes to the top secret research labs.

Of course I see now just how twisted and backwards it all was. Somehow, that day on Voren, I forced myself to still hold onto the belief that the Brotherhood was right. But it wasn't. The Brotherhood is even worse than the TAU.

I met you and Joëlle, and re-acquainted myself with K. When you were leaving Kronos, I followed you to make sure you didn't find out too much, or if you did, to eliminate you. I was still following Ryner's orders. I was meant to keep us close to Duhrnan, to make sure he wasn't going to betray his alliance with the Brotherhood, but also to keep a far enough distance that you wouldn't be able to find out we were involved. He must have considered offing me in some other way since the Director had failed, but when I told him about you and your interest in tracking the mothership, he decided I could still be useful a while longer.

Yes, I knew exactly where the mothership was then. I made sure we stayed close behind it at all times, close enough that I could intervene if Ryner gave the order, but far enough that you couldn't discover anything of the plot. That is until Duhrnan decided to attack the Titan-class warship. The distress signal messed me up. I didn't know what to do. Duhrnan got away with killing those people.

I should have done something different. But I don't know what we could have done against the mothership anyway.

I suggested we bring K along, not because I thought I'd need to activate her… simply because I-

I wanted to get to know her. I was already feeling conflicted.

Each day I spent on the Firebrand I felt closer to the three of you. There was a wholeness, a goodness in each one of you that had been lacking in all of my companions for the last few years. It was a light from the happy life I had before the attack on Rose. I was beginning to doubt myself, but I knew I couldn't betray the Brotherhood. I had spent so long working with them. And I had already let the base on Voren be attacked, not to mention the experiments I had done. "Anarchist's Land" looped in my head, telling me I was on the right path. I didn't think I was. But as far as I was concerned, I was in too deep. If I betrayed them now, I would be a target. They would murder me. And if the reality I didn't want to face about the Brotherhood was true, and it was evil, I was far beyond the point of redemption; I was too involved. So I followed my orders. I kept sabotaging our mission, hoping all of it would end soon and maybe something good would come of it all.

But then, Duhrnan attacked Astraloth.

I couldn't-

I couldn't believe…

…

I'm sorry.

I- I'm so sorry.

For everything that happened.

Forty-Four

Jonathan's face was wet. I stared at him and felt my heart sink into my stomach. He was heaving as he sobbed, choking on his own tears. He really needed to cry.

I looked away from him. My gaze fell to the stony floor. I didn't know what to say.

I breathed in slowly through my nose, gently closing my eyes. I tried to ignore Jonathan's wailing sobs.

"Thank you for telling me all of that," I said at last.

Jonathan sniffed, and wiped some tears from his eye and snot from his nose. He moaned. Then, breathing heavily but slowly through his mouth, he began to calm down. He inhaled through his nose, and swallowed. Just as I thought he had regained his composure, his face contorted in sorrow. He bent over and cried.

"It's hopeless!" he wailed. "You should have let me die! You should have killed me!"

I grabbed him firmly by the shoulders, and jostled him a little. His weary eye met mine. "You don't mean that," I said, then thought for a moment. "The waterfall… it's just an illusion. There's still a path back from this. A river to the perfect destiny-"

"How can you believe that?" he replied, shaking. "After all that's happened? After everything I've done?!"

My eyes darted to the darkness. Jonathan gasped. Something had pulled our attention away; a sound of movement, something heavy sliding along the rocks down the cavern.

"Wh- What was that?" Jonathan whispered urgently, rising to his feet.

We shined our lights down the dark tunnel, activating the flashlight settings on our holo-gauntlets. Particles of dry sand clouded in the cones of light we waved ahead of us. Something was there in the darkness, and the sound was getting louder.

"I don't know," I said quietly. I raised the E-gun cautiously to my eye. Then I remembered my eyepiece.

"Wait." We both said it at the exact same time, and exchanged a look. Jonathan's orange eye stood out to me; I could see the resemblance to K in his face, now that I was thinking about it. She really was a genetically modified clone of Jonathan. But now wasn't the time to think about that. We each raised a hand to our faces, I to my headpiece and Jonathan to his cybernetic eye. Two clicks later, and my visor's scanners were active, and Jonathan had switched to thermal vision.

We both froze. My visor highlighted a creature in faint green. They were on all fours, humanoid, and lithe. They had a tail, which flicked slowly back and forth…

"Omega!" I shouted. I was filled with an overwhelming sense of relief.

That didn't last long. Omega sprung up toward us, and thrust their arm forward. A yellow glow flashed in the shadows, heading straight toward us.

My furred ears shot back, and a bolt of adrenaline hit me. Jonathan moved at the last second, but I watched in horror as Omega's plasma shuriken struck him in the face.

Yellow sparks erupted from the collision, and a sharp zap punctuated the air. He screamed and fell to the floor, clutching his head. The shuriken lodged in the rock wall behind Jonathan. And Omega sprinted toward us, retrieving another throwing weapon from their belt.

I felt nauseated. I saw Omega running for Jonathan. I planted my feet on the cold stones in front of him, and aimed the glowing barrel of my gun at Omega.

"Stop!" I shrieked through clenched mandibles.

Omega breached our sphere of light, and crouched. Their smooth face gazed up at me with squinted black eyes, even as they gripped the floor with both clawed feet, their tail, and one hand. The other was poised to attack with another plasma weapon.

I panted, and Jonathan groaned behind me. I didn't dare to turn away from Omega and check him yet. I knew how deadly Omega could be in a flash.

Omega's red tongue stuck out like a snake tasting the air. They remained completely motionless. I noticed their skin colour had shifted to a dark purple, with hints of their natural greenish colour. It seemed like some kind of partial camouflage. They moved their angular lips and spoke. "I am here to eliminate the Brotherhood. If any member of the Brotherhood remains, the chance for peace in the galaxy is zero percent." They looked at Jonathan, then back to me. They narrowed their eyes. "I must keep the peace."

"But wait!" I cried. "Please, don't attack Jonathan!" My heart was pounding. "He's- He's quit the Brotherhood!" I glanced over my shoulder at him. "Look, Jonathan, I know you didn't say those exact words, but… help me out!"

Slowly, Jonathan, who was collapsed to the floor in his dusted black and white overcoat, shifted his body around so I could see his face. His left eye was shut tightly, his expression in a firm grimace, and his right eye, the cybernetic one, was entirely sliced across. There was no red glow, in fact half of the aperture was gone, the rest a mangled, flash-melted mess. Electric sparks flitted from the damaged implant, until at last with a click he deactivated the broken eye entirely, and exhaled. He shook his head and caught his breath, blinking several times with his one eye.

"Are you okay?" I asked.

He looked at me like I was a complete idiot. Then he turned to Omega. "It's true, I didn't say it… but…"

Omega and I waited for him to finish.

"I now quit the Brotherhood. I want no part of it," he said, disgusted. "I have wanted nothing more than to escape it for days. And I had my doubts for months." He looked Omega in the eye. "Deep down I never really thought I was right. I just thought… it couldn't be worse than the TAU." He ground his teeth together. "I was wrong."

Omega blinked. "I do not know what to do."

"Just, don't kill us," I said.

Omega hesitantly rose from their battle stance. "But my Commander has been captured, because of Jonathan's fake reinforcements. And K has been converted to the Brotherhood by him." They tilted their head to the side. "Why do you defend him?"

I looked between the two of them slowly. "Because- I believe everyone deserves a chance at redemption."

"Everyone?" they asked, perplexed.

Jonathan began to stand. "As much as I appreciate your optimism, I disagree, Osax," he said. "Ryner, and Duhrnan- They've gotten enough chances." He scowled.

Omega looked confused. "You actually want to stop them?"

Jonathan exhaled. "Yes," he said firmly. "In the past few days, I should have died countless times. Just now, even. But I haven't. There has got to be a reason for it." He touched his broken eye. "If you'll accept me as an honest ally, then I will do whatever I can to stop them both. I'll take K trying to kill me and your near-perfect throw as a final warning; I don't have any more chances. When I die, I want to make sure I'm on the right side." His lip formed a straight line, awaiting a response.

Omega took a long time to respond. I could practically see the gears turning in their head as they assessed the situation. At long last they reached out a hand to Jonathan, and I realized I had been holding my breath. Hesitantly, he stepped forward. He reached his hand out to shake theirs, somewhat inaccurately. Their hands met.

"I will accept you as an honest ally," said Omega. "But this is your final warning. If you betray us again, I will eliminate you."

Jonathan tried to smile, just as I tried to ignore the shiver that ran down my spine. We weren't killing each other right now. That was the important thing, I reminded myself.

Jonathan turned to me, and held out his hand. I took it and we shook. His grip was firm, though his arm was shaking. I laid my other hand on top of his and looked him in the eye.

"Consider us allies," I said. "Now let's get ourselves together and get moving."

I glanced at the Code-Alpha signal.

04:18:44:14

I shut my eyes. "We are running out of time," I said. "Things keep getting in the way of our primary objectives: stop the mothership, and stop the Shade Beam. This is one of those times. We need to prioritize. Step one, we need to get out of here. Step two, we need to save Joëlle, and we need to save K. Jonathan, I hope there's a way to reverse the 'Sheep's Clothing.'"

"There is," he said. "I have the deactivation symbols on my holo-gauntlet. All we need to do is get K to see them, and she will return to normal, with no memory of what happened." He paused, then pressed a few buttons on his gauntlet. "I'll send them to you, just in case."

I nodded. "Great!" He requested a file transfer, and I allowed it to proceed. I opened the symbols on my gauntlet to test them, and a series of abstract shapes began looping above my arm. That was a real sign of faith from Jonathan, and it cemented in my mind that despite anything which had transpired in the past, we were in this together, for the time being. We had so much to do, and a minuscule margin for error. "The plus side to all of this… is you, Jonathan."

"Me?" he said.

"We have unexpected challenges… and they are kind of your fault," I said. "But, up until now, you weren't really on our side. Imagine what we can accomplish with a Brotherhood insider working with us."

Jonathan's lip twitched into a shallow smile.

"We aren't going to get anywhere standing around," I said. "Let's see where this tunnel leads; maybe there is another exit. We can discuss plans on the way."

"Yes," said Omega.

"Al- Alright," said Jonathan.

We were an unlikely group. But we were all we had. I had no idea how we were going to pull it all off, stopping Duhrnan and the Brotherhood, and saving our friends, except that we had to take it one step at a time.

Forty-Five

It was slow going in the deep parts of the cave. To my initial surprise, it turned out that the entire cave system was quite large and seemed to go on for a long time. But after thinking about it, as we ventured into a brighter part of the cave where more of Malum's luminescent crystals grew, I realized that the landing zone we had found must have been made intentionally. The ground was so smooth, and the tunnel leading away from the pad was so level that it must have been carved out. Which meant the path must lead somewhere, even if it didn't lead to another exit.

Our footsteps echoed ahead and behind us in the tunnel. We brushed past hanging vines of purple and green, and I glanced into the corner and we all paused, gazing at the crumbling remains of an ancient pillar. It was half stuck in blue glowing crystals, and it was ornately carved. I immediately recognized the symbols as ancient Loro writing. I lifted my ears in excitement.

We kept going. Jonathan and Omega seemed wary of each other, (I couldn't blame them) and Jonathan kept stumbling on the path as it transitioned into ruins. With his eye damaged he was having more difficulty finding his way. But never once did he complain. He kept his lips tightly sealed, aside from the occasional grunt when he nearly slipped, but he knew better than to make a fuss about Omega's attack on him. I admit, I felt a sense of retribution was deserved for what he had done, and I couldn't help but feel it was poetic that the part of him which was destroyed was the cold, mechanical part, a device with only the ability to observe and judge the world in digital perfection, but not the heart to find love or meaning, or the truth of each of us that lies just under the surface of our physical bodies. That heart was still Jonathan's.

But my mind wandered back to Joëlle and K. Joëlle, along with her ship, was captured. Omega and Jonathan and I agreed that she was probably already a captive aboard Duhrnan's mothership. I found myself sweating at the thought that she would be harmed, but Jonathan pointed out to me that Duhrnan would find it much more amusing to draw out our suffering by keeping her safe. Isn't that part of why he broadcast the time of Earth's destruction? His greatest pleasure it seemed was giving people just enough hope, before crushing it utterly and replacing it with despair. He thrilled himself by playing with other people's emotions. He probably expected Omega and I to make a rescue attempt if we found our way out of the mountain caves. And he would be waiting.

But we were determined not to let him get his way. Somehow, we would save her.

K, on the other hand, must have still been at the landing site. That is, unless she climbed her way out, or found another way into the tunnels. But with her "Sheep's Clothing" programming, she was another pawn of Ryner. And since Ryner and Duhrnan were working together, we could assume that she would follow Duhrnan's orders, if he gave any. The one advantage we had, we agreed, was that we might be able to get to her first, and take her out of her trance.

A slow, stocky creature, no more than a foot tall, waddled away from us, swinging its yellow striped tail. We had just reached the summit of a large staircase in a massive open area. The ceiling was lit with glowing crystals. I saw the light of the sky shine through in beams from a long crevice which ripped through the violet mountains above. Water cascaded down into an underground lake beside the building from the mountain's ancient wound. We stood upon a structure of dusty stonework which resembled a massive temple, built and buried beneath the natural caves of the mountains above. It was as though the Loro had lived within the beating heart of the mountains. The stones were cool and dry under my feet. A cool breeze whistled in past the waterfalls, and carried on it a fragrant, fertile smell. The cave was full of patient, sleepy organisms, but the smell reminded me of the teeming, dangerous world above the surface.

Omega had reached the top of the stairs first, with an unsurprising elegance. As I waited for Jonathan to catch up, I closed my eyes and tilted my ears toward the sound of the water. Sunlight warmed my eyelids even as my lungs filled with crisp, fresh air. My ears tingled at the soothing white noise of the waterfall dripping and splashing below, and misting as it fell through the air.

"We should find the center of the ruins," I said after a long silence. "We may be able to learn something from the loro database, assuming there is one, and that it's still functioning."

Jonathan paused, panting. He pulled himself up to my level, and dusted off his coat. Omega watched him with their round, black eyes. Their legs were together and they stood with perfect posture.

Jonathan said, "What do you hope to learn from the ruins?"

I narrowed my eyes. "Duhrnan is a loro. I don't know how, but he must be. Maybe the ruins will help us find a weakness."

"That seems like a longshot," said Jonathan.

"Maybe," I said. "But we might as well take it. The database should be just up ahead, if I'm right. We can take a short rest. And we can come up with a plan to find K..."

Of course, I thought.

I gestured enthusiastically to Jonathan and Omega. "The tracking device!"

A smile crept across Jonathan's face.

Omega blinked. "That is how we will find K?"

"Her earpiece," I said. "She was wearing it in the battle. We can use it to track her. She's probably still wearing it. I wonder if she realized that by now... Jonathan, do you think-"

He shook his head. "No, I see no reason why she would have removed it. Unless she determined that wearing it conflicted with her orders. She probably doesn't realize that our aim might be to track her down and deactivate her. And I suppose we should keep it that way."

"Yeah?" I asked.

"Yes. Part of the 'Sheep's Clothing' means that she is programmed to prevent others from deactivating her... aside from her masters."

"So, what exactly does that mean?" I asked, nervously.

"If she knows what we're doing, then she'll just... close her eyes. If she doesn't see the deactivation symbols, she won't revert to her normal self. The alter-ego doesn't *want* to revert, unless her masters wish it."

I shivered. "Alright... well, when we do find her, our plan needs to be airtight, then. We'll have to surprise her."

"Remember," said Jonathan, "K's mind is split into two personalities. While some of her memories are cross-compatible, others are only accessible by one personality. Think of the activation symbols as a light switch. She can either be on, or off. And there is a unique set of symbols which she must see in order to be turned on, or off- one for each. The 'Sheep's Clothing' program was designed based on the idea that once the brain forms a strong enough connection with anything, a visual symbol in this case, it is *impossible* not to have a specific, predetermined reaction upon seeing it. It doesn't need to be a logical reaction. It just needs to be severely reinforced… which is why the program can only be applied to subjects like K, during a period of enhanced learning."

I nodded.

"But," he continued, "the point is, she can't control her reaction to the symbols. It's a reaction… not a response. So, it's really quite simple. If we get her to see the deactivation symbols, the old K- the real K- will return, and the Brotherhood agent will disappear… at least until she sees her activation symbols again. But if she's got her eyes shut, and she doesn't see the deactivation symbols… then she will not revert to her true self. It simply will never happen." His expression was grim.

Omega tilted their head to the side, curiously. "If K closes her eyes, can we not force them open?"

Jonathan and I sighed.

"In theory? Sure," I said.

"But that would mean getting close enough to her to do so," Jonathan chimed in. "She could rip any one of us apart with a flick of her wrist. We have to keep our distance until the exact right moment, then display the symbols so that she doesn't have a chance to react. She has to be looking at them when they are activated, or she might figure out what we're doing."

"But," said Omega, "with her eyes closed, K will not be able to defend herself. She will be easy to destroy."

I raised my hands up. "Omega. We don't want to kill her."

"But is she not a member of the Brotherhood?"

"Well…" I said.

"She has not quit the Brotherhood, like Jonathan," said Omega.

Jonathan stepped up next to them. "But if you kill her, you're also killing a hero. The K who volunteered to fight Duhrnan, and to protect the galaxy." His tone was firm. "The only way to stop the Brotherhood agent and save the hero is to deactivate her."

Omega waited, calculating. At last they nodded.

"Besides," said Jonathan, "I'm the one who activated her. If she dies because of it… I may as well be dead too."

My ears drooped. "Jonathan, don't say that."

He shrugged. "I wouldn't be able to live with myself. It's hard enough as it is."

We were shocked at what we found when we descended the stairs into the central chamber. Just like the ruins on Voren, a loro database connected to a pillar in the center. The room was massive with several columns holding up the ceiling, and ornately carved images and symbols covered every surface. Just like on Voren, a luminous liquid coursed through the indents of the carvings, green in colour, making the room dimly glow from every corner. But, contrasting the dusty remains of the ancient civilization, modern equipment, including computers, containers, desks, and cables littered the room, lit by white lamps mounted on tripods.

My skin began to crawl. There were corpses scattered throughout the room. Human bodies that were ripped apart, with clothing and armour scorched in places. I tried not to gag at the smell of decay that permeated the air, and I wished we were back atop the pyramid instead of inside. The bones had little flesh; they had rotted for some time now.

I screwed my eyes shut, fighting off the urge to puke. When I opened them again I breathed carefully through my mouth.

Omega's black eyes scanned the room, their lips frowning ever so slightly. At a glance, they seemed completely fine. But Jonathan on the other hand held his mouth open in disbelief, struggling to find words. His brows contorted in confusion, trying to make sense of the situation.

"Something terrible happened here." He spoke quietly, as if scared that something might be listening.

I spotted an insignia on the jacket of a nearby corpse. The cloth had been charred all over, but the symbol had been missed. It was an angry white skull, the symbol of the Brotherhood.

The sound of our footsteps and breath mingled with the faint hum of the researcher's computers, still active even since their users had perished months, maybe years ago. The entire room felt suffocating. The sickly green walls seemed to close in around us even as we stepped deeper into the open.

Jonathan and I bent over one of the bodies. The closer I got to it, the faster my heart raced. It was missing an arm and a leg. The skull was dry and blackened, as if all the hair had been burnt off. And just above the eye sockets was another hole. It had been punched straight through.

Jonathan shivered, and our eyes met.

"We should get out of here as soon as we can," I whispered.

Omega blinked. "Brotherhood members were killed here. But there is no sign that it was recent. We might not be in danger.”

Jonathan looked at them aghast. “I- Well, maybe you’re right, but...”

My heart skipped a beat. Something shifted on the other side of the room.

It must have.

No. I only imagined it.

“Jonathan, see if you can start tracking K’s earpiece. Now would be a good time to get reoriented.”

He gulped, and nodded slowly. Neither of us wanted to have to confront her, but anything seemed better than staying here.

“Osax... the Brotherhood would have been studying these ruins for a reason. It’ll take me a minute to calibrate the scanner- You might as well glance at what they were studying.”

I nodded. “Omega, keep an eye out for anything. I’m going to check out one of these computers.”

Omega locked eyes with me, and nodded. I thought I noticed some moisture on their skin, as though they’d begun to sweat slightly from anxiety. Strangely, that made me feel a little better. At least I wasn’t alone.

Jonathan fiddled with his holo-gauntlet in the dim light. Omega perched on a desk, surveying the room. I covered my nostrils, trying to filter out as much of the smell as I could, and stepped over a skeletal arm nestled between ancient loro debris.

I approached a solid computer screen. The monitor was black; I assumed it had automatically powered down from inactivity. But the computer it was attached to hummed faintly, and tiny lights blinked from it.

Hesitantly, I stretched out my fingers toward the mouse and keyboard. My hand shook, though I willed it to stay still. I brushed a layer of dust off the keyboard, and wiggled the mouse. Jonathan’s holo-gauntlet beeped behind me. A moment later, the computer screen activated.

There were multiple documents open at once, but my eyes immediately fell to an image file which was open in the center of the screen. It was colourless, clearly a loro image which had been recovered from the temple’s database. And it depicted a masked loro with four outstretched arms, standing on a stone, above a crowd of...

Valicorr.

“Hey-” I said. I waved Jonathan and Omega to my side, and they hurried over.

We all crowded around the computer screen. There were text notes attached to the image file, which must have been taken by one of the

Brotherhood researchers. Jonathan began to read segments of the notes aloud.

"It is evident that… the valicorr are not just random pirates… but instead… creations. Tools. Bioweapons, designed by the loro in a time long forgotten…"

I read, "The valicorr are indeed loyal to nothing but the loro. They are biologically imprisoned to follow their master's lead. They were created to be soldiers for the loro, so that no loro blood would be spilled in conflict…" I swallowed hard.

Omega glanced at Jonathan and I inquisitively, then continued where we had trailed off in their nasally voice. "Without the presence of their masters, valicorr will resort to violence and raids in order to satisfy their craving for purpose, as documented by the loro in ancient times. It is, after all, why they exist. It seems as though the loro had doubts about their decision to create the valicorr. Nonetheless, this is evidence that creating an army of bioweapon soldiers is indeed achievable. If only we were able to make contact with a loro, then perhaps through them we could become allies with the valicorr. But common knowledge suggests that the loro have entirely disappeared from the galaxy."

Omega stared at us silently. I looked into Jonathan's eye.

"The Brotherhood knew about this connection between the loro and the valicorr for some time now," I said. "Possibly years."

Jonathan was dumbfounded. "It seems that way. But they never told me." He sighed. "It makes sense though. That's how Duhrnan has got them all on a leash- The valicorr *must* obey him… It's their purpose."

If the valicorr were compelled to follow Duhrnan's lead, then his ability to command them made a lot more sense.

I shot Jonathan a glance. "I'm starting to feel like we're the only ones who *aren't* bioweapons." He exhaled shortly and smirked. I continued, "Jonathan, how close are we to tracking K?"

He lifted his holo-gauntlet, which projected a three-dimensional crude scan of the area. "It should have been able to lock on to her signal by now…" He tapped on some holographic buttons, and a bright dot appeared in the air.

Beep… Beep… Beep…

The gauntlet signalled that K was close to us.

Extremely close.

"What…" said Jonathan. He whirled around to face a door on the wall away from us, and Omega and I followed his gaze. Instinctively, I gripped the handle of Jonathan's pistol, and flicked it on. It whirred to life in a rising pitch. All our eyes were fixed on the shadowy door, outlined with glowing engravings on the walls beside it.

I rested my finger on the trigger of the E-gun. Sparks of energy began to froth at its barrel. I raised it up to my eye.

Beep. Beep. Beep.

My heart was racing. If it was K, could I even bring myself to shoot? What was our plan? How could we ensure that she would see the deactivation symbols? We would have to be quick.

Jonathan took a step back behind me and Omega. I glanced at the holographic map of the area. The glowing dot had stopped just behind the door. I turned back to face it. I held my breath, trying not to inhale the putrid air.

Sound exploded. Chunks of stone catapulted toward us, and I raised my arms to cover my face. Plumes of dust shrouded the doorway, and the glowing green liquid began to drain out from the archway onto the floor. As the dust began to clear, I caught sight of a figure. K stood alone, with a blank expression on her face. Her grey cloak hung from her spiked shoulders. Her horns pointed straight at us. Her holo-gauntlet was active. Just like Jonathan's, it showed a three-dimensional scan of the area, with two blinking points of light, right where Jonathan and I stood.

Forty-Six

K's hologram fizzled away, and she whipped her other hand up. Her lifeless eyes chilled me. Her automatic pistol flared to life, and a volley of scarlet energy bolts screamed toward me.

I gasped.

Omega shoved me. Heat seared my back as I toppled over and the computer desk beside me erupted in raging flames and smoke. Omega took a hit in the back and grimaced.

Jonathan screeched and ran for the cover of a nearby pillar. His foot caught on a cable he could barely see, and he tumbled hard into the stone floor. He scrambled behind the pillar, fresh blood seeping from his scraped cheek. The side of the pillar burst from an energy blast, and the green fluid began pooling on the floor.

I lay on my side. In a split second, Omega pounced toward K, smoke rising from where they were hit on the back of their shirt.

I watched Omega flip through the air. Their skin seemed to catch the red glow of K's laser blasts as they soared clean over them. Omega landed in a somersault, transferring their forward momentum into a run. Their tail flicked. They were about to barrel straight into K.

I panicked. Omega didn't stand a chance against K in close quarters.

I bolted upright and reached out to them. "Wait!"

K's lips were tightly pursed around her tusks. Her orange eyes seemed to glow with a deathly heat. She holstered her E-gun as Omega moved to tackle her. Her muscles were perfectly outlined in her leather jacket. Her bones spiked through her sleeves in vicious patterns. My eyes fell to the weapon at her waist. It was her retracted molecular sword. I flicked my gun toward her.

The gun trembled in my hands. In the hazy green ambience, Omega collided with K. I couldn't get a clear shot. And even if I could, I didn't want to hurt her.

Omega hammered both hands onto her shoulders, and grabbed tightly onto her spikes. K growled, and swung her arms forward to crush Omega against her chest, but they kicked off the ground with both legs and their tail. Their claws just cleared K's arms by an inch as they spun upside-down over her shoulders. They twisted in the air, and landed on K's back, with both feet pressed into her and their tail adhering to the cloak on her back. Their hands clutched the sides of K's head, and with the index and middle finger of each hand, they held K's eyelids open.

"Now!" Omega shouted flatly.

Jonathan moved to get out of hiding, but his boot slipped on the pool of luminous liquid at his feet. He splashed onto his hands, and coughed. "The symbols, Osax!"

So I lunged forward, and activated my holo-gauntlet. The abstract deactivation symbols flickered to life in a looping holographic display above my arm. *She just needs to look at them!*

K shut her eyes. She figured it out.

She slammed her torso forward and swung her head down. She reached her arms back and grabbed Omega's wrists. A second later, and Omega's body smashed into the stone floor.

K's eyes were shut tightly, but she was still holding onto Omega's wrists. She dropped one hand to her waist, and metal screeched as the blade extended. She pulled Omega's arm taught, and sliced down with the edge of the sword. Omega was silent.

I forgot to breathe. K growled furiously, and tossed Omega's severed arm against the wall. Then she kicked their bleeding body, which flew several feet and cracked against a piece of Brotherhood machinery. Then she panted, snarling, shifting her head from side to side.

Jonathan's eye was wide with terror, and he looked pale.

I stood completely still. K kept her eyes shut. But she was listening.

Jonathan knocked a stone to the side, and K turned on him. Light flashed, and smoke burst from the pillar. She brandished both sword and gun simultaneously. Jonathan was panting, and K fired again. He covered his head with his hands as pellets of energy ripped into the pillar he was hiding behind. Then he held his breath, and our eyes met.

K stalked slowly around the room. The sound of the glowing liquid trickling onto the floor from K's destruction was the only thing to be heard, aside from her footsteps. I kept my feet planted firmly on the cold stone. My ears twitched. I raised the E-gun as slowly as I could to my eye.

I felt heat coming from Omega's body, even though it was a few feet away from me. I couldn't help but look at them. Their left arm had been severed just above the elbow. The bleeding had already stopped, it seemed, and their skin was frantically shifting colours. Their eyes were closed.

I turned back to K. I tried to focus. I trained my eyes down the sights of the pistol. She was moving, but she was moving slowly. I knew I had to concentrate. The trigger was cool against my finger. I carefully pulled it, but it offered more resistance than I anticipated, and I hesitated. I held my breath. The sights realigned.

The air was electrified. The energy bolt collided directly with my target; K's pistol. It exploded, and clattered to the ground from K's hand.

She roared, and wound up to throw her sword.

My ears shot back. Not knowing what to do, I ducked and planted my hands on the cool floor. I felt the fur on my ears ripple in the wake of her sword as it spun and cut through the air above me and stuck into the far wall. A drop of blood landed on my cheek. My ear faintly stung, nicked from the sword.

Now at least she was unarmed. She was growling angrily, and waving her arms around. Jonathan gazed at me from his spot on the floor. I glanced to Omega's body. It was still pulsing with colour.

When I was sure Jonathan was looking my way, I gestured to him. I pointed to K, and started mouthing words. *He can't read skyther lips, Osax!* I thought, then stopped. I pointed to K, then to Jonathan. He stared at me confused.

I paused for a moment. The colour shifting on Omega's skin seemed to be dying down. I didn't know exactly how their regeneration worked, but I knew I had to bring them their detached arm. If they could reset bones, then maybe they could reconnect severed limbs. But judging from the fading colours on their body, it seemed like their regenerative energy might be time sensitive. If I didn't bring them their arm immediately, they might not ever get it back.

I looked back to Jonathan. He shrugged at me, and furrowed his brow.

I made sure K wasn't approaching and holstered my gun. Looking back at Jonathan, I pointed first to him. Then with the same hand, I made a fist. I stuck my index and middle fingers down as legs, and I wiggled them around, miming walking. Jonathan slowly nodded, perplexed, and pointed to himself. I nodded. Then with my other hand, I pointed to K. I turned that hand into another puppet. I mimed K walking slowly around while Jonathan was still. Then I shook Jonathan up and down, and made K turn to him. I made her chase him down as he moved, leading her away.

Slowly, as my message dawned on him, he nodded to me with pursed lips and apprehensive eyes.

My ears shot up in relief.

Jonathan slowly stood. He gave me one more look under his brow, and gulped.

"I'm the one you want, K."

K spun to face him, and her boots crunched on the floor as she approached him with surprising restraint. "You are not supposed to be alive," she said.

I inched my way around the other side of the pillar, trying to be as quiet as I could. Omega's arm was splayed against the wall where K had entered the room. I crept toward it.

Jonathan scowled. "Those aren't your words, K."

"Then who's words are they?" She said. Anger simmered beneath her calm exterior.

"Ryner's words. You were only programmed with them."

K stopped. "You don't know anything about Ryner."

Jonathan shook his head. "I know Ryner. He's the reason you've lost your mind."

K continued advancing, and Jonathan stumbled backwards, inching around the room.

I knelt down next to Omega's arm, and picked it up. The hand was limp and the skin was pale. I grimaced, and looked at the body. The colours were still changing, at a much slower rate now. I inched myself toward it.

K said, "I haven't lost my mind. I've recovered it." She paused. "You're the one who activated me. Yet now you want to undo it."

Jonathan replied. "Because it was a mistake. I never should have done it."

She smirked. "You're weak. You know you can't stop me, unless you trigger the 'Sheep's Clothing.' You desperately want to live." She licked her lips. "That's why you regret activating me."

He chuckled nervously, and backed into a desk. He quickly sidestepped over a pile of skeletal remains. "Living would be ideal, but no. Really, I want to bring you back."

"Bring me back?" she said. "And you think the *other* me is- what- the *real* me?" She snorted a laugh.

I felt a chill. A twisted glimmer of her old personality… I held my breath as I approached Omega.

Jonathan replied. "Of course I do. The other you *is* the real you. I would know." He frowned. "I made you."

I made it to Omega's body. Relief filled me. I shifted Omega's body so they were lying flat on their back, then I gently pressed their forearm up to the stub on their body. My eyes darted around their skin. The colour wavered between warm and cool.

My ears lifted. I could barely believe it. The skin around the severed area began to shift. Tendrils of skin opened up and reached out to one another. The arm was beginning to reconnect. My mandibles hung in astonishment as I witnessed this miracle. It was disgusting and beautiful at the same time. Heat surged from their body as it worked overtime to mend itself, and I slowly rose.

"You didn't make me," said K. "Ryner did."

Jonathan growled, "You were made from my DNA. I designed you. I was the one who first woke you into this world! And you're only around because I spared your life! You were reckless and afraid when you awoke. The Brotherhood would have had you killed, but I protected you!"

K shook her head. "No." Her voice cut deep. "You made me because Ryner wanted it. You protected me because Ryner wanted it. Everything you have done is exactly what Ryner wanted. Except for now. Now, you keep on living, even though Ryner wants you dead."

With her eyes still closed, she slammed her hands onto a desk and flung it toward where she thought Jonathan was. He dived to the floor, and the desk crashed against the wall. I needed to distract her; Jonathan had done so long enough, and he was navigating with only one eye.

"Stop!"

She spun and whipped a small boulder my way. I ducked, and it shattered behind me.

"Talcorosax," she uttered with disgust. "You're part of the problem. The prince of the skythers. Embedded in the backbone of this broken world order. The Brotherhood is the only destiny the galaxy deserves." Her words were venom. "You should have died along with Astraloth, and its rancid queen."

My knuckles turned white. *It's not your friend. She's not really K.*

Then I hatched an idea. A reckless idea, but an idea nonetheless…

I crept behind a pillar before speaking again. "Why would Ryner want you?" I said.

There was a moment of silence. "Ryner had me *made*. Of course he wants me. I'm his perfect creation."

"But you're far from perfect." My tone was mocking. "You- You're dying, aren't you? And you get headaches, and blackouts… That doesn't sound perfect to me. If I didn't know better, I'd say you were a mistake. You probably embarrass him. You probably couldn't catch me even if you tried."

That did the trick. She bellowed, and started running straight for me with her head down like a bull. I sprang to the side, and vaulted over a computer desk, knocking the monitor to the floor. The glass shattered. She drove her horns into the pillar I had been hiding behind, and it collapsed. Luminous liquid splashed everywhere, and she howled in pain as stones tumbled onto her back. The light from the ceiling began dripping out onto her. I panicked for a second, worried that she might not survive. But she stood in the shower of stones, covering her neck with her head down.

I regrouped next to Jonathan and gingerly we stepped over to Omega's body as K moaned. I watched the ceiling with intensity, looking for signs that the temple would cave in like it did on Voren… This was a gamble. But the ceiling held, and the debris stopped falling. K was heaving on her hands and knees.

Good. K wasn't dead.

Jonathan whispered. "We need to get Omega out of here, to heal!" He knelt and picked up Omega's body in his arms, careful of their mending wounds. Then he turned to me and frowned gravely.

"You go," I said. "I can get to her… somehow I can save K." Fire burned inside me.

He hesitated. "You are indeed brave, Osax." He eyed me with admiration. "Just, don't get yourself killed. I don't want to be alone after all this."

"I will bring her back."

We shared a brief gaze, then he turned and hurried toward a shadowy exit. I stomped a different direction and circled K.

It was just the two of us now.

"K!" I shouted.

She turned to face me, though her eyes were still shut. Blood dripped from her forehead. I activated the symbols around my holo-gauntlet.

"Can't you see Ryner is using you?" I said. "He'll toss you aside as soon as he is done with you, just like he did with Director Aali and with Jonathan. But I'm not going to use you. Real friends wouldn't do that."

She lunged for me, and I skirted around the room once more. My feet knocked against the punctured skull of a corpse. I grit my mandibles.

"You think you can appeal to me by pretending to be my friend?" she said. "It won't work."

"But," I said, "I am your friend. You know that, don't you?"

She bolted after me. I stumbled out of reach. The sound of our scampering echoed through the air.

"Heh," she chuckled, regaining her breath. "You think you're her friend?" She smirked with a sharp menace. "That's hilarious."

I was panting. "But we are friends."

"You lied to her."

"You know why I did that-"

"So what?!" She didn't even bother charging for me this time. "You... I don't see what she saw in you at all. You're an arrogant, self-important bastard with a toxic hero complex. You're weak- not just with a flimsy body. Everything makes you shake, and cry. And you're a filthy skyther, at that. You're disgusting. You're worthless."

She paralyzed me. Had she always felt this way about me?

No, she couldn't have. The real K couldn't think that. But what she was saying... it wasn't far from the truth, was it?

I trembled, and shut my eyes. I wouldn't let her words get to me. I thought of the moment we shared playing "Defenders of Earth" just a night ago. I remembered her consoling me on Kronos. I recalled our silent drive through the ice flats of Voren as the sun set, letting the calm sound of music fill the space and strengthen the unspoken bond that was forming between us. Her taunting words echoed the voices of demons inside my head. *Weak, unstable, emotional, worthless...* But I thought about the real K. I knew she cared about me. She had faith in me. Maybe that was enough. And I remembered what I promised her, just before the Brotherhood soldiers arrived. *I won't give up on you.*

"Please K, just look at the symbols. Please."

She shook her head slowly, eyes shut tight. "I have orders. I will not betray the Brotherhood."

My eyes were wet when I opened them again. My voice was barely more than a whisper. "It would be so easy for you. This isn't you."

She inhaled sharply. "I. Will. Not. Open. My. Eyes."

I knew she was telling the truth. I had to find another solution.

I glanced around the dead room, anxiety creeping up into my chest, nearly extinguishing the flame. The light from the ceiling had almost completely drained onto the floor, filling the cracks in the stones, and the spaces between bones, illuminating K and I in a haunting glow from beneath. *Not K,* I thought. There was no way I could convince, coerce, or confuse her into opening her eyes in front of me.

At last my eyes landed on her wrist as she waded vaguely toward me. And my ears shot up with tentative hope.

I had one last idea. But it meant I would have to flee.

"Fine," I growled as I slowly backed away.

She snarled in response, and leapt for me with arms outstretched. But I wasted no more time. I pivoted on the slick stone, and sprinted out of the room. It didn't matter where I was headed... I just needed to get away from her.

◆

With lungs ready to burst I sped down the winding halls of the underground temple. Almost at random, I skirted around corners and up and down crumbling stairs. I ran past more dead Brotherhood agents, kicking up dust as I sprinted. The halls were dark, lit only by my flashlight.

I slid across the smooth floor, my hands tracing a line across the textured wall until I came to an open archway, and I grabbed the carved frame and swung myself inside. Panting hard, I pressed my back up against the corner, and looked at my holo-gauntlet. This should be far enough.

The air was slightly less foul down here. I savoured every bit of oxygen I could get as I caught my breath. I stared at the holo-gauntlet.

I couldn't hear K, which meant she was far enough behind me that my plan might work. She must have realized that both Jonathan and I had gotten some significant distance, or at least that's what I was counting on. And if so, she'd have opened her eyes to find her way out.

There was one thing I was counting on... Our holo-gauntlets were paired!

Eagerly I fiddled with my computer. I was preparing to send the deactivation symbols to her gauntlet, and remotely open them in front of her. I figured catching her by surprise this way was the only way I could ensure she would see the symbols.

Transfer complete. All I had to do was press one glowing key on my arm, and her gauntlet would flash the symbols into the air. I wished I had thought of this sooner, before she found us and hurt Omega, but there was no sense dwelling on the past.

I waited in the blackness. The sound of breathing was my only comfort.

My gauntlet blinked. It informed me that K had just opened the short range scanner on her holo-gauntlet, and was continuing to track Jonathan and my earpieces. Which meant she would already be looking at her holo-gauntlet.

Without hesitation, I slammed my finger to the activation key. Though I couldn't see K, I knew her computer started projecting the deactivation symbols in front of her.

After a few seconds of breathless anticipation, I opened up a text file next to the symbols.

> K, are you there?

Seconds passed.

> K, are you there? what the hell is going on? osax
>
> were are you? i think i blacked out.

I stifled a cry. Almost immediately, tears of relief started streaming down my cheeks, and I shook my fists in the air with unrestrained excitement. I did it! She was back to normal! I almost couldn't believe it.

Hurriedly, I typed a response.

> You're already tracking our earpieces. Find
>
> Jonathan! I'll meet you there!
>
> what? but didnt he betray us?

I contemplated my response. I opened up the scanner and oriented myself to Jonathan's position. The scanner wasn't sophisticated enough to give a detailed map of the temple, as it couldn't fully penetrate all of the walls. So I wasn't totally sure how to get to him. But I at least knew the direction to start heading.

I startled myself when my foot caught on the bones of a Brotherhood technician, and they clattered across the floor, echoing loudly in the room. My eyes followed them out of the light, and I had a terrible realization. I wasn't the only thing breathing here in the darkness.

Forty-Seven

I swung my flashlight into the depth of the room. My breath puffed out in wispy clouds.

Something stirred in the back of the room. Something huge.

Panic struck me as I glanced down at the corpse in front of me. *Punctured skull… burn marks, limbs torn…* Just like the corpses in the central chamber. What did that remind me of?

I stumbled back over something as I inched my way out of the room and fell onto my rear. A white flake of organic material gently landed on my arm from above, and with wide eyes I jerked my flashlight to the ceiling. Attached to the ceiling were the dry, open remains of a massive cocoon-like skin, something shed by a monstrous creature during metamorphoses. Something that preferred the cool caves to the hot surface of the planet.

Two yellow eyes glowed in the shadows. The thing exhaled, and crawled toward me, hanging from the ceiling, stretching its limbs casually. It had been sleeping, but no longer. The eyes were positioned on either side of a long, sharp beak. Antennae-like whiskers shot out from its face. Boned horns jutted from its head, back, and limbs. It had jagged, curved claws, and a spiked spine. Its tail hovered behind it, and began to faintly pulse along with the creature's spine with an orange glow. It was impossible to get a grasp of the thing's shape, as its skin convulsed with each audible heartbeat. And I knew without question what it was.

It was a myrok. The apex predator of Malum. It was what had killed everyone here so long ago. And now its eyes were on me.

Just go! No time

I tried to warn K, but was cut off. Pain exploded from my wrist as a beam of searing orange light shot from its tail. My holo-gauntlet sparked out; it was utterly destroyed, the emitter on my wrist was no more than scrap metal now. I clutched my scorched wrist to my chest as I scrambled to my feet, and the myrok opened its beak wide enough to swallow me whole, howling. Its cry was both deep and screeching, and shook me to my core. The deafening sound echoed through the cavern. Its eyes were murderous.

I had no scanner, no light, and no way to contact anyone.

I bolted down the hall in pitch darkness. I was sweating profusely. I didn't dare stop to look back, but I could hear the clicking of its claws as it crawled after me like a spider.

I couldn't see anything. I traced my hand on the edge of the wall to give myself some orientation. Then my foot found nothing but air.

Helplessly, I yelped as I tumbled into the abyss. I hit something hard, and rolled. I was getting bruised all over as I tripped down a set of ancient stairs.

I crashed onto my back, and saw the myrok crest the top of the stairs by the faint glow of its tail. The tail got brighter. It was about to fire. I thought of the skull with its hair burnt off.

I willed my protesting muscles to move. A flash of light and heat grazed me, but I was fine. For the moment, at least.

I withdrew the pistol with my uninjured hand as I sprinted down the hall. It whined to life, and I began charging an energy bolt. The faint red glow began to increase in intensity, giving me barely enough light to see where I was stepping. The myrok clicked its claws on the walls after me.

After a few moments, my gun was going to burst. I swung my arm back, and looked over my shoulder. Thankfully, the myrok was a big target. I fired, and managed to hit the side of its face!

Smoke cleared, and it continued after me. It didn't even slow down.

My foot caught on a stone, and I fell to the ground. The myrok closed the gap between us within seconds, and skittered to the floor. It reared its head up, beak closed to a spear point. It was going to skewer me with one strike.

I'm going to die, I thought as I lay there, frozen. *And Duhrnan will never be stopped.* In that moment, I felt more frustrated than anything. After all that work, this was how it would end? I was too shocked to feel anything other than disappointment.

K disagreed. She shouted, and her sword flew threw the air. The myrok gurgled, and fell on its side, limbs flailing. K's sword stuck out from its back, deeply lodged between bony spikes. Our eyes met, and I was brought back to my senses.

"Osax!" She cried. She sprinted past the myrok, who was already beginning to rise, and picked me up, shouldering me with one arm. I coughed as she sped us both down the hall, glancing down periodically at her holo-gauntlet, which displayed Jonathan's position, and had just been tracking mine. My nostrils filled with the scent of sweat. I pressed my hands against her shoulder, relieving some of the pressure from my stomach against her spikes.

"You're not with Jonathan!" I said.

She leaped over a wide crevice in the floor, and I was jostled when she landed. I heard her say, "Yeah, you're welcome!"

She slid to a halt, and spun around, propping me on the ground. We shared a quick glance, and I couldn't help but lift my ears. Sure, we weren't out of danger yet, but my friend was back, and she'd just saved my life.

The myrok rounded the corner, and K kept her flashlight on it. She bent over and retrieved a large segment of collapsed wall. The myrok's tail flared, and K deflected the beam with the stone debris. As the myrok approached the crevice, K hurled the misshaped rock like a flying disc, and it collided with the myrok's legs, knocking it off the ceiling. It fell into the crevice.

"Yes!" I exclaimed. "K, you've got an incredible throw!"

She flashed me a grin. "I know."

"Actually, you almost killed me with it earlier," I said.

She looked at me confused. "What?"

Then we heard the sound of the myrok's footsteps echoing out from the pit.

"I'll explain later, come on! Let's find Omega and Jonathan, and get out of here!"

We kept running.

"Osax," she said as we kept pace with each other. "What happened? Jonathan betrayed us… but I must have blacked out right after that."

I hesitated. "You did…"

No, I thought. *You promised not to lie to her.*

"…didn't exactly black out," I finished.

She stared at me. "Then what the hell happened? Did I get sent through time or something?"

"No," I said. "You were activated. Jonathan was part of the Brotherhood, right? Well, he made you. And you have an alternate personality, one that is locked away in your subconscious, and is submissive to the Brotherhood's commands. You're a sleeper agent, though you don't even realize it. And you can be activated by being shown a specific set of symbols. Once that happens, your consciousness sort of flips, and the old you is essentially asleep until you get flipped back."

We ran in silence for a few seconds as she stared at me. "What the shit?!" She shook her head. "How long was I out?"

"A few hours."

"A few hours ago you found out Jonathan was a member of the Brotherhood, and he turned me into a subservient puppet thing, and yet we're trying to regroup with him? What happened in those few hours?!"

"We talked," I said. "And I listened."

"Are you part of the Brotherhood now?!"

"No!" I said. "He renounced the Brotherhood!" I shook my head. "Look, now's not a good time to explain. I trust him well enough. Despite everything he did, he risked his life to try to save you, and me."

"I don't know if that's a good enough excuse," K grumbled.

"Me neither!" I confessed. "But now isn't the time to make enemies. I believe he genuinely wants to help now, even if he was conflicted before."

K shook her head. "Well, if you say so..."

We were sprinting too hard to keep talking. A few minutes passed, and though we couldn't see the myrok, we could hear its movement echoing behind us. A horrible thought occurred to me then. Surely, it was faster than us. So why didn't it close in? Or shoot us with its tail? I could only think of one reason. It knew we were leading it to a larger meal.

At last we rounded a dark corner and reunited with Jonathan and Omega. Jonathan was shocked to see us, at once relieved to see K back to normal, and horrified at the new predicament with the myrok, which I hastily explained. Jonathan passed Omega's regenerating body to K, claiming his arms were aching and couldn't hold them any longer. Omega appeared fully mended, slowly regaining consciousness as we fled. K took their body with care, but kept her eyes trained warily on Jonathan. Even as this all happened, we quickened our pace through the shadows. Jonathan and I tried to navigate using his scanner to find the most direct route out of the ruins. We made our way back into natural caves, and at last we found a ray of sunlight beaming in at us, and the welcoming sweetness of fresh air. But the opening to the jungle was in the ceiling several meters up a shear face of the wall; we couldn't reach it.

The four of us stood at the foot of the wall, gazing up at the escape. We bathed in the warm light that reached us from beyond the forest canopy outside. Sounds of chirping and buzzing creatures filled my twitching ears. Sunlight! I could hardly believe it.

"That's our chance!" Jonathan exclaimed. "Quickly, how can we all climb out?!"

I scanned the wall. It was smooth, and sloped back up toward the opening. Not only that, but it was slick with water from the storm a few hours ago. There was a puddle at its base. A few purple vines snaked down the wall, but they looked treacherously flimsy. A tiny lizard blinked at us from the forest above, as if considering how it could help us, before scuttling away out of sight.

"K, what about your wrist cable?"

She nodded to me, then gently set Omega to their feet. Omega blinked wearily, and glanced between us, swaying from side to side. Jonathan and I stabilized them as K splashed into the puddle and fired her cable. The grappling hook soared up and out of the opening. It slid back into the cavern, and she tried again.

"Omega, how are you feeling?" I asked. Jonathan and I looked at their disoriented face with concern.

Their freckled skin was pale and nearly colourless. Our eyes met. "I am hungry," they said. "You saved me." They stared at me and Jonathan. "How… are you feeling, Osax?" They blinked.

I felt my mandibles tighten. Jonathan looked at me with furrowed brows.

"We need to leave, now," he said. "K! What's the situation?"

"What does it look like?!" She shouted back angrily. She retracted her wrist cable. It was useless. K looked at us, and I could tell gears were turning in her head.

Omega heard it first. Then Jonathan and I followed their stumbling gaze to the tunnel behind us.

Click, click, click.

The myrok had decided it was time to close in, and it was almost here.

"Gah!" Jonathan exclaimed. "K, block the tunnel!"

"No time!" She cried.

I shook my head. "Besides, myroks have super strength too. A barricade wouldn't stop it!"

K marched toward us. "Alright," she said, looking me in the eye. "Sorry if this hurts!"

K grabbed me by the chest with both hands, and hoisted me into the air. Before I had time to protest, she took a running start toward the opening. She flung her arms upward, and suddenly I was soaring through the air. My long limbs reached out in vain, trying to grab onto something or stabilize my twirling body.

"*Ah!*"

I burst into the colourful jungle and tumbled through the air. I landed on my back on a wet fern, with the wind knocked out of me. I looked up at the dense leaves and branches above me, and the dots of sunlight that snaked between them. Then my lungs filled with invigorating air, and the smell of petrichor. I got to my feet.

I heard Jonathan shout, "Hey, wait-" before screaming as he flew up out of the cave. His long coat swirled behind him. He rolled as he landed, and after a few seconds reoriented himself and groaned as he got to his feet.

I stepped over to the hole in the ground, and peered inside. K and Omega looked up at me.

"Come on!" I cried.

K grabbed Omega, and hurled them up out of the cave. Being Omega, I expected them to land gracefully like a cat, but instead they collapsed loudly onto their side next to me, and I winced. Then Jonathan jogged up next to us, and looked down the hole with me.

"Come on, K!" he shouted. "Jump!"

She hesitated. "I've never tried to jump this high!"

"You can do it!" he cheered. "Trust me! The capacity of your leg muscles- The power and leverage, in relation to your overall body mass, should allow you an acceleration fast enough-"

"Yeah, yeah!" she replied. She crouched, bending her legs generously.

"K," I said. "You can do it!"

She looked up at me, and smirked. "Thanks."

Energy burst against the wall, and K fell onto her side from the kinetic force of the impact. My heart stuttered. The myrok crawled toward her as the dust from its bio-laser cleared. Omega crawled to the edge of the hole, and gazed down at the scene.

I handed Jonathan his pistol. "Shoot it!" He grimaced, and fired bolts of energy down at the creature. The laser bullets seemed to melt into its body, completely ineffective. But Jonathan caught its attention. It reared its head up, gazing at us with its glowing yellow eyes. It wrenched its gaping beak open, and howled. There was an explosion of sound as the creatures all around the cave opening heard its cry, and suddenly sped off in all directions, wanting to be anywhere but here.

"K!" I cried. "Shoot your cable to me! I'll grab it!"

She gazed up at me. The myrok was distracted by us, but its body loomed over K's. She was in terrible danger. She raised her wrist up toward me and launched the grappling hook.

The cable whiffled through the air, and as it began to descend again I wrapped my fingers around it. Pain shot from the skin of my hands as the cable slid between my fingers. But I held the cable. My feet sank into the mud around the lip of the cave, and I reeled K up from the edge of the hole. Jonathan kept firing at the myrok, and its tail illuminated. The cable started retracting itself, and K used her legs to brace her ascent up the slippery incline. In a matter of seconds, she breached the surface, and she fell into my arms. We held each other, and I was filled with relief.

The myrok's energy beam fired up from the cave, and Jonathan yelped as he fell back, dropping the pistol into the hole. I let go of K, and bent over to help Jonathan to his feet. He was shaken, but unharmed.

"Go!"

Jonathan and I helped Omega stand, and we all started sprinting away into the trees. Jonathan was swift, running ahead of us all.

Then I heard K grunt in pain behind me, and I turned to see what was the matter. She was several meters behind. She clutched the sides of her head and moaned. She was blacking out. She shook, then her body went limp and she fell into the undergrowth. The myrok's front legs curled out over the rim of the hole, pulsing, and it dragged itself onto the surface. Its soulless eyes locked onto K.

My eyes were wide with terror. I had just brought her back, but K was in mortal danger. I wanted desperately to help, but I was unarmed. I clenched my fists, and inhaled slowly as my eyes narrowed. It didn't matter; I couldn't lose her again. My feet dug into the muddy soil beneath me as I poised myself to run for her. I had to try... Even if it was suicide to go up against the myrok... *I had to try!*

I took one step- then my arm was yanked back.

Omega threw me behind them, tripping me onto my side. Their tail flicked back and forth, and their body trembled for a brief moment. The colour of their skin began to warm slightly. They breathed in through their skin, keeping their lips tightly shut. They struggled to keep their composure, and I knew they had pulled me back for a grave reason. They were holding something in their hands- it was their belt of grenades.

"Omega!" I cried, wincing as I tried to stand. "Its skin is too resilient! And the blast will kill K!"

Omega replied flatly. "Not if I detonate them inside it."

The blood drained from my face. Omega was going to climb inside its mouth. "N- No, wait!" I stammered. I struggled to my feet. They turned to run, but I grabbed them by the arm. "That's suicide!" I cried.

Omega looked up at me. "I must. Or K will die. We all will. We cannot escape the myrok."

I shook them by the shoulders. "Omega! You won't survive! You weren't designed for this!"

The sun glinted off their large eyes. They looked at me, and it was as though a sudden clarity had filled their soul. They smiled slightly, and I could tell the smile was meant for me, to put me at ease. They spoke quietly, and surely. "And I was not created to make friends," they said. "Yet I did."

Omega shoved me to the ground with more speed than I could have predicted. When I sat upright, I saw them sprinting toward the myrok, their claws kicking up mud. The myrok's beak was raised above K, ready to strike. In a second, K would be dead. My chest constricted as I watched Omega trip on their approach. But they bolted up and whipped a hand forward, and threw a shuriken which grazed the myrok's cheek. Annoyed, it turned to face its new assailant, and shrieked to scare Omega off. Its beak opened wide… wide enough to swallow me whole. And Omega dove head first into its maw.

The creature gagged, and its beak shut. I was paralyzed. Then the ground shook from the explosion. The myrok's body quivered, then collapsed, still, and silent. Omega had done it. They'd saved us.

Jonathan panted past me, straight for K. I fell to my knees, staring at the corpse of the myrok. I gazed at my hands, and flexed my fingers weakly. I felt cold. If Omega had let me charge forward, the myrok would have killed me for sure. But instead, I was alive. We were alive.

And they were gone.

Forty-Eight

Silence filled every corner of the room.

The sun was low.

I sipped my drink. My ears lowered, and my eyes thoughtfully fell to the table, and the investigator's computer placed on the opposite side from me.

The investigator brushed a stray blonde lock aside, and leaned forward. Her blue eyes penetrated me. She frowned.

I basked in the silence, giving my voice a rest. The room was dimly lit by warm lamps. The sky was cloudy and the sun was low through the glass wall... the market would be closing soon. I knew I needed to return there, and buy more rations. *In a minute*, I thought.

"That's all for now," I said, standing up.

The investigator sighed, and gazed at me. "So, just like that?"

I blinked. "Just like what?"

"Omega. Dead. Just like that?"

I clenched my fists. "You could use a little more tact," I said.

"You as well," she retorted. She leaned back in her chair, stretching her arms up, and gazing at me.

My ears drooped. "I meant, Omega's passing affected me greatly. I would request that you broach such a topic with sensitivity." My voice was calm and quiet.

She was silent. She stood up, and adjusted her black uniform. "Alright. I'm sorry," she said. I eyed her carefully. "Thank you, Talcorosax, for continuing the story today, despite our conflict." She watched me curiously, then smirked. "I think I just get a little stir crazy, spending so long indoors. It makes me irritable." She chuckled nervously.

Seriously? I thought. *That's your excuse?*

"Of course," I replied, politely. "Now if you'll excuse me, I have other matters to attend to." I bowed farewell, in the skyther style. At least it felt good to pretend to be pleasant, for a moment. "Goodnight, Investigator." I said.

She folded her computer. "Shall we continue tomorrow?" she asked, gazing at me curiously.

I hesitated. "You really want to marathon this, don't you?"

She paused. "Well, the sooner we finish, the sooner I can get back to focusing on other things."

"Yes," I replied. "Of course. As will I, once the story is done. I have… a lot of things to do…" I trailed off, then nodded. "Yes, tomorrow morning, meet back here. There's still plenty left to tell. But with luck, by the time the sun sets tomorrow, I believe this business will be done. You'll be able to go tell the TAU you did your research on me, and everything checks out. And you'll have a nice audio-book of the story to listen to when you're feeling nostalgic."

She snorted a laugh. "Yes, of course." She waved goodbye, and as I turned to leave said, "Watch your back tonight, Talcorosax. In case those skythers come back."

My skin crawled as a chill ran down my spine. I was paralyzed.

I willed myself to face her. "Of course," I said, lifting my ears weakly. She held her computer tucked under her arm, and stood up straight as she gazed my way. "Thanks for the concern."

◆

Despite her warnings, I didn't run into any trouble in the market that night. I bought another two cases of rations, and averted my gaze from the people who took refuge beneath the signs, fighting to silence the voices in my head screaming *do more! You have resources! Try to help!* I could barely help myself. I barely wanted to.

I caught my breath atop the mountainside, absentmindedly scratching my chest fur. Still the TAU ships circled the sky. Still the city glowed beneath me. Still the cold embrace of the shadows beckoned me. My feet were cold against the rough stone, still damp from the rain the night before, which hadn't fully evaporated. I was tired- achingly exhausted- and I didn't want to waste any more time here. Anxiously I checked my holo-gauntlet for the fiftieth time since heading to the market. Still no reply from Fiona.

I placed the cases of rations next to the tree. The note I had left the night before was gone. My breath formed wispy clouds in the air as I let my eyes drag to the darkness of the forest, away from the city. Something stirred in the shadows.

"You can come out," I said. My voice was hoarse. "It's me."

There was no reply. Even the rustling ceased. There was no wind. Nothing stirred. I was caught between the glow of the city and the shadow. And I was alone. But I didn't want to be.

"Please," I begged. "Come out..." My voice was barely audible, and I choked back a sob. I held my hands in front of me. Were they even mine? They looked foreign to me, felt foreign, and even as I flexed them and willed myself to be present, I began to panic more and more. Reality was slipping away from me. I felt like I was stuck in some sort of limbo.

Breathing hard, I stumbled back to the summit, and gazed out at the city. It should have been a beautiful array of colours. And it *was*. I knew it was. But I couldn't feel it. I couldn't feel the colours. Time seemed to lag behind me, I was so tired. At least I was outside in the fresh air. I knew I should be sleeping, for my health, for any shred of hope that tomorrow might be better, but I wasn't. I wasn't sure I even could. A few stars stared back at me through a gap in the clouds. A tiny glimmer of hope, too far to reach.

I wondered if I should go and seek help. But from who? And what if it did more harm than good?

I lingered there for longer than I should, waiting for them to arrive. When I was certain they wouldn't, I began to scribble them a note.

"I hope these supplies aren't too late. And I need to ask a favour..."

Later, I lay for hours in my bed, watching television on my holo-gauntlet. It was the only light in the room. It felt good to numb myself. Well, no. That's not true. It just didn't feel bad... No. That isn't true either. It didn't feel scary. That's what it was. As long as I didn't think too hard about it, I was fine.

I flipped through the channels. There was a romantic drama. It was rather risque, featuring a romance between a skyther and a human. I didn't find out how it ended, cause I switched channels when the human fell into a coma following a hover-car accident. Not the kind of thing I wanted to see, yet leaving the story unfinished made me feel unresolved.

The local news droned on about an assault in the outskirts of the city. Someone had been hospitalized, apparently recovering. Someone else was arrested. Whatever. Then it switched to a new program, an informational video on what to do if you discover a bioweapon.

I leaned in. The narrator explained in the skyther tongue the dangers of bioweapons, reiterating that it is TAU law that any life forms biologically engineered for military or combat uses be immediately reported and turned into the authorities. "Bioweapons are a real threat to civilization," the voice said, "which is why the TAU have made them illegal. If you need any convincing, it was discovered by King Talcorosax himself that the valicorr were bioweapons created by the loro many millennia ago. Creating bioweapons is not only unethical, but it is also a crime. Housing a bioweapon is a crime as well. If you have any information about bioweapons, contact this code-signal to report directly to Round Table, the branch of TAU enforcers tasked with arresting bioweapons. Or, contact skyther police. Remember, Astraloth authorities have agreed to enforce these important laws in skyther space, in good faith, to uphold the treaty between Astraloth and Earth, and keep the galaxy safe."

I switched to a human crime show that was halfway through. The detective retrieved a piece of paper from a body, and waved it into the camera. "A letter from the assassin's leader!" His skyther assistant asked, in broken English, "Why they make writing, when can just send text?" The detective whirled around dramatically, and adjusted his glasses as he looked at the paper. "Don't be so naive, Toli. You can hack a computer... you can't hack paper!" Then the two were ambushed by a group of humans in black masks, armed with molecular swords. One of them said, "It's been a long time, Mister Baker. But now, I'm afraid, your time is up!" The music swelled as the image faded out.

A commercial popped up. There I was, sipping a can, decked out in combat gear. "Nothing beats a can of Galaxy Root Beer!" I said. "Galaxy Root Beer, you're a-"

I flicked a switch, and my holo-gauntlet shut off with a whine. It was well past midnight. I sighed, put my head in my hands. I felt freezing, so I pulled my messy sheets over my body. Why had I wasted so much time tonight? I was just stressed. I thought about the investigator. Tomorrow was going to be a long day, and I had a sinking feeling that whatever happened, by the end of it, things would be different. *Maybe change would be good,* said a tiny voice in my head. Then I shut my eyes, and tried not to think about waking up.

◆

The sun had barely risen. Bleary eyed, I slipped out of bed, and grabbed my holo-gauntlet before doing anything else. I checked for messages. Nothing. Then I activated my personal food synthesizer and scrolled through the logs of items I had recently synthesized until I found something that seemed mildly appealing. I sat on my bed and ate a small sandwich. It wasn't great, but it was something. The accompanying honeyed tea helped.

I took fifteen minutes to have a shower in my personal bathroom, and an extra few to dry off in the full body dryer which moved up and down blowing hot air on me. I grabbed a tiny brush and started cleaning my mandibles and teeth. I spat into the sink, and as I left the room the sink retracted into the wall on standby mode.

Back in my room, I glanced at myself in the mirror. My fur was a mess. My eyes were baggy. But I kind of felt like I recognized myself, for a second. So that was good. I just tried not to stare at myself too long. I was afraid the familiarity would wear off. In fact I felt like it already was beginning to. My brain wouldn't let me be too present… that would hurt too much. I had to stay detached. But I had to keep my wits about me today. I had to be on alert. I knew today was the day that the trap would be sprung. I was counting on it.

I reached up for my red coat on the clothes hooks, then remembered it was gone. I had left it with the skyther on the street. My hand hovered above the black hooded cloak which hung next to where my red coat used to be. The cloak Joëlle had given me. I held my hand there for a few seconds, contemplating what to do.

I took it off the hook, and flung it over my shoulders. The hood rested on my back, and the sides of the cape draped in front of my arms. I looked at myself in the mirror. I stood up straighter. I looked rugged, ready for adventure. I took in a deep breath. I reached my hands up to draw the hood over my head… then tore the thing off.

Without another glance, I tossed the cloak into a crumpled ball in the corner, and shut the door to my quarters as I left for the meeting room.

◆

We sat across from each other, a drink in each of our hands. We had already greeted each other. She hit the recording button. I glanced out the glass wall at the sun slowly rising. Then my eyes locked with the investigator's. She stared at me, a wicked smile spread across her face. She was excited this morning- excited that the story would be finishing today, as I had said it would the night before. I wasn't totally sure how I would get through everything in time, but I was tired of this charade. Everything was in place. I was eager to spring the trap.

I sipped my root beer, savouring the sound and the taste. "Alright," I said. "Let's not waste any more time."

Forty-Nine

Five hours after Omega's sacrifice, Jonathan, K and I found ourselves waiting atop another dusty plateau. The wind screeched across the plain, blowing sand up around our legs and into our faces. I sat with my hands bound behind my back with thick vines. K watched over me grimly, and Jonathan scanned the skies. But there was a reason we were there.

Jonathan and I had carried K's body away from the cave, and made our way as quickly as possible to higher levels above the heat of the jungle. None of us wanted to succumb to heat stroke, so that was our primary goal.

When K finally came to, we had to explain what happened. She was silent for nearly half an hour after hearing about what Omega had done, as we all searched for food and water in a part of the mountains, before finally speaking. And when she did speak, it was angrily, and it was directed at Jonathan.

K drilled him with questions about her past. She blamed him for everything bad that had happened. She said that if he hadn't betrayed us, Joëlle wouldn't be captive right now, and Omega wouldn't have died. She threatened to throw him off the cliff, though she restrained herself. Jonathan agreed with her. He broke down, blaming himself for all of the losses we had suffered. I hung my head in silence, and so did K. It took us a long time to find the strength to keep going. But eventually thirst drove us to climb deeper into the mountains, searching for the river that cascaded down the mountain's crevice to the underground temple.

Some time later, we found the stream in a glade of short trees upon the mountain, and each drank our share of the fresh water. It was remarkably fresh, delicious even, and I felt strength returning to me with each gulp. My nose filled with a sweet fragrance from tiny flowers that bloomed by the water. We splashed our faces to keep them cool in the heat of the three suns, and sat together on some stones in a circle, discussing what to do. K absentmindedly crushed rocks with her fingers, while Jonathan sat on his hands, and I drew lines in the gravel with a leafy stick.

We had between us no weapons, and only two working holo-gauntlets. Omega was gone. Joëlle was captive, presumably brought aboard Duhrnan's mothership, as Jonathan had commanded the Brotherhood reinforcements to do. And they had taken her there in the Firebrand, which meant we had no starship to help us either. We were stranded on Malum, with no supplies, no food, no reinforcements, and no weapons. The only thing we could do was attempt to contact someone, but even then, the range of our holo-gauntlets wouldn't be enough to leave the planet, even without the sporadic interference of Malum's atmosphere.

But none of us wanted to flee anyway. And as much as we all hated the idea, we quickly agreed that we only had one option, (unless you count giving up on saving Earth and trying to live the rest of our lives on Malum as an option, but we did not). There was only one choice, and if it worked, it wasn't a half bad idea. We had to turn ourselves in to the mothership.

If we were to save Joëlle, we'd have to find a way onto the mothership anyway. We scanned for her earpiece, but it was either beyond the range of our holo-gauntlets, or it was within a disruptive field of some kind. Our best assumption was that she was aboard the mothership. The safest way for us to get inside would be to let our enemies bring us on board. I squirmed at the thought of being captured by Duhrnan and his valicorr soldiers, let alone the Brotherhood allies, but I knew it was our best chance. Not only that, but we needed a way off the planet. Omega had mentioned Brotherhood outposts on Malum, so in theory we could infiltrate one and steal a ship if we wanted to flee. But again, we were unarmed. The chances of us finding an outpost and successfully executing that plan were minuscule.

We had one significant advantage, however. Jonathan and K were known members of the Brotherhood. Of course, previously, Ryner had ordered Director Aali to have Jonathan killed, and in turn Aali ordered K's alter ego to follow through on the command. Following that, Ryner obviously changed his mind about Jonathan and thought he could use him a little longer when he ordered him to watch us aboard the Firebrand. But it was clear the Brotherhood was not a transparent organization, even within its own ranks. The chances that someone aboard the mothership knew that Jonathan and K were rebels against the Brotherhood, or that if K was *really* activated she would kill Jonathan, were slim. So, the plan was to present me as a prisoner, one that Jonathan had secured with the help of his bioweapon, K, a sleeper agent who he had successfully activated, and was following his every command.

So K tied my hands with vines, the only thing we had available, and we made our way to a high plateau, with as little atmospheric interference as possible. Jonathan and K had been transmitting their coordinates for hours. The range of the signal was short, so we had to wait for a valicorr ship to fly by. Eventually however, a scout noticed us, and contacted Jonathan.

He turned to face K and I. His face was grim. "Duhrnan is coming," he said.

I exhaled. It was a strange feeling, one of both relief and dread. It was too late to change plans now.

K stepped toward Jonathan. "You know… if you decide to betray us once we get inside… I'm gonna kill you. I don't care if it gets me killed in the process- hell, I'm gonna die anyway, so-"

Jonathan raised his hands defensively. "K… I understand. I promise, I will not do anything to betray our mission."

K snorted angrily, and brushed some dust off her arms. "Like a promise from you means anything."

"Come on," I said. They turned to me. "We have to trust each other now. I know it's a lot to ask, but we need to trust one another. Like Joëlle would say… every good team is built on trust."

Jonathan and K pursed their lips, and glanced to each other. A moment passed.

Jonathan sighed. "I can't believe the mess we're in. You have no idea how sorry I am about everything."

K shook her head. "I have some idea. I know it's not sorry enough."

He frowned.

I stood up, my arms still tied. "Look," I said. "If you can't trust each other for our sake, then do it for Joëlle's." I paused. "Do it for Omega. They would want us to have the best chance of succeeding, and that means we have to be airtight in our faith in one another."

Jonathan nodded, and K sighed. At last, K reached out a hand to Jonathan. He hesitated, then grabbed her hand to shake.

"*Ow!*" He yelped.

K smirked. "What? It's just a handshake."

Jonathan pulled his hand back, and shook it in the air, staring at K.

"K!" I said. "Please!"

"What?!" She complained. "It's a lot better than he deserves!"

"I don't think he needs us threatening him anymore!"

K's lips curved into a thin frown.

Jonathan cleared his throat. "It's alright. You have every reason to hate me. And after Duhrnan is stopped, I will disappear. You'll never have to hear from me… never have to see my face again," he said. "But for now, I'm committed to saving Earth." He shook his head, a tear forming in his eye. His voice wavered. "Too many have already died. Too many have been used to fuel this machine of destruction and power. It's the least I can do, trying to redeem myself. And admit my wrongs."

"No, it's not the least you can do," I said. "You could have done nothing. And that's why I believe in you."

Jonathan turned to me, and I saw a spark of hope in his eyes. He smiled weakly.

K said, "Right. Well, I'm glad we have that sorted out. Alright, for now, I trust you. But don't forget my warning."

"I won't," he said.

K put her hand on my shoulder. Jonathan stepped up next to us. He put his hands on our shoulders and we huddled together in a circle, lowering our eyes and staring at the ground. We shared a deep breath.

"We need a win," I said. "Desperately. So desperately, our lives *literally* depend on it. But just like any creature that is backed into a corner, now isn't the time to hold back." I glanced at each of them. "We have no other option than to fight with all the heart, instinct, and quick thinking that we have. We've already been pushed past our limits, and that means that we can, and will, do anything necessary to win. This turn of events might be our key to stopping the mothership…"

A familiar flame kindled within me as I hatched an idea.

"Omega's sacrifice didn't just save our lives…" I narrowed my eyes. "I thought, coming to Malum, we would discover something about the loro that would help us stop Duhrnan. I was wrong… but it wasn't a waste. I knew destiny brought us here for a reason, and that reason was to find Omega. They, whether intentionally or not, gave us the key insight we need to stop the mothership." Tension was rising between us. Jonathan stared at me, and K breathed with a powerful calmness. "Just like the myrok, the mothership's armour is nearly impenetrable from the outside. But from the *inside*…"

The air was electrified around us. This was our chance.

"We're about to leap into the maw of the mothership," I said. "Obviously, we need to find a way to escape, and with Joëlle. But even if that's not possible… for the sake of the galaxy, we must take this opportunity to destroy the mothership from the inside. It may be our only chance. Once your cover is blown, we will only have so much time to take action, sabotage the starship, and escape with Joëlle."

We shared one last moment of silence, before I concluded.

"Let's go save the day."

We all nodded. Then Jonathan checked his scanner.

The mothership was almost here.

We waited for a few minutes as the great black spider descended on its invisible thread. Engulfed in shadow, we craned our necks toward the sky. A valicorr dropship, accompanied by four insect-like fighters, approached us. Heat blasted us from the engines of the dropship as it touched down, and valicorr soldiers in sleek black armour emerged, beckoning us to enter the shuttle. K shot me a glance, and winked, before resuming a stone-cold expression. She hoisted me up, and following Jonathan, shoved me onto the shuttle. I took in one last breath of fresh air before the shuttle doors closed, and I sat in silence next to Jonathan and K, bound, unarmed, and surrounded by valicorr. Their sets of three eyes were wet in the darkness, gazing at me curiously. They snarled quietly, baring their needle-like teeth. The seat was a cold metal. There were no windows, but I felt the shuttle lurch upwards. In just minutes, we would be aboard the mothership.

I thought about Voren. I thought about Astraloth. I thought about my mother. I thought about Omega.

We were almost within the heart of Duhrnan's domain. I clenched my fists in anticipation.

Fifty

My heart was beating hard. I glanced to Jonathan, hoping for some reassurance. But he was seated to my left, and couldn't see me with his robotic right eye being broken. Instead he breathed slowly, obviously trying to calm himself. I looked to K, and she was sitting perfectly straight- I didn't even know she could do that- and her face was almost completely neutral. Almost, except for a tiny hint of fear. Her horns stuck out on either side of her head, like some sort of blue demon. She didn't look my way, and I realized staring at her might make her uncomfortable, and her job a lot more challenging, so I averted my gaze. I looked forward, straight into the eyes of a valicorr soldier. Its pitch black sockets gazed into my soul, and it hissed through clenched teeth. It took a step toward me, and I leaned back in my seat. Though I stood around eight feet and the valicorr only seven, I was seated, so it loomed over me on its lanky digitigrade legs. The talons on its feet clawed at the metal floor of the shuttle.

Jonathan turned to it. "Back off," he said. "The prisoner is to be unharmed."

It twisted its head creepily toward him, and silently stepped backwards. The other valicorr kept their distance.

The shuttle touched down with a shake. The deep growl of the mothership's heart permeated the atmosphere and I felt a low vibration coursing through my body. Jonathan stood. K copied him, and lifted me to my feet. Then the doors of the shuttle opened, and we all stepped out onto a catwalk.

We had entered the mothership from a hangar on its underside, and the shuttle was clamped from the ceiling of the hangar. We stood on a silver catwalk that led towards a ledge, with doors lining the wall that led deeper into the mothership. The interior was lit with round white lights mounted on the walls and ceiling, and the walls were grey-purple.

The hangar was circular, with a massive door beneath us that lay open to the atmosphere of Malum. I looked down from the side of the catwalk at clouds, and the orange sand miles below. It made me dizzy, so I quickly stopped. Rows of catwalks and ships hanging from the ceiling lined the circular ledge, suspended in the air above the opening below us.

Valicorr officers stared at us blankly from above, through a high glass window on the far wall which led to a control room of some kind that oversaw the hangar. As we were led to the edge of the room, the bay door closed, sealing us inside the mothership. A valicorr approached us, with a scar across the grey skin of its face, adorned in purple and black clothing. And to my surprise, it spoke to us.

"Wellsworth," it rasped. "The Emperor demands your presence."

Jonathan cleared his throat, and stood up straighter, putting his arms behind his back. "Well, good," he said. "I'm sure he's happy to know that, as per Ryner's orders, I successfully neutralized the pests, and even brought one of them with me as a prisoner."

There were valicorr guards all around armed with wrist-mounted cannons and swords. The captain replied, "The Emperor will not be happy unless you follow me to his chambers. You must bring the bioweapon, and the prisoner."

Jonathan nodded. "Yes, of course." He opened his mouth to speak, and paused. "What of the other prisoner? Is Joëlle already with Duhrnan?"

The valicorr snapped its eyes to Jonathan, looking down at him. "I do not know what prisoner you speak of," it said. "Perhaps they are already dead."

"What are you talking about?!" I blurted. I stepped forward, and it took K a second to realize she was supposed to be restraining me. She grabbed my arm tightly, and held me in place.

The scarred valicorr hissed at me, then turned back to Jonathan. It said, "Keep this one quiet. We do not tolerate enemies aboard our sacred vessel. It only lives because the Emperor demands it." The valicorr looked at me, with anger burning in its eyes.

Jonathan nodded. "You heard them," he said to me. "Stay quiet." He stared at me with grave intensity.

"Duhrnan commands that the prisoner be placed in a holding chair." As the valicorr said this, two more pushed a hovering metal seat my way. Without warning, the valicorr cut my bonds, then shoved me so I was seated on the floating chair. They slammed my wrists to the arm wrests and my ankles to the metal legs of the hovering chair. A second later, metallic straps began to materialize over top of my limbs. The holding chair itself must have had some kind of nanotechnology, building solid restraints out of nanites, tiny robotic particles that were stored inside the chair.

Their footsteps echoed as the valicorr led us out of the hangar, and I looked back at K, who was pushing me forward in the floating chair. Her eyes darted to mine briefly, before returning ahead.

◆

We were led silently by six valicorr, plus the scarred one, through a maze of hallways, rooms, and elevators. Some of the walls sported glowing engravings, reminiscent of the central chambers of the loro ruins. *So,* I thought, *the mothership was designed by the loro.* It was all starting to make sense. If Duhrnan was a loro, and the valicorr were loro bioweapons designed to be servants of the loro, then of course the mothership was of loro design as well. That explained why the armour was so sophisticated, the size so impressive, and the weaponry so destructive. The loro didn't mess around… when they built something, they went all in.

I couldn't help but wonder how Duhrnan was the leader of the valicorr. He was so unstable. It didn't add up… where did he come from? What made him appear now? The loro were supposed to be extinct. I imagined him, his wild, frenetic demeanour… it was incongruous with the loro that I had studied. What were the chances that the first and only living loro that appeared would be Duhrnan? Nothing I had found in all my time as a loro researcher indicated that a majority, let alone any loro, were this evil, or volatile, or unsettled for that matter. Yet, because of the valicorr's DNA, they had no choice but to follow him, simply because he was a loro. It reminded me of the 'Sheep's Clothing' program.

My eyes were constantly darting around the greyish halls, looking for anything noteworthy, trying desperately to get my bearings. All of the markings and signage on the ship were written in ancient loro characters. K pushed me onward as I concentrated hard, trying to recall the symbols for words like 'power', 'generator', 'core', or anything similar, and seeing if I recognized those words on any of the walls. In order to sabotage the ship, we would first need to find the source of its power.

But before I could think any more about it, the valicorr halted before a large door.

Jonathan gulped. K glanced at me. Then Jonathan frowned, and glared at me. "Come on," he said, gruffly. He led us toward the door, which slid open into the ceiling automatically.

The thrum of the ship's engines reverberated through the floor as we entered the room. The door which we entered through was the only one in the room, and it slid shut behind us with a hiss. The floor was detailed with dimly glowing purple engravings. Ornate pillars stood on either side of a raised platform on the far side of the room. It held a towering throne, which faced away from us toward a massive window. The view revealed sky and clouds below as the mothership hovered in the atmosphere of Malum.

A drop of blood hit the floor from the ceiling, and I glanced up, ears peeling back. Duhrnan's furry beast was huddled, clinging to the ceiling, with something fleshy in its mouth. The massive monster's black and blue fur shimmered in the sunlight from outside. It had red accents on its face and back, and its six legs. The razor-sharp barb on its tail flicked back and forth, and its pure white eyes landed on me.

I started in my seat as it fell to the floor with a thud, and snarled at us, dropping the meat and revealing a set of jagged teeth. It must have been almost four meters long, and far too close for my liking. It raised its hackles, and lowered its muzzle to the ground, ready to pounce.

"Come, Lupaph!" Duhrnan's voice slithered out from behind the throne. The beast gave a low growl, then snatched up the chunk of meat and trotted around the room to him. I felt my blood beginning to boil.

The throne rotated to face us automatically, and Duhrnan stepped out of his seat on his digitigrade legs, rising up to my height. He wore purple, brown, and red robes, with black armour plates on his shoulders, arms, and torso. Hanging from his shoulders was a wide black cape, with a fancy collar around his neck. Four E-pistols adorned his legs, two on each side. His pale snout contorted into a freakishly wide grin of sharp teeth. His eyes were wide, and seemed to faintly glow violet. His four arms stretched up and outward as he rose, before falling to his sides. He inhaled through the slits of his nostrils. Then his eyes fell on me, and I felt a chill run down my spine.

I felt K's grip on my arm tighten.

Jonathan took a step toward him. "Emperor Duhrnan, it's an honour to finally meet you in person." He feigned a smile, but Duhrnan wasn't looking his way.

Ignoring him, Duhrnan pressed a button on his wrist, and several panels in the ceiling slid open. One by one, twelve drones hovered down from the ceiling, and began floating in the room, circling us. They were round black robots, with insect-like appendages sticking out at various angles. Duhrnan closed the gap between us, and reached up a hand to my face. He grabbed my cheeks with a cold set of fingers, and tilted his head to the side, grinning. "I've never seen a skyther up close before," he said.

"Yet you destroyed Astraloth!" I spat.

He recoiled, dropping his hand to his side. He looked genuinely upset, and wiped away my saliva from his clothing. Then his eyes narrowed. "You must be Talcorosax, son of the late Queen. Well I am Duhrnan." I flinched as he spat right back at me.

K lunged forward, and shoved Duhrnan back with a snarl. He stumbled backwards, and the monster behind him shot up, growling. In unison, the drones whined as yellow energy guns activated on each one, and they aimed at the three of us. Jonathan gestured to K.

"K!" he said. "You can… stop guarding the prisoner now." His eye was wide with intensity, and K glared at him, but relented. She resumed a neutral position, though I could tell she was clenching her jaw. So was I.

Duhrnan raised his two left hands toward the beast. "Be calm, Lupaph. All is well." He then turned his attention to Jonathan, and slowly crept toward him as the ship's engines hummed. He smiled ominously.

The three of us glanced around nervously at the drones. Duhrnan leaned forward as he paced back and forth, eyeing us. He grinned, clasping both sets of hands together. "Jonathan, Jonathan, Jonathan… You must make sure you keep a tight leash on that K, or things might get unpleasant." His words were venomous.

Jonathan breathed calmly. "Of course, Duhrnan."

I kept my mouth shut. Duhrnan and the beast watched us as the drones hovered around slowly, tiny yellow sparks flitting from their barrels.

Duhrnan stood up straight, and stretched his neck to each side, before sighing. He stepped up toward me, and I could sense K tensing. He reached a hand up to me and grabbed my headset, the earpiece which Joëlle had given to me. He removed it, looked at it, then placed it in Jonathan's hands. "Deal with this," he said. "Talcorosax will not need it anymore as a prisoner aboard this vessel."

Jonathan nodded, and put the headset inside his coat. I clenched my mandibles.

"Have Talcorosax escorted to the brig for now," said Duhrnan.

"It will be done," said Jonathan nervously.

I smelled blood as Lupaph rose onto its massive paws and barked at me. Duhrnan raised his hands. "Don't get too excited, Lupaph! I haven't decided how I want to play with him... yet! But when I'm done I'll be sure to give you the leftovers!"

Eyes wide, I glanced at the meat at Lupaph's feet, then to Jonathan. He shook his head at me silently. K trembled faintly, struggling to contain herself. I could tell she wanted nothing more than to grab Duhrnan by the chest and throw him out the window. But with those drones surrounding us, she knew that she wouldn't be fast enough to kill him without at least one of us getting hurt, or killed. Depending on how things went, it might be our only choice.

Jonathan hesitated. "While we were in the cave, Duhrnan, my cybernetic eye was damaged. I... left a replacement on the Firebrand, somewhere- Joëlle's ship. Could- could you direct me to it?"

Duhrnan whirled around, and took a few steps away from us. His tone was mocking. "Oh, Jonathan. I'm so sorry, but you must be confused. The Firebrand isn't aboard the flagship."

"What?" I blinked. *Then where is it?!*

Jonathan stuttered. "I- I ordered the Brotherhood troops to bring her to the mothership. They escaped on the Firebrand. They should have docked with the vessel hours ago."

Duhrnan faced us, frowning absently. "I don't know what happened to them." He paused, looking at his hands.

I was expecting him to say more, when suddenly, the door behind us opened. The scarred valicorr stepped forward, and kneeled before Duhrnan, who gazed down at it with disdain.

"Why the interruption?" Duhrnan asked impatiently.

The scarred one replied in a hoarse voice. As it spoke, Duhrnan stomped towards the valicorr, his cape flowing behind him. "My Emperor, Duhrnan... I do not know how-"

He bent over, and picked it up by the throat with his top two hands. He bared his teeth. "What. Do. You. Want?" It choked and coughed. I winced, unable to look away.

"A- A-" The valicorr struggled to speak. It almost looked like their three eyes were going to pop out. "Aszzt-"

"What is it?" Duhrnan whispered intensely, shaking the valicorr. "What is it?" His voice was like a whip.

At last, it coughed out a response. "Astraloth. Astraloth!"

Astraloth?! I leaned forward, restrained by the chair, ears raised in anticipation.

Duhrnan paused, then dropped the valicorr to the ground. It

scrambled onto its clawed feet.

"What about it?" Duhrnan growled.

"Astraloth..." the valicorr began, "Astraloth exists!"

Silence seeped into the room. Only the vibration of the ship could be heard.

"What?" I said. My mind was racing. "What do you mean?! Astraloth-"

"Quiet!" Duhrnan cried. Pain shot up from my cheek. His hand smacked me across the face. Blood dripped down my mandibles. My heart was racing.

Duhrnan turned to the valicorr. "That is impossible," he said. "I destroyed it. With the Shade Beam." He chuckled, then thrust his hands out triumphantly. "It vanished before the eyes of the galaxy!"

The valicorr was motionless. "Yes," it said bluntly. "But the planet reappeared. Astraloth exists!"

Fifty-One

Duhrnan marched past us, beyond the ring of drones, toward the window, and tapped his arm. The window darkened, and was replaced with a screen. It was displaying a video feed from a distant valicorr scout ship, orbiting… Astraloth!

I blinked, frozen to my seat. I gazed past Duhrnan's silhouette and stared at the image plastered on the wall. My home planet was there. Somehow, it wasn't destroyed by the Shade Beam. The four moons were in slightly different places, but Astraloth remained at their center. I could see both the red mass of the Thala nebula, and in a different section of space, the striking purple of the Toru nebula. Tears streamed down my face. It was miraculous. In that moment, I couldn't care less how it was possible. *Astraloth survived!*

I shut my eyes. The oceans, mountains, and trees of my home seemed to beam their energy right into my body. I thought of the orange avians, who's name I could never remember, and the regal athurlist, the apex predator of the jungles. I thought of my mother, Queen Suranos. She would be down on the planet, still alive. *Still alive!* Then I thought of the Great Temple, watching over my home city with its regal pillars and flowing rivers, and the great spheres-

The spheres of the Great Temple!

Somehow, the myths were real. They must have really had the power to protect Astraloth in its time of need. I was reeling in my seat. All my life, I took those stories for granted. But something saved Astraloth, and I could think of nothing else.

Duhrnan's head twitched to the side. Suddenly he groaned, clutching the side of his head, and he hunched over, moaning. His claws tightened around his skull.

The scarred one approached him, robes trailing the floor. "Emperor-"

Duhrnan whipped around, his eyes full of anger. Veins pulsed violently on his head. "To Astraloth. Maximum speed!" Spit frothed from his mouth.

The valicorr reached for their own holo-gauntlet, and after a brief moment, the window display shut off. The mothership tilted upwards toward space, and a moment later sky was replaced with a web of streaking stars. The entire ship shook like an earthquake- we were pushing speeds thought impossible via slipspace travel. I had to remind myself… the loro were more advanced than us.

The shaking kept growing, and the window seemed to burn in the image of each star, eventually turning pure white, until at last everything ceased with a bang. Astraloth was right in front of us. A thousand stars watched the mother spider descend toward its prey.

"Twelve percent energy remaining," the valicorr said.

"No matter," said Duhrnan, wiping the spit from his lips. "It's not as showy as the Shade Beam, but we only need a fraction of our reserves to wipe the surface of Astraloth clean. It's going to take a while, so we may as well begin!" He raised his hands to the air. "Power up the main cannons, and set a course for the surface! It doesn't matter where we begin… we'll glass everything. Eventually."

I strained against my wrists and ankles. "Bastard!" I shouted. "Can't you give it a rest?! Astraloth was peaceful to you. This war is entirely your doing! The universe is handing you a chance to make amends!" I bared my teeth. "You don't have to do this!"

Duhrnan stared at me. "And miss the chance to see your face as all life on Astraloth is squeezed dry?" he mocked. "I already missed it once. I don't want to make that mistake again!" He tilted his head to the side, and inhaled through the slits of his nose. "The quickest path from hope to despair… that is where true happiness resides."

I lowered my ears, tunnelling into him with my eyes. "I almost feel sorry for you, Duhrnan. You've clearly never felt real happiness."

He grinned. "How astute. But why would I need my own, when I can just take it from others?"

I grit my mandibles. "You're hopeless." Duhrnan shrugged.

Then I felt my spirits lift. Skyther fighters and cruisers began to emerge from the planet's surface. Their engines glowed red, each ship sleek and rounded, with triangular points sticking out the sides. A massive fleet of white starships rose up to challenge the valicorr vessel. A heroic act of defiance against Duhrnan. Astraloth wasn't going down without a fight.

We watched in silence for a brief moment as black fighters launched from the mothership. The ship hummed as the two fleets silently collided in a torrent of movement, lasers, and explosions. The stars were lit with a colourful show of energy blasts, like a deadly fireworks routine. I gripped the edge of my seat, as a harpoon of red lightning cut through one of the skyther cruisers from the mothership. They looked so small and insignificant from up here.

Duhrnan turned to the valicorr. "There is more resistance than I expected. Inform Ryner of the situation… tell him to bring his ship, the Silencer." The valicorr nodded, and left the room. "It seems our friend Ryner will be joining us, Jonathan." Duhrnan waved a hand to him. "Leave Talcorosax here with me. Now, take K, and leave us."

I gulped, and looked up to Jonathan and K.

Jonathan nodded. "Of course," he said. "Are you ready, K?" He began to remove his coat, casually, revealing a black jumpsuit and grey breastplate underneath.

K smirked, her orange eyes narrowed. "I was made ready."

Without warning, K kicked my hovering chair away to the left, and all at once the world went spinning. I tried not to get dizzy as I twirled outside the circle of drones, and bumped against the far wall. The holding chair levelled out and slowly spun like a buoyant object in water, and I watched the chaos unfold. Our survival hinged on the next few seconds.

Immediately after the kick, Jonathan ducked, and charged head first for Duhrnan, who spun around to face him. The circle of drones whined as their weapons charged. In a second they would fire on my unarmed companions.

K's arm shot to the side, and so did her wrist cable. Then she twisted her torso, flinging her arm in a wide arc. The cable whistled as it flew through the air like a supercharged tetherball. The cable itself knocked some of the drones aside, and the hook on the end smashed each drone it touched with vibrant bursts of fire. The drones were cut down by half in just a few seconds, and they focused onto K. The sheer force of K's arm turned her climbing gear into a deadly weapon, and she continued swinging it around like a flail.

Duhrnan drew his four pistols and spun each in his hand, just as Jonathan engaged with him. Before Duhrnan could get a clear shot, Jonathan threw his coat up onto his face, obscuring his vision. Duhrnan lifted his upper hands to the jacket, trying to peel it off. In the brief second of confusion, Jonathan kicked the gun in his lower-right hand clean out of his grip, and it soared through the air my direction. It clattered to the ground at my feet, and my ears lifted up. Duhrnan clawed at Jonathan's wrist. He tore the holo-gauntlet clean off. But as he did this, Jonathan grabbed the other gun with both hands, and twisted it out of Duhrnan's grasp.

"Yes!" I cheered from the sidelines.

K slammed more of the drones to the ground, disabling them, but she grimaced, grazed by a few bolts. Her armoured vest was smoking as she ducked behind one of the pillars. Meanwhile Duhrnan pulled the coat off his face, and fired his remaining two guns at Jonathan. Violet energy splintered off Jonathan's armour pads, and he stumbled back behind the other pillar. Duhrnan sneered, and squeezed down on Jonathan's holo-gauntlet. The device snapped between his fingers, and he dropped its remains to the floor.

"I must admit, Jonathan, I wasn't expecting this turn of events! You had been such a good little pawn up until now." He shook his head. "Tsk, tsk. What a naughty boy you are. Can't pick a side, so you keep betraying everyone. Your poor little head must hurt from confusion."

"Shut it, Duhrnan!" he replied. "The past is in the past. I know what side I'm on."

Jonathan fired at Duhrnan, who rolled behind the throne with agility almost comparable to Omega. Then my eyes landed on Lupaph.

The great beast had been stalking around, watching the fight, but its eyes fell on me, and it bared its teeth. Slowly, it began to approach.

Beads of sweat formed on my face. Frantically, with my arms and legs still tied, I swung my chest back and forth, tilting the hovering chair even as it tried to level itself. Each time, I dipped closer to the ground. At last, I heaved my body forward, and the chair flipped onto its front for a moment. I pulled my restrained hand toward the pistol. My fingers flicked open as I tried to grab it, but I accidentally knocked it a few feet away, gasping. I tucked my head, bouncing off the smooth floor. My ears flew forward as the chair swung back upright.

Lupaph's tail swivelled, and his crimson tongue fell to the floor. His teeth were red with blood. Our eyes met briefly, and I saw his body get ready to pounce. I grit my mandibles and looked at the gun, just a few feet away from me. Adrenaline coursed through my veins. I swung myself back to the floor.

I collided with the ground, face first, and shut my eyes. I bit down, and pushed myself back up with my fingers.

Gun in my mandibles, I bounced up. I opened my mouth, and

dropped the gun onto my lap.

Lupaph barked, and my ears shot back. He clawed six paws into the floor, and kicked off.

I thrust my pelvis out and rotated it, and the gun slid toward my twisting hand. My fingers fumbled for a second, spinning the gun so that I gripped the handle. My finger pressed against the trigger.

Crack!

Purple fumes wafted from the beast's head. Its body careened into me, and I bounced back, spinning against the wall.

"Lupaph!" Duhrnan yelled, staring at the lifeless body. Then he shrugged, and his lips curved to a smile. "Ah well. I can just make another."

A drone rose shakily from the ground, and the barrel of its gun twisted toward Jonathan. Then sparks flew from its side as it was punctured straight through by K's grappling hook. She extended the hooks, and it latched onto the drone's debris.

"Aw, hell yeah!" she said, as she pulled her newly weighted flail back to her.

Jonathan spoke loudly. "Give up, Duhrnan. You're outnumbered!"

At that, Duhrnan laughed. His voice lilted and soared through the room, ending in a cackle. "You should know never to say something like that. That kind of setup is irresistible!"

Duhrnan holstered his guns, and stepped out from behind the throne. His teeth were wide, and he opened his arms as he stepped gracefully toward the pillars. Jonathan fired his weapon, and purple bolts sparked against his armour. He laughed, and footsteps filled the room.

Valicorr soldiers poured into the room, and K and Jonathan scrambled around to the opposite sides of their cover. Yellow lasers spread across the room, igniting against the floor, pillars, and walls.

"Lookout!" I said, craning my neck.

Duhrnan ducked to the ground, and seemed to vanish. He *did* vanish! There was no trace of him. He must have been using the same cloaking technology as the shadow scout we found in the generator room on Voren.

Then something completely unexpected happened. The damaged drones lying around the room blasted metal guitar music from hidden speakers, laser lights, and mist. The room was a chaotic mess of sights and sounds, and my ears started to hurt. It was as though Duhrnan had packed an entire rock concert into his robots, and was just waiting for the moment to reveal it. I didn't know how to react to this absurd explosion of stimuli. But then I realized the brilliance of his plan- with so much ambient audio-visual noise, there was absolutely no way to determine where he was in the room. He cackled sadistically, his own voice amplified through the speakers of each drone, so the source couldn't be pinpointed.

The music was so loud I could hardly think. My chair slowly spun around, and I gazed into the glowing mist in the center of the room. Lasers, both deadly and harmless, flashed all around. I couldn't make out where anyone was.

I shut my eyes, trying to ignore the pounding of the drums in my head. The distorted guitar was impossible to ignore. I lost sense of direction, and time-

I felt myself being dragged backwards, and opened my eyes. Waves of heat streaked past me both directions. The metal music and Duhrnan's laughter faded in front of me as we passed through the arch of the door, which had been smashed open. Two valicorr emerged from the glowing mist, shrieking after us.

I snapped my mind back to the present moment, and flicked my wrist forward. A laser bolt soared towards me, and I flinched. Smoke and sparks burst from the holding chair just above my shoulder. I squinted my eyes, and pulled the trigger, not holding back. Bolt after bolt whizzed past the valicorr, even as more emerged. I hit a few of them, before I was jerked to the side as we turned a corner.

A door slid shut in front of me, and I heard K say behind me, "You know, Duhrnan was right!"

"What are you talking about?" replied Jonathan.

"'You're outnumbered?' I mean, come on, man! Don't say that kinda stuff!"

K spun me around. We were inside an elevator. Jonathan was slipping back into his coat, and K checked me over. "Osax! Are you hurt?"

I blinked, then exhaled. "Surprisingly, I'm alright. Though my face is probably bruised."

With her fingers, she ripped my restraints free, and I stepped out of the hover chair. The elevator floor was cold and hard. I twisted my body, stretching my limbs. "Thanks!"

"No worries, Sax!"

"Don't call me-"

"Sax, I know. Sorry-"

"Hey!" Jonathan interjected. "Where is Duhrnan?"

I looked him in the eye. "I have no idea. He turned invisible, just like

a valicorr shadow scout."

"Of course!" said Jonathan. "It's not valicorr technology-"

"It's loro tech," I said.

K said, "Yeah, yeah, whatever. So he's invisible. He's not our target though. We gotta blow this damn ship, right? Well now's our chance!"

I wracked my brain, looking at the symbols on the elevator's control panel. "There!" I said, pointing. "This one means energy! I bet it's the power generator!"

Jonathan nodded eagerly. His arm stretched out fully, and waved toward the button. K and I glanced to him. He stepped forward, and carefully pressed the button.

"What?" he said, staring at us. "Close one eye, see how good *your* depth perception is."

"Honestly, you're doing a pretty epic job for only having one eye," said K.

"…Thanks."

The elevator glided toward the "Energy" room, and we waited in silence. My eyes fell to K's makeshift flail, with the drone impaled on the end of it. I could hardly believe we made it out of the throne room alive.

"I can't believe we finally came face to face with Duhrnan," I said. "That was wild. I wasn't expecting the metal concert!"

Jonathan said, "He seems strangely fixated on using music to toy with people's emotions."

K shrugged. "Well, it worked! If he was trying to distract us, he did a great job."

"Yes," I said. "But he failed to kill us."

"True!" K smirked. "It was insane in there- I'm so glad I have this armour. Osax, did you see me swinging this around?!" She grinned, lifting the cable.

My ears lifted. "Yes, I did. You were great!"

K's eyes landed on Jonathan. "You know what I can't believe? In the chaos of that battle, you still found time to pick up your jacket."

He rubbed his collar defensively. "What? I love this coat."

"Good thinking, using it to blind Duhrnan for a second," I said.

His lips twitched into a smile. "Thank you." He bowed his head.

The elevator stopped, but the door didn't budge.

"They must have locked the door," I said. "K?"

"On it."

She took a step back, gripped the flail a few feet from its end and swung it twice. Then she slammed it against the door, busting it open.

The energy room was large, with a massive pillar in the center, presumably the ship's power regulator. It pulsed with energy every second. Computer terminals and doors ringed the walls, and several valicorr waited. We charged in, guns blazing, taking them by surprise. K flung her flail, throwing it into soldiers and computer terminals. Panting, we stood in the room, valicorr bodies around us. Connecting to a computer, K downloaded a map of the mothership onto her holo-gauntlet. My gauntlet was still destroyed from the myrok attack, and Duhrnan had crushed Jonathan's. I figured out how to lock the doors, though admittedly Duhrnan could probably override it if he wanted, and we puzzled over the regulator.

"We have to hurry," I said, "Astraloth is in danger, and the skyther fleet is being torn apart as we speak. We have to prime the ship to self destruct. That pillar regulates the ship's energy. If we destroy it, the cascade effect will gradually overload the ship with energy, resulting in system shutdowns, explosions, and once the energy surges to the engines, a slipspace fracture."

K looked at me. "Slipspace fracture?"

Jonathan interjected. "Space around the mothership, centered on the fracture's focal point in the engines, will crack like glass, accompanied by a fiery blast as the energy discharge ignites the fuel and any localized matter." He ran his fingers through his hair. "Basically, the mothership will explode, spectacularly.

"On top of that, leading up to the explosion, the energy buildup in the ship's communications system will begin to discharge, effectively turning this whole ship into a massive jamming unit. Meaning, our comms won't work until we get off the ship."

K nodded, and the three of us stood in silence. The gravity of the situation was beginning to settle on me. We stood at the center of the ship we had been hunting for weeks, on the precipice of retribution. Astraloth somehow escaped total destruction, yet was in the middle of another assault. The mothership was crawling with valicorr soldiers, and beyond it, a massive space battle raged on.

"How much time do you think we will have, after sabotaging the regulator?" I asked Jonathan.

He took in a deep breath. "It's impossible to know. But I would guess twenty minutes, maximum."

My ears lowered. K's expression hardened. Jonathan's eye darted between us. It didn't need to be said that if we were still aboard when the ship exploded, we all would die.

"Let's do it," said K. Then she swung the drone in her hand a few times, before launching it toward the central pillar. The pillar shattered, spewing sparks. The lights changed to a red colour, a klaxon sounded, and I smelled ozone.

I had never felt so powerful. At this point, there was nothing Duhrnan could do. The menacing arachnid that was the mothership was doomed. The first of our targets was finally destroyed. It was only a matter of time. I hated the smell of melting rubber and plastics, but this time, despite my better judgment for health concerns, I inhaled deeply, savouring the scent. It was a victorious smell.

Then my eyes fell to my companions, dimly glowing in the red hues. It was time to escape.

Fifty-Two

Jonathan, K and I hesitated in a long hall, gazing out a glass wall toward Astraloth, and the space battle that raged beyond. Fighters circled each other, launching volleys of energy bolts to and fro, and the larger skyther ships moved to attack the mothership. We lost our footing for a moment as the ship shuddered from an internal rupture, reminding us to keep moving toward a hangar. We needed to find an escape vessel, and fast. We were lucky that we hadn't run into many valicorr, but any we did see we didn't hesitate to shoot. It felt brutal, but it was our only chance for survival.

Another stream of red lightning lashed out from the mothership, ripping a skyther cruiser in half. I shook my head, astonished.

"Even while in a critical state, the mothership is still able to fire!"

K grabbed my arm. "Good thing it won't last long then. Come on!"

"Wait!" said Jonathan, raising his hand up. "Look!"

A massive beige battlecruiser suddenly blinked into orbit around the planet, from the direction of the Thala nebula. It was half the size of the mothership, but still significantly larger than a Titan-class cruiser, or any of the ships from Astraloth. It was blocky in shape, reminiscent of TAU designs, only it wasn't a TAU ship. It was larger than any TAU ship I had ever seen. And without warning, a downpour of lasers rained from it to the skyther ships. One by one, the ships split into flames, extinguished in a second by the vacuum of space.

"The Silencer..." Jonathan said.

I turned to face him. "That ship- Duhrnan mentioned it. It's Ryner's ship?"

Jonathan nodded gravely as a low rumble coursed through the vessel. Red emergency lights blinked all around us. "Ryner... he's here!" He pressed his hands up to the glass, gazing into the wide void of stars and starships. His breath condensed against the glass. "I can't believe it, but... This is our chance... to cut off the head of the snake! To end the Brotherhood, once and for all!" His fingers curled into fists.

K and I exchanged glances. "We need to get off this ship," she said. "How are we supposed to destroy Ryner's battlecruiser, anyway? It's armed to the teeth- look how it's cutting through those skyther fighters!"

My mind raced. The mothership rumbled once more. "We don't have much time..." I muttered.

Then the mothership fired another streaking bolt of crimson energy. Instantly, another skyther cruiser lost a chunk of its hull. Even as my heart was wrenched at the sight, I hatched an idea.

I turned to face my companions. "I know how we can destroy the Silencer, Ryner, and the Brotherhood." I gestured around us. "We use the mothership's lightning cannon."

K grinned. "You're insane, Osax. I love it."

"Right..." said Jonathan. "What about the escape part?"

"I... I don't know. K and I will find the controls to the cannon, while you find us a transport."

Jonathan cleared his throat. "I- Respectfully... No, Osax." There was a heaviness to his expression. "I should be the one to fire the cannon. That way, you both have the best chance at survival. You both, you run to the hangars and look for a transport. I will meet up with you... after I bring the Brotherhood down." He lowered his head. "Ryner *will* get what he deserves."

"But, what if you don't make it in time?" K asked, hesitantly.

Jonathan paused, gazing at the floor. "There's no time to discuss it!" he said at last. "We all knew the risks going into this. I-" He looked up at us. "I'll be alright. Just make sure you leave before the ship explodes. Whatever happens."

I nodded slowly. "Alright, Jonathan." I pointed to the map on K's holo-gauntlet. "Meet us in *this* hangar when you're done. Remember, our communicators won't function due to the mothership's overloaded communications system, so make sure you go to the right one!"

Jonathan nodded. "Of course. I'll meet you in that hangar, if I can." He stepped up to me, and clasped my shoulders. He smiled. "Osax... words cannot express how much you have inspired me."

I rested my hands on his shoulders. "And you continue to amaze me with your courage. Please, make it quick. I don't want to lose another friend."

His composure broke for a second as he tried not to cry. Then he turned to K. I could tell he wanted to hug her, though he didn't make a motion for it. "K," he said. "I'm so sorry for everything that has gone wrong in your life. I feel responsible for it all…"

"You're not responsible for everything," said K. "I'm responsible for a fair bit of it. Ryner for some of the worst of it…"

Jonathan sighed. "It might seem strange, K, but in case I never get another chance to say it… you… feel like family, to me. You- in a way, you're like my sister. Or, my daughter…" K was silent, and he shook his head. "Which would make me a horrible father… I know I don't deserve it, and it's not my right to have it, but I only wish we had gotten more time together. More time to know each other better."

K scoffed, nervously. "Well, we still can… after this."

He eyed her carefully, and forced a smile. "Right." He stared at the map on K's gauntlet, burning it into his mind. The ship boomed from deep within, and we could all feel it rumble. He held up the pistol in his hand, and gave us each one last look. "No time to lose."

Without another word, he pivoted, and sprinted down the hall toward the control room. I watched his coat trail behind him as he disappeared through a doorway.

K looked to me, and her brow furrowed. "First, I don't like him. Then he betrays us, and I hate him. I start to kinda like him, and then he goes off…"

"He'll make it," I said, eyes narrowing. "He'll make it."

◆

Valicorr filled the halls between us and the hangar, but we broke through them. Filled with a righteous rage, K and I were unstoppable as we made our way to the hangar. The klaxons blared obnoxiously as we sprinted down the halls, and in an empty chamber K stopped me, and told me to look outside.

The Silencer was disabled by a single blow from the mothership. Arcing energy of crimson lashed out like a whip, tearing the ship relentlessly to pieces. I gazed in awe at the sight. Ryner, the leader of the Brotherhood, and his flagship, were no more. Explosions consumed the debris of the battlecruiser as the mothership's weapon continued to strike it into ever smaller pieces. Jonathan had done it.

K and I cheered. The skyther forces which had broken off to attack the Silencer regrouped to battle the valicorr fighters. The ships sparkled in the glow of Astraloth's sun, like shells on a black beach. A tear dripped down my cheek. I knew the fight against Duhrnan wasn't over, with him and the Shade Beam still out there, but we had won two major victories in a single battle. The Brotherhood's leader was gone, and the mothership soon would be too. This was the most luck we'd had so far.

◆

Nearly out of breath, we approached the door to the hangar. I smelled something burning in the air, likely the wiring within the walls as the mothership's energy slowly surged outward from the generator. There was a tremor, and I caught myself on K's arm, despite her being shorter than me.

"Whoa! You alright?" she asked.

I let go of her, and steadied myself. "Sorry- I'm fine now. We have to move!"

When we entered the hanger, K and I slid to a halt at the sight of three valicorr who, like us, were rushing into the room, headed for a starship. They were too preoccupied with their own escape to pay us any attention. They each wore black jumpsuits over their bodies, and, curiously, each fidgeted with their own thick bracers that they fastened to their arms as we watched. With a beep, one of the valicorr's bracers emitted a pulse of light, analyzing the wearer's body. Liquid seeped out from the bracer, covering the valicorr's fingers, arms, torso… The liquid morphed into articulated plates, vacuum-sealed clothing, and even a helmet complete with a glass faceplate. Soon enough, their entire body was covered in a purple, protective spacesuit perfectly fitted to their body, with a miniaturized oxygen recycler on the back. The other two valicorr automatically geared up a moment after.

"Whoa," K and I marvelled. Apparently, loro nanotechnology was even more advanced than I could have thought. At this point though, not much more about the loro could really surprise me.

The three valicorr ran across the metal grating in their nano-suits, straight into a dropship. K and I jogged toward the edge, and gazed down at the hatch meters beneath us. It opened, and my adrenaline spiked looking at Astraloth below. Blue oceans, green and beige landscapes, and white clouds swirled together under me and I felt my head spin. I couldn't believe Astraloth was here. The hangar was shielded with a containment field, so none of the air was sucked out. But I could almost feel the pull of Astraloth's gravity, like a vortex reeling me in. Shakily, I backed away from the catwalk, fearing another tremor might send me tumbling down into space. The valicorr disengaged from their docking clamp, and swooped out of the hangar, passing through the containment field into the vacuum of space.

K scanned the room. There were six other shuttles hanging in a ring from the ceiling, each with their own catwalk. She looked at me, concerned. She could see how nauseated I felt.

"Hey," she said, quietly. "All of this is just hitting you now, huh?"

I nodded silently, with wide eyes. I could feel my heart thumping, and willed it to slow.

She reached out a hand, and gently urged me onward. "Come on, Osax. Let's hop on a ship, and wait for Jonathan!" She smiled softly.

My chest buzzed with warmth. I nodded slowly, as I took her hand. "O- Okay." *We can do this,* I thought.

Careful not to squeeze too hard, K led us toward one of the ships, and our feet clanked on the metal grating.

Then my vision started to flash and spin. I was blasted with heat, and tripped… right off the catwalk.

I felt my insides jerk horrifyingly upwards, and lost the pistol I had been holding. My ears were ringing. I tried to make sense of what was going on as my arms instinctively flailed, seeking anything to grab hold of. My fingers made contact with something leathery, and the tendons in my arms tensed. The weight of my body yanked on my outstretched arms, and I shut my eyes, forcing myself to hold on.

My hearing returned to the sound of the klaxons. Then my eyes began to focus.

My heart pounded. I clutched K's ankle, who in turn hung off the warped remains of the catwalk. I swung my head from side to side, ears dangling. Our ship fell apart into a fireball of gravity-bound debris before we could get to it. My eyes followed a chunk of the ship; the fireball fell straight toward Astraloth. The flames were choked out after passing the mothership's containment field.

I glanced up to the ledge, and my blood filled with rage. Durhnan stood on the opposite edge of the room, chuckling. His eyes met mine, and he grinned wildy. He held a fuming energy cannon in his right hands, while his left fiddled with his wrist.

K pulled us up onto the tilting catwalk with ease, helping me to my feet. We stood, and turned to face the Emperor. He watched from the other side of the circular room. The battle of Astraloth raged on beneath us.

"Hey, dickwad!" K mocked, "You missed!"

Duhrnan shook his head. "I wasn't trying to hit you. I just didn't want you to get on that ship."

"Then what the hell do you want?!" I screeched. I wished more than anything that I hadn't dropped the gun.

He tilted his head to the side, and a nano-suit began to form on his body after flashing a scan. His wide eyes narrowed. "I want you to die in the slipspace fracture. I want you to be responsible for it. I want you to kill yourself." He smirked viciously.

Duhrnan's suit finished construction with a sleek helmet over his face. Without a moment's hesitation, he pressed a button on his wrist, and one by one, the hangar's clamps disengaged. To my horror, the remaining shuttles fell around us. Duhrnan latched onto the nearest ship before it fell, and I trained my eyes on his descent. As the ships became smaller and smaller, Duhrnan entered his craft. A moment later its engines flared to life, and it peeled away from the battle, out of sight.

I breathed quickly, and my mandibles hung open. The hangar was empty of vehicles, and the ship shook violently. I couldn't look away from the ships drifting down, away from us. Then my eyes caught even more abandoned ships falling to Astraloth from other parts of the mothership. Duhrnan had emptied the hangars. Every single one.

"Oh shit," K muttered. She looked to me for ideas. "Osax?" I opened my mouth to speak, but couldn't find any words.

We ran off the damaged catwalk to the solid ledge. I scanned the room, and my eyes landed on the door from which we had seen the valicorr enter. A thought entered my mind, and a mix of hope and dread washed over me.

"There aren't any ships left," I said. "So we're not going to fly out of here."

K's mouth hung open. "Well what *are* we going to do?!" She gestured toward the wall. "The ship is gonna explode!"

I looked down at Astraloth below, then straight into her eyes. *This is a terrible idea,* I thought. But it was the only one I had.

"We're going to jump."

K stared at me as though I'd lost my mind.

◆

It turned out the nearest supply room was actually a fair distance from the hangar, but we found our way using the map on K's holo-gauntlet. It was a small room packed with weapons and equipment, and when we entered it was unoccupied. Loro bracers hung on the walls, and we each retrieved a nano-suit. The ship was vibrating constantly now in the glow of emergency lights, and the walls emitted a sharp hum, with a pitch and volume that slowly rose with each passing second. I was anxiously aware of how long it had been since we destroyed the power regulator; the ship could blow any minute. K and I glanced at each other as we fastened the devices to our wrists. Not quite knowing what I was doing, I pressed a button on mine and K's bracers.

A wave of light burst from each bracer, scanning the shape of our bodies. Then, silver liquid nanites began to crawl up my arm, and I watched as the same thing happened to K.

"Wh- Whoa!" K said, breathing quickly. By the time the liquid coating reached our necks, our arms had already morphed into solid purple material.

"It- It's okay!" I said, as the mask began to form around my face. K locked eyes with me, and we grabbed each others gloved hands. "These suits should be safe- The loro are the best engineers the galaxy has ever known." *Please be safe,* I thought. I shoved any doubts back down my throat.

The nanites reached my ankles, and I lifted each leg one at a time to let them seal around my feet. K did the same. I felt the nano-suit's boots magnetize with the floor. A glass faceplate covered my eyes, and my ears peeled back against my head. The helmet melded around my ears, sealing me in, and the world became muffled. K's helmet stretched around her bull-like horns, fully encompassing each one with a metallic substance. I exhaled, astonished. But we didn't have time to marvel over the loro's technology.

K's voice was muffled through her helmet. "Osax... what about Jonathan?"

I hesitated. "K- He's probably..." I didn't know how to say it.

She bowed her head. "I know." She frowned through the mask. "I just..."

The warning lights intensified, and the buzzing in the walls grew louder. Then, the lights popped, and the room dimmed, illuminated only by glowing engravings scattered about the walls and floor.

"We have to go," I said, trying not to think about Jonathan. "Let's get to the hull."

"I- I can't get at my holo-gauntlet with this damn suit covering it!" said K. "We don't have a map. Where do we go?"

I hesitated. "I remember your map said that this direction is the closest to the outside of the ship. But, we don't have time to find a hatch on our own!"

K thought for a moment. Then she cracked her knuckles. "Right. Then let's make one."

She charged the wall, and pummelled it with her fists. In a matter of seconds she had punched a sparking hole through it, straight into another room, and moved onto the next one. Before leaving, I snagged an E-pistol from the supply room. Heart racing, I followed her.

Eventually we popped into a dark hallway full of hissing valicorr, and as K bulldozed through to the next wall, I loosed a volley of bullets at them. There were too many to fight; I just needed to hold them off long enough for K to breach the next wall. Plasma blades ignited all around us as they charged, and a stray energy bolt hit me in the arm. K broke through, and as I followed her I glanced at my arm, which didn't hurt at all. The purple spacesuit was torn, but started to repair itself with silver liquid. The liquid solidified and the colour shifted back to purple. It was as if I had never been shot at all.

K broke a hole through the outer hull. Our boots clung to the metal beneath our feet, and I held onto K, who gripped the wall. We fought against the air which whistled violently out of the ship, sucked by the vacuum of space. K pulled us beside the opening, and we watched as our valicorr pursuers were whisked out through the breach in the wall. This section of the ship was quickly depressurizing.

K asked, "Are we really going to do this?! Can we even survive this?!" Her voice faded as she spoke.

"We won't survive if we stay here! But we might survive if we jump!"

"I guess you're right! Well, we..." her voice trailed off into silence as the last of the air escaped around us.

I hadn't anticipated this... The vibration of our voices could travel through our helmets and the air into our ears. But with no air left between us, there was no way we could hear each other. I couldn't hear anything outside my suit. The sound of my own breathing was deafening.

I tried to read her lips to no avail. I tapped the side of my helmet, and her lips stopped moving. Our eyes met. She nodded.

We climbed dizzyingly onto the outside hull of the mothership, turning ninety degrees. We stepped slowly. Our boots clung to the surface of the black spider, but my body felt weightless. I let my arms rest. It was like floating in water.

I glanced up, and my head began to spin. We were ringed by millions of stars, and they each looked infinitely far away. On the edges of my vision I saw the red and purple nebulas I was so familiar with. I watched in silent wonder as starships, big and small, clashed above our heads. Explosions and energy beams flared up all around us. When I looked to the side, I saw the debris of the Silencer as it slowly ascended toward the planet. The centrepiece was Astraloth, which loomed overhead. When I stared straight at it, it almost completely filled my vision, providing the stage for most of the battle. The sun illuminated most of the planet from this angle. My eyes traced the line of twilight on the planet. I couldn't believe my home was really there, or that just an hour ago I was still on Malum. My skin tingled ceaselessly. I could hear the fluids in my body pulsing.

K and I shared one last look.

She reached out to me. I let go of the pistol, which drifted away, took her hands, and took a deep breath. I could hear the low rumble of the mothership through my body as it quivered once more, ready to buckle. We couldn't waste any more time.

Together, we bent our knees and jumped. K's legs kicked off with immense force, and propelled us at a startling speed. We held onto each other tightly as we drifted away from the cold Ioro ship, straight toward Astraloth.

Fifty-Three

For a moment, all became silent. Not even the sound of my breath could be heard.

Gazing at the unblinking stars, it was as though the very lenses of my eyes had cracked in a hundred places as space around me seemed to distort and jut out at odd angles. I blinked, trying to reorient myself.

K and I faced each other, holding tightly to each other's arms as we flew upward toward the space battle, and the planet beyond. The visual distortion didn't seem to affect K as I watched her face tense. Our eyes met through the clear visors of our nano-suits.

Then blinding white light painted her underside, reflected off the armour covering her horns, arms, and every crevice of her suit. Despite there being no air around us- no path for a vibration to travel- a wave seemed to roll over us, shifting our bodies back and forth and sending us tumbling.

We had no way to stop ourselves from spinning, now that it had begun. There was no friction, no way for us to propel ourselves. As we drifted helplessly, my eyes fell to the mothership. It was obscured by a searing white sphere of energy. A moment later, and the cracks in reality seemed to reset themselves, first slowly, starting at the edges of the rupture, before accelerating, imploding back in on the mothership. At once the stars realigned, and the white glow was gone. The mothership had been sliced into countless pieces from inside out.

Then, in one final burst of light, the engines exploded. Rings of white energy expanded outward from the epicentre, and the blackened remains of the craft launched outward in all directions.

Relief bubbled in my chest. Where once a terrifying threat loomed, now there was only stardust and rubble. The mothership was no more.

K and I locked eyes. My eyes traced the shape of her face, her sturdy lip, her dark eyebrows, her tusks. Her eyes were wet, and I noticed tiny droplets roll off her eyelashes, floating around, quivering weightlessly within her helmet.

Jonathan.

I felt my own eyes well with tears. I shut them tightly, and forced my sorrow to the back of my mind.

Arcs of energy lit our visors. I glanced around frantically as we spun. The remaining valicorr fleet was entangled with Astraloth's defense force, and we soared through the center of the battle. Energy weapons fired silently all around us. Starships burst in flashes of fire before breaking apart, or were sent helplessly toward the planet. Time seemed to stretch on, and though I knew it was unlikely that we would be hit, I couldn't help but imagine a stray energy bolt searing me, breaking K and I apart, puncturing my suit.

I heard myself begin to hyperventilate, and willed myself to take deep, slow breaths. I unfocused my gaze, thinking about my breathing. The sound of it was deafening in my mask. Almost terrifying. Though I breathed slowly, my heart was firing like a machine gun.

Before long, the flickering lights of weaponry and destruction were behind us. I let out a sigh of relief. K's mouth hung open, her eyes flitting around as we spun. Then I felt warmth glowing on my skin.

I could make out the details of a distant cloud rushing toward us. A moment ago I felt we were drifting, but now we were decidedly plummeting. We spun once more and I caught sight of the starships far behind us, though the space they inhabited seemed to lighten as we fell into Astraloth's atmosphere.

K and I began to rattle. My visor began to change hues, engulfed in orange wisps of flame that licked the outside of my spacesuit. The temperature was making me sweat. I pulled myself closer to K, wrapping my arms around her. I tucked my helmet over her spiked shoulder.

The heat grew, and with it so did the flames. I felt myself getting lightheaded, fighting to hold on, both to K, and to my consciousness. My eyes focused tightly down to my forearm, which pulsed with heat. Tiny strips of armour melted into thin air from the friction, and those nanites which remained struggled to fill the gap before my suit was ruptured more seriously. We were still too high... If we lost the integrity of our suits- even if our bodies didn't begin to burn up- without our suit's oxygen we could suffocate. The air was still too thin up here.

But to my relief, the flames vanished. The loro suits maintained enough integrity.

If we had jumped from further away and had more time to build momentum it might have been a different story. But as it was, Astraloth's atmospheric drag slowed our descent quickly enough that we didn't burn up. And the loro nano-suits' compressive strength was high enough that we didn't explode against the atmosphere. I took a brief moment to be grateful for that. But I knew, even if these suits could survive atmospheric entry, we wouldn't survive contact with the ground at these speeds. We were still too high and moving too fast for me to make sense of the land below us, so instead I tried desperately to slow our fall.

Carefully, I moved my hands down K's arms until they met hers. We held hands, and I extended my body out horizontally, shooting my legs out into a star pattern, shaking against the whistling air. I hoped she would follow my movements, and thankfully she did. We kept our bodies outstretched, trying to create as much air resistance as possible. Until we got closer to the surface, we would have to slow our descent as much as we could. Then, seconds before landing, we would have to reposition ourselves depending on where we fell. If we hit water, our best bet would be to pierce the surface like a pencil- If we smacked the water we wouldn't be any better off than if we landed on concrete, because water doesn't compress. I wondered if K knew that, and what our chances of survival really were…

On the other hand, I thought, if we landed on something solid, our best bet would be to land firmly on our feet. While this would mean all of the force of our landing would be focused on our legs, they would at least absorb some of the momentum. The one thing we needed to avoid at all costs was landing head first; even face first might be better. Even in a best case scenario, with plenty of padding beneath us, having slowed as much as possible before contact, we would be injured. Seriously injured, in all likelihood, even if we could avoid death.

We passed below distant clouds. The sky was a bright blue beyond them. And the ground began to take shape below. As my eyes focused on the vast desert sands below us, I knew there was no real chance for survival. Sand wasn't the worst thing to land on, but we were still falling much too quickly.

My eyes caught sight of a wreckage which fell past us, bursting into the sandy dunes. Then another, a mile away. Plumes of sand rose where these pieces collided with the ground. Black chunks of debris fell all around us, shot to Astraloth from the mothership's explosion.

The sandy ground filled my vision. My heart pounded. Wind shrieked in my ears through the helmet. My fingers curled around K's. More and more pieces of the mothership dotted the ground as time passed. In just a few moments, so would our bodies, nothing more than lifeless debris.

At least we stopped the mothership, I thought, vaguely. I didn't have time to think anything else.

Then out of the corner of my eye I noticed a blur of motion. Something bright, not dark like the mothership's debris. I twisted my head to get a better look; it was a skyther ship!

Not just any skyther ship, but the Queen's sleek, spherical shuttle. My mother's starship! And it zoomed straight for us, kicking up sand as it flew. The sun danced on its shell.

In just ten seconds, K and I would breach the ground, splattered like insects. But suddenly, I felt a force pulling me back. Something was lifting us up, slowing our descent. Ten seconds passed, and though we still soared toward the glimmering yellow sand below, we hadn't yet hit it. K and I glanced to the white orb. As her starship flew closer to us, it slowed, matching our ever decreasing rate of descent as it approached us.

I tried to move my limbs, to brace myself for a landing, but found myself unable to budge. I jerked my body against an invisible force; only then did I realize what was happening. I glanced to the shuttle.

My mother must have been piloting her ship. I could hardly believe that she was alive, along with the planet. But somehow, she had found us! And in order to rescue us she was slowing our descent with her mind—with telekinesis! The concentration that required must have been immense. But it was working!

In my mind's eye, I saw her gaze. Her eyes were brilliant, shining with energy like the stars. Never before had I been so happy to be related to a psychic.

We were only several meters from the ground now, but I was no longer afraid. We were falling as gently as feathers now. I couldn't help but laugh. *We did it!* I thought. *We survived!*

And it was true. My mother had saved us. But…

With no warning, her shuttle exploded.

My eyes gaped in horror. A limb of the mothership had fallen from space like a spear, straight through the shuttle. It pierced through the starship like a knife through an eggshell. Then it jabbed the ground, and a shockwave of sand and wind blasted us away.

Our bodies fell, crashing the final distance to the slope of a dune below. We landed, I on my side, coughing as the air was pushed from my lungs and I rolled down the hill away from K. I caught myself weakly, hands digging in the soft sand, and gazed up at the sky. It darkened with a swarm of falling debris, all remains of the mothership, and beyond, the space battle continued above. But where my mother's ship should have been, a great ball of flame roared in the sky. White metal smouldered and spun through the air. The bulk of the Queen's vessel crashed behind the crest of the dune, and my veins seemed to freeze.

Pain pulsed through my body.

"No!" I coughed. Blood dripped from my mouth.

Legs quivering, I struggled to my feet. Coughing and panting, I rushed to the top of the hill. With each footstep I sank back into the sand, sliding away, struggling to propel myself onward. Ash and metal rained down upon the desert.

Before I reached the top of the dune, I glanced back toward K. She had tumbled a ways down the hill, and come to a halt. I paused, watching breathlessly. I saw her body move as she struggled to sit up. At least she was alive.

Then I crested the hill. The wreckage of my mother's ship spread out below me, blackening where fire roared around it. My gaze fell to the cockpit. I didn't wait a moment longer, and charged down the hill, running and sliding my way to the crash site.

Please don't be dead, I thought. *Please don't be dead.*

I ducked into the remains of the ship, haphazardly, barely conscious of the flames and smoke that engulfed my suit. The inside was barely recognizable, torn apart and scorched from the explosion. My nostrils filled with the scent of sweat, and the sound of crackling fire absently knocked on my helmet, beneath my panicked breathing.

I swallowed hard. *The door to the cockpit.*

I knew what I was going to find, but I didn't want to believe it. I had already begun to grieve her, thinking that Astraloth had been destroyed. And it was a miracle that it wasn't- that she had survived the Shade Beam's attack. I still didn't know how it happened. But to have her taken away once more was too much to bear.

I wrapped my fingers around the metal door, and slid it open. I stepped inside.

On the floor next to the pilot's chair was my mother. She was motionless, face down. Her regal robes of red, white, and gold were stained with blood. Though the ship had room for copilots, and a few extra skyther crew, there were no other bodies. Just Suranos. Just my mother.

I collapsed to her side. "Mom!" I screamed through my helmet. I yelled in Skorali. "*Mom?*"

My hands hovered over her body, shaking. Then I felt around my chin and neck, searching for a way to release my helmet. My fingers kept slipping on the purple metal. I whipped my hand to my wrist, jamming buttons on the device until the suit began to decompose, beginning with the helmet, melting back into the bracer.

Fire roared just beyond the doorway. The sun warmed us through a wide, shattered windshield. My eyes darted outside. The last of the mothership's pieces met the planet, scattered in the sand.

I rolled her onto her back, and leaned over her, bracing her head with my hand. Her tattooed face was etched with blood, her eyes half open. Then my eyes fell to her chest. A jagged piece of metal pierced through her fur. It was large, and lodged deep inside, right next to her heart. My vision blurred, and I wiped away some tears, sobbing.

"Mom," I said. "I'm sorry!" I pulled her up and hugged her tightly, my head resting on her shoulder. "Don't go! Please don't go!" I shut my eyes. "I thought I didn't need you, Mom, but I do!"

Her hand gently touched my face, and I gasped. I pulled away from her, and looked into her half-closed eyes. She struggled to open them, lifting her ears slightly. Her hand caressed my cheek as I held her. Her yellow irises contracted in the sunlight. "Talcorosax..." she whispered.

She clutched my hand.

"M- Mother-"

She lifted her ears weakly. "Osax... I'm dying."

"No! Mom- Don't go. Don't go! I know I don't deserve you- You were just trying to help me, you always were, and I... I just-"

"Shh..." she said, gently touching my mouth with her fingers. Her breath was faint.

"Please, don't leave me..." I was shaking. "Don't go."

"I must go," she said, warmly. Her voice was so quiet. So fragile. "No one lives forever-"

"But you can't die!" I cried. "You're not- You're too young. Astraloth needs you. *I* need you."

She pressed her hand against my mouth once more. "Shh, Osax. You are wrong."

"No-"

"Astraloth no longer needs me." Her eyes glimmered. "They need a hero, Osax. They need *you*."

My heart caught in my throat. "But, I can't do it without you, Mom. I just can't."

"Yes," she said calmly. "Yes, you can. I know you can."

She coughed violently.

"Mom!"

"Osax... child... do you forget? I can read your thoughts. I can feel your memories."

I clenched my mandibles, fighting back a sob.

She continued, "You have already done so much, believing that I was gone. You've proven yourself, Osax. You have met danger with skill... fear with courage... and despair, with hope. You didn't give up, even though you wanted to. I know you will save Earth, just like you saved Astraloth."

I shook my head. "I- I didn't save Astraloth, Mother. I just- How can I... I can't lose you, too! I can't do it alone!"

My voice cracked into sobs. I struggled to keep quieter than my mother's voice. I was desperate to hear her.

"Listen to me," she said gravely. Her eyes locked to mine. "You cannot change it. And what you cannot change, you must accept. I am out of time. But you... You can do it. You will not be alone. Do you hear me? Even when I'm gone... you *will not be alone.*" Her eyes left mine, and peered outside the window. I followed her gaze to the top of the sand dune.

With her nano-suit deactivated and blue face clear in the sun, K stood atop the hill, gazing down at me. A second later, two more figures appeared from the crest. I gazed in wonder. Jonathan's white coat blew in the wind as he limped, walking next to Joëlle, who trudged behind K, adorned in silvery power armour. I couldn't believe my eyes. Jonathan, and Joëlle.

Yes. Somehow, they had survived. And here they were. These people I had grown so fond of in such a short time... I knew they were each flawed human beings, but they looked angelic, like guardians descending from the heavens, watching over me. They approached the wreckage of the shuttle, searching for me.

I turned to face my mom. I lifted my ears, weakly. "I... I think I understand."

"Good," she said, smiling. "Osax..."

She coughed up some blood, and her breathing became shallower.

"Mom?"

Her eyes gently fell to mine. "I love you."

"I love you too, Mom..."

Her ears lifted.

Then her eyelids froze. I could hear the crackling fire, and the sound of my breath, but not hers. I held her close, and rocked back and forth, letting the truth of the situation flood into my core. There was no point in fighting it now. My mother was gone.

I didn't bother to conceal my emotions, belting them out over the flames even as my companions approached, and entered the wrecked shuttle. I had no idea how Jonathan and Joëlle had gotten here, but it was not time to ask questions. They crowded around us, my mother and I, watching the scene. For this moment, nothing could preoccupy me. I was fully present in sorrow.

But all moments pass, and eventually, the sobbing subsided. A solemn silence filled the room, and I rose from the floor.

I turned to face them. Jonathan, with his broken eye, and straightened lip… Joëlle, with her damp eyes, her quivering smile… And K, with her eyes of amber, and wild tusks on either side of a frown. They jolted me with emotion.

My gaze fell to the floor. Then I lifted my eyes, and reached my hands toward my friends. K stepped forward, and wrapped her arms around me carefully. Joëlle stepped up, and joined the group hug. Jonathan frowned, staring at us from the side.

"Oh, come on," said Joëlle in a hushed voice. She pulled Jonathan close. He broke down, tears streaming down his face as he leaned in, and wrapped his arms around me, Joëlle, and K.

I don't know how long we stood there, but it was a good long while.

Fifty-Four

The four of us stood atop the sandy dune, the sun beating on our backs. Desert stretched as far as the eye could see. And scattered around us in a mile radius were the chunks of the mothership. Dark fumes rose from each piece. I glanced down to the burning wreckage of the queen's ship behind us. My arms felt heavy, bearing the weight of her body.

K broke the silence. "Are you sure you don't want me to carry her?" She said.

"No," I said. "I can do it."

Jonathan gazed at me mournfully, but said nothing.

Joëlle's purple hair flicked in the wind, and she gestured down the side of the dune to another hunk of black metal, only it wasn't a wreckage. The Firebrand was nestled in the sand a ways down the hill; she must have landed it just after K and I touched down.

"Now there's a sight for sore eyes," said K.

Joëlle led the way, and I followed close behind. I could feel Jonathan and K's eyes on my back as we descended, my feet sinking into the hot sand with each step.

◆

After we entered the Firebrand I laid my mother's body upon one of the spare beds. I stared at her motionless face. Her eyes were closed, and she looked serene. My companions gathered around me, waiting for me to look at them or to say something. I trembled, and quickly turned away from my mother.

"I can't look at her anymore," I said.

Joëlle nodded. "Osax… I am so sorry." She frowned at me, eyes tilted with concern.

I couldn't look at her face either. The world seemed to shrink around me, and for a brief moment I forgot where I was. I was trying to process so much at once. I walked silently into the kitchen.

They followed me, watching warily as I raised a shaky hand toward the food synthesizer.

"Osax…?" K said.

Root beer filled my glass. I lifted it to my face and put my mouth around the straw. I closed my eyes and leaned my ears forward around the drink, sipping slowly. The sound tingled through my ears and for a moment I forgot myself. I felt strength returning to me as I drank.

I let out a sigh of relief, and turned to face everyone. "You have no idea how happy I am that you're all okay," I said.

Jonathan and Joëlle each smiled weakly.

K on the other hand, frowned. "But you're not," she said.

I raised my hand up. "I know you're concerned K. I know you all are. But please, right now, I don't want to be the center of attention. I… I'll be okay. Let's just- Just figure out what's next."

K sighed. "Osax. You can't just ask people not to care about you."

Joëlle cut in. "I think we all need some breathing room." She grabbed a glass of water for herself, and one for K. K took it, and began to drink. "Of course we should debrief in a few minutes. I'm going to get the Firebrand moving, and head for your home at the Great Temple, Osax. In the meantime, take a breather. Everyone… meet in the cockpit when you're ready to discuss what comes next."

I nodded, and so did K.

Suddenly Jonathan cried in pain, and fell against the wall. He winced, and grabbed at his thigh. I hadn't noticed before because his coat had covered it, but he was cut pretty badly, from the looks of it by a valicorr's plasma blade. It must have happened when he used the mothership's cannon to take out Ryner's starship. That must have been why he was limping.

"That looks bad," I said.

He glanced with his remaining eye toward us. "Joëlle, can you give me a hand?" he grunted. "I- I think it's worse than I thought. It… needs class-6 medical gel. Can you-"

Joëlle stormed past him toward the cockpit, not even looking his way. "I'm done helping you. You know where the medkits are," she said flatly.

K scoffed. "Hey, that was pretty cold!"

The door shut behind Joëlle, and Jonathan slid down into the corner of the wall, groaning. I put my glass of root beer down and knelt beside him. "K, can you get the medkit?"

"Uh…" she said.

Jonathan shook his head, gasping for air through the pain. "It's no use… K hates me. Rightly so."

"No," K said, furrowing her brows. "I don't. Actually… I'm glad you didn't die." Her face was rigid, but I recalled the tears I saw floating in her helmet after the mothership exploded.

Jonathan was silent for a moment. "R- Really?" He winced. "Then, would you please get some medical gel?"

She scratched her neck. "Heh, I uh… Don't know where the first aid kits are."

Jonathan and I looked at her, dumbfounded. "You were there when Joëlle gave the tour," I said.

"You think I payed attention to that?"

"But," said Jonathan, "you've been living in here for weeks."

She shrugged.

After a brief pause, I stood up, and hurried out of the room. "I'll get it," I said.

I came back with the medkit and knelt down to begin work on Jonathan's wound, but K cut me off.

"Osax… you take a break. I'll help him." There was something noble about the gleam in her eyes.

"Will you need any help?"

"I'm fine, Osax," she said, turning to Jonathan.

"Okay," I said, quietly. "I'll be in the cockpit."

I grabbed my soda and stepped out of the kitchen into the hall. When the door slid shut behind me and I was alone, I pressed my back against the wall, and shut my eyes. I sipped some more root beer, and tried to calm myself.

Then I heard K and Jonathan speaking quietly through the door.

"I just apply the gel directly and then wrap a bandage around it, right?" she said.

"Yes. Have you… never taken first aid?"

She snorted. "When would I have had time to do that?"

"I'm sorry… I didn't know what your education included, when you were being raised at the station. I thought it might have included first aid."

There was a pause before K replied. "For the one who made me, you sure weren't very involved in my life. I don't think I ever even met you until the attack on Voren."

"Well, we did meet, when you first awoke, and-"

"Yeah, but I don't remember it."

Another silence.

"Now I just apply the bandage?" K said.

"Yes, just don't make it too tight. *Ah!* Careful!"

"Sorry!"

"You could probably squeeze my leg clean off…"

"Yeah, I know. I'm trying not to."

"Is it that hard to restrain yourself…?"

"Are you talking mentally? Cause no. I don't want to hurt you… anymore. It's just hard to know my own strength sometimes." K sighed. "You need to lighten up."

"…But I'm… I'm responsible for so many bad things… How could you forgive me so easily?"

"Easily? Now that's a big assumption. I thought scientists didn't make assumptions."

"I..." Jonathan trailed off.

"I don't know, Jonathan. I don't know how I forgave Osax for what he did either. I think it had to do with me realizing that everyone else was constantly forgiving me, for everything I was doing… So I could forgive too. It wasn't really a choice, just kinda… happens."

"But you *deserve* forgiveness. Most of your mistakes were honest ones- accidents. Everything I did, everything I created, was bad."

"…But you made me," K said in a low voice.

"Yes," Jonathan said. "I did."

"Am I bad?"

"No."

K waited. "While I was falling to the planet, I thought about what you said. About being kind of like family."

"Did you?"

"Yeah. Maybe it's messed up- Maybe you're right and I'm not bad, but you are. Or maybe you're wrong and you're good and I'm the bad one. Or maybe we're both just both. Just a mix. Maybe everyone is."

"Maybe…"

"And I guess… well… When I was falling, I thought for sure I was gonna die. And I couldn't help but think how grateful I was that at least, in my short life, I got to make a friend before that happened. A real friend. Something I never thought I'd get to have." Her voice choked up a little.

"Osax?"

"Yeah."

Tears welled in my eyes.

"But then I thought, how sad is it that I never had a family?"
Eventually, K continued. "I dunno. Osax seems like he had a kind of
hard relationship with his mom. But obviously, he really cared about her.
And she cared about him. Maybe in a way only family can?"

"I don't know about that... Family can be a strong bond... I loved
my parents. I looked up to my dad... practically wanted to be him. But
sometimes, parents let you down. And sometimes... you let them
down..."

"Sure... but... I guess it would be cool to have a dad. Or a brother.
Or whatever. And I just kept wishing that if I survived the fall, somehow
I'd get to experience that feeling... of having a real family. Even if I'm
gonna pass out one of these days, and not wake up..."

Seconds passed.

"Jonathan...?" said K.

After a shaky sigh, he responded. "Thank you for tending my injuries.
For a first time, you did an excellent job."

"...I *am* a fast learner," she said. "Well, when I want to be. So...
anyway..."

"I think I'm good to stand now. Let's get to the cockpit. I don't want
to keep them waiting."

"Oh... okay. Then, I'm gonna grab something to eat first."

"An excellent idea. I'm starving."

"So..." said K, finally. "Since you created me... do you think... that
you might be able to cure me?"

I clenched my mandibles.

Jonathan sighed. "I... wish I could."

"Do you know what's wrong with me?"

"Not for certain, but I do have a theory... Your body is agitated at a
cellular level. It's what's responsible for your accelerated growth and
learning. It's what made the 'Sheep's Clothing' possible. I believe this
genetic alteration had unintended consequences, and that it's what's
causing the growths, and the headaches, and blackouts."

"Whoa," said K. "That's... weird."

"Theoretically, if I could neutralize the part of the cell that is causing
this..." Jonathan sighed. "But I don't even know if my theory is correct. I
don't have enough information, and I don't know how to get it-"

"Maybe you could use Osax's data, he's been taking scans..."

"You're right, K. Maybe I could."

Really? I thought. I don't know why I hadn't thought of it before. Jonathan probably had the expertise to really help K. I tried to restrain my excitement. She had a chance! Maybe if Jonathan and I worked together…

"Wait-" said Jonathan.

"What?"

"Osax's holo-gauntlet was destroyed. By the myrok. Remember?"

In my excitement, I had forgotten. I felt a crushing sensation in my chest. Neither of them said anything for a long while.

I left them to themselves, heading for the cockpit.

◆

When I sat down in the cockpit, Joëlle, still wearing her armour, was seated in the pilot's chair, silently looking at the landscapes which zoomed by below us as she flew the Firebrand.

I savoured the sweetness of my drink, and rested my aching muscles.

"What happened?" I asked finally.

"You mean how did I survive?"

"Yes," I said. "Joëlle… You were forced back onto the Firebrand by Brotherhood soldiers. They commandeered the ship. We thought for sure that you were captured and brought aboard Duhrnan's mothership. That's part of why we surrendered ourselves to Duhrnan. We were trying to rescue you."

"*I* was trying to rescue *you*!" She exclaimed. "The last thing I saw before being corralled onto the Firebrand was you, crawling through the smoke, surrounded by dead bodies. I thought Jonathan and K were going to kill you. I'm so glad they didn't!" She stared at me, a desperate look in her eyes. After a second, she regained her composure with a deep sigh.

"I'm glad you're okay too," I said, my ears tilting forward in attempt to show my compassion. "How did you escape after all?"

"Escape? Oh," she said. "The Brotherhood soldiers took off with the Firebrand, and locked me inside one of the cabins. I could hear them talking through the walls about how they were going to rendezvous with Duhrnan's ship. None of them even seemed to care that their companions had just been killed by Omega's grenades. It's almost like they were brainwashed. Completely emotionally detached.

"Anyway, I didn't waste any time. I activated the Firebrand's boarding defense mechanisms."

I blinked. "Defense mechanisms?"

She shot me a sidelong glance. "My holo-gauntlet has a direct link to the ship… kind of like how you linked your gauntlet with K's."

"Okay… but, what defense mechanisms?"

She smirked. "The oxygen recycler can actually synthesize a kind of sleeping gas… puts anyone- any human, at least- fast asleep after just a few breaths. Not sure how it works on skythers, but it's probably a similar effect."

I sat back in my chair, aghast. "So you could have put us all to sleep if you wanted at any time? Why didn't you tell any of us about that before?"

She trained her eyes on the horizon. The sun spilled in from the windshield, highlighting her face. "To be honest? I wanted to keep at least one card up my sleeve. I was pretty sure I could trust you all, but not completely." She rung her hands around the control levers. "Turns out I was right. I couldn't completely trust everyone."

My ears drooped. "You know Jonathan renounced the Brotherhood now, right?"

She sighed. "He said so. But does that really make up for everything he did? All that he is responsible for?" Her eyes drilled into me. "I don't think so."

She looked back ahead.

I cleared my throat. "So, you must have been able to vent the gas into all of the rooms of the ship except the one you were in, to put them all to sleep."

"Exactly," she said.

"But they were wearing helmets… Don't TAU helmets filter the air?"

"Yes, they do," she said. "But I know TAU technology. It took me a while to setup, but before I activated the sleeping gas, I rigged the Firebrand's computer to hack into their helmet's digital displays and their communications. I just blasted them with visual and auditory noise."

"Wow."

"And that's when I activated the gas." She paused. "Two of them got wise to what was happening, and kept their helmets on despite the noise. But they were practically incapacitated already. I vented the sleeping gas, and once it was clear, I unlocked my door and knocked those two out. The problem is, one of them fired a shot at me in the cockpit, and damaged the controls."

She gestured to the console in front of her, which looked scorched in places. Now that I was looking at it, I was sure that there were some different parts in place than there used to be.

"I made sure to engage the cloaking device as soon as possible. Then it was just a matter of flying the ship down to the surface, and throwing their bodies outside. It took me a few hours to repair the controls… it was technically flyable, but the controls were fighting me. I needed to replace parts, and re calibrate everything.

"After I finally reoriented myself and the ship, I suited up and activated the scanner. I wanted to see if you were still alive. To my surprise, I pinpointed all three of your communicators clustered together, somewhere in the mountains.

"The signal was spotty, but I did what I could to rush to you as soon as possible. I knew you were in great danger as Jonathan and K's captives." She lowered her gaze. "So I locked onto the tracker in your eyepiece, and set full throttle.

"What did we miss?" K said, barging into the room with Jonathan. They each held sandwiches in their hands. K took a seat next to me on the right side of the cockpit, and Jonathan limped to the far chair on the left. Joëlle kept her back facing him.

"Just telling Osax how I put all the Brotherhood soldiers to sleep using gasses, and took control of the Firebrand."

"Badass," said K.

Joëlle chuckled. "Thanks, K."

K leaned forward, munching loudly on her sandwich. "So how'd you and Jonathan get here?" she mumbled.

Joëlle replied, "Well, I was tracking Osax's eyepiece, which led me to hover, cloaked, beneath the mothership. When I noticed it suddenly course correct and jump into slipspace, I made sure to fly close enough that I was caught in its slipstream. I had no idea where it was going, but I wasn't about to give up on Osax. So it dragged the Firebrand along into orbit around Astraloth.

"At that point, I thought you and Jonathan were both enemies. So I didn't bother following your earpiece, K, when the ship started to self destruct and you split off from the others. According to my instruments, Jonathan must have had Osax captured, because both their signals were so close together.

"Wait, what happened to your eyepiece?" K asked.

I glanced to Jonathan. He paused, then jerked his hand up, indicating she should wait just a second. Then he reached into his coat pocket, and retrieved my headset.

"Right," she said. "Duhrnan made you take it off him before everything went down."

Joëlle said, "So when I saw Osax's signal enter a hangar after all of the ships had been ejected, I flew in for a desperate rescue attempt. To my surprise, I only found Jonathan." She gave him a sidelong glance. "I let him onboard."

"For which I am eternally grateful," he said.

"As you should be." She turned back to us. "After that, Jonathan explained that he renounced the Brotherhood, and that you were a sleeper agent, K, but that your mind was restored. So I started tracking you. Which is when I saw your signal plummeting to the surface of the planet."

"We tried to get here in time to catch you," said Jonathan. "Or something… But we weren't fast enough." He turned to Joëlle. "K told me Suranos saved them with telekinesis."

K glanced to me. "It's the only explanation."

"You're right, K," I said. "She saved our lives."

Joëlle exhaled. "That's amazing…"

The room fell quiet.

"Somehow, we all made it out alive," said Jonathan.

"Except you told me Omega sacrificed themself fighting a myrok…" said Joëlle.

"Well- Yes…"

I hung my head. "It's true."

We shared a moment of silence. Then Joëlle said, "It's strange, but… I miss them already."

"So do I." I said.

"Me too," said K, to everyone's surprise.

Clouds wafted past overhead, and green landscapes shot by below. The Firebrand hummed steadily.

"But…" I began, "here we are. The four of us." We exchanged glances, even Jonathan and Joëlle. "I don't know if it was skill and determination, or just luck, but we made it out alive. And Joëlle, we did it. We destroyed the mothership!"

Slowly, she smiled to herself, a deep, warm smile. "God, I can hardly believe it. But you're right. Despite everything…" She spun her chair away from the window so she could see us all just by turning her head, then she cleared her throat. At last she grinned. "Mission accomplished, team."

"Woo!" K cried, crumbs flying from her mouth. Instinctively, my ears tilted away from her line of fire. "Hell yeah! We showed that bastard who's boss!"

"Though, it wasn't without losses…" I mumbled.

Jonathan interjected, "Our mission isn't over. Duhrnan escaped. The Shade Beam is still out there. The timer is still ticking."

K looked at us, dumbfounded. She shook her head, gesturing with her sandwich. "Can we just celebrate a little? For once?"

I looked at her, willing my ears to lift. "You're right. It's… not all bad. We did some amazing things." I couldn't keep my ears up, despite my efforts.

She frowned, and slumped over, sighing heavily. "Okay, you don't have to pretend. A lot of bad shit happened."

Joëlle stated, "There's got to be a balance between grief for our losses and joy for our successes. We have to give space for both."

After a brief silence, Jonathan and I nodded in agreement.

Then I noticed just how heavy my body felt. "I think you three should celebrate. I… need to lie down."

"Okay," said K, watching me as I stood.

"Let me know when we arrive at the temple," I said quickly.

Joëlle nodded. "Will do, Osax. Hang in there."

◆

Hazily, I stumbled into mine and K's room of the ship. I took a few minutes removing the pieces of armour I had been wearing for the past several hours, and carefully removed the loro nano-suit from my wrist, placing it gently on the counter. I'd have to send that, along with K's, to the loro research community and report my findings. I flopped onto the bed, dimming the lights in the room. I couldn't help but think that if we hadn't destroyed the mothership, mom would still be alive. It was a piece of debris from the ship which destroyed her vessel; it was a piece of debris that killed her. I could hardly believe she was dead. And I could hardly believe we were on Astraloth. In fact, nothing felt real. I shut my eyes, and it made no difference. It was as though I was in a fever dream. I was so glad that Jonathan and Joëlle were here, that they had survived. But even that I couldn't believe. My skin felt hot, my thoughts disturbing. I wanted to cry, but I couldn't.

Soon we'll be home, I repeated in my head, over and over. *Soon we'll be home.* Then my thoughts wandered to the floating spheres of the Great Temple. Somehow, they must have saved Astraloth from the Shade Beam. We were on Astraloth right now, after all. But how exactly had it happened?

With eyes tightly shut, I forced myself to focus on that thought. It was a good distraction; something miraculous to be eager about.

◆

We arrived at the Great Temple; the floral pyramids watched over the city like sentries, but to my astonishment, they stood entirely exposed to the sun. The great floating spheres were gone, as if they had vanished into thin air.

The Firebrand's ramp hissed open. We stepped onto a platform protruding from the exposed middle of the pyramid, soaking in the sunlight that beamed down on us from above. Crisp air rustled the leaves of the trees that covered the sloping roofs of the pyramids. Water filtered down the canals of the temple, cascading on either side of a bridge which connected our landing pad to the pillared, open midsection of the pyramid. I held my mother, scooped up in my arms. We caught the attention of some skyther guards, adorned in their ceremonial armour, who rushed over, and started speaking to me in Skorali. I don't remember what was said. I was too overwhelmed. But they were in shock, unaware that Suranos had even left the temple in the first place.

My arms were shaky, so I passed my mother to the guards. The skyther fleet returned from space after driving the last of the valicorr fighters away. Astraloth was safe.

The High Priest of the temple, Kaia, upon learning what had happened to my mother, told me I would need to be inaugurated as king. Then I broke down. I apologized to my companions, and to the skythers. I told the High Priest that there was no time. I held up Duhrnan's timer so she could clearly see. I told her that for now, she would have to lead the people in my mother's stead.

She nodded, slowly and solemnly, clearly distressed to see me acting this way. Distressed about the turn of events.

We, the High Priest, my companions, a few guards, and I, stood under the ceiling of the upper half of the temple. My mother's body had been taken away. Around the temple, starships flew to and fro at a distance.

A cool breeze wafted between the pillars. Kaia's wistful eyes watched us sorrowfully from under a red hat. She grew up at the temple like me, was only a few cycles older than me, and had recently taken her place as High Priest after the last one had passed away peacefully. Her crimson robes waved in the breeze, made of a thin fabric. Her mandibles twitched in the silence. None of us knew what to do or say.

At last, I took in a deep breath through my nose. I looked up at her. "Kaia," I said, in English so the humans could understand us.

Gracefully, she stood up straighter. "Osax…"

"What happened to Astraloth?" I said. "It should have been destroyed. But it wasn't. And the spheres are gone. Were the stories really true?"

She bowed her head. "Yes, Osax. The stories of the spheres were true. In our time of need, Astraloth was protected by them."

Silence lingered. My gaze lowered, as I tried to process what I was hearing. Obviously Astraloth had been saved… obviously the stories were true. But somehow, that didn't make it easy to believe.

"How?" K asked, taking a step forward. "What actually happened?"

Kaia hesitated. K and I exchanged glances. Jonathan, who had his head down, shifted his eye back and forth across the crowd. Joëlle crossed her arms.

"High Priest," she said, "please tell us. We need to know."

She gazed past us, and responded. "*He* will help you."

I heard someone approaching from behind, and the hairs on the back of my head began to rise. We all turned to face the figure. It was a skyther clad in grey armour, and a white helmet which masked his face. He wore a black hooded cloak which draped over his shoulders and head. He paused just a few feet away from us.

"If you follow me," he said, "I will tell you how it happened."

Fifty-Five

We sat around a circular table in a small meeting room deep in the temple. Kaia was busy elsewhere in the temple. It was just Joëlle, Jonathan, K and I, plus the mysterious skyther. He hadn't removed his helmet, and when I asked for his name, he didn't respond. Kaia seemed to trust him, so I thought I should give him a chance. Though we were seated, he stood watching over us. All was quiet.

"Are you sure we can trust him?" Jonathan said, not bothering to be secretive.

I lowered my ears. "Kaia trusts him. And my mom trusted her. And I trust my mom."

A moment passed where we all waited, staring at the skyther.

"First things first," he said. "How did Astraloth survive? I'll tell you."

His gaze shifted between us as he stared through the black visor on his white helm. "Astraloth was sent forward in time."

Jaws dropped all around the table.

K scoffed loudly. "What, you expect us to believe that?"

"Why not?" I said, cautiously. "We all saw the planet disappear... yet we're standing on it now." I lifted my ears slowly as the gears turned in my head. "Come to think of it, when I saw the Shade Beam fire, I thought I saw the planet disappear just before the weapon hit it."

The figure slowly lowered his head. "It's true. The spheres floating above the Great Temple... they housed the ability to send the entire planet of Astraloth forward in time, approximately two and a half days into the future." He paused. "That's how Astraloth survived. It stopped existing just before the Shade Beam hit... but only for two and a half days."

Jonathan started chuckling, quietly at first, then louder. We all turned to him. He kept laughing, looking at us with perplexion and amusement at the same time. "Time travel?" he said at last. "That's not possible!"

Joëlle shook her head. "Actually, Jonathan, it is possible... at least, it's theoretically possible. Well, there are plenty of theories about how to travel through time, both forward and backward-"

"But it's not possible in *practice!*" He exclaimed. "Theories are one thing, but time travel is nothing more than that. A theory. It's never been documented." He ran his fingers through his hair, spiking it up.

Joëlle put her hands on her hips, sitting up. "Just because it hasn't been documented doesn't mean it's impossible."

"What would you know about it?" he asked. "You're not a scientist!"

"No," she said. "But, I actually have read a lot about time travel. It's a bit of a hobby of mine." He stared at her, and she began to blush. Then she scowled. "What, you mean you're *not* interested in time travel?"

He scoffed. "Actually, I am, I just-"

"That's enough!" K yelled. Her fists slammed onto the table, and everyone fell back. She hit it with such force that a chunk of it broke off and sprang back soaring over her head. It crashed into the wall, right next to the skyther, who sidestepped just enough to avoid it. He was the only one who hadn't flinched. Even K did.

K looked at the table, and her face slowly morphed into a shy smile. "Oops. I was just trying to get your attention."

They were silent.

"Just... don't break too many *more* tables, alright?" I said.

She nodded sheepishly.

"So that's it?" said Jonathan. "Astraloth travelled through time?" He looked at us each individually. "I concede, perhaps it is possible. But... why did you wait to gather us all in this room, specifically, before telling us?"

The skyther sighed. "I just wanted some privacy," he said. "So... what is your plan now? What's the next step in fighting Duhrnan?"

"Wait," I said. "I still have questions. How were the spheres activated. Is it manual? If so, how did the people know when to-"

"I'll answer your questions in a minute." He cut me off sharply. "Jonathan, you had some thoughts about the next move... about how to stop the Shade Beam. Why don't you share them?"

Our eyes fell to Jonathan, who looked at the skyther with confusion. "How did you..."

"Are you psychic?" K asked. "Like Suranos?"

The skyther tensed. "Just, pretend I'm not here right now."

I raised an ear. "That's... kind of hard to do."

"I understand completely," he said. "But there's no time to lose- No time to argue. The countdown is still going. Now, Jonathan, what did you want to talk to everyone about?"

Jonathan turned to look at me, eyes narrowed. I shrugged. He cleared his throat.

"Well, 'Mr. Mysterious' is right... I did have some thoughts I wanted to share, while we were flying over here. About how to stop the Shade Beam."

We all leaned in. "Go on," said Joëlle, impatiently.

His gaze fell to the table. "Back on Voren, at the facility where the Shade beam was made... Where we all met... Where K was made, in the secret Brotherhood labs beneath the base, lies a computer." He looked up at us. "We don't know much about the Shade Beam, but I know it's heavily armoured. Which means, if we are planning to destroy it, we will need to find a weakness..."

"Why don't we just board it and blow it up from the inside, like we did the mothership?" K asked.

"Maybe that would work. But we don't know if it will, and we wouldn't know how to. We don't have the schematics. We don't know what its weak point is." He raised his finger up. "But, if we can access the main computer on Voren, deep in the secret labs, we should be able to download the schematics for the Shade Beam and analyze them for any weaknesses. Then it would just be a matter of actually taking the thing down."

The thought of going back to Voren now intrigued me. "Jonathan, that's a great idea."

He bowed his head, and sighed. "Yes... except for a couple major flaws."

"What flaws?" asked Joëlle.

"In order to get into the computer we need a Brotherhood access code."

"Wouldn't you have that?" I asked.

"Yes," he said, "But the code for the computer is over three hundred characters long. I never memorized it... for obvious reasons."

"Yeesh," said K. "Somebody in the Brotherhood's compensating for something." She glanced around, smirking. "Not funny? Alright."

"Did you have the access code saved onto your holo-gauntlet?" I asked.

"Yes, I did!" he exclaimed. "But in the battle with Duhrnan, he pried it from my wrist." He pulled back his coat to reveal the bare sleeves of his undersuit. "I... wasn't sure I should even tell you about the computer, because I knew we didn't have a way to access it."

Joëlle spoke up. "It might be a long code, Jonathan, but we can hack it. A computer could try every combination of characters in no time at all."

"Right, I thought of that too," he said, "before I remembered that the Brotherhood computer is programmed with a smart AI that is designed to self destruct the memory banks if it detects someone is trying to hack into it. Same thing if we try to manually remove the memory core. We can only access it with the code."

"Phew..." said K, slumping into her seat. "Way to get us excited."

I leaned forward. "If we try fighting the Shade Beam without a plan, we don't stand a real chance at stopping it before Earth is vaporized. Even with the mothership gone, there's probably a fleet of valicorr fighters ready to defend it. And we all know Duhrnan is fully capable of following through on his threat." I shut my eyes, concentrating. "Maybe we can enlist the TAU's help? Maybe they could help us figure out how to crack the code, since it's human technology-"

"No!" Jonathan cried, leaping from his seat. "No, if they get involved with the research labs... No, Osax. I won't allow it."

"But-"

"If I show them the labs, they'll destroy... everything. I can't let that happen."

I raised an eyebrow. "I thought you regretted all of your experiments..."

Jonathan sighed. He looked to K. "The cause may have been wrong... but the experiments themselves are not."

K's brow furrowed, and her mouth opened. "Wait, are you saying... Back on Voren, are there more people like me?"

Jonathan gulped. "Yes. Though I halted the experiments after you were awoken. If I'm not mistaken, all of the other clones should still be in stasis pods."

K was shocked. "How many more?"

"Three... three-hundred."

"Three-*hundred?!*" K shouted. My ears peeled back.

"An army of bioweapons, created by the Brotherhood. The TAU would undoubtedly consider them a threat." I glanced to K. She shook her head in disbelief. "We're not bringing the TAU into this."

Joëlle pointed to herself with her thumb. "...I'm part of the TAU."

"You're different," Jonathan said. "You know K… You understand why it would be wrong to kill the others."

"Maybe it was wrong to make them in the first place," she said.

"Hey!" K exclaimed. "Maybe it was wrong for your parents to have you, huh? I don't think you can make judgments about who's life is right and who's is wrong!"

Joëlle was stunned. "Sorry, K. That's not what I meant."

"Damn right it's not," she replied.

"Let's stay focused," Joëlle said. "Was the access code saved anywhere else?"

Jonathan shrugged. "I'm sure other Brotherhood agents may have had it saved somewhere… possibly. But I can't think of any-"

"Director Aali!" I blurted. "Could he have had the code on his holo-gauntlet?"

Jonathan nodded. "Maybe. But… I know his holo-gauntlet was rigged up using the same technology as the main computer, so we'd have to find the password to his gauntlet first, or risk wiping *its* memory. And knowing him, I'll bet he just had it memorized."

I put my head in my hands. "So, it's hopeless?"

The skyther removed the hood from his head, though the mask remained. "Now you understand what's at stake, and you understand that you need Jonathan's Brotherhood access code."

"Do you have a solution?" I asked, plainly.

The skyther nodded. "I do. And now, I can answer your questions about Astraloth and the spheres."

I tilted my head, confused. "Okay… But why did you want us to jump around between subjects of conversation? It seems unconventional… and needlessly complex."

He raised his hands in defense. "Trust me. It needed to happen this way."

"Why?"

"It just did. Now, I believe you were wondering about how the spheres were activated?"

I nodded slowly. "I can believe that the spheres sent Astraloth into the future… but was the activation manual? Only a living being would have the context and judgment to determine when it was appropriate to use such a defense, and send Astraloth forward in time."

"You are correct," said the skyther. "The spheres were activated manually, by Queen Suranos."

"So, she must have been tuned into the Code-Alpha signal just before the Shade Beam fired. Duhrnan even counted down to the shot- it would have been easy to predict."

"It would have," he said, "if she had been able to access the signal. But when the Shade Beam arrived in the system, it was accompanied by another battlecruiser... the Silencer."

"Ryner's ship!" Jonathan exclaimed. "It gets it's name for a reason, you know. The Silencer houses a powerful array of directed jamming devices. Point it at a planet, and the Silencer could block all communications and scanners to or from the surface."

I said, "The Silencer jammed communications around Astraloth, so nobody on the planet even knew of Duhrnan's broadcast or the Shade Beam before it fired?"

"Correct." The skyther said.

"Then how did my mother know when to activate the spheres?"

"Because you told her exactly when Duhrnan fired the Shade Beam."

"What...?"

Everything seemed to slow as the skyther reached his hands up to his white helmet, and slowly lifted it. Then it all made sense- in a kind of way which made no sense at all. He dropped the helmet to the floor, revealing his pale face, the white hairs of his fur, and his amber eyes. A face I knew all too well.

"Osax?!" K said, staring at the skyther. "But... You-"

K, Jonathan, and Joëlle each took turns staring at me, and the skyther in front of us. The skyther and I locked eyes. He looked just like me, and as I stared at him, I took in the details of his attire. His black cloak slid behind, off his shoulders; it was the same cloak Joëlle had given to me, the same one I was wearing that very moment. His armour too, was the same. I could see the same scorch marks that adorned the shoulder, the same damage in all the same places. His ears wobbled in the same way I noticed my own did when I glanced in the mirror, and he stood with one hand on his hip, gazing at me with an expression that held the same self-consciousness I was feeling that very moment as he looked at me.

"Are you a clone?" Jonathan asked.

We both shook our heads.

"No," he said.

"He can't be," I said.

"But then..." Joëlle said, before grinning. "A causal loop!" She jumped up out of her seat. "I can't believe it! This is the craziest day of my life!" She squealed with excitement. "Oh my god, I never thought I'd get to witness something like this!"

It was hard to pry my gaze away from the other me, standing just feet away on the other side of the table, shuffling awkwardly.

"Wait!" said K. "Osax is right there, but you- You're Osax too!" She pointed at the skyther. "What the hell happened?"

Osax looked at K, and lifted his ears slightly. He said, "It's... alright K. I am Osax. Your friend. The same Osax as him." He pointed to me.

K and I locked eyes. She looked confused. I tried to hide my own confusion. Then I turned back to Osax. "It's weird to see you... to see myself like this."

"I know," he said. "Completely bizarre. It's like looking into a mirror, except-"

"...except I don't know what you're thinking," I said.

He exhaled. Then he scanned the room, looking at each of my friends... each of *his* friends. "This time travel business is actually a little more complicated than just sending the planet into the future." His eyes narrowed, and I tried not to focus on how strange it was to see myself talking and moving without my own will. It was a true out of body experience. "The second part of the defense, part of what makes it work, is this device."

He retrieved a small golden orb from a pouch on his leg, about the size of a baseball. At a glance, it looked like a plain sphere, but I caught sight of an indent which ringed the sphere, cutting it in half, and several buttons. He held it up in his hand so all could see. "The spheres of the Great Temple, when activated, send Astraloth into the future. But this time ball, given to me by my mother... sends its user into the past."

Not a sound was made. *Sends someone into the past?* I thought. *So, this other me...*

"That's how you're here. You used that to travel backwards through time." I said.

He nodded slowly, staring at me. "I used it... and you're going to. Soon."

I lowered my gaze. "What..."

He continued. "If Astraloth was ever to be threatened, it would be saved before anyone even knew it needed to be. By sending someone back in time to before the moment of destruction, the leader of Astraloth would know precisely when to use the spheres and send Astraloth into the future, evading whatever threat there was, and essentially waiting until the threat passed." He paused. "That is exactly what happened. I used this orb to travel back in time to before Duhrnan's attack, warn Suranos of the attack, and ensure that Astraloth was safe."

"I'm confused…" said K. "Which one happened first? Did you go back in time first? Or did Astraloth go forward in time?"

I puzzled over that for a moment, before the other me responded. "Actually, Joëlle, you explained it best."

She flashed him a strange look. "But I didn't…" Then she chuckled to herself. "Right… to you, this conversation has already happened!"

"I'm confused," said K.

"Trust me," said Osax, "It makes sense. Joëlle?"

"Right," she said, taking her seat once more. "Forget everything you think you know about time travel, alright?"

We waited. After a moment, I nodded. "Alright."

"Okay. What we are dealing with is a very specific kind of time travel. It's called a causal loop."

"Okay," said K. "Time loop. Got it."

"Actually, it's *not* a time loop. That's something else."

Jonathan eyed her carefully. "What's a time loop, then?"

She ran her fingers through her hair. "A time loop is when a span of time is repeated, sometimes more than once. Whenever time resets, everyone involved in the time loop would theoretically re-experience events. But as I said, we're witnessing a *causal loop*, not a time loop."

"So, what's that?" K asked.

Joëlle rubbed her chin thoughtfully. "A causal loop is completely different. Time isn't repeating itself. What a causal loop implies is that two separate events are both cause and effect for one another."

"How can two events cause each other?" I asked.

"Well, think about it," she said, leaning forward, her eyes glimmering with excitement. "Astraloth survived Duhrnan's attack only because Osax was able to travel back in time and warn Suranos of the Shade Beam. But, Osax was only able to travel back in time because Astraloth wasn't destroyed by the Shade Beam. Astraloth surviving caused Osax to travel back in time, which caused Astraloth to survive, which caused Osax to travel back in time… You get the idea."

K frowned. "That sounds like a time loop to me."

"It's not. Time itself hasn't looped at all… but cause and effect has. It's circular causation."

I looked up at the other me. He eyed me knowingly.

Jonathan put his head in his hands. "Okay, Joëlle. Explain to me this: These two events, Osax travelling back in time, and Astraloth being saved… they cause each other. But what caused the loop to happen in the first place? It doesn't make any sense… Because as you said, if

Astraloth had been destroyed, then Osax wouldn't have been able to travel back in time, because this 'time ball' Suranos supposedly gave him would have been destroyed too… right?"

"Yes, *if* Astraloth had been destroyed," she said.

"But when Durhnan fired the Shade Beam, it *would* have been destroyed, because Osax wouldn't have been able to travel from the future, because Astraloth would have been destroyed! So how could this possibly be what happened?"

"Jonathan," said Osax, "you're thinking in terms of cause and effect as we commonly understand it. But this causal loop operates on a fundamentally different understanding of spacetime. You can't use the same kind of logic to explain it-"

"But that's absurd!" he protested. "The order of events would result in Duhrnan arriving at Astraloth and destroying it with the Shade beam. If Astraloth was destroyed, we never would have wound up back here. Therefore, Osax couldn't have gone back in time… Therefore he couldn't have saved Astraloth. Therefore-"

"Jonathan!" Joëlle shouted. "You're logic is backwards."

"No, my logic is sound. There must be another explanation for Astraloth's reappearance."

"How do you explain that other me being here?" I said, gesturing to Osax.

"I make a good point," he said. "Joëlle?"

"Let me set the record straight," she said. "A causal loop is self-originating. Meaning, it doesn't follow standard cause and effect." Joëlle hesitated for a moment. "As I said, it follows strict circular causation. Your logic, Jonathan, is flawed, because by the time Duhrnan arrived with the Shade Beam, Osax had already travelled back in time. Well… not quite." She motioned to me. "Obviously, Osax hasn't travelled back in time, yet, or he wouldn't be here." She motioned to the other me. "That Osax has experienced it already. But as far as the flow of time for the rest of us goes… What really happened first was Osax *arrived* from the future.

"After that, Astraloth was saved… ironically by travelling to the future, though that detail is irrelevant to the causal loop itself."

"I think I understand," I said.

The other me turned to face Jonathan. "I know it's confusing, but it actually makes sense, in its own way." He raised his hand up. "You're going to say 'If time travel were real, people would have done it a long time ago.'"

"Wh-" Jonathan stuttered. "How did you know- But how could you have known I was going to say that, when I haven't said it? By Joëlle's thinking, even if you were basing it on having heard this exact conversation the first time around, I never said it, which means you wouldn't have been able to know-"

"But I just heard *myself* say it," I said. "Self-originating… I know that you were going to say that now, not because you actually did, but because I just heard myself tell me!"

The other me tilted their ears slyly, gesturing to me in approval.

Joëlle spoke up. "See? In a causal loop, events aren't the only things which can be self-originating. Knowledge can be too. And theoretically, so can objects. But it looks like we don't have any self originating objects…"

"Good grief," said Jonathan, slumping in his chair. "I don't think I could take any more complications."

"Put bluntly," said Joëlle, "Everything within the causal loop happened, and will happen, because of itself. You can try to think your way out of it until your brain hurts, but it won't help. Osax knew what to say there cause he heard himself say it already… he's not psychic, he couldn't actually read your mind. He just remembered that part of this conversation. Don't worry too much, Jonathan. Cause and effect should return to a normal linear sequence once the causal loop ends. Which will happen once we reach the loop's furthest boundary in chronological time, when Osax departs *for* the past. Which, to us, hasn't happened yet. Even though its effects have."

"Alright, Joëlle, alright," Jonathan resigned. He said to the other me, "I believe you, Osax."

We all took a moment to breathe, and rest our voices. I remembered what my mother had said to me, in her last moments. *I know you will save Earth, just like you saved Astraloth.* Just like I saved Astraloth… I met eyes with myself. His face looked tired, straining to keep his eyes open. He struggled to appear strong, to encourage me. My gaze fell to the device at his fingertips. I believed him. And I knew I was about to time travel.

I rose from the table, pushed my chair in. "I'm going to travel back in time to warn Mom about Duhrnan's attack. But that's not all." I pointed to the ball, a fire igniting within. "Can you send me back to the night when the Firebrand stopped here for repairs?"

Osax smirked, nodding. "Of course I can. This little device can send you through space, as well. You're going to appear outside the city, just to make sure no one witnesses it happening. We don't want to alarm anyone."

"Wait, can I use it too? I want to come along!" K said.

"It can only send one person. And, it's a one time use deal. It will disintegrate like the spheres of the Great Temple did." He shook his head. "Sorry, K. He has to do it alone."

I watched his fingers carefully pressing against the sphere, and a holographic display projected out from it in blue. He adjusted settings for time, and location, written in Skorali. I made sure to commit his motions to memory, trying to learn how to use the device by watching him. I couldn't help but feel myself bubbling with excitement.

Joëlle said, "What are you going to do with the Firebrand?"

"Nothing, but I need us all to be on the planet when I arrive. I'm going to get Jonathan's code," I stated.

Jonathan's lip twitched into a smile. "Now there's an idea… The code is lost now, but back then I still had my gauntlet. You'll need to somehow get a hold of my holo-gauntlet…"

"And I'll need a holo-gauntlet of my own, to copy the code onto."

"Here, use mine!" said K, unstrapping the device from her wrist. She stood up. I reached out to her hand, grabbing the device, and she placed her other hand on mine for a second. "And make sure you don't get hurt, or die or something. You need to come back safe, okay?"

The other me lifted his ears, laughing. "K, it's alright. I'm right here."

"Oh… I guess you are…" she said. "Hey, if you need to unlock my holo-gauntlet, my password is 'K'."

We all stared at her. She shrugged.

"What? It's easy to remember!"

Jonathan chimed in as I strapped K's holo-gauntlet to my wrist. "You'll need my password as well, to access my gauntlet. It's 'kovu is not scar', the first letter of each word is capitalized, and the 'O's are zeros. And no spaces."

"Got it," I said, saving the password to a document on K's holo-gauntlet. I noticed Joëlle giving him a strange look.

"…Is your password a reference to the Lion King?" she asked.

He blushed. "What? I love old cartoons! When I was a kid my dad brought home an archive of old movies from the turn of the millennium. Besides, I've been using that password since my mom set up my first q-mail account when I was-"

"I just didn't think you'd be the kind of person to watch musicals made for kids."

"Well, your hobby is reading about time travel, mine is old cartoons."

She snorted a laugh. "Yes, I read scientific theories, you watch cartoon animals-"

"What, don't tell me you hate cartoons! I mean, you caught what my password was referencing, so you must have seen the movie too…"

"You're right. You know, if I'm being honest, that movie is one of my fav-"

"Guys," said K, struggling to restrain herself. "Osax is about to *travel through time.*"

Jonathan and Joëlle stopped talking.

I laughed. "I admit… this feels pretty strange. But I'm glad you're all here to send me off."

Jonathan stood up. He reached out to shake my hand, and I returned the gesture. "It is strange, saying goodbye, when you're also right next to us." He glanced at the other me briefly. "But, you're still departing on an important mission. So good luck."

"Thank you," I said.

Joëlle shook my hand next. "See you… well, right now."

I chuckled. "I guess you will. And I'll see you…"

"In a few days," said Osax.

I nodded.

"So what are you waiting for?" said K.

I turned to face the other me, and stepped toward them. I reached my hand to his. He gave me the ball. Our fingers touched. It was a strange feeling.

"It's ready," he said. "Just twist the two halves. That will send you backwards through time, outside the city."

"Okay," I said, taking one last look at everyone. "Just, two more questions before I go."

"Right…" he said. "The first one, I'll explain when you get back. Or rather… you'll find out along the way."

"Oh… okay…" I said, hesitantly.

"What? What was the question?" K asked.

Osax replied, "'Who created the spheres?' Don't worry, I'll explain it. But not right now, because-"

"Because you didn't," I said. My head was spinning. "Alright. I get it."

"I know Joëlle explained the causal loop," he said, "but I don't want to take any chances and purposefully try messing things up now. What if it broke the loop?"

"That's not technically possible," Joëlle said.

"Okay. Final question. Do I succeed? Do I get the code?"

He stared at me, blankly, mandibles hanging slightly.

Doubts started to fill my mind. Why didn't he respond?

"Maybe… maybe I can't do this," I said.

His eyes locked to mine, and I saw a fire burning within him. "You can," he said. Then he thrust his hands onto mine, twisting each half of the ball before I could react. I looked down at my hands as he withdrew his; the gold ball disintegrated, and I felt my body heat up. K's voice faded in my ears and my eyes were blinded with light. I shut them, and suddenly felt wind on my back. I was falling through the air.

Fifty-Six

"I was wondering when we'd get to this bit," said the investigator.

I leaned back in my chair. Astraloth's sun beamed in warmly through the window. Our meeting room at the Great Temple was well lit and comfortable, if a bit stuffy. I had been munching on a bowl of noodles while narrating the last bit of the story, but I set the bowl back onto the table. The investigator had her own lunch, a wrap of some kind, which she hadn't touched at all. We had taken a break just before I launched into the discussion my companions and I had with my future self, and it seemed the conversation was too intriguing for her to eat through.

"I'll bet that this part of my story is one of the most contested, and curious parts to those who have heard the rumours."

The investigator's sharp grin flashed across her face. "It's the part of the story that is the least plausible- Yet we all know it's true. Everyone on Astraloth experienced the time leap into the future, but you're the only one who travelled to the past. That must have been a wild experience."

I raised an eyebrow, flexing my fingers as I leaned forward, stretching my back. "Of course it was. And if you didn't interrupt, I was just about to explain the experience, in detail."

She rolled her eyes. "I had barely interrupted since beginning today. Cut me some slack, please." After a pause, she smiled slyly. "...Your Highness."

"Alright, fair enough. But if you have anything else you want to say, you may as well say it now, to avoid further interruptions." I tried to keep my face calm, but I was straining my eyes, scanning her expression for the slightest signs of deception. Maybe now would be another chance to figure out what she was plotting.

She leaned back, and I held my breath. "There is something I have been wondering about," she said at last.

This could be a clue.

"Yes?" I said, innocently.

She pointed to me, and paused, finding the words. "Something about your storytelling… it makes no sense."

I felt the hairs on my back begin to rise with tension. "Oh?" I said, forcing myself to sound calm. *What is she getting at?*

"I've noticed when you describe distances, you constantly switch between meters and feet. You do know those are two different systems of measurement, right?"

Oh, I thought, and all of the tension left my body. I had to restrain myself from laughing. I had worked myself up for nothing.

"When I was on Earth, I learned both metric and imperial systems, but never distinguished them very much. It seemed like the people of Earth flipped constantly on what they preferred, so…"

"Metric is definitely the superior measurement system. It makes more sense with a base ten numerical system."

I stared at her. "I could use the Lexer system, since I know it better, but I feel that would just confuse you."

She sighed. "If that's a skyther measurement system, then I'll pass. Just… stick with flip flopping."

I smiled, and bowed in feigned gratitude. "Alright, if I'm to finish the story today, we shouldn't waste much time."

Fifty-Seven

"Oof!"

I landed on dirt and dewy grass. Dull pain shot from my back. My eyes were blurry, and I felt the blood pumping in my head. I chose to take a moment and catch my breath, blinking until I could see again. I raised my hands up above my face. The time ball was gone. Beyond my fingers the stars shined brightly against a deep blue sky. I was bathed in light from two of Astraloth's moons.

I sat up. I was surrounded by small trees. Each breath I took filled my nostrils with a fragrant, invigorating scent of the flora surrounding the city. Pushing against my knees, I stood, and dusted myself off. The pain in my back subsided as I stretched my muscles. I wasn't sure exactly where I was, but I knew I must be near the city.

It worked, I thought. *It worked!*

I roared with laughter, startling a flock of birds from their perch in a nearby tree. It was too late to go back now. My fists shot to the sky.

"WOO!"

I couldn't believe the relief I felt as I realized I had just bought myself time to relax. Quickly, I signed into K's holo-gauntlet and tuned into the Code-Alpha emergency signal. There was no transmission. Nothing.

I sighed deeply. I hadn't realized just how much that timer had been bothering me. Of course, I knew that my feeling of freedom was superficial. Inevitably, Duhrnan was going to attack, and I'd be prisoner to those feelings of anxiety once more. And I still had a time limit, albeit a new one.

I deactivated the gauntlet and clenched my fists, lifting my eyes forward. I had to get the access code from Jonathan, or we'd be relying too much on luck to stop the Shade Beam. And I had to do it before the

Firebrand left in the morning.

Putting one hand in front of the other, I climbed halfway up one of the nearby trees. From there, I caught sight of the massive, floating spheres of the Great Temple. I had my heading.

◆

I ran through the forest and made my way to the beach that edged the city. My feet kicked up sand as I ran, and the orange glow of distant streetlights and buildings came into view. I slowed to a walk, suddenly feeling self conscious. If I ran into anyone, I didn't want to draw too much attention to myself. I glanced across the water as I walked carefully along the edge of the beach, heading toward a hill in the distance which would take me up into the city. From there, I would make my way to the temple, I thought. I pulled the black hood over my head, and caught sight of the crimson nebula which coloured the horizon. The Thala nebula.

That's where it was made, I thought. *The Shade Beam.* And suddenly, I remembered the mysterious shape that our scanners had picked up behind the Shade Beam when we were in the nebula. It must have been a massive ship, that much I already knew, but I finally realized what ship it was. The Silencer!

I stopped, staring at the nebula. It finally made sense, and I was happy to have an answer to that lingering mystery, even if by then I had almost forgotten it. Ryner and Duhrnan must have coordinated their meeting in the nebula. And if the Silencer was there at the attack on Astraloth as the other me had said… well, it made sense that it would be hiding in the Thala nebula, close enough to strike out at Astraloth at a moments notice. Duhrnan had probably outfitted the Silencer with a loro slipspace engine... And Ryner had sped to Duhrnan's aid when the mothership attacked the planet as well; it must have been using the nebula to hide from any unwanted attention.

I lifted my ears in satisfaction, remembering the chunks of the ship falling to Astraloth, utterly destroyed. I was glad I'd never meet Ryner. The sound of the waves gently crashing against the beach was like a soothing melody for my ears.

Then my gaze fell to a figure swimming in the water, and I froze. Adrenaline pumped into my veins. It was me!

"G-" I mumbled. I had to say something. *He's looking right at me!* "Great night for a swim!" I called out.

But I had only misread his silhouette. *Osax, you idiot, he* wasn't *looking at you before, but now he is!* He started swimming closer to me, trying to get a better look. *Act casual,* I thought.

"Yes..." I heard myself say, hesitantly. "The water is quite nice tonight."

I didn't want him to realize it was me, and panic. So I tried to lower my voice, and sound as friendly as possible. Slowly, I began to back away from the edge of the water. "Not many people come down and swim here this time of year," I declared. "I admire your spirit."

"Th- Thank you," he said.

He was getting closer, still gazing at me. I began walking away, but since I started a conversation, I felt like I had to keep it going. "So many people these days, too caught up in machines, and the future and the past. Nice to see a fellow present-liver." I had no idea what I was saying. "To live so carefree, swimming in the calm of the night... Must be a good life."

I could barely make out the gleam of moonlight in his- in *my*- eyes. And I remembered everything that was going through my head that night. I had felt so exhausted, so wound up and anxious and concerned.

He had no idea what he was about to go through. So I paused, and pondered what to say.

At last, I spoke simply. "Enjoy this moment, alright?"

He kept gazing my way, but I spun around, and made my way quickly up the hill. When I was sure I was out of sight, I exhaled a sigh of relief.

◆

I left the sea breeze behind and wove through the streets of the city, conscious now of another time limit. If I was going to sneak into the Firebrand and find Jonathan's holo-gauntlet, it would be much more difficult to do so without being spotted once the other me returned to it. I couldn't remember exactly how long I had spent that night in the water, but I guessed I had about thirty minutes.

I made it to the base of the Great Temple, and craned my neck toward the red sphere which loomed above, floating at its point. I scanned the temple as I climbed the steps, passing water canals, and paths which branched off of the stairs leading into the temple. Off to my right, several floors above me, I saw the Firebrand landed on a docking platform which stuck out from another staircase. That's where I needed to go.

I glanced up the staircase I was climbing, and noticed a patrol of guards. They had clearly seen me already. I slowed my jog to a walk, trying to look casual. I removed my hood, and lifted my ears, trying to smile at them.

"Good evening," I said in Skorali.

"Prince Talcorosax," said one of them, bowing their head. I bowed and waved as they passed, saying farewell.

As soon as they were behind me, I put the hood back on, and kept running.

Once I had climbed to the same height as the Firebrand, I paused. There was no convenient path from here to the landing pad on which it rested. I would have to enter the temple, or else climb across the rooftop gardens.

Then I heard K's unmistakable laugh bellowing from above. I glanced up, and caught sight of her, Joëlle, and my mother, Suranos, descending the steps above me. I felt hollow at the sight of her. Without any more hesitation, I jumped over the edge of the stairs into the rooftop garden, ducking behind the trees and bushes. I waited breathlessly as they passed, unaware of my presence. I knew I had to warn my mother about Duhrnan's attack… but I didn't want to do it before the Firebrand left the planet, in case it changed how she interacted with Joëlle or K.

"…But how can those balls protect the planet?" K asked. "They're just balls. Giant balls, I admit, but still."

My mother laughed. I tried to be grateful that I could see her once more. The sound of her laughter was so familiar and so comforting. But I knew the times I had left to hear it were numbered, and I felt like I was being stabbed in the stomach.

She said, "I wish I could satisfy your curiosity, K, but that is a secret I must keep for myself."

"Aw, can't you trust me?" K said.

They passed by the bush I was hiding behind. My mother looked so graceful and strong as she led K and Joëlle down the steps.

After they passed, I realized a flaw in my logic. If the causal loop meant everything up until the moment I travelled back in time was already determined, then did it even matter if I stepped out onto the stairs and told my mother, right then and there, of the attack? I could warn Suranos whenever I wanted, and it wouldn't change a thing. According to Joëlle, there was no way anything I did could change the outcome.

I shut my eyes, feeling a headache coming on. If everything within the loop was predestined, did any of my choices matter? I pondered this for a moment. Did it mean that even my thoughts were already decided?

I tried not to think about it. I could hardly believe any of this was happening, but I had to press on.

I turned away from the stairs, toward the Firebrand, and started making my way across the rooftop garden, ducking under branches and over roots of great trees. A water canal rushed below me to my right. Soon enough I had made it to the platform with the Firebrand, and after making sure there weren't any guards nearby, I pulled myself up onto it, panting in the cool air.

There were no other ships docked here, just the Firebrand. Curiously, the ramp was open. Maybe Jonathan had gone out? This was the perfect time to search for his holo-gauntlet!

◆

I crept inside the starship, leaving the ramp open. I tiptoed cautiously deeper into the ship, and entered the kitchen. The light was on, but there was no one there.

I entered the hall which led to his room, and found the lights on there as well, and his door ajar. My heart rate began to increase. Silently, I crept up to the doorway and peaked inside. The bunks were empty. The bottom one had sheets which had been tossed about haphazardly. I scanned the computer desk for his holo-gauntlet, but it wasn't there.

My eyes fell to the bedside table. It was a small box with multiple drawers; every one of the Firebrand's crew's quarters had one. Unfortunately, the holo-gauntlet wasn't atop it either, but he might have been storing it inside. I bolted into the room, and knelt by the drawers.

Holding my breath, my ears dangled against the bedside table as I opened the drawers, looking for the holo-gauntlet. They were stuffed with random gear, which looked to be mostly Joëlle's; there were things like batteries, and tiny devices she kept but didn't know where to store. But I also saw Jonathan's sleek black pistol and holster, and next to it, an intriguing silver device.

Curious, I reached my hand into the drawer, and held it up between two of my fingers. It was only a few inches in size, a small ball-like structure suspended in a metallic plate. I recognized the aperture design in the center of the ball, and realized I was holding Jonathan's cybernetic eye.

Something moved in the hall. Then I remembered Jonathan wouldn't have left the Firebrand that night at all; he was too afraid of his mind being read by Suranos and his allegiance being revealed. *I* must have been the one who left the ramp open.

Panic hit me. Jonathan must still be inside the Firebrand. *He's in the hall!*

I stood up, slamming the drawer closed with my leg. I knew there was no way I could leave the room in time, so I stepped away from the drawer, and said, "Jonathan?" as though I had been looking for him.

Just then, he turned the corner into the room, and jumped with surprise.

"Ah!" He wasn't wearing his signature black and white long coat and gloves. Instead he wore a light blue set of pyjamas. But when my eyes scanned his wrist, to my dismay, I saw he was still wearing his holo-gauntlet. The thin device was securely strapped to his wrist.

His eyes were wide with shock; both eyes, including his prosthetic which glowed a clear red. I fumbled with the eye in my fingers, tucking it behind my back. It must have been a spare.

"What are you doing?" he demanded.

"I- Sorry!" I exclaimed. He entered the room, and I exchanged places with him, standing in the doorway now. "I was looking for you-"

"Why were you in my room?" he snapped. His lip formed a straight line, his brow creased. His cybernetic eye twisted, focusing on my face, taking in every detail.

I felt myself begin to perspire. "I- The, uh… Ramp was open?" I hesitated. "I was just concerned about you, I thought something had happened…"

He ran both hands through his hair, breathing slowly, with his eyes shut. "I was just using the bathroom. You probably just forgot to shut the ramp when you came in."

I grabbed the door frame with one hand and leaned into it casually. "When I came in?"

"When I got up, I noticed you were gone. You weren't in your room, or the kitchen. I assumed you were out," he said.

"Oh!" I said. I chuckled. "Yep, you're right. I did just come back a minute ago… Ha ha… yeah, you- You're probably right, I probably just forgot to shut the ramp." I shook my head at myself. "I sure can be… silly."

He eyed me suspiciously. "…Right."

"Well!" I said, standing upright. "Since you're good… I'm gonna try to get some sleep."

"You don't seem tired," he said, in a low voice.

"Well…"

"Hey," he said, pointing at me.

I was paralyzed. A drop of sweat dripped down my mandible. "Yeah?"

He stepped up right next to me, looking up at me. He reached out his hands toward my arm. I was still gripping his cybernetic eye, and I twitched the hand that held it away from him, keeping it behind my back. I could feel his breath on my chest.

He grabbed my cloak, rubbing it between his fingers. "Isn't this Joëlle's cloak?" he said.

I took a step away from him, and replied. "Oh, yeah, she's letting me borrow it." She didn't give me the cloak until after we left Astraloth. He looked at me strangely. "Isn't... Isn't she the best?" I added, trying to keep my smile genuine.

His cheeks began to flush a little, and his gaze lowered. "...She's a good leader." Then he frowned, and looked haggard.

"Hey, if you think so, why don't you tell her how you feel?" I said. "She'll probably appreciate it."

He smiled weakly. "Maybe you're right, Osax." He waved at me dismissively, clearly exhausted. "Have a good sleep..."

He shut the door behind himself. Somehow, he didn't suspect anything! Or, at least he didn't bother pursuing me any further.

Then my ears drooped and my spirits sank. I missed my chance! There was no way I could get his holo-gauntlet now. Even if he took it off, he had it locked in his room. And even if I could find a way to sneak in without waking him, pretty soon the other me would return to the Firebrand. *And hatch the brilliant idea to cure K with placebo,* I thought, feeling embarrassed for myself. There's no way I wouldn't have noticed if another me was sneaking around the Firebrand. By dawn, K and Joëlle would return, and after breakfast, the ship would depart. And I knew I had to stay on Astraloth to warn my mother about the Shade Beam, which meant once they left, that was it. I briefly considered stowing away aboard the ship and waiting for the opportune moment to download the access code. But the ship was too small for me to stay aboard undetected for days. *Besides,* I thought, *I need to make sure Astraloth is safe.*

◆

I stepped outside of the ship, and caught sight of a figure exiting the temple. He turned onto the walkway which led to the landing pad. It was a skyther, dripping wet, with relaxed ears, gazing up at the night sky as he walked.

My heart skipped a beat and I bolted behind the Firebrand's ramp. It was me again!

I heard the ramp rattle under his feet as he stepped inside. I chuckled to myself, realizing I had nothing to worry about. I had no memory of seeing myself that night, which meant that I couldn't be noticed by him now, according to the nature of the causal loop.

Everything within the causal loop happened, and will happen, because of itself. You can try to think your way out of it until your brain hurts, but it won't help. Joëlle's words echoed in my brain. I needed to remember that.

My thoughts spiralled back in time to when I made K's pills. Well, technically it was forward in time, by a few minutes, but it was a while ago in my memory. I cursed my previous self for spending tonight synthesizing those damn sugar pills for K. At least I had been well intentioned…

It gave me an idea. It wouldn't help me get Jonathan's access code, but maybe I could solve another issue.

I remembered the conversation between Jonathan and K. If Jonathan had my scans of K's brain to assist him, he might be able to help her and stop her from dying… I didn't know what to do with the data, but Jonathan was the one who created her. Maybe he could use it better than I could.

The ramp closed, and I walked away from the Firebrand. I hopped off the platform onto a lower level of the floral roof, and nestled myself in there. I activated K's holo-gauntlet, and got to work.

Using K's computer, I remotely opened my own holo-gauntlet, which I remembered leaving in my room while I was in the kitchen working on the pills. Our holo-gauntlets were paired, so I would have no trouble downloading all of the scans of her brain to K's gauntlet. But that would only include the scans I took before we left Astraloth.

So I scheduled a file transfer to take place in five days. It would copy the folder of K's brain scans to a hidden folder on her gauntlet. That way, more of the scans would be saved than if I had just downloaded the data which my computer had tonight.

My ears perked up, and I checked K's gauntlet on my wrist, searching for the hidden folder. There it was, and all of the scans I had taken of her brain were intact, successfully transferred in the past without either of our knowledge. Or, the future, technically. My eyes narrowed and my ears lifted. I felt pretty clever.

Fifty-Eight

I thought about entering the temple and sleeping in my room that night, since I knew the other me wouldn't be using it. But I knew that was a risky move, so instead I climbed my way down the temple through the gardens and entered the city. I wandered the streets with my cloak drawn tightly over my face and no real destination. The market was closed, but I decided to wander through anyway.

I tried to ignore the fact that I failed to get the code. The other me hadn't wanted to answer when I asked if I succeeded. Knowing myself, it was because I hadn't. So I resigned to my fate. I figured I wasn't meant to get the code after all, but at least I tried. I'd worry about that later.

I slipped the cybernetic eye into a pouch on my leg; there was no easy way I could return it to Jonathan tonight without revealing I had been going through his things. But at least I could hold onto it until meeting up with him in the future; I was certain he'd be glad to replace his damaged eye with this one.

A few skythers walked the streets. I could hear their footsteps as a group of friends passed by, joking and laughing loudly. They paid me little attention, their ears lifted in joy. They had no idea what was about to happen to the planet, or the galaxy, with Duhrnan's threat. And despite everything, I smiled to myself… For once, I was the one who had all the secrets. I took my time, enjoying the feeling of the rough stones beneath my feet, the warmth of the cloak on my shoulders, and the feeling of the air whistling quietly through my fingers. I only wished I had someone I could talk to about what I was feeling; excited, nervous, grateful, and in awe. I stretched my arms up, yawning. The stars were beautiful and vibrant. For now, I was free.

I admit, it was surreal being back on Astraloth. Not only after seeing it destroyed- or thinking it was destroyed, at least- but knowing that I was reliving a day which I had already spent on the planet somewhere else.

I passed by friendly faces, orange lampposts, alleys and trees. I pondered where I might sleep that night. My sleep schedule had been ruined by the poison coma I had on Malum. Between then and now I had only slept once, for six hours. And now I'd been sent back in time from day to night. Talk about jet lag. Regardless, I had too much adrenaline in me to fall asleep.

◆

I came-to in a field of tall grass just outside the city, with barely any memory of how I got there. I think I had wandered for hours, and decided to stargaze where there was less light pollution. I guess my stamina wasn't as good as I had thought. My face warmed in the sun, and as I sat up the grass rippled around me. I rubbed my sore neck and shoulders in vain.

My stomach growled, I was thirsty, and I had to relieve myself. Not to mention, I realized it had been days since I had a shower. Grass clung to my cloak when I stood, and I attempted to brush it off. Everything smelled vaguely dry. I guessed it was already midday.

I stared at the city, and the Great Temple at its center. *The spheres.* It was time to talk to my mother. By now, the Firebrand would have left.

I synced my holo-gauntlet's time with the standard time of the city, and cross-referenced it with my record of the exact time when the Shade Beam fired. I had exactly three days between now and then to warn my mother. And to say goodbye.

I stumbled through the field. The sun was blinding. I thought about my mother, and my body quivered. Suddenly, I felt I was surrounded by flames. She was in my arms, limp, bleeding from the chest.

I keeled over, retching.

Everything was spinning. I shut my eyes, breathing shakily.

Three days before Astraloth would be sent to the future.

And then… no more than an hour before my mother would die.

I couldn't move. I knew I had to warn her. And I wanted to spend this time with her, to cherish it, to show her how much she mattered to me. But I was terrified. I was terrified of seeing her face.

I needed the causal loop to be over. And yet I wanted more than anything for time to stretch on forever. I couldn't handle knowing how much time she had left.

I forced myself to concentrate on my breathing. In and out. I tried to slow it down, to slow my heart. The shaking began to subside.

I raised my eyes to the temple, and I knew if I didn't go now, I might not have the courage to meet with my mother until the three days were already used up. And if I missed my chance to see her again, before our time was up, I didn't know how I could live with myself. So I put one foot in front of the other. I would find a public washroom, buy some food in the market, and then make my way to the temple when I was ready.

◆

I scaled the temple in a haze. It was a bright, warm day. Everything seemed so picturesque, and the colours of the city and trees seemed to pop, with the crimson spheres as the centrepiece, floating high above the floral pyramids.

I quickened my pace. Along the steps and around the temple were royal guards who recognized me. They watched in confusion as I passed. I paid them no mind.

What if my mother didn't believe me?

She'll understand, I told myself. *She can read your mind.*

But she'll know that she's going to die, as well.

I entered the cut out center of the pyramid and scanned the open area for anyone I recognized. There, a ways to my right, the High Priest, Kaia. Her flowing skirt and hat were unmistakable.

She stared at me in shock and confusion when I stopped at her feet, panting.

"Take me to Suranos," I heaved.

She blinked, perplexed. "Prince Talcorosax-" Her cheeks began to flush.

"Please!" I pleaded. "I can't waste any more time!"

She nodded, and turned, leading the way. "She's meditating right now, I believe, in her sanctuary."

I was sweating. "That doesn't matter… she'll want to hear what I have to say."

"Weren't you leaving this morning on your friend's starship?"

"Yes," I said. "I'll explain when we find my mother."

◆

Sitting on her knees in a circular room was my mother. She was alone when Kaia and I entered the ornate shrine, wearing white robes on a soft carpet. The room was warmly lit from all sides, and my mother seemed to glow. Her back faced us, and she sat motionless.

My hands began to shake.

"My Queen," said Kaia in a gentle voice. "Your son is here to see you."

Suranos rose and faced us. Her yellow eyes locked onto mine, and they quivered. I could almost see my memories of the past few days flooding into her as she, whether intentionally or not, peered into my mind.

I thought of falling to Astraloth, and of her coming to save us. I thought of her ship exploding. I thought of our last conversation together, and of her death. I could see my mother's face contort, shifting, struggling to maintain composure as these images and emotions entered her. Her tattooed face squinted at me.

Kaia simply watched us both with wide eyes. My mother stepped up to me carefully, not breaking eye contact. Her face shifted between concern, pity, and compassion.

I trembled. I opened my mouth to speak, but choked on my words. *Be strong,* I thought. *Be strong!* But despite my efforts, tears trickled down my cheeks.

"I'm sorry, Mom," I said. "I'm sorry that I got mad at you."

"It's alright, my child!" she said, her ears tilting with compassion. Then she grabbed my hands from my sides, and squeezed them, bringing herself close. I looked up at her. Then she pulled me in for a hug, and I buried my face in her chest. Her fur was soft and comforting, and I felt the tension leave my arms as I sobbed into her. We held each other for a long time.

Not long enough.

She pulled herself away from me. "…You are not from this time," she said slowly.

I shook my head, scared to make a sound because I knew if I tried to speak I would only cry.

Kaia ventured hesitantly, "You do not mean… that Prince Talcorosax used the ancient artifacts?"

She nodded. "Yes, Kaia. Osax is a visitor from the future."

I looked at Kaia, and nodded quickly. "I've come to warn you about Duhrnan-"

"Duhrnan?" Kaia asked, tilting her head to the side.

"Yes," I said, wiping my face with my wrist. "There's a lot to explain."

Sitting cross-legged on the floor, we talked for hours. Eventually I concluded my story, and Kaia and my mother were both on the same page. I told them everything about the attack... even about my mother's death.

Kaia was shocked. Not by the time travel- it seemed that her and the queen were the only two who knew the truth about the spheres of Astraloth- but she was shocked at hearing of my mother's death.

"Is there no way to stop it?" Kaia asked. "Must you die?"

My mother lifted her ears, calmly. "All things must die, eventually. Though few have the chance to know exactly when, and how."

"But," I said, "Mom, you know exactly how you died... or, will die... doesn't that mean you can do things differently this time?"

She smiled at me. "Osax... if I am to save you and K from dying, I will need to concentrate on nothing else. Slowing your falls with telekinesis... that will not be an easy feat."

"You can do it," I said, encouragingly. "Can't you avoid the mothership's debris at the same time?"

She rested a hand on my leg. "I will try, Osax."

I felt my heart sink. Deep down, I knew: it was hopeless to try to change the outcome.

I asked about the spheres, to change the subject. My mother explained that all of the time travel technology was unearthed over one thousand years ago on one of the moons of Astraloth, when skyther's had just finished perfecting interplanetary flight. They were clearly the product of an ancient civilization, but according to my mother, *not* the loro.

I was aghast. "You mean, all this time, we've had evidence of another ancient civilization? People who travelled the stars before us... and they're not the loro?"

Kaia and Suranos looked nervous.

"You can see why we never spoke of this to the TAU," said Kaia. "And why we never made these discoveries public. To share this knowledge would undermine the effectiveness of the defense. If our enemies knew that we could send our planet into the future-"

"But why hasn't anyone heard about these other people. Do they even have a name?" I asked.

Suranos replied, "The spheres were practically the only evidence we ever found of such a civilization, along with instructions on how to use them. It was not hard to hide their existence."

I gazed at them, perplexed.

Kaia continued where my mother had left off. "The spheres were towed back to Astraloth and installed per the instructions. For hundreds of years, a trusted few have tried to reverse engineer the technology, but it is too complex. Even our best engineers cannot comprehend the internal structure of these devices."

"Yet you put your trust in them," I said. "How did you know they would work?"

"The device you used to travel here from the future- the time ball… There were once two of them. An early king thought it was worth the risk to use one as a test. When it truly did send him back in time, he was convinced of the sphere's power, and tried to erase any knowledge of the spheres from the public to keep their power secret. He hid what he could of the technology beneath the surface of Astraloth, though he kept the spheres floating above the Great Temple as a symbol of worship. As for the true abilities of the spheres, only rumours remained."

"You mean there are more spheres hidden below the planet's surface?" I asked.

Kaia bowed her head, and my mother nodded. If I hadn't just experienced time travel first hand, I likely would have had a harder time believing everything they said. But before I could puzzle over the ancients who must have created the spheres, my mother interjected.

"So, we have a few days before Duhrnan will attack." She lifted her ears at me. "What would you like to do, Osax?"

My gaze fell to the floor. I tried to keep my body still, but my arms started shaking again. I tried to control my breathing, but it started to slip away from me. "I don't know…" I whispered.

The three of us sat in silence as I pondered her question.

"I think I just want to spend time with you."

Fifty-Nine

I wish I could say I remembered those days with vivid clarity. I wish I could say that I soaked in all of the time my mother and I spent together, talking, wandering the city, and sharing stories and feelings. I wish I could say those moments will be with me forever. But for the most part, it was all a hazy blur. There was a looming, foreboding feeling, pressing down on my chest in each slow moment. Every time the sun set, I felt like it was harder to breathe. Every time I woke, I anticipated the day with quiet dread. There was nothing for me to do but wait. We spoke softly to each other. I tried not to cry. My mother never cried.

On our final night together, we stayed up talking and gazing at the stars across the horizon. We sat at the top of the temple on a flat stone surface no more than six meters wide. One of the great spheres floated high above us, but we could see the entire city below, and the horizon stretched on in all directions. We could see both the Toru and Thala nebulas, purple and red clouds of streaking colour, peaking up from the horizon line.

The stars twinkled in a clear sky. It was so clear in fact, and we were high enough from the lights of the city below, that I could see a bright swathe of stars, clustered together, spilling across the sky. It was the center of the Milky Way galaxy. I thought of Voren, of Malum, of Olympus, and of all the other planets in the galaxy. I thought of Earth.

For a moment, I felt so small. One hundred billion stars burned in our galaxy. And I had the nerve to care about the destruction of a single planet that would be eaten whole countless times by even the smallest of them. To think I was concerned about losing a single life… the life of my mother. Or K.

But I was. Of course I was.

Duhrnan had to be stopped. *But what can I do against him?*

"You can fight," my mother said, breaking the silence.

A cool breeze whistled through our ears, which dangled in the wind. We sat side by side with our legs hanging over the edge of the platform.

I gazed at her. "Fighting is what gets you killed," I said. "Yes, we destroy the mothership… but Duhrnan gets away, and you- You die. Sure I can fight, but can we really stop Duhrnan? Can I really stop the Shade Beam? I couldn't even get Jonathan's access code, and now it's lost forever. We don't have any backup plans. Our whole mission, it's- It's probably impossible."

My mother nearly said something. She closed her eyes for a moment, then opened them and looked toward me.

"Osax, soon you will be the leader of the skythers, as I am now. You must realize the weight of this responsibility." She paused. "Everyone is going to look up to you. They will look to you for guidance and for answers. Your every word will have the power to change people's hearts. To change their lives."

I lowered my head. "I can hardly believe it," I muttered. "I don't *want* to believe it."

"You must believe. Believe in yourself."

I was silent.

After a moment, she rested her hand on mine. "I remember when you were just a little boy," she said, her eyes squinting. "Before you spoke. One day when you were taken to the park by your guardian, something happened. You came back different."

I looked at her puzzled. "You… you mean…"

"Yes," she said. "The time when you witnessed a gang harassing a boy."

I was surprised to hear her talking about that memory.

"It was almost all you would think about, for a while," she said. "And it was then I knew you were destined to do great things, Osax."

I frowned. "Why? I didn't do anything impressive. I couldn't even stop them."

"No," she said. "You couldn't. You were just a child." She looked me in the eye. "But you showed something which can't be easily taught… compassion. Empathy. And a deep kind, at that. I knew then that your life wasn't going to be an easy one… Those who feel deeply, hurt deeply. But then again, who's life is easy?" She sighed. "There is so much I wish I could tell you, Osax. So many stories."

I felt tears returning. "You can, Mom. If you just make sure to-"

"No, Osax. You know that's not true." Her voice was quiet and unshakable.

I shut my eyes. "I want to hear your stories, Mom. I want to know everything…"

"And I want to share it all," she said. "But, even if I were to live for a hundred more years, I'd never be able to share everything." She tapped her chest with her fingers. "My life is my own experience. And your life is yours, too. Try as we might, we will never be truly capable of sharing it all."

I slumped. "That's a sad thought," I said.

She sighed. "Yes, it may be. But sadness is not wrong. And in sadness, you may find more connection than you know. And in connection, find life itself." She lifted her ears, and gently placed her fingers beneath my mandibles, lifting my head. Our eyes met.

"We are all made up of stars and cycles," she said. "The same particles and energies are shared by all things. And there is a constant shifting. Even in stillness, there is motion. The planet is spinning, and gliding around the sun, which in turn weaves through the galaxy in a cluster of stars. And the galaxy drifts through space. And beyond? Who knows?"

She paused briefly, collecting her thoughts. "Even if we are in some way destined to forever be separate, we are also in some way one and the same. Life is paradoxical in that sense."

I looked away from her. "I don't know what the point of it all is," I said. "This causal loop has got me thinking… If everything within it is predetermined, what about life beyond the loop? Is everything already written? Do my choices even matter?" I sighed. "If- If you're really going to die tomorrow, and there's nothing I can do about it… I just don't know. What's the point in trying at all?"

"If you seek peace, you first must accept that you cannot control everything."

"I know I can't control *everything*," I said, "but can I even change *anything*? If my fate has already been decided…"

"Fate is a mysterious thing," she said, after a long silence. "Neither humans nor skythers have ever come to agreement about whether or not it is real."

"Yeah," I said.

"But, we can agree that consciousness is real?"

"I guess," I said.

"As real as anything," she said. "And I find comfort in that."

There was a long silence.

"You remember the stories of our ancestors?" she asked, finally.

I winced. "…Yes," I said. I knew where this was going.

"When I die, I am going to join them," she said. "I will be watching over Astraloth with the ones who came before." She pointed to the Toru nebula's purple glow. I thought for a moment I saw it shifting. "That is where they reside, remember?"

"I remember," I said.

She grabbed my hand, and held it gently. "Your life is your own, Osax. But I will always be with you when you need me."

I tried to contain myself, but broke down into tears, and leaned into her. We hugged for a long time.

"I love you, Mom," I said.

"I love you too," she said. "More than you know."

By dawn, Duhrnan would attack, and we would have to activate the spheres, and our time together would be over. So I tried to force myself to stay up as late as I could. But eventually, my mother told me she would need to be well rested in order to have the focus to save K and I from falling to our deaths. She was so practical about it.

Reluctantly, I wished her a good night. I thought of sleeping in my room, but instead asked if I could sleep on the floor of hers. Of course she welcomed me there, and I was filled with a grateful warmth. Finally, I synthesized some sleeping pills for myself; there was no way I'd fall asleep naturally that night.

◆

In the morning we made our preparations. My mother showed me to a hidden place, deep below the temple, in the vaults. She recovered the golden time ball, and gave it to me. I placed it in a pouch on my leg. Then she retrieved another device; it was a silver sphere. She told me it was the activation key for Astraloth's defense mechanism. I glanced at the time. We had fifteen minutes.

The time passed in a blur, and my mother and I met up with Kaia on the outside of the Temple, gazing up at the blue sky. I set up my own timer, counting down on my holo-gauntlet to the exact moment that Duhrnan would fire the Shade Beam.

To think at this very moment I was also sipping root beer in the cockpit of the Firebrand, laughing with Joëlle, Jonathan, and K…

The moment came, and Suranos twisted the activation key. The sky turned white, and I lost my balance. When the colour returned, the sun was in a different place in the sky, and I glanced up at the spheres of the temple. Like a dried up sandcastle caught in the wind, they blew apart, dissolving into nothing.

I opened K's holo-gauntlet and tuned into the Code-Alpha signal.

04:11:53:52

We had done it. We had travelled to the future.

"Duhrnan's mothership will be here in minutes," I said, turning to my mother. "His starship was made by the loro. And apparently they can travel across the galaxy in a matter of seconds, when they want to." My heart was pounding.

"I know," she said. "It's time to deploy the fleet."

Using her holo-gauntlet, Suranos sent a broadcast across Astraloth, hastily explaining what had happened. Then she asked all combat ready pilots to take to the stars with haste, for in a few minutes, we would be under attack. Even as the entire planet reeled from the jarring time leap, and soldiers scrambled to their ships, Suranos continued to speak into her gauntlet, explaining the situation. I was astonished at her ability to rally everyone so quickly, but perhaps what she said the night before was right. When I became leader of the skythers, perhaps I too would be able to lead people with words alone.

One by one, white starships rose up from around the city, and from landing pads scattered across the temple. Skyther pilots and marines ran to and fro, suddenly aware that something big had just happened, and their queen was calling on them to defend Astraloth. Few questions were asked. Suranos' message was clear; we didn't have time to discuss it until our attackers were repelled.

But everyone knew the myths of Astraloth's defense. And with the sun suddenly shifting in the sky, and the spheres of the Great Temple vanishing, and my mother's broadcast, they found it surprisingly easy to believe that we had just been sent into the future, even if it all felt like one strange, collective dream.

I found myself on my mother's personal landing pad, watching her prepare to leave. Clouds had rolled in from beyond the mountains on the edge of the horizon. The air was cool, but the sun was hot.

Hundreds of white fighters and battleships rose to the sky and beyond, not just from our city, but in clusters of tiny shapes rising from every direction beyond the curve of the planet.

Far on the horizon, I saw a faint blue shape, growing slightly larger each second. It was the mothership, hovering far above a distant part of the planet, coloured by the sky. And the fleet was converging to confront it.

I strained my eyes to watch what was happening, but it was too far away for me to make out any details. I forced a sigh, in a vain attempt to expel my nervousness.

I turned to my mother, who waited for a second as the ramp to her spherical, white shuttle extended to the floor. She turned to face me. I found it hard to swallow.

"Well," she said in Skorali. "It's time."

I stepped a pace toward her, and wrapped my arms around her. "Good luck, Mom," I said. I sounded weak. Not like a King. I felt ashamed of it.

She pulled away so she could look at my face, grasping my shoulders. "Thank you," she said. "Remember, soon enough you'll be back with your friends. They will be here for you. Especially K. Whether or not she says it, she cares for you."

"I know," I said, awkwardly. "And then we'll be... doing something. Trying to find a way to stop Duhrnan."

She lifted her ears. "If there's anyone who can save Earth, it's my son, Osax. My son." She smiled warmly. Then she retrieved the silver activation key, and handed it to me. I took it graciously, holding it with both hands. "Keep this safe," she said.

I nodded.

I felt my insides beginning to twist. I didn't know how much longer I could drag this on.

Silently, she nodded at me. "I need to go, if I'm to save you and K."

"Wait," I said, "Why don't you bring anyone else along with you? Maybe if you had a copilot-"

"You saw the shuttle get destroyed," she said. "I'd only be risking their lives."

"But maybe-"

"No, Osax." She said. "It won't change a thing."

I frowned.

"It's alright," she said. "I've accepted it. I'm happy that my final moments will be protecting you."

I will not cry, I said to myself. *I've done that enough already.*

Suranos touched my face gently. "Do not berate yourself for crying, Osax. It does not make you weak."

"Okay," I said, shakily.

She stepped away, then crossed one arm over her chest to her shoulder. She bowed low, and waved her hand away from her body. I returned the gesture, bowing farewell.

She hesitated for only a second, and I thought I saw her eyes glimmer with wetness. Then, before I could look at her face any longer, she turned away and entered her shuttle, not looking back. A moment later I was blasted with warm air as the engines flared to life, venting heat from slits on the bottom of the shuttle. Shining, the ship thrummed and lifted into the air.

I ran to the edge of the platform, following the shuttle with my eyes. It sped off like a torpedo in the direction of the space battle, but stayed low within the atmosphere.

I stood on the edge, watching until my mother and her ship became too small for me to see with the naked eye.

Then I heard footsteps behind me, and whirled around. It was Kaia.

"Talcorosax… Is there anything you need?" Her eyes were full of remorse, as though she wished more than anything that she could help me. I felt her fingers gently touch my arm.

"I just need to be alone for a while."

"Wait," she said, as I began to pass her. She held up a white helmet. "I wanted to give this to you," she said.

I blinked. "Why? What is it?"

"It was your father's. He was a great hero to the people before he died."

"I know he was," I said.

"Now that you are the last of your family, Suranos would have wanted you to have it," she said. "But there was too much else going on for her to think of it. So, I decided to bring it to you myself."

Shoving the silver activation key into my pouch, I took the helmet graciously. It had been kept in great condition.

"I never really knew my father," I said.

"I know," said Kaia. "I was young, too, when he died. But you certainly remind me of his memory."

"Thank you," I said, bowing my head. "Kaia, in an hour, the Firebrand will return with me and my friends."

"Yes?"

"They'll ask about what happened, but… Don't tell them. I'll do it."

She lowered her gaze. "Of course, your majesty."

"Please," I said. "Just call me Osax."

She lifted her ears, and her cheeks flushed. Then I walked past her, determined to wander until the Firebrand returned to the temple.

Sixty

In the small meeting room with Jonathan, K, and Joëlle, after a discussion about time travel, my slightly younger self hesitated with the time ball in his hands. "Maybe… maybe I can't do this," he said.

"You can," I said. Then I twisted the ball in his hands and he vanished in a flash of light as the device disintegrated.

K shouted. "Hey! What the hell are you doing? He changed his mind! He didn't want to go!"

Her orange eyes were sharp against her blue skin. "It's fine, K. I needed to do it. I just… needed some assistance. From myself. Besides, it's done now. And I turned out alright."

She sat down in her chair, shaking her head. "Ugh, this is so confusing."

Joëlle smirked, brushing aside a stray purple lock. "Don't worry, K. Now that Osax has left for the past, the causal loop is done. It's over."

Everyone sighed collectively. I walked around the table to where I had been sitting before, and pulled the seat out. I sat down, and placed my father's helmet on the table in front of me.

"Thanks for bearing with me through all of that," I said.

Jonathan stared at me with one eye. "So… you travelled back in time, and now the causal loop is done. So, who created the spheres?"

"Right," I said. I told them what Kaia and my mother had said. "So," I continued, "That was the last time ball. And since we can't replicate the technology, there aren't going to be any more."

Jonathan stretched his arms back, exhaling. He spiked his hair with his fingers. "I'm going to be honest, I'm glad to hear that. We shouldn't be messing with things we don't understand."

"Says the guy who joined a terrorist organization and started trying to create bioweapons," said K, smirking.

"I- Well..." Jonathan sighed. "Fair point."

Joëlle leaned forward, ignoring Jonathan. "Isn't it odd that these spheres are the only evidence of the civilization they came from, and that they even came with instructions that the skythers could understand?"

I blinked. "Yes... it is strange."

"Maybe they're not an ancient civilization at all?" she said. "If they're the ones who invented time travel, who says they had to do it in the past?"

We sat in a humble silence.

"You're right," I said. "Maybe the spheres were planted on the moon for us to find them in the past. Maybe they were invented by... By skythers in the future."

"Now that's just crazy," said K. "That doesn't make any sense."

To my surprise, Jonathan spoke up next, defending the idea. "It makes as much sense as the causal loop we just witnessed. But we'll never know. It's only speculation. And even if they were created by skythers from the future, it would have to be so far in the future that none of us will live long enough to see it."

"What I don't understand is why Astraloth never mentioned this to the TAU," said Joëlle, not bothering to look at Jonathan. "Doesn't it break the treaty?"

"No," I said. "The spheres were discovered long before humans and skythers ever encountered each other. If the treaty were retroactive for all technological discoveries ever made, then both Astraloth and the TAU would be in breach of it for countless items."

"Fair enough," she said. "But it still seems like a big secret to keep from your allies."

"That's because it is," I said, my eyes narrowing. "But it doesn't matter now. The spheres are gone. There will be no more travelling backwards through time."

"What about forwards in time?" asked Jonathan. "You said there were some more time spheres hidden beneath the surface of the planet."

I shrugged. "Who's to say whether or not they disintegrated when Astraloth leapt to the future?"

"Well, you could check," he continued. "Besides, if there were originally two time balls to send a messenger into the past, to be used in conjunction with Astraloth's defense, then wouldn't there be two sets of spheres to send Astraloth into the future?"

He had a point. "You might be right. But now's not the time to check.

We need to talk about the Shade Beam."

Everyone shuffled in their seats.

K leaned forward onto her bulky, spiked forearms. She flexed her fingers, and her eyes shifted between us. "Well, Osax? Did you get the code?"

I shook my head.

"Dammit!" Jonathan cried. "That was my only idea."

"That's a shame," said Joëlle, trying to hide her unease. "We'll just have to find some other way to fight the Shade Beam."

"But if we can't search the schematics for a weakness, what are we going to do?" asked K. "Dammit Osax, your plan got me excited for a few minutes there."

I sighed. "I know, I let you all down. But believe me, I tried. Jonathan was wearing his holo-gauntlet on his wrist, and when he went to bed he locked the door."

"So, it's Jonathan's fault," said K.

"What isn't his fault?" Joëlle muttered, her shoulders tensing.

He raised his hands in defense. "What, you expect me to have magically known that I needed to let Osax steal my holo-gauntlet in the past, so that when I decided to abandon the Brotherhood and stop Duhrnan we would have a chance at destroying the Shade Beam?"

K shrugged. "It would have helped, yeah."

"I do have some good news," I said, trying to raise their spirits. I activated K's holo-gauntlet, and opened up the scans of her brain, displaying the holographic images of K's brain above my arm.

K met eyes with me. Her lips curled into a smile, and I felt my ears lift. "Aw, Osax! That's probably not even going to help me, you know. But that's- It's thoughtful of you."

"Osax," said Jonathan. "Can you send those scans to me? I... want to see if I can help K, as well."

"Of course," I said. "Well, you can get K to do it, later. I should return this to her." I removed the device from my wrist and gave it to K.

Joëlle smiled at me. "You know, you are sweet, Osax."

Jonathan lowered his gaze, and I caught sight of his damaged eye.

"Oh!" I exclaimed. I reached into my pocket, and retrieved his spare eye. "I, uh... accidentally stole this from you."

He lifted his head, and then his eye widened and a grin spread across his face. "Osax! You bastard, I remember now! That night, I lost my spare eye! You were acting so strange! It was you!" He laughed, then scrambled, leaning over the table to me. "Give it here!"

He snatched it from my hand before I could react. I couldn't help but smile seeing Jonathan so energetic.

He put his head down, and fiddled with the metal plate around his damaged eye, until the center piece popped out. A moment later, he fitted the spare eye to his face. He looked up, smiling, and flicked a switch. His eye began to glow white.

"Wow, it's not red!" said K.

"It's colour changing, just like my old one," he said.

"So wait-" said K. "You intentionally had a red eye this whole time?"

"So?"

"Isn't that, like… obviously the evil thing to do? Red eyes?"

"It's just a colour," he said. "I like red. Besides, some people have red eyes naturally. It's not evil."

"White suits you too," I said.

He was going to fiddle with his eye some more, but at hearing this lowered his hand. "Thanks. You know, the light doesn't actually do anything. It just looks cool."

I laughed.

Then he jerked his body to a halt and a look of concentration came over his face. He snapped his fingers together, and smiled. "I've got it!"

"What?" said K, leaning in.

He touched his cybernetic eye. "Ah!" he said. There was a clicking sound, and then he leaned back, continuing to fiddle with the device attached to his face. He closed his left eye, and the aperture on his right shut as well. He grinned. "There we go…" We all stared at him in silence before he opened his eyes, and looked at us, still smiling. "My eye implant- It has a storage component. Whenever I am looking at something, the device automatically saves a snapshot, once every second!"

"Uh…" said Joëlle. "That's unnerving."

"Yeah, dude, that's creepy as hell!" said K.

He raised his hands in defense. "Call it what you will, but don't blame me; I didn't design the prosthetic myself. That was a feature I wouldn't have wanted, but it came with the eye, and otherwise this prosthetic is the best in its class-" His cheeks began to flush. "I- I don't need to explain my choices about my body to anyone, anyway. The point is, I can use this to find the brotherhood access code! I *know* I looked at the code using this eye before, which means it's just a matter of searching through its memory!"

Excitement hit me like a crashing wave, and I almost jumped out of my seat. "So we still have a chance!" I cried. "Jonathan, that's some brilliant thinking!"

"Ha ha! Thank you, Osax!" He shut his eyes again. "The images are sent directly into my brain, so, it's a little disorienting. I can't concentrate on anything else while I'm browsing through my eye's image gallery. But with luck, I should be able to find it in a few hours."

"It'll take us a while to fly from Astraloth to Voren where the schematics are hidden," I said. "Maybe you can look for the code on the way?"

"Good point," he said.

I stood up from my chair and checked the Code-Alpha signal.

04:09:34:33

My brows furrowed. "We don't have any time to lose." K, Jonathan, and Joëlle each stood from their own seats. "Alright, Joëlle. Is the Firebrand ready?"

She frowned and stared at the floor. "...Yes," she said, after an awkwardly long pause. She looked up at me, and her face told me she had just come to an important decision. "But you need to find your own transport to Voren."

I felt like I had just been punched in the gut. Jonathan and K stared at her, utterly confused. No one knew what to say.

"Why?" I asked finally.

She looked me square in the eye. "You're the King now. You should have no trouble acquiring a transport to Voren. In the meantime, I'm going to take the Firebrand to the TAU fleets at Olympus and speak with the admirals, maybe conduct some repairs on the weapons system." She couldn't resist the urge to give K a quick glance, though I know she didn't mean to make her feel bad. "They need to know what we know. And I'll make sure that the fleets reconvene over Earth. We'll wait for your return there with the schematics. And once we analyze them, we'll come up with a plan to destroy the Shade Beam and save Earth from the valicorr.

"Besides," she paused. "I don't think I can work with a member of the Brotherhood."

Jonathan's lip twitched. "I-"

"I don't wanna hear it!" Joëlle snapped.

"But, I'm not-"

"You betrayed us," she said. "But I still saved your life. Don't ask for anything more."

His mouth hung open. Then he shut it, and frowned as his gaze fell to the table.

I opened my mouth to speak, but Joëlle cut me off.

"Just because you forgave him doesn't mean I have to," she stated. "Even ignoring everything he did before we met him, it's because of him that Omega is dead right now. You wouldn't have been trapped in a cave with a myrok in the first place." She scowled. "I don't want him aboard my ship anymore."

I noticed K clenching her firsts, but she stayed silent. She bit her bottom lip.

I sighed. "Alright, Joëlle. You go to the fleets. I will tell the skyther fleets to meet with the TAU over Earth. We need to stand together if we are to defend our galaxy from Durhnan. Then Jonathan, K and I will get the schematics from Voren, and return as soon as possible so they can be analyzed," I said, though my heart was heavy. We had only just reunited. I didn't want us to split up again. And I didn't want to leave the Firebrand; it had just started to feel like home to me.

It was never your home. The thoughts invaded my mind. And for a moment I was back in the freezing air of Voren, with a black sky above me as missiles detonated in vicious flames and the tower where her team was trapped crumbled away into the abyss.

She was never your friend. She could never really like you, after what you did. After what you let happen. The voice in my head cut me like a molecular sword. I forced myself to ignore it.

I stepped a pace toward her around the table, and reached out a hand for her to shake. "It's been an honour getting to know you."

She wrapped her fingers around my hand, and squeezed firmly. I could tell she was holding something back behind her eyes. "Be careful, Osax. Contact me if you need anything. We all should leave at once."

She halted on her way out the door. Facing me, she gave the skyther bow, which I returned. Then she glanced back at K, who stared at her sadly. "See you around, K," she said.

Then she disappeared.

Jonathan hung his head in shame. K sighed. I stood silently as my thoughts wandered back to the frigid snowfields of Voren. We had no time to lose.

"My mother had a spare ship," I said, flatly. "We can use that."

Sixty-One

Joëlle left with the Firebrand to meet with the TAU fleets, and I piloted one of my mothers- one of *my*- spare shuttles. It was identical in design to the vehicle my mother had flown, a smooth sphere as white as snow.

Neither Jonathan nor K had ever flown a skyther ship before, and they were too exhausted and stressed to want to learn now. Nevertheless, I taught Jonathan basic skyther ship controls in case we found ourselves in a situation where I was unable to fly it. I would have taught K too, but she slumped in the corner and played games on her holo-gauntlet for most of the ride, complaining about an ongoing headache which seemed to get worse with each passing hour. I was worried about her.

But I tried to keep my mind distracted from K, and everything else. While I was at the helm, I turned off autopilot for as long as I could before getting tired. I flew manually, making constant micro adjustments. My fingers grazed the plastic buttons and control sticks and I went into a bit of a trance. It helped keep my mind off everything else. Even with a sleep break in between, a day and a half seemed to easily slip by, there for the briefest of moments, and then gone.

We had just entered Voren's solar system and the stars stretched back into place after exiting slipspace. I sat alone in the cockpit, fingers curled around the control sticks. I gazed through the window, and inhaled at the sight of the tiny white planet against a vast blackness. I shuffled in my seat as my consciousness returned from its mindless wandering to the present moment. I flexed my fingers and mandibles. My ears twitched. The cockpit still smelled like fresh plastic.

I heard the door open over the faint whine of the engine and swivelled in my chair to see K step inside the room, holding a bowl full of strange red fruits. They were small, somewhat cone-shaped, and dotted with tiny seeds.

"Wait!" I exclaimed. "You can't eat in here!"

I felt silly for startling her with my sudden movements. Her eyebrows creased with concern. "Why? What's wrong?"

I hesitated for a moment. "Oh..." I leaned back in my seat, trying to relax my shoulders. "My mother never let me bring food into the cockpit. She would always scold me if I did, saying that she didn't want crumbs on the controls or on the floor." I scratched behind my ears. "I guess..."

"It's okay," said K, backing away. "I'll eat in the dining area."

"No, it's alright. Forget what I said. You can eat in here."

She smirked. "Whatever you say, Osax."

There were three seats in the room, I took the pilot's seat in the center. K plopped onto one of the side seats, and spun the chair so she could see me. She kicked off her boots to get comfortable. The cockpit was small, and our seats were close together.

Her horns pointed toward me as she leaned forward, resting her elbows on her knees, casually holding the bowl of fruits in one hand while she picked at it with her other. I could see veins pulsing against the blue skin of her forehead, which was dotted with pale ridges of bone. She forced a half-smile as she looked at me, munching away at the bite-sized fruits.

"How's your head?" I asked cautiously.

She gestured vaguely with her hand, before grabbing another fruit and popping it in her mouth. "The strawberries are helping. Kinda." She snorted. "Taste good, at least."

I relaxed in my seat, and lifted my ears. "How did you get those, anyway?"

"Downloaded a food-synthesizer recipe on my holo-gauntlet," she said. "Then plugged it in, and voilà! Synthesized strawberries." She held the bowl up to my face, and I had to back away slightly so she didn't smack my jaw with them. "Wanna try 'em?"

I smirked. "I'm up for the challenge." I grabbed one of the fruits carefully between my fingers and examined it. Then I popped it into my mouth. It was sweet, soft, and quite juicy. "That is actually delicious," I said. "Where do they come from?"

"Earth, apparently," said K. Then her eyes fell to the floor. "Of course I've never had a properly grown strawberry. You know, that would be a pretty cool experience." She looked up at me. "To eat some food that was grown in the wild. Rather than something made by a machine." She bit into another strawberry, savouring it. "I wonder if you can notice the difference, you know?"

I smiled warmly, leaning forward onto my knees. "Well, I can certainly notice the difference between real fruits from Astraloth, and the synthesized stuff. But that doesn't mean synthesized stuff is bad." I inhaled. "Hey, after we stop Duhrnan for good... let's do that."

She sat up, and raised a brow. "Do what?"

"Go to Earth," I said, my ears lifting. "Find a wild strawberry, and eat it. Cut it in half, if we need to share."

She grinned. "I'm pretty sure they grow on bushes, so if we found one, we'd probably find a bunch."

"Perfect," I said.

She grabbed my dangling hand, and squeezed it carefully. "Let's do it," she said. "After all of this is over... you and I are gonna be dining on wild strawberries."

We sat there in silence for a few moments. And a deep, but simple truth began to dawn between us...

"K-"

"Osax-" she cut me off, and let go of my hand.

We each snorted a laugh as we tried to let the other speak. "You go on," I said.

"Okay," she said. "I was thinking about Omega."

I felt my ears skew at an angle, but I remained silent.

"They sacrificed themself for us. For me." She said. "It's noble. But it seemed odd to me. They only knew us for a day. Why would they die for us?"

"I don't know."

"Well," she continued, "I think the answer is actually really simple. They realized that connections are what make life meaningful." She stared at me. "Omega spent their whole life following orders, hardly even questioning their existence. They thought they were made to kill the Brotherhood. And maybe that is why they were made, but maybe it's not why they were meant to exist... you know?"

I nodded. "Maybe."

"And, we were kind of Omega's first friends. Their first people. And even in that short time, their world must have changed so dramatically... They found us dying, struggling to fight the elements. And they chose- They *chose*- to help us. To nurture us back to health. Complete strangers. Omega felt something, some kind of calling to do more than just go through the motions, to do more than just follow orders, to do more than just kill. They chose to heal. To protect. To step into the unknown.

And maybe, despite all of their physical prowess and coordination, even despite their abilities of regeneration, that really was Omega's greatest super power. That they were willing to change."

I nodded slowly. "Wow, K. I don't know what to say."

She smirked. "Yeah, I guess it sounded pretty cool. But where I'm going with this is, I-" She held her breath for a second. "I want to find my purpose. Beyond just fighting things, you know? I was made to be a bioweapon. But even Jonathan had a change of heart... maybe I can change too. Maybe I can get through my condition. Maybe I'll have a chance to live a full life."

I smiled. "I think you will, K. You've already grown so much since I've known you, and we've only known each other for a few weeks."

"It's crazy, right?" She said, scratching her head. "Cause, I was thinking... One thing I don't wanna change is- I don't-" She sighed shortly, then paused. Her orange eyes locked with mine. "I don't wanna say goodbye to you, after this is all over," she said. "I don't know what's going to happen. But..."

I felt a warmth rising in my heart. "K, don't worry," I said. I grabbed her hand firmly, and lifted it up so our palms were clasped together. "You are my friend. And I see no reason why we can't keep being friends after this is done."

She smiled. "We're friends," she said. "Maybe best friends. Can I say best friends forever?"

I laughed. "Sure! Best friends forever."

She let go of my hand, and laughed, shaking her head. "Actually that- That sounds weird when you say it, but... The sentiment is there. Yeah. You matter to me. That's the main thing."

"And you matter to me." I paused, ears reaching for the ceiling. "So after this is over, wild strawberries?"

She smirked. "Wild strawberries."

Jonathan stepped into the room, standing straight as his head swivelled between us and his coat trailed behind him. "Hey, we arrived at the planet, why did no one tell me?"

"I- Sorry," I said. "K and I were just relaxing before-"

"We don't have *time* to relax!" he stated. "Chop chop, people. Osax, take us in please. Need I remind you of the time pressure?"

"Give us a break!" said K and I in unison.

He sighed. "Whatever. I'm not angry, I'm just stressed."

"Fair enough," I stated, and I faced forward. I grabbed the controls and flew us toward Voren. Jonathan sighed once more, and took the remaining seat.

"Hey," said K. "You shaved your moustache!"

I glanced over to him. She was right. His upper lip was free of hair.

He nodded. "Yes. It was time for a change."

"See?" said K, gesturing to me. "Change." Then she turned to Jonathan, who looked a little confused, and said. "It looks good."

Sixty-Two

The exit ramp hissed loudly as it lowered to the snow-covered docking bay. With Jonathan and K on either side of me dressed in thermal suits just like I was, I stepped onto the platform. Wind blasted my face, and flecks of snow swarmed me, eagerly clinging to my fur and clothes in the sideways gust. Everything was white.

My feet crunched into the snow, and I squinted. With each exhale, our breaths condensed into clouds of fog, which were quickly whisked away by the weather. I craned my neck, gazing up at the hazy spire of grey before us. I'd landed us on the same platform which the TAU shuttle had dropped me off on weeks ago. It was even more stormy now than it had been then.

Unease crept into my chest. Being here felt wrong.

I turned back to face my companions, forcing myself to ignore the thought. Jonathan wore a blue cloak over his coat, which was lined with fur on the inside. With his gloved hands, he gripped each side of the furry hood and held it tightly over each side of his face, which was covered with a fabric mask. His cybernetic eye shone a pure white light. K wore a thick furry jacket, and had wrapped a thermal scarf around her bald head, face, and neck. The cold was even getting to me already, but they both looked like they could barely stand it.

"Let's get inside, quick," I said. They nodded hurriedly, and marched with me across the snowy bridge toward the entrance to the facility.

K grunted faintly, clutching the side of her head. "Ow..."

I wrapped my arm around her shoulder, and helped her inside.

When the door shut behind us, the base felt eerily quiet. The lights were all on, and the hallway felt warm. The power generator had been left on.

I shivered, but not from the cold. The smell of decay wafted in from somewhere deeper. It looked like a TAU outpost, but now this place was a graveyard.

"Come on," K grunted impatiently, unwrapping the scarf from her head. "Take us to those secret labs, or whatever."

Jonathan gave her a sidelong glance, removing the fabric covering his mouth, and the hood from his head. He shut his eyes. "Follow me."

Jonathan took the lead. We wandered through the facility, and quickly found signs of the valicorr attack. Charred and blasted bits of architecture, broken glass, and human bodies littered the place. I grit my mandibles.

I gazed out a glass wall toward the white horizon. The snow was so thick that I could barely see anything. I closed my eyes and remembered the screech of that giant monster chasing K and I in the hover-car. Its pale-blue teeth. Its raw strength.

My gaze fell back to Jonathan, who led the way a few paces ahead of me. Could that monster have been one of Jonathan's earlier experiments? The blue-tinged bones, and super strength... It reminded me of K. I thought about asking him, but decided not to. Now didn't seem like a good time.

Then I caught sight of the ruined base of a tower. It was the eastern tower, where Joëlle's squad had been killed. The air choked in my lungs...

"Osax?"

Jonathan's voice snapped me back to reality. I nodded, and followed him and K into an elevator. We stood in silence as it descended. I tried not to think about that man's arm slipping from my grasp back in the elevator shaft, falling into darkness, or the tormented face of his wife.

I tried not to think about Omega. About my mother.

We destroyed the mothership, I thought. I shut my eyes, and forced myself to imagine something else. The feeling of the ocean lapping at my feet. The sound of fizzy soda bubbling in a glass between my ears. The sight of stars, stretched out across Astraloth's sky.

I took a deep breath, and shakily exhaled. Then I opened my eyes and met K's, who had been watching me with a silent, concerned frown. She smiled faintly, and I felt okay. I lifted my ears.

The elevator stopped well below the surface of the planet. It was absolutely quiet down here. Jonathan entered an access code, and the door opened to a dimly lit room.

He led us through the halls, which were uncomfortably thin. The ceilings were only seven feet tall; tall enough for most humans, but I had to duck my head a little to walk around. I felt myself getting a little claustrophobic. We were deep underground.

Even down here, there were signs of battle. TAU scientists lay dead around every corner, and plasma scoring from valicorr E-guns and swords decorated the walls. Or I guess they were Brotherhood scientists. Maybe now it didn't matter...

"So, the valicorr fought all the way down here," I said. "They stole the plans for the Shade Beam, but I hadn't really considered how until now. Did they hack into the main computer?"

Jonathan replied. "Ryner had me send them an access code, so they could steal the Shade Beam prototype and its plans from the computer."

K scoffed. "You mean you just gave the code to the valicorr?"

"I'm not proud of it," he said.

K growled, clenching her fists. "You- You let all of this happen, didn't you?!"

"If Jonathan didn't do it, Ryner would have just killed him, and gotten someone else to," I said. "Or he would have done it himself. It's not like Jonathan had much of a choice, right?"

K shut her eyes, groaning. She clutched her head. Her veins pulsed quickly. "Yeah, you're right. Ryner would have made the attack happen." She grit her teeth. "Even so-"

Jonathan frowned. "Even so, I still feel responsible..."

K rubbed her temple. "I don't understand it, anyway. Ryner's whole plan... he gave so much power to Duhrnan, letting him take the Shade Beam. Why would he do that?"

"He wanted to create an enemy for the galaxy, so he gave Duhrnan the power to threaten it. But he intended to betray Duhrnan, eventually. He wanted to make the Brotherhood look like the heroes by taking down the valicorr." Jonathan said.

"But really," I said, "the Brotherhood was working with the valicorr the whole time."

Jonathan sighed. "It's all a huge mess. I can hardly believe I was part of it now."

"I know," I sympathized. "But that's not the point right now. We need to get the plans for the Shade Beam, and reunite with the fleets over Earth. Duhrnan will bring the weapon to Earth, and likely an army along with it. We don't have much time." I shuffled nervously. Really, I just didn't like being down here.

"Well," said Jonathan, stopping at a door, "this is the computer room."

The door slid open, and we stepped inside. I had to duck low under the doorway. Then I felt my heart get caught in my throat.

The room smelled of ozone and death. Human bodies lay strewn about, and sparks flew from the flickering ceiling lights. The room was full of metal computer consoles which lined the walls, and each one had been slashed across with a plasma sword.

"No," I said. "It can't be- Jonathan, is the computer...?"

"It's fine," he said, hesitantly. "The valicorr must have slashed up the consoles, hoping to destroy them, and the memory banks along with them. But these are just access terminals. The main computer's physical storage is located in another room."

I exhaled a sigh of relief. "Then we need to access the memory directly-"

"No," Jonathan cut in. "Remember, if we tamper with the physical memory storage and are detected by the computer it will self-destruct the entire database. We just need to find another terminal to input the access code, and I know where we can look."

Eagerly, he slipped past me, and as I turned in the doorway, K and I exchanged a glance. Since I was crouching, our faces were much closer than usual.

She smirked, playfully. "Come on, Osax." Then she sped after Jonathan, and I followed.

We passed many unlabelled doors, but eventually Jonathan stopped at one, giving K and I time to catch up.

Jonathan exhaled. "Welcome to my secret laboratory," he said. Then he punched in a code on the door, and it hummed open.

Blue lights flickered on in the room before us. We stepped out onto a catwalk which ringed the massive room. We entered on the top floor. It was a long, rectangular room with dark grey walls, and a three dimensional grid of grated walkways running through the center. The air was much cooler in here, and immediately I noticed our breaths condensing into faint wisps as we exhaled.

Suspended from the ceiling in countless rows and columns between the walkways were metal pods. Each pod had a glass door from which blue light shone. Many of the pods were empty, but even from a distance I could make out a humanoid shape inside one, then two. More than I could count.

"Wow," K marvelled.

Jonathan led us through the room to a silver lift which carried us down to the bottom floor, below the walkways and all but the bottom row of stasis pods. I noticed that this room seemed untouched from the battle. There were no scorch marks, no obvious signs of damage, and most importantly no bodies. I lay my hands atop the railing of the lift, and when I lifted my fingers I'd wiped a large amount of dust from the surface.

"No one has been here for a long time, have they?" I asked.

Jonathan shook his head. "After K awoke and I realized how wrong it was to continue with the experiments, I shut down the labs. Everyone who worked here moved onto different projects at the facility."

"And Ryner was okay with that?" I asked. "He let you shut down the labs?"

Jonathan's lip tightened. "I guess by the time I shut down the labs, he'd already gotten what he wanted from my experiments." He looked uneasy, as though the thought upset him. I couldn't blame him.

We stepped off the lift. He led us straight through the middle of the dark room, past rows of pods, many of which were empty. But most contained a human, just like K. They were blue skinned, horned, muscular, and all shared some of her and Jonathan's features. Each one looked a little different. The horns grew in different shapes and sizes, the bone ridges appeared in different formations, and each body's form was unique despite their similarities.

I glanced to K. Her gaze wandered up and around the entire room. I could only imagine what she was thinking.

"So, this is where I was made?" K wondered. She stopped, gazing up at the array of pods.

Jonathan and I stopped too, turning to look at her. "Yes," he replied.

"And there are three hundred others, waiting in those stasis pods?" she said quietly.

Jonathan nodded slowly. "Yes. Each one is a genetically engineered clone using my DNA as a baseline. But they are all unique. To accelerate the process of designing the perfect weapon and make full use of our facilities here, I thought we should make an entire batch of bioweapons, each with slight variations in genetic makeup. By testing each individually and comparing results and findings, we could quickly narrow down potential problems and solutions."

I followed K to a nearby pod. There was another being inside, just behind the glass. They looked like they might have been K's sibling, and in a way, I suppose they were. Their eyes were closed, and their expression neutral. They stood inside the pod with their arms, legs, and forehead held in place by straps. They were lit from the bottom of the pod by blue light which weirdly highlighted their features. K gently placed her hand on the glass, and leaned in to get a better look.

"Careful-" said Jonathan.

"I'm being careful," K retorted. "I just... She looks almost just like me. Even the horns... but they're not quite the same." Silence filled the air. "They're just like me..."

I tried to find something to say, but all I could manage was, "Amazing..."

We each stood in silence not knowing what to say, until K turned to Jonathan with a determined look on her face.

"What's going to happen to them?" Her voice was clear.

He pursed his lips. "I don't know." He stared at her solemnly. "I really don't know."

"You created a people," I stated, the gravity of it all finally dawning on me. "K, and her siblings... they amount to something of a new species-"

"Hey! *I'm* human!" said K, indignantly. She glowered at me, and I recoiled.

"I- I didn't mean it like that, K. You're human! But, you know... you are different."

Her expression softened. "Yeah, guess you're right, Osax." Then she looked back at her sister in the pod. "We're human... but we are different."

Jonathan spun around, facing away from us. His neck craned as he looked up at the array of pods and clones. "None of them have ever been awakened, because... the galaxy isn't ready for them. They are too powerful. Too different. And furthermore, they were intended to be weapons used by the Brotherhood. If the TAU knew of their existence, they would want them exterminated."

"But the TAU didn't want to kill me," said K.

"You're a single anomaly in their eyes. The TAU probably isn't too afraid of you on your own. But if they knew your origins, and if they knew about the other clones..." He cleared his throat nervously.

K winced, and clutched her head. "Ah, jeez!" Her veins pulsed violently.

I felt myself involuntarily wincing as well. "You don't look so good," I said. "The headache is getting worse, isn't it?"

She nodded, inhaling sharply.

Jonathan stepped toward her. "There are pills you can take to relieve headaches; some of them work very well on humans, and while your DNA is different it shouldn't be so-"

"Yeah, I'm kinda turned off of pills for a while," she growled, clearly agitated. "We've been talking too long, lets go get the plans."

"Right," Jonathan said. He sped off across the room, and I walked up to K. I wrapped my arm around her shoulder, and helped her walk.

"I can walk just fine, Osax," she said, glancing up at me.

"Sorry," I replied sheepishly, withdrawing my arm.

We walked in silence for a moment.

"Actually," she said, still clutching her head, "you can keep helping me." She gave me a sidelong glance.

I placed my hand on her shoulder again, and guided her gently. We caught up with Jonathan through the doorway to another room.

It was a small, cozy office for one, and Jonathan plopped onto a swivelling chair. He grabbed the edges of a wide desk and used it to roll his seat forward. There were several computer monitors mounted on the wall on adjustable armatures. Jonathan flicked a few switches and the computer screens flashed on. The computer terminal whirred and hummed as it came to life, and Jonathan immediately began typing in the access code.

"This is going to take some time," he said.

"Yes, a three hundred character string of numerals would take a while to input. It's not incredibly efficient," I said. "What if you need to access something from the memory core quickly?"

He snorted a laugh. "*Someone* thought it was a good security system. And with the Brotherhood, sometimes it's impossible to pin who's responsible for what decisions. I thought about complaining many times though, trust me."

Then K groaned, and my ears shot back. "Ugh, my head," she said. "This is seriously bad right now..."

"What can I do to help?" I asked, trying to sound calm. Jonathan was too focused on the code to pay attention.

K shielded her eyes from the white lights of the office. "It's too bright in here. I'm gonna wait outside."

She made for the exit, and I followed her, watching as she stumbled clumsily to the doorway. *She's fine,* I thought. *This is just another headache. She hasn't even passed out. She's gone through worse.*

The sound of Jonathan's typing was completely muffled as we shut the door behind us. We waited outside the office in the blue-tinged bay of clone pods. We sat with our knees up and our backs against the wall next to the door, side by side. She kept groaning and blinking. I was eyeing her carefully, trying to breathe slowly to maintain some control over my adrenaline levels. But watching her wince in pain and begin to sweat was making me nervous. *Everything's fine,* I told myself.

"...How are you holding up?" I gulped.

K screwed her eyes shut, and she pulled her knees in closer. Her fingers massaged her temples in vain. Then drool seeped from her lips and around her pronounced tusk-like teeth. A wave rippled out from her core, and she collapsed to the floor with a thud.

My heart stuttered.

"K?!" I shrieked.

I scrambled on my hands and knees, and rolled her onto her side. She was completely limp. I couldn't see the veins on her head anymore. One of her eyes was half open. They were completely still. Her lips were parted slightly. My breath fogged as I panted in panic. But I couldn't see any comforting cloud of breath coming from her mouth.

My hands scrambled to her wrist, pressing, feeling for a pulse. Nothing. I tried her neck.

Seconds passed.

Nothing.

The door hissed open, and Jonathan stepped out with a smile on his face. "I've got the schematics!"

"K's dying!" I cried.

His eyes lit up with fear, and his mouth dropped. In a flash he was by her side with me. I was too panicked to think of what to do, but Jonathan whipped out his holo-gauntlet and started scanning her. I couldn't look away from her body. She looked dead. I willed my muscles to stay still, but they started shaking.

"She's..." Jonathan swallowed hard, and looked up at me. Our eyes met, and I saw tears welling in his eye.

"She can't be," I said. "She *can't be dead!*"

Not her too, I thought. *Not now.* I wasn't even sobbing, but tears started to stream down my face. My heart hurt. Actually hurt. I jammed my thumbs into my thighs until they hurt as well, trying to distract myself.

Jonathan was breathing heavily. He scanned the room frantically. "Osax, listen to me." We locked eyes. "Help me get her into one of the pods."

"Okay," I said, shaking.

My muscles felt sore all of a sudden. The two of us bent over, and grabbed K by the shoulders. We lifted her heavy body off the ground and carried her to one of the empty pods. Her head bobbed, and her feet dragged across the floor.

Jonathan let go of her, and I held her full weight in my arms. Her head draped back over my arm, and I stared at her blank face, my ears dangling on either side of her head. We stopped next to the pod, and the corners of my vision began to darken as I hyperventilated. The pod beeped coldly as Jonathan punched in a code. Then gas vented from it, and the glass door swung open.

Jonathan grabbed K's arm, and together we carefully moved her body into the pod. Jonathan started strapping her limbs and head in place, and I tried to help.

"Will this help her?" I asked.

With the last strap in place, he quickly shut the door on her. He pressed a few buttons on the side of the pod, and it lit up from within with a blue light. There was a high whining sound from the stasis pod.

I pressed my fingers against the pod, then let my face fall against it. My nose pressed against the cool glass as I looked at K, suddenly so distant seeming in the weird light of the pod. My breath fogged up the glass, and I stayed there, breathing quickly.

Jonathan replied. "I don't know, Osax. My scanner said... that her heart had stopped."

"I know." I felt like I was going to sob. I stared at her, unblinking. It was so sudden. How could she be gone?

Jonathan laid a hand on the glass as well, peering in at her. He frowned, and though his lip quivered, he didn't cry. He was straining not to. "I just thought, maybe... If her body is in stasis then her condition won't worsen, so maybe..." He breathed a shaky sigh and finally a tear rolled down his cheek. "I don't know..."

Then I sank to my knees. I whimpered, my hands sliding and sticking to the glass as I fell, and lowered my gaze. I curled inward. I couldn't stop myself from crying.

"You can't be gone, K," I muttered. "It's not fair. It's not fair. It's not fair."

Sixty-Three

The investigator's eyes trained on me.

I tried to hold my body still and fight the shaking. I shut my eyes tightly. *Breathe.* Five seconds passed. Ten.

I exhaled for another ten seconds. Then I inhaled once more. With each slow breath, I pulled myself closer into the present moment, and away from the memory. Colour returned to my vision. My muscles felt shaky, yet they remained still.

"What's wrong?" said the investigator. Her face was barely concerned; instead she wore an expression of confusion, as if she could hardly understand my reaction. When I saw her expression, my stomach twisted into a knot of rage. How could she not understand my grief? Didn't she know by now how much K mattered to me? Hadn't she been listening?

My eyes narrowed, and suddenly my blood boiled. Under her hat her eyes watched me with a quiet menace. My fingers tightened around my glass as I watched her.

Had she no compassion? She was not my friend. She was not my ally. And in that moment, my grief and depression were replaced with wrath. I fought to contain it within me, but I could feel it beaming out from my eyes. She flinched when our eyes met.

"Nothing is wrong," I lied.

"Alright," she said calmly. She adjusted her hat and glanced outside, breaking eye contact. The sun was beginning to set behind the distant mountains across the water. Astraloth's moons spun slowly around the planet. As the glow of the sun began to fade in the sky, the purple and red nebulas started to come into view. Massive TAU ships circled above the city.

"So," she continued, looking back my way. "K died. You and

Jonathan put her into one of the Brotherhood's stasis pods. Then what happened? You retrieved the plans to the Shade Beam. And you only had so much time until Duhrnan would use it to attack Earth, as he had threatened. So what did you do?"

"Well," I said, "I looked at the timer, and I told Jonathan that we needed to leave. Then he broke down crying. He told me that he couldn't leave K. That he needed to take care of her. That he was responsible for her. That he needed to find a way to save her, somehow." My eyes fell to the table. I lifted my glass to my mouth and slurped on the straw, but it was long since empty.

"So you left Voren by yourself?"

"Yes. I got back in my ship and took off towards Earth to meet with Joëlle and the fleets."

"Leaving Jonathan and K behind on Voren?"

"Yes," I said.

She leaned forward. "When a reconnaissance team went to the base on Voren weeks later, they found it completely abandoned. No sign of Jonathan, K, or any of the clones."

I nodded. "Yes, I know."

"The secret labs were completely empty. No one was there."

I nodded once more.

The investigator tilted her head. "Are you saying that you had nothing to do with their vanishing?"

I sighed deeply. "I was just as shocked as everyone else to hear that the base was empty."

"So you have had no contact with Jonathan since leaving Voren?"

"Not since leaving Voren."

"You know that harbouring a bioweapon is illegal now, and aiding a Brotherhood agent- even one who claims to have renounced the Brotherhood- is a crime. Your contact and closeness with K and Jonathan puts you in an awkward position, as you can probably imagine..."

"That was the last time I saw them," I stated firmly. "I have had no contact with Jonathan since that day. And he hasn't tried to contact me either."

After a moment of silence, the investigator relaxed in her seat. She eyed me carefully, but she seemed convinced. And I caught sight of a strange smile creeping across her face. She looked excited. Perhaps this was what she needed to hear this whole time.

"Alright," she said. "I believe you."

"Good," I said. "Is that all you needed to hear? Should I stop the story?"

"No, please go on, your majesty." she said. "I want to know what your experience at Earth was like, when the attack happened. After that... I think I'll have everything I need, and you can finally rest." Her eyes were like a snake's.

I breathed out a shaky sigh, watching her carefully. She believed me. But I could tell her confidence was growing. The story was almost done. The trap was ready to be sprung, and I was walking right into it.

"Excellent," I said. "I'm eager to conclude the story... it would have felt strange to stop so close to the end." As I spoke, I subtly activated my holo-gauntlet beneath the table. I needed to send a message.

A second later the message was sent. Everything was in place. I only hoped that I knew what I was getting myself into.

I shuffled in my seat, and cleared my throat. "More refreshments?" I asked. She nodded, and I stood from my seat and walked to a small food synthesizer in the corner of the room. I took a few moments to generate a fresh root beer for me and coffee for her. I could feel her eyes on me.

"No servants today?" she asked. "Come to think of it, the temple has been rather empty since this morning."

"Oh," I said, trying to keep a calm expression. I gave her the drink, and returned to my seat. "Yes, it is a special holiday for us skythers, today. The temple is empty today because of it, aside from us of course, and a few essential workers in the lower levels." I forced a smile. "The quiet is nice, is it not?"

She had no trouble smirking at this. "Yes. It is nice indeed. I'd love to learn more about skyther culture some day," she said. She looked immensely pleased. "But for now, I'm just eager to hear the end of this story. It would be *great* to finish it today."

"Then let's get back to it."

Sixty-Four

I woke blearily in the white bedroom of my mother's starship to a faint beeping sound coming from the cockpit. There was no comforting sound of my friends chatting in the next room. No smell of food cooking in the kitchen. No sign of anyone, except for me, alone in the vastness of space.

I tumbled out of bed, and before doing anything else, I checked the time on the Code-Alpha signal.

01:00:14:56

I shut my eyes for a moment. I could hardly believe what my life had been for the past eight or nine days... I couldn't remember how long it had been since seeing Duhrnan's threat. I had more time to prepare for the attack on Earth than anyone else, but I still didn't feel ready. We had one day left. It wasn't enough time, but I'm not sure if any amount of time would have been.

My fur was a mess. I threw on my armour and black cloak, and stumbled into the cockpit.

When I entered the dark room, overhead lights activated, and the grey wall above the controls faded until it was a window. I peered out at the stars stretching before me, pooling around my starship. Then I took a seat, and flicked off the alarm which had been warning me that I was about to exit slipspace. I tapped a button on the ship's computer and a holographic display awoke in front of me, showing the detailed schematics of the Shade Beam. I sighed deeply, and curled my fingers into fists.

The ship's engines lowered in pitch, slowing, and space beyond the windshield snapped back into place. Before me was a blue and green planet; planet Earth glowed with the light of its sun. And I could see a mass of starships gathering on the far side of the planet, in the direction of its moon.

I inhaled the scent of fresh plastic, and wrapped my fingers around the controls, gently skirting around its orbit.

My gaze fell to Earth. I could make out the continents behind the swirling white clouds. Slowly I crested its shadow side, passing a silver satellite, and continued to fly toward the glowing white moon and the armada of battlecruisers that gathered there.

I shut my eyes and breathed slowly.

Then I pressed my finger into a plastic button on the dashboard, activating my communications channel.

"Joëlle," I said shakily. "I'm back. Where are you?"

◆

I was escorted to the Kronos by a squadron of TAU fighters. Joëlle was waiting for me in the hangar when my ship touched down. The hangar was full of commotion, with military officials and soldiers bustling about, but as I stepped out of my ship and my feet pressed onto the smooth, cool floor, our eyes met.

She ran over to me, decked out in her combat gear, as usual. She was smiling, and her purple dreads bounced with each step. She shoved her way through the crowd.

I walked toward her, blinking, overwhelmed by the bright lights of the hangar, and the deafening sound of the ships taking off and landing. I had only awoken minutes ago.

"Osax!" Joëlle said. "You made it!"

I nodded silently as she reached me. I looked down at her, and she looked up at me. People passed all around us. I remembered when we first met, in the vehicle bay at the base on Voren. Before all of this happened.

"Did you do it?"

"Yes," I said. I held my arm out and activated my gauntlet. The schematics hovered above my hand, and we both stared at the translucent form of the Shade Beam as it slowly spun in the air between us. People had already been looking my way, being the only skyther in the room, but now a crowd circled us, watching. They were all here to defend Earth.

The massive room seemed to quiet. Joëlle's brown eyes gazed into me.

"Osax? Where's K? And Jonathan?"

I lowered my hands slowly, and my head and ears curled downward. The hologram disappeared. I screwed my eyes shut and clenched my fists.

I could feel all their eyes on me. In the blackness of my mind I could see Omega, K, and my mother. I felt the heat of a fiery explosion, yet my hands felt cold, like they were pressed up against the glass of K's stasis pod. Her expressionless face filled my mind.

"...They're gone."

"What?" said Joëlle.

"K's heart stopped. Jonathan put her in a stasis pod, but..." I nearly gagged, trying to hold back a sob. Tears welled in my eyes, and ran down my cheeks, and I tasted salt. My body began to shake.

I breathed in slowly, and after a few seconds, I rubbed my eyes and face, blinking them open. I looked at Joëlle.

"He stayed behind," I said.

Joëlle looked stunned. "I don't know what to say... I didn't expect anything to happen when you were down there, it seemed like a perfectly safe mission-"

"It was," I said, shaking my head. "It was perfectly safe. But there was nothing we could do. K just... She just-" I exhaled sharply, and bowed my head, tensing my shoulders and arms.

I felt Joëlle's hand on my arm. "Osax..."

"I'm fine," I said, pulling away. I wiped my face once more, and looked away from her toward the opening in the hangar. I stared at the planet beside us. "I'm fine."

"Are you sure?" she asked, hesitantly.

"I'm fine!" I blurted, whipping around to face her. My arm shot out, pointing toward Earth. "Duhrnan will arrive in twenty-four hours to destroy Earth! How I feel doesn't matter! All that matters is that we stop Duhrnan, and destroy the Shade Beam. We *need* to destroy it!"

I panted. Saliva dripped from my mandibles. Joëlle recoiled, clearly hurt, and I was hit with a pang of guilt.

Then I heard the voice of my old friend, Fiona. "You're right, Talcorosax."

The crowd parted behind Joëlle, and the admiral walked through the opening. She approached us waving her robotic hand my way, and I tried to relax my posture.

"Fiona," I said, bowing slightly.

"Admiral," said Joëlle.

Fiona nodded to us each. Her eyes carried heavy bags beneath them, and she looked exhausted, but forced a smile nonetheless. "You've got the schematics?"

I nodded.

"Then follow me. We need that analyzed, ASAP."

◆

00:14:23:54

I was alone on the observation deck, waiting for the analysts to complete their work, when Joëlle climbed into the dome-shaped lounge, breathing quickly.

"They found a weakness!" she declared.

I glanced over to her, then uncurled my legs and swung them over the side of the couch. I inhaled slowly. My limbs felt heavy.

"K was here, you know."

"What?"

"In this room, with me. Weeks ago now, but still... She was right here." I looked up at the glass dome above us. Thousands of white dots sparkled before my eyes, but they felt so cold.

Joëlle hesitated, taking a step toward me. I was only vaguely aware of her presence. "Osax... Do you want to talk about it? We have a bit of time..."

"Look," I said, avoiding her question. Joëlle followed my gaze.

Just then a fleet of skyther ships had arrived in orbit around Earth, and began their rendezvous with the TAU army.

"So you called for Astraloth's aid," said Joëlle.

"Of course I did," I said. "Stopping Duhrnan is a matter of galactic importance. We're eager to come to Earth's aid."

"Even though the TAU built the Shade Beam without telling the skythers?"

"Yes," I said. "We don't have time to be angry with the TAU right now. We need to work together."

Joëlle nodded. "I agree. I'm glad you see it that way," she said. "You know, just because some humans are bad, doesn't mean we all are. I know from what you've seen we probably all seem selfish, or evil. But we're not. I can't help that you've had some bad examples though, what with the people who made the Shade Beam, and the Brotherhood, and Jonathan-"

"Jonathan isn't evil," I snapped.

Joëlle sighed. "I don't- I don't know... Maybe you're right, but... he betrayed us. He would have had us all killed. I don't know how you can forgive him."

"Well, I can't make you forgive him." I stated.

"True." Joëlle frowned. "I *want* to forgive him... But... Well, now he's gone."

"He's on Voren. He's not gone."

"For now he's on Voren, but he'll probably fly off into uncharted space soon," she said.

I blinked. "What do you mean?"

"Back on the Firebrand, before Duhrnan attacked Astraloth and we followed him to Malum, he kept telling me about how he wanted to take a starship and fly off into the stars... to start a new life away from galactic society. He wanted to build a home on a distant planet and forget about the troubles of politics and the military. I asked him why he hadn't done it already, and he said he still had other obligations... That he had some hope for the world." She tightened her jaw. "I think he was talking about the Brotherhood... and now that Ryner is dead, and the Brotherhood must be scattered, he probably doesn't have any reason to stick around. Being a member of the Brotherhood, even if he betrayed them, he's technically a fugitive, too, so..."

"He said he would look after K."

She shrugged. "Maybe he will. When he told me about his dream, I asked if he'd be lonely. 'Not if you come with me,' he said." She chuckled, weakly. "I guess if he brings K..."

"But she's not a-" I exhaled. "She's in a stasis pod. She wouldn't be much company."

"What's the difference to Jonathan, being alone on Voren or alone somewhere else?"

I shrugged, and then sat in silence. My gaze fell to the floor and my mind began to wander.

"Hey," said Joëlle, retaking my attention. "Come to the mission briefing with me. Please."

I met eyes with her. There was such intensity in her gaze; a firestorm of emotion, but she kept it so well contained behind her eyes.

"Okay," I said. "Let's go."

◆

00:13:52:12

The briefing room was circular, and almost funnel shaped, with rows of benches descending closer to the middle. The benches were full of humans in military uniforms. In the center was a small platform for Admiral Fiona to stand on as she presented the findings and outlined her ship, and the fleet's mission. Meetings just like this were being held on every cruiser in the TAU fleet as we spoke, in preparation for the upcoming battle.

The admiral pointed with a holographic stick at the schematics of the Shade Beam which displayed in the center of the room, just beside her on the platform, projected from holographic generators on the floor and ceiling. Joëlle sat next to me in the front row, and I leaned on my hands, elbows pressed into my knees. My legs were restless, constantly shaking. I had become accustomed to the smell of plastic mixing with the synthetic atmosphere of my mother's ship, meant to mimic the air makeup of Astraloth, but Kronos' air smelled strangely like Earth.

We were eight minutes into the briefing, and every minute that passed felt agonizingly slow.

"...and its shielding system should be fully functional." Fiona pointed to the outside hull of the ship. "This means that it cannot be damaged from the outside."

The Shade Beam looked like a gargantuan grey cone. The main barrel of the weapon was a small opening on the flat side of the larger end, but the hull was outfitted with countless auto-turrets for taking down smaller assailants.

I raised my hand. Fiona looked at me, and raised an eyebrow. I got the sense that I wasn't supposed to interrupt the presentation, but I had never been to a TAU military briefing before and no one had actually told me the rules.

Fiona cleared her throat. "King Talcorosax, would you like to add something to the briefing?"

Everyone's eyes shifted to me, and I stood up cautiously. "We've had to deal with this before. Duhrnan's mothership had a shielding system which couldn't be penetrated. Instead we had to enter and sabotage the ship from the inside, so that it could self destruct. That's how we destroyed the mothership, and that's how we'll destroy the Shade Beam." I lifted my head high, scanning the room. Hesitant faces looked back at me. "Sorry to interrupt, Fiona, but we don't have much time. There must be a way to get aboard the ship. That's what we need to know."

The attention of the room turned back to her. She shifted onto her robotic foot, and took in a deep breath. "Thank you, King Talcorosax." She turned her attention outward. "What the skyther King said is true; our only chance at destroying the Shade Beam is to destroy it from the inside. But our analysts have discovered that there *is* no docking bay. There are no entrances. There is no interior of the vessel."

Although surely everyone in the crowd intended to be silent and attentive, they all began to murmur at once and the room erupted with sound.

"What do you mean?" I asked. "What about the pilots? How do they get onboard to control the ship?"

Fiona's blonde hair flicked around from beneath her hat as she turned to me. "There are no pilots. The Shade Beam flies itself." She pointed toward the center of the hologram, and it expanded, zooming in until a vague orange glow appeared. "This is the ship's brain. An organic structure embedded within the core of the ship's systems, it receives commands from an external source, but can think for itself. It's a form of artificial intelligence."

A bioweapon, I thought.

"Our strategists considered ways to destroy the brain, thus disabling the Shade Beam entirely. But there is no way to do so from the outside, so we are met with the same problem."

"Then what do we do?!" cried one of the pilots in the back. His voice was met with a chorus of agreement and fear. The tension in the air was thick.

Fiona raised her hands to silence the crowd. "There is *one* way to destroy the Shade Beam."

I leaned forward. She pointed to the front of the cannon. I didn't like where this was going.

"The barrel of the weapon is thirty-six meters wide, and it's a straight shot to the power source of the ship. If we can hit the core directly with a high-impact weapon, such as an energy-missile, it should do enough damage to overload the core and self destruct. That means firing straight down the barrel of the gun."

The room fell silent.

"The Shade Beam's cannon is sealed at all times to compensate for this, aside from when the weapon is about to fire." She pointed to the hologram. The muzzle looked small when compared to the overall size of the ship. An animation played showing the covering of the barrel splitting into countless triangular pieces which folded outward from the center of the circle until the barrel was completely clear.

"Twenty-five of the fleet's ships will be outfitted with a guided E-missile strong enough to destroy the core and set off the reaction which will destroy the Shade Beam. The fleet only has the twenty-five missiles, and each one will be assigned to an elite starfighter. That means those twenty-five ships are our only shot at saving Earth.

"RT Officer Joëlle," she said.

"Yes, Sir?" Joëlle replied.

"You are the best pilot aboard this ship, and I'm assigning you to be the Kronos' E-missile bomber."

"Aye, aye," Joëlle said. She seemed surprisingly calm. I turn my gaze to the floor, brows furrowed as the admiral continued her briefing.

"The rest of the fleet will be tasked with fending off Duhrnan's army and protecting you and the other bombers. The missiles have already been programmed with the Shade Beam's core as the target, and the appropriate flight path down the shaft of the cannon. Each missile has a smart AI that should be able to find its way to the core if you are in front of the cannon and within five hundred meters of its opening when you launch your missile.

"The covering opens sixty-four seconds before the cannon fires. It takes approximately three and a half seconds for a high impact E-missile to fly the entire length of the barrel, from the tip to the core. Longer if you are firing from a bit of a distance. That means you and the bombers have at most sixty seconds to react to the cannon opening its maw. Miss your shot, and the Shade Beam gets a chance to fire at Earth.

"One more thing," said Fiona. "You have specific orders, Joëlle. Your ship has a cloaking device- unique among the fleet. Use it once the fighting begins to protect yourself and the E-missile. Only uncloak once you are in place, and it is time to launch the bomb."

"Yes Admiral," said Joëlle.

Fiona turned her attention to the room at large. "Now I'm sure you've all heard the rumours about Astraloth, and yes, it's true, as King Talcorosax told me; the planet survived the Shade Beam's attack by being sent forward in time. Unfortunately for us, Earth doesn't have that kind of defense mechanism. If the Shade Beam fires, Earth *will* be disintegrated. Entire species will go extinct. Ecosystems will be lost forever. Billions will die, and even those who were able to evacuate will never get to go back home.

"So make sure it doesn't get a chance to fire. Your squad captains have more details. This is not a drill, and it sure as hell isn't going to be easy. But you're the best of the best- That's why you're in this room. So go. Do your best."

◆

00:11:02:54

In the hangar, preparations were going swiftly. Beeping hover-lifts zigzagged between jogging pilots and soldiers in blue uniforms. Engineers and mechanics worked together to perform system checks and maintenance on a squadron of fighters. I watched from my seat on a metal crate as a group of three mechanics on a rising hover lift worked with Joëlle to install the E-missile to the top of the Firebrand. A few more mechanics carrying toolboxes and spare parts exited the ramp of the Firebrand, and I followed their gaze to the front of its sleek silhouette. The four E-guns at its front swivelled left and right, then up and down. I could make out another mechanic on the inside, behind the red-tinted windshield. He was operating the newly repaired weapon controls, and lifted his hand to flash the mechanics outside a thumbs up, before standing from his seat and making his way out.

Joëlle climbed down a service ladder which was driven away toward the next ship, followed by the mechanics on their hovering platform. She brushed aside some violet hair, and met my eyes. My ears lifted slightly as she smiled my way.

She took a seat on a crate next to me, and we both stared at the Firebrand. Mounted in the center of the Firebrand's roof was the E-missile, a three-foot long and one-foot wide cylindrical bomb which tapered at the front. It was equipped with an energy propulsion engine, and was held in place by thick metal clamps.

"The missile is installed and linked up with the ship's computer system," said Joëlle over the clamour of the vehicle bay. "The Firebrand is looking good. She's all ready."

I nodded. "How about you?" I asked. "Are you ready?"

"Well, we have eleven hours," she said, checking the Code-Alpha emergency broadcast on her holo-gauntlet. "I'm planning to sleep soon. That'll give me a good eight hours of sleep, plus some to prepare once I wake up."

I nodded in agreement. "That's a good plan. I should do the same... if I can manage to."

She sighed, and we sat in silence. I noticed her flick toward the fleets outside. White skyther ships drifted about, mingling with the grey and blue TAU vessels. I could tell Joëlle was eyeing the skyther battlecruisers.

"Why aren't you there with them?" she asked. "You're their leader now, after all."

My ears drooped. "Maybe, but I'm not a military leader. And I never asked to be King. I haven't even had my coronation ceremony yet."

"I know," she said. "But... I think you've really come into yourself, in terms of leadership. I think you should go to them."

I stood up. "I... understand," I said. I looked away from her. "You never could forgive me for what I did, could you?"

"What?" Joëlle said. "I just don't understand why you're still here, when your people are out there."

I closed my eyes. "Maybe *you* are my people. But I guess you could never forgive me for what I did on Voren..." My body felt so weak. I could hear Joëlle breathing behind me, contemplating her response.

"Osax..." she said, slowly. "I could use a copilot. If you want to help..."

I slowly turned to face her, with half-closed eyes and lowered ears. She gazed up at me with a thin lip and sorrowful eyes. I sighed shakily.

"I let you down, Joëlle. I let your team die. They were like your family-"

"Osax," she interrupted, raising a hand. Something shifted in her eyes. "I- The thing is..." She frowned. "I should have told you sooner. You know, my squad... those people- They weren't really like a family to me."

I titled my head, perplexed. "But you said-"

"I know I said that," she replied. "And I wanted that to be true. But to be honest I hardly knew them. That's why I never talked about them. They were a group of other RTs who had known each other for a long time. *They* were like a family, but, I was new. Their new leader. We had only been working together for a few months, and none of them really warmed up to me, as much as I wanted the company. Obviously it's hard when people die under your command, but- Really, I've never felt comfortable being alone. And I knew I would be, when the tower was destroyed. My chances at becoming close with them were gone. And I'd have to continue on all by myself until I found a new team." She screwed her eyes shut and held her breath. "I have monophobia."

"Monophobia?" I asked.

"It's a catch-all term for the fear of being alone." She scratched her head awkwardly. "For me, I notice it usually when I'm alone at home, or in space... Or just anticipating being alone."

"Interesting," I said. "And... that's why you let us all come aboard your space ship so readily."

She gulped nervously. "That was definitely part of it, yes. But I also knew I needed help tracking the mothership. And," she said, looking into my eyes, "you ended up really caring for me. I can see that." Her eyes were damp. "Even Jonathan cared, as much as I hate to admit it."

She was opening up to me.

"I think K cared too," I said.

Joëlle looked away, towards the planet and the ships which gathered around it.

I looked at her carefully. "But if you don't want to be alone," I said, "why did you tell me I should leave?"

"Because I'm working through it," she said. "I don't want to be controlled by fear. I know logically that I can handle things on my own. Fear isn't logical, but I know I can overcome it through exposure. Back on Malum, I had to save myself from the Brotherhood agents, and then I had to save you, on my own. It didn't go exactly as I planned, since I found Jonathan instead of you, but I realized then that I don't need other people to feel safe."

I nodded, and my ears lifted. "You have always seemed strong and independent to me, Joëlle."

"I guess the secret is I don't often feel that way," she said. "Anyway, that's not the point. I'm telling you this because you *are* my team, Osax. And you're my friend. And I don't need your help, but I could use it, and I do want it."

Slowly, I sat back down on the crate next to her. "Alright, Joëlle," I said. "I'll be your copilot. I was hoping I would be anyway."

She smiled, and wiped away a tear. When her hand fell back to her side, her grin flared with confidence. "Okay. Well, I need to sleep; you probably want to go back to your ship-"

"No, actually," I said. "I'd rather sleep in the Firebrand."

She smirked. "Aren't the beds a little small for you?"

"I got used to them," I said. Then I gestured to the white orb I had flown here in. "And that ship doesn't feel like mine. It still feels like my mother's."

She nodded. "Right. Well, you're welcome to stay on the Firebrand." She glanced toward the ship. "I think she misses you."

◆

00:02:13:45

My eyes fluttered open, gazing straight up at the bottom of the bunk above me. My body lay motionless. The Firebrand's familiar humming made me feel calm. I sat up in the dim light of my room. I inhaled, breathing in the scent of my blankets. They smelled like me. They hadn't been washed since Joëlle took us all aboard her ship when we left the Kronos weeks ago. Which meant the bed above me probably still smelled like K.

I shook my head as a heaviness pulled against my heart. K was gone. I couldn't believe it.

I swung my legs over the side of the bed, and my eyes landed on the bedside table. A tiny wrist device lay there: the loro nano-suit I had stolen from Duhrnan's mothership. I had forgotten about it entirely until then, and wondered then what happened to K's suit. Maybe she was still wearing it.

My ears sagged, and I stood up. I began to put on my armour, and pulled Joëlle's black cloak over my shoulders.

◆

00:01:10:13

In the cockpit of the Firebrand, Joëlle and I swallowed the last bites of breakfast. The lights in the cockpit blinked innocently. Joëlle wore her silvery-blue armour, "just in case," but her helmet rested on the floor by her chair. I placed my now empty glass of root beer on the counter to my side. It only took me a few seconds to drink it all.

I exhaled. "How are you holding up?" I asked, turning to her.

She shot me a sidelong glance. "I'm- What kind of question is that?" She snorted. "I'm fine, Osax. Just a completely normal day- Nothing to worry about." Her sarcastic tone was exaggerated.

"Fair enough," I said, shuffling in my seat. "I'm... I'm with you, you know."

She smiled at me softly. "Thanks."

My holo-gauntlet beeped, alerting me to a new message.

"The admiral wants to speak with me, I'll be right back."

Joëlle nodded. "Alright, Osax."

◆

00:01:08:12

Outside in the hangar, Fiona greeted me. We stood beneath the Firebrand; my mother's ship was parked not far away. The hangar was beginning to empty as starfighter pilots took off to regroup out in space.

"Talcorosax," she said gruffly, "what are you doing?" Her gaze challenged me, and she spoke quietly. She had taken me away from the remaining starships, and we stood alone in the center of the room.

I furrowed my brow. "What do you mean? I'm going to help Joëlle.

I'm going to help fight the-"

She waved her hands in my face. "This isn't a joke." She frowned. "People are going to die. We might all die."

"I know," I said, sternly. "That's why I need to help!"

"But you're the King of Astraloth! If you die, who will lead the-"

"No! Don't tell me what to do," I exclaimed. "You're all risking your lives to defend Earth because you choose too. Well, for a time Earth was my home too! And I'm going to protect it as well. You need all the help you can get. You might need me."

Fiona's face froze. Then she sighed, closing her eyes briefly. She looked so tired. "Friend," she said. "I just want you to be safe."

"No one is safe while Duhrnan is still out there and the Shade Beam still exists," I said.

We stared at each other for several seconds. At last Fiona replied. "Okay."

"Okay."

"But you know this is basically a suicide mission?"

"It's suicide *not* to fight," I said. "We have to."

She pursed her lips. "True."

◆

00:00:01:15

We had been waiting in formation for nearly an hour.

We didn't know where the valicorr would appear, so the combined armies of Earth and Astraloth formed a wide net-like shield that covered the entire planet, protecting it from all sides. The ships were spaced relatively evenly.

Some people had wondered whether Duhrnan would actually follow through on his threat. But I was certain he would show up. I was certain that he wanted the fleets to converge. He wanted to wipe out all our military strength in one motion. And he was such a glutton for drama; of course he wanted to stage the biggest space battle our societies had ever seen, and utterly destroy us. But he didn't know that we had the plans to the Shade Beam. He didn't know we had a chance, however small it was.

When Duhrnan arrived, the fleets would orbit the Earth and converge on his army. The twenty-five bombers outfitted with E-missiles, like the Firebrand, would make their way as fast as possible to the Shade Beam and try to block its cannon, covered by the rest of the fleet. Joëlle's computer showed a list of the twenty-four other bombers. Next to each ship on the computer display was a blinking green word "OKAY" representing the live signal feed we were receiving from each vessel.

We would wait for the Shade Beam to start its firing sequence, and then launch the guided E-missiles down its barrel, destroying the weapon.

I scratched my chest fur nervously, standing in the cockpit of the Firebrand just behind Joëlle who sat in the pilot's seat.

"Now might be a good time to take a seat," she said. I nodded, and sat down beside her at the weapons console.

We stared out the windshield. We were just one tiny piece of the network of ships that hovered above Earth, but we were an important one. Skyther and human vessels surrounded us to our left and right as we looked out toward space, away from the Earth at our flank. The sun beamed in at us, illuminating the cockpit in a bright white light, casting dark shadows on the wall behind us. Thousands of stars shone unblinking in the blackness, and all was quiet except for the hum of the ship and the faint communications of the fleet coming through Joëlle's helmet.

I watched the blocky white numbers of the countdown. There were only seconds left, and then Duhrnan would arrive, and the fight for Earth would begin.

00:00:00:03

00:00:00:02

00:00:00:01

I tightened my grip on the weapon controls, and held my breath.

Sixty-Five

The hairs on the back of my neck straightened, and my knuckles turned white as I gripped the weapon controls. The timer reached zero, and after a second the Code-Alpha signal went dead. The hologram fizzled out, and for a single moment no one breathed. Joëlle and I peeled our eyes and scanned the stars beyond. Our grid of ships waited with backs turned to Earth, waiting, waiting...

Then they came.

On all sides of the planet a swarm of valicorr starfighters warped into view. Yellow glows appeared from their energy weapons, and like a flash flood the space around us was hit with wave after wave of dazzling laser bolts.

"This is it!" I cried, leaning forward. It was impossible to tell how many ships there were, but they were closing in fast.

"Get ready!" I could barely see Joëlle's face from behind the visor of her helmet. She shoved the throttle forward, and the hum of the engine grew louder, rising in pitch. I couldn't feel any motion, but I saw us accelerate to a blistering speed. The Firebrand felt smooth as butter.

Three valicorr fighters streaked toward us, weapons blazing. I glanced at the targeting computer in front of me, adjusted the cannons, and pulled back on the trigger until it clicked.

Blue pellets of energy fired from each gun, barrelling into one of the fighters and exploding in violent flames. We soared through the debris and clear to the other side of the enemy lines.

"Woo!" Adrenaline surged through me as I cheered, lifting my fist to the air.

Joëlle slammed the controls to the side, spinning us around as we drifted away from the planet. The battle came into view just ahead of our windshield. Every ship was in motion, every weapon trying to find a clear shot. Grey TAU cruisers turned slowly, unleashing volleys of fire upon the valicorr ships. But some were too slow, exploding in streaks of flame as Duhrnan's army strafed past, shedding their own torrent of lasers. Interspersed between these moments of chaos, I caught sight of the white carriers of Astraloth closing in on their attackers. Red spears of energy shot out in rhythmic bursts, piercing through the swarm of wasps. Between it all, skyther and TAU fighters wove together in a dizzying motion, hunting the valicorr fighters with a bold vengeance.

Ships were being lost on both sides, but...

"It looks like we're winning!" I said, nearly jumping from my seat.

"Stay focused!" Joëlle yelled, and swerved to avoid a valicorr fighter who broke off to attack us. I jolted into action and fired back, destroying the ship in an instant.

Joëlle activated the Firebrand's cloaking device. Our weapons couldn't fire while the cloak was active, but our signals were no longer traceable.

"The Shade Beam hasn't arrived yet," said Joëlle, glancing my way from beneath her helmet. "Until it does we need to stay clear from the worst of the battle. Once it arrives, we fly straight to it and wait for its cannon to open, just like the other bombers."

"And then launch the missile before it gets a chance to disintegrate Earth," I said, breathing deeply. "I've got my eye on the scanner..."

At least twenty valicorr battleships, each the size of a Titan-class cruiser, exited slipspace in a cluster not far from the Firebrand, headed for Earth. Then a moment later, a massive cone-shaped vessel appeared between them.

My adrenaline spiked. "The Shade Beam!" I cried.

"I see it!"

The engines whined as we flew like a dart to the cluster of enemy ships, and our target. The Shade Beam loomed with a palpable malice, and I imagined a beating heart at its center with bolts of red lightning arcing out in the dark chasm where it resided. A twisted, malevolent life force within a monstrosity of metal. A true weapon with no compassion—only the cold calculations of destruction.

The fleet admiral's voice came through the ship's communicator, commanding all vessels to converge in front of the Shade Beam. Everyone, humans and skythers alike, pushed their engines to the limit.

I tightened my grip on the controls as the Shade Beam grew larger in my view, and we came closer to the beetle-like warships that surrounded it. I watched in horror as the battleships unleashed their fury, breaking through the first wave of our defences with ease.

I clenched my jaw. "Has the Shade Beam begun its firing process yet?" I asked, as we flew closer.

"Not yet," Joëlle replied. "The cannon is still shielded. We need to get closer first, anyway."

Then I heard faint voices in Joëlle's headset. She turned to me, eyes wide.

"I'm getting reports that Duhrnan is leading the attack in some sort of elite starfighter." She looked out the windshield into the fray. "Look!"

She pointed in front of the Shade Beam, and I could see several Titan-class cruisers and skyther warships forming a shield in front of the weapon. They were taking heavy fire from the Shade Beam's escorts. Earth's defenders continued to rally around the weapon, pulling out from other sides of the planet, but so did the valicorr. The entire battle was converging on this one point, and the space between ships was shrinking, making maneuvering difficult.

Then I saw what Joëlle was pointing at. A deep purple ship, as large as three regular starfighters, hovering around a TAU cruiser. Red lightning lashed out from its underside, slowly slicing the cruiser apart.

"It must be another loro ship," I said.

Joëlle eyed the destruction Duhrnan's fighter was causing, then exhaled shortly. "It's not our mission to take him out. We need to be ready for the Shade Beam when it opens its maw."

Then I felt my blood freeze over. He wasn't just tearing apart any ship. His red beam had just cut the word KRONOS in half, sending a chunk of the hull to drift through space.

I pointed at the half-destroyed Titan-class cruiser. "Joëlle! He's attacking the Kronos! We have to stop him!"

She hesitated. Then she furrowed her brow. "No, Osax! The Shade Beam is our priority!"

"Fiona's still aboard!" I yelled. "She'll die!" I looked at the scanner, my body tensing. "The other bombers are en route. We have a cloaking device. We can fly in close and surprise him!" *Not Fiona*, I thought. *Please, not her too!*

Joëlle checked her scanner as explosions around us lit the cockpit's interior. "There are fifteen bombers in position already..." I glanced at the computer. Three of the twenty-four bomber's readings had already changed to "NO SIGNAL" in red text.

I stared into her eyes. "Please, Joëlle. We can turn around if the other bombers get damaged."

She scrunched up her face. Then she breathed out, and changed course. She locked eyes with me, and smirked wildly. "Alright. Time to stop that monster, once and for all."

I felt my blood ignite.

Undetected, we swerved by ships, energy bolts, and explosions. We approached the Kronos, which had just lost another large section of its hull that had been haphazardly sliced off by Duhrnan's purple fighter. He was dismantling the Kronos almost single-handedly.

His ship was wide and thin like a crescent blade, with a black windshield in front, and four jagged prongs that shot out the back. From its underside, red light arced toward the Kronos, and where it hit the grey TAU hull splintered and depressurized. A squadron of black valicorr fighters circled Duhrnan's ship, blasting the Kronos' gun turrets and any TAU or skyther ships that flew close to him. Any of them, except for us.

"When I deactivate the cloaking device, the weapons system will regain power," said Joëlle. She shot me a fiery look. "That's when you shoot him, got it?"

"Got it." I said, eyes narrowing on my target.

Duhrnan's ship flew up towards the bridge, completely unaware of us hovering behind him. The Shade Beam was slowly encroaching behind us, as well as a flock of valicorr fighters and battleships. But my mind was only on Duhrnan.

He closed the distance toward the wide window of the Kronos' bridge, clearly savouring each moment. *That's where Fiona would be!* I thought. I flashed Joëlle a look, and she nodded.

"Now!" She said, disabling the cloaking device.

I leaned forward in my seat, pulling the trigger tight until my fingers hurt. My eyes were glued to Duhrnan's ship, intense rage burning in my chest and arms. The underside of his vehicle began to glow red. Then the Firebrand roared, and blue bolts of light exploded on his hull. Smouldering, it spun out of control, bouncing harmlessly against the hull of the Kronos and spinning out of sight, into the chaos that surrounded us.

I shouted in triumph. Joëlle cheered. We were close enough to what remained of the Kronos that I could see people standing in the bridge through the window. They were staring at us in shock and wonder.

Joëlle and I were riding the highs of adrenaline, grinning. I tapped my holo-gauntlet, calling the admiral.

"Fiona! Are you alright?" I asked.

I caught sight of a figure in a black, grey and blue uniform in the window, holding an active holo-gauntlet to her mouth. Fiona's voice came through my gauntlet. "Half the ship is gone, but what remains is holding, for the moment. And I see we have you to thank for it!" I lifted my ears. She continued, "Now, reactivate your cloak and go! Stop the Shade Beam!"

Then the Firebrand shook and groaned. Lights flickered, and I could hear something sparking. We spun out of control. Something had hit us from above.

"Dammit!" Joëlle reactivated the cloaking device, and took us away from the Kronos. We were floating in the middle of the chaos, between the shield of cruisers and the Shade Beam. We were surrounded by dogfighting fighters, but with the cloaking device active again we were as safe as we could be.

A gentle alarm beeped at us, and Joëlle opened up a holographic display of the Firebrand. The image of the ship spun slowly. I scanned for anything indicating damage or malfunction. The clamps holding the E-missile on top of the Firebrand's exterior were blinking red.

I looked at the weapons console. The missile's guidance system seemed unaffected, but the computer was telling me that the firing mechanism was jammed.

"Joëlle, the missile was hit. The clamps- The firing mechanism is melted shut!"

Joëlle swore, then tried to calm herself. "Well, look on the bright side... At least the explosive casing wasn't damaged, or we would be vapour by now."

I put my head in my hands and began rubbing my temples furiously. "I guess there's nothing we can do..."

She opened up her scanner. "Every one of the remaining bombers is in position. We just have to leave it up to them."

"Alright," I said, lowering my hands and gazing out at the battle beyond. Joëlle turned the ship so we faced the Shade Beam and its entourage of warships. I took in a slow breath, calming myself. "At least we were able to save part of the Kronos."

Then the valicorr warships let loose a volley of energy bolts, and ships began to splinter with energy all around us.

I had to shield my eyes as blue flames erupted in massive spheres of light, coming from tiny TAU starfighters scattered about in front of the Shade Beam. The windshield was hit with a spray of silver particles and dust from the vaporized vehicles, which slid over the window like flecks of sand in the wind. I leaned over, gazing at the computer screen. One by one, the bomber's signals flickered to red, until every single ship displayed the same thing, and I felt a chill roll over my body.

We were the only ones left.

I looked up at the Shade Beam. It was moving straight toward us, its cannon aimed directly for the Earth which waited behind us. I knew what was at stake. My eyes fell to the weapons console, warning me of the jammed missile. I knew I needed to get it free before the Shade Beam fired. We were Earth's last hope. I clutched at my chest, and stared at the weapon before me. I stood up from my seat, compelled by a power seemingly beyond me to rise up against the darkness.

I reached my hand out to Joëlle. "Give me your molecular sword."

Joëlle spun to face me. "What? Osax, what are you doing?"

"Take us in close," I said, eyes narrowing. "I'm going to cut the missile free. Keep in contact via comms."

"Wait! Uh- Okay!" Joëlle quickly reached to her belt. She held her sword, and hesitated, looking me in the eye. "Don't lose this-"

"Why would I?" I replied.

She raised an eyebrow. "Osax, *please*. I've given you weapons before. How many guns and swords have you dropped or lost in the past few weeks? Have you managed to hold onto a single one?"

"Uh-"

"No. You always end up losing them." She smirked.

Hurriedly, I glanced to the battle outside, then back to her. "Whatever! We don't have time Joëlle." Then I added, "I won't lose it!"

She winked, and tossed me her deactivated molecular sword. Then she turned her attention back to the controls, and I slipped out of the room, the door hissing shut behind me.

I ran through the Firebrand to my quarters and lunged for the bedside table, gripping the sword. The loro nano-suit was right where I'd left it, and I strapped it to my wrist as quickly as possible. *Glad I didn't send you away for research just yet,* I thought. It flashed brightly as it scanned my body, and silvery liquid nanites began to slip over my arm and chest.

"How do you plan-"

"The loro nano-suit," I said. "I'm going to use the escape hatch to get on top of the ship, and pry the missile free manually." I sped through the Firebrand, and found my way to the escape hatch airlock. The door shut behind me, and as the nano-suit sealed itself over my face and ears, muffling the hum of the ship, I started the depressurization sequence.

"You- Osax..." Joëlle's voice trailed off in my earpiece.

"Yes?"

"...I believe in you."

◆

I crawled, clawing my way onto the top of the Firebrand, and the hatch shut closed behind me. My hands quivered, grasping at nothing on the surface of the ship. The balls of my feet magnetized to the surface. Lights and explosions flickered in the sleek reflections of the hull inches away from my shielded face. I could only hear my breath, painfully loud in my ears.

Slowly I rose, pushing myself to my feet. I stood isolated on the hull. Behind me was the Earth, and countless TAU and skyther ships. Around me, the battle raged on in densely clustered struggles. And in front of me, the Shade Beam's flat face watched me with amusement. I stared at the cannon's barrel at its center. Slowly, unmistakably, the covering of the cannon began to open until I could see straight down the weapons shaft, to a dimly glowing orb in the center of the ship.

"Osax! The Shade Beam!"

"I know," I said quietly. I didn't have much time.

A ship exploded right next to the Firebrand as I stepped toward the E-missile, and the Firebrand swerved. I knelt down next to the missile and began to assess the damage. There were two metal clamps holding the missile in place, each one a solid arm that contracted around the bomb and held it to the Firebrand. I just needed to cut them free.

I held my arm up, and activated Joëlle's molecular sword. Metal plates shifted into place. Sunlight reflected off the silver blade, and I knelt down.

My heart was beating quickly. I tried to shut out blinking lights in the space surrounding me. I trained my eyes on the bomb, and with a shaking hand I move the blade to the base of one of the clamps.

I hadn't realized I was holding my breath until the chunk of cut metal drifted harmlessly away from the bomb. My hands were shaking.

One down, one to go.

I glanced up at the Shade Beam. It was almost upon us. I felt my gaze being sucked down its throat to the core, whose light had flared up now. We were caught in a ray of light that glowed in the dust and debris of countless shattered starships; a spotlight shone straight from the Shade Beam's cannon. A blackness began to mix into the orb of light at the cannon's core, like ink in a glass of water. Somehow I knew when the light faded the Shade Beam would fire, and all would be lost.

"Osax?" Joëlle's voice came through my earpiece.

"Almost got it," I said, straining as I bent over the rocket, reaching for the final clamp. I aimed my sword down toward it...

My visor lit up with the explosion of a ship in front of us. A chunk of engine debris careened toward the Firebrand, and Joëlle took us into a spin. We missed the debris, but I lurched forward and sparks flew in front of my eyes.

When the Firebrand levelled out, I looked down at the missile. It had a keypad and computer panel attached to its side for calibrating the guidance system. Sparks flitted out from the incision I had accidentally made straight across it. The tiny computer screen cracked and flickered, struggling to show me its plain message. My heart leapt to my throat.

GUIDANCE ERROR!!! GUIDANCE ERROR!!!

"Osax?! What happened to the E-missile!?"

I swallowed hard. "I may have just cut through the guidance system..."

"What?!" Joëlle panted. "Then we need to get out of here-"

"No!" I yelled, clenching my fists until they hurt. I knelt down and wrapped one arm around the missile, bracing it against the Firebrand's hull as I cut the final restraint free. The metal piece drifted up weightlessly, and I pushed it so it floated away out of my face, leaning on the missile. "I need to fire it manually."

"Osax, are you out of your mind?!"

"It's the only option!" I shouted.

I glanced at Joëlle's sword in my hand. *Sorry!* I thought. Then I let go of the sword and clung to the Firebrand with all my strength, holding the sparking missile wrapped under one arm. Sweat trickled down my forehead, and I gazed ahead at the maw of the Shade Beam. The core was fading, vibrating with a dark energy. My visor flickered with the lights around me. I glanced back at the blue and green planet one last time. "How do I manually start the missile's engine?!"

"You don't!"

"Then can you launch it?"

"Ignition should be linked to the Firebrand still-"

"Then do it when I say so!"

"But you'll get burned by the rocket-"

"This suit survived atmospheric entry!" I shouted. "If we don't try, we're dead anyway!"

"Okay!" she said, her voice wavering. "Tell me when to fire!"

I leaned over, placing my eye just behind the edge of the missile. I could feel the blood pumping through my veins. With both hands I angled the rocket carefully, lining it up so it faced straight down the barrel of the Shade Beam. The core was almost entirely dark now, with only a faint trickle of light coming through. I knew I only had seconds to fire.

I opened my mouth to tell Joëlle I was ready.

Suddenly, a smoking purple vessel swooped down directly in front of us, obscuring my shot. It was Duhrnan's fighter. He had tracked us down, despite us being cloaked, and his ship glowed with a crackling red light...

Then the Firebrand bared its teeth and blue energy crunched into his vessel. The purple starfighter cracked into chunks of smouldering debris which shot out in every direction, and a luminous energy cloud bristled in its place for a moment. The path cleared just enough, and aiming through the wreckage I realigned my shot. I gently held the missile in place against the Firebrand. There was no more time.

"Do it, Joëlle!"

I was blinded by light. I braced myself as the rocket flew from my fingertips and blasted back against me. Then it was gone, flying toward the Shade Beam's great chasm.

I was transfixed. Time stopped. The world fell away, and all I could see was the glow of the E-missile soaring towards the shaft of the Shade Beam. It cleared the opening. I strained to see if it would impact against the edges of the shaft...

It found its mark.

The core lit up like a star, and I had to shield my eyes. I could see the weapon begin to disintegrate as waves of its own energy seeped to its edges. Then it all turned to light and heat. The Shade Beam burned itself up in the blink of an eye.

It was done.

The Firebrand soared through the debris of Duhrnan's ship, and I exhaled a sigh of relief. When I tried to inhale, the wind was knocked out of me. Something from Duhrnan's ship crashed into my chest and threw me off the Firebrand, and I was now tumbling helplessly through space. I looked down; something held onto my leg.

Fear gripped me. Duhrnan, in his own nano-suit, pulled me down with all four of his arms so our masked faces were level. I struggled in his grasp, heart beating quickly.

I flailed my arms at him, battering his head with my fists, but he grabbed my wrists with his two lower arms and forced them away. Our eyes met. He was frenzied. He was screaming silently in his helmet, baring his teeth. My ears were constrained in my helmet, but the muscles involuntarily shot back. We were falling through space.

He held me tight with three arms, and bashed my helmet with his fourth. Again and again, he smashed against the translucent nanite visor. Stars and explosions spun around us. I wriggled and kicked at him with my legs. My head began to throb with pain, and crimson droplets of blood began to weightlessly float inside my helmet; I wasn't sure where I was bleeding.

Then he punched my helmet, and my ears screeched with the whistling of air escaping my suit. I gasped, peering through the crack in my visor. The nanites struggled to repair the breach, and Duhrnan reeled back for another swing.

My head jerked back and I shut my eyes. My skull reverberated as Duhrnan jammed his fingers through the crack in my visor, and pulled. He tore half of my visor off. Air was sucked from my helmet.

I knew I only had a short time to live without a suit, but if Duhrnan kept hold of me, there was no chance I would survive. My fingers curled around his hand, reaching for his wrist...

I pressed hard on the buttons of his nano-suit until it started to liquefy. Panicking, Duhrnan let go of me, and reached for his wrist. Without thinking, I planted both of my feet against his body and pushed off, sending us drifting in opposite directions. I watched him flailing helplessly as he tumbled away into the darkness.

I raised my hands to my broken mask and shut my eyes, trying to cover the hole. The suit had lost a fair amount of mass, and was struggling to repair itself. My breathing was strained, and frantic. I wasn't getting enough air, and my face was beginning to freeze. I was dying.

But we had won. The timer was gone. Earth was saved. The Shade Beam was destroyed. I peered out from behind my hands, and watched the valicorr ships being overwhelmed, one by one. The warm glow of the sun against the remaining fleet, against the blue planet. The stars, welcoming me home. *Sleep now,* they whispered to me. *Return to us, and sleep.*

Sixty-Six

"But you survived, obviously," said the investigator.
"Yes," I replied. "Of course I did."

Sixty-Seven

I awoke on a warm bed, unaware of how long I had been unconscious. My eyelids gently opened, and I blinked several times. My body felt stiff, my vision was blurry, and I was breathing through a mask. I tried to lift my arms and glanced at my hand. The loro suit had been removed but I was still wearing my armour underneath. Whoever had saved me didn't have time to change me into more comfortable clothes.

A wizened looking skyther in a skintight jumpsuit peered over me, blocking the bright overhead lights. His ears were gently tied together with a white ribbon behind his head so they didn't brush against me as he inspected me, but they lifted, and his eyes squinted when he saw me open mine.

"Oh, thank goodness," he said to himself in Skorali. His voice was soothing and gentle. "His highness is alright," he said, smiling.

"Where-" I murmured in English, then switched to Skorali. "Where am I?"

He looked me in the eye, his face lined with wrinkles. His ears tilted forward slightly. "You're aboard Aquiloss. One of the skyther battlecruisers. I'm the head medical officer-"

My eyes shot open, and I sat up, looking around in panicked confusion. "Where's K?! Is she alright?!"

The doctor tilted his head to one side. "I- I'm sorry, your majesty. I don't know."

Images and memory washed into my mind. The feeling of the cool glass of K's stasis pod. Jonathan's silent tears, streaming down his face. My mandibles hung open in shock. I felt my eyes becoming wet, and my gaze drifted down, as I remembered. She was gone.

The doctor helpfully placed a hand on my arm. "Talcorosax," he said warmly, "you may feel a little disoriented for a while. It's a completely normal part of recovery."

"Oh..." I mumbled. "Okay..."

A door hissed open to my right. My mind absently pieced together the medical equipment that adorned the white room as my eyes traced a line to the open doorway.

"Osax!" Joëlle squealed with relief as she rushed into the room. I barely had time to lift my ears before she wrapped her arms around me in a tight squeeze.

"Oh, be gentle, please!" The doctor spoke English now, and lifted his hand hesitantly, unsure if he should break up the moment.

Joëlle's cheek pressed against mine, and I shut my eyes, smiling. Warmth filled my heart, and I began to chuckle faintly. She pulled away, grinning, and I wiped my eyes.

"Joëlle... Did you..." She looked at me shyly from the side of my hospital bed, and the doctor cleared his throat.

"Your friend saved you, Talcorosax. She pulled you aboard her ship and brought you here for recovery."

I turned back to Joëlle. "You saved my life," I said. I bowed my head in reverence. "I am indebted to you."

"All you owe me is a new sword." She laughed.

My face hurt as my eyes squinted in a smile. "Oh, right. Sorry, Joëlle."

"Don't worry about it, I'm only joking," she said. She couldn't contain herself, smiling ear to ear. "Without your help we wouldn't have been able to save Earth. After the Shade Beam was destroyed, the valicorr were disoriented. Our fleets were able to destroy most of the remaining ships. I thought it only fair that you might want a chance to visit the planet again, after you worked so hard to save it." She winked at me.

I lifted my ears. "We... we really did it." I let myself flop backwards onto the pillow, and gazed up, relaxing my muscles. My heart was beating calmly. Duhrnan had been stopped.

"I would like that," I said, my head spinning. "But maybe... not right away. I feel kind of dizzy..."

The gentle doctor smiled. "You were drifting through space for at least a minute. A human likely wouldn't have been able to survive that long, but-"

"...But it's a good thing you're a skyther," said Joëlle, smiling.

I laughed. "I can't help being me," I said. I met her brown eyes, and reached a hand over to her.

"And I'm glad for that," she said. "Only you would be so crazy, and only someone so crazy could have freed that missile." She grabbed my hand gently in both of hers. "We did it, Osax." Her eyes seemed to sparkle.

I shut my eyes. "We did it."

◆

You know the rest, I'm sure. Cleanup on Earth is still ongoing, even six months after the battle. There was plenty of debris that fell to the planet from the destroyed ships. Most of the major damage was cleared up in just a few weeks; humans are resourceful, and I had my people help as well. My coronation happened just a week after the battle of Earth, and in my first weeks as the king I wanted to make sure to uphold good relations with the TAU.

I supposed some of the slowness can be attributed to the protests and rallying that have been going on there. Now that the Shade Beam is destroyed, people are wondering why it was even made in the first place. Of course, the Brotherhood's involvement in it was brought to light, and everyone who worked at the base on Voren, (plus many others in the TAU) were investigated, and charged if found guilty. The base itself was investigated weeks after the battle, as part of the TAU's response to the public backlash. I had hoped Jonathan would still be there, but... he had disappeared along with the stasis pods, as you mentioned earlier, investigator.

I was asked to comment on the events but, well, to be honest I didn't have the emotional energy to dive into it all so soon. I shared the important details, about the Brotherhood, and of course I shared my discoveries about the loro with the research community, who in turn made the findings public. I turned in the loro nano-suit for research, and brought in an entire team of loro archaeologists, humans and skythers, to gather the debris from Duhrnan's mothership on Astraloth, and begin their research. If we're ever able to replicate the loro's slipspace drive, space travel would become nearly instantaneous...

But I digress. When the research community went public about the valicorr's connection to the loro as bioweapons, and word got out about the Brotherhood's experiments with people such as K, and when the public found out the Shade Beam itself was a bioweapon, petitions to make bioweapons illegal came flooding in. The TAU, to make amends for the wrongs they had done, recalled all bioweapons, ceased any experiments with them, and made their very existence illegal. I complied, of course, and so it became part of our treaty... I could see the benefits. And I didn't want to cause any conflict with the TAU.

And people started telling stories about the battle of Earth. Joëlle and I became renowned heroes. Everywhere I went on Earth, people would cheer and thank me for what I had done, or ask me incredulously if the stories were true. I was approached by companies seeking endorsement, charity organizations, and all sorts of people just wanting to speak with me. Some people even said that I was proof that the TAU needed to change, because they'd needed a skyther to save their planet. I reminded them that Joëlle, a human, was the one piloting the Firebrand, a ship who's name also became renowned, and that she'd also saved my life. I heard sales of the Ranger-Class gunship skyrocketed. I started seeing Firebrand themed craft beers, adorned with art of the black and red ship, and Firebrand t-shirts with a skyther standing on top, and the words "Stronger Together" written on the bottom. That was a popular design... though nobody ever asked me if I was okay with it being made. I was, so it didn't really matter, I guess...

◆

Anyway, I was invited to a ceremony by the Cardinal of the TAU to be held on Earth. I'm not sure if you were there; thousands of people attended. It was a memorial for those lost in the battle of Earth, and also an award ceremony. As the King of Astraloth it would have been rude to say no.

Joëlle and I stood on a platform surrounded by thousands of people. The Fleet Admiral droned on about our exemplary service. The other admirals stood in line, watching us. Fiona nodded to me, smiling with approval.

The Fleet Admiral gave us each a golden medal, symbolizing our valour and thanking us for our service. I had to duck for them to fit the ribbon over my head. It was meant to be somewhat of a solemn ceremony, with restrained clapping if anything, but when the Admiral gave us our medals the crowd roared with cheers and whistles. It was all too much.

Some time after the ceremony, Joëlle and I sat silently at a quaint café. I grabbed a glass bottle of root beer from the soda cooler, and paid for it at the counter. Then I squished into my seat next to Joëlle, and we gazed out the window at the humans wandering the street.

"It feels wrong," I said, sipping my drink. My eyes narrowed.

Joëlle looked at me, puzzled. "What feels wrong?"

"We got medals. There was a whole ceremony and everything. But Jonathan and K got nothing. No recognition. They were... they were our team."

Joëlle sighed. Quiet rock music played over the café's speaker system. "I'm trying my best to just forget them," she said, and took a sip of her hot chocolate.

I felt betrayed, and a pang of anger simmered in me. I glared at her. "How could you say that? They risked their lives for us, more than once. They risked their lives for Earth, and for Astraloth. They-"

"Osax, will you cool it?" she interrupted, agitated. "Jonathan betrayed us. He was part of the Brotherhood. That's not gonna change. And he could have done something to stop the Shade Beam before Duhrnan got hold of it-"

"You don't *know* that," I said. "Maybe there was nothing he could do. He made mistakes, but he did the best he could to make up for them."

She shrugged, and her eyes darkened. "He never even contacted you... or me, after the battle. He cared more about his experiments. He just vanished with them, after all."

My mandibles twitched. "He couldn't contact us. He's considered a criminal now. It would have been dangerous for him."

She frowned. "But he- He could have tried. Even if he- I just thought he-" She shut her eyes, and sighed in frustration. "I thought he liked me. And then he betrayed us. And maybe someday I could forgive him for that, but... I was starting to come around to your perspective Osax, but he..." She closed herself off, her face hardening. "He vanished without a word. He didn't even contact me."

My ears drooped, and my eyes narrowed. "I'll bet he was trying to keep you safe, by not contacting you. I think he liked you too-"

She whipped her hand toward me. "Don't you even *say* that, Osax! Implying he cut contact with me because he *cared?!*"

I placed my hands on the table. "It's not like you gave him much reason to call you! He was going through so much shame and guilt for what he had done, offering insider information on the Brotherhood, which we needed to stop the Shade Beam, volunteering for suicide missions and apologizing every chance he got, just to make up for his mistakes, and you spat in his face at every chance! You didn't see what he was going through. You weren't there in the cave on Malum- You weren't there on the mothership-"

"*No I wasn't!*" she cried, tears forming in her eyes. She stood up from her seat. "I wasn't, because Jonathan betrayed me, and I was taken hostage on my own ship! God, Osax! I had to fight for myself! I had to do it all on my own, because of him!"

I stood up too, slamming my chair behind me. "Fine! But what about K?!" I shouted. "I'm just saying she deserves to be remembered for the good she did, not for the intentions of her creators-"

"Oh, you mean Jonathan's intentions?" she spat. "Yeah, the reason K isn't remembered as a hero is his fault, too-"

"No!" I said. "He stayed behind on Voren to help her! He wanted to figure out how-"

"Settle down you two!" said the owner of the café. "Or take it outside! This isn't an arena, and I won't tolerate fighting."

I glanced his way, then turned back to Joëlle. I grabbed my things hurriedly, and spoke quietly. "I can't believe you hate him so much."

"Well I can't believe you can't see how much he hurt me! He left you, but you're still defending him." She crossed her arms defiantly. "I'm your friend, and I'm still right here with you. Why can't you see it my way? Why can't you let go of him?"

"Because he's my friend, too!" I said, shooting her a glance.

"He left you, Osax." She shook her head. "He abandoned you too."

"You don't understand-"

"I understand that you're holding onto an image of Jonathan that is false, and it's putting a wedge between us-"

I looked her square in the eye. "If that's what you believe, then maybe we can't be friends after all," I said, darkly.

She blinked, her mouth hanging open for a second in shock. Clearly she was hurt. Then she shut her mouth. "Fine," she growled. "At least being alone, fending for myself taught me that I don't need anyone's help," she said, sarcastically. "That's one thing I can thank him for."

I locked eyes with her. "Well, if you really don't need people, then why am I here with you?"

She frowned at me. "Wait, Osax, please. *We're friends.*"

"I thought we were," I said, and stormed out of the café.

And that's the last time I spoke with her.

Sixty-Eight

Starlight and moonlight shone silver beams through the window to my right. I flexed my fingers, feeling at once a great release and a swelling tension in my body. The room was dimly lit, my glass long empty. I had told the story well into the night. TAU ships circled above the Great Temple, blinking in the darkness, and I waited, watching the investigator slip a stray bit of blonde hair back under her pristine hat. The story was done.

"Is that it?" asked the investigator, shuffling anxiously. Her lips twitched, and a shallow smile spread across her face. "Can I finally leave?" She eyed me, teasingly.

I nodded. "I am finished, investigator."

She yawned, and reached her arms up to the ceiling, stretching. "That's a bit of a downer to end on, you know," she said. She replayed the last bit of the recording.

"And that's the last time I spoke with her." My voice sounded so sad.

She smirked at me wickedly. "Might want to revise the ending so it's a little happier, you know, for your ancestors."

My ears drooped, and I clenched my fists, glancing at the nebula in the sky. "You have no idea what you're talking about," I said, bitterly. I bit my mandibles.

I stood from my seat. Leaves rustled on the rooftop garden outside the window. Clouds were gathering overhead. I eyed her, then glanced to the door that led to the hall. I swallowed, then checked my holo-gauntlet.

"But really," asked the investigator, packing her computer away into a case, "have you not had any contact with Joëlle since then?"

"No," I said. "We had a falling out..."

She forced a frown, nodding. "I'm sorry to hear that," she said. My eyes narrowed. She was so pleased with herself, and her acting was so fake at this point.

I gestured to the door graciously, grinding my mandibles. "The Temple is still empty. Our holiday doesn't end until sunrise. The other skythers won't be back until tomorrow, so..."

"I see," said the investigator. She lowered her head slightly, and checked her holo-gauntlet discretely under the table. Casually, I glanced toward the window. I could see her gauntlet in the reflection; she opened a local area scanner, tuned for life signs.

Satisfied, she deactivated her gauntlet, and cleared her throat, standing up with a smile. "Look at the time!" she said. "Well, I must say, King Talcorosax, this has been an unforgettable couple of days here."

I met eyes with her, watching suspiciously. "Indeed," I said flatly. "Would you like me to escort you out of the Temple?"

"Oh," she said. "That would be much appreciated, your highness."

I bowed gently, then turned away from her and approached the exit door.

I heard her approaching me from behind.

Then I felt something cold against my back. My skin crawled as I heard the unmistakable whine of an E-gun powering up.

"Don't move." Her voice was cold.

I stood completely motionless. My heart rate began to increase. I was completely unarmed. Her E-pistol was pressed hard against my back.

"What-" I began. "What are you doing?" I asked, timidly.

She snorted a laugh. "Oh, 'Osax,' you made this too easy!" She cackled. "All alone in the Temple? No one around to notice if something were to happen to you?"

I began to tremble slightly. "I- I don't understand..."

"Of course you don't understand!" She couldn't stop herself from laughing. "You, all this time, you really believed I was sent by the TAU?" She paused. "Get on your knees!"

I complied, shakily. The floor was hard against my bones. With her gun still at my back, she leaned her head over my shoulder, and grinned viciously.

"B- But, if you're not with the TAU..." I trailed off.

"Talcorosax," she whispered. "I'm with the Brotherhood." Her voice was like a snake.

My veins swelled with adrenaline. My ears sank in fear. "But, the Brotherhood were defeated! The TAU purged them from their ranks."

"Not all of them," she hissed.

"What-" I shook, panting. "What is your plan? Why are you here? Why did you listen to my story if you were just planning to take me hostage?"

She laughed. "Oh my. You really fell for it." She chuckled. "You're *so* weak. Weak, and idiotic-"

"Don't insult me!" I shouted.

She pressed the gun harder against my back. "Oh no, your highness. You're not in control now." She leaned her head over my shoulder once more. "Now you have to listen to *my* story."

I clenched my fists, growling slightly. That seemed to make her even more content.

Good, I thought.

"You're a hero, Osax," she said. "Just like you said. People worship you. Not only are you the King of Astraloth... you're the saviour of Earth. Everywhere you go, people are willing to wait on you hand and foot. Heavens, they'll do anything you say." She chuckled. "Well, not us, of course. But that's beside the point." Her voice was sharp, like a knife. "You have power, Osax. You just don't know how to use it. But your image... your identity could command the galaxy, if wielded correctly."

"My... my image?"

"Precisely," she said. "Your mother said it well enough. What was it? 'Your every word will have the power to change people's hearts.' Well, she was right, more than she probably knew."

I grimaced. "What do you plan to do with me?"

"Oh, my story isn't done," she said, scoffing. "You had me listen to your sob-story for days. At least give me a few minutes to gloat about *my* accomplishments.

"You see," she continued, "the Brotherhood wasn't too happy when you destroyed the Silencer. We were going to stop the Shade Beam ourselves. And we would have used that praise to seize power, and usher in a new change for the world."

"You couldn't have stopped Duhrnan even if you tried," I spat. "We only succeeded because of our teamwork, our trust. The Brotherhood is built on lies. We won because we believed in one another-"

"Fool," she said. "You succeeded because of dumb luck. In any case, your victory certainly put us at a loss... but Ryner had other plans in motion." Her lips spread in a freakish grin.

"What... plans?" I asked, trembling.

"Oh, you would like to know, wouldn't you?" She roared with laughter. "I see no reason why I can't tell you. You're going to die soon, anyway." She paused. "Oh, it feels *so* good to finally get this off my chest..." She couldn't stop laughing. "You remember the 'Sheep's Clothing?'"

"Of course I-"

"Now imagine a world where the leaders of the galaxy all agreed on everything. Wouldn't everything be so perfect? So peaceful? Everything would be run so smoothly, decisions would be made without conflict. But that kind of ideal isn't possible, is it? Because some people know what's right and others don't. But, what if the leaders of the world *did* agree? What if they agreed, because they were all controlled by the same person?"

My spine tingled, and a shiver ran through my body. My ears tensed. "You mean-"

"Yes. What if the Brotherhood were to replace you with a clone... one we could control? A wolf grown wearing 'Sheep's Clothing.' He would be our sentinel, watching over the skythers."

My heart skipped a beat.

I looked back at her, over my shoulder, arms tense. Her gun pressed against my back. "You mean to kill me, and send a sleeper agent doppelganger to the throne of Astraloth in my place? One who works for the Brotherhood? So the Brotherhood can control Astraloth?"

She sighed with satisfaction. "Now you're getting it," she said. "Do you see why I had to hear your whole story?" she asked. "Why I couldn't settle for just some of it?"

"No," I said, honestly.

She rolled her eyes. "I came here to assess your social life."

I blinked.

"If you were socially isolated," she said, "it would be no problem replacing you with a clone. There wouldn't be any one to notice minor discrepancies." She giggled through her teeth. "Well, turns out you're all alone; it really won't be a problem. But when I heard about the skyther's ability to recount stories word for word, I knew that I had to stick around for the long haul. Every detail of your story needed to be recorded-"

"That's why your motivations seemed to shift," I growled. "You were just saying whatever you could to make me finish my story."

"Precisely," she said. "Bravo, you're figuring it out! I just needed a recording of your story, direct from you, to feed into your clone's brain. That way if your replacement ever got asked about what happened during your finest hours, he would have a response." She smirked. "Clever, aren't I?"

I felt my blood begin to boil with rage. "You're sickening," I said. "Can't you see that whoever is leading the Brotherhood will just use these clones to get whatever they want? Your leader isn't benevolent. Whoever they are-"

"Oh, and I supposed you've met Ryner?" She paused, mocking me. "Oh, that's right, I remember. You haven't met him, you said so yourself."

I scoffed. "Ryner is dead. He was on the Silencer when we destroyed it-"

"Wrong," she said. "He survived."

Though I had never seen him, images of a tall, gaunt man filled my mind. With wispy hair, he stood in the darkness, hands outstretched. Thin threads dangled from each finger, and at the bottom of each thread was the cross of a puppet. Those puppets had more threads, spiralling down to even more puppets. A whirlpool of tangled wire connecting hundreds of puppets together, being sucked closer and closer to the center of a black hole, while Ryner laughed...

I looked back at her, aghast. "How," I said. "After hearing my entire story; after hearing about Jonathan... how can you still work for the Brotherhood? How can you believe that they have anything to offer you?" I was enraged, for her sake. "You know Ryner will kill you once he's done with you! How can you be so blind?! How can you still follow him?!"

She stared at me with malice in her eyes. "I live for the Brotherhood," she said, plainly.

I stared into her eyes. Her face seemed somehow distorted and lifeless... like K, when she had been 'activated.'

You've already been replaced. The thought hit me, and a creeping sensation rippled through my body. The TAU *had* purged their forces of the Brotherhood. But without their knowledge, their personnel were slowly being replaced by sleeper agent clones. My eyes shifted to the window, and the fleet of TAU ships that circled overhead like vultures.

"Yes," she said, noticing my gaze. "They're Brotherhood too. In fact, our entire fleet is hovering in Astraloth's atmosphere right now. So don't think about trying to escape. You have nowhere to run. And now that you know our plan, we will have to kill you if you try to flee. It will be easier to make a clone with live tissue, but we can use your corpse if necessary..." She smirked. "And by the way, if you send for help, we *will* bomb the city."

My heart stuttered. "No..."

"Yes," she said, ominously. "Now get up. You will come with me to my ship."

I stood cautiously, shaking. "Where will you take me?"

"To the planet Viperion," she said.

"Viperion?"

"That picture you found on our researcher's computer on Malum? With the loro, standing above the valicorr? That was taken on Viperion, at the loro's old valicorr cloning facility. Which is now our home base. The labs there are perfectly suited for our needs." She gazed at me, smugly. "Now, move."

She pressed the gun into my back, and I moved with her. She opened the door, and we stepped out into the hall.

Our footsteps echoed as we walked down the empty corridor. I waited tensely. *Now would be a good time...*

Suddenly, in a flash of movement, a red-tipped tail swung down from the ceiling and swiped the E-gun clean out of the investigator's hands.

"What-"

Without missing a beat, I spun around as soon as she was disarmed, and with a solid fist punched her hard in the gut.

"Oof!"

Her hat flew off her head, and she stumbled backwards onto the floor, completely shocked. I couldn't help but lift my ears and squint in delicious vengeance.

"Hah!" I exclaimed. Then I turned my gaze upward.

They dropped from the ceiling with surprising grace. Omega effortlessly transferred the gun from their adhesive tail to their right arm. Their left arm was a stump at the elbow, the colours faintly shifting at the end. They wore a skyther skirt around their waist; their chest, arms, and face were exposed. They gripped the carpet gently with their paw-like feet, their tail flicking around with excitement. Their black, circular eyes blinked innocently, and their lips curved into a smile as they inhaled through the spotted skin of their face.

"There is your favour," they said flatly, their red tongue flicking out.

I couldn't help but grin. "Right on time, too," I said. They had come to my rescue after all. Omega aimed the gun at the investigator, who crawled backwards in fear, glancing between us. It felt so good to have them here with me.

"What?" She stared at me. "But you were so scared-"

"I was pretending," I said, breathing calmly and smirking.

"How did you know?" she asked. "How did you plan this?" She

looked genuinely confused.

"The skyther muggers," I said. "I never told anyone about them. But you knew."

She slowly shut her eyes and clenched her mouth shut. "Dammit," she said.

"I bet you hired them to capture me for cloning, before realizing you might need to hear my whole story... I guess it's hard to call off a band of mercenaries when you hire them anonymously." I hesitated. "Or maybe you would have been fine with capturing me prematurely." I shrugged. "Well, they failed, anyway. And now, thanks to Omega, so did you."

"But-" she said. "But, you said Omega-"

"I said Omega detonated a belt of grenades inside a myrok," I replied. "Which is true." Omega, eyes fixed on the investigator, nodded in agreement. "I may have left out the part where, weeks after the battle of Earth, they called me from an abandoned Brotherhood base on Malum, asking for help, and I picked them up and brought them back here."

"But, how?" asked the investigator. "How did they survive?"

"I was designed to survive," said Omega in their nasally, monotone voice. "My cells were clustered together inside the skin of the myrok; I regenerated and crawled out."

The investigator's face scrunched up in disgust. "Why didn't you tell me during the story?"

"Because some heartless TAU politician agreed that people should be judged based on how they were born, rather than who they are," I said. "And as a bioweapon I had to keep Omega a secret, even from a TAU investigator. Not that I really believed you were one."

The investigator stared at me, then slowly smirked. "So," she said. "You *are* a liar."

I stood up taller. "If it means protecting my friends and upholding my morals... then yes." I smiled, confidently. I knelt down beside her, and removed her holo-gauntlet. I turned and passed it to Omega.

Then searing heat blasted my shoulder, and I yelped in pain. My heart jolted as I spun around to face the investigator. She had withdrawn a hidden E-pistol from her uniform pocket, and shot me in the back.

Without a moments hesitation, Omega fired. A bolt of energy hit the investigator. She collapsed, motionless.

My knees buckled, and I panted. The pain throbbed in my shoulder, and I was having difficulty concentrating. Omega knelt beside me, tilting their head to the side. "You are hurt," they said.

"Yeah- Ah!" I winced. "Omega, we have to go," I said.

They blinked at me inquisitively. "Where?"

Omega helped me stand in the dim, carpeted hall. My left arm felt limp, and I decided not to try moving it for at least a few minutes. I met Omega's eyes. "To stop the Brotherhood, to stop Ryner and put an end to this," I said. "To the planet Viperion." I started walking down the hall, and Omega, looking once at the investigator's body, decided to follow me. "I should have known the Brotherhood would still be around..."

I started jogging, Omega keeping pace. "But," said Omega, "You will miss the skyther holiday."

I waved my right hand dismissively. "I made it up," I said.

Omega blinked. "You made it up?"

"Yes," I said, panting. "I ordered the workers at the Temple to take a few days off. I wanted the investigator to feel as comfortable as possible so she would definitely spring her trap," I said. "I was hoping she'd gloat about her plans... I can hardly believe it worked!"

Omega looked forward, easily keeping pace with me. "You are clever."

"Thanks."

"And thank you for looking after me," said Omega. They tilted their head toward me.

"Of course, Omega," I said. I was hit with a pang of regret. "Sorry I couldn't bring you food as soon as I wanted to," I said. "Those muggers blasted one of the containers, and I gave the other one to a skyther, who looked like he needed it..."

"It is alright," they said. "I survived."

"That you did, Omega," I said, eyes forward. "That you did."

Sixty-Nine

Omega and I ran side by side. Our destination was my private room, and the landing pad which connected to it. My starship was docked there, ready for take off at any moment. Even though I was waiting for the investigator to jump me, I hadn't anticipated that she was part of the Brotherhood, or that I would be compelled to take off from Astraloth so soon.

I was deep in thought, and after a few minutes of silence, Omega spoke as we rounded a corner and continued up a flight of stairs.

"The Brotherhood must be stopped," they said. "If any member of the Brotherhood remains, the chance for peace in the galaxy is zero percent." Their skirt trailed behind them as they deftly ascended the stairs, gun in hand.

"I get what you mean," I said, eyes narrowing. "And that's exactly what we're gonna do."

I thought about what the investigator had said. "If the Brotherhood isn't stopped, then pretty soon our entire galaxy will be living in a controlled, dystopian society." I shuddered to think of it... The Cardinal of the TAU, replaced by a puppet. Myself, replaced by an agent of the Brotherhood. Where would they stop? Military officials? School teachers? Police officers? *They won't stop...*

I ground my mandibles together. "Ryner never believed the world needed fixing," I growled. "That's just the lie he told his followers to ensnare them. All along, the only thing he wanted was control. Absolute domination over everything."

"Then Ryner sounds like Duhrnan," said Omega.

At last we came to the doorway of my private room, and I froze. The door was ajar, and soldiers equipped with E-rifles and TAU armour were searching the place, checking drawers and inspecting the furniture. I was angry at their audacity to invade my personal space... but there plan had been to steal my identity and kill me, so I shouldn't have been surprised. One of them held a small silver orb in their hand; it was the device to send Astraloth to the future!

Beyond them was a glass door to the outside, and beyond that was a thin bridge to my private landing pad. The white sphere of my ship waited with four landing poles sticking out from the bottom to stabilize it. It was just out of reach, shining in the moonlight that snaked through the clouds. Rain pelted the ship and the platform outside.

Before I could react, the Brotherhood agents saw me. They lifted their rifles, and red energy flitted from the ends of their barrels. Electric hums shrieked, and I dove away from the doorway. Lasers burst into smoke on the wall behind me, and I grunted in pain as I landed on my bad arm. I seized up for a moment, curling into a ball and breathing heavily.

One of the soldiers whipped a hand to his helmet. "Don't let the king escape. Converge on his landing pad-"

Omega leapt straight into the room. As they soared through the air, they pointed their gun to the farthest soldier, the one making the call, and shot him in the chest, sending him to the floor, silent. As they approached the ground, they curled their legs up to their chest, leaning back, and coiled their tail. Then they pushed off the ground with their tail, maintaining their forward momentum and bounding straight at another two soldiers who stood next to each other. Laser bolts flew past Omega, blasting the walls. They planted their bare claws onto the chest of each soldier. The Brotherhood agents slammed onto the floor, pinned by Omega's feet. Two other soldiers remained standing, and they whirled to shoot Omega, who continued in a roll, ripping the rifle from one of the prone soldier's hands as they somersaulted with their tail. Then they righted themselves on the other side of the soldiers near the glass door, spinning as they ended their movement in a crouch. In one motion, they shot one of the standing soldiers, and using their tail threw the rifle straight into the other's head.

My mandibles dropped.

Omega killed another soldier who tried to rise, and the room went still. Once again, I felt incredibly glad that they were on my side.

I scrambled to my feet, and ran into the room. Omega waited with perfect posture, eyeing me expectantly as their tail flicked to the side. I saw the rain outside, and my eyes fell to my coat rack. My eyepiece hung on its spokes; without hesitation I grabbed the familiar device and fitted it to my head.

The black cloak Joëlle had given me lay crumpled on the floor in the corner. But when I saw the cloak I didn't feel a horrible, twisting, sinking sensation in my chest like I had for the past several months. Instead I felt the opposite. I knelt beside it, and my fingers gently brushed the textured cloth, and I caught sight of the rips and tears I knew so well. Nothing had changed... why did I feel different? I grabbed the cloak and threw it over my shoulders. I pulled the hood over my head, and pulled my ears through the holes I had cut into it. I felt like my heart lifted.

Then, cloak billowing behind me, I rushed over to one of the soldiers. In his hand was the silver activation sphere; the device that could activate the hidden underground spheres of Astraloth, and send the planet forward in time once more.

I lifted it to my eye level, and gazed at it, eyes sparkling. "I can't leave *you* lying around, in case more Brotherhood agents arrive," I said to myself.

Omega replied. "It would not be good if Astraloth were sent to the future unintentionally."

"Yeah," I agreed, shoving the orb into my pocket and making for the glass door. "I really should have hidden it in a safer place. There are only enough underground spheres for one more leap to the future, anyway. Gotta make it count."

"You have no weapons," said Omega, as I pressed a button and opened the sliding glass door. They gestured to the Brotherhood bodies.

"I have some on the ship," I said. "Come on!"

My heart burned with a righteous fury. Maybe it was just the adrenaline and endorphins, but I felt so alive sprinting onto the rain slicked bridge. Omega was right behind me. The sky was full of clouds, and rain stung my eyes, but there were a few patches of open stars, and I could see the violet glow of the Toru nebula. My gaze lingered there for a moment. I felt my mother's presence with me. *You will not be alone.* My legs pressed powerfully into the floor, propelling me forward with splashing steps. I looked back over my shoulder at the verdant pyramid, and Omega running just behind me.

Then a spray of explosive bullets cut into the bridge between us. Heat and light scorched me, and I stumbled back, shielding my eyes. The lasers came from a Titan-class cruiser that loomed over the temple.

I crouched low to keep my balance as the ground shifted beneath me. The explosions cleared and left only the white noise of rainfall. The bridge collapsed, and Omega was thrown back toward the slope of the temple. Standing on the landing pad, I strained my eyes and saw them catch onto a tree branch in the darkness below.

Then my stomach lurched. The landing pad was held up by a thin tower, which was beginning to sway and creak. The platform was tipping.

Heart pounding, I ran for my ship. My foot slipped on the tilted, wet flooring, and I crashed onto my left arm, crying out in pain. I heard the sound of TAU fighters swooping in to capture me, and willed myself to stand. I glanced up at the Titan-class cruiser, and saw its weapons begin to glow.

I activated my holo-gauntlet, and the white sphere's bottom opened up into a ramp. Bright blue explosions chased me to the entrance of the ship. My ears were ringing as I stepped inside, and the ship began to screech as its landing pads scraped against the tilting platform. The ship was sliding off.

Without hesitating I dashed toward the cockpit. I could hear my heartbeat in my head. The ship was accelerating, screaming as it slid towards the edge of the skewed landing pad. The front of the ship was leaning forward, and I braced myself on the door frame of the cockpit just as it slid off the tower.

My ears shot behind me. I gazed down into the cockpit. The ground rushed toward the windshield. I couldn't swallow. The ship was falling face first to the bottom of the Great Temple where civilians panicked, staring up at the chaos suddenly erupting above them. Not knowing what to do, I clenched the door frame with my fingers, my feet slipping on the vertical flooring. I felt weightless; I needed to start the engines...

I pulled myself through the door with both arms. My left shoulder screamed with pain. I misjudged my angle, and bounced against the central chair with a grunt, rolling over onto the windshield. The activation sphere fell out of my pocket, drifting through the air as the ship fell. No time to look down- I reached for the controls from a backwards angle, bracing myself for impact.

The engines hummed to life with a click, and I felt myself press hard against the windshield as the ship decelerated to a steady hovering position. The activation sphere clanked to the floor, and I laughed wildly. *Not today, Brotherhood!*

The ship began to rotate, levelling itself out, and I climbed off the windshield and the controls, and into the pilot's seat. I shook my body, then grabbed the controls, and looked outside as the front slowly lifted up. A skyther man stood on the sidewalk a meter in front of the window, staring at me with a look of utter surprise on his face; his mandibles were open and his ears had shot backwards, flat against his head. The ship was hovering just inches from the ground.

I lifted my ears awkwardly, and waved a hand to the skyther. Then I activated the window's shield so it turned solid white from the outside. I rose to the sky. I needed to get out of here. I would have to leave Omega behind for now...

The Temple fell away as I approached the clouds. I inhaled deeply. I pulled the soaking hood from my head, ears dripping onto my chair. The scent of fresh plastic filled my nose. Several TAU fighters looped around to intercept me, and the Titan-class cruiser turned ominously to face me. But I had dealt with worse.

"Is that all you got?" I mocked, feeling unstoppable.

Then my shoulders tensed. One by one, twelve more Titan-class cruisers emerged from the clouds. Dazzling darts of lightning lit the sky, and thunder rolled over me. Muffled raindrops rapped at the window. Hordes of starfighters took off from the hangars of the battlecruisers, and set their sights on me. I sighed and shook my head.

"Okay," I said, my voice strained. "Fair enough."

Seventy

Lightning and laser bolts arced through the sky. The air bellowed with rumbling cracks of energy. Another second, and my ship would be ripped apart by the Brotherhood's volley of bullets.

My ears shot up as I took the ship into a steep dive. The rain was blasted off my window in the wind, and I pulled back on the controls, curving back upwards and away from the city, towards the ocean.

That's right, I thought. *Chase me over here!*

I skimmed the choppy waves with the bottom of my spherical shuttle, leaving a wake of white foam. Water stretched onward before me, and the Brotherhood's fleet closed in behind.

I pushed the throttle to the maximum speed my ship could handle in the atmosphere without exploding against the air resistance. At least I wasn't piloting a cube, but nevertheless my ship wasn't the most aerodynamic. First and foremost, it was a space vessel.

The water splashed around me with the impact of their weapons, and I wished I was back on the Firebrand with a cloaking device to mask my signal. But no. I was in a shining white orb, with no cloaking device, and no weapons. At least I had a shielding system to deflect energy weapons-

A direct hit. I shook in my seat. I checked the dashboard; my energy shields had just dropped to three percent integrity. One more hit would take me out, and then I would crash into the waves like a stone, sinking deeper, deeper, gasping for air as water poured into my damaged hull...

I knew I wouldn't be able to escape them if I stayed in the atmosphere. I checked my scanners, and I could see the fighters closing in around me like a pack of wolves on the hunt. Only these wolves were brainwashed and made of steel, could fly, and could spit fire.

I had to get away from them.

Thunder rolled over the dark ocean waves, and I considered my chances at escape. I needed to get to the planet Viperion, and stop Ryner's plan of galactic domination. I needed to destroy the loro cloning factory there. If I didn't, then the Brotherhood would surely take control of the galaxy, one person at a time. Ryner would become like a twisted god.

My eyes narrowed and I seemed to swallow the energy of the storm. I couldn't let that happen. But I realized, even if I was able to get out into space and make a slipspace jump to Viperion, the Brotherhood would be right on my tail. They would easily be able to track me there, and then I would be in the same situation, only I'd be fleeing from their attack ships over enemy territory. I wouldn't survive...

I twisted to the side, narrowly avoiding a flock of purple sea birds that spiralled out of my way, squawking. When I levelled out, I heard something hard clatter against the wall, rolling along the floor. My eyes landed on it. The silver activation sphere...

That's it, I thought with a rush of excitement. Then I bent over and scooped up the device, placing it on my lap. I pulled a hairpin turn and shot to the clouds. I would have to be fast.

If I slowed down then I might be hit by the lightning; everyone knew that flying through Astraloth's storms could be deadly. On Earth, negative lightning was far more common, but most of the lightning strikes that happened on Astraloth were positively charged due to the makeup of the clouds, making them significantly stronger, farther reaching, and more unpredictable. Our ships were at risk because protection that could defend against negative lightning wouldn't necessarily protect against positive lightning.

I reached the clouds, and the Titan-class cruisers struggled to turn and follow me, lightning dancing around them. Out of the corner of my eye, I saw one of the cloud-covered cruisers get struck with a bolt of Astraloth's fury. A second after the light faded it began to plummet, sickeningly. I looked forward at the whirling clouds between me and the stars, and the zapping forks of blue that lit my path, and I felt my heart skip a beat, my head spinning.

I couldn't bear to look, so I shut my eyes, and accelerated into the storm.

My ship whined, and I held on tight. The storm sounded like cannons, firing on all sides. I couldn't stop, couldn't look back. I needed to get out of the storm before it decided to take me in its jaws.

Beyond that, I needed to clear the atmosphere before my pursuers could, for my plan to work.

I gasped. With a great amount of luck, I passed above the clouds and the rain, unscathed. I exhaled with relief, though I wasn't quite out of it yet. Their ships would be right behind me.

Darkness surrounded me, and in the shadow of the planet my cockpit flickered with the glow of red sprites- fleeting crimson flares of lightning that stretched up from the tops of the clouds toward the edge of the atmosphere. I didn't worry about them though, the sprites were hardly dangerous. Instead, I accelerated even more, soaring up and away from Astraloth.

I spun my ship around so I faced Astraloth while I sped away from it. The Brotherhood ships were still fighting with the storm. Now was my chance.

I took the silver activation device in my hands, and twisted it. The dark planet blinked away, and I jumped when I felt the device in my hands begin to disintegrate.

Heart pounding, I let myself relax back into the pilot's seat. The silver orb faded into nothing and I knew the hidden time spheres below the planet's surface would be spent now, too. I rested my now empty hands on my chest, ruffling my fur, still damp from the rain.

Then my chest constricted. A streak of blue lit my cockpit, and I saw that one of their fighters had made it out of the atmosphere before Astraloth disappeared, and it was showering my ship with lasers.

Without thinking, I leaned forward, shooting myself toward the grey starfighter. I knew I couldn't run from the ship forever; sooner or later it would shoot me down unless I destroyed it first. The thing is I didn't have any weapons, but I did have mass...

It tried to evade me, but my shuttle crashed into its underside. The Brotherhood starfighter burst into flames against my hull, and my ship vibrated. Then the shaking stopped.

I let out a sigh of relief. I was no longer being chased, and while my shields were gone and my white hull was now scorched black in places, I was alive.

◆

I vaguely lamented that I had just altered the entire population of Astraloth's off-world correspondence by two and a half days... With luck I'd be back safe and sound to take care of things by the time the planet reappeared. *This is the last time, I promise,* I thought to myself. Then I inhaled deeply. I probably wouldn't make it back. The cockpit smelled like wet fur and plastic.

I opened up my ship's map of the galaxy, and searched for the planet Viperion. There, on the far edge of the Milky Way, held to the galaxy's core by a thread of gravity, the planet hid. It was a rogue planet; it had no star, instead orbiting the galaxy directly, on its own.

It had been named like countless other planets from a distant observatory, but never explored. The Brotherhood, with their research on Malum, must have discovered information about the loro cloning facility there.

But wouldn't the valicorr have fought back against them? Unless that's where they made first contact with Duhrnan and came to an alliance...

I grit my mandibles. This is exactly why our people had agreed that any knowledge of the loro needed to be shared publicly, why it was a crime to keep discoveries of the loro hidden.

The stars watched me, floating alone between Astraloth's moons. The purple and red nebulas glowed fiercely in the dark of space. I flexed my fingers and toes, stretched my back, and without a second thought engaged the slipspace engine. Everything stretched, and pooled back behind my vessel as I shot towards the edge of the galaxy. I didn't know how, but I was going to stop Ryner, once and for all. I had to.

But I wasn't sure I could do it alone.

I glanced at the communications console in front of me. I could use the Code-Alpha signal and warn the galaxy of the Brotherhood's threat. I could tell everyone what had happened, and ask the TAU and skythers to come to my aid at Viperion, and my message would be heard across the galaxy.

My hand froze above the console. *No*, I thought. *If I use the Code-Alpha signal, the Brotherhood will know I'm coming. They will have time to escape. They'll slink back into hiding, and I will have missed my chance to stop them.*

I put my hands on my lap, and sat back into my chair, contemplating my options.

I nearly leapt from my seat when my holo-gauntlet began ringing. It was Fiona.

Instinctively I moved to answer her call, but I stopped myself. The device beeped while I hesitated. She was probably returning my call from the other day... but could I really trust her? I knew I could trust the real Fiona, and I wanted more than anything to call out for help right now. But for all I knew, she had already been replaced.

I shivered, and let the call go to the answering machine. I sat in the silence, gazing at the warping stars before my eyes. I could call Joëlle, but I couldn't be sure that she was herself, either... And Omega wouldn't exist again until Astraloth reappeared.

No. There was only one person I could trust, and though I didn't know if they would answer, I knew I had to try calling.

Beep. Beep. Beep.

"The device you are attempting to call is unavailable. Please leave a message."

I exhaled into the receiver. "Jonathan," I said. "It's Osax.

"I know we haven't talked in months, since I left Voren..." I shut my eyes, and swallowed hard. "I don't know where you are. Maybe you won't get this in time, or maybe you won't want to risk helping me, but I need help. It's about the Brotherhood..."

I continued talking for several minutes, explaining in my message everything that had just happened, that the Brotherhood had adapted Jonathan's research into a new sinister project, and that they planned to replace me and countless others with sleeper agents.

"...They want galactic domination," I said. "And I'm determined to do what I can to stop them. Which is why I'm on my way to Viperion right now."

I closed my eyes, my head in my hands. "I know coming to help me is putting yourself at risk in more ways than one- The Brotherhood will want to kill you, the TAU will want you arrested... But you're the only one I can trust." I inhaled deeply. "Please, Jonathan."

I shook my head. *What am I doing? He wanted to get away from the troubles of the galaxy. He's not going to respond.*

I sat up. "You're the only one who knows about this, except for Omega. And they're still on Astraloth, surrounded by Brotherhood ships. Though, Astraloth won't appear again for a few days...

"In any case... If you don't hear anything from me in a week, and you don't hear anything about the Brotherhood on the news, but people are still talking about me... then it means I've failed, and already been replaced."

I felt my throat clench. "If that happens... Please, Jonathan. Do something... Anything... if you can. And if I never speak with you again... then good luck."

Beep.

I stood up from my chair, and rummaged under the desk. In a hidden compartment, I retrieved a sleek E-pistol, and a curved molecular sword. I holstered each weapon to my belt, and tried to calm myself, adjusting the eyepiece I wore. Then I found the ship's medical gel, and applied some to my shoulder.

When I was done, I returned to the cockpit, trying to ignore the sting of my wound. Thoughts orbited my mind like an asteroid belt. I stood next to my seat, watching the stretching stars. I knew in my heart that, at long last, this was the final destination. This would be the end of my journey. It would take several hours, and then I would reach Viperion. And whether I liked it or not, I was going alone.

I clenched my fists, and a fire burned in my eyes. I talked to the warping stars that seemed to stare my way telling them with more confidence than I felt, "I'm ready."

Seventy-One

Viperion. A dark orb of purple and red. The debris of ancient loro satellites orbited the planet like undead sentinels of an ancient society. Behind me, the Milky Way shined with innumerous stars. But ahead, beyond Viperion, was the edge of the galaxy, and with it a haunting blackness, devoid of stars, at least none my eyes could see. I was at the ends of the world as I knew it. I grit my mandibles, and my shuttle hummed as I descended toward the rogue planet.

I was leaving behind everything I had ever known.

In the thick atmosphere of the ancient loro planet, I skirted low across the rocky, dusty terrain, so that my signals would be refracted and I would be harder to spot. The surface of the planet was sheer and jagged, with sparkling, sweeping spires of purple and reddish glass. In only a few sparse places could I see any chance there might be life between the craters of glass; tiny, darkly coloured pools of water that may have hidden some struggling bacteria. But otherwise, there was no sign of life. There was no wind. The planet was holding its breath.

My ship hummed, and I inhaled the scent of plastic and sweet soda. I slurped at a glass of root beer, drinking in the sound and taste. I wanted to enjoy it, since for all I knew it might be the last time I ever got to.

It was hard to tear my eyes away from the ghostly landscape ahead of me. I was skirting over the brighter side of the planet, but it was a far cry from daylight. With no star close by, instead this shadow of a world was lit not by a rising sun, but the rising of the galaxy. From here, the stars of the Milky Way looked so clustered together. I had to dim the interior lights of my shuttle to let my eyes adjust to the eternal night.

I was tracking a large energy signature on the surface of the planet with my scanner. It could only have been the valicorr cloning facility, and the Brotherhood's hideout. The signal blinked at me. I was almost at my destination.

I closed my eyes, but nothing stirred in my mind. No comforting thoughts or images showed themselves. I was all alone in the quiet darkness.

A wide purple structure covered in jagged spires emerged from the crest of a hill. It was adorned with dim lights and I could almost hear the hum of energy coming from it. I dared not fly my ship any closer; if the Brotherhood detected my vessel, then I would surely be destroyed. From here I would have to go on foot.

I touched my ship down, nestled behind a sloping wall of dark glass. I opened the shuttle's exit ramp, then flicked a few switches with my finger, until the entire ship powered down. No lights, no sounds. I blinked in the dark cockpit, then activated a dim flashlight from my holo-gauntlet to lead the way. I drew my E-pistol, but kept it powered off just in case the signal could be detected by their scanners as I approached, and with my cape trailing behind me I navigated out of the dark shuttle and stepped outside.

My feet gripped against the cold, smooth ground. I filled my lungs with brisk air, and made my way to the lower side of the smooth glass barrier I'd hidden behind.

I took a moment to peer out over the lip. I was on the edge of a barren, sparkling hill that sloped down toward the massive cloning facility. The base was adorned with gun turrets, and I could see a lone Brotherhood ship landed not far from the structure, barely illuminated by the galaxy that hung in the sky. This was definitely the place.

I deactivated my flashlight and holo-gauntlet, so that I wouldn't be emitting any signals. Then I vaulted silently over the ridge and slid down toward the structure. I scrambled as quietly as I could toward an almost hidden doorway at the base of the building. There were no patrols, no guards stationed at the base. And why would there be? Who would they be expecting to arrive at Viperion?

I hoped they weren't expecting anyone.

I racked my brain, trying to decipher the buttons on the door's control panel. Then I punched in a sequence, and the door slid open.

With one last look up at the Milky Way, I slipped into the illuminated hallway.

◆

I traced my fingers along the walls and their ornate glowing engravings. The interior was dim, but much brighter than the outside of the planet. So far, I hadn't met any signs of the Brotherhood aside from the ship outside, nor had I seen any valicorr. What the investigator had said must have been true; the Brotherhood's entire fleet was flying over Astraloth. I felt lucky that I had been able to escape them.

But clearly, judging from the ship outside, someone was here.

I scanned the dark walls and doorways for any loro symbols that could point me in the direction of the main power generator. Just like the mothership, my plan was to set this base to self destruct. I knew that a facility like this on such a remote planet would require an immense power source, and that meant something I could exploit. A power generator strong enough to charge this entire station would also be powerful enough to blow the whole thing up. At least that's what I was counting on.

I briefly paused, considering that I was trying to destroy a massive structure of loro architecture, and what a loss that might be to the research community... But I couldn't allow the Brotherhood to use the cloning facilities for their nefarious purpose. I clenched my mandibles, and kept walking, my footsteps echoing in the silence.

Then, faintly, I heard the sounds of machinery up ahead. Cautiously, I turned a corner, following the sound into a glowing corridor.

The corridor was made of a translucent material, and it formed an encased bridge through the center of a gigantic room. I gazed in wonder through the glass. Like a massive factory, thousands of transparent pods were being carried across zigzagging lines that crossed through the room. The walls and ceilings were adorned with bright lights that illuminated the sorting room. Mechanical wall-mounted arms grabbed and sorted the pods, pushing them to new conveyors that carried them out of the room. The pods were filled with fluids, and the bony bodies of half-grown valicorr.

I recoiled at the sight, furrowing my nose. My head was reeling, my furred ears dangling low. I was witnessing the dark legacy of the loro right before my eyes; machines that manipulated life, all in the name of war and dominance. I wished it weren't true, but it was as clear as day.

But, I thought, *they're making more valicorr... Why would the Brotherhood do that? Unless...*

I shook my head, and gripped my pistol firmly, aware of the sweat beading on my face. It didn't matter why. Either way, I needed to destroy this base and stop it from churning out more monsters, whether they were valicorr soldiers or sleeper agents for the Brotherhood.

◆

As I continued deeper into the hideout, I began to see signs of human technology. Brotherhood computers and wires were placed in seemingly random places in the hallways. Disordered TAU machinery filled the rooms. I stepped more quietly now, aware that I was passing through a section of the base that was directly used by the Brotherhood. But it was uncharacteristically scattered and unorganized. The place felt abandoned, even though clearly there was a Brotherhood presence here...

I peered into an open doorway, and saw a wide, empty room. Loro furniture had been pushed aside, and the space had been haphazardly converted into a cloning lab. Clearly though, the technology in this room was of human design. There was no one inside the room, but I shuddered as my eyes wandered between the two empty pods at the far wall, and the operating table in the center. The tanks at the back were at least nine feet tall. I had a sinking feeling that this was where they planned to clone me.

I felt a sudden creeping sensation that I was being watched.

I spun around, and powered on my E-gun with a whine. Breathing heavily, I peered down the dimly lit halls. I could only hear my own breath, could only see my own reflection against the walls.

I held my breath.

Nothing.

Hastily, I crept further down the hall, and entered an elevator shaft. I caught sight of the loro symbol for energy, and pressed the corresponding button. The door slid shut, and I felt the elevator begin its descent, letting out a sigh of relief.

My ears twitched, and my heart began to race. I thought I heard the sound of breathing beside me.

I looked to my side, but all I saw was the wall of the elevator. I couldn't hear anything.

Then the elevator stopped moving, the door opened, and my attention was fixated on the sight in front of me.

I stepped out into the heart of the machine. The power generator was lit on all sides by orange pads of light. The room was spherical, and I stood on a metal catwalk that extended towards the glowing power core in the middle of the room. There was a net of catwalks that connected together like a spider-web, with perfectly spaced spokes coming out from the central platform and extending to doors on other sides of the room.

The pillar in the center reminded me of the energy regulator in the loro mothership. I knew that if I could damage it I'd trigger a similar cascade effect, overloading the station with energy, ultimately resulting in an explosion that would destroy the cloning facility in its entirety.

But the room wasn't empty. In front of the power regulator, on a thin, folding chair, sat a man. He was young, with pale skin. He was tall for a human, thin, and with a gaunt, shaved face. His hair was long, pale, and wispy. He wore all black clothing, with a black long coat, boots, gloves, and a collar that hugged his wiry neck. He sat calmly, with both arms resting on his chair, which faced me directly. Black, rectangular glasses outlined his eyes, and his lips curved into a shallow smile.

Instinctively, my ears shot back and I lifted my E-gun toward his chest, sparks flitting from the barrel. He sat several meters away from me, and didn't even flinch at my act of aggression. Instead, he waved with his hand from the arm rest, and said in a quiet voice, "Welcome, Talcorosax."

Seventy-Two

"Ryner," I growled. My eyes narrowed to focus on the sinister man before me. His gaunt features were outlined with an orange glow from the light panels that lined the sphere. My finger rested against the trigger of my pistol, which I aimed squarely at his heart. The air down here smelled at once musty and electrified.

Ryner remained seated for the moment, smiling casually at me. He had a reservedness to him that felt somehow all the more unsettling. He didn't appear armed, though I suspected he hid a weapon beneath his long black coat. He was motionless, and we stared each other down from either end of the thin catwalk.

He began to speak. "There's no reason why we can't-"

"Give me *one* good reason I shouldn't shoot you in the heart, right now!" I hissed. The generator hummed in the absence of our voices. I was dead serious, and to make sure he understood, I began charging a bolt of energy. My weapon began to glow brighter, its whine rising in pitch.

At this, he raised his hands, and his smile disappeared. "Wait!" Even his yell was quiet, almost meek sounding. "I thought you and I could talk!"

My mandibles twitched. The barrel of my gun began to spit sparks. I hesitated for a moment...

Pain shot from my leg, and I collapsed to the metal grating. Something had kicked the back of my knee, forcing my leg to buckle. My E-pistol discharged harmlessly against the far wall, and the weapon clattered from my hands, bouncing off the catwalk to the bottom of the room, far out of reach.

I struggled to my feet and turned to face my attacker, but there was nothing there. I heard Ryner's voice behind me, roaring with laughter. Then a flicker of movement-

The wind was knocked out of me, and I stumbled backwards, coughing, fumbling for the railings of the catwalk.

"Oh my," said Ryner, softly. "It's sad that you fell for that."

With my back to Ryner, I took a combat stance, ready to defend. Then I swung a fist forward and hit something tangible. I yelped as my arm was grabbed, twisted, and slammed against the railing by a shimmering invisible force. The catwalk rang from the impact, and the side of my hand tingled.

"Turn him around so he can see me," said Ryner over the hum of the generator.

Fear gripped me. I was forced to my knees. My arms were held helplessly behind my back, and I was positioned in front of Ryner. I struggled against my invisible captor.

"How's that?" said a chillingly familiar voice from behind my ear.

My skin seemed to prickle with rage. "Duhrnan!" I twisted my neck around, and his body uncloaked into view behind me. He survived the battle of Earth- He must have been saved by one of the valicorr ships.

He grinned at me hungrily. I could feel the heat of his breath on my face. His hands squeezed my arms together behind my back.

"Well done, Duhrnan," said Ryner, cutting through my thoughts.. "You were finally able to stop him." He stood from his seat, casually brushing his gloved hands together. He took a few steps along the catwalk toward us. "Talcorosax is an elusive one, isn't he?"

"Just lucky," said Duhrnan, his tone mocking. "I almost killed him above Earth... He should have died in the explosion of my ship above Astraloth-"

"Well he didn't, and he's been a nuisance ever since," snapped Ryner. Then he turned his back to me and Duhrnan. He sighed, almost as if he was disappointed. "It's time. Kill him," he said, coldly.

My heart skipped a beat.

"*I* should have died?" I said, trying to distract them. I twisted my hands, reaching my fingers toward the handle of the molecular sword at my waist... *Keep talking, Osax!*

I fixed Ryner with my most arrogant gaze, and seemed to catch his attention. "You should have died above Astraloth, not me. We ripped your ship apart!"

Ryner's eyes landed on me with a look of disgust. "I wasn't on the Silencer during that battle."

"Then where were you?" I asked, my voice accusing.

He rolled his eyes and scoffed. He had no answer. "Duhrnan. Kill him. Now."

The tips of my fingers grazed the hilt of my sword, but slipped off. I couldn't grab hold. My heart was pounding, and I struggled against Duhrnan's grip.

"No." Duhrnan's voice was calm. Eerily calm.

"What-" Ryner began.

"Not yet. I'm not done with him," said Duhrnan, ominously. "I want to *enjoy* my revenge." He pulled his face close to mine as he said this, and I struggled to stay focused, grasping at the handle...

Ryner turned to us, and stood completely still. He looked unamused, silhouetted against the power regulator that pulsed in the center of the room. "This is not a request," said Ryner. "I *compel you* to kill him!" He thrust his arm toward Duhrnan and a flickering set of holographic symbols appeared in front of his hand. Just like the symbols Jonathan used to activate K.

I froze. Suddenly it all made sense. The Brotherhood hadn't just stumbled across the last living loro and made an alliance with him. There *were* no loro left. They were extinct, just like the research suggested. But Duhrnan was clearly alive.

...The only way it could work was if the "Sheep's Clothing" was integrated during the early phase of accelerated learning... I remembered Jonathan's words. If Ryner was using the "Sheep's Clothing" on Duhrnan, then it meant that Duhrnan was a pawn, created by the Brotherhood from the beginning. He was a sleeper agent. He must have been cloned using DNA from some loro remains the Brotherhood had discovered... That explained how he was even alive in our time, and why he was so unlike the loro I had studied. He was raised by the Brotherhood to be their weapon. Come to think of it, I had never heard him speak the loro language. His fascination with music only explored human genres. He had no connection to loro culture. His starships and technology must have just been relics the Brotherhood had found and given to him.

The blood drained from my face as I stared at the symbols in front of Ryner's hand. Duhrnan was being activated. Which meant that he would have to obey Ryner. Which meant he was about to kill me.

Except he didn't. Instead, he laughed, which somehow felt even more horrifying than I could have imagined. Ryner lowered his hand, staring at Duhrnan in confusion.

"I-" he muttered. "I don't understand." Fear crept into his voice, and the gaunt man stepped backwards, away from Duhrnan and I, staring at the wickedly sharp grin hovering next to my shoulder.

"How charming," said Duhrnan. "But I believe you've got our dynamic a little confused, dear Ryner." Then he lifted one of his four hands from my arms. His own set of symbols began to display in front of his hand, and confusingly, Ryner's eyes glazed over when he saw them. The black-clad man lost all tension in his body, standing completely neutral. His face became blank. He was *Duhrnan's* puppet. Duhrnan began to whistle some kind of cheerful melody.

Never mind that, I thought. My blood burned, and with only one of Duhrnan's hands restraining my arm, I wrenched my hand free, and pulled it to the hilt of my sword. Now was my chance!

Metal screeched into a solid blade, and Duhrnan let out a howl. I sliced the blade up and backwards, cutting him clean across the torso, blue blood trickling from his wound to the bottom of the room below. Now free from his grasp, I whirled around, sword in hand, crouching low. Ryner waited behind me like a zombie, and Duhrnan clutched at his wounds with his four hands, grimacing. He stared at me through wide eye slits.

I panted. I held the thin, curved sword in both of my hands. My eyes narrowed on my nemesis. "You-" I said, gathering my thoughts. "You're not a real loro."

Duhrnan braced himself on the railing with two of his arms. His other two covered the bleeding line I had slashed across his chest. Despite the apparent pain he was in, he raised his head up to the ceiling, and laughed.

"Oh, how astute," he coughed.

I grimaced, gazing at him in the orange glow of the room. The power regulator hummed. We stood in silence, staring at each other. Duhrnan eyed me with a pained, yet amused expression.

"You were created by the Brotherhood," I mused. "All this time, you were just a pawn..."

Duhrnan grinned at this. "Oh, that's what they intended, yes," he said, his voice like a snake's. Then he turned to Ryner. "But Ryner didn't know if the 'Sheep's Clothing' project would work on a loro. He'd never met one, after all."

My eyes narrowed, my mind racing. "Ryner created you with the intent to brainwash you so you would follow his orders... but it didn't work?"

Duhrnan clapped lazily with two of his hands, smiling strangely. "Oh, Talcorosax, you genius. You figured it out." He chuckled. "*Of course* it didn't work," he snapped. "But I knew what they were trying to do to me... The experiments were agony. I was all too aware... so I played along."

"You pretended to be under Ryner's control?"

"Yes," he said, immense pride in his voice. "I did what I could to survive!" He clutched the railing with his hands, and began to pull himself closer to me. I took a step back without thinking. "The Brotherhood taught me about life. About control. That's what it all is, after all," he said. "A struggle for control." He sounded desperate.

I stepped back, and startled myself when I backed up into something. I whirled around, and glanced down at Ryner, standing motionless. A chill ran down my spine.

"Ryner wanted me because I'm a loro. That's all. He wanted a way to control the valicorr, and he knew that they would listen to a loro..." I turned back to face Duhrnan, and he frowned, his eye twitching. He continued, "He had plans, too many to count, all convoluted, all with the goal of giving him the most power, the most control. Like his plan to build the Shade Beam." Duhrnan giggled. "Oh, yes. Even in the beginning, at the colony on Rose, Ryner was twisting the TAU's arm to construct the Shade Beam. But when the valicorr attacked it threw off his plans, and he knew he would have to start over, and find some protection from the valicorr." Duhrnan pointed at himself. Then he bared his teeth in a horrifying smile. "You did kill him, you know. The third or fourth Ryner, I can't remember. He *was* aboard the Silencer when you destroyed it." He inhaled through the slits of his nostrils. "And he still has all those plans in his head. Only, now they're mine."

"You," I declared. "You've been controlling Ryner. *You're* the leader of the Brotherhood!"

"I told you," he sneered wickedly. "I'm the Emperor of this galaxy."

Adrenaline jolted my body. I'd heard enough. I pressed my feet into the cold grating and rushed for Duhrnan, with the curved point of my sword angled toward his head. He was responsible for everything. The valicorr, the Brotherhood, the Shade Beam. *Everything.* I screamed with rage. I thrust my sword toward his throat.

I saw him push off the railings, and begin to flip himself over me just as his cloaking device re-engaged and his image disappeared. He was invisible again; I narrowly missed my lunge.

I spun around, swinging the sword wide. Something fizzled in the air in front of my sword, and a few drops of blue blood shot to the side of the blade. I'd cut him, but only barely.

I panted, listening to the hum of the power core. His footsteps echoed through the catwalks, but I couldn't quite figure out where he was.

My ears shot forward in aggression. Then my mandibles twitched. He was stalling me. I needed to stop Duhrnan, but I also needed to destroy the base.

I turned to the power regulator, and started toward it, sword raised.

Durhnan yelled, "Shoot him!"

My ears recoiled. Ryner sprang into action, withdrawing a slender pistol from his coat. He flashed his gun toward me, and I flinched.

The energy bolt hit me in the leg. My mind was overcome with pain. Smoke rising from the wound, I crashed onto my side. I held onto the sword with all my strength.

I landed right next to Ryner, and the central pillar. Having followed his order, he now stood over me with an empty expression. I tried to stand, but my leg seared with pain. Then Ryner's chair lifted off the ground, and flew straight at my face.

Blood streamed from my nose, and I blinked, trying to reorient myself. My face hurt, and I tried to sit up. My heart was racing.

Duhrnan's invisible foot stomped down on my hand, pinning my sword to the ground. I screamed in pain. He raised the chair up, getting reading for another strike.

"I should have killed you back on my ship!" he screeched. Then he slammed me once more.

Pain rippled out from my face, and I tasted blood. My ears trailed against the cool metal grating. Sweat dotted my face and arms. My eyes were watering, and I couldn't focus them. I struggled to move my arm, my legs kicking limply.

"No," I gurgled. "I won't let you..."

"Won't let me what?!" Duhrnan shouted. "I'm in control! I'm in control!" He smashed me once more.

This time, I managed to block the swing with my free arm, but it sent pain up through my shoulder where I had been shot the day before, and I bit my mandibles together to fight the shaking. The world went spinning.

"I won't let you hurt anyone anymore!" I yelled with a white-hot rage. I mustered all my strength, yelling through the pain in my muscles.

I grabbed onto the chair with one hand and started pushing it back against him, sitting up despite his invisible weight. My body was shaking, but I kept rising. Pain pulsed through my arm. Then I wrenched my right hand out from under his foot, and swung my sword wildly toward his body. I cut deep.

He cried, and stumbled back. A severed arm appeared and fell to the floor with a thud. Then he breathlessly shrieked.

"Kill him!"

I tried to roll myself up to my feet, but Ryner was on me in the blink of an eye. My back smacked against the floor. He pinned my shoulders to the ground, straddling me, and stared at me blankly. My heart stuttered. Then he raised his gun and pressed it into my chest. I was too shocked to even close my eyes. In just a moment, my heart would explode.

Then with a searing burst of heat and light, Ryner was blasted off me.

I sat up, and glanced at Ryner's corpse which lay smouldering beside me. He had been pierced in the side by an E-gun. My ears shot up and I turned my bloody head. *It can't be!*

Tears welled in my eyes. I didn't know how, but standing on the far side of the room, gun still smoking, was Joëlle. Her tattooed face wore an expression of intense concentration beneath her helmet. She wore her silver-blue armour, and held an E-rifle in her hands. But my heart nearly skipped a beat when I saw who stood behind her.

"K-" I said. My eyes were wide with tears, my ears lifting. Everything fell away in that moment. All the pain was gone. She stepped into the room, wearing a grey cloak over her spiked shoulders, her combat boots and vest. Her horns faced my way. Her skin looked so blue, vibrant like the sky of Astraloth. Her muscles looked so strong. She looked so *alive.* Jonathan must have found a way to revive her! Her lips frowned with concern. But her orange eyes met mine, and lit up like a glowing ember.

"Osax!" She yelled. Her voice! *Her voice!* In that moment, it was the best sound in the galaxy.

Then, Jonathan stepped into view from behind K. His holo-gauntlet displayed a local scanner. He must have gotten my message, contacted Joëlle, and tracked my eyepiece here with her and K! His coat trailed behind him as he moved. He lifted an E-pistol to his robotic eye, which glowed a deep crimson. He closed his other eye, his lip twitched into a straight line, and he pulled back on the trigger without hesitation.

Red energy arced through the room from his gun, electrifying the air, and impacting against something invisible. Duhrnan bellowed with pain. Then Jonathan fired again, and again, until Duhrnan's cloaking device was too damaged to function, and he appeared before us. He collapsed to his knees, resting on his three remaining arms, struggling with each breath, utter despair on his face.

K rushed into the room, followed by Jonathan and Joëlle.

"Osax!" K said, panic stricken. "Shit, are you okay?" She knelt down beside me, and wrapped her arm under my back, helping me sit up. I gazed into her eyes.

"K..." I murmured. I lifted a hand up to her face, and gently stroked her cheek. I was too overwhelmed. She smiled at me, and her eyes welled with tears. "You're alive..."

Her eyes squinted with joy. "Yeah," she said, softly. "Jonathan cured me. He couldn't have done it without your scans..."

"It's true," said Jonathan, smiling as he approached, spiking his hair with his fingers. The aperture of his robotic eye twisted and blinked.

"Hey, Osax," said Joëlle, softly. She removed her helmet, dark brown locks of hair spilling out, and met my eyes with a shallow smile. Then her eyes landed on the sword I gripped in my hands. She smirked. "So you could hold onto *your* sword, just not mine." Her eyes seemed to glimmer, teasingly.

I was overwhelmed with emotion, and barely knew what to say. All I could manage was, "You're here, Joëlle..."

"Why?" Duhrnan cut in, grabbing our attention, chuckling even as he coughed up blood, barely holding himself up. "Why bother coming to save him?"

K shot him a disgusted look, wiping her eyes. "Do I really need to explain it to you?" Letting go of me, she stood up and stared him down. She snorted, and cracked her knuckles, ready to pulverize him.

He rolled over onto his back, and the four of us gazed at him. "But, nothing in this world matters," he said, wheezing. "In the end, nothing matters. Nothing matters..."

"You're wrong," I said. I struggled to my feet.

K bared her teeth. "It's time you payed for everything you've done, Duhrnan!" She growled and took a step toward him, clenching her fists.

Suddenly compelled by something within me, I lunged forward and grabbed her arm with both hands, pulling her back. She stopped and stared at me, anger burning in her eyes, confusion on her face. I felt Jonathan and Joëlle's puzzled eyes on my back.

"Osax," she said. "What are you doing? Why are you stopping me?"

"Let me speak to him," I pleaded. I gazed into K's orange eyes, which softened a little. Her expression was concerned. Her lips parted to speak, but seeing the intensity in my stare, she hesitated.

"Okay," she said. Her lips twitched, then her face hardened. She stepped aside, making a path for me on the catwalk.

"Careful, Osax..." said Joëlle, eyeing me, her gun ready.

Jonathan simply stared, blinking. He kept his gun armed and raised toward Duhrnan.

K held onto my arm, and I gently pulled away from her. I nodded to her for reassurance. Then I limped over toward Duhrnan, who lay on his back in the middle of the catwalk, barely alive, missing an arm. My ears drooped. The sheer loneliness of the station seemed suffocating. I knew, with my friends at my side, that we had already won. But Duhrnan still clung to life by a thread.

"The world isn't meaningless. I refuse to believe that."

He laughed, though it was barely audible.

"You," I began, "must have been so tormented. Created by the Brotherhood, treated like an object, like a weapon. Your first experiences of the world were so distorted, and violent. You never had a companion, a friend..." I wiped away the tears from my eyes, breathing shakily as I stood on a wounded leg.

He stopped laughing, staring up at me with an open mouth.

Joëlle's voice cut through the air. "Osax, we should kill him, now!"

My ears drooped.

"We can't trust him," said Jonathan, frowning gravely.

I glanced back at them. K was frozen in place, her expression solemn. Her skin glowed with the orange light of the room. I still could hardly believe she was here, but seeing her gave me strength.

I shut my eyes. Then I turned back to Duhrnan. He looked so pitiful sprawled on the floor, bleeding, breathing shallowly. I glanced at my bloody sword. Then I deactivated it, and it slid back into the handle which I placed on my belt.

I continued, the power regulator thrumming behind me. "All your life, you've been fighting in a struggle for control... But the truth is, no one can control everything. But that's okay. You can let go. You can learn. You can grow. You could even love."

Duhrnan shuffled, eyeing me. "What do you mean?" He croaked. His pale snout twitched with apprehension.

I knelt down next to him. "We are all made up of stars and cycles," I said, finally understanding the words of my mother. A warm glow seemed to radiate from me. "Energy. That's what connects us. We are the energy of life; each one of us. Even if you were made, and not born. It takes courage to live, but the courage is there, in the very fibers of our being. The audacity of our cells to take in energy and multiply, to communicate, to die and multiply again. The boldness of our lungs to expand and fill with air and extract the oxygen as part of the ecosystem that is each of our bodies. The bravery that is the very nature of existence; a fearlessness embedded in our atoms, in the stars, and in every space between. You can tap into it. You don't have to be bound to the obsession of your creators."

He simply stared at me. "I don't understand."

I lifted my ears, weakly. "I just mean... the Brotherhood has to end. But maybe, this can be your beginning."

"Osax..." said K, nervously.

I looked into Duhrnan's eyes, and felt the eyes of my friends on my back. He stared back at me. I couldn't read his expression. But I felt a deep serenity coming from my heart. This was the end. My enemy's fate in my hands. My final test. The fire in my heart began to cool.

I reached out my right hand to him. "What do you say?" I asked gently. "Maybe I can save you, too." I waited there for a brief moment.

Slowly he lifted his right hand, and the space between our hands grew smaller. Our fingers touched. We clasped hands.

Then his face morphed into a twisted snarl, and with another hand, he reached down to his belt.

He screamed, "I hate you!" A plasma knife ignited in his hands, and he cut straight through my bicep.

Searing pain blinded me, and I fell backwards with a cry. The world was a haze. My companions yelled, and sprang into action. K grabbed me under my shoulders, and dragged me away from Duhrnan, who stood up with startling speed. He raised his hand, ready to throw the dagger into Jonathan's chest, but Joëlle blasted his arm, and he dropped the weapon. Then Jonathan and Joëlle each shot him in the chest, and he stopped breathing. At once, Duhrnan fell to the floor with a thud. The life left his body.

Then I looked down at my arm... or where it should have been.

My right arm was severed just below the shoulder. Luckily, I wasn't bleeding, because the plasma had cauterized the wound. But I was reeling in shock, struggling to stay conscious and present.

My companions surrounded me. I was vaguely aware of each of their faces.

"Oh my god, Osax!" Joëlle cried, shock plastering her face. "Your arm!"

Jonathan stared at me with a straightened lip. "You'll be alright," he said, warily. "You'll be alright."

"I'm fine," I said, though I clearly wasn't.

K knelt down beside me, and clutched my other hand with her

fingers. Tears trickled down her azure cheeks. "Why did you do that, Osax? Why?"

I closed my eyes. "I had to," I smiled. "I had to give him a chance. I had to try to save him."

K sobbed, and pulled me into her arms, careful not to crush me. "I could have stopped him," she lamented.

"Don't blame yourself," I replied, my head spinning. "It was my choice. I had to try."

K shut her eyes tightly, and she held me close.

I was enveloped in her warmth. I could hear her beating heart. I wondered then if I would survive my wounds, but I wasn't afraid of dying in that moment. Joëlle and Jonathan knelt down beside me, and wrapped their arms around in a group hug. We were united again. Warmth radiated from us, and despite the shock and pain, I felt a swelling hope in my chest, as though I was floating on a white cloud.

"I think I'm going to be okay," I mumbled.

"We- We need to destroy this base," said Joëlle, trying to regain her composure as she pulled away from the hug. "K?"

K let go of me, draping me in Jonathan's arms for a moment. She stood powerfully and wiped her eyes. "On it."

I shut my eyes. The room rumbled, and I was vaguely aware of an alarm, warning of the cloning facility's imminent destruction. I thought about Duhrnan. About the valicorr. About the Brotherhood. The base itself seemed to groan and howl from deep within, struggling to keep itself alive, to keep the Brotherhood alive, to keep the valicorr alive even as its own power began to spread out from the generator and overload everything with energy. But this was the end, here at the edge of the galaxy. The end of the journey. The dark deceit was over. And I felt my consciousness slipping away...

Seventy-Three

"Stay with me," said K through clenched teeth. "Come on Osax, stay with me!"

I was draped in her arms as she, along with Joëlle and Jonathan, dashed out of the elevator, and through the dim halls. A pulsing red emergency light lit the place, and my ears stung with the sounding alarms. My mind dwelled on the bodies of Duhrnan and Ryner that we left in the core of the base. We were leaving them behind. Soon it would all be behind us...

I wrapped my left arm around K's waist, and tried to flex my right fingers. But they weren't there. I could almost feel my arm through the pain, but it was gone. My white ears flapped as K ran.

I clutched K's vest, and gazed up at her face. "I'm with you," I managed.

At that, she turned her eyes toward me, and bared a bittersweet smile. "Good," she said. "Good." Her eyes were damp, and the orange contrasted vibrantly with her blue skin.

I fought to keep my eyes open as I was jostled, carried out of the base. We ran past Brotherhood computers and cloning equipment, no doubt the site at which most of the current Brotherhood agents were created.

Then we passed through the glass corridor that ran through the center of the valicorr sorting room. The machines had halted, and aside from a low rumbling that came from deep within the base, everything was still. Each pod hung motionless, each mechanical arm stopped dead. I exhaled in relief.

Time passed unperceived, bobbing up and down in K's arms. We stepped out into the black daylight of Viperion, and as my head rested, draped over her arm, I gazed up at the sky. A great swathe of stars beckoned me back to the center of the galaxy, to my home. The sheer beauty of the galaxy was unbearable, and I was filled with light.

Then heat, light, and sound erupted from the core of the base. The cloning facility shattered, going up in flames. We climbed to the edge of the glass ridge, and I could feel the warmth of the enormous bonfire even from fifty meters away. I stared from K's arms, Jonathan and Joëlle at our side. A blanket of flames licked the dark sky, stirring up a sighing wind. The planet exhaled, finally free of its burden. The beauty of the Milky Way shone upon the exposed flames, and the evil that was there was burned away. At once, the atmosphere was filled with a whispering peace.

I pulled myself closer to K, and we cried. All four of us. Jonathan took Joëlle's hand, and they exchanged a wordless stare, smiling and weeping silently. Our hair, and fur, ruffled gently in the fire's gale. I was reeling with pain and joy and relief. My eyes followed a cluster of glowing ash that flew up to kiss the stars.

Joëlle sighed deeply, and pulled Jonathan closer to her, so she could rest her head on his shoulder with a wide smile and closed eyes. He stiffened his shoulders when she did this, but eventually relaxed, and blushing, rested his head on hers. Hand in hand, tears rolled down his cheek as he smiled. I was so surprised, but so happy to see Joëlle here, and to see them able to express their compassion together. I watched them silently for a few moments.

"You two," I marvelled. They looked my way, and Jonathan lifted his head, shuffling awkwardly, still smiling. "Joëlle," I said, looking at her. "You... How did you..."

Joëlle's eyes seemed to sparkle. "You mean how did I find you?"

I nodded. K and Joëlle looked expectantly at Jonathan, who cleared his throat.

"Well," said Jonathan, thoughtfully. "When I received your plea for help, I knew I had to come to Viperion and support you, Osax." He met eyes with me, his robotic aperture focusing on my face. "When a friend asks for help... Well, I need to be there for them."

I lifted my ears. Their faces glowed with orange firelight as they looked between each other.

"We were eager to help," said K, baring her tusks in a grin. "Even though coming out of hiding was a danger to us, both being criminals now." She grit her teeth. "But it was worth it. Of course it was-"

"And we had the transport we stole from the hidden labs on Voren," said Jonathan. I tilted my ears in curiosity. "I- I guess there's a lot to explain," he said, his eyes darkening. "After you left Voren to defend

Earth, I loaded all of the stasis pods onto a TAU cargo vessel that was hidden in the snow there. I took the ship, along with all of the clones, including K, and I flew it off world." He paused. "I knew the TAU would come for me sooner or later, and if they found us there, they would surely arrest me and kill everyone else, just for being associated with the Brotherhood..."

"I thought that was why you left," I said. I coughed, and my nose twitched.

"In any case," K interjected, "Jonathan found a remote planet to park the ship, and dedicated his time to finding a way to cure and revive me." She grinned. "It worked, Osax! He was able to help me!"

"How?" I asked, my ears lifting. "That's wonderful!"

Jonathan smiled warmly, his coat trailing in the breeze. "It wouldn't have been possible without your scans, Osax," he said. "I was able to use the scans, along with my own research, to determine which genes were causing the destructive growths. They were linked to K's accelerated learning. Then it was a matter of developing a bio-screening system that would neutralize that part of the cell while K was in stasis." He sighed. "It took me a few months, but I was determined..."

"You dedicated months of your life to trying to save her?" I asked, astonished. I sniffed back some tears. Then I looked up into K's smiling face above me.

She looked down at me in her arms. "Turns out he's not a completely shit dad after all," she said.

"Hey!" Jonathan protested, but he was smiling.

I thought about Jonathan, all by himself aboard a TAU vessel full of frozen clones like K, barely sleeping, pouring over his work to save her. Hiding from the TAU, and from the skyther government...

"That's why I never contacted you," I said. "I knew you wanted to hide away."

"I didn't want to," he said, "but I had to. And that's why I never contacted you either- I didn't want to put you, or Joëlle, at unnecessary risk by being connected to me." A shadow passed over his eyes. "It didn't help that Round Table was put in charge of capturing bioweapons."

Joëlle frowned, still holding Jonathan's hand in the firelight. "I... I understand why you wouldn't feel safe contacting me."

Jonathan smiled, weakly. "I'm still sorry... I wasn't sure that you'd want to hear from me, anyway, even if it was safe for us to talk..."

Joëlle turned to me and said, "But he did contact me, after getting your message. He told me everything, even played your message for me.

And I knew I had to come help you." Her eyes fell away. "You know, you could have called me directly, too-"

"I wanted to!" I said. "I really did, Joëlle. But the Brotherhood had already replaced an entire fleet of the TAU with sleeper agents. I couldn't be sure if they had gotten to you or not..."

I gazed into her brown eyes. She looked deeply disturbed at this. "That *does* make sense. I understand." Then she smirked. "So, if you wanted to reach out to me... I guess that means..."

"We're friends," I said. "If you want, I mean," I added awkwardly. "I'm really sorry about what happened back on Earth, how we ended things..."

Her eyes lit up. "You've always been my friend, Osax," she said.

My ears lifted.

"Anyway," said Jonathan, "K and I wanted to help, but we only had a clunky TAU cargo ship. We needed something more suited for a daring adventure. We needed the Firebrand." His eyes lowered sheepishly. "And... I wanted to contact Joëlle, even if it was dangerous."

"Yeah," said K. "She could have ratted us out, and sent an entire fleet of TAU to arrest or kill us."

"But I didn't!" said Joëlle.

Slowly, disbelieving, it dawned on me. "Joëlle, you could be considered a criminal now, for helping Jonathan and K."

She nodded, solemnly.

Their three sets of eyes were all on me, and I felt myself beginning to shake. "You... you all put yourselves in great danger... just because-"

"For you," said K. "That's something we all have in common. We all care about you."

"And about saving the galaxy," added Joëlle, helpfully.

"And stopping the Brotherhood," said Jonathan.

The Milky Way reflected in my eyes, and an overwhelming sense of love swelled inside me.

"Well, we did it," I declared. "We saved the galaxy."

K grinned. "Hell yeah we did." We met eyes. "I'm so glad you survived... when we got your message, I..." She shook her head, eyes watering. "I was so worried."

I felt myself choke back a cry. "But you-" I began. "*You're* alive! I can't- I can't believe..." I started sobbing, then winced, snorting out blood. My head started to spin, and I went to steady myself on K's shoulder with my right hand, but felt it wasn't there, which made me more nauseated. The stars whirled above me.

"Aw, Osax!" said K, wiping the blood from my nose. "We need to get you to a doctor." She was so *gentle*, and despite everything, I felt safe in her arms. Our eyes met once more "I'll be here," she said. "I'm with you."

"Right," said Jonathan.

"Come on," said Joëlle. "The Firebrand is this way!"

Then I closed my eyes, and let my friends carry me back to the light.

Seventy-Four

That was six months ago.

I leaned on the railing of a high balcony with my cybernetic arm. It was the kind of day where the sky was practically singing with colour. The clouds were gorgeously full and white, and each one seemed to crackle with a silent energy. I'd be surprised if there wasn't some dry lightning tonight.

I flexed the metallic fingers of my right hand, and glanced down at it. The sun glinted off my silver arm. Even after six months, it still felt a little strange. But it was surprisingly comfortable. I could feel the cool breeze against it, could feel the railing. I was almost as nimble with my new arm as I had been with my old now. I took in a breath of fragrant, fresh air through my nose, and blinked my eyes closed for a moment.

When I exhaled, I opened my eyes and gazed out across the landscape towards the sea and the mountains beyond, listening to the sounds of the wind rustling through the trees and bushes on the gardens above and below me. There was a lot of bustling down below at the base of the Great Temple, and sunlight sparkled off the ships that hummed across the sky. It was a busy day today, but otherwise just an ordinary one. My furred ears dangled at a skewed angle in the breeze. I glanced at one of the other pyramids of the temple, and for the briefest of moments, I was surprised not to see a great sphere floating above it. In a way, skythers, like humans, could adapt to change quite quickly, even if it wasn't always easy. But at the same time, sometimes I'd think I was used to something, and then a year later still be surprised by it.

Flapping wings punctuated the air, and my ears twitched toward it. I trained my eyes on a large, orange bird. He landed gracefully on the railing, just a few feet away from me. I'd begun to suspect that it was always the same bird who I saw on this balcony, stopping by to greet me. It made me feel like we had a special bond. I wondered if he recognized me the same way I recognized him.

"Hello again," I said softly, in Skorali. I tried not to move too much; I didn't want to scare him off. "It's good to see you."

I smiled, taking in the details of his feathered plume, and sharp talons. He surveyed the city with a quiet attentiveness, and I felt strangely akin to this bird. He watched over everyone like a noble sentinel. Then I turned my gaze outward, following his example.

There were no TAU ships in sight. When Astraloth reappeared, the Brotherhood fleet had been apprehended by a TAU force that Joëlle had rallied. I was brought to the Great Temple and my wounds were treated there. K, Jonathan, Joëlle, and Omega all waited there with me, and I granted them safe haven at the temple while I recovered. Keeping their involvement secret at that point would have been pointless, and we were all tired of hiding.

After I regained my strength, I told my story to the galaxy. Everything about the Brotherhood, about Duhrnan, and Ryner, was laid bare before the public. And I argued that, while the creation of bioweapons may be unethical, their right to exist as life forms was no less than ours, humans or skythers alike. And the TAU listened. They abolished the laws that made bioweapons illegal. They pardoned Joëlle for knowingly aiding Jonathan and K, when they all helped me on Viperion. Now, K and Omega were free to be citizens of the TAU. And of course they were free to exist in skyther lands as well.

My eyes darkened a little, thinking about K and Jonathan. She was technically a free citizen, but Jonathan...

"Osax?" said Kaia, startling me and the bird, who took off into the sky. She had a way of sneaking up on me while I was deep in thought. Her red skirt drifted in the breeze. It was a warm day, so we were both topless. I turned to face her, ruffling my chest fur casually, and lifted my ears. Her cheeks seemed to flush a little when our eyes met. We had gotten much closer over the past year since I became King; we spent a lot more time together since I got back from Viperion, and everything changed.

"Yes, Kaia?" I said.

"I'm sorry, I didn't mean to startle you."

"It's alright," I replied. "I was just deep in thought, that's all."

She tilted her head to the side. Her ears dangled, and her cat-like nose twitched. Her deep blue eyes met mine. "Were you thinking about

Jonathan and K again?"

I sighed. "Yes."

Kaia stepped up to me, and placed a hand on my metallic arm. I could feel her fingers gently pressing onto my body- it still felt a little strange that the arm *was* my body.

"You wish they could live here?" she asked.

I turned away from her, and gazed down at the city. "Yes," I said. My fur shook in the wind. "I understand why Jonathan can't. And I understand why K chose to go with him. They have three hundred people to look after. But it would be so much easier if they could come out of hiding. I don't want to have to keep visiting them in secret."

"Well," she said, helpfully. "Maybe you can offer them a place on Astraloth. It's within your power." She blinked at me, her eyes filled with caring. "The TAU haven't forgiven Jonathan, but..."

"I know," I said, meeting her gaze. "The TAU doesn't control Astraloth." I glanced back down at the city, and my ears relaxed. My eyes caught sight of the old urban market district. I was happy to see the new corporate restrictions in place. The neon signs and billboards had been removed, and the place was once again a centre for local produce and the arts. The people there, humans and skythers alike, seemed much happier now, with the freedom to give their attention to whatever they wanted, and the newfound quiet of the place. Now it was a place that put life at its center, rather than money. I couldn't undo that damned root beer commercial I'd been paid to star in, but I could stop it from praying on poor citizens, stealing their attention with the hope of taking their money, too. With the advertisements gone, that was a little bit of skyther culture put back into place.

"It's not the TAU that are stopping me," I said at last.

"It's not?"

"I've offered Jonathan and K a place on Astraloth," I said. "I don't care what the TAU think. I know I have friends there who will back me up. And the people of Earth, for the most part, really look up to me. A lot of people have forgiven Jonathan after hearing the story, even if he's not officially pardoned."

Kaia put her hands on her wide hips, and breathed in the crisp air. "Then what *is* stopping you?"

"K," I said.

"Oh?"

"She's happy," I said, gazing up at the sky. "Her and Jonathan, they've finally found a planet. A place to raise their people." I lifted my ears, thinking about it. "Jonathan said 'it's great, really. Just imagine Earth, but a little smaller. A lot smaller, actually.'"

Kaia laughed warmly, her eyes squinting. "That's wonderful."

"Yes, it is."

"Have they come up with a name for them, yet?" Kaia asked, wondering about the clones.

I shook my head. "The last time I called them, K suggested 'The Sisterhood', but I think she was joking. Then she said 'What about the Blumans? Cause- We- Cause we're blue! Blue humans!' She laughed, then shook her head, and Jonathan chimed in with his response. 'I don't think that's quite it but... ah, yes. What about Bloomers? Because, they'll be blooming, like... ugh... no, that's not right.'-"

"...It sounds like you're starting into another story," Kaia giggled.

I laughed, gesturing with my robotic hand. "Oh. I just meant to say, they're still picking a name."

She smiled at me. "Did you have any suggestions?"

"I said to them, 'Why not just call them "Alphas?"' K nodded in agreement. 'Yeah, that's a perfect name. If they're anything like me, then we're *definitely* alpha.' Jonathan smirked thoughtfully. 'Yes,' he said, 'Alpha, like alphabet. Like K's name. It makes sense. But we can't rush into a decision like this...'"

Kaia brushed a loose bit of fur from my shoulder. "You're clearly thinking about them a lot," she said.

I smiled. "Of course I am. They're my friends."

"More like family," she said, her eyes sparkling.

I turned around to face her, leaning my back against the railing. "So, Kaia, were you just checking up on me? Or did you have something to tell me?"

She eyed me shyly. She'd been doing that more and more recently, as we became closer friends. "I wanted to talk to you, Osax, because I enjoy your company. But I also wanted to tell you that someone is here to see you."

I bolted upright. "Is it Joëlle? She's early-"

"Actually, it's someone else," she interjected.

I was perplexed. I wasn't expecting anyone else to visit today. "Oh. Well, I guess I shouldn't keep them waiting. Will you show me to them?"

"Of course," said Kaia. "They're on the open floor of the temple.

◆

515

The air blew calmly through my ears, past the pillars that held up the top half of the pyramid. Skythers walked to and fro as Kaia led me, skirt trailing behind her...

I caught sight of the homeless skyther I'd given rations to nearly half a cycle ago in the pouring rain of the market. He saw me, and lifted his ears in joy. "Osax!" he said, stepping up to me. He wore a nice set of clean, fresh clothes, with my old red coat tied around his waist. His chest fur was well groomed, and his face wrinkled with happiness.

"Tallor," I said, greeting my friend with a bow. He returned the gesture. "How is the temple treating you today?"

"Very well, of course," he replied, in Skorali. His fingers grasped at the red coat at his waist. I noted that he kept it with him at almost all times, and it made me blush. "And how are you on this beautiful day?"

I lifted my ears, genuinely. "I am well. Quite well."

Tallor nodded at me, as other skythers bustled about, and Kaia waited. "My friends from the market- I brought some more to stay here at the temple. I hope that's alright!"

"I'm glad!" I said. "We have the space and the resources. There's no reason why our people should be going hungry in the streets." I bowed to him. "I'd love to chat more, Tallor, but I'm going to meet someone. Perhaps another time-"

"Don't let me keep you, then," he said, and he bowed farewell. "Thank you again."

I returned the bow, and continued after Kaia.

◆

A human woman stood alone in the cut out section of the temple, next to a thick pillar. The skythers gave her a wide berth. My mandibles twitched. I thought I recognized her, as she looked up and around the temple with wide eyes, but I couldn't quite recall her face... I shifted my weight from leg to leg, pressing my feet into the cool stone of the temple.

Kaia nodded in her direction, and so I cleared my throat and stepped up to her. She gazed up at me. I introduced myself in English.

"Hello there. I am King Osax. I was told you wished to see me?" I stood straight.

She looked stunned for a moment. "Oh, your- your majesty..."

She was struggling to find the words, so after a moment, I continued. "I feel like I recognize you, but I can't remember from where..."

She locked eyes with me, and her expression turned grim. She had dark hair that she wore in a bun. Her clothes were business casual. I didn't recognize any of the details, yet still she seemed somehow familiar.

"Voren," she said. "I- You met me on Voren." She bowed her head slightly. Involuntarily, my ears shot back in defense. She saw this, and sputtered, "I- I didn't know the base was being run by the Brotherhood. I was never part of that!"

I nodded slowly, my heart rate normalizing. "I believe you." I waited expectantly.

She lowered her gaze. "Ah. Well, thank you." She cleared her throat, and I could tell she was nervous. I tilted my head in confusion. Her eyes were wet.

"You were there, in the elevator," she said. "I wanted to thank you, for saving my life."

I was stunned. She gazed up at me.

"I... of course," I said. That was a painful memory... That poor scientist had slipped from my grasp, into the depths of the shaft. I shut my eyes tight. I had done my best, but the failure there had been a great source of self-hate for me. I opened my eyes, vaguely bracing for more of a sting.

"I know you couldn't save everyone," she continued, as if reading my thoughts. "But you helped me get out of there, along with most of the others trapped in the elevator." She chuckled shyly, and looked away. "I didn't get a chance to thank you. So, after we were all taken back to Olympus, I did my research. My wife, she's a loro researcher, so I asked her to help me track you down, cause I knew that's why you were there and I thought she might have heard of you... Then I found out you were the prince, and I doubted I'd ever get the chance to meet you. But here I am!"

My heart eased. I smiled, bowing my head slightly. "I'm glad I was able to help," I said.

"W- wait," she said. Then she reached into a large pocket on her leg. "Our son, Steven, he's a big fan; he drew this picture for you."

She held up a piece of paper. On it was a crudely drawn skyther, coloured in bright crayons. He wore a black cape and held a silver circle in his hands, which he lifted up above his head. Silver stars dotted the background. My name was written in gold crayon in shaky handwriting. When I saw it, I don't know why, by my eyes watered.

"Of course, you probably don't want it, it's just a kid's drawing. He's eight," she continued. "I had to come by the Great Temple, for a business trip. He asked me to give this to you, and, well, I couldn't say no." She held the drawing up to me, awkwardly.

Kaia watched, standing politely still, but I could feel her smile on me. Gently, I took the drawing from the woman's hands. "Tell Steven I think he is a great artist," I said, quietly.

Her face lit up. "Oh, he'll *love* that! If it's not too much to ask, would you pose for a photo?" She was already retrieving her camera.

I smiled with my eyes. "Of course."

I knelt down and held the drawing next to my face, giving my best smile. The woman stepped back a pace, and snapped a photograph. Then I stood up, and looked once more at the drawing, at the skyther's orange-crayon eyes.

"What was your name?" I asked, looking back to her.

"Julia," she said. "Julia Gilbert."

I bowed to her deeply. "Thank you for sharing this with me, Julia Gilbert."

She grinned. "Thank *you* for humouring me. And saving my life." She checked the time on her holo-gauntlet, and hastily added, "I have to go, or I'll be late for a meeting. The main reason I came to Astraloth!" She chuckled nervously, then waved. "Thank you again!"

"My pleasure!" I called out as she walked quickly away, and down the stairs out of sight.

I turned to Kaia. Her ears were shaking as she struggled to contain herself. She said quietly in Skorali, "That was so sweet. So adorable."

"Yes. Yes, it was." I nodded, looking at the drawing of me. He may have been a disproportionate, two-dimensional figure, but he stood with a heroic posture, and I couldn't help but smile.

◆

In my quarters, I sat on my bed with my knees up, my back against the wall. I was staring at my holo-gauntlet, listening to it beep. I was warmed by sunlight from outside. My ears lifted when the call connected.

A holographic image of K shimmered into view above my arm. She was wearing a tank top and some work gloves. It was still a bit strange to see her in civilian clothes since she used to spend so much time wearing weapons and pieces of armour. Her horns looked bigger than when I had first met her, and it was hard to tell but I thought her muscles did too.

She smirked at me. "Hey, Osax!"

"K," I said. "Glad you picked up. I just wanted to check in-"

She swivelled her head at the sudden sound of a muffled crash, followed by Jonathan cursing faintly in the background. K grimaced, looking at whatever accident had caused the noise.

"Shit!" she said, before darting away from the communications terminal. I was left staring at a holographic wall for a few seconds before she came back into view, panting. "Sorry-"

"Something wrong?" I asked. "Is Jonathan okay?"

She chuckled and waved her hand dismissively. "Yeah he's fine, just dropped a crate of supplies." She scratched behind her horns. "We're uh, actually pretty busy prepping for tonight."

I leaned back, and slid down so I was laying on my bed. "Yeah, I'll bet. Well, if now's a bad time I can hang up."

She shrugged. "Yeah... it's not a great time to be honest. But, you're still coming, right?"

I nodded. "Yes. Just waiting for Joëlle to arrive, and then we'll be on our way. It should only take us half a day-"

"Ooh, has the Firebrand got one of those fancy new slipspace engines installed?" She grinned. "I'd love to see it!"

"Yeah, Joëlle was telling me about it. Based on loro tech salvaged from the battle of Astraloth, apparently."

"Crazy," she said, shaking her head in astonishment. "To think the remains of that mothership are being put to good use... I'm glad."

Her orange eyes shifted to the side, staring at whatever Jonathan was doing beyond my view. I got the sense I should really let them get organized, so I said, "Hey, K, I'll let you go for now."

She looked back at me. "Alright. Well, don't take too long, I want to show you what I've been working on! Jonathan's got the food synthesizers set up, but I wanted to try my hand growing something naturally... Yesterday I started setting up a garden!"

"Really?" I said. "That's great, K. What kind of garden?"

"Well, right now I've just planted some flowers I got from Astraloth. Gonna see how they grow. But I hope to start planting food someday. I dunno, I'm really new to this- it's a challenge not to crush the plants with my hands." She smirked. Then I heard Jonathan calling for her, asking for help lifting something. She gave me a look, and joked, "Man, Jonathan is so weak, he can't lift anything."

I snorted a laugh. "Yeah, easy for you to say. Don't forget, some of us are just mortals!"

She cackled. "You're all *insects* before the almighty god of strength, K! Ha ha!" She grinned, and I stared into her eyes... as best as I could through the hologram.

"Careful, K, you're starting to sound like a super-villain," I remarked.

"You're just scared cause you know I could beat you in a fight. You might be tall, but you're almost as weak as Jonathan!"

"You always have to bring the insults into it, huh?" I replied.

She grinned. "Hey, you know you love me anyway!"

I nodded thoughtfully. "You're right." I smiled. "I do."

"I know, Osax," she laughed. "It's pretty obvious."

"Yeah," I replied. "Sometimes though, it's worth saying."

"Well," she said, "I'd better go before Jonathan breaks his back trying to lift a pencil." She gave me one last look before hanging up. "Love you too, Osax!"

Beep.

I rested my body, and gazed at the ceiling.

◆

Back in my washroom, I groomed my fur with a tiny comb. The full-body mirror defogged itself swiftly as I gazed into my own eyes with stark recognition, and sighed. My black pupils narrowed slightly, and I brushed one of my ears back as I straightened the fur. I was full of excitement. Joëlle would be here any minute.

Someone knocked on the door, and a nasally voice followed. "Osax. Joëlle is here."

Hurriedly, I put the comb away and pulled my clothes on. The door hissed shut behind me as I stepped back into my private room.

Omega waited there for me. A year after their heroic sacrifice on Malum, their body had fully regenerated now, and they stood with their arms at their sides. They clawed the carpet with their feet, tail flicking back and forth. Sunlight painted us and the room with a bright glow, pouring in from the glass door that led to the landing pad. I peered out at the dock, which had been repaired months ago. The Firebrand had just touched down, sunlight glinting off the textured hull. Its engines were still fuming with heat.

I grinned at Omega. "What are you waiting for? Let's go!" I said.

I followed Omega outside. Fresh air filled my senses, and the colours of the city below were full of life. We made our way eagerly across the narrow bridge to the landing pad, where the Firebrand waited. The ship's exit ramp lowered with a quiet hiss, and Joëlle, hair freshly dyed a striking blue, stepped out onto the pad, waving.

Tonight, I'd be sleeping on a familiar bed aboard the Firebrand, on our way through slipspace toward the planet where Jonathan and K prepared to raise the Alphas. They were going to wake the first few clones soon, and wanted Joëlle, Omega and I to be there with them when it happened. It was a strange situation, but hardly the strangest thing I'd experienced in my life. I often wondered about the spheres of the Great Temple, about what really happened to the loro in ancient history, and, more pressingly, about the future. I didn't know what the future held. But I knew that, at least for now, things were alright. Good, even.

I folded my arms, and sighed. Sometimes, I wished K would visit me more. Every so often we would call each other, or visit and play games, and talk about life. But it was more than enough just to know that she was alive. I knew she found a calling preparing to raise her sisters. She was eager to help teach them. And she wanted to give Jonathan company while he worked to take responsibility for the life he had created. She told me that once things settled down there, she'd come back to Astraloth. We could take a trip to Earth, and go exploring through the wild lands, searching for strawberries.

I looked forward to that.

Jonathan and Joëlle had worked through a lot over the past half year. They visited each other every couple of weeks. I didn't really know if they ever were upfront about their feelings... That wasn't my business. But I was comforted to know that they had forgiven each other for the past. It must have been difficult to do.

And Joëlle and I saw each other every now and then, as well. We reminisced about the past, though we didn't always have the emotional energy to talk about Duhrnan. I was glad to be her friend, though she chose to spend much of her time these days alone. That was one experience we shared. We'd both learned how to believe in ourselves, and how to be happy on our own. Strangely, I found that made having friends much easier, too.

I sat next to Joëlle and Omega in the cockpit of the Firebrand, with a refreshing glass of soda in my hands. The ship hummed and whirred, and Joëlle fiddled with the controls as we drifted above Astraloth. The Toru nebula coloured the black of space like a luminous purple ink, and I could feel the presence of my mother. My ears perked up, my eyes glazing over as I wondered about the past, and the future. I was eager to see Jonathan and K. I missed them, but it wouldn't be long before we were all together.

I found solace knowing that I wasn't alone. Even in solitude, the same energy that gave me life was found all across the galaxy, in countless stars, in countless life forms. And in a way that meant I was always connected to others. Even my cybernetic arm was full of a living energy, in a way. And my friends, the humans, carried a bit of that light in them too. Even Duhrnan had, though I doubt he ever realized it. We can struggle so hard to feel connected to something, when the truth is we always are, and we always have been. Just being alive is enough; it doesn't matter if you are born or made. We are not merely visitors to this world, but part of it.

Joëlle activated the slipspace drive, and I was brought back into the moment. The Firebrand seemed to yawn as it stretched into slipspace. The smell of Joëlle's coffee wafted into my nose, and I could feel the warmth of my companions by my side. I leaned forward in my seat, my ears perking up. Clutching the seat with my silver hand, my eyes fixed on the stars ahead. In a flash, they shot back into brilliant streams of light, and we tore off into stars, embraced by the fathomless wonder of the galaxy.

Author's Note

Spending so much time with skythers was certainly interesting.

Since I was a young kid I wanted to be an author. I was inspired by Kenneth Oppel's work, and the Chronicles of Ancient Darkness by Michelle Paver, which is still my favourite book series. I started many novels, all the way back in middle school, but this is the first one I had the pleasure of finishing.

Osax, K, Jonathan, and Joëlle have been with me for many years. They had their roots in characters from a sci-fi roleplaying game that I wrote for my brother Bayden and twin sister Ashlyn. The original Osax was invented by Ashlyn, and the original K invented by Bayden. Their antics and banter served as the inspiration for the characters you know from the book, and while many things about the characters and story are different, some things stayed the same. I began the process of adapting that game into a story a long time ago, originally planning to make it into a web comic. But one day I decided I wanted to write it as a novel.

I want to thank Ashlyn and Bayden. Without them this story would not exist the way it does, and my life would be a lot less interesting, exciting, and fun.

I'd like to thank Shay, who was among the first to read *Sentinel* and share feedback and encouragement with me.

I'm grateful for Candace and Taryn who also showed me a lot of support and helped me improve upon certain aspects of the story and characterization.

I am also grateful for Katree, who helped me process through many of the doubts I faced as I worked through the final steps of this writing process.

And of course, I am grateful for you. For reading my story. I have always been fascinated and enthralled by stories about heroes, and I hope that you found some wonder and excitement following along with Osax's tale.

Now, onto new adventures!

-Seb Woodland

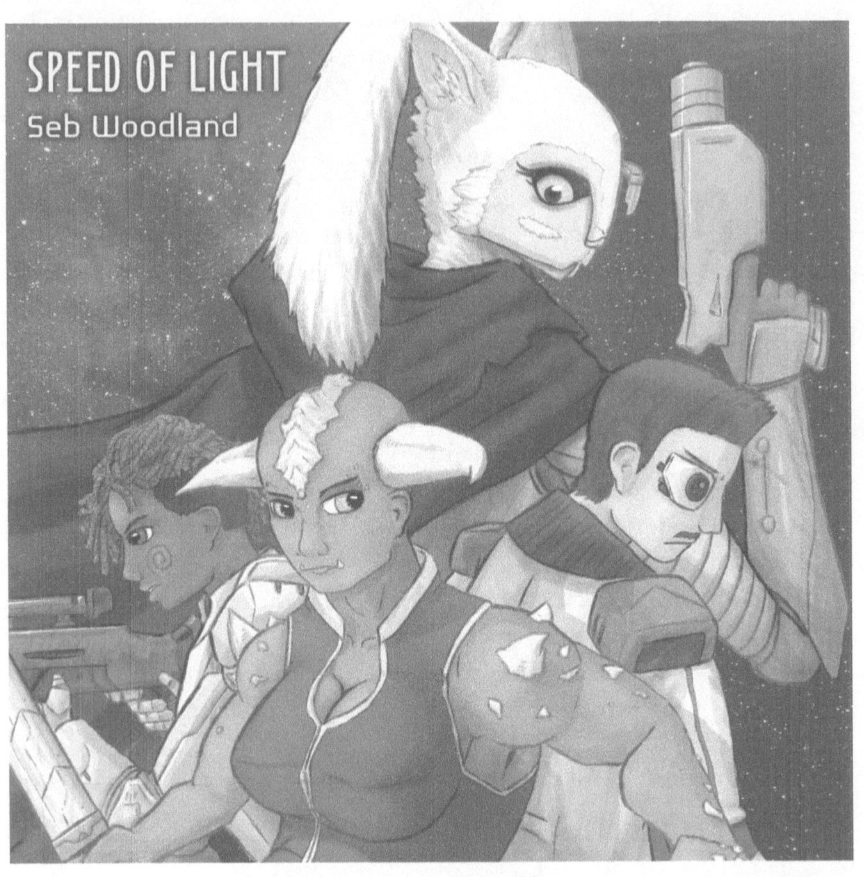

Check out the *Sentinel* song, "Speed of Light"
by Seb Woodland!

https://sebwoodland.bandcamp.com/track/speed-of-light

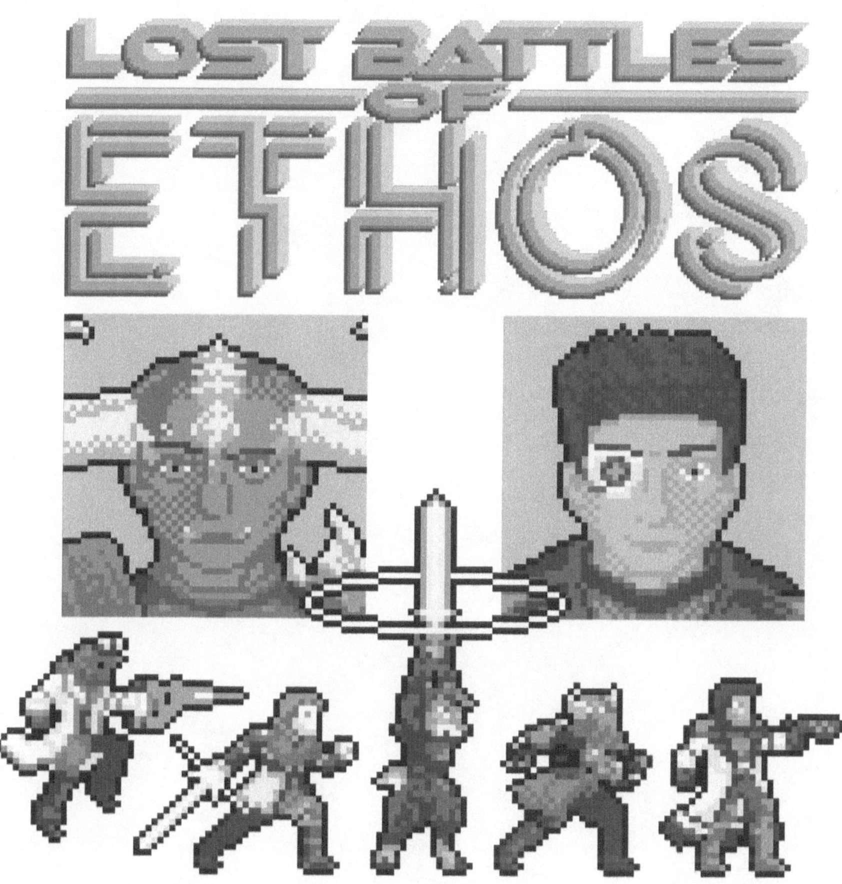

Look for Twin Tales Games' *"Lost Battles of Ethos"*,
a zany coop video game set in an alternate galaxy, starring
Laltus Emmerdar. Featuring *Sentinel* characters Jonathan and K, as
well as a cast of new heroes.
Expected 2022-2023

9 781777 914509